USA TODAY BESTSELLING AUTHOR

OLIVIA WILDENSTEIN

COLD LITTLE GAMES

THE COMPLETE SERIES

For information contact :
OLIVIA WILDENSTEIN
http://oliviawildenstein.com

Cover design by *Sarah Anderson*
Editing by *Jessica Nelson & Becky Stephens*

To my mother and her twin sister,
Aster and Ivy are not you, but you did inspire
The Masterpiecers with your amazing talent
with a needle & thread.

To my father,
thank you for raising me in a world
filled with the timeless beauty of Art.

ONE

Age is not a one-size-fits-all number. I'm seventeen, but there isn't a single seventeen-year-old out there to whom I can relate. Not even my twin sister, Ivy.

She enjoys being seventeen. She says it's not something you can change, so you might as well accept it. Even though I have a fake ID that says I'm older—which I made when I was fifteen so I could go see R-rated movies without a chaperone—there's no forging my real age.

I'm dying to be older, to be done with high school, to leave home for good, to get out of Kokomo. Ivy says she wants to live in New York, so I guess that's where we'll head when school's over. I don't really care where we end up, as long as it's far away from Mom, and as long as Ivy and I are together. We can't live apart, the two of us.

Just as I think about my twin, she bursts into the house, shaking spring rain off her umbrella. Ivy's not a fan of rain, but that's because it ruins her shoes and makes her hair frizz.

"I saw Dr. Frank today."

I lower my gaze to the bolognaise sauce. It makes a strange gurgling sound as it cooks, like a live animal drowning, but it's only ground beef. Ground beef isn't alive. Besides, there's more tomato than meat, because meat is too expensive. "Why did you see her?"

"I passed her in the street, Asty. On East Markland Ave. She stopped by Jo-Ann's to buy yarn for a scarf she's knitting."

I put down the wooden spoon. "What did she tell you?"

"She didn't tell me anything." Ivy shivers and dries her hands on a kitchen towel. "Do you like her?"

"She's nice."

Ivy's wet blonde locks glint under the cone-shaped ceiling lamp. "Do you feel like she's helping you?"

I shrug. "Sure." My twin is convinced I need help, so I keep weekly appointments with Dr. Frank, after which I swallow pills she prescribes. Not every day, but often enough to appease Ivy.

"She said you were more forthcoming than at the beginning of the year."

"I thought she didn't tell you anything…"

Ivy narrows her blue eyes that are a deeper shade than mine. "She didn't give me any specifics, Asty. Anyway, I'm so late. I hope Mom won't be mad. The salesclerk took forever cutting the samples."

"When has Mom ever been mad at you?"

Ivy winces. I smile to lessen her guilt. Mom likes Ivy; she doesn't like me. It's one of the only things that's not a secret in our family.

My twin retreats toward the veranda where Mom works around the clock, sewing quilts based on pictures customers send her. They're well made—I'll give her that much—but I don't understand how people can pay a couple hundred bucks for fabric copies of photographs. They should blow up their pictures and frame them. It would make more financial sense. I suppose most people don't have much financial sense.

Through the closed door, I hear my sister and mother speak, but I don't hear what they say. I put a lid on the tomato-meat sauce, turn the heat to low, and go take my shower while no one's occupying our only bathroom. I spend extra long under the hot spray, letting the water rinse away the scent of dried sweat from this morning's PE class. Some girls take showers in school; I don't. I always keep my gym clothes on underneath my school clothes, so I don't have to parade around in the nude.

Wrapped in my towel, I pad back into the kitchen to check on the sauce, which has thickened. Sometimes I feel like a witch, like cooking is magical. I throw together all these different ingredients and they bind in the most extraordinary fashion to create something new.

I put the pasta to boil, cross the small living room toward the adjoining veranda, and knuckle the closed door. "Dinner will be ready in five."

I don't know if they hear me because an audiobook is playing inside. They're always listening to books on tape. I wonder if it's to mask their conversations or if it's because they don't have much to tell each other.

I try the doorknob. I'm surprised when it gives. Mom usually locks her door. I peek inside. "Dinner will be ready—"

Mom shuts the bottom drawer of her sewing table with her foot. The soft bang echoes against the glass walls of the veranda.

Ivy glances up at me, blue eyes wide. The waning evening light cuts a gilded path across the bright room, making Ivy's hair shimmer gold and Mom's gray hair shine silver.

"Dinner's almost ready," I say.

"I'm not hungry," Mom says. "Besides, I need to finish this for Friday." She gestures toward the fabric pooled at her feet.

Disappointment fills my stomach. I'm not hungry either, but I want us to sit at the table like a normal family. Even if it's merely pretend.

"Ivy?" I ask hopefully.

"I really should—"

My face crumples.

She folds what she's working on in half and then folds that half into more halves until it's just a tiny square of blue satin. Over the metallic drone of the sewing machine, she says, "I really should eat." She walks out and pulls the door shut behind us. "Want me to set the ta—" She stops in front of the small wooden table I've already set for three. I even clipped a couple branches from the button-bush outside the veranda and put them in a water glass. The glossy green leaves give the table a splash of chicness. Ivy loves chic things.

"This is…lovely," she tells me.

Her words penetrate and linger in the tomato-and-garlic-scented air long after she's spoken them.

Steam blasts my face as I drain the pasta. "What does Mom keep in that drawer?"

"What drawer?" Ivy grabs a carton of milk from the fridge and pours herself a glass. She sniffs it before drinking, then searches for the expiration date. "Wow. This is a week old."

"Does it smell bad?"

"No, but it's a week old," she repeats as though I didn't hear her the first time.

Mom doesn't want us throwing out food until it smells. It's one of the few things we agree on, one of the few things she and Ivy *don't* agree on. This shared value hasn't brought Mom and me closer though.

"They put so many preservatives in stuff today. It's probably still okay to drink," I reassure my twin.

"Not taking that risk." She pours the milk into the sink, nose still wrinkled.

As the ribbon of white vanishes down the drain, I hear the nickels and dimes it cost clatter down along with it. I remain silent. I don't want to sound like Mom, always nagging Ivy about being wasteful.

I set two steaming bowls on our placemats. "So, what's in Mom's bottom drawer?"

Ivy drags her hand through her straightened curls. I rubbed some serum on mine like my sister taught me, but it did nothing to tame the frizz. I probably didn't put enough in, but I don't like putting unnatural stuff on my body. Taking medication for my mood swings is poisonous enough. I only take it every other day, but Ivy doesn't know that. She'd be really angry if she knew.

"Rolls of fabric," she answers.

"Then why does she lock it?"

She wraps a gigantic mouthful of pasta around the tines of her fork and shovels it inside her mouth. "This is really *really* good," she says after swallowing.

Pride inflates my chest and satiates my hollow belly better than food ever could. But then I think of Mom's eternally locked drawer and suspicion supplants pride.

"Is it really only fabric?"

"Yes." Her voice sounds like an eye roll. "Aren't you going to eat?"

Pensive, I pick up my fork and dig into the gloppy red mess that feels like my life. This mess, though, I can make disappear. The turmoil inside me, that won't go away until Mom does.

Or until I do.

TWO

JOSH

"The sun feels so damn good. Classes should take place on the quad." I nudge Ivy, who's sitting cross-legged next to me.

"That's an idea," she mumbles, not paying attention.

"Vitamin D's good for the brain." I glance at my friend, who's bent over her phone. "It also makes facial hair grow. Did you know that?"

"Uh-huh. Yeah. Totally."

"Stop checking your Instagram feed and listen to me, Redd."

Ivy puts her phone away. "I wasn't checking my Instagram feed. I was reading about the new reality TV competition that's starting this summer. *The Masterpiecers.*"

"What are people competing for?"

"Getting a free ride to the art school."

"Is that the place you want to go to?"

"Yeah. But unless I get a scholarship, there's no way I can afford it." She rolls onto her back. "I can't believe you're already done with your second year of college. That's insane."

I smile, feeling a quick rush of satisfaction. "One more year to go." I'm taking a bunch of summer credits to finish in three years, so I can apply to become a cop.

"Officer Cooper." Ivy makes a face. "Still sounds weird."

"Why?"

"*Because*. You'll be a law enforcer. You'll have a badge, and a gun, and stuff."

"Which will come in handy to get you out of trouble."

She snorts. "Like I ever get into trouble."

"Um. Have you forgotten the time you stole a pack of watermelon bubblegum from under the cash register of the CVS, and the salesclerk caught you?"

"Because Mom wouldn't buy it for me."

"And then Aster took the blame."

She rumples her forehead. "That was horrible of me."

Silence stretches between us as we both recollect the shopping expedition that started as an excursion to the movies—her mother wasn't actually taking us to see a movie; she was dropping us off for the afternoon because she had *stuff* to do—and ended with a slap that sent Aster skidding sideways and collapsing onto the sidewalk. I didn't have a cell phone back then since I was only nine, but I told their mom to leave before I had a passerby call the cops.

Mom was away at a baking conference in New York. She'd been planning that trip for so long that I hadn't called her, but I'd phoned my dad from a concerned bystander's cell. He came to pick us up and took us home.

Mom returned that night too—Dad had called her even though I'd told him not to—and she'd stormed off to pay Mrs. Redd a visit. To this day, I'm not sure what happened, but Ivy and Aster ended up staying with us for ten days.

"Shouldn't have brought that up," I mutter.

Ivy bites her lower lip.

"At least we got a prolonged sleepover out of it."

The bell rings in the squat rectangular building behind us, signaling Ivy's lunch period is over. "Man, that felt quick."

"Time flies when you're with me."

She stands up and dusts the back of her jean cutoffs. "Why are you here anyway? Don't you have sun on your campus?"

"I'm taking Aster to the DMV to get her driver's license in an hour. Wanna come?"

"In New York, no one drives."

"This is Kokomo, not New York."

"But one day, I'll be in New York. You just wait and see."

Ivy is stubborn, ambitious, and overflowing with talent, so I don't doubt that one day she'll get what she wants. *Everything* she wants. I don't think she'd ever settle for anything less. We're kindred spirits in that way.

She readjusts the red bandana she's sporting to keep her hair back. "Bye, Joshy."

I roll my eyes. "Gotta stop calling me that. I'm not twelve anymore."

"You'll always be twelve to me."

"Go away. You're gonna get detention." I lie back down. "Plus, you're blocking my sun." We grin at each other.

She leaves, and I plug my earphones into my phone to listen to music while I wait for the other twin.

I MUST'VE FALLEN ASLEEP, because when I look up, Aster's crouched beside me, her incredibly light eyes roaming over my face.

"How long have you been laying out here?" she asks, prodding the skin on my jaw with her fingers. "You're lobster-red."

I heave myself up. "It'll turn into a tan."

"Burning is really bad for you, Josh."

"Thanks for the heads-up, *Mom*."

"I'm serious. I don't want you to get cancer."

"I don't want to get cancer either." I smile at her and take out the now-silent earphones. "Ready?"

"I think so."

As we walk over to my car, which I parked in the school lot, I notice her narrow shoulders are pulled tight, and her lips are squeezed into a line straighter than the markings of my parking spot. "What's up?"

"Remember that Pac-Man game I programmed for Ivy at the beginning of the year?"

Back at the beginning of the school year, Aster impersonated Ivy during an IT test. She's really good with computers, unlike Ivy. If she'd kept the code simple instead of adding cool features, the girls would probably have gotten away with it. Long story short, they got caught.

"The principal doesn't want to remove the low marks from our GPAs."

"That sucks."

She clicks her seatbelt on. "It especially sucks for Ivy. Her GPA's not that good. She spends too much time sewing with Mom instead of studying." She sucks in a breath and twists toward me, cheeks flushed. "Maybe I should record our classes. She loves listening to stuff when she sews. Then at least she could keep up with the curriculum."

I squeeze Aster's hand once before gripping my steering wheel. "You're so considerate."

Her cheeks become beet-red at my compliment.

"Look at that...our skin tones match," I tease.

She doesn't laugh. Instead she faces her window.

I didn't mean to make her feel bad, but I don't apologize because it'll fluster her more. Instead, I pump the volume of the stereo up until Jay Z's killer rhythm rocks the car and drowns out the awkwardness.

After three songs, I turn the volume back down and ask, "So who you going to Junior Prom with?"

She looks over at me. "I'm not going."

"Why not?"

"Because."

"That's not a good answer."

She picks a piece of lint off her baggy jeans. I don't know if it's her new medication, but she's lost weight. My forearm is larger than both of her thighs put together. Maybe I'm exaggerating, but she's definitely too skinny. After she passes her test, I'll take her for a celebratory donut run at Mom's bakery. She'll like that.

"Why aren't you going?"

"Because I don't have a dress."

"I'm sure Mom has a dress you could borrow."

She shoots me a horrified look.

"Oh, come on, Mom has great taste."

"I can't wear one of her dresses. What if someone pours punch over it? Or—"

"Sounds to me like you're making excuses."

"I'm not. Besides, Ivy's going with Sean, and I don't have a date."

I brake in the middle of the street. Thankfully there's no traffic. I pull over to the curb.

Aster frowns. "Aren't we a little far to park?"

I get out of the car, jog around the front, and sweep open her door. And then I get down on one knee. "Aster Redd, will you take me to Junior Prom?"

Her expression goes from shocked to crazy shocked. Even her mouth gapes.

I add, "Please?"

"Josh, you don't have to—"

"Redd, I want to! Come on. I promise to make it fun." When she still hasn't said anything, I add, "And I really do miss high school dances. It's the only part of the high school experience I miss." I don't, but Aster will go if she thinks she's doing me a favor.

She smiles. "Okay." Her full lips part wider over her perfect white teeth. "Okay, I'll go with you." A woman pushing a stroller passes by us. "Better get up before someone thinks you're proposing," she whispers.

When Aster smiles, she really is the most beautiful girl ever. She morphs back into the pigtail-wearing girl I chased through my granddaddy's sunflower field, the girl who shrieked when her sister asked to go higher on the tire swing, the girl who pressed a palm against her mouth when she laughed.

I almost forget she's like my sister, and I also almost forget she was diagnosed with schizophrenia five years ago.

THREE

Moments like the afternoon I went to the DMV breed fragile dreams. Dreams of love and a blissful future bursting with exquisite reds, sunny yellows, and cobalt blues.

For the millionth time since Josh asked me to prom, I close my eyes and replay his proposal. I shouldn't read too much into it, but what if—

Ivy barrels into our shared bedroom.

I sit up in bed.

She's holding something behind her back.

When she doesn't say anything, I ask, "What's going on?"

"I heard you're going to the dance."

I imagine Josh told her. I wonder if he told her how he asked me. The thought makes a blush crawl over my jaw. I toy with my hair, twisting it into a long, coarse rope. "Yeah."

"I'm so glad because I made you this"—she pulls out something from behind her back—"and I would've hated to see it to go to waste."

The loveliest dress hangs from her outstretched fingers. It's fluid, sky blue, and shiny, like Springhill Lake on cloudless days.

"You made that for me?"

She grins even wider and nods.

I peel myself off my bed and walk around the brown sandals I kicked off when I came into my bedroom.

"Try it on."

I hesitate to take it from her. I'm afraid to soil its beauty with my indelicate fingers.

"I've been dying to see it worn."

I turn around to pull off my T-shirt. Ivy doesn't mind stripping when I'm around, but I don't like being naked or in my underwear in front of anyone.

"Hands up," she says.

I raise my arms, and she drops the floor-length dress over my head. It trickles over my skin like warm water. I wiggle out of my cargo shorts once the dress settles.

Ivy opens the closet door so I can glimpse my reflection in the long mirror. My eyes heat up.

My sister's smile transforms into a frown. "Do you hate it?" she asks softly.

Hate it? I spin around toward her. "Are you kidding?" I whisper hoarsely. "It's the most beautiful dress I've ever worn."

She rolls her eyes, but a pleased blush pinks her cheeks. "Wait till I get really good."

"You're already really good. You're way better than really good."

She doesn't say anything for a while. Simply observes the satiny sheen of the fabric and the way it drapes over my light brown skin and jutting bones. "You could be a model."

I let out a soft snort. "Please."

"I'm serious, Asty."

I watch my reflection again. The girl in the mirror seems unfamiliar and yet completely familiar. It's Ivy; not me. The girl in the liquid dress is confident and stylish, the sort who would capture a boy's attention.

Trapped butterflies flutter inside my belly. Whoever said hearts were in chests never truly felt nervous and excited.

I squeeze my sister tightly against me. And then I cry because it's the nicest thing she's done for me in a long time. Not that she's ever unkind, but this is the pinnacle of kindness.

"Wait. What will *you* wear?" I ask, pressing away.

"I made the same in red."

The butterflies perform backflips. *She doesn't mind looking like me*. For some reason *that* makes me even happier than the prospect of Josh seeing me in such a stunning dress.

"And if anyone asks, they're BCBG originals. I sewed labels into them."

I don't know what a *BCBG original* is, but it seems important to Ivy, so I commit it to memory. In case someone asks. Although I doubt it.

No one ever talks to me in school.

ALTHOUGH I NEVER WEAR MAKEUP, Ivy adds mascara to my lashes and bright pink lipstick to my mouth. She's even relaxed my hair so that it falls in supple curls over my bare shoulders. Hers is blow-dried completely straight and dips down her spine in a swath of gold.

Between the shininess of her dress and the glittery oil she's rubbed over her collarbone, she resembles a bronze statuette of a goddess. Plus, she has on these high-heeled silver pumps worthy of one of those shops I would never dare enter at the mall because there are too many zeros on the price tag.

"I found them at Goodwill and spray-painted them silver." She grimaces. "Can you tell? Do they look cheap?"

"Nothing looks cheap on you."

"Yeah, yeah." She swats my arm, shakes her head. "What shoes are you wearing?" She starts rifling through my half of the closet. It doesn't take her long to discover that I only own two pairs of shoes: my beat-up Converses and the pair of brown sandals that are a size too small.

"Should I wear my sandals?"

Ivy bites her lower lip. "You know what, let's be fashion-forward and wear Converses."

"But...but your shoes are so pretty."

"Yeah, but they're not comfortable." She slides her feet out. "Want to try them on?"

I shake my head. I could never wear heels. I'd trip and fall, and I don't need more people pointing and staring.

She sets them neatly on the closet floor and pulls out her Converses. They're identical to mine, except hers are black instead of cream—the shoes were a Christmas present from Josh's parents.

When we make our way into the living room to wait for our dates, Mom's on the couch watching TV, fingers moving instinctively over patches of fabric. Sewing is second nature to her, like computer keyboards are to me.

"We won't be home late." Ivy walks toward the kitchen and grabs a carton of orange juice. She pours out two glasses and hands one to me. "What do you think of the dresses?" Holding her drink out so it doesn't spill, Ivy twirls.

Mom looks away from the TV screen, takes in my sister from head to toe. She doesn't speak for a little while, merely runs her light blue eyes up and down and across my sister as though checking for a foiled stitch or an uneven hemline. "It's beautiful on you, Ivy."

"Isn't the blue stunning on Aster?"

As though remembering there are two of us, Mom's gaze surfs over to me. Her milky forehead crinkles like parchment paper. "Would look better if she actually ate something."

She often talks to me in the third person. I think she believes it'll offend me less if the criticism is delivered indirectly. A tiny frown clouds my twin's face. I lay a hand on her forearm.

Gaze stuck to my salient collarbone, she adds, "But the color's nice on her." Her eyes crawl up to mine and linger. Sadness gusts though them and sparkles like the dust motes suspended in the sunset light slanting through the living room window. Sometimes, I feel like there are a million things Mom wants to tell me but doesn't dare, or simply can't. Like two magnets, we repel each other.

The doorbell rings.

"Sean taking both of you?" she asks.

"No. Josh's taking Aster."

"Josh asked you?" Her translucent eyebrows arch.

I nod as Ivy pulls the door open.

"Is his mother making him?" Mom asks.

Josh stands on our doormat in a fitted navy tux that seems barely able to contain his pecs.

My heart gallops as his eyes meet mine.

"Hi, Mrs. Redd," he says tightly. "Ives." He saves my name for last. "Aster." It rolls off his tongue like a deep gasp, like a prolonged heartbeat.

"Can you even breathe?" Ivy asks him, patting his stomach.

He unbuttons his jacket. "Barely." He winks. "The rental shop was out of suits, so I borrowed my cousin Vinny's wedding suit."

Headlights ignite our street, and then a red Toyota parks next to Josh's Camry.

"Whoa!" Sean gasps when he spots Ivy.

Sean has greasy blond hair. Every time I see him, I want to wash his long bangs or chop them off. But who am I to give tonsorial advice to anyone? Most of the time, I can't be bothered to style my own hair.

"Lookin' hot, girls."

Girls.

I blink.

He means me too.

"Eyes off my date, Braxton," Josh says, wrapping an arm around my waist.

"Bye, Mom," Ivy yells right before shutting our front door.

Some mothers would be snapping pictures or doling out unwanted sexual advice, but not our mother. I think she's glad when we get out of her sight, out of her house. When I menstruated at eleven, she told me to avoid getting knocked up, but that was it. No birds-and-bees conversations. No dating guidance. Not that I would've wanted any from her—after all, she wasn't able to keep our dad around—but advice would've shown she cared.

Josh opens the door for me, and I get in. When we pull away from our street, he says, "And by the way, Mom is *not* making me take you."

FOUR

JOSH

I really don't like Mrs. Redd. She isn't fit to be a mother.

I've thought that since the first time I met the twins in the McDonald's jungle gym. While my parents ordered me a McFlurry—I still ate those back then—I dove into the ball pool. Instead of landing on squashy plastic, I landed on something sharp and trembling. I dug through the balls, sending them shooting against the net, until I unburied this tiny body with a shock of wild blonde curls and tears streaming down her cheeks.

That was the first time I laid eyes on Aster Redd.

I remember thinking her tears were my fault, that somehow, I hurt her when I landed on her. At eight, I weighed as much as a thirteen-year-old. Once she calmed down, she explained she was crying because she couldn't surface from the balls. Her eyes had been so red that her blue irises appeared radioactive.

A second later, her lookalike trundled down the slide, waded through the multi-colored balls in a panic, and heaved her sister into a sitting position. I blinked a bunch of times, then muttered how much they resembled each other, and identical huge grins slashed their faces.

We played together until my parents said it was time to go, and then, as I was putting on my shoes, I asked Aster and Ivy if they were leaving too. They said they were waiting for their mother to come back. Mom asked when that would be, and they shrugged their knobby shoulders.

Their mother had up and left them there all by themselves. "They're five-year-olds!" I remember Mom telling Dad, puffing her cheeks out, way more furious than when I'd used my sled to glide down our stairs a month before.

Dad bought the twins and me Happy Meals as we waited for their mother. By nightfall, my parents packed us all into the suburban, excusing themselves for not having booster seats. The twins stared at Mom as though she'd sprouted a jetpack. They didn't know what booster seats were.

After sticking us all in front of the TV—*Ninja Turtles* was on—Mom called the cops. They arrived soon after. Even though I found them intimidating at first, they showed us their badges and let us touch them, and the woman cop, Jackie, told us about a robber they'd just caught trying to shoplift a gumball machine.

That was the day I decided I would become a cop. For the badge, but also because capturing bad guys stealing gumball machines sounded like fun.

From that day on, Mom, along with a bunch of appointed social workers, visited the Redd household regularly.

The girls know they can run to my mother with their problems. But they run to me instead. They know I would do anything for them. Same way I know they would do anything for me.

I glance over at Aster, who's toying with the blue silk of her dress. She looks like a siren tonight, like a movie star, like one of those flowers that bloom only after sundown. Guys will be checking her out. I clasp the steering wheel tighter.

Aster doesn't fare well with attention. Maybe I should suggest we go hang out at my place or something. "You sure you want to go in there?" I ask, as I park next to the gymnasium.

She spins her head toward me, eyes wide, panicked. "Y-you don't want to take—"

I gather her hand in mine. "I *want* to take you, but I don't want you to be uncomfortable."

"As long as you're with me, it'll be okay."

"We can go home whenever you want."

I let go of her hand, and we get out of the car. Dozens of students are hanging out outside. Red dots glow in the darkness. Cigarettes.

As we walk past them, the looks start.

I latch on to Aster's hand. She tips her head up toward me. I'm usually good at reading her, but her emotions are muffled tonight. Or maybe I'm paying too much attention to everyone else to focus on what she's feeling.

I get a few *heys* and a couple of fist bumps. I've been gone two years, yet people remember me.

Gazes slide up and down Aster's body. I tuck her closer to me.

"Nice dress, Ivy," Luke says, sidling up to my date. Luke and Ivy dated millions of years ago. He's still into her, but the feeling isn't mutual.

"Aster," she corrects him softly.

"What?" he asks.

"I'm Aster. Not Ivy," she murmurs.

Luke does a double take. "Serious?"

"Yes, Luke, *serious*." It's Ivy who says this. I didn't even notice she'd caught up to us.

Sean wears a trace of lipstick on his jaw.

Ivy grins at Luke, who's still standing there dumbstruck, eyes volleying between the two sisters.

Ivy smiles at his bewilderment. Or maybe it's swapping spit with Sean that's made her smile. Aster, though, has become rigid as a log. She's never been a fan of attention, especially since it was almost always negative. I know a thing or two about being bullied, since I was the butt of jokes during my chubby days. It was a long time ago, but the sting and the nickname—Hamster—never went away.

"Say the word, and we go home," I whisper in Aster's ear.

She shivers, combs a lock of hair back. "It's okay. I'm okay. Let's go inside."

"We don't have to."

Determination tightens her features. "I want to."

The enormous room vibrates with the sound of drums, electric guitar, and the high-pitched voices of the three girls on the makeshift stage. The school hired a band, like they usually do, but unlike at previous events, these chicks rock. They play a song from One Republic, but they've tweaked the rhythm, and it's catchy.

Ivy and Sean make a beeline toward the dance floor, where they melt into the crowd.

"Is Ivy dating Sean?" I ask Aster over the sound of the music.

"I don't think so, or if they are, she hasn't told me."

"Or it started tonight," I say. "Ivy tells you everything."

"Does she?" Aster looks up at me.

"Yes. She does." The mashed bodies remind me of the last time I partied on that dance floor. I feel like such a different person now. Confident and chill. I have college to thank for that.

"Are you jealous?" Aster's voice sends my gaze soaring back to her.

"Jealous? Of Sean?"

She bites her bottom lip and nods.

"I'm not jealous. Ivy's like my sister." I almost add *like you are*. But I don't.

I'm not sure why.

I spot a group of guys standing by the bar, ogling Aster. I narrow my eyes at them, but they don't look away. Instead, they whisper among themselves.

"Want to dance?" I ask her.

"Sure."

I lead her onto the dance floor and twirl her, and then I let her go. Aster has awesome rhythm. I'm actually surprised by how good she is. "Have you been taking dance lessons?"

"What?" she asks.

Her hands are in the air and she's swaying to the new song. I dip my face closer to her ear and repeat my question.

She shakes her head.

"Well, you're really good," I say.

She spins her face, probably to tell me I'm being too nice. That's her usual line when I give her a compliment. Before she can get the words out, before I can tell her to stop putting herself down, our lips brush. Startled, she pulls away, and so do I.

For the next half hour, although we remain on the dance floor together, the gap between our bodies stays as wide as the tube slide in the MacDonald's jungle gym.

I bridge some of the distance to tell her my parents are thinking of putting a Jacuzzi in our backyard. "Wouldn't that be awesome?"

Her eyes are a little red, which makes her irises stand out.

"Aster, are you okay?"

Her lashes lower. She nods, but there's no weight to her nod. I grip her hand and lead her off the dance floor. Her fingers are lax in mine. When we're away from the crowd, I tilt her head up.

"What's wrong?"

She closes her eyes. "I want to go home."

"Okay. Let me tell Ives we're going. Wait for me here okay?"

She nods, then folds her arms in front of her. I don't want to leave her alone, but I need to find Ivy, and I'm pretty sure she's sandwiched in the crowd. I don't want Aster to get locked between bodies and feel as though she's floundering again, stuck.

I find Ivy slow-dancing with Sean to a song that definitely doesn't warrant a slow dance, faces squished together. I tap her shoulder.

"I'm going to take Aster home. She's tired."

She angles her face to the side. "Did someone say something to her?"

"No."

"You promise?"

"I promise."

"Okay. Tell her I'll be home soon anyway."

"Not too soon," Sean says.

She smiles even though her face is full of concern. "Thanks for taking her home, Josh."

I rake my hand through my hair. "Of course."

She gives me a hug. "I mean it."

Before I let her go, I add, "Be good."

"Don't worry."

"I always worry."

"Well don't. At least not about me." She winks and turns back toward Sean.

I walk back to where I left Aster, but she's no longer there. Panic stirs in my gut. I check the bathroom and ask a couple of girls waiting in line if they've seen her.

One of them asks, "Who's Aster?"

"The weird twin," another one says.

My fingers jam into a fist.

One of her friends must feel my anger, because she adds, "Chill out. She's not here."

I run back into the gym and scan the dark crowd for blonde hair and a blue dress. I see a lot of blonde and blue, but I don't see Aster. Crazy thoughts catapult through my mind. What if a dude forced her to dance with him? Or maybe someone made fun of her and she's hiding in a corner of the gym?

After one last sweep of the room, I push out the doors into the warm Kokomoan night. My eyes snap to my car. A slender figure is standing rigidly next to it.

I sprint over to her. "Why are you out here?"

"I...too many people were staring at me." She's wringing her hands together.

I want to catch her hands and squeeze them in mine and tell her that everyone was checking her out because she was the prettiest girl in the gym tonight, but I don't do or say any of these things. "I think I'm too old for high school dances."

"Sorry."

"Why are you sorry?"

"For making you go."

I step closer to her. "You didn't make me go; *I* made *you* go. If anyone should be sorry it's me." Her head is tipped toward me, and her wide blue eyes shimmer. "Are you crying?"

She blinks, and one of her hands comes up and presses against her eyes, smudging her black eye makeup. I bet Ivy put it on her, because Aster doesn't usually wear makeup. "No."

I know she's lying, and yet I don't ask her why or who made her cry, because deep down I'm aware of the answer.

Me.

I made her go to a dance she didn't feel comfortable attending.

I thought I was doing her a favor when I offered to take her, but favors should make people happy. Coming tonight *did not* make her happy.

FIVE

Aster

"There's something wrong with Mom," I tell Josh in a low voice when I stop by his mother's bakery.

It's been three weeks since he kissed me. He hasn't mentioned it; I haven't either. I think he's afraid to start something with me, afraid it might complicate our friendship if it doesn't work out. Deep down, I'm afraid too. I can't lose Josh. He's everything that's right in my life. Like Ivy. Although she's also a reminder of everything that's wrong with it. It's not her fault that she's perfect and smart and beautiful. Just like my imperfections aren't any fault of mine. They come down to genetics and love. We might be twins, but we didn't receive the same number of good genes or the same amount of tenderness. I made my peace with this inequality a long time ago.

"What do you mean there's something wrong with her?" Josh asks.

I look down at the plate of mini donuts he's placed in front of me. There are three. The glazed, golden buoys of dough remind me of Josh, Ivy, and me. "The world isn't fair," I say, thinking about my faulty genetic predisposition.

"Aster?" His voice is so sharp I look up into his tanned, chiseled face. He turned twenty not long ago and has a man's face now. "What do you mean there's something wrong with your mother?"

"I think she wants to kill me," I whisper this so as not to alarm his mother, who's serving some customers a few feet away.

He jerks up straighter. "What?"

I press my lips together. "Inside her sewing room, she has this drawer she keeps locked. Yesterday, I was clipping the buttonbush when I saw her open it, pull something hard and black from inside. It looked like a gun."

"A gun? Why would she have a gun? Is she afraid of someone?"

I bristle at his suggestion. "I would never harm her."

His long dark lashes repeatedly sweep up and down over his dazzling green eyes. "I didn't mean to protect herself from you. I meant to protect herself from someone else."

"You think someone's after her?"

"Have you asked her?"

"I was afraid to bring it up. Afraid she might move it if I mentioned seeing it. I'd rather she didn't know I'm aware of it."

"We have to ask Ivy."

I shake my head slowly. "No."

"Why not?"

"Ivy and Mom are close, Josh."

"Don't you trust your sister?"

"Of course I do. I trust that she's protecting me. I trust that she's controlling and monitoring the situation. You know Mom's not always *there*, right?"

His forehead ridges, either in surprise or in concern. Maybe it's both.

"She's schizophrenic," I whisper across the small round table. "But don't tell your mom. I don't want to worry her."

He glances at his mother. For a second, I think he'll tell her, but his mouth doesn't open, his lips don't shift. Everything in his face tightens. "I won't tell her."

"Thank you." My gaze dips to his lips, and my pulse swarms and hums inside my veins. I close my eyes to harness the desire to lay my lips on his. "I need to get some groceries. I'm making pizza tonight. You want to come over?"

"I can't tonight."

I probably scared him with my talk of guns and schizophrenia. What sane person would willingly enter a house with an unbalanced, weapon-toting woman? Even though Josh wants to be a cop, he's not one, yet. I start to push away from the table when he says, "You didn't eat anything, Aster."

I stare at the donuts. "Right. I forgot." I'm not hungry, but I pluck one off the plate and bite into it. I swallow without chewing, then gulp down the second half. In seconds, I make the remaining two donuts vanish as well. I don't want Maggie to think I'm ungrateful for the free food she's always giving me.

I kiss Josh's bristly cheek and fill myself with his warm, liquid citrus scent. He smells like grapefruit juice and sunflowers, like rainstorms on a summer day. I smile at him, and then I smile at Maggie and leave the small bakery, holding the door open for a little girl with uneven pigtails. She darts in on a purple scooter, wispy hair ribboning behind her. Her mother ducks in behind her, thanking me for holding the door. She has kind eyes and a gentle smile. She must be a good mother.

Déjà vu gels inside my brain like the foam spray I used in our bathroom last month to suppress an ant infestation. But it can't be a déjà vu because I've never seen this little girl *or* her mother. It's a vision of my future. One day I'll have a little pigtailed girl. I feel it in my gut.

I gaze back at Josh.

His eyes are on me.

Did he experience the same déjà vu? I dare to wonder if he'll be her father.

His gaze skims the top of the little girl's head, which doesn't quite reach the marble countertop, then returns to mine. Something gleams in his eyes.

He feels it too.

I want to stay with him, but I have to take care of my sister and mother. Someone has to do the grocery shopping. Our cupboards and refrigerator don't magically replenish themselves. So I leave, the baby-pink awning of Little Cakes fluttering over my head like a swaddle cloth.

I stare up. At its pinkness. And then I stare beyond it, at the pieces of blue sky visible behind the gray and white buildings of Kokomo, and thank whoever's up there for giving me visions of better things to come.

The name Violet forms inside my mind like a delicate soap bubble.

I don't know anyone by that name, which leads me to guess that it's another sign, another vision.

Violet will be my daughter's name.

Violet.

Violet.

Violet.

It plays on a loop inside my mind like a lullaby. It beats against my eardrums like a heartbeat.

Her heartbeat.

Clinging to the fragile gift bestowed upon me, I fill a basket with dry pasta and a few fresh items. I don't go overboard in the produce aisles because vegetables and fruit are expensive, but I grab a few peaches for Ivy. They're her favorite. I pick up some bananas for Mom, making sure they're still streaked green. She hates when they've ripened and bruised, even though she'll still eat them.

After paying, I return to my new car. It's a third-hand Honda with rattling suspension and shedding paint, but it's mine, which makes it the most precious thing I own. When I'm behind the wheel, cruising down roads with air conditioning licking the tip of my nose, I feel like the luckiest girl alive, like my new purchase was the first step toward success and change, like I can escape Kokomo. But I can't. I could never leave Ivy and Josh.

Stopped at the traffic light, I swivel and imagine a car seat strapped behind me. I love babies, but never considered having one before. Now, I can't stop thinking about Violet. I can't stop wondering if she'll have a little mole over her upper lip like I do. Are moles genetic?

A car honks behind me. I twist back around and find the light has changed to green. I press on the gas pedal and shoot through the intersection. A few blocks from home, I spot a woman exiting a shop. What snags my attention is the strawberry-blonde-grayness of her hair and the wispy texture of it. This woman has the exact same hair as Mom. When she turns around, I realize it *is* Mom.

I pull up by the curb and am about to call out to her and offer her a ride home, when I get sidetracked by the name of the place: PSYCHIC READINGS BY DONNA. It's written in pink neon lights set against a beaded curtain. Outside, two squares of AstroTurf have been laid out and topped with flashy orange furniture: two chairs and a small table.

Mom's laid her bag down on the table and is rifling through it. She hasn't spotted me yet. If I leave now, she might not even see the car.

But I'm a good daughter.

Even if she's not a good mother.

I lean over the passenger seat to roll down the window. "Mom!" I call out.

Her face jerks up, and her eyes, like laser beams, settle on me.

"Do you want a ride home?"

She walks over to the car, bends, and peers through the window. "Were you following me, Aster?"

I'm taken aback. "No. I was on my way home."

She grunts. Her mental disease makes her distrustful.

I gesture to the grocery bag in the backseat. After scrutinizing it lengthily, she opens the door and gets in, placing her enormous purse on her lap. I wonder if the gun's inside. I try to glimpse the contents, but she pulls it tighter against her.

I zip my gaze back to the road and pull away from the curb. "Did Donna give you some good insights into your future?" I don't know if she'll answer me, but it beats the stale silence. I should be used to it after seventeen years.

"I didn't ask about my future."

"Oh." I glance at her.

"I inquired after Ivy's. She's going to have great success one day. Lots of money. It'll pour down over her. And she saw twin towers."

"You mean like Ivy and me?"

"I mean like *the* twin towers."

"Mom, they crashed down during 9/11."

"I'm not an idiot." Her blue eyes have soaked up the shadows of the car. "Of course they crashed down back in 2001, but they still represent New York to a lot of people. The fact that the psychic saw them means New York is in Ivy's future."

Mom's always dreamed of living in the Big Apple, and she almost did, but then she got pregnant with us. She reminds us that we ruined her dream at least once a year. Usually, it's on our birthday, which is four days before Christmas. Her sorrow colors the rest of holidays in various shades of dull gray.

"And me? Did the psychic say anything about me?" I dare ask.

Mom blinks, which blunts the sparkle. "I didn't ask about you."

I suck at my teeth. I don't want to care, but I do. Sadness coils through me, laces around my belly and squeezes it like butcher twine.

"I always felt Ivy was going to do well for herself, but having confirmation is reassuring."

I'm so tempted to say *She's a psychic, Mom. Psychics are not higher beings.*

They're money-grubbing, cunning people who possess an affinity for human psychology. I don't say any of this though.

During the rest of the car ride, while Mom drones on about Ivy's magnificent future, I think of my unborn baby girl.

Of my little Violet.

The sweet girl whose smiles will erase all the badness from my world.

SIX

JOSH

I call Ivy the minute Aster leaves the bakery and ask her about the gun. Mom's standing next to me. She keeps one eye on her seated customers and the other on my drumming fingers.

"Gun?" Ivy exclaims. "Aster thinks Mom has a gun?"

"Yeah."

"Why would Mom have a gun?"

"I don't know, Ivy."

I hear her walk around the apartment. "Where did Aster say she saw it?"

"In the sewing room. In your mother's locked drawer."

"She only keeps fabric in there."

"Under lock and key?"

Mom's bright red lips are pursed in worry.

"Only reason someone would lock anything up is to keep it away from others," I say.

"I know it sounds weird, but"—I hear something scrape and swoosh on her end—"Mom's weird. Look, I don't have the key, but when she gets home, I'll ask her to open it so I can check."

"You think she'll open it?"

"If she has nothing to hide, yeah."

The door chimes, so Mom bustles back behind the marble countertop to serve her customer.

I shove my hand through my hair, tugging at the short roots. "Ives, is it me or is Aster acting a little strange?"

"Strange how?"

"Distracted. Apprehensive."

A long pause. "Yes. Ever since the dance. I thought something might have happened between the two of you, but I didn't want to pry."

"Nothing happened." I sigh. "Has she been taking her pills?"

"Let me check." Her footsteps echo through the receiver. "Seems like she has. But maybe she's been flushing them down the toilet." She exhales a whistling breath. "What am I supposed to do, Josh? Grind them up in her food and feed them to her?"

"You need to talk to her. Maybe she has been taking them, but they're losing their effect. If that's the case, you need to get her on new ones." She doesn't say anything for such a long time, I add, "Or I can get her new ones. You're not alone, Ives. I'm here too. Never forget that."

She breathes. Just breathes. "Sometimes, I really want to leave this place. Hit the road and go somewhere. Anywhere. Preferably New York, but really, I'd take *anywhere*." Her voice wobbles. "I want to run away from both of them." Her low, gravelly voice sends a shiver up my spine.

"How about you stay at my house for a few days? You and Aster both?"

"That'd be nice. Are you sure Maggie wouldn't mind?"

"Mom's fine with it. She's giving me a thumbs-up." She's actually plating a brightly frosted cupcake, but I know she'll be okay with my impromptu invite. The girls have stayed over often in the past twelve years. "Call me later okay? After you check the drawer…" I remind her in case talking about her sister's and mother's conditions has made her forget about the gun.

I spend the next few hours helping Mom clean the bakery. As we lock up, Ivy calls me back.

"There's no gun," she says in a hushed voice.

I hold my eyes closed for a second. "You're sure?"

"Yes. And Aster confessed to having stopped her meds."

I squeeze the bridge of my nose and sigh.

"Yeah," she says softly.

"You want me to come over?"

"I think it might be overwhelming. Let me talk to her."

"Okay." I finally open my eyes.

Mom's staring at me, keys still dangling from her hand. Worry tracks concern into her laugh lines. She always complains about having wrinkles, but then Dad reminds her that not everyone gets to have them, that it's a great privilege to age, and she becomes okay with them.

"Is Aster okay?" Mom asks me.

I lower my phone and murmur back, "She will be."

Ivy and I will make sure of that.

AS DAD FIRES up the barbecue, I sit on the porch swing next to Ivy. She has her legs tucked underneath her and is staring at the screen of her cell phone. An old guy is revealing the identity of the contestants on the televised art competition she was telling me about.

Aster's in the kitchen with my mother. They're frosting Mom's world-famous blackout cake.

"Did you secretly apply?" I nod toward her screen.

"You have to be eighteen. So next year."

I watch the pictures of the nominees appear on her screen, but it's really boring, so I get off the swing and join my apron-clad father at the grill. He's talking with Jackie, the responding officer on that long-ago night who told us about the gumball machine theft.

At the beginning, my parents' and Jackie's interaction revolved around the twins' well-being. Then Jackie started joining our post-church Sunday brunches and over-the-top Thanksgivings.

I dig a bottle of water out of the cooler and gulp half of it down. It's late, but still so freaking hot. I run the bottle over the nape of my neck to cool down, then discuss Dad's latest construction projects. He runs a concrete finishing company started by my grandfather. He'd like me to take over, which is one of the reasons I'm getting a business degree, but I'd still rather be a cop.

"We landed the Discoli landfill commission," he tells me.

The Discolis own the largest private trash-collecting company in Indiana. There are rumors that trash isn't their only line of business. But their other line of business isn't legit, and thus no one talks about it.

"You don't say," Jackie says, sipping her beer.

"Don't start, Jackie."

She lifts one palm and holds it out in front of her. "I didn't say anything."

"Are they looking to cover dead bodies with cement?" I ask.

Dad's eyes grow as wide as the Portobello mushroom caps laid on the grill. "Joshua Cooper!" he exclaims, gaze zipping from Jackie to me.

"What?"

"That's not nice."

The Discolis are mafia. Everyone knows it.

Jackie grins at me. "That's my boy."

"I can see you've been rubbing off on him," Dad grumbles.

"How are they paying you?" I ask him.

"What do you mean?"

"Cash? Wire transfer? Gold bars?"

"Ha ha. By check."

"Uh-huh." Jackie winks at me. "You'll show me those checks, right? And you'll let me know if you find any bodies below the cement?"

I chuckle.

Dad sets the long metal tongs down on a mound of raw sausages and marinated lamb chops. "The checks will be certified. I would never accept anything else." He stares between Jackie and me. "It's a big project, which means a big paycheck. One the company could use right now."

I frown. "Are we in the red?"

"We're okay, but there are a lot of salaries and the market's been slow. I couldn't turn down the deal."

No one says no to the Discolis anyway. Either the money's too good to refuse or your life is too valuable to give up. There is no dream death, but ending up face down in a landfill is pretty much the worst conceivable kind, and that usually happens when you turn that family down.

"I'm not judging," Jackie says. "I'm simply wary of that bunch. Comes with the job."

"Did you tell Mom?" I ask.

Dad's cheek dimples as though he were biting it. He probably is. Although he and Mom discuss everything, and I mean *everything*—full-disclosure-no-secrets-everything—Mom fears the Discolis, like most Kokomoans. When she found out I was enrolled in the same summer camp as their son five years back, she told me to stay the hell away from him. Mom never curses, so using the word *hell* really marked me. Not that I would've hung out with the dude. He's a conceited prick who buys alliances with wads of dirty cash.

Dad's eyes dart behind Jackie. "I'm going to tell her. Eventually. Don't—"

"I won't say anything, but tell her," Jackie says.

I nod my agreement.

He runs a hand through hair that's the same brown as mine, but longer. He used to wear it in a ponytail, but thankfully chopped it off when I hit thirteen. "Not tonight," he says.

Mom crosses the lawn toward us, clutching a cake stand topped with a monstrous chocolate creation. There must be close to ten thousand calories in that thing.

"And people wonder why I used to be fat," I say, as she puts it down on the table, filling the humid air with the heady aroma of cocoa and butter.

Mom swats the back of my head. "You were never fat."

I snort. "Right. I was *pudgy*." I was fat.

Arms braced around a bowl of salad, Aster walks over to us.

"I think just smelling that thing is adding pounds to my waistline," I joke.

"I'll eat your share," Aster says, grinning up at me. "I'm starving."

"Glad to see you got your appetite back," I tell her.

I'm not really talking about her desire to eat cake though; I'm talking about her desire to live, to indulge. Ivy managed to get her back on her meds forty-eight hours ago by promising to get rid of their mother's "gun."

Already, Aster's a different person. Happier, almost serene. Her eyes are as cloudless as the dusky sky above us, and her smile as shiny as the sun poking through our picket fence. I want to freeze this moment, store it for the days that aren't as clear and bright.

If only her pills were a cure instead of Band-Aids, but there is no cure for schizophrenia.

SEVEN

Aster

Today is Mom's birthday.

She hates celebrating it, yet every year, Ivy and I make it a point to do something special for her. This year, we're taking her out to a fancy restaurant. It's Ivy's idea. I wouldn't have dared set foot in La Finestra otherwise. I wear the blue dress Ivy made me for Junior Prom.

When Mom walks into the apartment, both Ivy and I spring off the couch and sing Happy Birthday.

She claps her hand over her heart—well, over her handbag that she carries against her torso. "You scared me!"

Ivy smiles. "Sorry, Mom."

"Are you going somewhere?" she asks, brows knitting on her freckled forehead.

"Yes. And so are you," Ivy tells her. "We're taking you to dinner."

"Oh." Mom's eyes are so wide, I can't tell if the idea is shocking or appealing.

"Whenever you're ready," I tell her, pushing a strand of unruly hair off my face and locking it behind my ear.

"Okay." She eyes us again. "Why is Aster dressed like she's about to attend a red-carpet event?"

I suddenly feel self-conscious about wearing a floor-length dress.

"It's a nice restaurant," Ivy says.

"*You're* not wearing a gown," Mom comments.

"I felt like a skirt tonight." Ivy darts a glance my way. "But I'm probably underdressed."

"I don't have anything fancy to wear."

"What about the Diane Von Furstenberg wrap dress we bought you last year?" Ivy suggests.

"I sold it."

My sister's disappointment leaches the pinkness from her cheeks. "Oh." She swallows hard. "You didn't like it?"

"It was nice, but I owed someone money."

She probably had to pay that Donna lady or another psychic. "You can wear my dress, Mom," I offer. "I'm sure I have something else—"

Mom grimaces. "You're a size minus zero, Aster. Besides, I like pants better." Still holding her bag close to her chest, she walks through the living room and disappears down the corridor.

When I hear her door close, I whisper, "Is it me, or was she holding on to her bag awfully tight?"

"She sold our present," Ivy mumbles.

I sigh, then wrap my arms around my sister and hug her gently.

"Promise you'll never sell the dress I made you." Her voice is hoarse.

"Are you kidding me? Never! It's the most beautiful thing I own!"

She hiccups.

I hold her tighter. "I solemnly swear to keep it forever and ever." When I sense her breathing has evened out, I release her. "I should probably go clean up the backseat of my car before we head out."

"I'll help."

In the time it takes Mom to get ready, Ivy and I have rid my backseat of two empty pastry boxes and vacuumed the dried crumbs stockpiled in the groove between the seat cushion and the backrest.

"You look really pretty, Mom," I say.

For once, she's put on makeup, tinting her diaphanous lashes black and her pale lips mauve.

A blush highlights her freckles, adding another layer of color to her features. "Thank you."

During the drive over, Mom and Ivy discuss a new idea for a quilt while I focus on getting us to the restaurant.

The radio purrs a Christina Aguilera song in the background. I want to turn up the volume but am afraid to disturb the ongoing conversation. In my head, I sing along, and the music fills me, making me feel as light as a dandelion floret.

It was the song playing in the gym when Josh and I kissed.

We still haven't discussed it. I'm waiting for him to mention it, but maybe I'll have to bring it up. I wonder if I should do it over the phone or in person. I weigh the pros and cons of both. When we reach our destination, I still haven't made up my mind.

Mom presses her lips together before entering the dimly lit Italian restaurant. I feel as nervous as she does. The only one who seems perfectly at ease in our fancy surroundings is Ivy. I swear, my sister was born in the wrong family, but by God am I happy she was born in mine. I don't know how I would've survived if it had only been Mom and me.

Dripping candles are the main source of light in the small eatery. The effect is sultry, even though it makes scoping out diners' plates near impossible. I can't tell mozzarella from chicken. I rely on my sense of smell, and inhale the air that's flecked with paprika, fresh herbs, fried dough, and melted cheese. My stomach growls.

We are shown to a small table against a wall covered in flowery wallpaper. It reminds me of the butterfly print on our bedroom walls. The familiarity slackens the tension in my shoulders. I slide into one of the chairs and take the tendered menu.

As Mom and Ivy decide what to order, I slip my hand inside the little knit bag and discreetly count the twenties I peeled out of my pillowcase. Ivy contributed one and Maggie another—her present to my mother. I count five. I was sure I'd brought six. Could one have fallen out?

Cold blood prickles my face as I search the floor next to my feet for a folded green bill. I find none. And then I remember…

I used it to fill my car's fuel tank.

The realization tumbles on me like the Olympic bar Josh lifts at his gym, crushing, embarrassing, worrying.

Most entrées are priced between fifteen and twenty dollars so I wait for Mom and Ivy to order. My choice will be based on what I can afford.

Our waitress comes over with a pitcher of iced water, which she pours generously into our long-stemmed glasses. "Are you ready to order, ladies?"

Ivy nods. She selects the lentil soup—$9—followed by the spaghetti carbonara —$19—while Mom asks for the buffalo mozzarella—$13—and the truffle linguini. I gulp when I notice the twenty-seven-dollar price tag.

"I'll have the chocolate soufflé for dessert," Ivy says. $6.

"And I'll take the tiramisu." $7.

Twenty-nine dollars left.

"And I'll have a glass of Prosecco," Mom tells the waitress. I quickly scan the price of Prosecco by the glass. $7.50. "And one glass of the Pinot Grigio with my pasta." $5.

I factor tax and tip. That leaves me with five dollars.

I don't see anything for five dollars.

"How much is a green salad?" I ask.

"Five-fifty."

Her answer crushes me all over again. With trembling hands, I hand the waitress my menu, blink, lashes sweeping back hot tears. "I'm not really hungry," I mumble.

"Aster, you have to eat," Ivy says.

Ivy must not realize I used one of the twenties to buy gas. Because I don't want to make her feel guilty, I repeat the line of not being hungry, and add, "I'll just have some bread."

"Bread is extra."

I wince. "A lot extra?"

"Two-fifty."

"Great," I say.

"She's struggling with anorexia," Mom tells the waitress.

A lump forms in my throat. I seize my sweaty glass of water and drink heavily.

"Mom," Ivy whispers, but Mom tells me how unhealthy it is, that it's a real disease. She enumerates all the effects it will have on my body.

I'll lose my teeth and hair.

My brain will be damaged.

My muscles will deteriorate.

I'll become infertile.

The vision I had of my baby girl settles over me like a balm. I focus everything I feel, everything I am on my precious progeny.

IVY INSISTED on sharing her spaghetti carbonara with me. She must have remembered our stop at the gas station, must have done the math and realized my refusal to eat had nothing to do with anorexia.

It was the best pasta dish I have ever eaten. My taste buds are still swimming in the richness of the sauce, in the saltiness of the crisp bacon pieces, in the creaminess of the Parmesan. I spend most of the ride home recreating the recipe in my mind so I can make it tomorrow. By the time we pull into our driveway, I have the list of ingredients etched inside my brain.

Cream.

Peas.

Parmesan.

Bacon.

"Watch out!"

Mom's shriek startles me out of my grocery list. Startles me, period. Something thuds underneath the car's front left tire.

I brake.

I don't dare move. None of us move. For long seconds, the only sound inside the car is our heavy, shuddering breaths.

I hit something.

Something soft.

Small.

I hope it's not one of our neighbor's children. I pray to God—if there is one—that it's not a child. I will die if I killed an innocent human being.

After an excruciating eternity, I click my seatbelt off. It releases me in slow motion.

I close my eyes, take three deep breaths, then push my door open.

Slowly, I lower myself to the ground. The pavement digs into my palms and bare knees. Soft mewing makes bile rise in my throat.

I crane my neck, spot a tiny form writhing in the shadows.

Not a child.

The crumpled body shudders, the fur shivers.

I catch the glint of glow-in-the-dark eyes and silver fur. It's a cat.

"Shit," Ivy says, crouching down beside me.

Sweat trickles down the nape of my neck, soaks into the blue silk of my dress. Her curse word doesn't begin to describe the horror of the situation.

"That's Mr. Mancini's cat," she adds.

"Is it still alive?" Mom asks, coming around the car.

"Yeah," Ivy says, "but I don't think for long. Shit."

I'm going to be sick. Vomit rises up my throat. I jolt out of my crouch and rush to the buttonbush plant and hurl my delicious meal. I taste the cream; it's bitter now. I taste the bacon; lumpy. I taste the pasta; bland and slimy.

"We have to put it out of its misery," Ivy says.

Rubbing my mouth against my bare forearm, I walk back toward the scene of the crime. "I'll go"—my throat clenches—"I'll go get Mr. Mancini."

"I got it," Mom says.

For the first time in my life, I look upon her with gratitude. She's going to help me. She's going to make this moment less terrible. She'll take care of my cruel error. Fix it.

"Thank you," I whisper, at the same time as Ivy says, "How?"

I gape at my bleak-faced twin, then gape at my mother. *Right. How?* Mom pulls something out of her bag.

Something dark and sharp.

Something that goes bang in the black night.

EIGHT

JOSH

I don't think I've ever run so fast.

"Stay with me," I tell Aster over the phone as I jump over a curb, legs and arms pumping like karate chops. I lent my car to a buddy, and my parents drove over to a friend's house in the next town over, so there was no vehicle in my driveway. I thought about calling a cab, but didn't want to wait, so I started running the two miles separating me from the twins.

"She shot it." Aster's voice is a horrified whisper.

A loud voice barks through the phone.

"Our upstairs' neighbor is threatening to call the cops," she whimpers.

"It's going to be all right," I reassure her.

From what I gather, Aster ran over their neighbor's cat, and then her mother put it out of its misery with the gun Ivy told me she didn't own. Aster was right. Her mother has a gun.

None of us took her seriously.

"Is Mr. Mancini still there?" I ask through labored breaths. I thought I was in good shape, but I can barely breathe.

"He's talking with Mom," she murmurs. There are tears in her voice. I can hear them. They coat her vocal cords in something hot and thick.

"I'm almost there. Where's Ivy?"

"She's talking to the neighbors."

"Okay. Hold on. I'm around the corner." I skip over a low hedge and hang a sharp left on Mulberry Street.

Moonlight outlines six dark figures.

Aster clutches her phone with one hand and hugs her waist with the other. Sobs make her dress tremble like a ribbon.

I lower my cell phone, then crush her against me. She soaks the collar of my already-damp T-shirt with tears. I rub her back, and then, when I feel she's calmed down, I pull away. Tucking her hand in mine, I guide her toward the others.

Mr. Mancini's hunched over a small, curled form lying in a black puddle.

"Hey," I tell Ivy softly. Then, I nod to the middle-aged couple who lives over the Redds' apartment. They stand in matching navy bathrobes and matching white slippers. The man's arms are folded tightly over his chest, while his wife just looks spooked with her wide eyes and half-open mouth. She's holding her phone in her hands. "Did you call the cops?" I ask them.

"Not yet, but this crazy woman has a gun."

Mrs. Redd spears him with a look. "Which I used to fix a dire situation."

"Do you even have a license to carry?" the man asks.

"Of course I do." A nerve ticks in her freckled jaw.

"I don't feel safe knowing you have a gun," he says.

"Oh, come on, everyone on this fucking street has a gun," Mrs. Redd says.

"Where is it?" I ask.

Ivy points to her mother's right hand. It's a Glock. Those don't come with safeties—Jackie taught me about guns. And Mrs. Redd's index finger is still dangerously close to the trigger. So as not to alarm anyone, I ask if I can take it from her.

She jerks her hand up. I take an involuntary step back. Actually, it's totally voluntary. After all, she's aiming a gun straight at me. I raise my palms.

"Take it." She all but throws it at me.

Releasing Aster's hand, I rip it from Mrs. Redd's fingers and eject the magazine, then stuff both inside my pockets. Not that I think it will accidentally fire but why risk it?

"We should call the police, Steve," the wife tells her husband. "I'm going to call them." She starts typing numbers on her phone.

"Please…please don't," I say. "There's no more threat. I'll take the gun to the precinct—"

"Who says she don't have another one stashed away?" the man asks.

"I don't have another one." Mrs. Redd's voice is angry. A little wobbly.

"Please don't involve the police?" Ivy pleads. "Please. They'll take her away. Please."

Her series of pleases rattles their resolve. "Mr. Mancini, you want us to call the cops?"

Mr. Mancini lets out a wheezing sound. "No. It's all right. Thank you for your concern." His gaze brushes over them, then over me, then returns to the crumpled mass of fur at his feet. "Bullet," he whispers, his voice hoarse. I think he's telling me how the cat died, but then he says it again—"Oh, Bullet"—and I recall it's the feline's name.

The neighbors finally return upstairs, grumbling loudly.

Ivy releases a sigh of relief while I contemplate how I can help Mr. Mancini. I spy a cardboard box in the neighbors' trashcan. I wrestle it out and bring it over.

The old man straightens and lifts slick, perplexed eyes toward me, then toward the box. I put the box down and, trying my hardest not to flinch or gag, I slide my fingers under the cat's weightless, broken body.

Sticky, hot blood coats my hands, runs through my fingers, drips over the gray pavement. As delicately as possible, I place the cat in the cardboard box.

I breathe through my mouth to avoid smelling the blood that's everywhere. "Mrs. Redd, could I use your sink to wash my hands?"

She makes no move to open her front door. Aster leads me inside. As I step over the threshold, Ivy asks Mr. Mancini if he's going to press charges. I don't catch his answer.

Could he press charges? He could probably ask for money, but they don't have any, and he knows it. *Crap*. I rush to the kitchen sink and use a heap of soap. Way more than necessary. My hands still don't feel clean when I dry them against my sweatpants.

I grab an upturned glass from the cupboard over the sink and fill it with cold water that I gulp down. And then I pour a second glass for Aster and force her to sit on the couch and drink it.

"I'll be right back. Stay here." I jog back out.

Mancini's crossing the street toward his apartment. The box is no longer there, so I assume he took Bullet with him.

"What did he say?" I ask Ivy.

"He says it was an accident." Her blue eyes are wide, but neither red like her sister's, nor vacant like her mother's. "It *was* an accident."

The car was; the bullet wasn't. I don't bring this up. Besides, I doubt the cat could've survived the weight of Aster's car. Even if it really had nine lives.

Ivy rubs the arms of her bobbing mother. "Mom, it's okay."

"Get her inside, Ives," I say softly. "I'll go see Mr. Mancini."

"I need to clean up the blood."

"I'll do it after. Go."

She leads her mother inside.

As I walk across the street, the weapon bangs against my thigh.

Mancini's door is ajar. Still, I knock. On his dining room table rests the box. I can't see Bullet from my vantage point—not that I want to. "Mr. Mancini, can I help with something?"

He's half-in, half-out of a closet. Things crash and thud inside. He mumbles curse words. Finally, he turns around, a shovel in his knobby fingers. "Let me do that," I offer, walking over to him. "Where do you want the hole?"

"In the backyard," he croaks. "Under the lilac tree."

I extricate the shovel from his trembling hands, then stride out and around the house to his small backyard. There is only one tree back there, thin-trunked and loaded with white blossoms that suffuse the night air.

Lifting weights three times a week makes shoveling the soft earth swift. In ten minutes, the hole is deep enough for the box. I return to the house to get Mancini.

He's sitting at his kitchen table, fingers intertwined, forehead lowered. Maybe he's praying.

I clear my throat so I don't startle him. "It's ready."

"Thank you." He presses away from the table, folds the flaps of the cardboard box, then reverentially gathers it in his arms and carries it out. I follow him with the shovel.

He sets the box down in the little hole, tears a cluster of white blossoms from a branch of the lilac tree, and lays it on top of Bullet's final resting place. "He was my daughter's cat. Never liked the thing at first. But then she left, and he stayed, and"—his voice snags—"and well, I grew attached to the mangy fur ball. He was loyal as hell. Mark my words, Josh, animals are better than people. They'll like you with all your goddamn flaws, and they won't leave…" The old man makes a noise that sounds like a choked howl.

I sniffle. I'm not sure if it's the tree or Mancini's emotional eulogy. Maybe it's both. I rub my eyes with the back of my hands, then ask if he's ready for me to pack the earth around the box.

"I'll do it, Joshua. Thank you. Now go see to the women. They need you more than I do."

The twins' old neighbor always struck me as a hardened widower who cared more about his NRA membership than about real people. Tonight, though, I see another facet of the man: kindness.

"Thanks for not pressing charges." I give him the shovel.

He nods and wraps arthritic fingers around the wooden handle. "Wasn't premeditated."

I let out a heavy breath and leave the man alone with his lost friend.

When I step back into the twins' house, it's quiet. Ivy's making tea in the kitchen while Aster and her mom sit on opposite ends of the L-shaped couch, gazes cast downward. None of them speak. Shell-shocked. Lost in thought.

"She *did* have a gun," I murmur to Ivy. The electric kettle gushes, drowning out my voice. I don't mean to sound accusing, but I realize that's exactly how I sound.

She twists a long lock of blonde hair over and over around her finger. "I know."

"Does she really have a license to carry?"

Ivy shakes her head no just as the kettle clicks off.

"Where'd she get it?" This comes out louder than intended.

"I found it in the pocket of one of my coats," Mrs. Redd answers, her voice ringing through the quiet apartment.

I spin around like a swizzle stick.

Aster once told me their mother had a passion for coats: fur, trench, leather, wool. She had several of each. Winters in Kokomo are glacial, but does a person need that many coats? Surely not. Especially when her daughters can barely afford one good one.

"I was cleaning my closet"—she's bobbing forward and back, forward and back—"when I felt a bulge in a pocket."

"Where did it come from?"

"Don't know." Her voice shakes in time with her swaying body. "Someone must have planted it there."

Ivy walks out of the kitchen gripping a mug of tea. She sets it in front of her mother on the coffee table, then grabs her hands and whispers words I can't hear.

"Why would someone put a gun in your closet?" I ask, coming to sit next to Aster, who seems frozen in place. She hasn't looked up once since I walked in.

"To frame me." She stares at Aster. "Someone must want to frame me." She's no longer bobbing. She's suddenly calm. "Maybe it's been used in a murder." She says this so flatly it makes my back snap straight and trails cold fingers of fear up my spine.

I lay a shaky hand on the gun concealed in my sweatpants. What if it *is* a murder weapon? It has my prints all over it now. I shove the thought away. Jackie would believe me when I tell her I never fired it. "Have you checked who it's registered to?"

"No. I didn't want to go asking too many questions," she says, still fixing Aster with a dead-eyed stare. Does Mrs. Redd know her daughter told me about the gun?

Aster's head jerks up. "Then why were you carrying it around?"

"Because I couldn't very well leave it here. Social services are already crawling up my ass. If they found a gun, they'd haul me off to the nuthouse."

Ivy gasps; Aster doesn't make a single sound.

"But perhaps that's what you want, Aster."

Aster's body stiffens until she is only a stack of bones, no more soft flesh.

"Mom!" Ivy drops her mother's hands and stares at her in horror.

"What? You don't think your sister's capable of that? Don't you see how she's always watching us? Always listening to us?"

A tear courses down Aster's gaunt cheek. And then another. And another. I wrap an arm around her shoulder and pull her in close.

I'm shaking now, but out of anger. If my mother heard this accusation, she'd wring Mrs. Redd's scrawny, pasty neck. "Your daughter would never do that to you."

She snorts. "You should be careful who you trust, Joshua."

I tighten my hold on Aster, then whisper in her ear, "Go pack a bag."

Aster squeezes her lips together, squeezes her lids closed, squeezes my hand. And then she gets up and walks to her bedroom.

I meet Ivy's gaze. She stands up and follows Aster. I hear them talk quietly.

"My daughter's not right in the head. And she has it out for me. I bet she planted that weapon in my closet."

"She still wouldn't do that," I repeat.

"She has money to pay for a fancy dinner. She probably has money to buy a gun. You have any clue where she's getting all that money?"

"Tips from waitressing jobs. Aster's a hard worker."

"Waitresses don't make that much money. Unless they're offering additional services."

Her insinuation raises my hackles. "Aster's never prostituted herself," I hiss.

"And you would know that how, Joshua? Are you *always* with her? Don't you have a life?"

Blood pumps furiously in my veins. I stand up, curl my fingers into fists, lock them at my sides.

"Are you going to hit me?" she asks.

"I would never hit a woman." Right now, I'm willing to make an exception.

"Are you screwing my daughter, Joshua?"

I'm too startled by her question to answer. Besides, it's none of her business.

"'Cause if you are, and you knock her up, you're in charge of her *and* the baby."

I hope the look I give her is as cutting as the pocketknife Dad keeps in the glovebox of his car.

"I'm ready," Aster says softly.

I hold out a hand, praying she didn't hear her mother's last comment.

Aster hoists her backpack over her shoulder. It looks heavier than she does. I pluck it off her arm and carry it. "You want to come too?" I ask Ivy who's standing in the little hallway.

She shoots me a longing look. "Mom needs me."

Trapping Aster's icy hand, I head out the door. I feel bad leaving my friend behind with this monster, but I know Ivy can control her mother. She's like a horse whisperer, but for schizophrenics. She's one of the only people who can soothe Aster when she goes off her meds.

Her meds.

I don't ask her if she took them. She doesn't need me reminding her of the only connection she has with her mother.

NINE

After

I don't want to go home. I want to stay with Josh, Maggie, and Stewart forever. But I miss Ivy. And I don't want to impose on this kind family. I make up the guest room after I wake, tucking the sheets in, shaking out the flowery comforter, and fluffing up the pillows until the bed looks pristine.

I take my backpack into the closest bathroom—Josh's. The mirror's still foggy from his shower, and the tiled walls smell citrusy like him. I fill my lungs with his soothing scent, let it envelop my skin like a silken robe.

I rub the fog off the mirror. My lids are puffy and my under-eye circles are almost purple, as though I've been punched. In a way, Mom's blame was a jab. A jab to the heart, not to the face, but emotions always leak into faces.

I hate her so much.

And yet, all that hatred has never funneled into the Machiavellian scheme I'm accused of. All I would have to do to have Mom taken away is show up in a hospital after one of our feuds. She stabbed my hand with a fork once. I still have four tiny, white scars under the knuckle of my right middle finger. She's locked me in the hallway closet more times than I care to remember. Once, she left me there the entire day. I ended up peeing myself, which won me name calling after she let me out.

I bet she bought the gun herself. To play the victim.

I need to find whom it's licensed to, that's what I need to do. Today.

I forgo a shower, but wash my face and tie my hair up. I dig through my backpack for my clothes—a white T-shirt and a pair of khaki drawstring shorts that I have to tighten so much they bunch unflatteringly around my waist. Thankfully, the T-shirt is long enough to hide the bunched effect.

I find my phone in the zippered pocket of my bag. It has six percent battery left, enough to read Ivy's many messages asking me how I am, how I feel, how sorry she is Mom took it out on me, how Mom's calmed down, how she's willing to apologize.

I can't forgive her, Ivy, I type back. ***Not this time. I'll come back, but I'll only come back for you. Not for her.***

Seconds later, Ivy texts me: ***You forgot your medication.***

I stare at her words.

I'm done taking drugs. It clouds my judgment. Besides, I don't really need it. I'm depressed sometimes, but it's because of Mom. If my home life was like Josh's, I wouldn't need to take happiness pills; I would simply be happy.

I turn off my phone and toss it back into my pack. When I get out of the bathroom, bag slung over my shoulder, I head downstairs but stop before reaching the landing. I hear Josh and his mom talking softly. He's telling her about last night. I hear the word gun.

"We have to call the authorities, Mom."

"They'll be eighteen in five months. If we call the police now, they might separate the girls, place them in worse homes."

No home can be worse than mine. They might be as terrible, though. Mom doesn't sexually abuse us, but what she does is also abuse.

"They might even send them to other towns, other states. They have one more year of high school. Uprooting them now would rattle their studies."

Why can't Josh's parents act as our legal guardians? I've never dared ask Josh or his mother because I didn't want to impose.

They stop talking so suddenly I worry they know I'm listening. I descend the last few steps to the landing. Maggie is grabbing her car keys and purse from a hook on the foyer wall.

She smiles at me, and I freeze in my tracks. Her kindness makes me regret eavesdropping. "Did you sleep well, honey?"

"Very well."

"I'm so glad to hear that. I have to get going, but Josh is in the kitchen." Right before leaving, she asks, "Want to help me make *sole à la normande* tonight?"

"Yes!" I hope my enthusiasm doesn't come off as desperation, but the thought of cooking, learning something new, is enthralling.

She chuckles. "Great. I'll see you later. Have a great day, hun."

When the door clicks shut, I head into the kitchen, where Josh is drinking tea. "Hey."

His eyes run over my face a mile a minute. He's trying to guess how I feel by my appearance. I look worse than I feel. "Mom let me off work today," he finally says.

"I need to buy something for Mr. Mancini." I twist my lips up. "I'm not sure what though. I kind of suck at guy gifts. Can you help me?"

He nods. For a while, the only noise comes from the AC vent blowing cool air over our heads. The tips of his short brown hair flutter.

"Aster?"

"Yeah."

"I ran the serial number of the gun last night on this website." His Adam's apple bobs in his freshly shaven throat. "The ATF—"

"The what?"

"It's an electronic tracing system for weapons."

"Oh."

"Anyway, the response came back a few minutes ago. It was bought in Noblesville at Gus's Guns." He pauses. Probably to give me a second to come to terms with the fact that Noblesville is the next town over. "I called them to find out if they were open, and they are. I was going to head there—"

"I'm coming with you."

"You don't have to."

"You don't want me to come with you?"

"I don't want to pressure you. You're under enough stress."

I smile to appease him. He worries about me too much. "I *want* to come with you."

He swallows, and his Adam's apple joggles again. "'Kay."

"Should we leave now?"

"I made you French toast."

"You…?" The rest of my words become suspended when I spot the plate of golden brown triangles.

Josh made me breakfast.

He cooked for me.

"Yeah. Mom supervised the whole thing though." He gestures toward the white marble dining table in the corner. It sits underneath an enormous silver lampshade that seems to have been salvaged from a ship. When I still haven't moved toward it, he says, "I ate some, and I didn't die, so you should be all right."

I laugh.

I walk over to the table and dig in, lifting large forkfuls into my mouth and chewing quickly, but savoring each morsel. I taste egg, maple syrup, and love. "Don't tell Maggie, but you might just cook better than her."

Josh joins me at the table with his tea. "Flatterer."

"Honest."

"Uh-huh." The intensity with which he observes me makes me blush. "I'm sorry I didn't believe you."

I shrug. "It's okay."

"No, it's not okay." His eyes are as green as moss this morning, and his brown hair gleams copper in the sunlight inundating the eat-in kitchen. "Ivy wanted you to call her."

I drop my gaze to my plate. "My phone died."

"You can use mine." He slides his cell toward me.

I eye it reluctantly. "I don't feel like calling her right now."

For a long moment, he stays silent, and I eat.

Everything vanishes from my plate into my mouth.

Josh cocks an eyebrow. "Are you mad at her for staying with your mother?"

"No. She needed to stay with Mom."

I take my plate to the sink and wash off the sticky remnants. My stomach burbles. I can't tell if I'm still hungry or if I ate too fast.

"You never told me how dinner went last night," Josh says.

I'm happy I have my back to him. "It went great."

"Really?"

I squeeze my eyes shut. "Yes." Even though my plate is clean, the water's still running. I'm afraid that if I turn off the tap, he'll hear my heightened pulse.

A hand settles gently on my shoulder and squeezes even more gently. In spite of the softness of Josh's touch, I jump. And then, I shiver. He doesn't raise his hand. He keeps it right on my sharp joint, bleeding delicious heat into my cold skin.

"Ivy told me you didn't order anything."

I don't answer, because if I do, he'll pity me, and that might change the way he's been looking at me since the dance.

The water stops gushing.

His other hand traps my free shoulder and spins me around slowly. "Aster?"

Slowly, I lift my lids. His tea-warmed breath tickles the tip of my nose. "I wasn't hungry last night."

He sighs, and it rumbles in the air between us. I lick my lips. His gaze drops to them, but then he releases me and turns away, his jaw pink.

TEN

JOSH

What am I doing? What the hell am I doing? I glance at Aster sitting in the passenger seat of my Camry. She's staring out the window. I sit up straighter. I've been having lots of indecent thoughts about her recently. She's starred in several dreams. I know it's her and not Ivy because the girl in my sleep has a small mole over her mouth like Aster. And Cindy Crawford. But the girl in those dreams was definitely not Cindy. Cindy does not have kinky blonde hair. Nor does she have lagoon-blue eyes.

I wonder if Aster knows how pretty she is.

My guess is no.

If she did, she wouldn't be hiding behind frumpy clothes.

She wouldn't be hanging out with me. The Hamster.

Sure, I'm not fat anymore, but she probably remembers me like that. And that memory must stain the way she sees me now.

She catches me gaping. Like a juvenile idiot, I blush.

Real men don't blush.

I try to think dampening thoughts. Mancini and his cat pop into my head. That cools me right down. It even propels a shudder down my spine. "You could get him a book about trees and flowers. He seems to like trees." He knew what type of tree grew in his backyard.

Old people like horticulture, don't they?

"Who's *him*?"

Right. "Mr. Mancini."

"That's a good idea. Maybe I can get him a landscaping book and a thriller. He has so many guns. I'm sure he likes thrillers."

"Good idea."

We drive the rest of the way in silence, both lost in our respective thoughts. I pump up the music and roll down my window. Sunny air licks my bare forearm, soothing after my crappy night. We arrive in Noblesville around lunchtime. The pavement wobbles from the humid heat.

I follow my phone's GPS to the firearm shop on 16th Street and park in the reserved lot.

As I click off my seatbelt, Aster asks, "What if it's stolen, Josh? Or what if it *was* used in a murder? Will they arrest us?"

I grab my nylon gym bag. I stuffed the gun in there this morning. "They wouldn't have any grounds for an arrest." That's a lie, though. We should've taken the gun to a police precinct. We shouldn't have kept it, much less driven around the state with it. I touch Aster's hand. It's stiff and feels as cold as the air spitting out of my AC. "It'll be all right, Asty. I promise."

Finally, she takes her seatbelt off and joins me on the other side of the car. Together we walk into the shop.

I suspect the owner is a big-game hunter. Every inch of the back wall is covered in rifles—from stainless synthetics to heavy wooden ones to automatics. But it's not as much the array of guns as the row of animal trophies—from heads to full bodies—cluttering the entrance. Even though the beasts are stuffed, their glassy eyes seem to follow us as we make our way to the glass counter that houses the handguns.

One other customer's in the shop. He's got his cap on backwards and his face is scruffy with a curly, red beard.

"Lydia!" the salesman showing him the rifles yells.

A woman scurries out the back, ruminating a wad of chewing gum. "Hiya. What can I help you kids with?"

"I ran an ATF trace on a gun in my possession, and the serial number matched a sale that came from this shop," I say.

"Come again? You have a gun but ran an ATF trace?"

"*Her* mom found a gun, and *I* ran a trace on it to figure where it came from."

The store's gotten awfully quiet.

"If it ain't yours, you need to take it to a precinct," Lydia says.

Aster shifts next to me.

"And we will," I say in a crisp voice, "but first, we were hoping you could tell us who you sold it to. That's all."

Lydia splays both her palms on the glass countertop. "Why?" The tips of her nails are sharpened to a point and lacquered purple. She could gouge someone's eye out with those.

"Because her mother isn't fit to carry a gun, so if she managed to procure herself one, she could probably procure herself more. And that's damnright frightening."

"Downright," Aster whispers.

"Huh?"

"Downright. Not damnright. Forget it," Aster mumbles.

"Did she threaten you with it, dear?" Lydia asks Aster.

Aster's bottom lip quivers. "She did."

"I'm sorry to hear that." The woman sighs, presses off the counter. "Can you kids show me some ID?"

I dig my driver's license out of my wallet and hand it over.

"I left mine in the car," Aster says. "I'll go get it. Josh, the keys?"

I give it to her, and she walks back through the forest of dead animals.

"Your girlfriend really got threatened by her mom?"

First instinct is to correct her—Aster isn't my girlfriend. She *is* my girl friend though. In the scope of things, it doesn't matter. "Yeah."

"Have you told the police?"

"Not yet."

"You better do it quick, son. I've seen these situations, and they can turn nasty. Sometimes fatal."

Silence fills the store. I shoot my gaze to the cap-wearing customer. He looks down fast and asks the salesman to see the lightest rifle they carry.

"Can I see the trace?" Lydia asks, dragging my attention back to her.

I dig the print-out from my bag, careful to keep the gun out of sight, and slap it on the counter. Blowing a humongous pink bubble, she picks up the printout, squints at the serial number, then enters it into the shop's computer.

Aster's back, driver's license in hand. "Here."

Lydia reaches for Aster's ID, glimpses at it, then whips her gaze back up toward us. Or more precisely, toward Aster.

I frown. "What?"

"The gun's in her name."

"What?" Aster cranes her neck to see the computer screen but it's one of those that's dark from an angle.

Color drains from my face. "*Her* name?" I pivot toward Aster. The wheels spin in my head, as fast as a gun barrel. And like a gun barrel, each chamber contains some harmful thought. "It's registered to you?"

"To another Aster. Not to me." Beads of perspiration form on her small nose. That happens when she's frightened or when she's stressed out.

Which is it at that moment? Fear or anxiety?

ELEVEN

Josh gapes at me in a way that makes the hair on my arms rise. He thinks I bought the gun. Tears scald my eyes. I don't blink because I don't want them to drip out. Instead, I tilt my face toward the beige popcorn ceiling so the tears slide back in.

Lydia smacks the gum around in her mouth. "Well it says here the gun's registered to Aster—"

"Lydia!" the rifle salesman says sharply. "That's enough."

It startles her so much that she swallows her gum and starts coughing.

"I'll take over from here. You take care of Mr. Conrath." He stalks over to us. "Do you have the gun with you?"

"No."

I gape at Josh. He never lies! It's a great sin in his family. It's even worse than cursing.

"We're not stupid enough to drive around with a stolen weapon," Josh adds.

"Where is it?"

"I locked it up in my parents' safe."

I study my brown, too-small sandals. I'm not a good liar. I'm not even a good co-liar. If the salesman checks my face, he'll understand Josh is being deceitful.

"Then I can't help you."

"Super customer service you guys got here," Josh says.

"We respect our customers' privacy"—he glares at Lydia, who starts wheezing. Maybe the gum got stuck in her airway—"so yeah, I agree, we provide excellent service, young man. Now, if you please. We have *actual* customers who need our help."

Josh and the salesman have a staring competition while Lydia chugs a bottle of water in great, wet gulps.

"Do the last names match?" Josh tries.

"Look, kid, I remember who bought the gun, and it wasn't her."

Knuckles whitening around the handle of his nylon bag, Josh swipes our IDs off the countertop and springs out of the shop. I rush out after him.

He waits for me by the car. I walk to the passenger side and tug on my door handle but it's still locked.

"You have the keys, Aster."

I pat my back pocket. Find the mini dumbbell keychain. I beep the Camry open, then get in and drop the keys in the drink holder, next to a half-eaten tube of Mentos.

He twists the key in the ignition but doesn't move the gearshift out of park. His eyes are closed and his nostrils flare. He must be trying to calm down. "Did you have someone buy it?"

"What?"

"The gun, Aster. It was in your name. Did you ask someone to buy it for you?"

My molars grind at his harsh accusation. I lock my arms in front of my pulsating chest and angle my body away from his.

"Aster." He tries to touch my arm, but I shift away before his hand can settle.

"I can't believe you would think that." My voice sounds flimsy, weak…like me.

"The gun's registered in your—"

"It's registered to someone called Aster!" I shake my head.

He drags his hands through his hair and pulls at the roots. His biceps bulge in his Metallica T-shirt.

"I'm not the only person named Aster in this world," I add, although I shouldn't have to.

He sighs, releases his hair. "You think your mom used your name to buy it?"

"I. Don't. Know."

Tension and regret writhe within his jade irises. "I'm sorry." Josh cups my cheeks. Makes me look at him. "Please forgive me."

I swallow hard. "You hurt me."

He presses his forehead against mine. "I'm so sorry." His words vibrate against my nose. With his thumbs, he whisks away my tears. "I hate myself right now."

"You know I could never stay mad at you, but you—"

He hushes me with a brush of his finger against my lips.

A shiver shoots all the way down my throat and creates concentric ripples inside my heaving chest. "…hurt me." I'm surprised I manage to finish my sentence when Josh's mouth is so close to mine. If I tilt my head up, our lips will meet.

I don't move, though, because his accusation pulses inside my mind like a bee sting.

I slide my face out of his warm palms. The air vents cool my cheeks. "Why did you lie about having the gun?"

"Because they would've taken it away from us." He studies his gear shift. "And I'm holding out hope that the police can tell us who this...*other* Aster is."

AFTER JOSH DROPS me off on my street, I cross the road and ring Mr. Mancini's doorbell. He comes outside in a pair of olive-green cargo shorts and a black T-shirt that has several small holes along the collar and in the hem. Perhaps I should've gotten him mothballs instead of books.

He stares at me without saying a word, his eyes swollen and pink like rosebuds.

"I got you this. It won't bring Bullet back, but it might help ease your pain." I hand him my gift-wrapped present.

He doesn't take it from me. He must hate me. Hate my entreaty. I'm so ashamed I drop my gaze to his doormat that reads: *The neighbors have better stuff.* I doubt he picked it. He doesn't strike me as humorous. Plus, on this street, no one has better stuff.

When he still doesn't take the gift from me, I crouch and place it on the word *neighbors* and flee. He's still standing outside, motionless, when I let myself inside my house.

I've decided to confront my mother.

Her studio door is closed. A husky man's voice trickles out through the thin wood door. I listen, wondering if Mom has company. It's been a long time since she's brought home a man.

The voice takes a high-pitched tone.

Audiobook.

I knock softly. "Mom?"

The sound shuts off with a click.

I try the doorknob but it's locked.

Footsteps resound on the other side.

The door creaks open.

Mom's haggard eyes fix on me. "What?"

I jerk backward from the crispness of her voice. "You registered the gun in my name."

Her pupils pulse against their light backdrop. We have the same eye color, except hers is a crueler shade than mine. "Are you testing my patience?"

The key she wears around her neck swings against her shapeless white blouse. It's the key to all her secrets. Sometimes, I think it's the key to her heart, but then I remember she doesn't have one.

"The gun was registered to Aster. Why did you put my name—"

"I didn't buy a gun!" She jabs her index finger against my collarbone repeatedly. "Are you thick?"

I jerk backward.

"Have you called child services yet?" she asks, breathing hard.

"What?"

She slaps her forehead. "Of course you didn't. You're not eighteen yet." She gives me an ugly smile full of pretty teeth. "I'm not a perfect mother, Aster, but you're not a perfect daughter either."

I recoil.

"Thank God we have Ivy," she says.

I try to peek behind her to see if my sister's there, but the gap's not wide enough. And it's getting narrower. I place my palm on the door to keep it open so that my last words can penetrate. "You are so mean."

She snorts softly. "The world's a mean place, Aster. Get that through your head. Everything it gives, it takes back. You're not too young to understand that. Learn it. It'll hurt less." And then she shuts the door in my face.

The air whooshes against me.

I'm too shocked to cry.

On autopilot, I walk toward my bedroom and grab clean clothes because there's no way in hell I'm staying in this goddamn house. After I repack my backpack, I write Ivy a note to tell her I'm okay, that I'm going back to see Josh, and that I love her. I text Josh to tell him I'm ready. He answers right back: ***Still at the precinct. Be there in fifteen.***

Since I don't want to breathe the same tainted air as my mother, I sit on our front stoop to wait.

I look up at the stars twinkling in the purpling sky and wonder what my father could've seen in my mother. I bet she was nice with him at first, and then, when he saw her true face, it drove him away. Even though she loves to tell us it was her pregnancy that made him run. I think she's lying. I think Dad wanted us. Who wouldn't want innocent babies?

As I take in my sleepy neighborhood, I stroke my abdomen and think of baby Violet.

A dog barks in someone's backyard.

Will my daughter like dogs?

Simmering tomato sauce and sautéed onions flavor the dusky air.

Will she enjoy my cooking?

A TV blares from a living room.

A cartoon.

Headlights from a shiny Jeep splash the low hedge lining our front yard and then Mr. Mancini's doormat.

My present is no longer there.

TWELVE

JOSH

"Can I subpoena information from a store?" I ask Jackie, dropping into the chair across from her desk at the precinct.

"Come again?"

At this hour, the precinct is almost empty.

"Say someone bought something, and to buy it, that person needed to give some personal information, can I subpoena that information?"

Her penciled-in eyebrows shoot upward. "Have you been accused of something, Josh?"

"No! Why would you think that?"

"Because subpoenas are used in court cases."

I lock my fingers together, lean forward, balancing my forearms on my thighs. "I'm not facing any accusations or anything."

"Then why are you talking about subpoenas?"

"I just thought…" My shoulders tense up. "I just thought I could compel someone to give me information legally."

"What information do you need?"

"I can't tell you."

"Josh, you're scaring me, and I'm a cop. I'm tough to scare. What information do you need?"

I chew on my bottom lip. I can tell her? Right? But then, this tiny part of me yells, *What if Aster bought the gun?* Even Jackie won't be able to protect her then. "Forget it. I'll look it up online."

"You know you can trust me."

I nod as I get up.

"If this was dangerous, you'd tell me, right?"

My jaw prickles. "Yes," I lie.

She stares into my face a good, long while. "You're a good kid, Josh, but a bad liar."

She's right. I suck at lying.

ON WHITEPAGES.COM, I look up people with the name Aster. I'm not sure whether I'm supposed to be looking at last names or first names. I add Indiana in the location tab. Only seven Asters left, including Aster Redd.

I start calling the numbers listed below the names. I don't start by asking if they have a license to carry. I ask if they know a woman named Rose Redd. The first guy I phone asks me if this is a prank call. I tell him, *no. Rose Redd?* he repeats incredulously. *Yeah, Rose Redd,* I repeat abrasively.

Even though I'm not the one who picked Mrs. Redd's first name, I take his mocking tone personally.

"Nope," he says. "Don't know any Roses."

I try the next ones. Call each of them up. Two don't answer, so I leave voicemails, and the two others have never heard of a Rose Redd, or been to Noblesville *or* Kokomo.

The following day, I call the two who didn't answer. This time I reach one of them. A woman. Rachel Aster. A ninety-seven-year old nursing home resident. She apologizes for not returning my call, but a rectal exam had her feeling woozy. I grimace, tell her I'm sorry for her pain, I hope she recovers quickly. There's no recovery at her age for colon cancer, but heck, because her cells are so old, the disease is spreading slowly. Doctor told her it could be months before she dies. I pace around my bedroom as she tells me about how her grandkids don't come visit often and asks if I visit my grandparents often. I spent a week in April with them. And I'm planning another trip soon. And then they're coming up here for Thanksgiving, and—

And then I stop talking. I'm supposed to be finding the owner of a gun, not discussing my family relationships with a complete—albeit friendly—stranger.

Unable to hang up on someone, I keep talking to Rachel for another *fifteen minutes* until she finally tells me she's late for her game of euchre. Before disconnecting, she makes me swear to call my grandmother today. Never know if they'll be there tomorrow. I promise I will.

I take a breather after that. Go eat two bananas. Chug down a diet Red Bull.

A half hour later, I try the last Aster again. The only other Aster who carries the name as a first name: Aster Colson.

She doesn't answer so I text her, Hi. My name is Joshua Cooper. Do you know a woman named Rose Redd?

I type the name in Google. Find out Aster Colson owns a security firm in Indiana. I click on the Bio tab of the webpage. A picture of a man with a shaved head, light brown skin, and a thick neck materializes on my monitor. I know it's stupid, but the fact that he's a man stuns me more than the fact he's ex-military.

Soft rasping at my bedroom door startles me.

I shut down my browser. "Who is it?"

"It's Aster." She cracks the door open. "They want me to come back tomorrow. They liked me." She was filling in for a waitress at the old diner on Fulham Street.

I rub the heels of my hands into my eyes. "That's great."

"Yeah. I made all of eighteen dollars in tips today. I can almost take you to a movie tonight."

"Take me? *I* do the taking." Her reddening cheeks make me realize how it sounds. Like I'm asking her on a date. My palms are moist, so I rub them against my pant legs. "Want to go to a movie with me tonight?"

Her gaze drops to my beige carpet that's whiter in spots where I used bleach to get dirt stains out. I thought Mom would applaud my initiative, but I ended up damaging it instead of fixing it. Although proud of me, she advised me to check with her next time I felt like housekeeping.

"Sure. Should we—" Aster fingers a little hole in her black leggings. "Should I ask Ivy too?"

"No." I whip the word out way too fast. Desperate much? I'm tempted to slap my forehead but clutch the chair's armrests instead. "I want to make it up to you. You know"—I shrug—"because of my assumption yesterday."

Her mouth bursts apart with the softest gasp. Maybe I shouldn't have reminded her. Maybe she's already put it past her.

"*We're the Millers* looks good," she suggests.

"Yeah it does. Let me see what time it's playing."

I check the local movie theater for showings.

"Did you find anything?" She sits cross-legged on my bed and tips her pointy chin toward my monitor.

"It's playing at seven-thirty."

"I meant about *Aster*?"

I'm tempted to show her Colson's picture. Ask her if she's ever seen him. For some reason, I shake my head.

She sighs. "Maybe we should go back to the gun shop. Maybe if we give them the gun, they'll give us the person's full name."

"What if it's *your* full name?"

"Then we'll know for sure it was Mom who bought it." She taps the floor with the rubber sole of her Converse. "The police really ran the serial number and found nothing?"

"Yeah. They got directed to the same website where I ran the ATF trace."

Aster thinks I showed Jackie the gun because that's what I told her. But if I'd shown it to Jackie, and she'd traced it back to Aster…*my* Aster— I shudder just thinking about it.

Even though Aster blames her mother, a tiny part of me still wonders if Aster commissioned someone to buy it for her. She doesn't have many friends—just me really—but she told me she met a girl in her shrink's waiting room. A girl with hairy legs and a nose piercing who never speaks. What if it's a lie though? What if she *does* speak? What if they've had conversations? About guns, for example?

Aster stretches her neck to the side. It cracks. "You'd think the police would have their own database."

"You'd think."

"Explains why gun control is so crappy in this country."

"Yeah."

She sighs. "My feet are killing me, and I smell like stale fries. I'm going to go shower and lie down for a bit." She rises from my bed, but pauses in my doorway. "We are going to the movies, right?"

"Yeah. I mean, if you want to."

Her eyes linger on mine. "I want to."

A small current passes between us, zaps me, zips up my spine, stiffens my neck. We've gone to the movies together hundreds of times, so why does this time feel different?

THIRTEEN

I spend a long time in front of the mirror, attempting to smooth my curls with the coconut butter I found in the Coopers' pantry. It's greasy, but it makes my hair shiny and gives it an exotic smell, as though I've frolicked on a sandy beach full of sunshine. I twist in front of the mirror, my glossy locks clumping together. I probably put on an insane amount, but it's too late to take a shower and shampoo it out.

If only Ivy helped me. She's so good at all this. But I haven't even called my sister today, and she hasn't called me either.

I finger-comb my hair some more, then screw the lid back on the glass jar of the nut butter and exit the bathroom, hiding the tub underneath the uneven hem of my T-shirt. It wasn't always uneven, but Ivy did the laundry once and hung it to dry with a clip, which stretched out the fabric. It's not unwearable, but then again, what do I know of fashion?

Maybe I look awful. I wish I could ask Ivy…

I'm about to go downstairs when I hear Josh talking with his parents. I double back to my room and stuff the glass jar underneath my pillow. Then I head down, trying to push out the nervousness fueling the thunderous pounding of my heart.

"I'm ready to go."

All three Coopers stare at me.

"Don't you look pretty tonight," Josh's father tells me.

"And you smell so good," adds Maggie, sniffing the air. "Like coconut. Hmm. That gives me an idea for a pound cake."

"Honey," Stewart says, "you're off work."

She leans over the table and pecks his lips. "You're never off work when you work for yourself."

"*I* work for myself."

"And the Discolis."

The shells of his ears glow bright red. "They hired me."

"I was teasing you. My work is just so much more fun than yours." Maggie leans over, but before she can place another kiss on her husband's lips, Josh's voice halts her.

"Guys, I'm right here."

Maggie grins wickedly. "Aren't the people who made you allowed to express their love for each other?"

"Yeah, but in private. Yeesh." Josh rolls his eyes.

If there ever was an ideal couple, the Coopers are it. Perfect and loving and responsible. They never left their five-year-old behind at home while they ran errands. They never told him how inconvenient his birth was to their career. They never used cruelty to harden him.

"We gotta go. Movie starts in fifteen." Even though Josh complains about his parents' PDA, I don't think he actually minds it.

"I love your parents," I tell him as we make our way out to his car.

His hands are stuffed in his track pants. "Yeah. I got lucky."

"I want what they have."

He glances at me. "What? You don't want what *your* parents had?"

"That's a paltry joke, Josh."

"Paltry?"

"Mean."

"Yeah. I'm sorry."

As he starts driving, he repeats the word *paltry* a couple times. That's how he teaches himself things. He has to say them a couple times, and then they're cemented in him. I usually only need to read or hear something once to learn it.

"I'm sorry, Asty. That was really *poultry* of me."

My mouth splits into a smile. "Paltry with an A. Not poultry."

He clucks, then winks. "I know. Just wanted to see you smile."

WE FIND seats easily in the nearly empty theater. A large bucket of popcorn rests on my lap. Every now and again, Josh's hand sneaks into the bucket, and like one of his dad's diggers, scoops popcorn out.

The trailers begin. I love trailers. I like anything that's exciting and forthcoming. It's not that I don't appreciate the present—like right now, sitting in a dark movie theater with the boy I've had a crush on for ten years: that's pretty amazing

—but I live for the future. I know it'll be better, because it can't possibly be worse.

My hand collides with Josh's in the popcorn bucket.

He doesn't pull his hand out, even though his fingers aren't ploughing through the puffy kernels. Something must be distracting him.

My gaze climbs up to his.

He's staring straight back.

The bright glow of the screen makes his eyes sparkle like black emeralds shimmering in a forgotten pirate chest. Before I can ask him why he's looking at me, his hand arcs out of the bucket and settles on the nape of my neck. Grains of salt transfer from his palm to my skin.

Without hesitation, he brings his lips down on mine, and stars shoot around me. His mouth is soft and warm and tastes like salt and butter. His tongue, though, is not soft. It prods my lips open and slides in, seeking my own tongue hungrily.

I've been holding out for this kiss forever, and yet, instead of reciprocating, I become stiller than a mummy. And then the moment is over, and Josh is saying, "I'm sorry," but I'm the one who's sorry.

If I don't reach out now, if I don't bridge the space between our faces, if I don't let him know that kissing me is fine, better than fine, he will never do it again, and I can't live in a world where Josh doesn't kiss me anymore.

I lay a hand on the hot band of skin above his T-shirt collar and pull him to me. And then, breaking out of my tight, hard shell, *I* kiss *him*. *I* touch my tongue to his. *I* knock my teeth into his.

This time, he's the one who doesn't respond, yet I keep stroking his tongue, his teeth, his lips, because I want a reaction.

I *need* a reaction.

I press my mouth against his harder, crush my fingertips into his skin, then rub them gently over the downward peak of silky, shorn hair that dips toward his spine.

Finally, as though I've found the correct combination, he comes alive and reacts with more heat and tenderness than I could ever have wished for.

FOURTEEN

JOSH

I hold Aster's hand tight throughout the whole movie. And I kiss her again.

My heart is scrambling to beat normally. *That girl.* I don't know what it is about her, besides the fact that she's hot, but I'm so attracted to her. Maybe it's the way she makes me feel: needed. Or maybe it's our shared past.

After the movie is over—a movie that I'll have to watch again because I have no clue what went down—we're still kissing. The lights are bright now, and the room is almost empty. Two staff members walk in with brooms and standing dustpans.

I shift away from Aster, let go of her hand. Her cheeks are flushed and her mouth is taillight-red. She stands and waits for me to stand too, but I need to readjust myself before I rise. I don't want her to notice the bulge in my jeans.

I focus on the cleaning crew to quiet down.

It takes a couple seconds but it works. I stand up and walk behind Aster, my gaze drifting from the ends of her hair to the dimples in her lower back that peek out of her lopsided T-shirt.

I ask if she wants to grab a kebab at the Turkish place next door. It's crowded, so we get ours to go and walk through the flowery alleys of Highland Park. When we reach the deserted playground, Aster sits on a red plastic swing. She's still eating her kebab, while I've finished mine and balled the aluminum foil. I toss it into a bin, pretending it's a free throw. My aluminum missile sinks right into the center of the bin.

Swinging gently, Aster seals the aluminum edges around her kebab and lays it in the sand at her feet.

I latch on to the chains of her swing and steady her. Her giant blue eyes climb up to my face. A tiny glob of tahini is stuck to her upper lip, right next to her mole. I lean down and lick it off.

And then I'm kissing her again.

I tug her up, take her seat on the swing, then pull her down onto my lap.

Slowly, I dig my sneaks into the ground and push, giving the swing momentum.

"You think Ivy"—Aster swallows—"you think she'll mind that we…we…?"

"Made out?" I finish for her. "Why would Ivy mind?"

"She might find it weird."

"So what? We don't need her permission." Her hair curtains off half her face, yet I still see her reddened cheeks. "We don't need anyone's permission." I tuck the wall of hair behind her ear, but it springs back out. I gather it in my hand, all of her hair, and twist it away, and then I apply light pressure to the back of her head to bring her face closer to mine. "Kiss me again."

Her mouth curves into a dazzling smile that floods her eyes. They shine, brighter than the moon overhead.

Aster isn't my first kiss, but she's the first girl I've kissed whom I know inside out.

She blinks and a tear tumbles down her cheek.

My heart holds still. "Are you crying?"

She nods.

"Why?"

"Because…I didn't think you felt the same way I did."

"Aster Redd…I—" I'm about to say the L-word, but that'll scare her. It scares me. "I've *always* liked you."

She sniffles. Smiles. But she's still crying.

"Don't cry." She's always been sensitive, but she seems especially emotional tonight. I can't help but wonder if she's taking her mood stabilizers. Then again, she's a girl, and girls are emotional. "I don't want you to cry every time I kiss you," I say softly.

"Every time?"

"You didn't think this was a one-off, did you?"

More tears traipse down. I let go of her hair to whisk the wetness off her cheeks with my thumbs, and then I kiss her forehead and pull her close, until her head is resting in the crook of my neck.

"Aster Redd, if it's okay with you, I'd like to kiss you every day from now on."

She sniffs again. "You don't have to ask permission."

"Men should always ask a woman's permission to kiss them."

She grins, then whispers, "Okay. You have my permission."

TONIGHT IS one of those times I wished I weren't living with my parents anymore, but it makes no financial sense to pay for room and board when I live a couple miles from campus.

Holding onto Aster's hand, I lead her up the stairs of my quiet house—Mom and Dad always go to bed early. I should probably part ways with her in front of the guest bedroom, but I don't.

I sit down on the bed and pat the spot next to me. She lowers herself, as stiff as a knitting needle.

"I don't want to have sex with you," I blurt out, so she'll relax.

She blinks, lets out a soft gasp. "You don't?"

"Tonight. I mean, tonight. I didn't take you in here to…you know, take advantage of you"—I rub the nape of my neck—"or anything."

Whoa. I sound like such a loser. I squeeze my eyes shut and massage them with my balled fingers, wishing I could rub the stupidity right out of me. Aster scoots closer to me, her sharp hipbone digging into my thigh. "As long as you want to make love to me someday, then I'm okay with waiting."

Wait, *what?* Did I just ask her to wait for me? I don't want to wait. I haven't had any action in months. I'm more than willing and ready to go. I'm about to tell her all of that—well, except the part where I haven't had sex in so long—but I bite my tongue.

Literally, I bite it.

This is Aster. Not some random girl I picked up next to a beer keg at a frat house party.

I want our first time to be special.

Before I can make more of a fool of myself, she lays one hand on my jaw and nudges my mouth open with hers. And then she's straddling me, and I fall backward on the bed. My breath rips right out of me for two reasons.

One, that was hot. Her taking charge.

Two, my head hits something hard that's not the headboard. I reach beneath the pillow and pull out a glass jar.

"Coconut butter," I read out loud. "Why do you have coconut butter under your pillow?" Aster is a messy person, but food—well not food, a condiment—in bed is a bit weird, even for her.

"I tossed it there before leaving. It must've rolled underneath the pillow." She's so flustered, her words tumble out and her face floods with color.

Smiling, I place it on the nightstand, brush away the black leggings that hang half on half off the comforter, then pull her against me and remind her of what we were doing. She's gone stiff again, and it takes my hands running up and down her spine several times to loosen her, to make her forget about the interruption.

My phone vibrates in my jeans. I don't want to stop, but I yank my phone out of my pocket. I'm about to pitch it onto the nightstand when I read the text message: ***Never heard of Rose.***

Aster Colson's finally answered me. *Great timing, dude.*

Aster slides off me. "Who's that?"

Instead of lying, I tell her about my furtive investigation, about my lead. I look for disappointment in her eyes but find none. She's not mad. But our conversation has definitely killed the mood. She's thinking about the gun.

"You think my mother knows—*knew*—another Aster than myself?" she asks.

I pull her against me, kiss her forehead. "It's possible, right? I mean, you're not the only one with the name."

But it would be quite the coincidence.

A pretty major coincidence.

The wheels spin inside my head so hard and fast I'm afraid an actual grating sound is coming from my ears.

To show Jackie, or not to show her?

To return to the gun shop, or not to return?

"How's that friend of yours from the doctor's office? You know the girl with the hairy legs?" I murmur into Aster's coconut-y curls, hoping it can spur a memory…or a confession.

She doesn't answer me. I press her lightly away so I can see her face.

She's fast asleep.

FIFTEEN

After

The day after Josh and I start dating, I return home.

I do it for Ivy.

She took the bus over to Josh's house. Told me that Mom's psychiatrist readjusted her meds. That Mom is doing better. Has become calmer.

"She woke up asking if you'd died," Ivy tells me as I drive us to a place that should feel like home but doesn't.

Home has never been a place.

Home has always been people.

Home is Ivy and Josh.

Ivy is the hearth that warms the walls my arms form around us, and Josh is our roof, our floor, the one who keeps us sheltered and grounded.

"Asking or hoping?" I ask.

"What?" Ivy's hair is twisted into a bun atop her head and wrapped with a piece of gold silk that matches her hair color. The sun always burnishes her hair in the summer. I don't like to sit in direct sunlight, but Ivy does. She takes real pleasure in laying out.

"Nothing."

I take a right on our street. Although a great rainstorm washed over Kokomo this morning, blowing rubbery leaves off thick branches, gluing them to car windshields, our driveway still seems blemished with Bullet's ruby-black blood. The stain is in my mind, indelible, however much rain falls over my town and over my body.

"How's Mr. Mancini?" I glance over at his front door.

"Haven't seen him."

"I'll go visit him later. Want to come?"

"Sure."

I turn the car off, but stay inside.

"Asty, Mom loves you. In her own way." Ivy clasps my hand in hers. "She would never *hope* for your death."

So my sister did hear me.

"Besides, I forbid you to leave me. What would I do without my better half?"

My eyes heat up. "I *did* leave you. The moment things got hard, I left."

"Asty, I'm not mad at you for going with Josh. You needed space to process all that happened, and so did Mom." Ivy bites her lip. "Can I ask you something, though? Mom mentioned that the last time you talked, you asked her about someone called Aster?"

"I wasn't asking about myself, if that's your question."

Ivy studies the mold-speckled wall of our apartment building through the windshield. "You didn't take your medication with you to Josh's."

I yank my hand out of hers. "You all believe my world will start spinning out of control if I stop gulping down my pills, but all they do is numb me. Make Mom's abuse sufferable. Make the world a little shinier."

Ivy's copper skin pales.

"The gun's registered to an *Aster*, and that Aster isn't me. Josh asked Jackie to run the serial number through the police database." I lie because I want Ivy to stop looking at me like I'm some sad lost puppy. "I'll bet you anything Mom stashed that gun in her drawer and has been keeping it there."

Ivy's mouth slackens.

"You said you saw rolls of fabric in there. Who locks up fabric? Want to know what I think? I think she hid the gun inside the rolls of fabric."

Ivy sucks in a breath. "You think?"

"Why would she lock up fabric?"

My twin's gaze shifts downward. Is there something she's not telling me?

Perhaps there's no fabric at all in the drawer.

Perhaps my sister lied to me.

I study her hooded eyes and pressed lips in silence. "Show me what's inside."

Her eyes sweep up to mine. "You don't believe me?"

"Do you ever believe *me*?"

She clicks her seatbelt off and pushes the door open. "I've just been through hell with Mom. Don't you put me through hell too." She gets out and shuts the door.

Reluctantly, I step out of the car and follow her. "You're turning this around."

She spins on her wedge sneakers, throws her hands in the air. "You turned it around first!"

All I want is a glimpse into Mom's damn drawer. If she isn't hiding anything, why am I not allowed a peek? "I'm sorry. I believe you."

After a moment, she says, "Okay," and walks into the house. I wonder if I should've told her about Josh. He's her friend too after all. But part of me is keeping this secret tucked away. What if she's against our relationship? What if she's disgusted? Josh and I are close, almost like siblings.

Or worse…

What if she's jealous? Has she ever thought of Josh that way?

I double back to the Honda and pop the trunk open to grab my backpack. As I hoist it out, a forest-green Jeep parks in front of Mancini's house.

Did he buy a new car? No one comes out. I squint to make out the driver, but the glass is tinted. Maybe it's his daughter. Maybe she heard about his loss and came down for a visit. Or up. I'm not sure where she lives.

"Aster?" Ivy calls out. She stands in the open doorway of our house. "Are you coming?"

"Yeah." I shut the trunk of my car and brace myself to enter the place I hate above all others, to see the person I fear above all others.

SIXTEEN

JOSH

It's been a week since I kissed Aster. A week since she kissed me back. A week during which we've kissed a lot. But never in public. At least not in front of people we know like my parents, Ivy, or my college buddies. Neither of us have told anyone about what we're doing. When I ask Aster if it bothers her, she says no. She likes keeping things to herself. Frankly, so do I.

As I wait in front of her school with a foil-wrapped BLT from the deli—Aster's favorite sandwich—I text Jackie to tell her I'll be a little late. I asked her to meet me at Mom's bakery. I didn't tell her why I wanted to see her. Just that it has to do with my visit to the precinct the other day and my question about subpoenas. I've decided to tell her about the gun. She'll know what to do.

I spot Ivy first. She's walking arm-in-arm with Felicity Suell. I feel a pang of dismay that she's friends with Felicity. I know for a fact that the chick bullied Aster back in middle school. Granted, people change, but Felicity, with her high-pitched giggles and dramatic hair flipping, acts exactly the same as she did back then. She lost the braces but not the attitude.

The second Ivy notices me, she walks over. "Hey!"

"Good first day?"

"Yeah. Best ever."

I arch an eyebrow. "*Best ever*?"

"I'm a senior. This is the beginning of the end."

"And there's a party at my house this weekend," Felicity shoots in. "Wanna join, Josh? We'd love to have some real men around." Her hand skims over my bicep. "Plus, you could bring some of your friends. Preferably of the male gender."

I shrug her off. "Is Aster going?"

Ivy scrunches her nose. "Probably not."

"Is she invited?" I ask her, but it's Felicity who answers.

"Whole senior class is invited. I'm even letting some juniors in on the fun. I have a *big* house. But you know that."

Felicity's mansion is the second largest estate in Kokomo after the Discolis'. While the latter live in a palace surrounded by a moat and castle-worthy gardens, the Suells own four acres of land with a private tennis court and a grotto-style outdoor pool.

I hooked up with Felicity's French cousin in that pool.

Aster chooses that moment to pop out of the school doors. I shove the memory as far away as I can. I shouldn't be thinking about other girls. The second her gaze alights upon me, her tense features smooth out and she smiles. But then she sees Felicity, and Aster's face falls a little. Cautiously she approaches us, fingers wrapped tight around her backpack straps.

"We were just talking to Josh about the party at my house this weekend," Felicity tells her. "Anyway, I gotta go. I have cheerleading practice in twenty minutes. You should totally try out, Ivy. I've seen you dance. You've got moves, girl."

Ivy blushes and smiles. Felicity smacks a kiss on Ivy's cheek, then starts leaving but spins around. "FYI, Manon will be there, Josh. Apparently schools in France don't start for another two weeks." She winks and leaves, putting me in a really uncomfortable situation.

"Was that the girl you had sex with in Felicity's pool?" Ivy asks.

I tug on the neck of my wife-beater that seems made out of chainmail. "I didn't have sex with her."

Aster's studying her brown sandals. Her toes poke out over the sole.

"Sorry. *You made out with*," Ivy says, emphasizing each word.

I jerk my head back up. "Can we not discuss my exes?"

Ivy's eyebrows slant on her forehead.

Aster still hasn't looked up, which is starting to worry me.

I offer her the foil-wrapped sandwich. "I got you a BLT."

She raises her head. Relaxes the death grip she's exerting on her backpack. She still doesn't take my offering though.

I pluck her hand off the strap and place the ball of warm foil inside her palm. I keep my hand on hers, hoping it will get her thinking about something other than my hook-up with Felicity's cousin. Hoping it will remind her that Manon means nothing to me. Nothing compared to what *she*—Aster Redd—means to me.

"Asty, you don't need to go to this party," Ivy tells her, misunderstanding her sister's sudden tension.

Aster smiles at her twin. "I know. I might have to work on Friday anyway…"

Ivy smiles back, and then becomes distracted. "Hold on a sec. I just want to ask Stephanie if she managed to switch into my AP Math class." Ivy trots over to a girl with auburn hair and a mask of freckles that gives the impression she's always tanned.

"Are *you* going to the party?" Aster asks me.

"I'd rather take you out to dinner. Unless you really are working."

Patches of flushed skin burn on her cheeks and neck. For a moment, she looks like one of her mother's quilts, made of various silks and cottons and threads. "I'd rather have dinner with you."

My heart thumps as we gaze at each other in silence. "BLT's still warm," I remind her.

Her crystal-clear eyes drop to the forgotten ball of foil in her hand. She unwraps it as though it were some delicately packaged present, and then she lifts it to her mouth and takes a large bite. I watch her lips move. When her tongue darts out to lick her lips, a ton of fantasies spiral through my mind.

Most of them do not involve a sandwich.

Most of them involve her and me and darkness. Semi-darkness. Not total darkness. I want to see her body, not simply feel it. I want to see those transparent eyes of hers rake me in while the rest of her takes me in.

Whoa.

Dinner.

It's only dinner.

From the corner of my eye, I spy Ivy heading back our way. I plunk my hands into my sweatpants' pockets and push the fabric out so she doesn't notice the effect my dirty mind just had on my body.

"Can we stop by Goodwill on our way home?" Ivy asks. "I want to see if I can dig up something to wear to the party."

Aster nods. "Want half my sandwich?"

"You're not hungry anymore?" Ivy asks.

Aster shakes her head, so her twin snatches the sandwich and scarfs it down. The girl can eat. I'm pretty sure she eats more than me. But she's never had weight problems.

"I should get going. I have a meeting with a study group in twenty at the campus library."

"Thanks for coming," Aster says, her voice as soft as the flower she was named after.

"About that, why *are* you here? Not that I'm not happy to see you," Ivy says.

"Just wanted to check up on my two favorite girls."

Ivy grins. "No wonder you can't find a girlfriend. Who'd want to be third best? Actually fourth best. Maggie's third, right?"

"Maybe I have a girlfriend," I interject.

Ivy's eyes become as wide as the rims on my car. "That you haven't told us about?"

Shoot. I glance over at Aster for help, even though I'm not sure how she can dig me out of the hole I flung myself into. "I said *maybe*," I mumble.

"I think I'm being followed," Aster says suddenly, gaze on the parking lot beyond me.

"What?" Ivy blurts out, shielding her eyes to see the object of her twin's attention.

"What makes you think that?" I ask, spinning to scan the rows of cars.

"The forest-green Jeep over there. It was in front of our house last week. Well, in front of Mr. Mancini's house. And it was also in front of the diner when I got off my shift a couple days ago."

"Are you sure?" I ask, adrenaline spiking through my veins.

She nods.

Without a second thought, I take off toward the parked Jeep.

"Josh, stop!" Ivy yells. "Come on. Let's not do anything brash—"

I don't stop.

A hand wraps around my forearm, tugs me back. The manicured nails tell me it's Ivy. Aster never polishes her nails. "Slow down a sec."

Aster hasn't moved. She's still standing in the spot where we left her.

"Why would anyone be following her?" Ivy asks in a hushed voice.

"Because of the gun."

"How would they even know she has it? And how the heck would they know where she lives?"

"We took the gun to the shop where it was purchased. We had to show them some ID."

Ivy chews on her lip. Her fingers loosen on my arm but stay put. "Okay. So there's an actual possibility that my sister's *not* being paranoid…?" Ivy half-asks, half-states.

I hadn't even considered this. I think back on the time she was certain one of her mother's exes was trying to kill her. She hadn't reacted when he'd choked on a piece of meat—neither had she performed the Heimlich maneuver nor had she phoned 9-1-1—which had led him to call her a psychopath. Which in turn had led her mother to shake her so hard, it had left bruises on her upper arms.

By the time she told me the story, the *asshole*—God knows I don't use curse words lightly—had left, and so had the twins' mother, who'd gone after him to salvage their effed-up relationship.

Again, the twins had stayed with my family for a prolonged time. Thirteen days.

For weeks after that, Aster was certain the man was tailing her. Both Ivy and I took her seriously at first, never left her alone, but it turned out the guy had been sent to jail for racketeering shortly after the break-up.

That was around the time Aster was first diagnosed with schizophrenia.

One of the symptoms is paranoia.

"Well, it can't hurt to see who's inside the car," I mumble.

But no one's inside the car.

A cross dangles from the rearview mirror and a *Baby on Board* sticker decorates the bumper. Even though the glass is tinted, I make out two car seats and various toys. This does not strike me as the car of a vengeful gun-owner.

As I think this, a woman in heels teeters toward us, holding one infant in her arms and dragging another by the hand. She has a dinosaur sticker stuck to the hem of her dress.

"Can I help you?" Her tone tells me she's not looking to help us; she's looking to find out what we want with her car.

"Sorry, ma'am. My cousin has the same car. I thought he'd come to pick us up." I hate how easily lies are coming to me.

She shrugs. "Happens. Jeeps are popular." One of her kids screeches. "Since you're standing right there, mind getting the door?"

She beeps the car open, and I draw the door wide. She all but tosses the infant into the car seat, loops all these different straps around his flailing arms and legs, then kicks the door closed with her heel and goes around the car to get her other kid settled.

"Is it five o'clock yet?" she asks.

"No, ma'am, it's three-thirty."

"Must be five o'clock somewhere," she rambles, getting inside her car. And then she's pulling out of her spot so quick, Ivy and I have to jump out of the way.

"What happens at five?" I ask Ivy.

"Beats me."

As the Jeep exits the parking lot, I think of the man who almost choked on his meat. "Has Aster been taking her pills?" I ask.

"I don't think so. You know she hates it when I check."

"Can you check?"

"I'm going to have to." A rush of air escapes her lungs. "I hate playing bad cop all the time."

I touch Ivy's shoulder.

"Why can't I have normal worries? Like what I'm going to wear to school tomorrow, and who has the hots for whom?"

"'Cause you're exceptional. Not normal."

"That was *super* cheesy." She rolls her eyes.

"Cheesy's my middle name."

"I thought it was Hamster."

"Shut up."

"No, you shut up," she says, laughing.

I crack a grin. "I never thought it would make me laugh someday." But then I look back at Aster, and my glee wilts.

How am I going to tell her no one's following her? That it's all in her head? I ask Ivy this before returning to Aster.

"We're not going to tell her anything," she answers.

"I don't want to lie to her."

"And I don't want to hurt her. Sometimes, going along with someone's imaginings is kinder than challenging them."

Sadly, she's right.

"We need to get her back on her pills," Ivy adds with a sigh. "She'll be all right then."

On my way back to Aster, I text Jackie that I'm going to have to meet her some other time. I don't give her a reason because the reason scares the hell out of me.

I stash my phone back into my jeans. Aster's become chalk-white. I squeeze her hand, search her blue eyes.

I want to tell her she can stop making things up.

I want to tell her I'll keep her secret.

I want to tell her I understand why she did it.

I want to tell her I'm not mad at her for lying to me, for making me believe the Aster who bought the gun was someone other than her.

SEVENTEEN

While Ivy browses through the shelves of Goodwill, I stand by the shop window, peering out onto the parking lot.

"What do you think of these?" she asks me.

I glance at the pair of sandals clutched in her hands.

"They're nice," I say distractedly. At least I think they're nice. Why is she asking me? I'm not good with this sort of thing.

I go back to watching for the green Jeep. I can feel it's there, somewhere. Ivy and Josh saw a woman with two kids getting into the one in front of school, but I bet that was a ploy to lead me astray…to make me feel safe when I'm not.

"I'm ready to go. You want anything?" Ivy asks.

I finally turn away from the window and meet her at the cash register.

"That'll be twelve dollars," the salesperson says.

I start peeling money out of my Velcro wallet when Ivy's voice stops me.

"What are you doing?" she asks.

"Paying."

"I can see that, but why?"

"Isn't that—" I was going to say, *why I'm here*, but it might hurt my sister's feelings, so I rephrase it. "As a back-to-school present?" I fish out twelve singles.

"Aster," she says, pushing my hand away, "I got this."

"How?"

"I sewed some curtains for Miss Norbert over the weekend. She paid me two hundred dollars."

I blink. "You made two hundred dollars?"

"Yep." Ivy smiles proudly.

I'm too shocked to smile.

When we walk out of the shop, Ivy hands me the shopping bag. "They're for you." She tips her head to my feet.

Again, I blink. "You bought shoes for me?"

"One day, when I get famous, I'll buy you super nice ones…like, from Coach."

Her generosity stuns me into silence. I take the shoes out of the bag and really study them this time, run my fingers over each gold grommet and each black strap. Slowly, I crouch and take off the ones I'm wearing.

My feet are streaked with red indentations and blisters. Ivy winces at the sight, while I breathe a sigh of relief. I put the new ones on, tugging up the back zippers, waiting for them to pinch or press on some tender bone in my foot, but they don't. Instead of digging into my flesh, the leather straps are smooth and supple.

"I don't know what to say, Ivy."

"Just say you like them. You do, right?"

As I stand back up, my eyes brim with tears that end up spilling over.

Ivy pulls me into a hug. "I didn't mean to make you cry."

I sniffle. "Thank you."

"You're welcome, sis. Now let's go home. I promised Mom I'd help her hem her new quilt."

During the entire walk back home, I stare at my shoes.

While she tells me Sean asked her out on another date, I stare at my shoes.

While Ivy recommends I take medication I don't need, I stare at my shoes.

While I take said medication, I stare at my shoes.

Afraid they will vanish if I take them off, I keep them on to sleep.

KEEPING my car key wedged between my index and middle finger, I walk into Dr. Frank's office building. Ever since the Jeep started tailing me, I'm careful. Jackie once told me you could do serious damage with a key, so that's my weapon of choice.

The afternoon light is muted from the thick cover of clouds hanging over Kokomo. I wish it would rain already. I hate the stillness, the mugginess, the wait. The imminent storm reminds me of the stalking Jeep.

I ring the doctor's doorbell—because a little plaque on the door says *ring before entering*—then draw open the unlocked door. I'm early, so I sit on the brown corduroy couch by the window and scan the row of parked cars below. There's no Jeep, yet I feel as though I'm being watched.

I don't put my car key away. Instead, I inspect its sloping, jagged edges, and it makes me think of the key hanging around Mom's neck.

I slide my phone out of my backpack, open up a search page, and type: *Easy way to copy a key at home.*

I find a tutorial video that uses a lighter, clear packing tape, scissors, and a box of Tic Tacs. I watch it three times. By the third, I have it memorized. I put my phone away just as Dr. Frank's office door opens.

She ushers a young boy with severe acne and greasy black hair through the waiting room. I wonder what's wrong with him. Perhaps nothing. Perhaps he's like me and a concerned parent or sibling believes he needs someone to talk to.

"Aster, you can go inside. I'll be right there." Dr. Frank smiles that mouthful of ochre teeth that always makes me cringe.

She's pretty nice otherwise, but her teeth…

I put my phone and car key away in my backpack, then sling my bag over my shoulder. As I walk toward the gaping door, I pass the girl with the hairy legs. She stares unblinkingly back at me.

Sometimes, I want to ask her what's wrong, because—unlike me and the boy who just left—there's definitely something wrong with her. It's written all over her face.

I lower myself into the crackled, leather La-Z-Boy across from the flowery armchair Dr. Frank always sits in. Once she made us switch seats, and it really threw me. I wonder if she's made the boy switch seats yet. And then I wonder what chair the girl in the waiting room favors.

Dr. Frank returns, short, gray ponytail swooshing around the back of her head like a feather duster.

"What's wrong with her?" I ask.

"*Her*?" Dr. Frank takes a seat, pulls her yellow notebook out.

"The girl with the hairy legs in your waiting room. Why doesn't she shave her legs? Is it a fashion statement or is she afraid of sharp blades?"

"Oh…*her*." Dr. Frank nods. "Perhaps she wants to be different? What do you think?"

I arch a brow. *Diagnosing is your job, not mine.* "I think she might be afraid of sharp blades."

"Are you afraid of sharp blades?"

"Me? No."

"Have you ever used any to harm yourself?"

I tried cutting myself once. To let out the darkness Mom filled me with. But nothing came out except blood. I don't tell Dr. Frank because I would never do it again, so there's no point in worrying her about it. I simply shake my head.

"How have you been feeling lately, Aster?" she asks.

I show her the new shoes Ivy bought me. Tell her that Josh kissed me. I don't tell her about the gun *or* the Jeep.

"These are wonderful occurrences." Dr. Frank flashes me that yellow smile of hers.

I try not to wince. It's rude to make people feel self-conscious. If my mother were the one sitting across from the doctor, she would already have made a comment. I pride myself on being nothing like Mom.

Dr. Frank dips her head toward the wall mirror behind me. Each session, she makes me stand up in front of it and tell my reflection five things I like about myself, external or internal. I usually get stuck at two. But she doesn't like it when I stop, so I always make three things up.

I stand up, letting my backpack tumble to my feet, and walk over to the wall. "My eyes. My beauty mark." I always say those two because I really do like my eyes, and Josh likes my beauty mark, so it must be nice. "I like the way my sandals fit on my feet." I stare at my reflection, at my blonde corkscrew curls that puff up around my cheekbones. I've already mentioned them in sessions, even though I'm not crazy about them. I bite my lip, observe my straight, white teeth. So unlike Mom's crooked ones. Thinking about my mother reminds me of the video tutorial I watched back in the waiting room. "My industriousness. And I like that I'm proactive."

Five. There. Done.

I return to my seat, fold one leg underneath me, and sit. "Those last two are new."

"The sandals too."

"The sandals too," she concedes, "but let's talk about those last two. How have you been industrious and proactive?"

Since I don't care to divulge my plan, I tell her I've been collecting recipes and testing them out regularly, and the results have been delicious.

Dr. Frank takes notes. At some point, she stands up, walks to her hang window, pulls it up, and lights a cigarette. She blows a cone of smoke through the side of her mouth.

The glowing embers remind me of the lighter I'll need to buy at CVS, along with Tic Tacs, sharp scissors, and clear packing tape. During the rest of my session, these four items scroll through my mind on a loop.

EIGHTEEN

JOSH

A dark green Jeep idles outside my gym.

Right next to my Camry.

Heart blasting, I stare around me, but the street is deserted. I walk around the Jeep. Take in the bumper sticker, the car seats, the messy backseat. What are the odds that the mother with the dinosaur sticker glued to her clothes is a member of my gym?

I jog back inside the gym. Few people are working out right now, and she's not one of them. Maybe she's in the locker room?

I burst into the women's changing room. One woman is unclipping her bra but stops when she spots me in the doorway. She stares at me, horrified. I take in the corridor-like space, listen for the sound of a shower or of a toilet flushing. It's quiet.

"Is anyone else in here?" I ask the flushed lady.

She snatches a towel from the bench to cover herself and shakes her head.

I mumble a quick apology, then head back out, scanning the room again. The woman I met in front of the twins' school isn't here. When I walk back out of the gym, I almost punch the hood of my car.

The Jeep's gone! It's freaking gone. *Poof.* Gone! I grab onto the roots of my hair, yank hard. How could I be so dumb? I should've waited. Stupid. That's what I am. *Stupid.*

The nape of my neck prickles as though I am being watched. My gaze zooms over the darkening street. Sure enough, I spot the Jeep's receding taillights. I leap into my car and crush the gas pedal, reversing out of my spot way too quickly.

Tires squealing, I take off in the direction of the Jeep. I turn the corner at full throttle. The car almost tips over, I'm pushing it so hard. I don't even care if I get fined for speeding. Jackie won't let a ticket stick once I explain my reason for burning rubber.

The Jeep turns left at the next intersection.

The left lane is clogged with cars, so I careen up my lane, then spin my wheel to the left just as the turn arrow becomes yellow. The car I cut off honks at me. Whatever. I made the light.

I've almost caught up with the Jeep, but it's weaving in and out of lanes. The woman knows I'm on her tail. She makes a sharp right, wheels biting into a curb. That's sure to destroy her rims.

I go after her.

The road ahead is a dead-end. I have her cornered.

But suddenly, the crazy woman starts backing up, at full throttle no less. Before she can convert my car into an accordion, I drive into the nearest yard, crushing an abandoned tricycle. The Jeep rockets back onto the main road, then lurches out of sight.

"Fuck!" I punch my steering wheel with an open hand. I owe my mother's curse jar another quarter.

I wrench my seatbelt off my chest and get out of the Camry to pull the squashed trike out from under my suspension. I don't want to roll over it a second time. Deep down, I'm also sort of hoping it's not totally broken, but the handle is bent parallel to the seat.

I let out a sigh that sounds an awful lot like a growl. I get back into the car and pull off the grass before returning to assess the rest of the damage—the lawn is ripped and bruised and will need to be reseeded, and there's a dent in the hedge lining the owner's walkway.

Still fuming, I walk to the front door and ring the doorbell. I hope the people will be reasonable and accept my offer to fix their yard myself. If they press charges, it'll cost me way more than the stupid chase was worth.

I still can't believe she got away!

It's a young girl who answers, a toddler sitting on her hip like a koala. I explain my little mishap. She explains she's the babysitter, that the parents aren't home yet. I leave my phone number with her.

I am an orb of nervous energy, overheated like the bare lightbulb that popped in our garage yesterday. The worst part though, is that I'm starting to doubt my cop potential. I should've been able to handle that car. Instead, I got out of its fucking way—*ping*.

I stop walking.

I still have the gun—*this* is what she's after.

She'll be back for it.

And this time, I'll be ready.

NINETEEN

The sky turned a burnt orange tonight, tinting the gray pavement the color of desert dunes and the hedges the color of molten chocolate. I wonder if Ivy saw it. She loves sunsets.

When I walk into the house, I find Mom in front of the TV, fingers laying listlessly on her lap, eyes wide open, zombie-like. My first thought is that she's dead. I check for a bullet wound, but remember Josh has the gun. Then again, if she procured herself *one* gun, she could probably buy another.

She doesn't turn toward me, and her chest isn't rising.

Maybe she overdosed.

I get this sick feeling inside my stomach, like I've swallowed a bag of nails and the pointy tips are embedding themselves inside the fleshy lining. I've always wished my mother would go away, but I never wished for her to die. I—

"What?" she huffs.

My heart kicks around in my chest.

She's not dead.

I should be relieved but I'm not. I'm—

"Why are you looking at me like that?"

I shut my gaping mouth, then slowly open it again to form words…a sentence. "I'm just surprised you're not working."

"I deserve a break sometimes."

I painted my toes bubblegum pink. I thought I used Ivy's nail polish, but she told me all her nail polishes are on top of our dresser, not in the bathroom where I found the pink one. I was going to rub it off before Mom noticed I borrowed something of hers, but there was no nail polish remover.

I squeeze the CVS bag in my hand. Pink acetone sloshes in its plastic bottle, clinking against the Tic Tac box, the scissors, the lighter, the roll of packing tape.

I should've used the nail polish remover before entering the apartment, but I assumed Mom would be in her studio, working, not on the couch, vegetating.

The ceiling light isn't on, so I doubt she can see my painted toenails. Still, I step toward the couch and tuck my feet underneath its base.

"Do you know where Ivy is?" she asks me.

"I thought she'd be here."

Mom frowns. "Well, she isn't."

I try moving but my bones feel like they've fused together. "Want something to eat? I was about to make dinner…"

Mom tilts her head down. "Sure, but don't make anything too fancy. I know Maggie loves her complicated, unpronounceable French dishes, but you should be able to pronounce what you eat."

I walk briskly to the fridge and pull it open to see what's inside. Grated cheddar. Half a carton of cream. Half a head of lettuce. Orange juice. "Penne with cream sauce?"

"Okay." Making sure Mom's attention is on the lit screen again, I edge back out of the kitchen and walk down the narrow corridor to the bathroom. As soon as I'm inside, I ball some cotton, soak it in the remover, and strip my nails of their pretty pinkness. I place the bottle on one of the shelves and am about to close the mirrored door when I spy a bottle of sleeping pills. I shake out a few, then screw the lid back on and replace the bottle. I toss the used cotton in the toilet and flush it down, then stop by my room to stow the rest of my purchases inside my underwear drawer.

Pills stuffed snugly inside my jeans' pocket, I return to the kitchen to make dinner.

"YOU LIKE IT?" I tip my chin toward Mom's almost-empty bowl.

The tines of her fork scour the thick ceramic, scraping up the last lumps of congealed sauce. "You put in too much cheese, but I was hungry."

I want to ask why she can't simply say *yes it was good,* or *thank you for making dinner, Aster*. How hard is it to say something nice? Does she think it will make her appear weak or soft? Or does she think it will weaken *me*? She's wrong. Kindness makes people stronger; it makes people believe in themselves; it makes them feel necessary and important—and I don't mean conceited, I mean useful.

"I wanted to speak to you about the gun," she says suddenly.

My spine tautens. Is she going to accuse me again? Ask why I did it? Will she listen when I tell her…again…that even though my name was on the registration, it wasn't mine?

She shuts her eyes, rubs her forehead, massages her temples. "*I* bought it."

I gape at her. This feels like an apology. Mom never apologizes.

Her lids come up. She looks at me, then beyond me at the door. "If you tell Ivy, I'll deny it."

I've managed to wedge my mouth closed even though the aftershock of her words lingers. "Why?"

"Because I felt unsafe. We live on the ground floor. We're only women—"

"I didn't mean, why did you buy it? I meant, why did you pin it on me?"

She takes a deep breath, wipes the back of her hand across her eyes. "I thought I was losing Ivy to you."

I don't tell her, *it's not a competition, Mom*, because I'm acutely aware that it is…it always has been. Mom and I have constantly jousted for Ivy's affection and attention, because winning them gives us purpose and importance.

I toy with a loose thread on the hem of my T-shirt. "How did you get them to put my name on the registration?"

She sucks on her bottom lip and glances over at the TV. "I asked a friend to buy the gun."

"And her name happened to be Aster like me?"

"Funny, huh?"

She's lying. I feel it in my bones. She must've found my fake ID and used it.

She yawns. "Why do I feel so tired?"

My cheeks flush with color that I pray she doesn't spot.

Over the next five minutes, her lids lower as though tiny weights were attached to her translucent lashes. I think about the sleeping pills I ground into her sauce and the handful of cheese I added at the last minute, worried she would detect the chalky flavor or powdery texture.

When she falls asleep, I don't feel an ounce of regret for what I have done or for what I'm about to do.

I carry our empty bowls of pasta into the kitchen, pour scalding water over Mom's to erase all traces of the pills. The sound of the tap running doesn't bother her sleep. What if she never awakens? What if I put too many pills?

No. She'll be fine, I reason. I only used three. Four at the most.

After I set the bowls to dry on the rack, I go collect my supplies from my bedroom. With shaky fingers, I empty the orange Tic Tacs right into my drawer, then cut out one of the sides of the box. I bring my makeshift tools into the living room and lay them out on the coffee table like a surgeon about to operate.

Drool leaks out of Mom's mouth. I scoot closer to her.

My breathing stills, but not my heart.

The key is tucked inside her blouse. I hoist the string up. When the glare of the TV screen glints off the metal, I suck in my breath. I carefully liberate it from the blouse. I cut a piece of clear packing tape, but because my fingers shake, it folds on itself. I crumple it and cut off another piece, this time more carefully.

I stick it to the edge of the coffee table, then cut out two more strips—backups—and tape them to the table also. Next, I grab the lighter. Praying the scent of fire won't wake Mom, I hold the key away from her flammable shirt and warm the metal. It heats up so quickly, it singes my index finger and thumb. I almost drop the key, but if I drop it now, it'll wake Mom, so I endure the burn. Once the metal has blackened, I toss the lighter on the cushion next to me and wait for the key to cool down.

Sweat drips down the sides of my face, beads on my nose. I don't wipe it away. After enough time has passed, I seize one of the pieces of tape and press the sticky side against the metal.

Like in the tutorial, a blackened imprint appears on the clear tape. I set the key down against Mom's rising chest, then carefully glue the tape on the section of Tic Tac box. Latching on to the scissors, I reverentially swipe the square of plastic from the table and return to my bedroom. I don't have a lock on my door, so I keep my back against it as I cut out each crenellated edge.

More perspiration forms on my face, drips into my mouth, salty and wet like tears. I barely breathe as I incise the plastic. Closing one eye, I hold my creation up to the ceiling light to inspect my handiwork. I snip off a tiny piece of excess clear plastic, then inspect my intricate design again. This time the plastic shape matches up to the black imprint perfectly. How I managed this with shaky fingers is an absolute miracle.

My heart leaps against the ramparts of my chest. Mom will never be able to hide anything from me again. Not a gun, not anything.

I set the scissors aside on the bookshelf, on top of a pile of dog-eared Western romance paperbacks I recovered from a trash bin, and open my bedroom door, wincing when it creaks.

I ball my fingers, making a protective fist around my plastic key. The grooves and indents bite into my skin. Heart pumping madly, I creep back into the living room. Mom's eyes are still shut, her chest still rising evenly, the key still resting on her cheap blouse.

I tread quietly to her studio and am about to let myself in when Mom makes a loud snorting sound.

I drop my hands back to my sides, lurch away from the door like a ballerina. Panic rises, tangy like vomit, in my throat. Mom stirs, moves her head from side to side. I wait for her lids to spring upward; I wait for her pallid gaze to set on me; for her thin mouth to pinch.

My fists feel like rocks against my hips, hard in spite of their wobbliness. Mom's lids remain shut, and then she's immobile again.

For long seconds, all I do is breathe. Try to return some oxygen to my depleted lungs before they shrivel like the first strip of packing tape. When I feel calmer, I edge toward the studio again.

With clammy fingers that no longer feel attached to my palms, I turn the doorknob, and press the door open, then slide my quivering body inside and shut the door softly behind me. I don't spin the twist lock because it always makes a sharp grating noise, like a bullet.

I tiptoe across the room and kneel in front of the drawer. And then, whispering a little prayer, I fit the piece of plastic into the lock.

It slides right in.

TWENTY

JOSH

The sweat on my temples has turned icy by the time I pull out of the dead-end street. I lower my window to let the warm night air dry the frosty dampness. I'm also hoping it will ease my nerves. Thaw me out like a microwave defrosts frozen stuff.

My knuckles are bone-white. My fingers too. I relax my death grip on my steering wheel, but I don't unsquash my lips. I drive to Aster's. I need to tell her I trust her. That I never meant not to trust her.

No, I won't tell her that. It will only hurt her.

I try calling to tell her I'm coming over, but she doesn't answer her cell. So I dial her home number. It rings and rings.

Scenarios start spooling through my mind.

Wild scenarios.

The crazy lady in the green Jeep went to Aster's house. Driving me off the road was a diversion. She's going to hold Aster hostage until I hand over the gun. She must be working with Rose. Maybe she's another patient of Rose's shrink, because who drives someone off the road? Who stalks teenagers?

I think about her kids. Pity them. Cracked people shouldn't be allowed to raise children.

Yet they do.

Everyday.

Everywhere.

I think of Aster and Ivy and all they've endured.

I call Aster's phone. Nothing. I call Ivy.

"She's at home, Josh. Why?"

I don't tell her why. I don't want to worry her.

"Just looking for her."

"Okay. Well I need to get back to studying. I'll see you later?"

"Yeah. Maybe."

I hang up, then phone the Redds' home phone again. Still no one picks up.

Heart thundering, I speed down the shadowy roads toward Mulberry Street.

TWENTY-ONE

Mom's standing in the doorway of her studio, one hand on the knob, the other on the doorframe. Even though no light is on, her eyes blaze in the obscurity.

Ivy always jokes the ringtone of our house phone is loud enough to wake the dead. I don't know about the dead, but it woke Mom.

I slam her special drawer shut and rip the plastic key out of the lock, and then I stand to face the retaliation that's sure to be vicious.

My gaze darts to the big pair of scissors tucked into a shelf on her sewing table. I don't take them, but make sure they're within reach.

Mom sways into the room, woozy with sleep.

I feel like I have a sharp blade inside my chest instead of a heart. Mom's hand comes up and arcs through the air toward my cheek. When it comes down, my face flies sideways. My skin smarts and prickles and burns.

I don't cry.

"How dare you, Aster? How dare you!" She grabs my wrist, forces my fingers open, then rips the serrated piece of plastic out of my fingers.

In the moonlight, she studies it. And then she hits me again.

This time, I fold like a chopped tree trunk. My knees and palms hit the ground first. And then my head knocks into the hard and cold five-star base of Ivy's chair.

The world turns ghost-white, then chrome-yellow, before crackling back to its hushed blueness.

"I've always respected your privacy. Always. I never pried. Never went inside your bedroom. Never looked through your stuff. But if that's how you want to play it, then that's how we'll play it."

She takes off toward the living room, spidery legs no longer affected by the drugs. I scramble to my feet and run after her. She makes it to my room before I do. She pulls open the dresser's top drawer, yanks out handfuls of clothes, and throws them around. Orange Tic Tacs flutter out like confetti. She closes her fingers around the little porcelain box containing my milk teeth. I grab onto her arm before she can lob it at the floor.

"Mom, stop! I didn't see anything! I didn't see anything!"

She doesn't stop. Wrenches her arm out of my grasp and throws my keepsake box. It soars through the air and lands on a pile of dirty clothes I planned to wash later.

Mom yanks open the next drawer. Ivy's candy-colored clothes spray around us like the cool water from the sprinklers we used to run through on sticky summer days. Rooted to the ground, I watch as Mom sweeps her arm across the dresser top, sending all of Ivy's nail polishes crashing to the floor. A framed baby picture of Ivy and me sails down next. The glass fractures, falls in big shards around the silver frame.

When Mom edges toward my bookcase, I stand before it, like a warrior guarding her soldiers. I extend my arms. Yell for her to stop. She advances toward me, fury burning in her narrowed eyes.

"Mrs. Redd!"

I fling my attention to the doorway.

Josh is here.

I blink to make sure my mind isn't playing tricks on me.

He's really here.

Josh has come to help me.

"How—" I croak. I want to ask how he knew I needed him, but the words die when Mom's hands jerk me aside. I collide into the wall like a ragdoll. Josh lunges toward me, catches me while Mom wreaks havoc, tossing my books, ripping pages, shredding them.

Though my head is swimming, though my eyes burn, though Josh is trying to shelter me behind his broad body, I keep my eyes on my ravaged possessions.

Mom's eyes meet mine over Josh's shoulder. They gleam with surprise? Fear? Understanding? "You are not worthy of his name," she says, voice as thick and tense as the air pulsating between our three bodies.

Without looking away from my face, she picks up the fallen scissors, shreds my plastic key into tiny, clear slivers, and flings the shards at me, but they hit Josh's chest instead.

Flit down to his feet.

"Let's go," he says roughly.

Rivers of tears course over my cheeks, drip off my chin.

I stop putting up resistance and let Josh guide me out of my devastated room.

"You betrayed me, Aster," Mom bellows, following us into the living room.

I wince. I want to answer, "You betrayed me first," but my lips tremble too much to form words. I keep my eyes on my shuffling feet, on the flashing grommets of my sandals, as I walk.

"How?" I ask him once I'm sitting in his car. "How did you know to come?"

Green eyes fixed on the road, he says, "I just felt it."

I smile. In spite of the horror of tonight, in spite of my tumbling tears, I smile.

Josh felt me.

He felt *me*.

TWENTY-TWO

JOSH

After Aster falls asleep in the guest bedroom, I head downstairs to where Mom and Jackie are having a glass of wine.

When I thundered into the house, cradling Aster against me, when they took in her bloated, tear-streaked face, the green bulge on her forehead, they fell terribly quiet. They didn't try to intercept her and sit her down for questioning.

They knew.

They just knew.

The years have connected us in wordless ways.

"She needs to be placed in an institution. She's a danger to her children and a danger to herself," I tell them, grinding my fingers into fists. "Aster can't go back there."

Mom's placed her hand over my shoulder. She's trying to soothe me, but her effort is wasted. I am beyond manic tonight. Like a pressure cooker, I've reached my boiling point. Anger spews from every pore on my body.

"Six months, Josh. Six months," Mom's saying.

"Did you not see the bruise on Aster's forehead?" I'm shaking. "That woman is crazy! She needs to be interred."

"Interned," Jackie says quietly. "I'm pretty sure we'd get arrested if we buried Rose."

I stare at her. "What are you talking about?"

A laugh erupts from Mom. She claps her palm against her mouth, but it only mutes the bubbling sound. "I'm sorry. Nerves." And then she's crying laughing.

And I still don't get what's going on.

Jackie bites her lip. "Josh, does Aster want to press charges?"

"I didn't ask her." After a beat where the only sound is my mother's dying laughter, I ask, "Can she?"

"Does Rose have a gun?" Jackie asks.

"What?" I go still. "How—" My words die out when she flicks her gaze to Mom. "How do *you* know, Mom?"

She wipes her eyes, smudging some of her mascara. "The phone call in front of the bakery. You asked Ivy if Rose had a gun, and then a couple nights later, Aster's at our house and I guessed something was going on. So I called Ivy and she told me about Mr. Mancini's cat."

"You knew all along?"

Mom's sober again. She nods.

"And you?" I ask the cop in street clothes nursing a glass of wine.

She takes a deep breath, pushes her glass of wine away, leans her forearms against the white marble kitchen island. "I guessed something was going on when you dropped by the precinct, but I didn't know it had to do with a gun until right now."

"Ivy says the gun's registered to her sister," Mom adds.

"Yeah," I answer, "but Aster didn't buy it."

"Are we sure of that?" Mom asks.

"'Cause if she did, Josh," Jackie putts in, "then she must've forged an ID to fake her age, and, well, that's not going to help once we get the twins in front of a judge."

"She didn't buy it!" I repeat, hating that they don't trust Aster.

"How can you be sure?" Jackie asks.

"Because I am." Maybe they'd stop asking questions if I told them that a car drove me off the road tonight, that it's been tailing Aster ever since we stopped by the firearms shop. But what's the point in panicking Mom? Besides, I don't want to get the police involved.

I started this mess when I ran the trace; I will finish this mess. Even if it means running down my street, waving a gun in my hand. If the crazy Jeep lady knows where Aster lives, she knows where I live too.

"Does Rose still have the gun?" Jackie asks.

"No."

"Where is it?"

"I gave it back to the shop."

"Why'd you do that?" Jackie says, springing away from the countertop. "You should've given it to me, Josh. It's evidence."

"Evidence? There was no murder..." I say. Besides Mancini's cat. *Poor creature.*

"But if Rose used it to threaten her daughters—"

I interrupt Jackie. "It'll be her word against theirs."

Suddenly, the door bursts open. I expect to see my dad but it's Ivy. She careens into the kitchen, skin pasty and mouth gaping open. "What the hell happened at my house? Where's Aster?" Her voice is so harsh I'm afraid it'll wake up her twin. "Why'd she trash our room?"

"*She* didn't. It was your mom."

She jolts back, blinks. "But Mom said…"

"That it was Aster?" I finish for her. Shake my head. "Your mom blames your sister for everything that's wrong in her life."

"But—" Ivy gapes at Jackie and Mom. "Why would she do that?"

"Aster wouldn't tell me what happened." I tried to get her to talk but she was too stressed out to utter a single word. "I'm surprised your mom didn't tell you."

"She said Aster flipped out."

"I was there, Ivy. It was your mom who *flipped out*."

My friend mulls this over, then asks, "Where is Aster?"

"Upstairs. Sleeping."

Ivy fords across the kitchen. I'm about to stop her but think Aster will be glad to see her sister.

"She's not going back there. I won't let her."

Ivy freezes.

"And you shouldn't go back there either. You're not safe."

"What are we supposed to do? Get tossed into the foster care system for six months?"

"You can move in with us," Mom says. It's not the first time she's offered them refuge.

"We can't, Maggie. You've been more than kind over the years, have done more than anyone has ever done for us, but we can't just abandon our mother. She's not well. She wouldn't survive without us."

"Aster won't survive *with* her," I say.

"I never forced Aster to come home with me. Never."

"Yet she comes back each time *for* you."

"But I don't ask her to."

I snort. "She cares about you more than she cares about anyone!"

"Calm down, Josh," Mom says.

I toss my hands in the air. "How am I supposed to calm down?"

Mom, Jackie, and Ivy exchange a look. And then Ivy turns the corner and heads up the stairs. Her light footsteps resonate against our carpeted pine floors and then fade once she enters the guestroom.

"I'll stop by their apartment on my way home," Jackie says in a low voice, tugging her coat from the hook by our front door.

"Will you arrest her?" I ask.

She lowers her gaze to the umbrella stand, thanks Mom for the wine, then leaves without answering me.

"Have you had dinner yet, honey?" Mom asks after Jackie leaves.

I shake my head.

"Do you want me to make you a plate?"

I drag my hands down the sides of my face. "Yes. No. I don't know."

Shoulders pinched, she opens the oven door, scoops roasted meat and carrots onto a plate, then places it in front of me. "You mind if I wait for your dad? He doesn't like eating alone."

I shake my head, shovel down the food that tastes hot.

Ivy comes down a few moments after I finish eating. She hasn't regained much color. If anything, she seems more gray than white. "She won't tell me what happened," she says softly, then sighs as she takes a seat next to me. She places her hand on top of mine, squeezes it. "Thank you for bringing her here. I don't know what we would do without you in our lives." She bumps her shoulder into mine.

And for the first time since I left the gym, I breathe a little easier.

"It might be the new meds," Ivy says. "That made Mom act"—she swallows—"the way she did."

I don't believe it has anything to do with her medication.

"She said something strange tonight," I suddenly say.

"Who?"

"Your mom."

"Mom? Say something strange?"

It's a paltry attempt at a joke, but I smile a little. "She told Aster: *you are not worthy of his name*. What does that mean?"

"God's name?" Mom suggests, dipping her lips into her glass of wine.

"Rose isn't religious."

"It's weird, but not the weirdest thing she's ever said. Recently she told me I was going to marry a man who'll live among horses and chickens."

"What?" I ask.

"Yeah. Apparently, her psychic told her I'm going to get hitched to a farmer." She grins widely, and it gives her cheeks some pinkness. "Me. The girl who dreams of living in a big city. Who dreams of fame and fortune."

I chuckle. "You'll just be fortunate if you can find a man who can deal with your passion for sewing."

"Hey!" Ivy flicks me.

I laugh now.

A wide grin splitting her face, Ivy continues telling stories we already know. Stories of the strange things her mother has done and said over the years. And it humanizes that hateful woman, but it doesn't spark any forgiveness in me.

Broken people shouldn't try to break others.

TWENTY-THREE

Josh's scent is everywhere. I pull in a lungful of air from my dark bedroom. I swear I can smell him, and yet, when was the last time he laid in my bed?

My bed.

My bedroom.

Mom.

My lids slam up in time with my upper body. Sitting, I blink to make out my surroundings. I'm not in my bed, not in my house. I find Josh lying on his stomach, head on the pillow next to mine, wearing gray boxers and a Metallica T-shirt.

Heat snakes through me. Like a belly-dancer, it writhes and fills each corner of my soul with warmth and love. Gently, so as not to wake him, I lie back down and snuggle against him.

Visions of the evening file through my mind. They feel surreal. Half dream, half nightmare. Even though my audacity was punished brutally, squashed and shattered, it thrills me. I've never felt so strong and cunning, able to accomplish anything. Yes, I have no more key, but deep down, I know that if I ever have doubts about what Mom hides inside her drawer, I can make a new one.

I've done it once. I can do it again.

Besides, tonight, I learned one other thing.

A thing of vital importance to me.

Ivy didn't lie to me. Inside Mom's drawer, there really were only rolls of fabric. Glittery, soft, crinkly, beaded. I'm not sure why she locks them up, but then again, I'm not sure why my mother does most things.

Well, besides to drive a wedge between Ivy and me.

She failed.

She will always fail at that.

Nothing could ever separate Ivy and me.

You can't chop one person in two and hope one half stays alive and not the other. Human bodies don't work like that. Ivy and me, we're one. She cannot make us two.

Audacious and victorious.

I trail my fingers over Josh's bent arm, over the fine hairs bleached by the sun, over the soft skin burnished by the long hot summer. I touch the smooth, tanned planes of his face next. And then I get bolder and press my lips against his.

His mouth softens against mine. His lips move against mine. Soon, his breathing intensifies, and his hands skate over my skin. He shifts onto his side, opens his eyes.

"Hey."

"Hey," I whisper through tipped-up lips.

He touches my forehead lightly, and it smarts. The memory of the base of Ivy's chair flashes through my mind then back out.

Thank you, I mouth. *And not simply for tonight but for the last four thousand three hundred and eighty days of our lives.*

I don't say this out loud, but I think it as I press him onto his back and straddle him.

The butterflies have returned in numbers tonight, and they are performing backflips inside my belly. Tonight, I am made entirely of butterflies. There are no more contemplations and emotions inside of me, no more considerations and decisions.

Only instinct and need.

Only the man I've landed on.

Or rather the one who landed on me twelve years ago.

TWENTY-FOUR

JOSH

Aster and I have decided to tell Ivy about us. She'll do the telling while I drive the gun over to the precinct. I plan on handing it over to Jackie and letting her investigate its provenance. Hopefully it will lead to the arrest of psycho Jeep-lady.

As I take the street that leads to the precinct, I catch a glimpse of dark green in my rearview mirror.

"Unbelievable," I whisper. The woman just won't stop.

I ogle my phone. It would be a good time to call Jackie. She'd come out and arrest Jeep-lady right then and there.

Instead, I keep driving. When I turn right on South Lafountain, and the Jeep turns right, I know I've got it hooked to my bumper. Exhilaration throttles through me.

I know exactly how I'm going to trap Jeep-lady.

Even though I detailed my car three days ago, I hang a left in the middle of the block and pull into Mason's Drive-Through Car Wash. The Jeep slows to a crawl further down and enters the Walgreen's parking lot. It's no longer in my field of vision, but I'm pretty sure it won't be going anywhere until *I* go somewhere.

The white Toyota in front of me enters the car wash. I go ahead and purchase a token from the drive-through attendant. From the looks of his pimply skin and sparse chin hairs, I assume he's sixteen, give or take a year. The guy eyes my car, frowns—he must notice the Camry doesn't need a wash—but takes my money anyway. Maybe he thinks I'm OCD or something.

I drive onto the automated rails, then jump out, hauling my gym bag.

"What are you doing?" the dude asks, wide-eyed.

I jerk my chin toward Walgreen's. "I'm working undercover, and I need your help." I haven't put in my token yet. "Drive my car through the wash, then head into the Walgreen's lot and park it. I'll meet you there."

"You serious, man?"

"Yeah. I called for backup but they're fifteen minutes out." Surprise and doubt mash on the attendant's face.

"Can I see your badge?"

"No time for that. Here." I shove the keys in his hands. "This is a matter of national security."

He blinks.

I lay a reassuring palm on his scrawny arm. "You got this. Just stay in the car, all right?"

Finally, he moves. Straight for the open door of the Camry. After he gets in and shuts the door, I insert the token and then run around the large white building.

I edge around the side until I can see the back of the Walgreen lot.

I watch the Jeep.

Detect a presence inside.

I feel like Led Zeppelin's drummer is inside my chest, beating my heart like he used to pound his drums.

I text Jackie: ***Rendezvous Walgreens on South Lafountain***. I toss the bag and the phone on the ground, and dig out the gun, sliding it into my jeans' waistband.

And then I wait some more.

My nostrils pulse with furious breaths.

I see the front hood of my car pop out of the car wash, and then, exactly like I asked, the attendant drives onto South Lafountain and takes a sharp left into the adjacent lot.

Knowing Jeep-lady's attention will be on my car, I race across the concrete field toward the back end of the lot like a running back and slide-lunge behind the first parked car. Ducking, I dash from one car to the next until I've arrived next to the Jeep.

With slick fingers, I grab the gun from my waistband, and slurping in an insane amount of air and courage, I jerk upright and point the gun at the passenger window.

The person at the wheel startles, but not as much as I do when I make out the face of my stalker through the tinted window.

TWENTY-FIVE

There are so many things I want to tell my sister. And in time, I'll tell her everything, but some will have to wait until we no longer live under Mom's roof.

Ivy picks a piece of crumble off the top of her raspberry muffin. We are sitting in Maggie's bakery that's overrun with pudgy-limbed toddlers and their legging-clad mothers. We should be in school, but we spent our morning picking up the debris inside our bedroom and salvaging our possessions after Mom locked herself in her studio.

Ivy told me Mom felt bad about what she'd done, that she'd panicked because she couldn't find her key and thought I'd taken it. But then she'd located it. It was wedged between the couch cushions.

I'm not sure why she lied. Perhaps she did it because she felt guilty about the gun she pinned on me. Or perhaps she didn't mention my plastic key because she thought it undermined her authority.

"She told me she asked a friend to buy her the gun for protection," my twin says.

"She used my fake ID," I say.

"She said her friend was called—"

"You fell for that?"

Ivy gapes at me. Slowly, she wipes the astonishment off her face with a sigh. "I'm sorry, Asty. I wish she'd used mine."

When I made my ID, I made my sister a matching one. She doesn't use it to sneak into R-rated movies, though; she uses it to buy beer and get into clubs.

I raise a stiff smile. "I'm glad she didn't involve you."

Ivy smiles back, and it's like peering at a mirror, because her smile is as strained as mine, and her eyes are as puffy as mine, and her skin is as sallow as mine. Neither of us slept much last night.

Funny thing is though, last night was possibly the worst and best of my life.

"I need to tell you something," I say, nibbling on my nails that are already bitten to the quick.

"You're going to press charges?"

"What?" When I get that she means Mom, I look down. "I haven't decided yet."

I haven't decided because I feel like I owe Mom for her discretion. I never thought I would owe my mother for anything besides giving me life.

Ivy's forehead is creased. "I don't think she would survive losing us."

"Losing *you*," I correct.

Ivy doesn't correct me. She takes a bite of her muffin instead and chews slowly, pensively.

I feel Maggie watching us from behind the counter. I give her a quick smile to reassure her that everything's okay. Her brightly painted lips bend upward in response. When her attention drifts back to the customer pointing to the tray of red velvet cupcakes, I lean across the small round table so the next thing I tell my sister will reach her ears and hers alone. "There's something else I need to tell you."

Ivy's gaze detaches from the moist, flecked confection in her hands.

"Josh and I, we're…we're together."

The half-eaten muffin tumbles out of her fingers and onto the plate. After a beat, she blurts out, "Like a couple?"

I nod.

Her blue eyes widen and fix on my identical ones. She gapes at me so long without saying a word that I think she's mad.

My stomach flip-flops. "Are you angry?"

"Angry?" She straightens. "No. Just…surprised. How long has this been going on?"

"Almost two weeks."

"Two weeks!" she squeaks.

I nod.

She makes a face. "That's why he's been acting so bizarre lately. Coming to school with BLTs and—"

"I really love him, you know?" A blush creeps up my throat, splatters my jaw, paints my cheeks red.

For a moment, she doesn't say anything, and no emotion registers on her face. "I know. I do too. Not in that way, though. Don't worry." She catches my drumming fingers in hers and squeezes them hard. "I'm so happy for you guys. This is the best news I've had in a while."

I scrutinize her face to make sure she's not lying to reassure me. There is true joy in her gaze.

She leans over, whispers conspiratorially. "Have you told Maggie?"

"Not yet. We wanted to tell you first."

She grins. "I'm happy you did. It means a lot to me."

Just like her approval means everything to me.

"So...how did it happen?" she asks.

I'm about to tell her about the movies, when I spy an abandoned magazine on the table next to ours. It sits beside an empty porcelain mug marred by lipstick-stains. I reach over and pick up the magazine.

On the glossy page, staring wide-eyed back at me, hairy legs pulled into her chest, sits the girl from Dr. Frank's waiting room.

"Aster?" Ivy says, trying to catch my attention.

I point to her. "I know her. She goes to see Dr. Frank too."

Ivy's gaze roams over the page and a small groove appears between her eyebrows. "Are you sure?"

"How many girls with hairy legs do you know?"

"Not many, but this looks like an advertisement. Which probably means she's a model."

Being different is okay is written in a pretty yellow font over the girl's troubled face.

She sits the same way at Dr. Frank's waiting room. With her legs pulled up underneath her chin. "She must be a spokesperson."

My sister frowns. "Maybe. Anyway, tell me about your first date."

I flip the magazine over, replacing the girl's sad eyes with my sister's happy ones.

TWENTY-SIX

JOSH

I gape at the man in the driver's seat as he lowers the passenger window. Keeping my gun trained on him, I search the backseat for the crazy mother who ran me off the road. Only thing back there are the two car seats. "Where's the…where is she?"

"Can you put the gun away, Joshua?"

I swing my gaze back to him, squeeze the gun tighter, put my finger on the trigger. He knows my name.

"I'll explain, but not at gunpoint. You either lower the gun and get in, or I will back out of here, and you'll stay in the dark."

"I have a gun. You don't. You don't get to make the rules."

Out of nowhere, he points a pistol pimped out with a long cylindrical silencer at me. "Get in the car before your friend over there calls the cops."

"They're already on the way."

"Then I'll be on mine."

He reverses the car. I jolt backward. Before he can roll off, I lunge toward the passenger door. "Okay. Okay. Let me get my car keys."

"No time."

The distant wail of sirens pierces the quiet afternoon.

Shooting the drive-through attendant an apologetic look, I jump into the Jeep. Although the dude's face isn't completely unfamiliar, I can't place him. He's put his gun down, but I haven't. I glide one of my hands over my jeans' back pocket to grab my phone, but it's not there.

I left it in my gym bag!

Heart banging, I curse my stupidity, then wrap my hand back around the gun. "Do we know each other?" My voice rings in my ears.

"Put the gun away," he says, his voice a low rumble.

"Hell, no."

He spins the wheel of the Jeep so hard the velocity pins me to the door and unbalances my aim. He seizes the gun from my clammy fingers with such little effort I wonder if I was even holding on to it.

"Kids shouldn't play with guns."

"But psycho stalkers should?"

One side of his mouth hitches up. "Psycho stalker?"

"You've been following us with your sidekick. You even used children to lure us into thinking—"

"My wife isn't my sidekick, and my kids aren't bait."

"But—"

"I've been using her car while mine's in the shop."

It hits me why he's familiar. "You're that security guard! Aster Colson!"

"Private agent, not security guard."

Even his voice sounds familiar, but that's impossible. And yet—

I'm jerked around in my seat. Snapping out of my trance, I look around. We're in the middle of a deserted construction site. He slides the Jeep underneath the metal foundations of a building as huge as my old high school.

Cold sweat beads on my upper lip.

He's brought me here to kill me.

Instead of thinking up ways of escaping, I think of my mother, Aster, Ivy, and Dad, and hope they'll think I was kidnapped. If they know I willingly jumped into a car with a madman, they'll be so disappointed. On the upside, it might make my death easier on them.

I can already hear my eulogy: "He wasn't very bright, but he was kind."

I blink away my macabre thoughts. I'm not dying today. *Nope. Not ready.*

I run through what Jackie taught me about criminals. The best way to distract them is to keep them talking. Hostage negotiation was her specialty back in the day. "The owner of the gun shop called you and told you about me and Aster?"

He puts the car in park, then glances at me. His hand is on the Glock. He's stroking the barrel as though it were a woman's thigh.

He doesn't seem to be listening to me, so I continue, "Why did you chase us around instead of simply asking us for your gun back? You out of jobs or something?"

"You ask a lot of questions."

"You said you'd explain."

He stops stroking the gun, looks up. His eyes are startlingly blue in contrast to his light brown skin. He reminds me of that baseball player. What's his name again—

"I've been searching for this gun a long time," he says, interrupting my straying thoughts.

This is *so not* the time to think about who he reminds me of.

"I thought I'd lost it but..." His gaze lands on something beyond me.

I shift around in my seat, relief and fear warring inside my torso. Has someone come to help him, or help me?

There's no one there.

Anxiety crawls up my throat like a worm on Ritalin. "But what?"

"But now I know it was stolen from me. By a woman no less. Not that I have anything against women."

"You mean *Rose* stole your gun?"

"Rose," he repeats softly. "Can't believe she's the one who stole my gun...." A wan smile settles over his lips.

"How do you even know her?"

He tilts his head down, studies me with his intensely bright eyes. I blink because I think I'm seeing Ivy. She always makes that face when she's considering something. "We had a thing almost twenty years ago," he finally says. "I was on leave back then, so it didn't last long. Two weeks." He lowers his eyes to the gun, studies its lines and contours. "And I didn't ring your doorbell, Joshua, because I needed to understand what two kids were doing with my gun. Especially since one of them had my name. So when my buddy gave me Aster's address—Mulberry Street—I drove out there. And then you text me asking if I know a Rose Redd. And everything falls into place." His gaze locks onto mine. "I didn't mean to scare you kids, but I didn't want to leave my gun in some stranger's possession. I'd never declared it lost or stolen, so if it was ever used, it would've been one hell of a shitfest."

"Rose never mentioned you," I say.

"I don't think I was worth mentioning." Something akin to regret makes his eyes murky. "You see, I lied to her. Told her I sold fabric because that's what she liked. I even bought her all these colorful rolls of satin and beaded silks to make myself feel better about lying." He snorts, even though a small smile plays on his lips. "And how does the woman repay me? She steals my gun. She was cunning, that one." He rubs his hand over his closely-cropped hair. "Have I answered all your questions, Joshua?"

A realization squirms into my brain. Rose said, *You don't deserve his name.* Could *his* refer to the man sitting across from me? As though I'd been sleeping and someone poured a bucket of iced water over me, I wake up.

Like, really wake up.

"You're their father," I whisper-yell-gasp.

"What?" He shakes his head. "No."

"Yes!" This is why he looked familiar! Not because of his website photo, not because he resembled a baseball player, but because of the color of his eyes, the angles of his jawline, the shape of his mouth, the shade of his skin.

"Those twins aren't mine."

"One of them even has *your* name!"

His pupils throb. "Rose would've told me—"

"Not if she was scared of you."

"Scared of me?"

"What sort of fabric salesman carries a gun?" I say way too loudly, but it's hard to contain my excitement. "When Rose found your gun, she must've freaked, and when she got pregnant, well, she probably thought she was protecting her daughters by not involving you." The tension that's been oozing inside me for the past few weeks finally diffuses. "There's no doubt in my mind that you're their father!" I declare, feeling more winded than when I lift for two hours straight.

This time, he doesn't contradict me. He merely sits there, mute and dumbfounded.

The sky darkens outside. Jackie must be wigging out. I hope she hasn't called Mom. I can't bear to think what state my mother is in if she believes I was abducted.

"We should get back," I say.

Aster doesn't react. *Aster*...Not sure what weirds me out more, the fact that he's named Aster too, or the fact that he's the twins' long-lost father.

"They'll be so excited to meet—"

"No."

"What?"

"No, Joshua. I can't."

"Can't what? Be their father? It's not a choice...it's a fact."

"I already have a family." His voice sounds as shrill as Ivy's when she freaks out over something.

"But they need you. Their mother, she isn't...well."

"Not my problem."

I feel like he sucker-punched me.

"Besides, I bet Rose slept with a lot of men back then. They could be someone else's girls."

I toss my hands in the air. "They *look* like you!"

"They look like their mom."

I frown. Out of all the reasons not to claim paternity, that is the dumbest. Rose is pale and freckled and has limp hair. "They look nothing like their mother. Run a genetic test. You'll see."

His nostrils pulse. "I'm not running any genetic tests."

"So what? You're just going to drop me off by my car and disappear? You have a website. I know your car's—well, your wife's car's—license number. I know your phone number."

"Are you threatening me? Because I don't do well with threats." The sleeve of his black nylon jacket lifts an inch and reveals a streak of blue-black ink on his wrist. I bet the man's covered in tattoos.

I shift in my seat, suddenly uncomfortable sharing air with a gun-toting, tattooed ex-soldier. I bet he was a SEAL. "All I'm saying is if *I* can find you, *they* can find you."

"They'd have to know where to look."

He raises the gun, points it at me. The tendons in his hands shift underneath his skin.

I keep my shoulders squared and force the panic off my face.

He dips his head down again. "I also know where *you* live Josh. I know how much you care about your mom. I know your dad's working on a project for the Discolis." He pauses. "It's real easy to make death appear accidental."

The blood drains from my face.

"Now, you're going to forget you ever saw me. You're going to wipe our conversation out of that lively mind of yours, and you're going to tell everyone you tossed this gun in Wildcat Creek."

"Or what—you'll kill me?" I square my shoulders. "I wonder what your wife would think if she knew you refused to even meet your daughters. She'd probably take your kids—you know those two, sweet little boys you deigned to recognize—she'll take them away. What woman wants a man without balls?" I'm pushing him hard. With a gun in my face, it's a dangerous move. But the twins have wanted to find their father for so—

Aster's arm locks around my neck, and the gun presses against my temple. The metal tip is cold, and pulses. Or maybe it's my forehead that throbs. Air trickles sluggishly through my throat, tacky like cough syrup, and soon I start gasping. I try to move, but he jams the gun harder. It'll probably leave a bruise. Unless he pulls the trigger. A bruise will be the least of my worries then.

"Going to shoot me to shut me up?" I wheeze.

"It would be a good solution, but I have a better one that doesn't require reupholstering yet another car."

When he mentioned his car was in the shop, I imagined he meant it was banged up, not soiled with blood and guts.

Chills fire up my spine and spread to my arms. I think of Mrs. Redd, of how brave and smart she was to keep her daughters a secret from a man like him. Not that one right erases the sum of her wrongs, but at least now—if I ever make it out of this car—I'll be able to share air with her without wishing her dead.

Aster speaks to me slowly, or maybe his words sound slurred because of how little oxygen is hitting my brain. "If *anyone* ever comes knocking on my door…be it the police or one of the Redd women…then I'll pay one of your parents a surprise visit."

I stare at the man holding me at gunpoint, and the knot of feelings untangles until only one sentiment is left: disappointment. "You don't deserve them."

Keeping the gun leveled on my face, he relaxes his grip on my neck and reaches over me for my door handle. He clicks it open, then shoves me out so hard, I stumble out and flop to my knees. I cough, retch, cough some more. The door swings shut, and then the car swerves out of the construction site.

I twist my neck, massage it. I spit. Hatred and anger thicken inside me, restoring some of my dignity.

Finally, I stand up.

I have no clue where I am, yet I know I can find my way back to the twins just like I knew I could uncover the origin of the gun.

As I walk, I kick Aster Colson out of my head.

Rid myself of his voice that sounded too much like Ivy's.

Purge my mind of his face that looked too much like Aster's.

I kick a pebble out of my way, and it arches and plummets noiselessly back down, vanishing in a sea of other upturned rocks. Like everything else in this life, what comes up must go down. I'll forget Aster Colson like I've already forgotten that stupid pebble.

EPILOGUE

DECEMBER 21, 2013

Josh and I have been dating for four glorious months.

I used to wish time would move faster, but not anymore. Now I wish each minute lasted a month.

I stand beside him in Maggie's candle-lit bakery, rubbing my clammy hands on the white-and-gray *ombré* dress he bought me for my birthday. He gave it to me merely an hour ago and instructed me to wear it right away. I told him it was too nice, too much for me. He shut me up with a kiss.

Stephanie, who's waiting for Ivy next to a little group of my sister's friends, glances my way. She smiles. She probably feels like she has to. After all, this party is for me, too.

"You think she's coming?" I ask Josh, tearing my eyes away from the hot-pink tulle eyesore Stephanie's sporting.

"Your sister? Miss a party? Especially a party in her honor?" He rolls his eyes. "Of course she's coming."

"I'm not talking about my sister."

He steals my hand from my side and clasps it between his soft, warm palms. "It's your birthday."

"She's missed a lot of them."

Ever since I discovered Mom's hidden treasure—a bunch of fabric rolls—she has avoided me. Not that I've set foot inside my home since the incident. I always idle out front in my car as I wait for Ivy.

I drive my sister to school every morning and drive her back every afternoon so she never has to take the bus or hike the now-frozen, blustery streets.

For months now, the only contact I've had with Mom is visual—through the veranda window. She sits in front of her sewing machine while I sit in front of my steering wheel. We watch each other until Ivy appears. I think Mom regrets alienating me. Or at least I hope she does. I don't dare ask Ivy because what if I'm wrong? What if Mom appreciates my absence?

Sometimes, ignorance truly is bliss.

"There they are," Josh murmurs.

I stiffen as Maggie parks in front of the bakery, then peer through the darkness to make out the number of bodies in the car.

I only see two.

Mom didn't come.

Josh wraps an arm around my waist and pulls me tighter against him, but I press him gently away because his parents are here. They know we're dating, but I'm still squeamish about PDA around them.

As my sister enters the glowing bakery, Stephanie, Sean, and her other friends squeal her name and capture her in giant hugs. They act as though they haven't seen her in days, as though they weren't just sitting next to her in class hours ago.

Finally, Ivy makes it to me. She takes in my dress and her mouth gapes a little. "Where did you get that?"

I try to answer her, but my emotions have tangled around my vocal cords.

Josh must have answered her question because Ivy says, "You have really good taste for a man."

"Not sure whether to take that as a compliment or not."

Ivy winks at him. "Definitely a compliment. I doubt my farmer husband will give me such pretty dresses. He'll probably give me overalls or cowboy boots."

"What farmer husband?" I ask.

Ivy and Josh exchange a conspiratorial look.

I feel left out, and it hurts. "Did you get married?"

"Of course not!" Ivy tells me about Mom's fortuneteller.

A prickling sensation bubbles behind my breastbone. Does Ivy know Mom never asked about me? "Why didn't she come?"

My question leeches the rosiness from my sister's skin. "She had to finish a project." My twin tucks a long, silky strand of hair behind her ear. "Christmastime is always busy for her."

Her lie vibrates in my bones. She's making excuses for Mom. I blink away tears. Why do I even care? I'm eighteen. As soon as tomorrow, I can emancipate myself from this woman.

Josh's father arrives with a platter full of rainbow-colored glasses. "Who wants to try one of my sparkling mocktails?"

Ivy pouts. "What? No champagne?"

"Not until you're twenty-one, young lady. Three more years to go," he says loudly. He tips his head toward Jackie who's helping Maggie light the candles on our cake.

When we turned fifteen, Stewart let us try beer. Sometimes, when Maggie's not paying attention, he'll sneak us a sip of his wine.

Ivy rolls her eyes, then goes for a pink glass, but he says, "Take the blue." And then he tells me, "Yours is the green, Aster."

I frown. Ivy wears a matching expression.

"Yellow for you, Josh."

Ivy picks the blue glass off the platter and takes a sip. Her frown transforms into a smile.

He whispers, "I added a splash of champagne to yours, but don't you dare tell your friends. *Or* Jackie. I don't feel like being arrested tonight."

"You're the best," Ivy quips.

"Happy birthday, sweethearts," he says, kissing Ivy's cheek, then mine.

I think he's been sampling his "mocktails," because his jaw is ruddy and his eyes shiny.

He waltzes away, distributing colorful glasses to the people who've come to celebrate our birthday. Well, Ivy's birthday. If it had only been mine, none of them would have come.

I dip my lips into my glass. The bubbles burst against my palate, then descend like pop rocks down my throat. I don't really taste the champagne because of all the fruit juice mixed into it, but halfway through my glass, I feel it.

I've become as light as a soap bubble, and Mom's absence doesn't irk me anymore.

The room breaks out in song as Maggie carries a blazing sheet cake decorated with tiny purple marzipan flowers and green buttercream leafy vines. Our namesakes.

Ivy sidles next to me and links her arm through mine while Josh holds his phone out to take pictures.

Everyone's still singing.

"Did you make a wish, sis?" Ivy asks.

I look over at Josh, then back at Ivy.

I wish for us to be together forever.

I nod. "You?"

She nods, after which we blow out the candles.

Everyone claps.

While Jackie and Maggie start cutting up the cake in even squares, Ivy hands me a small, giftwrapped present.

I blink up at my sister, flushing. "I didn't get you anything."

"You don't need to get me anything, Asty."

"I do."

"Open it."

I tear the paper open to find a glossy paperback. I suck in a breath, trace the title with my fingertip.

Hopeless.

"The bookstore lady said it was a really good love story," Ivy says as I flip to the back matter and devour the synopsis.

"Thank you so much." My voice sounds strangled. "Tell me something you want. Please."

She bites her lip. "There is *one* thing."

I hope I can afford it. Ivy likes pretty things.

"Can you promise not to file charges against Mom?"

The book slides out of my fingers.

Neither Ivy nor I move to pick it up.

"Please, Asty. Don't have Mom taken away because you can now. School will be over in six months, and then you can leave…"

Ivy says more words, but they're flushed out by the loudness of the ones she's just spoken.

You can leave.

Not *we*.

You.

I've never felt lonelier in my life. "She didn't even come tonight. She doesn't care about me."

Ivy touches my shoulder. "She had to work."

"Don't lie for her! If she'd shown up, I might've…"

"Might've what?"

I was about to say *forgiven her*, but that's not true. I could never forgive my mother for her cruelty. "Might've reconsidered," I finally say.

Ivy's nostrils flare. "Asty, she said she'd kill herself if they tried to take her away."

More than her cruelty, what I can't forgive her for is turning me into someone cruel, someone who wishes death upon another human being, someone who can drug a person to uncover their secrets without feeling guilt.

That is not who I want to be.

"Maggie said you could stay with them until the fall," Ivy says, "and then you'll live on a campus somewhere. You're so smart, you'll get a full scholarship. I'm sure of it…"

I chose not to apply to colleges—something I haven't told either Ivy or Josh—because I want to start working. I want to make money so I can afford my own place. And then I'll go back to studying.

Josh is suddenly next to us. "Your entourage requests your presence," he tells Ivy, nodding in Stephanie's direction.

Ivy studies me a long time, awaiting my answer. I don't give her one because I don't want to lie to my sister.

Not on her birthday.

She turns her attention to Josh, and silent words travel between them. Or maybe they speak. My ears are buzzing.

When Ivy goes to her friends, I walk toward the door of the bakery and step out into the freezing night. I hug my arms around me to keep the cold air off my bare skin.

The door chimes a second later. A heavy coat falls over my shoulders.

"What happened?" Josh asks.

I pull his coat tighter around my shoulders, but still I shiver. "Mom won."

A crease appears between his eyebrows.

"Ivy asked me not file any charges against her."

He takes this in slowly, thoughtfully. "You don't need to press charges. You can emancipate yourself now."

"But what about Ivy? Mom could hurt her…"

"Ivy's a big girl."

"I don't want to do this alone," I croak.

"I'm right here." He pulls one of my hands away from my arm and twines his fingers through mine, then repeats the motion until both my hands are trapped in his.

Warmth flashes through me.

I love this boy so much.

If only his declaration could wipe away the pain of Ivy's wish.

Blinding headlights flood the street and then a car drives slowly by the bakery.

A dark green Jeep.

I inch toward Josh. I wish I was fearless, but I'm full of fears. "Mom's friend is back." My whisper curls like smoke through the frigid air.

Josh, who had his back to the road, spins around.

Mom made a friend in her shrink's waiting room, a friend whom she paid to buy a gun in my name. Jeep-lady swore to Josh she'd helped Mom because, being a single mother herself, she understood Mom's fears of living in a ground floor apartment unarmed.

"Why is she back?" I whisper again.

He shields me with his body until the car has vanished in the dark night. "Wasn't her." His voice is hard. He turns back toward me. "It wasn't her, Aster."

I run my gaze over his face a great many times to figure out if he's telling me this to reassure me or if it's the truth. "Maybe she doesn't believe you tossed the gun."

"I swear it wasn't her. I know the license plate by heart. It was another Jeep."

He pulls me into his arms and nestles his nose against my hair.

"No one's going to hurt you anymore. No one. That's my birthday present to you. To always protect you."

I lay my cheek in the crook of Josh's neck and smile. "You know, when I dream of my father, I dream he says those exact words to me." Josh's quick pulse nips my ear. "You think he would've protected me if he'd known about me?"

Josh doesn't say anything for so long I wonder if he's heard my question. I'm about to ask him again when he says, "You don't need a father. You have me."

Underneath the flapping pink awning and the canopy of stars, without caring who's watching us, I kiss him. "You know what I wished for before blowing out my candles?" I ask him once I've pulled away.

"Don't tell me or it won't happen."

Even though I burn to tell him, I swallow down my wish and lock it deep inside of me.

COLD LITTLE GAMES

BOOK 2

COLD LITTLE GAMES

USA TODAY BESTSELLING AUTHOR

OLIVIA WILDENSTEIN

ONE

Our mother used to say that Ivy sucked all the good from the womb and I was left with the scraps. I hate to think she was right about anything, but my twin sister *is* exceptional.

"You're going to do so well," I tell Ivy, squeezing her hand.

"No touching," barks the guard watching over us.

It's just the two of us in the visitation room.

Ivy yanks her hand out of mine. "I don't know about *so well*, but I'm going to do my best." She links her fingers together in a business-like manner. "Has Josh come to see you yet?"

"No."

"He told me he spoke to your warden about letting you watch the show. You have his permission to look at it whenever you want."

I give her a weak smile. "That'll be the highlight of my day."

She runs her nail underneath the peeling, synthetic wood surface of the table.

"I'm happy you came to see me," I say.

Her gaze sticks to the tabletop. It's as though she doesn't dare look up at me. I think she's afraid to cry. "Was it really an accident, Aster?" Her voice is so faint that I have to strain to make out her words.

"Yes."

"You promise me—"

"Yes," I say. "Stop worrying about this. By the time you come home, it will be ancient history."

She bites her lip.

"Now go *make* history," I tell her.

"I'll probably be disqualified after the first round."

I shake my head. "Can you stop putting yourself down? You are *so* talented. So much more than all the other contestants."

"But this isn't only about talent."

If only I could curve the outer corners of her lips into a smile like I do at work with my computer cursor.

When her eyes twitch down to my hands, I slip both inside my jumpsuit pockets. "There's something I wanted to give you before the show," I tell her.

"What?"

"Just a little present."

"What is it?"

"If I tell you, it'll ruin the surprise." I drop my voice to a whisper. "It's in my underwear drawer. Where I kept my baby teeth."

She stays silent and still for so long that I shift around on the rigid iron chair. Suddenly, she stands. "I have to go home to pack."

"Already?"

She nods. "Before I go, though, you have to sign something for me." She heads over to the guard stationed in the corner.

As I watch her, the tips of my coarse curls brush against my gray jumpsuit. Ivy's hair is much longer than mine, and much softer. She styled mine once like hers—she even tried to teach me—but I have no patience with brushes and serums and creams. Besides, as much as I love my twin, at nineteen, we're past the age where it's cute to look identical.

After a quick exchange, she returns with his pen. She digs out a folded piece of paper from the back pocket of her skinny jeans and smooths it out on the desk. "The show sent me some extra forms to fill out. They need the signature from my next of kin in case something goes wrong."

My mouth goes dry. "It's an art competition…what could go wrong?"

"It's just a formality, Asty." She sticks the pen in my hand.

"But—"

"Nothing will go wrong." Her gaze softens. She knows I can never say no to her when she looks at me like that. "I promise."

I push out the breath I'm holding and study the paper. It's all fine print.

Ivy points to the signature line. "I've already read it. It's legalese. Disclaimers. The usual."

I bite my lip, and look back up at her. She's checking the round white wall clock, so I hurry to scratch my name on the dotted line. "Here."

She tugs the sheet away from me and folds it back into her pocket. "Are you eating? You look skeletal."

I study the sharpness of my wrist bones. They do look like they're about to pierce my skin.

When she doesn't sit back down, I say, "It's time, isn't it?" I don't want her to leave, even though I encouraged her to go.

She nods.

I stand up, hoping for a hug, but instead, she lifts the pen from my hand and walks over to the guard to return it.

Over her shoulder, she calls out, "You take care, all right, Asty?" Her voice catches on my name.

I smile even though I didn't get my hug. Just like she didn't give me one yesterday when she came to visit. Maybe with the whole "no-touching-the-prisoner" rule, she doesn't know she's allowed to hug me on her way out. I keep the smile on my face long after she's gone, just in case she returns. She doesn't, but I don't hold it against her. Ivy has trouble with separation.

She was a mess when Mom was committed fifteen months ago. She was an even bigger mess when I was arrested.

TWO

Ivy

With both Mom and Aster gone, our tiny, ground floor apartment is quiet, too quiet. I toss my keys onto our Formica kitchen countertop and head to Aster's room, which we shared before I moved into Mom's. The butterfly wallpaper is yellowed in spots and peeling, but Aster doesn't want to replace it. She hates change. She also hates order. I trip over a lone sneaker, catching myself on her white wooden dresser. Swearing under my breath, I pull open the top drawer and comb through her all-black cotton underwear until my fingertips touch a piece of cool porcelain—the tiny box Mom bought her to keep her baby teeth in when she was six. I have a matching one. Something jiggles inside. I pop the tarnished latch. Among an array of tiny dead teeth lies Aster's present.

My first impulse is to stuff the box back inside the drawer, but then I think of the police. What if they search our place and find it?

"Shit, Aster, where did you get this?" I mutter.

I snap the box closed and tread back out, hopping over an old sock that didn't make it into the hamper. I grab the large red bag I'm taking to New York, empty it, and head to the adjacent veranda Mom used as her studio. It's the only room in the apartment I feel happy in, perhaps because it's filled with colorful fabric and drenched in natural light.

I find a spool of red thread, a needle, and my seam rippers, and set to work. Ten minutes later, the porcelain box has vanished inside the lining, cushioned by the foam inserts Mom used for texture in all of her quilts. A part of me feels guilty for transforming her last creation into a bag, but another part feels reassured to bring a piece of her with me on this trip.

A car honks outside, making me jump. At the window I see a forest-green cab parked in front. My ride to the airport. I knuckle the window to get the driver's attention and hold out my open hand to signal five minutes. I race back to my room, place all of my belongings inside the mended bag, check that all the lights are off, that the fridge is empty, and turning back one last time, walk off into the unknown.

INDIANAPOLIS HAS SHRUNK. The backyard pools are drops of turquoise and the vehicles are miniature toy cars rolling over looping, white-dotted highways. I strain to make out the site of Aster's jail and think I spot it when a voice crackles over the loudspeakers, focusing my attention back inside the plane.

"Hi, folks. So it looks like our trip is going to be uneventful. Just the way I like it." The pilot guffaws. "We should be touching down in Newark at around 5:30 p.m. The weather in New York City is clear and sunny and in the high eighties. You should see the city coming up on your right thirty minutes before landing. I'll be sure to remind you. Sit back, relax, and have a pleasant flight."

"What can I get you to drink?" the stewardess asks me. "Champagne, orange juice, water?"

I'm tempted to have the champagne, but she must know I'm underage. "Sparkling water would be great."

When she leaves, I flick my gaze to the compartment overhead where I stuffed my bag. I'd been worried about going through airport security, but it turned out fine. I go back to staring at the world below.

"First time on a plane?" She's already back.

"Yes."

"I can always tell when someone's a sky virgin. I'm perceptive like that." She hands me the glass of water and a small packet of cashews. "Have I seen you somewhere before? Your face looks awfully familiar."

"I'm one of the contestants on the Masterpiecers," I say so that she doesn't come to another conclusion.

The frown on her face fades. "Of course! And here I thought they chartered private jets for their contestants."

"I think they do for the winners. But flying business is—"

"Can I get your autograph?" She thrusts a cocktail napkin and a ballpoint pen at me.

"Sure," I say, and scribble my name—Ivy Redd—on the napkin before handing it back to her.

"I'll be rooting for you, Miss…" Her voice trails off as she studies my name, and the frown gusts across her face again. Thankfully, someone's call button draws her away.

When she stops by my row later, I've put my headphones on even though I'm not listening to music; I just don't want her to talk to me. To make my intentions clearer, I fasten my attention to the window and the empty sky beyond until we land.

As I step off the plane, she whispers something in the other stewardess's ear, but holds her thumbs up nonetheless. She's probably figured out whom I'm related to. It's not much of a secret, especially now that I've willingly stepped into the spotlight and splashed our family name on every tabloid in the United States. I pass by a newsstand and spot my face, alongside the other competitors' in a Brady Bunch composition on the cover of People Magazine. I don't purchase it. I'd rather not read what is being said about me and I already know everything there is to know about my adversaries.

With no suitcase to wait for, I breeze past the luggage carousels and find the person sent to pick me up. He's carrying a sign with my first name. No last name so as not to attract too much attention.

"Is this all?" He points to my duffle bag.

"Yes."

"I suppose they're going to be lending you clothes," he says.

"Yes." They mentioned it in the exhaustive packet they sent me two weeks ago.

"How was the trip?" he asks.

"Fine."

He tries to pluck my bag off my shoulder, but I hold on tight.

"It's not heavy," I tell him.

We walk through the crowded terminal toward the glass doors.

"First time in New York?" he asks.

I nod.

"You're going to love it. Supposed to be great weather all week."

"Don't think I'll be getting out much."

"Right," he says, just as his phone rings. "Yes…I'll pick him up too…okay, ma'am."

He stops and doubles back toward the terminal, signaling for me to follow him.

"Another contestant?" I ask.

He shakes his head. "Woo-hoo! Mister Jackson!"

A man in a tailored suit clutching a rolling black leather case catches sight of him and treads our way. Because he's on the phone, he greets the driver with a silent nod. He doesn't greet me, though. But I suppose that a judge can't greet a contestant, because Brook Jackson is none other than one of the Masterpiecers' judges.

Brook walks alongside the driver, crossing the car lanes. I follow close behind. We arrive in front of a big black car whose trunk pops open without anyone touching it. The driver sets Brook's wheelie case in.

"Want to put yours in the back?" he asks me.

That's when Brook realizes I'm there and finally hangs up. Dark brows pulled together, he slips the phone into the breast pocket of his jacket. "I'm sorry. I didn't realize you were with us." He looks at the driver and then down at the sign that carries my name. "Ivy," he reads out loud. His gaze snaps up to my face. His skin has gone a few shades lighter. He scans the parking lot. "Carl!"

"Yes, sir."

"Get the girl another ride," Brook says.

"On it." The driver raises his cell phone to his ear.

"Judges and contestants can't be seen together! Who was in charge of this planning?" Brook is so loud that a few people stare.

Carl covers the mouthpiece. "Mrs. Raynoir, sir. She told me to pick you up since I was already at the airport."

Brook shakes his head a great many times, yet his dark hair is gelled back so stiffly, it doesn't budge.

"Danny, buddy, I got a customer in the parking lot of terminal A," Carl says. "Needs immediate pickup. You free? Great. Usual spot."

"This could've been a disaster. If the paparazzi—"

"You better get in the car, sir," Carl says, disconnecting. He tips his head toward two men with large cameras poised in midair. "They're here."

Brook lunges into the backseat and shuts the door just as the two men barrel across the busy car lanes toward us. They stop inches away from my face. I can nearly feel the cool glass of their lenses. I hear the *click, click* of the shutters. It mirrors the *blink, blink* of my eyelids. Carl grabs my arm and yanks me away from them just as a black sedan pulls up. He opens the door and pushes me in. Before I've even straightened upright, the door closes and the car swerves away.

The new driver is chuckling. "Never loaded up a customer so fast and I'm used to working with stars. Movie stars. Music stars. You name it, I've driven it."

I turn around to look at the paparazzi. Their cameras are aimed at the car.

"They got their money shot, sweets," he says. "Your pretty little face will be everywhere by tonight."

"It's already everywhere."

He eyes me in the rearview mirror. "Everyone's been waiting for Lucky Number Eight."

"Lucky?"

"That's what the media calls you. Lucky Number Eight. You know...because the person they picked before you was disqualified, and you got the spot."

"I suppose I did luck out," I say as we pull up next to a tollbooth.

He lowers his window and hands the woman in the booth a ten dollar bill. As he waits for his change, he turns to peer at me. His hair is gray at the temples and his eyebrows are so bushy, some hairs are curling. "You're prettier in person."

"Thank you."

He spins back toward the toll officer to pocket his change. "So which contestant are you the most worried about?"

"I'm not worried."

"Confident little thing, huh? And pretty. Got a boyfriend?"

"Not yet." I pick at a loose thread on my bag and pull on it. It bunches up the seam and finally rips off. I'm left with a small hole which I'll have to mend...like everything else in my life.

His phone rings. "Yello," he shouts. "All good, chief. On our way to the Met... yup...ETA is forty-five minutes...you can count on me."

He pops his phone into the cup holder and shoots the car onto the highway, just missing a yellow cab. He slams on his brakes and hits his horn, insults the taxi driver, and then crosses three lanes in one go. Nauseated, I lower the window and stare out at the crackling blue city looming in the distance.

My bag is on my knees. I don't shift it to my feet. Instead, I pull it closer to me, because it smells like home, like fabric softener, like Mom. Aster never liked our mother. She reproached her everything: our lack of money, of clothes, of food. But it wasn't Mom's fault. She tried her best. Her fingers bled from trying her best.

I caress the wine-colored spot along the seam; a drop of dried blood Mom never had time to wash off.

THREE

When Ivy left, it hit me that I wouldn't see her for ten days. *Ten!* I've never been apart from my sister for that long. I must look really glum because a woman with red dreadlocks keeps staring at me in the cafeteria. In the past two days, no one has bothered talking to me…which is fine. I don't feel chatty. Besides, there's no point in making friends. I'll be gone soon.

Dreadlocks chews her food and gawks. Frankly, it's annoying. For a moment, I pretend she's not there, but it becomes unbearable. I'm about to go off on her when I hear my name called out.

"Aster Redd, you got a visitor."

A visitor? I wipe the surprise off my face before Dreadlocks can spot it. Why wouldn't I have visitors? I know people. I quickly grab my tray, dump the half-eaten contents, and set it on the shelving. Then I stride through the metal detector and past the guard who's holding the door open for me. I imagine I'm going through a portal that will lead me out of here, but I end up in a sterile corridor irradiated by zinging strips of too-bright neon.

Through the glass door of the visitation area, I can make out Josh's familiar broad shoulders. When the guard buzzes me through the door, I hurry to where he's sitting and plop down. He's dressed in his police uniform and sports dark circles beneath his green eyes.

"Hi," I say, my voice a little airy from the thrill of seeing him. Even though we're no longer together, I can't help my heart from beating faster in his presence. I've loved him since we were five and have never stopped, not even after the awful morning six months ago…not even after we decided to take a break from each other.

"Hey." He scans my face. It practically feels as though he's touching it.

I shiver. His hands were always so soft, so much softer than mine. Then again, at the pizzeria where I serve and do the dishes, I have my hands in water half the day.

"The chief okayed my involvement."

I let out a sigh of relief.

"Look"—he takes the little notepad peeking out of his shirt pocket and the tiny ballpoint pen hooked into the spiral binding. It's the one I bought him when we were still together. The ink tip comes out when you shake it—"I really don't feel like you're telling me everything, so let's go over this again."

"But I—"

"Just humor me."

"Fine." I look down at the chipped edge of the table. "I was counting up tips when this guy walked in to pick up his takeout. Everyone had left."

"You mean all the customers?"

"I mean *everyone*. I was in charge of locking up."

"What did he order?"

I fling my gaze back up to his. "A pepperoni pizza."

His eyes hover over mine. "I dropped by the pizzeria and asked Abby for a receipt. She didn't find anything. Not even a credit card slip."

"He paid cash."

"What about the receipt?"

"It must be there. She must not have looked well."

Josh rubs the back of his short brown hair. "So he bought a pepperoni pizza... then what?"

"As he was paying, I thought I recognized him from somewhere. It took me a second to realize it was from that file you keep on your desk."

He sighs and it resonates deep inside his chest. "Which you shouldn't have seen."

"But I did. He was a wanted criminal."

"Granted, but you're not a detective, Aster."

"I know, but he was right there."

"You should've called me."

"I tried."

"No, you didn't."

"I did."

"Aster," he growls.

"Okay, fine. I didn't. But that's only because he was getting into his car. So I locked up fast and got into mine. My cell phone didn't have any more battery."

Josh fixes me so intensely that I fold my arms in front of my chest.

"I got him. Isn't that what matters?" I ask.

"He was wanted alive."

"He tried to yank me out of the car. I reacted." My heart's beating faster, pumping blood that feels like fire through my body. "I didn't think I'd killed him. It was an accident."

"Was it?" he whispers loudly.

"Yes! I'm not a murderer, Josh."

He fixes me as though trying to x-ray my scalp to peer inside my mind. "I got an anonymous tip."

"An anonymous tip?"

He nods and leans his muscular forearms onto the fake wood table. Josh spends equal time at the gym and at work. For the longest time, I thought he would become a sports coach instead of an officer. "Someone saw you that night. They called in to say a small Honda had a large, bloodied crack in the windshield, and the girl at the wheel was nervous and apparently cold. Covered in some blanket."

"I admitted I hit a man. And I'm allowed to have been cold. I was in shock."

"What did the blanket look like?"

"I don't know. Blue."

"He said it was multi-colored."

"It was dark out. He couldn't have seen."

"Was it one of Ivy's quilts?"

I shake my head.

"Where's the blanket now?"

"Probably still in my car."

"It wasn't. I checked."

"Then someone took it out. Why is this even important? Troy Mann is what's important."

He smacks his palms against the table, which makes me jump. It also makes the guard in the corner stop picking at his cuticles to stare at us. The sound reminds me of my mother's palm colliding with my face, leaving a glaring red imprint that would begin fading just in time for the next slap. "That's not the point, Aster. You can't go around killing people."

My saliva suddenly feels like plaster, thick and dry. "But he was yelling at me. He tried to strangle me."

"You should've driven away," he says, his tone more sad than angry.

"I would've lost him, Josh."

"I'd rather you lost him. Instead, I—we—might lose you, Aster."

"I'm right here," I say, wrapping my hands around his.

"No touching," the guard snaps.

I glare at him, but let go.

"What happened after you hit him?" Josh asks.

"I drove off." I smelled the blood through the shattered windshield. "I threw up, so I went home to take a shower." I swallow. "You know me, I hate blood. Especially since…" I don't mention the awful morning. Josh was there. He remembers.

He shakes the small pen. The ink tip slides back in. He shakes it again. It slides back out. He does this several more times before asking, "You didn't take anything from the crime scene, did you?"

I shoot my gaze downward. "No," I say, peering down at my cracked nails. They're all so short. Except the one on my right pinky. That one is long and sharp. It's the only one that never breaks. The one on my left hand is torn off like the others. My pinky nails are like Ivy and me—one's stronger than the other.

"The police report states there was dirt underneath your nails."

I ball my hands and burrow them underneath my armpit. "My keys fell in the potted plant by the door, because my hands were shaking. I had to dig them out."

He eyes me in silence. "Aster…"

His voice is so soft I'm expecting him to tell me he loves me, reassure me that he's going to get me out, that—

"Tell me the truth."

"That's what I'm doing!"

"I know you well enough to know when you're lying, and you're lying. I can't help you if you don't help me."

"You never believe me anyway," I say. My vision is clouding. "You didn't believe me that morning in the park and you don't believe me now." Josh's face wobbles. The entire room wobbles. There are two, three, four guards. An optical illusion. "This conversation's over." I'm about to stand, but Josh grabs my arm and squeezes it.

"It's not over."

"Take your hands off me," I say coolly, since the guard is suddenly totally useless.

"Aster, please…" His voice has dropped to a whisper. "Please…stay. I didn't mean to upset you."

"Thanks for making them approve the TV channel."

His overly tanned forehead scrunches up again. He's going to have skin cancer someday and he'll deserve it.

I shrug his hand off. Accompanied by the guard, I leave and count the number of footsteps it takes to reach the dayroom and the little screen that will make the next few days bearable.

FOUR

Ivy

I haven't been sleeping much since Aster entered the Indiana Department of Correction, so I doze off in the back of the sedan, which makes me miss my first glimpse of the city. When I wake up, I don't feel rested, but I don't feel as horrid as I've felt this past week.

I take in Manhattan. The waning sun softens the sharp edges of the buildings. Gray, white, beige, glass, and metal collide in a lovely, linear landscape. I snap a mental picture of everything to reproduce with fabric when I get home…or maybe on the show.

The car lurches to a stop at a red light. Danny spins around. "Oh, you're not sleeping! I was worried I was going to have to wake you. I hate interrupting someone's peace. Although you didn't sound too peaceful."

I frown.

"You were mumbling all these things."

"Like what?"

"I couldn't understand much. Heard the words *man* and *quilt* a couple times."

I concentrate on the outside world to forget my inside world.

"Must be the stress from the competition," he says when I don't speak for a long time.

"Yeah."

When we pull up, there are swarms of people with flailing arms and smartphones propped in the air.

"Ready, sweets?"

"Ready."

He smiles and hops out his door to open mine. "I got your back." He extends one arm.

"I'm good," I tell him, pushing out of the car, but he keeps his arm over me anyway. The stench of wool and perspiration prickles my nostrils.

I hear my name. It's being screamed left and right. I also hear *number eight* hollered. I raise my eyes and get lost in the grand stone building before me. Voices and street noise die away. It's just me and the block-long museum I've longed to visit since my early teens.

"My wife just saw us on the news," the driver says, pocketing his phone. "She'd like an autograph. Can you do me the honor?" He already has a pen and a dollar bill out.

As we push into the museum, I sign my name across the creased green and white paper.

"Break a leg, Eight."

And then he leaves through the revolving doors and I'm alone in the mammoth entrance, underneath a row of carved columns holding up a mezzanine. I step further inside, looking up and around like Charlie when he entered Willy Wonka's chocolate factory. The walls stretch up neck-breakingly high, vaulting together into giant arches and wrapping around magnificent skylights. The octagonal desk at the center of the space has been turned into a giant vase enclosing a landscaped mound of orchids, peonies, and calla lilies.

"Thought you'd never make it." A woman in jeans, a black tee, and a headpiece is standing right in front of me.

I didn't hear her approach.

"We got to get going. The show starts in an hour. Follow me. Number Eight's in the building, Jeb." I don't see anyone else around, so I assume she's speaking into her mic. When we arrive in front of an elevator, she says, "I'm Cara, your assistant." The doors open and we step in, and then they close and we're whisked away from the beautiful lobby. "You'll be on the third floor throughout most of the competition. The other floors are off limits, unless you're escorted there. Receptions and events will take place in the Temple Room. I'll be accompanying you everywhere." She pushes her short, bottle-blonde hair behind her ear to clear her mouthpiece. Her roots are shockingly black.

The elevator pings and the doors open. Cara goes right. I follow. We continue down a short hallway toward an open doorway. The walls inside the vast room are wainscoted wood with a repetition of pale rectangular patches at eye level—probably where paintings were hung.

"They removed the artwork for insurance reasons," she explains when she notices me studying the walls. "Your prep table's over there. Number eight."

There are eight stations with the same three-sided mirrors adorned with round light bulbs. The numbers stick out above the top of the mirrors, large and gold—impossible to miss. People are milling around. Most are dressed casually and sport the same headpieces as my assistant, though I spot some sitting in front of the vanities—other contestants. Two of them turn to glance at me. The third doesn't turn, but his eyes follow me in the mirror. In spite of the light shining into them, they're dark, practically black.

"Over here will be your living quarters," Cara is saying.

We weave out of the room into a contiguous one. A long band of beige fabric stretches from floor to ceiling, spanning the entire width of the stripped gallery. We penetrate a flap in the middle. It's a tent, but not just any tent—it's something out of Shakespeare's *A Midsummer Night's Dream*. The entrance is paved with a forest of potted trees strung up with twinkling lights. There's a white oval table on one side of the garden, and a living area made up of a long couch and plush armchairs on the other.

I trail after Cara down a grassy corridor lined with the same lit trees. Every fifteen feet or so, there's a zippered flap with a large number painted in silver. Number eight's the last one.

"Your room," Cara announces, unzipping the entrance.

We leave the garden theme behind, and enter a luxurious bedroom. It's hard to believe we're still in a tent, what with the hardwood floors, the velvet upholstered headboard, the king-size bed, and the mirrored bathroom in the back.

I must look awed, because Cara smirks. "Nice, huh?"

I nod.

"Okay…so before I go, I need your cell phone and any other electronic devices you might've brought with you."

I dig my phone from the front pocket of my duffle and give it to her.

"Nothing else?" she asks, brows drawing together over her large brown eyes.

"Can't afford anything else"—I give her a wide smile—"yet."

"You can unpack later." She eyes my bag. "Your stylists are waiting by your station. Go out in a bathrobe and slippers." She juts her chin to the bathroom wall where a white robe is hanging. "I'll pick you up and take you to the venue as soon as you're ready. See you in a few."

The second she vanishes, I drop my bag on the bed and sprawl out on the comforter. The duvet is so soft, it molds around my body. I don't want to move; it's heaven.

A shrill, "All contestants to the dressing room!" echoes from a concealed speaker. I pry myself off the bed, wondering if someone saw me, but the zipper is shut tight and there are no cameras on the cloth ceiling—at least none that are apparent. It was probably an announcement meant for everyone. I kick off my sneakers and strip. And then I look at the mess, and it reminds me of Aster, and I don't want to be reminded of her right now, so I fold everything up and place it neatly on the wooden bench at the foot of the bed.

As I wait for the shower to heat up, I tie my hair up. In the mirror over the sink, I see Aster staring back at me with her haunted blue eyes. I fling the door of the shower open to allow the steam out. When it has completely blurred my reflection, I step inside and breathe. It feels like breathing fire and yet it's the freshest breath of air I've had since leaving Indiana.

Too soon, I get out and dry myself in the honeycomb bathrobe that is softer than cashmere. I wonder if I'll get to take it home. The number eight is stitched on the breast pocket in silver thread. The slippers are fuzzy and thin-soled. They fit a little big, but stay put. Casting one last glance around, I return to the grassy hallway and retrace my steps to the makeup room.

"About time," a woman with black hair all the way down to her waist says. "I'll be your makeup artist for the duration of the show. Amy, get your ass over here. We have thirty minutes left to get her ready!"

A twenty-something girl with pink hair and extra-wide hips scampers over with an apron full of pins and brushes. "Hi," she says, smiling warmly.

"Get to work," the makeup artist tells her as she wipes my face with a damp cotton disc.

Amy's smile evaporates. In silence, she yanks my hair, while the other one stabs at my face with brushes and pencils.

"Is this the first time you've worked this competition?" I ask.

"Look up," the makeup artist says. I still don't know her name. Then she adds, "I've been here since the beginning. I was assigned to the past two winners."

"Wow," Amy whispers.

"I only work with winners," she adds, looking straight at my reflection. "Let's hope you won't break my streak, Eight."

"I have every intention of winning."

Amy pulls on my hair as she brushes it, bringing moisture to my eyes. "This is my first time."

"And your last if you make our contestant cry and ruin my work."

"Oops…sorry, Leila. She has *a lot* of hair," Amy says.

I do. I have a proper mane, like my sister. Unlike Aster, though, I brush mine out religiously and coat my strands with gloss and softener. If I didn't, they would tangle and look like the frizzy mess she doesn't mind sporting. We assume we got our hair from our father. We never met him, gone long before we were born, but apparently he was a handsome, dark-skinned man with a strong southern accent. Although Mom wasn't a romantic, she loved our father. She never straight-out said it, but when I took an interest in stitching quilts, she unlocked the bottom drawer of her sewing table for me, and I understood…I understood so many things about my mother that day.

"Time?" Cara's right behind me. I can see her in the mirror.

"Five," Leila says.

"Okay, good. I'll go inform Jeb." She walks back out of the gallery.

The blow-dryer shuts off. Amy made my hair stick straight. I raise my hand to feel it. It's smoother and softer than I've ever managed to achieve.

Leila rubs something into my cheekbones. It makes them shimmer like copper. "Your outfit's in the dressing room. Amy will show you."

Amy leads me to a curtained room with a purple velvet pouf and a floor-length mirror. I let the bathrobe fall to the floor, which makes Amy blush. People are so funny about nudity. We're all just flesh and bones.

"Arms up," she says, staring at the blue material she's clutching.

She pulls the gown over me, making sure her fingers don't graze my skin. The cool satin feels divine. I touch it, and it reminds me of the first quilt my mother showed me how to stitch.

"Same color as your eyes," Amy says, pulling me back into the present.

It's the exact same shade, which looks striking against my skin. Especially around the waist where there are large cutouts lined with blue stones. She hands me a pair of silver platforms. With them on, the hem of the dress barely brushes the carpeted floor.

"Jewelry," she says, plopping a big silver ring and a pair of earrings in the palm of my hand. I slip the ring on, and then hook the blue chandelier earrings through my lobes.

I swing my head from side to side to admire my reflection. "Are the stones real?"

"I think so."

Cara pops her head into the makeshift dressing room. "Good. You're dressed. Let's go."

The remaining people in the room stare at me as I traipse out. The attention gives me such a rush that I feel as though I'm walking on air. We return to the lobby, turn left, and walk by the mountain of flowers toward a wing of dimly lit corridors filled with Egyptian treasures. We tread so quickly that I don't have time to take everything in. Not that I can concentrate on much else than the imminent introduction ceremony. When I hear music and loud voices, my heart somersaults and I forget all about the artifacts and statues.

"Most of the events will take place in the Sackler wing," Cara explains.

The music is getting louder. We're getting closer.

"It's where they keep the Temple of Dendur," she continues.

"The Temple of what?"

"Dendur. A gift from Egypt to the United States in 1965."

"A real temple?" I ask.

She nods. "It's something," she says, just as we veer through a disproportionately small entranceway—disproportionate because the room stretching beyond it is majestic, rising thirty or forty feet high with a twinkling, glass-paneled ceiling that echoes the vertiginous slanted wall of windows framing Central Park. I can still make it out even though the sky is dimming.

Dominic Bacci stands on an elevated stone platform between two structures—a thick pale arch, and a larger, columned structure covered in chiseled hieroglyphs and animal carvings that crop up in the warm glow of the overhanging projectors. To his right, on a gold bench, sit Josephine and Brook, and behind him sit the other contestants. A hundred—or perhaps more—round tables dripping with candlelight, white flowers, fine china, and jewel-toned spectators girdle the stage and the sharp, U-shaped pool filled with coins.

"Go," Cara whispers, giving me a little shove into the room.

Shoulders held back, I step from obscurity into the light. Dominic spots me right away.

"Eight! Lucky number eight, you made it!" His voice erupts out of his microphone.

Everyone spins in their seat to stare. I put on my best smile and strut toward Dominic, the icy satin dancing against my naked skin. I set aside Aster and the mess that awaits me in Kokomo, and focus on this dream that has become a reality. One tiny dream bobbing in a raging sea of nightmares.

FIVE

W*ow*. I'm not sure if I say this out loud or not. I don't really care. The only two people in proximity are Dreadlocks, who gaped at me in the cafeteria, and another girl with a thick body and a black mullet. Most of the other inmates are busy reading or playing board games.

Dreadlocks swivels her head from the screen to me so many times that I snap at her. "What?"

After a beat she says, "You look a lot like that chick in the blue dress. What gives?"

"She's my twin," I admit, although we don't even look alike anymore. They made her into some sort of Hollywood siren while I resemble Frankenstein's daughter.

"What did I tell you, Cheyenne?" Dreadlocks scoots to the edge of the couch, bends at the waist, and holds out her hand. "Pay up."

The hefty chick—Cheyenne—digs into the top of the V-neck tee she wears beneath her prison-issue jumpsuit and slaps a hand-rolled cigarette into Dreadlocks' palm. I expect a prison guard to intervene, but the one present is too busy twirling the knobs on her walkie-talkie.

"I'm Gillian, but you can call me Gill," Dreadlocks says, settling back into the battered couch.

"Aster," I say, leaning away from her until the armrest jabs into my ribs.

"What you in for?" she asks.

"Nothing."

"That must've been some pretty ugly nothin'," Cheyenne pipes in.

"Self-defense."

One of Gill's orange eyebrows hikes up her freckled forehead. "They locked you up here for self-defense?"

"Yeah. To await my trial."

"Are you some repeat offender?" Gill asks.

"No."

"Flight risk?" Gill continues.

"No." When she pops her mouth open again, I say, "You mind? I'm trying to listen to the show."

"Thank you!" a suave voice explodes out of a microphone. "Your presence at the third annual Masterpiecers games proves that we're doing something right." The voice belongs to Dominic Bacci, art patron extraordinaire and creator of the Masterpiecers, the famed finishing school for artists, dealers, and collectors.

Dominic makes a few jokes, throwing out chalky smiles left and right. Everyone laughs, especially the women—I can tell because it's high-pitched. He's a tabloid favorite and an international celebrity. At sixty-three years old, even though his hair's turned silver and his skin's a bit creased, he attracts women of all ages.

"Before we introduce you to this year's lucky eight, Josephine and I—" He doesn't get to finish his sentence as another wave of applause ricochets against the slanted glass wall.

Josephine Raynoir, Dominic's second-in-command, stands up and waves to the room. Then she gracefully lowers herself back onto the judges' golden bench. Her silver pantsuit is as shiny as the diamond lariat that dips down the length of her bare back. She's fifty but looks thirty, with white blonde hair cut with such precision that her hairdresser must use laser beams.

"Dominic's such a sleazeball," Gill mumbles.

"I'd do him," Cheyenne says.

"You'd do anyone with a pulse."

"I wouldn't do you, Firehead."

"Good. You're not my type," Gill tells her.

"Will you two please shut up?" I say, my tone sharp.

Dominic Bacci taps his microphone to recapture everyone's attention. "Josephine and I want to welcome this year's top graduate—" Applause. Dominic raises his voice and continues, "Brook Jackson—" Hollers. Dominic smiles, out of pride or habit I'm not sure. "To this year's panel."

Brook rises and bows to either side of the room. Deep dimples crease his jaw, which is covered in an afternoon shadow.

When Brook sits back down and the audience quiets, Dominic walks over to a blonde whose face is so shiny, she looks like she has plastic skin. "Now let's begin with introductions. Lincoln Vega, please stand, my dear."

She does, her beaded dress swooshing to her feet and gleaming like the lopsided neon sign above the pizza joint where I used to waitress.

"Lincoln is an avid art connoisseur, who, at twenty, dreams of becoming the next Picasso. I even read in your application that you recreated his *Demoiselles d'Avignon* in chalk in a subway station. Shoot us the picture, Jeb."

The stupendously huge screens dotting the room fill with the image.

"That's quite a lot of talent. I even suspect not all would be lost if you don't win. Right, Delancey?"

"Who the fuck is Delancey?" Cheyenne asks.

As though Dominic heard her, he adds, "Delancey's a talent scout. He's launched many a career. Are your parents watching us tonight?"

Lincoln is grinning so widely that I expect her to give a shout-out to her parents. She doesn't. "Mom's dead. But if my dad's alive, maybe."

Dominic cringes. "How indelicate of me."

She gives him a sweet smile. "It's fine, Mister Bacci."

The camera swirls around the room, closing in on certain spectators' faces as they utter *awws* and *poor girl*. Then it's back on Lincoln whose green-gold eyes glimmer. She's either about to cry or loving the attention. I'd put money on the latter. There's something about her that blocks my sympathy. Possibly her cool, polished exterior. She makes me think of a slab of marble and you can't feel bad for marble.

I catch Josephine inspecting her. Unlike the others, she's not gushing.

"Heard the female judge was a lesbo. Is that true, Firehead?" Cheyenne asks.

"Just because I like women doesn't mean I know all the lesbians out there," Gillian says.

I'm about to shush them when Dominic introduces the next contestant. "Herrick. That's an uncommon name," he says.

"I'm an uncommon man." He wears eyeliner and a burgundy floral scarf that he keeps petting.

"Quite true." Dominic smiles. "At the ripe old age of nine, Herrick was so taken with Michelangelo, he reproduced the Sistine Chapel fresco on his bedroom ceiling. Then, if I'm not mistaken, you redecorated your parents' entire house."

Herrick grins. His teeth are like Chiclets, large and rectangular. "You're not mistaken."

"Any pictures, Jeb?" Dominic asks. The screens flicker with a lengthy slideshow of Herrick's house.

"That's nasty," Cheyenne says, picking her nose.

I agree with her. I wonder what Ivy thinks. I wish the camera would move to her, but it stays on Herrick's smug face. He caresses his black pompadour hairstyle as he chats with Dominic about his expectations of the competition. I zone out because Cheyenne's now feeding herself the booger. I clamp my teeth together to avoid regurgitating my tasteless breakfast.

Next up, Nathan Stein. Forty-three years old. Sad eyes and shaggy brown hair. When I first saw his picture on TV the day they announced the contenders of this art competition, I thought he was some homeless man. Now, with clean clothes and a shave, he looks less unkempt. He still looks sad though. I learn he's the descendent of an art dealer whose family was robbed by the Nazis during the Second World War.

"Art. It's in my blood," he says.

"I hear you," Dominic says. "So tragic what happened to your family…to the world." Dominic's still smiling, which is totally weird. Maybe it's some nervous tic, like someone laughing at a funeral. "You know, that's one of the reasons our school was created. To protect art dealers and safeguard their collections." After a brisk shake of his head, he adds, "So tragic." Then he squeezes Nathan's shoulder. "Well, best of luck, my friend."

Applause. He walks across the stage to the next person, a boy around my age.

"We have a very special contestant this year." He pauses for effect. "Ladies and gentlemen…"

Drumroll. There's an actual live drumroll. It comes from the mammoth orchestra positioned against one of the walls.

"Brook," Dominic calls out. The youngest judge snaps to attention, raking his hand through his shiny black hair. "You want to come and introduce your little brother?"

"No fucking way! I didn't realize they were related," Gill says.

I knew. Ivy told me. She learned everything there was to know about her competitors.

Brook grins and gets up, covering the short distance in long, fluid strides. He takes the microphone from Dominic and drapes his arm around the boy's shoulders. "As you all know, the school has a strict one-person-per-family rule. However, Chase shares my passion for art and artists. Don't you, little brother?"

Chase nods, even though it looks painful for him to do so.

"When he told our parents two years ago that he wanted to follow in the family footsteps, our father tried to dissuade him. What did he suggest you do again?"

"Investment banking," Chase answers flatly, shrugging his brother's arm off.

A flicker of emotion crosses Brook's face, betraying some underlying animosity between the brothers. I wonder if it has to do with the school's one family member policy.

"*Ooh*. Investment banking. *Bo*-ring," Dominic says, leaning over Chase to speak in the microphone that Brook is now clutching with both hands.

Chase gives a crooked smile. "It could've been worse. He could've suggested auditing."

Laughter.

Chase's face stays impassive, but he stands up a little straighter. He's shorter than Brook, and definitely not as handsome. Still, he's good-looking with his purposely-messy brown hair and dark eyes; he's just not the god his brother is. Sort of like Ivy and me.

"So," Brook continues, "he sends in his application and *bam*! Josephine insists he be a part of this year's competition."

"But it wasn't all excitement and entrechats," Dominic adds, performing a sort of hop kick before landing like a ballerina with his feet angled sideways and his knees bent. The audience laughs. "There was still the issue of no siblings," he says, panting slightly.

"Before the winners were publicly announced, there was much, much deliberation," Brook says. "But since Chase is here with us tonight, you can imagine what Dominic's answer was."

"Yes," Dominic exclaims, seizing the microphone. "I said yes!"

Chase sort of smiles but I can tell he's nervous. He keeps stretching his fingers and folding them into fists. The camera pans onto his face, so close that I notice he has long, sweeping lashes.

"Best of luck, Chase." While Brook returns to the judges' bench, Dominic reaches Maxine's side. "Now, let me introduce you to contestant number five, Maxine Specter."

She gives the audience a wave and a smile. She looks nice and bland, like Special K. Ivy will have no trouble taking her out.

"Maxine has a funny story to share with you tonight," Dominic says. "The story of how she got here."

Maxine touches the brown fuzz growing on her head. "Oh, no…I couldn't possibly—"

Dominic cuts her off. "Oh, yes, yes, yes."

Blushing, she nibbles on her lower lip, and then gulps in a big breath. "Daisy Dukes."

"Ah…Daisy Dukes. I *love* Daisy Dukes," Dominic says, which makes a bunch of people in the audience hoot.

"I mean the shots," Maxine adds.

"Of course. Me too." Big theatrical wink. I can nearly hear his eyelid open and shut.

"I had twelve of them—" she says.

"The drinks," he clarifies. I think everyone got it, but *hey*, it's his show.

"They're teeny tiny, but *really* strong. That's why—"

"What's in them?" Dominic interjects.

"Um…I'm not sure."

"Can someone find out and mix some up? I think we could all use a *tiny* Daisy Duke. Except Chase, Lincoln, and Miss Ivy over there."

The camera perches on my sister's face. I scoot closer to the edge of the couch, hungry for a glimpse of her. The armrest practically pops out one of my ribs. Too soon, they're back to filming Maxine.

"So tell us how a drink landed you on my show."

She clears her throat. "When I got home, after the bar, I was reading my emails. Among them was one my mother had forwarded me with a link to the application form. My parents are great art enthusiasts—I was raised around art. Some children have musical mobiles hanging over their cribs…I had an authentic Calder."

Subtle tittering erupts which relaxes the stiff line of Maxine's shoulder blades.

"Anyway, I thought I'd make Mom and Dad proud so I filled in the application and emailed it. I'm not really sure what I wrote in it though."

"Whatever you wrote in it got our attention, so assume it was great! Did you celebrate with a haircut?"

She winces, the corners of her large eyes crinkling. "That was a bet. I told my best friend that if you guys accepted me, I would shave off my hair. I really didn't think I'd win."

He grins. "Can I touch it?" he asks, already running his palm over her scalp. "Ooh…it's so soft."

Maxine hoists up a smile that doesn't reach her eyes.

"Can I call you Daisy from now on?"

Her face crinkles with a clumsy smile. "S-sure."

"Good luck then, Daisy."

He starts walking to the next contestant, but doubles back to stroke her cropped hair. Maxine goes crimson. Dominic winks and scampers off.

"And in this corner, we have world famous hooligan, J.J.!"

Ivy told me J.J. became famous after he spray-painted the corridor of his dorm in college. At first, he was fined, but then the principal decided it made the drab cement more attractive, so he dropped his complaint and commissioned him to repaint the rest of the hallways. After he graduated, other colleges called on him to enliven their bland atmospheres.

"How many schools have you spray-painted to this day?" Dominic asks.

"Three. I'm working on number four."

The screens around them are displaying his work. It's actually pretty neat, with all the colors and the oddball characters.

"Promise not to paint over any walls in this place or we'll get into serious trouble."

J.J. smiles. "Promise, dude."

"Shall we shake on it?" Dominic suggests, jutting out his hand.

Chuckling, J.J. shakes it.

"Josephine, do we have insurance?" Dominic asks, twisting around, still holding J.J.'s palm.

She smiles complacently.

"Phew." He lets go of J.J. and makes a big show of swiping his brow. "Best of luck to you, my friend."

"Thanks, man." J.J. is very West Coast, totally chill and totally tanned.

"And now…a woman who needs no introduction."

I think I'm about to see my sister, and my body goes as rigid as the rusty bars of my cell. *Don't bring it up, Dominic. Don't bring* me *up!*

SIX

Ivy

"Miss America 2000!"

People clap. The woman closest to me smiles and gives the cupped-hand pageant wave. Seriously, who invented such a pathetic gesture?

"Maria Axela," Dominic says, proffering his arm.

She latches on to it and rises, her black lace dress swinging around her knees. Even though she's in her mid-thirties, Maria exudes a voluptuous childishness with her perky breasts, flat waist, and pouty red lips.

"So tell us, Maria, what made a former beauty queen enter an art competition?"

"What made me enter?" she repeats in a thick Hispanic accent. "It's quite simple really. I'm not just nice to look at"—she winks—"I'm skilled."

"Jeb? Can you—"

Before Dominic even finishes his sentence, the screens light up with Maria's work. Sixteen paintings of pageant winners. I stare along with everyone else, thinking that whoever told her she was skilled should be shot. The oil paintings are poor renditions of chirpy girls in sequins. I scan the room. Everyone seems captivated—everyone except for Brook. He's staring at me. When our eyes meet, he jerks his gaze back to the screen, a little color staining his jaw.

"I don't know what's more beautiful…the women who pose, or your execution of them," Dominic says. He tucks a few more words into her ear, which make her glossy lips pull up. "A big round of applause for the Masterpiecers' first beauty queen contestant."

Maria sits back down, while I sit up straighter.

"And last but not least, please welcome a young and extraordinarily talented girl, Miss Ivy Redd."

I grin as I stand. Dominic's already at my side. He smells like a bottle of cologne, and something stronger—stale and vinegary. Day-old Merlot?

"This girl has created something truly original. Quilts! And I'm not talking old-timey ones, but fresh, modern works inspired by cityscapes, nature, basically everything she observes around her. Jeb?"

I watch the projected images of my work, a sense of pride stirring deep within me. Blown up and bright, my pieces look magical.

"So tell us what or who inspired you?"

"My mother," I say into the mic Dominic is holding up to my mouth. "She made quilts. Incredibly colorful landscapes with silk and tassels and chiffon."

"Like yours?"

"In a way. Although, I favor abstract over figurative."

"Do you stitch them by hand?"

"Of course. I have to feel the fabric, the thread, the needle. I need complete control over the process."

I'm eager for him to ask to buy one. I think he just might, when a waiter scuttles onto the stage, rudely interrupting us. He's carrying a silver platter covered in shot glasses. The liquid inside is amber with smoke curling out of it.

"Is that what I think it is?" Dominic asks the waiter, forgetting all about me.

"Daisy Dukes, sir," the man says, extending the platter.

Dominic grabs a glass and holds it up. "Daisy, to you, my dear." He's about to drink it, but stops. "Isn't there a saying that people who drink alone are drunks?" His smile widens and he gestures for the waiter to distribute the glasses.

He starts with me. I'm about to grab a random one when he points to a small glass that isn't fuming. Frustrated, I take it.

"Everyone has a shot glass?" Dominic asks. "Bottoms up!" Just as I tip my glass toward my lips, Dominic hollers, "Wait! Ivy, no!"

I jolt and spill some juice. It trickles down my forearm and soaks into the immaculate satin.

"Hers is simply *du jus*, Dominic," Josephine says with a strong French accent. "It's not even the same color as this"—she sniffs it and her nose wrinkles—"*concoction*."

He claps his hand over his chest emphatically. "And here I thought I was going to get in trouble with the authorities." His comment receives laughs.

I stare at the expanding wet spot on my thigh. Why did Dominic single me out? Chase and Lincoln are underage too.

"Now I *really* need this." He bares his rows of pearly whites like a shark. "Ready?"

There's a hum of assent. Elbows lift, necks snap backward.

Josephine puckers her painted lips. "That's *dégoûtant*."

Dominic smiles and shakes his head. "Don't mind her, Daisy. She thinks everything's awful if it's not French."

"You're such a *baladin*, Dominic," Josephine says.

"That means *catch* in French," he ping-pongs back.

"*Non*." The corners of her mouth lift briefly. "It means comedian."

"And this, ladies and gentlemen, is why I've never gotten romantically entangled with this beautiful woman. We don't speak the same language." Dominic flings his shot glass to the waiter who just catches it. "Now, where were we?"

"The last contestant!" people answer back jovially.

"Oh, yes. The last contestant. Ivy, anything you'd like to add at this time? Perhaps you'd like to send out a greeting to a family member?"

"No." I hope Aster won't get offended, but I don't feel like bringing her up.

He tips his head to the side. "Well then, best of luck to you, *Mademoiselle* Redd!"

Luck is overrated. Relying on it would be like trying to climb a fir tree by holding on to its pinecones. Dumb.

"May the best one win!" Dominic exclaims.

The orchestra on the side of the room breaks into the Masterpiecers' anthem, a melody about beauty and emotion and vision—or so Dominic explained the first time the show aired two summers back. It's pretty, but a little too mournful.

"Thank you all for coming," Dominic announces once the music dims. "Now enjoy your dinner and don't get to bed too late. Tomorrow's event will begin at 10 a.m. sharp in the main hall. Contestants, it's picture time!"

As we file off the stage underneath expanding applause, my stomach grumbles, the packet of nuts from the plane long gone. I smell fresh baked, buttery rolls and something rich and spicy. I fill my lungs with the aroma to ward off the hunger.

I meet some curious gazes as I walk out. I smile to appear forthcoming. Cara's there when I walk out, standing next to seven other people with head mics and informal apparel—the other assistants, I suppose. They all come to join us.

"How's that stain?" she asks.

I'd nearly forgotten about *that* stain. The fabric is darker. "Should I change before the group shot?"

"No. They'll probably have you stand in the back."

I clench my jaw. "They could have me sit down. It's barely noticeable if the fabric is bunched up."

"I don't choose, but it's a possibility," Cara says as we walk back through the Egyptian artifact-filled rooms toward the grand hall with the domed skylights.

It's full of people—security guards lining the walls, the camera crew, a guy with a shaved head prepping a large camera on a tripod, and faceless others milling about, adjusting furniture, strobes, reflectors, and the angle of an enormous painting they must be using as a backdrop. I feel like I'm on a movie set. It reminds me of my childhood fantasy of becoming an actress, which I grew out of during adolescence when I discovered my talent with needles and thread.

Cara leans in as we arrive on the set, so close that her blonde bob grazes my chin. "The photographer's really famous."

I stop myself from scratching the spot her hair brushed to avoid blemishing my skin with red claw marks.

"Works for all the fashion magazines," she continues.

It still tickles, but I keep my nails at bay and focus on the photographer. He does look familiar with his smooth head and handlebar moustache.

"Patrick Veingarten," she says.

He's not just famous; he's a legend.

"Dominic, my friend, it's been ages," Patrick says. They smack kisses on each other's cheeks. "Ravishing, as always, my dear Josephine," he says, lifting one of her white hands to his lips. "And if it isn't the Masterpiecers' most beloved graduate," he tells Brook, clapping his back.

"You mean the one who stuck around." Brook smiles and his dimples appear.

Patrick chuckles.

"So what are you thinking?" Dominic asks Patrick, gesturing to eight ornate golden frames.

"You'll see," Patrick begins. His gaze scans all of our faces before perching on mine. He strides toward me and takes my elbow. "Let's start with you."

He has swirls of light green and brown in his eyes, like slow-churned, mint chocolate chip ice cream.

"I hope my camera will do you justice," he adds with a wink.

"Where would you like me?"

"Somewhere more private," he whispers inside my ear.

I replace the snort frothing up with a subtle titter, which I hope will win me a spot in the foreground of the picture.

"Why don't you sit here?" he says.

Ka-ching. I lower myself into a rose-colored velvet chair that's angled sideways, cross my legs, and straighten my back.

"Too stiff. Too stiff," he says. "Let yourself go a little, Ivy. Think languid, just pleased, but still ravenous. I'm sure you know how to do that."

I hear someone grunt, which makes everything tighten up inside of me, from my ligaments to my veins. I look for the source and find Lincoln scrutinizing me, arms crossed in front of her chest. She's just jealous I was chosen first. I breathe in deeply and do as I'm told.

"Now tilt your head to the side."

I let my eyes go unfocused to blur the ogling faces around me, then slowly, I unfold and refold my legs, lay my forearms on the stuffed armrests, and loll my head against the soft velvet imagining it's one of my mother's quilts.

"Get the oval frame in front of her," Patrick yells to one of his assistants. It's so large it encases all of me. He steps back to observe the effect. After a long minute, he breathes, "Perfect…a true work of art." He admires me for so long that my confidence skyrockets. Coupled with my roiling hunger, I feel like I'm floating, hovering over the rest of the contestants on a cloud as gilded as the frame outlining me.

"Next," he yells.

I skid off my cloud, and land with a thump in the deafening room.

Leisurely, Patrick positions the others, bestowing upon them the same admiration he afforded me. Stupid me for feeling singled out. Patrick's appreciative of his work, not of his subjects. He scatters the judges among the framed contestants and instructs them to act as though they were appraising our value. Brook, who's supposed to be assessing my worth, is looking everywhere but at me. I'm pretty sure I make him uncomfortable.

While the strobe lighting blinks on and off, making a popping sound each time, the assistants orbit around us, slanting reflectors and readjusting the frames.

Patrick steps out from behind his camera. "Perfect. No one touch anything!

Brook, I'm sure your shoes are valuable, but eyes on Ivy please. Everyone else, stay in position."

With one click, we are immortalized.

SEVEN

I return to my cell with my head so full of my sister that I don't mind she didn't send me a verbal shout-out. We're twins—we have other ways of communicating. When she smiled, I knew it was for me.

I also don't mind all the attention I'm getting tonight. Let them stare at the new girl. Let them get an eyeful. Soon, I'll be gone. Ivy will take me to New York with her. I'll be able to quit my job at the pizzeria and focus on what I love best: graphic design.

A bell rings through the sterile hallway signaling that the cells are about to be bolted for the night. I hurry into my room just as the automated gates begin grinding against their built-in rails to lock us up like lab rats. The shrill sound reminds me of the garbage truck that used to beep every morning at five sharp while it backed into our street. Never thought I'd be nostalgic for the sound of a garbage truck.

I brush my teeth and splash cool water over my face from the sink in the room I thankfully don't need to share with anyone. As soon as my head hits the pillow, I fall asleep, but wake long before dawn. I fish out the book that I keep underneath my pillow to make it more substantial. I don't have a flashlight, so I angle the cream pages toward my barred window through which trickles the faint glow of the perimeter lighting.

I borrowed the book from the prison library. It's the story of a Southern white woman's love affair with one of her father's slaves. Sometimes, I wonder if my ancestors were slaves too. I'll never know. My mother had no stories about my father. I remember asking her how long they'd known each other before she had us. Her answer was always a huff and a flick of her wrist. Then again, my mother was no storyteller. There were no bedtime fables when we were children and no dinnertime tales. Rare were the times when we all sat around a table for a meal anyway.

I realize I've read the same paragraph three times, so I put the book away and fall back asleep. It's the shrill ringing and metal grating that rouses me. I rub the sleep out of my eyes, but it feels counterproductive, like I'm pressing fistfuls of sand into them.

I use the toilet quickly, feeling exposed now that the lights are on and the other inmates have started filing out of their cells. I stretch the T-shirt I've slept in over my knees to hide more skin. Before even washing my hands, I race to the bed and yank on my jumpsuit.

Breakfast is the usual: bland oatmeal. It goes down okay and doesn't come up, unlike some of the other stuff they serve. I take my food back to a deserted table and wolf it down because I want to go to the dayroom to see my sister. Unfortunately, Gill spots me and strides over. She sets her tray down right in front of mine.

"In a hurry, A?" she asks.

"A?"

"It's better than Ass."

I narrow my eyes. "My name's Aster. Not Ass. Not A."

"O-*kay*," she says, scrunching up her lips. "Don't get your jumpsuit in a twist. I was just trying to be friendly."

"I don't need a friend." When she smirks, I add, "I'll be out of here by next week. No point in making friends."

"Breaking out so soon?"

"No. I'll be released so soon," I say.

"Yeah. Keep thinking that if it helps you sleep at night."

"It was an accident. I'm not some criminal."

"I'm pretty sure killing a man makes you a criminal."

I glare at her. "Just shut up."

"Or what? You'll kill me too? Aster, if they thought you were the victim, you wouldn't be locked up with the likes of me. Wanna know what I did?" She's smiling. It's grotesque. Her teeth are crooked—all of them.

"I don't care what you did."

She sets her pointy elbows on the table and knots her finger together. "You're not even a little curious?"

I shake my head and gulp down the remaining cooked cereal even though it has the texture of wet cement. And then I'm on my feet, tray in hand, about to make a run for the door when one of the guards marches my way. He has rolls of fat bulging over his waistband.

"Inmate Redd."

The cafeteria goes quiet—too quiet. Sure enough, everyone's gaping.

"I'm here to escort you to your appointment with the psychiatrist," he says.

"Now?" I exclaim.

The guard lets out a thick laugh. "No, tomorrow."

There's snickering.

"Yes now. Let's go!"

"But—"

He hunches over and leans in so close that his nose is nearly against mine. "Do you want to end up in the tank instead of in your cozy little cell? Because I can make that happen."

I swallow hard. "No, sir."

His breath smells like stale cigarettes. It makes my eyes water. After a few painfully putrid seconds, he pulls away and starts for the door. Gill smirks. I would give her the finger if I weren't afraid of how she would retaliate—because isn't that what people do to each other on all those prison shows?

I peek at the clock on the wall right before going through the metal detector that checks for stolen cutlery. Eight thirty. I have another hour before the show starts, although I'll miss the preparation.

"Is this a routine appointment?" I dare ask the guard.

He turns to look at me, lips hoisted up on one side like skewed blinds. "Yeah. Your mani-pedi's right after."

Seven days. I focus on that. In one week—if the district attorney hasn't already set a court date and a bail amount—Ivy will come home and find a way to set me free. She promised and she always holds her promises.

"Here we are, princess," he says, rapping against a glazed glass door. "Have fun."

The door swings open to reveal a woman in a tweed skirt suit. She seems way too chic to work in a prison. "Hi. My name is Robyn." She holds out her hand.

I shake it quickly, barely pressing down, then stride into the room past her. There are two large windows overlooking the barbed wire fence and the dense forest beyond.

"Please take a seat." Robyn has lines around her mouth and eyes.

I sit facing the windows. She sits across from me, a dark outline against the stark light.

"Would you like a glass of water?"

"No."

"So, Aster, tell me…how are you adjusting?"

I shrug. "Fine."

"Are the other inmates treating you nicely?"

"Yeah. Whatever." The small talk is making my skin itch, so I cut to the chase. "Why am I here?"

"I'd like us to discuss how you're feeling."

"Awesome, thank you. Can I go now?"

"Sarcasm denotes distress. Are you distressed about being here or over the events of August 17th?"

"Is anyone not distressed about being locked up in prison?"

"So it isn't August 17th that has you so upset?"

"Of course I'm upset about *involuntarily* killing a man," I say with a huff. "Just like I was *distressed* when I ran over my neighbor's cat two years ago. It sucks."

"You sound more distraught about the cat."

"The cat was innocent. It didn't deserve it."

"But the man did?"

"Troy Mann had ties with the mafia. He was a bad man. He killed people. So forgive me if I sound cold, but killing him—involuntarily," I add, "is probably a good thing for humanity."

"Let's talk about that then."

"Fine."

She flicks her gaze to the folder resting on her lap. "After you saw Troy Mann at the pizzeria, you followed him back to his motel without alerting the authorities. Is this correct?"

"Yes," I say.

"Why?"

"So he wouldn't get away."

"Why didn't you call the cops?"

"They wouldn't have come in time."

"What did you think you would do once you found out where he lived?"

"I wasn't thinking that far ahead."

She scribbles in the file. "Once you got to the motel, why didn't you phone the police?"

"My cell had no more battery."

Again, she takes note of what I say. "So he got out of his car and walked over to your window?"

"Yes. He'd noticed I was following him. He threatened me."

"What were his exact words?"

"He told me he would break some bones in my body if I didn't leave straight away and forget I ever saw him. He said he would hurt Ivy if I called the cops," I say in a hushed voice, rolling the scratchy fabric of my jumpsuit between my thumb and index finger. Ivy used to do that on a frayed and yellowed piece of quilt to soothe herself. It worked for her so perhaps it'll work for me. After a few minutes, I don't feel better.

"The cops didn't find a pizza box in his car. Do you know why that is?"

"He tossed it out on his way home. From his car window."

Her already lined forehead puckers even more. I count nine wrinkles. "Into a bin or on the sidewalk?"

"In a bin."

"Do you remember where that bin was?"

I shake my head. My breathing is too shallow. I focus on dragging it out. "I was focused on not losing him."

"No cross streets come to mind? Store awnings?"

"It was ten-thirty. It was dark and everything was closed."

She shuts the folder. "How do you feel about your sister leaving for an art competition three days later?"

"I forced her to go. It's her chance, and I won't take that away from her. Plus we need the money."

Robyn holds my gaze. "But how did it make you *feel*?"

"I miss her."

"Do you feel like she abandoned you?"

"Didn't you hear what I just said? *I* forced her to go. She would've stayed if I'd asked her to."

"Are you certain about that?"

"Yes."

She stares at me, then stands up. "This was a good session, Aster."

"That's it? We're done?"

"For today. I'll see you next week. Same time?"

"I won't be here anymore."

"Is that right?" One of her eyebrows lifts. "Well then, feel free to stop by before you leave. I'm here every day from ten to four."

"Sure." *Not.*

As I rise, she extends her hand. I don't shake it, so she lowers it to the file she's clutching against her chest. A paper's sticking out. I catch the word *nervous*.

"Good-bye, Aster."

I walk out of her office on autopilot, distracted by those seven letters. If I'm nervous, then I'm in trouble.

EIGHT

Ivy

Thanks to the sleeping tablets I picked up in the pharmacy on my way to the airport, I sleep deeply and dreamlessly and wake only because I hear birds chirping. It takes me a second to remember I'm inside a museum, and then another to activate my brain and realize that tweeting birds isn't normal. But then, this is the Masterpiecers—the school defies normalcy. They very well could have actual birds. They have real grass and small trees outside our tents.

"Ten minutes to hair and makeup," I hear someone call out from the grassy hallway.

I tie up my hair and jump into the shower. Too soon, I hop out and don the bathrobe someone's already replaced. While I brush my teeth, I search for a fresh pair of underwear in my duffel, but my bag is empty. Someone unpacked it!

I throw the toothbrush on the bed, and with both hands, feel the bottom of the bag, trying to locate the lump. When I touch it, a whoosh of air tears out of my lungs. Willing my heart to quiet, I grab a thong from a drawer and tug it on underneath the bathrobe. Still agitated, I head to the prep wing, bypassing the breakfast spread.

Lincoln and Herrick are already seated. Both have people working on them. I meander toward my station where Leila and Amy are waiting, and sit, bobbing my right knee up and down, up and down.

The bright bulbs are blinding, yet I notice Cara's reflection in the mirror. She's wearing a head mic. "Cup of coffee, tea, green juice?"

"Green juice," I say.

When she leaves, Leila tapes a picture to the mirror, her long black hair swinging around her waist. "That's your look for today."

I stare at the picture. "Is the photo in black and white?"

"Nope." She smacks a piece of gum around in her mouth. "They just want your skin to be pale."

Amy leans in toward the picture and then sways back like a bamboo. "That's some serious hair teasing."

By the time they're done with me, I look spooky and electrocuted. Thankfully, I'm not the only one. Chase also resembles an albino macaque. We even wear matching outfits: white tights and white V-necks.

The others look different. Lincoln is doll-like in her polka-dot dress. She has rouge on her cheeks and cherry-colored lip-gloss.

Maria, the ex-beauty queen, is literally washed out, her dark skin and clothes have been bleached, down to her clogs that are also gray.

Herrick's skin has been tinged pea green, like the hulk, and his clothes are orange.

Maxine sports a yellow wig over her buzz-cut, dark purple circles under her eyes, a red clown nose, and a pair of ripped Daisy Dukes.

Nathan's longish hair is pulled into a ponytail and he's wearing a pair of round bifocals that emphasize his sad eyes. His shirt is oddly buttoned and his tie's on crooked.

And J.J. looks like a yeti. They glued whiskers to his tanned face and stuffed him in some furry outfit.

I'm thinking that my accouterment isn't the worst when Dominic bursts into the room. "Is everyone—" He doesn't finish his sentence. "Fabulous! Now hurry and eat some breakfast. Make it substantial. You're skipping lunch." As he heads toward Jeb—who's practically as short as Aster's prison warden—he calls out, "I want you all in the main hall in fifteen for the announcement of today's episode!"

"Hey, Ivy," comes a voice from behind.

I turn to find Brook in a black suit and black shirt opened at the collar. "And here I was afraid I wasn't recognizable anymore."

He chuckles, which makes him appear somewhat kinder.

"So what are we doing today?" I ask him.

"Can't tell you."

"Really? Not even a hint?"

"Not even a hint." His dark eyes crinkle at the corners, penetrating but not as abrasive as last night.

"I should go eat something," I say.

He gestures toward the panel of fabric delineating our quarters. "After you."

My seven opponents are chatting while gobbling down plates piled high with slices of bread and golden pastries. Maxine and Nathan seem to be hitting it off. She's propped up on the arm of the couch and Nathan's standing inches away, laughing. Every so often, his eyes dart to the hem of her Daisy Dukes.

"Morning, everyone," Brook says with a smile.

As he enquires as to how they slept, I head to the buffet to pick up a piece of toast, which I slather in cream cheese and strawberry jam. There are pieces of real fruit in this jam, unlike the dollar brand Mom used to buy that was basically red goop with strawberry extract. Quickly, I load up a second slice just as someone from the camera crew arrives and barks, "Last touch-ups and we're a go. Come on, people."

I gulp it down, wishing I'd had time to grab a cinnamon roll or a banana from the buffet. Food going to waste—especially such incredibly expensive food—is a pet peeve of mine. Mom was like that too, although she took it to another level. She would skim the green fluff from expired yogurts and scrape the mold off sliced Wonderbread. Aster, on the other hand, would rather starve. Mom used to think she was anorexic, but she's just not interested in food and forgets to eat.

Once our makeup artists fix what needs fixing, we file out of the third floor and take the wide staircase down to the darkened main hall. They've covered all the windows—even the round ones on the ceiling—and turned off all the lights. Spotlights suddenly flare up and settle on each one of us, plunging the cavernous space beyond in total inky blackness. I blink, but avoid squinting because I'm being filmed. Instead, I call upon my other senses as though they were insect feelers. From the thundering applause resounding against the tall stone walls, I can tell that hundreds of people are gathered in the lobby, and from the heady scent of caffeine, I can tell that breakfast is in full swing down here as well.

"Today, we begin with a show," Dominic says. "A great, great show. In our métier, we call it performance art." He spins around to face us. "For those of you who've never heard of it, forfeit this instant!"

Is he serious?

Dominic guffaws. "I'm kidding. Who fell for it?" His eyes shine as they scan each of our faces. "Don't tell me you all knew what I was talking about?" Still no one speaks. "Well then, this should be a breeze for all of you. Music, maestro."

The orchestra plays the opening notes to the Masterpiecers' theme song.

"Lights!" Dominic exclaims over the music.

Large spotlights blaze, illuminating seven square forms cloaked in heavy emerald velvet. Dominic raises his hands, palms facing up, as though making an offering to the gods, and the velvet is pulled off, shimmying like the glossy leaves of the buttonbush shrubs bordering our ground floor apartment. The fabric pools to the side of enormous glass cubes in which various pieces of furniture have been deposited: chairs, desks, a bar, a human-sized hamster wheel. One's even filled with dirt.

"Contestants, your stages!" Dominic bellows, his voice rife with delight. "Herrick Hawk, for the next eight hours, you will be a carrot. You will stand in dirt. You will not talk. You will not move. But please, don't forget to breathe," he adds with a bark of laughter.

The green makeup does little to hide Herrick's revulsion. When he finally moves, it's in slow motion. One of the stage hands props a ladder against the side of his dirt-filled glass cage to help him scale the wall. He lands noiselessly on the thick earth. He doesn't insert himself in the hole they dug against one of the sides. He's probably waiting until he has to.

"Maria, my dear, I hope you enjoy knitting," Dominic continues, wrapping one arm around the former beauty queen's waist.

"Not especially," she says.

"Well that's too bad, because"—he shoves her toward a cube with a chair in the middle and a basket full of electric blue yarn—"you will be knitting a scarf for the next eight hours."

"*Que bueno*," she mumbles, advancing toward her box.

"Daisy. Darling Daisy," he tells Maxine. "Guess which stage I've had readied for you."

She points to the one with the bar.

"Good girl. You'll pretend to pour yourself shots and drink them."

He grins. She doesn't.

He turns to Lincoln, who's smoothing down her gold hair. "You see that stage with the wooden vat and all the wands sticking out of it?"

She nods.

"That's all yours, sweetheart. You will enchant us with bubbles of all sizes. It will be beautiful."

She smirks as she leaves. I wouldn't have minded blowing bubbles dressed as Lolita for a few hours.

I stare at what's left: the hamster wheel, a desk with a stool and a thick leather-bound book, and a glass cube with two chairs facing each other. I hope I get the desk, but I don't. It becomes Nathan's. He must read the entire book. I'm jealous until I hear it's an encyclopedia on plants and seeds.

J.J., unsurprisingly, is awarded the hamster cage. The whiskers gave it away.

"Chase and Ivy, you will look at each other for the next eight hours. You may blink, but no looking at anything or anyone else. Studies have shown it's extraordinarily intimate when it lasts for four minutes," Dominic says, which makes me grunt. "No one's ever studied the effect of eight hours, though."

I'm sure it will have the opposite effect. When I spot Lincoln toying with her bubble wands, I'm envious. Why didn't they stick her in here with Chase? I walk ahead of him, threading myself through the thick crowd, and take a seat on one of the transparent chairs, bracing myself for complete boredom.

"Can I get a countdown?" I hear Dominic ask.

I stare around me one last time before I'm stuck with Chase's pale face. The crowd starts counting down from ten to one. My gaze locks on Brook's. He's standing right outside our cube, his arms folded in front of his chest.

"Three…two…one…show time!" everyone chants.

Cara seals the door of our cube, and then, it's just me and Chase. There's no more noise except that of my breath whooshing past my parted lips.

The first hour is the most painful. My eyes are sore, and my bottom, in spite of relentlessly shifting around in the plastic chair, smarts. My nostrils keep flaring from Chase's oily, green smell that makes me think of muddy grass after a rainfall. But the physical agony is nothing compared to the displeasure of being scrutinized by him. His eyes feel like the sheets of icy rain that fall over Kokomo in autumn. I hope mine feel the same.

After the second hour, it gets easier because my vision has gone unfocused. I've shut down. My breathing has slowed and my soreness has receded. I stare unseeingly at Chase. My peripheral attention is on the world outside the glass cube. People point as they mill around our *stages*, and discuss our quiet showcases. One presence never shifts though: Brook.

When hour number three is announced, my stomach growls so loudly that I think Chase hears it. I will it to stop. It does by hour four. I feel light now. By hour five, I'm floating, more clear-headed than a Buddhist monk who's been meditating his entire life. At least, that's what I imagine meditating monks feel like. I have no clue.

Hour six, it gets easy. Staring into Chase's dark irises is hypnotic.

Hour seven. Something strange happens. There's shrieking. A lot of it. I'm so tempted to turn to see what's going on. Maybe it's some ploy to break us. The crowd around our box migrates to another part of the room. *Okay...*maybe it's not a test. I strain to listen to the world outside. I make out Dominic's voice and metal hitting the floor. The squealing resumes, and then it gets quiet again. Eerily so. I look at Chase—I mean really look at him—to see if he knows what's happening, but his features are set in stone.

It's finally hour eight. If I was floating three hours ago, now I have an out of body experience. I'm soaring over the glass ceiling, watching myself watch Chase. It's overwhelming and extraordinary. I'm not sure if it's my empty stomach or the silence, but this tranquil strength envelops me. It's so powerful that I shiver, and so wonderful that I smile. And for the first time in months, I feel like everything is going to be okay again.

Chase looks stiffer than he did at the beginning. There's tension in his arms and shoulders. Even his legs, which are splayed out in front of him, are as rigid as tree trunks. He hasn't stirred in the past hour, yet there's this vein on his temple that's been pumping feverishly, as though his pulse were racing. My blood, on the other hand, is syrup, sluggishly sliding underneath my skin.

Loud music suddenly fills the vaulted room. It's followed by Dominic's voice announcing that the contest has been completed. Chase's lips unbolt, and he rips his eyes off mine. I can almost feel the tear. He springs out of his chair and marches out of the glass cube without a word.

I'm offended.

"You may return to your tents and relax for an hour." Dominic's voice rings too loudly.

Chin up, I rise and thread myself through the applauding crowd, my irritation at Chase's brisk exit dissipating. I don't want to rest; I want to stay here and lap up the praise the spectators are distilling on me as I pass by them.

Someone grabs my elbow. At first, I smile, thinking it's a fan, but then I spot Cara. "Lost your way?"

"I'm not tired."

"Contestants can't mingle." She all but drags me to the stairs.

I shake her off with the energy brought on by the compliments. "That's a stupid rule."

"Yeah, but it's a rule. Up we go," she says.

I go up a few stairs, but turn back and take one last, longing look around. As my gaze surfs over the crowd, I catch sight of a man with dark hair and an orange tie. He's watching me with great interest. Too much interest. Then again, I'm sort of a star now.

NINE

I've just spent several hours in front of a tiny television screen. My eyes are raw, my legs stiff, and I'm ravenous. The oatmeal might have tasted like cement, but it wasn't, and there's now a gaping void in my stomach. The food will suck tonight, like it sucks all the time, but I'm so hungry I don't care. I could eat the polyester fill of my pillow. I head to the cafeteria along with the hordes of other inmates. I spot fiery red dreadlocks ahead of me, so I slow down. Maybe if I wait for Gill to sit first, she won't join me.

I take my time gathering my meal. Finally, Gill sits next to fat Cheyenne and two other women who do not look particularly friendly. She catches me staring, so I turn my attention to the opposite side of the room where I find a table occupied solely by a white-haired woman whose advanced age leads me to believe she's inoffensive. I place my tray next to hers and take a seat.

The mashed potatoes are lumpy, the piece of meat appears as appetizing as a shoe sole, and the boiled carrot, with its green leaf, resembles Herrick. I squash the tender orange flesh with the tines of my fork. My stomach growls, so I gobble it down along with the watery potatoes. I have more trouble with the meat. The blunt knife doesn't even pierce the steak, so I pick it up and tear off chunks with my teeth.

My least favorite time of day comes after dinner. Ironically, it used to be my favorite back home: shower time. I sorely miss the privacy of my bathroom. Tightening a tiny, scratchy towel around my body and keeping my prison-issue flip-flops on, I head to the salmon-tiled communal shower where the grout has turned a nasty shade of tobacco.

Most of the prisoners use this time to socialize. Definitely not me. I'm in and out so quickly that I don't press the shower button more than once for water. I still have foam on my thighs and calves. I sponge it up with the coarse towel and don my gray uniform.

"Can I be escorted back to the dayroom?" I ask the guard on duty.

She narrows her eyes.

"Officer Cooper got me special permission. It's in my file," I tell her.

"Is that so?"

I nod.

She holds out her palm. I stare at it so long, that she says, "A twenty will do."

"Twenty what?"

"What do you think?"

"You want me to bribe you?"

"It's called payment for services rendered."

Right. "I don't have any money on me."

"That's a shame."

"But Josh—I mean Officer Cooper got—"

She's twisting her long neck left and right. "Don't see *him* nowhere."

My nostrils flare. My first reflex is to dig through my pocket for my cell phone. Then I remember that it was confiscated because I'm in fucking prison. The guard turns her back to me to survey the palette of naked bodies on display.

Desperation hits me so hard that an idea—probably an awful one—materializes in my brain. "I have a proposition for you," I say, coming around to stand in front of her.

She cocks her head to the side. "I'm listening."

"My sister's competing in the Masterpiecers. You know, that show about—"

"I know it." She scrutinizes my face. "That's why you look familiar. You're related to that girl, Lucky Little Eight, or whatever the media calls her."

"Her name's Ivy."

"What's your offer?"

"I'll give you some of the prize money."

"She hasn't won yet."

"But she will. I know my sister. She always gets what she wants."

"How much are we talking?"

"A hundred dollars."

She snorts. "Isn't the prize a hundred thousand?"

"Yeah, but I'll need bail money, and Ivy will want to keep some—"

"Five thousand."

"Five thousand?" I choke out.

"Take it or leave it."

My bargaining skills are nil, but I can't just hand over five thousand bucks. Then again, we're talking about imaginary money. Once I'm out, I'll never see this woman again so she can hang on to her imaginary payday.

"For that price, I get permission to watch the show whenever I want."

"Aren't you a little wheeler and dealer? Fine. But—"

My mouth goes dry.

"If your sister gets disqualified," she says, "you'll still owe me the money."

Cold sweat gathers on the nape of my neck. I remind myself that it's pretend money, like the one Ivy and I bartered when we played on the faded Monopoly board my mother once brought back from the flea market. We'd had to make play-dough houses and hotels, and cut and write our own chance cards and property deeds, but at least we had the board, the dice, the bills, and the metal tokens. It gave us something to do on dreary, rainy afternoons.

"Fine," I finally say.

She smiles. "Kim!"

A short woman with a long, coarse braid trots over.

"Gotta escort a prisoner. Take over."

The walk to the dayroom is quick and quiet in spite of the pointed looks the guard keeps firing my way. I wish she'd stop. I wish everyone would just stop looking at me.

She buzzes the door open. The TV's already on. I can hear two commentators rehashing the day's event.

"Hey, Redd," she calls out as I hurry in.

"Yeah?"

A crooked smile lights up her face. "I always collect."

When I nod, she leaves, and the anthem booms out of the stereo in time with the door banging shut.

"Welcome ba-ack!" Dominic singsongs. He's holding his mic so close to his lips that it looks as though he's French-kissing it. "Tonight is an unusual night, because, usually, there's a vote among the judges and among the audience to decide who gets the boot. Tonight, we didn't have to deliberate. Performance art wasn't Maria's forte. Or maybe it was the knitting…"

Laughter warbles out of the dark pit of people seated around the raised stone platform. It's scornful, which makes me angry, but my anger recedes when I spot my sister. Her face resembles burnished copper, and her lips have been painted a bright red. When they curve into a smile, I feel an overwhelming sense of pride.

"That's my sister," I say to no one, but Ivy must hear me because she winks. I wink back, and then settle down to watch.

TEN

Ivy

"You're late," Leila says when I arrive at my station the next morning, yawning and stretching.

I didn't fall asleep until really late—or maybe really early. With no windows and no clock, I couldn't tell what time it was.

"Get in the chair. We have forty minutes left. Amy!" Leila's shaking, even her slick-straight hair is vibrating.

"Herrick just arrived," I point out.

"I don't give a shit about Herrick. I give a shit about you. Why are your eyes so puffy? Didn't you sleep?" From the way she mutters this, I take it she's not asking. She pulls a little tube from her makeup trunk and rubs a dollop of its content across both my lids. It burns like ice.

"What the hell is that?" I exclaim.

"Hopefully, a miracle," she says. "Now don't move until I'm done."

While Leila brushes and stabs my face with crayons and mascara wands, Amy blasts my locks with hot air. No one talks. Chase is at the next station getting primped. Although his gaze is locked on the mirror, the line of his shoulders tightens as though he senses I'm looking. Last night, over dinner, I was tempted to ask him what his problem was, but that would exhibit insecurities, and New York Ivy has *no* insecurities. Powder wafts into my right eye and it tears up. I blink, but it still waters.

Leila grumbles as she swabs my lash line with a Q-tip. "Look up."

Finally, I'm ready. My hair has been slicked down. It reaches far below my shoulder blades and shines like spun gold. The amethyst powder on my lids makes my eyes appear bluer and hooded instead of swollen from lack of sleep.

"Tonight, six-thirty sharp. Not a minute later." And then she's gone.

"What's her problem?" I ask Amy, who's masticating her lip.

She gathers my hair in a high ponytail and wraps a ribbon around it. "Leila's a perfectionist."

"So am I. It doesn't mean you have to be nasty with people."

"Why aren't you dressed yet?" Cara exclaims, stopping by my station.

"She'll be ready in five minutes," Amy tells her.

"Just hurry. I put your clothes in the dressing area."

On the purple velvet pouf, my assistant has laid out a pair of light jeans, a pearl-colored shirt, and white sneakers. I pull on the jeans while Amy helps me with the blouse, careful that it doesn't snag on the ribbon in my hair or pick up pigment from my skin. I tie up my sneakers and reemerge after a glimpse of myself in the floor-length mirror.

Cara is checking her bulky, neon-orange rubber wristwatch, the sort of watch I drooled over as a pre-teen. Now I aspire to sleeker ones, preferably metal and preferably brand-named. If I win the prize money, I'll buy myself a diamond watch. And exotic fabrics from India. Maybe I'll even go to India.

As my mind travels to faraway destinations, my feet travel down one flight of stairs to a bright and grand hall with wall-to-wall oil paintings and statues. As I approach, the crowd parts to let me through. I hop onto a makeshift podium covered in navy fabric and join the lineup of contestants. The Masterpiecers' anthem plays and quiets the straggling voices.

Once the music stops, Dominic, who's clutching a large glass jar, explains today's test: solving a riddle that will lead us to a specific work of art. "Each contestant will take a piece of paper from this container. Under no circumstance can you show anyone besides Jeb. Jeb will film your riddles, then broadcast them to our faithful viewers. Now, let's start with the girls."

Lincoln goes first, then Maxine, and then me. As soon as I unfold my paper, my gaze flies over the riddle.

"My luminaries were shaped by bees and human blood."

WHAT THE HECK ARE LUMINARIES? *Lights?*

A camera pops up in front of me, pressing down toward the paper like a dog snout. After everyone's picked a riddle, and it's been videotaped, Dominic says, "Ladies and gentlemen, please remember that you are *not* to help our contestants. You may follow them on their hunt, but do not offer clues or answer questions, or they will be eliminated. Understood?"

A loud *yes* resounds.

Dominic grins. "The works you are looking for are on this floor and this floor only."

I'm about to pounce off the stage when Lincoln asks, "Do all our riddles lead to different ones?"

"Of course," Dominic says.

"Can we jot down thoughts?" Nathan asks.

"No pen, no paper. Use your minds," Dominic tells him, tapping his temple. "Ready?"

"Yes," I say along with the others.

"Let day number two begin," he exclaims

Lincoln leaps off the stage first and barges through the dense crowd of cocktail-attired people gathered in the long hallway, clearing a path for the rest of us. After we've all funneled through, the audience seams together and turns to follow. Heels and soles pound the floor. Most spectators keep out of our way, but some get so close, the camera crew has to corral them back. I try to ignore the rubberneckers as I move around the museum, but they're always there, gaping, pointing, and whispering. It's distracting. I remind myself that they are the people who made this competition possible with their money and their connections. Without them, I wouldn't be here. The thought makes their presence more bearable.

A painting captures my attention. It's a seascape of crimson-hued waves thrashing against a large wooden boat with a setting sun in the background. The sun is a luminary, right? And the water is red, like blood. But there are no bees, so I move on.

As I tread through the chain of galleries, I glimpse a lot of suns and stars and moons, several lampposts and light bulbs, a hefty dose of oozing blood, but not a single painting containing bees. After an hour, I collapse on a banquette. Somewhere along the way, I managed to lose the camera crew and the audience.

"My luminaries were shaped by bees and human blood," I whisper, hoping that saying it out loud will help me make sense of it. It doesn't. Checking that no one is around, I keep talking to myself, because too many ideas are playing leapfrog in my brain. "Okay. So…the light source was made by bees and blood. Maybe I'm not looking for bees and blood in the art. Maybe just light sources."

I sound silly…I sound like Mom. Always talking out loud to herself. I bat my lashes to dispel the sudden moisture caking my eyes and find myself staring right into a camera. *Shoot.* I strap on a confident mask that quickly decomposes when a rush of excitement booms out of an adjoining gallery making the camera crew race out.

I lean my head back and close my eyes. Slowly, I tap my skull against the wooden headrest, hoping I can knock the answer into my brain.

Can bees produce light?

Can honey produce light?

Or pollen? Pollen is yellow? Could pollen be considered light?

What makes some bugs light up?

"Think synonyms," I hear someone tell me.

I snap my lids up to find Brook sitting next to me.

"Trying to get me eliminated?" I ask, my heart bumping around my ribcage. The gallery is empty save for the two of us.

"No," he says quietly. "Synonyms are the foundation of a riddle. It's a fact, not a clue."

After a minute of silence, curiosity gets the better of me. "Who solved theirs?"

"Believe it or not…Daisy."

"Daisy?"

"I mean Maxine."

"No, I know who Daisy is. I'm just surprised—I thought it would be your brother."

Brook's eyes darken. "He's still searching."

"He'll get it soon enough."

"He *is* pretty obstinate," Brook continues.

"I can tell."

"This is his chance to get what he wants."

I smirk. "If he wins, will he be allowed to attend the Masterpiecers or does he just get the hundred grand?"

"He'll be allowed to attend."

"Won't that destroy the school's policy?"

"It will complicate it," he says as I stare at the Jackson Pollock in front of me. The paint splatters remind me of the last quilt I sewed. I used splatters of silk and velvet instead of paint. "Is your sister also artistic?"

"No. Not in the least."

He's looking at the Pollock too. "You don't talk about her."

"I came to compete in an art show, not to discuss my family."

"Fair enough."

"Now can you please leave so I can concentrate?"

"I'll be quiet."

I'm about to tell him that it's his presence I find troublesome, when I hear footsteps. My pulse skyrockets. I leap up and away from Brook before anyone can assume I was cheating.

Chase is standing in the large doorway.

Brook rises slowly and walks over to him. "How are you holding up?"

"I thought the contestants weren't supposed to speak with judges or people from the audience," Chase says curtly. The vein on his temple lobe throbs.

"I can ask how you're doing."

"Is that what you were asking Ivy? How she was *doing*?" His accusatory tone makes me livid.

"Yes." Brook pushes a shiny lock of black hair off his forehead. "I wasn't giving her any clues, if that's what you're worried about."

No one speaks and no one moves. The large gallery suddenly feels oppressive. I pretend to examine a painting when I hear loud applause.

"Another winner. You two better hurry up," Brook says, brushing past his brother.

I walk off in the opposite direction. There's no way I'm spending any more time cooped up in a room with Chase. Plus my painting's not here. There are no light sources in any of the pieces hanging on the wall. As I cross the entire south wing, I start the unscrambling process anew.

Bees can't produce light.

Blood can't either.

What's synonymous with bees? Besides bugs and honey.

Pollen…honeycombs…buzz. I keep buzz in mind. *Filaments buzz.*

Or maybe it's a painting that was buzzed about.

Maybe it's a painting that was killed for!

My pulse quickens because I think I'm onto something. I commit this thought to memory then move on to the verb.

What's tantamount to shaped?

Formed. I try it out in the riddle.

My luminaries were formed by bees and blood.

Ugh! It doesn't make more sense. I think up more synonyms. My brain halts on the verb *molded.*

My luminaries were molded by bees and blood.

My nose wrinkles at the idea of a painting fashioned with blood. A few years back, a painting *was* made with excrement, so maybe there's one made with blood and dead bees. I check the label affixed to the wall in front of me. It's a Dubuffet created with plaster, oil, tar, and sand. Tar…weird. I didn't know artists used tar. The next painting is a combination of acrylic and wax. I get this niggling in my skull and read it again. *Wax*. Bees make wax.

I check the work associated with the plaque, but can't find anything resembling a light source. It's a painting representing waves or squiggly lines. Not my painting.

A shift in the air alerts me to a presence. It's Nathan. His forehead glistens with sweat. Either he's been running or he's nervous. From the way he fidgets with his belt buckle, I decide it's the latter. Another round of applause erupts somewhere in the museum. I tick off my fingers. Three. I think of what Lincoln said, about us chasing the same painting and start wandering off toward the din. Just in case. When I get to the gallery, I find J.J. beaming in front of a Persian rug. *Yeah…*I don't think our riddles are linked.

"Ivy? Did you solve yours?" Dominic asks. He's standing right next to the graffiti artist.

Josephine and Brook watch me, and so does the audience. One of the cameras is poised on my face.

I put on a smile. "Almost."

Willing my knees not to shake, I walk out of the gallery and look at all of the paintings made with beeswax. I now understand the sneakers. The museum is a maze. I begin jogging, grazing the walls so that I can read the insignias without stopping. When I spot the word wax again, I stop to examine the subject matter: a self-portrait with no source of light. But still, I don't move. I study it and something clicks. It's textured, like the Dubuffet! *Of course.* That's what wax does. It makes my quest easier now, as I only stop in front of paintings that have relief.

A loud clamor resonates. *Four.* There are two spots left. I pick up the pace. There's a painting that takes up an entire wall. It's huge. And has tons of texture and color. I desperately try to locate something akin to luminaries or blood. But unless blood is neon pink and luminaries are dandelions, it's not it. My stomach lets out an angry growl that mirrors how my mind is feeling.

As I rip through yet another gallery, I hear a new commotion. *Five!* How is everyone done and not me? Their riddles must have been easier than mine! One spot to go. One spot. *One.* My rubber soles pound the floor. I cross Nathan's path.

His eyes are as bright as his cheeks. He's running with a purpose. That's when I begin to lose hope. I'm tempted to trip him, but that's not going to help me.

I watch him disappear into the adjacent room, his footsteps ringing like a ticking time bomb. I suck in a breath and focus on the artwork around me to snuff out the ticking. Nothing resembles a freaking light source. There's a painting with a bunch of geometric shapes, there's another that looks like some blown-up Japanese calligraphy, there's a white flag, there's a—

I twist back toward the flag. It's white, but textured. And there are stars on it. Stars are light sources, right? I dash to the plaque, heart crashing against my ribcage. *Encaustic oil, newsprint, and charcoal.* Many had to die to unite America. I have my blood and my luminaries…

"What the hell is encaustic?" I say out loud.

"Wax."

The only other person around is Chase, and he's staring at another painting. Did I imagine his voice?

"Wax?" I repeat.

He doesn't answer. He doesn't even look at me. Maybe it was some ruse to make me fail. Chase would never help me. *Would he?* I stare at the flag and think that it fits my riddle.

A noise rises not far away. Nathan's stupid sweaty face pops into my mind and I sprint toward the clamor.

It has to be the flag.

"I got it!" I yell the second I enter the gallery.

I notice pity staining the onlookers' faces. And then I notice Nathan standing beside Dominic, beaming like a stop sign.

He got it before me.

ELEVEN

Every inch of skin on my body burns as though it were being doused in acid.

"Nathan. Your answer?" Dominic asks.

The camera moves off Ivy's face onto Nathan's. I don't care about his face. I care about Ivy's. Only Ivy.

"Looks like someone doesn't win after all," the long-necked guard says. Ever since I promised her the money, she's been bursting into the dayroom to catch segments of the show.

"It's not over," I tell her. It can't be. Ivy's the best.

The camera slides back to her. She's bleached all emotion from her face, but I know she's unwell. I can feel it through our twin connection.

"*The Love Letter* by Jean Honoré Fragonard," Nathan says, his face as shiny as a glazed donut.

Dominic shakes his head as though he has a fly buzzing around it. "No, Nathan. That's not it."

It takes a few seconds for the smile to tumble off Nathan's lips, as though each cell of skin is repositioning itself.

"I'm sorry." Dominic pats him on the back. "Ivy? What do you have for us?"

She doesn't move. I spring to the edge of the couch. "Come on, Ivy," I whisper.

Giraffe-neck smirks.

"What's the answer to your riddle, sweetheart?" Dominic asks.

She moves forward, carving a path toward the master of ceremony. Once next to him, she says, "*White Flag* by Jasper Johns." Her voice is steady.

Dominic hisses, hiking up his lips and baring his teeth like a hyena.

My hope shatters like the ornament Mom threw at my head during our last Christmas together.

"Is that your final answer?" he asks.

Her gaze coasts over the crowd, over me, but the rest of her face remains impassive. "Yes."

Dominic begins to clap, and then everyone claps, and I realize her answer was correct and Dominic was just being an asshole. My emotions are all over the place, like the shimmery painted glass fragments that embedded themselves in my skin. Nathan swipes his eyes. He's crying. I want to care, but I don't.

The TV switches off.

"What did you do that for?" I exclaim, twisting toward the guard. "It's not done!"

"For today, it is. Recreation time."

"I don't want to go to the yard."

The guard smirks. "And I don't want to babysit you, but I do it anyway."

"I'm paying you."

"I let you skip lunch already. Now get your ass to the yard before I do away with your little privilege."

I grind my teeth together and get up. The enclosed prison ground is full of people. Some are just hanging in groups on the grassy part; others are doing pull-ups on metal bars like caged monkeys. Half of them are crazy. I wonder if they arrived like this or if prison turned them into wackos.

The temperature is sweltering. For a second, I tilt my face up to absorb the sun, but then it's too hot. I look for shade, but there is none. Shade would be too much of a luxury. I walk over to a deserted strip of dusty pale sand and drop down. First I sit, but it's awkward just sitting there, being stared at by the entire prison population, so I roll back and close my eyes, and replay today's show.

When I don't feel the sting of the sun, I snap my lids up. Sure enough, Gill and Cheyenne are standing above me.

"The princess finally joins us," Cheyenne says.

"Tired of watching your little game show?" Gill asks.

"It's done."

"*Aww*...did your pwetty little sister lose already?" Cheyenne asks.

My jaw clenches. "No. Can you move? You're blocking the sun." I'd rather get sunburned, charred even, than endure another minute of scrutiny.

"I'm blockin' her sun," Cheyenne repeats, distorting her voice. I don't know if she thinks she sounds like me, but she doesn't. She just sounds like an idiot. "Get any darker and you'll turn black. That's Firehead's type."

Gill shoots her a look, which makes Cheyenne wobble away. I'm hoping Gill will go away too, but she doesn't. Instead, she lies down next to me. I scoot a few inches away. It disrupts the sand that floats up like a dust moat and cakes my face.

"Ever heard of personal space," I mutter.

"Chill. I'm not gonna jump you."

We don't talk for a few minutes, but I can feel she's there, her body vibrating inches away from mine. I roll up. She watches me, but doesn't move.

"You have sand in your hair," she says.

"Whatever. I'll wash it out," I say, patting it to get rid of any excess.

I scan the yard. Women hang out in racial clusters. I realize I wouldn't fit in anywhere. I'm too light for the African American group and too black for the whites. I stare at Gill, suddenly aware she must be breaking some code by hanging with a mixed girl.

I tip my chin toward the group Cheyenne has returned to. "Shouldn't you be with them?"

"Why?"

"You're white."

She snorts. "I don't believe in segregation."

For some reason, her answer makes me hate her a tiny bit less. "Because your ex was black."

She shrugs. "That's part of it."

"What happened?"

Gill turns to her side and props her head up on a bent arm. "*Now* you want to know?"

"Actually, I don't." I rub my hands together and watch as a little puff of dust disperses in the air in front of me, glimmering in the bright sun.

"She hurt me, so I hurt her," Gill says.

I stop rubbing my hands.

"I found her hooking up with another chick. In our bed. I got mad. I threw the girl out, and then we had a fight and I left."

I frown. "And then?"

"And then I went to the bar where I worked. It's in a crap neighborhood, so the owner keeps a handgun under the register. I took it and went home. She was sleeping."

"And you shot her?" I exclaim.

"No, I fucked her with the gun." She gives me a wry smile. "Of course I shot her. She hurt me. She broke my heart."

I swallow. It feels as though the dust has coated my mouth and throat. "But now she's gone."

"And she can never hurt me, or anyone else, ever again."

There's something hard and shiny in Gill's eyes, like congealed tears.

"It wasn't the first time she'd two-timed me, you know. She did it with a guy too. Said she was making sure she liked women best. I believed her." She's biting her bottom lip with her buckteeth. "You know what they say: 'Fool me once, shame on me. Fool me twice, shame on you.'"

"Isn't it the other way around?"

She narrows her eyes. "No. It's just like I said it."

I drop it because arguing a quote is pointless.

"Now you know my story. Out with yours."

Although I don't want to talk about it again, I know she won't let it go, so I tell her what I told everyone else.

I don't tell her the real story.

TWELVE

Ivy

After bidding farewell to Nathan, who left shortly after the evening announcement, we are sent back to our wing for dinner. I want to skip the meal, but I don't think I could sleep yet. I'm way too wired—probably because I tasted the sour tang of elimination today.

I take my seat at the table that is now set for six. There's music tonight; it's soft and throaty and fills the room. An animation is playing in the middle of the white glass top: a video of a graffiti artist creating deceptive murals full of *trompe-l'oeil*. As I watch him, my fingers itch with the fire to create. They long for my spools of thread and my collection of rainbow-hued fabrics. I rub my thumb and index finger together, feeling the slightly hardened skin, and ideas for new panoramas spring to mind.

"So that was fun," Lincoln says, her hazel eyes gleaming.

Herrick pulls up the lapel of his purple velvet dinner jacket. "Yes. And easy."

A waiter deposits a fancy salad in front of me. Just a few leaves stick out from underneath a pile of cubed white cheese, diced beets, and halved cherry tomatoes.

I sense Chase's eyes on me. After feeling them for eight hours, I could feel them anywhere—probably even in a congested subway station. I look up from my plate and glare back.

"Hey, Maxine, how'd you guess so quick?" J.J. asks, chewing with his mouth open. The salad dressing tinged pink from the beets is frothing around his neon white teeth. It's disgusting, yet fascinating—and a good distraction from Chase.

"I used to write riddles for candy companies. You know, the ones they print on the inside of the wrappers."

"How'd you get into that?" he asks.

"An ex-boyfriend. He worked in marketing and got me the job," she says, toying with the thin gold hoops hooked into her earlobes that reach her chin.

"That's cool."

"Yeah. But there's not much use for it in the real world."

"Except for today," J.J. says. He's taken another bite, and again, his mouth is wide open.

"Can you keep your mouth shut while you chew, J.J.?" Herrick asks.

J.J. wipes his mouth with his wrist. "Should I be worried that you're staring at my lips?"

"Don't flatter yourself," Herrick says.

"And here I was afraid the zipper of my tent would shoot up in the middle of the night and other zippers would shoot down."

"I wouldn't say those things if I were you, J.J.," Chase says. "You heard why contestant number eight got disqualified?"

"Ivy got disqualified?"

"Obviously not, surfer boy," Lincoln says.

"The one whose spot Ivy…took," Chase says.

"Pictures got him disqualified, not me," I counter, my voice as sharp as the pointy blade of my seamripper.

"What pictures?" J.J. asks.

Lincoln pushes a curled lock of blonde hair behind her ear. "God, what planet are you from?"

"I don't follow the news."

"Really?" Maxine says.

"If something's important, I'll hear about it."

"It's pretty ironic, though, isn't it?" Chase says, unfolding his arms.

"That I don't read the news?" J.J. asks, sponging the crumbled cheese with a piece of bread.

"No, dickhead." Lincoln rolls her eyes.

"That a white supremacist was replaced by Ivy," Chase says.

I lock eyes with him. "Why?" I ask, daring him to voice his thoughts.

He doesn't, and silence settles over the room.

After a long minute of heated glaring, I lean back. "I didn't rig the competition. I was chosen. Based on my application. On my skill. But perhaps you did, Chase. After all, your brother's a judge. How difficult could it have been for him to get Josephine and Dominic to endorse your application?"

"You don't know the first thing about me and my brother," he says, his voice low and rough.

"I know he got into the school, and you didn't."

"Because he was older. He applied first."

I lean forward, the silver sequins of my shorts digging into my bare thighs. "Is that the reason, or is he just better than you?"

Chase's eyes grow dimmer, like pieces of sky filling with rainclouds. "Is that what Brook was telling you during the riddle hunt? That he's better than me?"

"Brook?" Lincoln pipes in. "You spoke to him during the test?"

Chase nods. I'm tempted to kill him for bringing it up. I'm sure I would feel no remorse.

"Cheating, Redd?" Lincoln asks.

"Of course not!"

"Then why were you talking with my brother?" Chase asks.

And why did you give me the definition of encaustic? "We were talking about *you*," I spit out.

His thick eyebrows arch up.

"*Ooh*...this is getting interesting," Herrick says, tapping his shiny black nails on the tabletop.

"Brook was telling me how badly you wanted to get into his school. Basically, he pleaded with me to let you win," I say, stretching the truth, hoping Chase is too proud to check. "How's that for fraternal love?" I scan the faces of my enemies. "Wouldn't be surprised if he came to all of you at some point to ask you to go easy on Chase."

A hush falls over the table. Chase's complexion has gone paler. For a second, I think he's going to leave, but he doesn't. I don't know if it's because he's hungry for the second course that's just been brought out, or because he's trying to prove a point.

I spear a broccoli floret and place it on my tongue. Still looking at him, I chew. No one speaks. The clatter of forks and knives and the low music break the otherwise stifling silence. It's only after the plates are cleared that someone speaks.

"I wonder what they'll have us do tomorrow." Lincoln is plaiting her side pony, but doesn't tie the ends, so when she releases them, her hair unravels and ricochets the subdued light from the sconces mounted on the canvas walls.

"Maybe they'll have us make something! That would be so dope," J.J. says.

"Not for me and Chase," Maxine says, ever the considerate one. "Unless you know how to paint or something," she adds, her cheeks flushing.

"No," he says. "But I'm sure they'd find something else for us to do. Maybe auction off what you make."

"Ever sold anything, Chase?" Herrick asks.

He nods.

J.J.'s laminated shirt gives his black eyes a feral gleam. "What?"

"A thirty seven million dollar painting."

Intrigued, I sit up, my scratchy silver sequin shorts scraping my bare thighs again.

"Thirty seven million?" Lincoln chokes out. Either a piece of the fancy multigrain and olive cracker she's eating or the price tag went down the wrong way.

Herrick places his elbows on the table and knots his fingers underneath his chin. "What was it?"

Chase is leaning back with his arms crossed. "That's classified."

"Oh, come on, dude, you can tell us," J.J. says.

Chase shakes his head. "You can't reveal that sort of information, or you lose your clients. Confidentiality's a primal rule of art dealing."

"Good thing I don't want to deal then," J.J. says.

"How much did you make out of that sale?" I find myself asking.

He raises his eyes to mine, his incredibly dense lashes sweeping up arrogantly. "My commission was ten percent."

"Are you fucking kidding me, dude? Three and a half mill!" J.J.'s interested again. "Maybe I *should* deal."

"I'm a firm believer that if you do anything for the money, you won't do it well," Chase says.

I grunt. "That's easy for you to say when you have the money."

His dark gaze brushes mine.

"Was it a piece your family owned?" Maxine asks.

"No. Only Brook's allowed to dig into the family vault. My dad's not even licensed to sell anymore. Masterpiecers' rules. It was a piece from Christie's. I worked there one summer."

Dessert arrives. Vanilla soufflé. "I could really get used to this place," Maxine says, picking up her fork and piercing the crisp top. It deflates slowly, the edges folding into the gooey center.

"I propose a little toast." Herrick raises his glass of wine. Maxine and J.J. follow suit while Lincoln, Chase, and I lift our glasses of sparkling water. "To fun, to knowledge, and to ambition."

Everyone's about to drink when Lincoln blurts out, "Better look into someone's eyes, Ivy, or you're going to have seven years of bad sex."

Even though I'm not superstitious, I stare into the only set of eyes looking back: Chase's.

"I need more wine," Herrick calls out, but no one comes. He spots the decanter on the buffet behind us and grabs it.

"I think I'm going to call it a night." Lincoln pushes back from the table. "Sweet dreams."

After she leaves, J.J. asks, "Anyone want her dessert?"

It's still golden and puffed.

"I'm stuffed," Maxine says.

Even though I'm not usually one to turn down food, I don't think my stomach can stretch anymore, so I shake my head.

Herrick nurses his glass of wine. "It's all yours."

As J.J. seizes Lincoln's soufflé, Maxine nudges me. "We're being filmed," she whispers. She budges her eyeballs to the left, toward a camera with a glowing red dot that's hooked into the corner of the tented ceiling.

"Duh," Herrick says. "They mentioned it in one of the files they sent us. We had to sign off on it. Didn't you read it?"

"I hate fine print," Maxine says.

Herrick shrugs. "We're on a reality TV show. It's standard."

"Does it record our conversations or just our images?" Maxine asks.

"Just our images," Herrick says, downing the last of his wine. He smiles and waves at the camera.

After a beat, I ask, "Are there cameras in our rooms?"

Herrick smirks. "You got something to hide, Ivy?"

"My body, for one."

"Suddenly modest, Redd?" Herrick asks.

I suck in an air-conditioned-loaded breath that makes my lungs flame like rayon on fire. "What's that supposed to mean?"

"My stylist told me you were quite comfortable with nudity," he says.

"And how would your stylist know that?" I ask.

"She heard it from the girl who does your hair."

"I'd be comfortable too if I had a body like hers," Maxine says, squeezing my forearm.

I snap my arm out of her grasp. Before she can fumble for an apology—because Maxine strikes me as a person who apologizes for everything—I repeat my unanswered question. "Are there cameras in our rooms?"

"No. That would be an invasion of privacy," Chase says.

Good. Then no one caught me freaking out over what I've hidden in my bag.

THIRTEEN

"Why is everyone watching me?" I ask Gill over breakfast the following morning.

Gill turns to take in the entire room. "Because you're still the new girl."

"How long do you stay the new girl?"

"Until there's a new girl," she says matter-of-factly. "Few weeks would be my guess."

"Thank God I'll be out in a few days then."

She loops one of her brassy dreads around her finger. "Still believe that?"

"Of course I still believe that!" My temper flares, which attracts more attention. I lower my voice. "I didn't do anything wrong."

The tall guard with the potbelly approaches our table. I wrap my feet around the legs of the bench, an old habit left over from school.

"Inmate Redd, the shrink wants to see you again."

Could he speak any louder? "Why?"

"'Cause she has a crush on you." He lets out a yip of laughter that reminds me of the sound of an injured dog. When I don't laugh, he clears his throat. "I didn't ask, but I think it's because something's wrong with you. Would you like me to go find out?" He smiles.

I grumble as I get up.

"I heard your sister was almost eliminated last night." I bet he's trying to rile me up.

"Well, she wasn't."

"I'm betting Chase Jackson's going to win."

"Good for you," I say.

We tread down another hallway in silence. The walk seems endless this morning.

"You really believe your sister has a chance?"

"Of course!"

"They do call her Lucky Number Eight, don't they?"

"Apparently."

"I heard the guy—you know, the racist dude—I heard he lawyered up and everything."

"Good for him."

"Claims the photos were doctored."

"Of course he does."

"You might get a new roommate soon."

My brain attempts to make the connection between doctored photos and new roommates. When it does, I stop walking.

"Guess who suspect number one is?" He waggles his brows. One of them is slashed by an old scar, which he probably got for being an asshole.

"Ivy didn't do anything," I say, starting back up.

"She's still suspect *numero uno*."

I whirl around on my flip-flops, and my brittle hair—there's no freaking conditioner on this side of hell—flogs my cold cheek. "My sister is good. Real good. She had nothing to do with it."

"I didn't come up with it. I saw it on CNN. If you stopped watching that show of yours and started watching the news, you'd have heard it too."

"Is everything all right out here?" Robyn asks. She's leaning against the shiny, thick crust of eggshell paint coating her doorframe.

"Fine," I say, storming past her into the office. I bet she now thinks I'm irritable on top of being nervous.

I drop down on the couch—the one facing the window—and fold my arms. Anger is ticking through me. I focus on my breathing to relax. It doesn't work, so I press my fingertips against my temples and think of the song Ivy hums to me when I'm out of sorts. That usually quiets me. When it doesn't, I let my hands fall back against my thighs.

"Tell me what's going on, Aster." She's sitting now, legs crossed neatly.

"The guard was making stupid accusations."

"What sort of accusations?" she asks. The beet-colored silk scarf tucked into the collar of her navy blouse makes her look old.

"That my sister got someone kicked off the show to take his place."

"Whose place?"

I frown. Doesn't she know anything? "That contestant who got disqualified because he was racist."

"Tell me more about this contestant."

"He attended a white supremacist meeting with swastikas inked on either side of his face."

"Do white supremacists frighten you?" she asks.

"I'm part black, so yeah."

"Have you ever been threatened because of your skin color?"

"I was insulted."

"What did they say?"

"They called us—"

"Us?"

"Ivy and me."

"I thought it was only you."

"I'm a twin," I say matter-of-factly. *How dense is this woman?* "They called us brownies, half-breeds, bounty bars."

"How did your sister react to the slander?"

"She told me not to listen to it."

"But you did?"

"It was hard not too. They were saying it to my face."

"But not to Ivy's?"

"To hers too, but she didn't care, so after a while, they stopped harassing her and just harassed me."

"So your sister wasn't treated the same way you were?"

"People respected her."

"And they didn't respect you?"

"No."

She nods, jots something down, then flips to another page in my file. "I asked to see you today because I'd like to talk about your mother."

"My mother?"

"We didn't talk about her yet."

"I hate her. She hates me. End of story."

Robyn's pen scratches the paper on her lap.

"What are you writing? That I'm delusional about my feelings for my mother? That she's really a caring person, but I'm not worth caring for?"

She looks up. "Is that how you feel? That you're not worth caring for?"

I don't want to answer this woman who keeps asking irritating questions and extrapolating.

"Aster, did you feel you weren't worth caring for?" she repeats.

"My sister loves me. Josh too."

"Josh?"

"My boyfriend."

"And your mother?"

"My mother's screwed up in the head! I don't give a crap what she thinks of me!" My nostrils flare. I can feel them expand. I stare down the bridge of my nose expecting to see smoke curling out.

"What do you mean, *screwed up in the head*?"

I wrench my gaze back up. "Isn't that in my file?"

"It is, but I don't care what's in your file. I want to know what's in your mind."

"You don't care what's in my file?"

"That's what I said. Now tell me…why do you think your mother hated you?"

"She threw stuff at me all the time. She slapped me. She even locked me in the hallway closet once…all day, and then when I peed myself because I couldn't hold it in any longer, she called me horrible things."

"Did she ever insult or hurt Ivy?"

"No. Ivy was her little princess. She taught her how to sew. Never taught me. Never even let me come into the room where she worked. But Ivy could. She could go anywhere, touch anything." I shove my parched locks behind my ears, but they don't hold and spring right back like metal coils. "I was the odd one out. She told me once she wished I were dead. She hated me. Told me I had screws loose. She was the one with the fucking loose screws. She didn't even know it. I had to schedule an intervention to have her committed. Ivy was pissed, but she didn't see how bad Mom had become. She didn't understand what stage four schizophrenia meant."

I wring my hands together, remembering that June morning perfectly. It was hot—stiflingly hot—and it wasn't even eight o'clock. Ivy had just come in from a run and was chugging orange juice from a carton in the fridge when our doorbell rang. She got to the door first. The shocked look on her face when she swung it open and found Mom's shrink flanked by a police officer brandishing a court order will forever stay ingrained in my memory. Ivy hated me then. She hated that I'd gone to see a judge behind her back. She hated that I'd shown a doctor the bruises Mom inflicted on me. She didn't understand how scared I'd become that, one day, one of those bruises would end my life.

Mom spared my sister because she held so much promise. Ivy was going to save our family, that's what Mom always said. Not me. I was going to be its downfall.

"It took my sister a long time to forgive me," I tell Robyn. "Sometimes, I think she hasn't completely forgiven me."

"Have you asked her?"

"She said it was in Mom's best interest…that I did the right thing."

"So what makes you think she hasn't forgiven you?"

"I don't know. Little things. Like she goes to visit her behind my back. She took up sewing like her. She left me here." My cheeks are dry, yet I feel like they should be wet, because my heart's been cracked open like a walnut.

The therapist scoots to the edge of her chair. The file flops open on her lap, but the pages are blank. She'll probably fill them out the second I leave. "Aster, you told me that *you* encouraged your sister to go to New York."

I suck in a sharp breath. It feels like a knife sliding down my throat. "You know I take care of her?"

Robyn frowns at the change of subject, but scoots back in her armchair. "No. I don't know."

"Yeah."

"How do you take care of her?"

"She doesn't know how to cook, so I cook for her."

"How else do you provide?"

"She's an artist, so I work two jobs."

"Is that how you paid your mother's institution bills?"

"No. The government covers those."

Her forehead creases, which makes her eyebrows arch up like furry rainbows. "The government only allocated a small amount of money to your mother."

I frown. "Then who's paying for it?"

"Do you have any other family?"

"No."

"Then my guess is that your sister took care of the bills."

"My sister? But she's never made a dime!"

"Are you sure about that?"

Am I sure? "Of course!" But I'm not. How was Ivy making money? Was she selling her quilts? Wouldn't she have told me if she were? *Oh, God, no…* My sister couldn't have been involved with Troy Mann, could she?

"Aster? Are you all right?"

"I'd like to talk to Officer Joshua Cooper," I say.

"What would you like to talk to him about?"

"Something. Can you get in contact with him?"

"I can ask the warden if he can arrange something." After a few quiet minutes, she stands. "I would like to schedule another session tomorrow. Same time?"

"Will you contact Officer Cooper?"

"Yes."

"Then okay. I'll be here tomorrow." I stand to leave. "We're done, right?"

She nods, so I start toward the frosted glass door. As I pull it open, I hear her call out, "We made good progress today."

I agree. Finding out my sister was making money behind my back is progress.

FOURTEEN

Ivy

I feel like a zombie this morning. I'm so tired that I nearly stride right into a wall of glass. Thankfully, Maxine warns me right before I face-plant. Three glass cubes have been erected in the makeup wing, similar to the ones they'd used for the performance art test. Inside each, they've set up a long glass desk and three chairs. I suspect it's for today's challenge.

As we're primped and dressed, my attention wanders to the other contestants and lingers on Chase. Even though the tents are fabric and fabric absorbs noise, I heard him move around his room last night. I even saw light flicker on and off. His makeup artist is applying concealer to his face, which leads me to believe the shadows underneath his eyes rival mine. What could keep Chase Jackson awake? I doubt it's stress. Even if he loses, it won't change much to his gilded life. I bet his parents would still be proud of him. *His parents.* Are they in the audience? Chase's gaze lands on mine, so I snap my attention to my reflection in the mirror.

Amy's humming to herself as she teases my hair and pins it into an elaborate half-up, half-down 'do. And Leila's her usual bright self—not. She snaps my chin up and pokes a black pencil into my lower lash line. I bite my lip and blink. I'd ask her to be more gentle were I not terrified she'd be even less so. Her kohl-smeared gaze shifts from one side of my face to the other to inspect her handiwork. When she puckers her lips, I brace myself for more pain.

Ten minutes later, I'm released from my torture chair and stuffed into a sleeveless, knee-length dress with a beaded collar. The high-heeled sandals I have to wear will give me blisters. The only positive aspect of the strappy heels is that they probably signify I won't be racing around the museum like some headless chicken.

Dominic checks in on us like he does each morning before we have breakfast. But this morning, it isn't to make sure we're ready. "Ivy, a word." He gestures to a glass cube.

The others all glance our way, but leave for breakfast. Dominic shuts the door behind us.

"Our school was built on an honor code, which every student swears allegiance to the day they enroll. *Inter se credimus*. Do you know what it means?"

I feel heart palpitations in my jaw. Did Chase tell him he gave me a hint yesterday? "I'm guessing something about giving credit," I say, although I know that's not it.

I try to block out the curious gazes of the crew members filming us while Dominic jiggles his head left to right.

"Not exactly. It means, *In each other we trust*. Now, I hate myself for having to ask this..." He's dropped his voice although I doubt anyone can hear us. "I wouldn't even bring this up, but it's all over the news." Despite the layer of foundation on his cheeks, Dominic's face looks like a crumpled sepia photograph.

My entire body pulses. Even my eyes have trouble focusing. I see everything double. "What's on the news?"

"That you might've had a hand in eliminating the former eighth contestant."

All at once, relief and astonishment catapult through me. The two emotions are so different that they make my body go still and throb more fiercely. "I had nothing to do with his elimination."

"You don't know how relieved I am to hear you say that. I'll have you know, I didn't believe it for a second." He lays a hand on my shoulder and squeezes it, then rubs it a little, then squeezes it again. "I'll prepare the press release and we'll go over it before you face the"—he suddenly looks around and releases my shoulder—"cameras. Okay?"

"Okay."

"And with Brook. Yesterday. During the test. Someone told us they saw you talking."

Someone. I grunt. I bet that someone is Chase. For a flimsy second, I'm tempted to tell him about the latter's unwelcomed clue, to have *him* disqualified—but then I come to my senses. I would be too. I seal my lips shut and add that information to the long list of secrets I have bottled up. If only I could just get rid of them all, throw them into some mental well and watch them sink.

"We were discussing the school," I say.

A smile appears on Dominic's face and then vanishes and then returns, like a flickering light bulb. "So not your riddle?"

"No. Not my riddle."

He exhales such a deep breath that his skin regains some of its firmness. "Good. That's what he said too. Good."

And then I'm allowed to go to breakfast, but the knot in my stomach is so tight that everything I swallow tastes like chalk. After wolfing down two croissants, I perch myself on one of the armchairs and sip scorching coffee. I don't partake in any conversations. I don't answer questions about what Dominic wanted. The only person not enquiring about my clandestine meeting—unsurprisingly—is Chase. *Bastard.*

Someone from the camera crew bursts in to inform us that it's show time. Accompanied by our assistants, we return to the Temple Room. The anthem is already playing as we file onto the platform between the two Egyptian relics. Instead of tables, they've set up rows of tourmaline-colored velvet chairs. The audience is already seated, gold paddles dangling from their clapping hands.

Josephine and Brook are standing side by side on the far right. His face is pulled tight, a bit like Josephine's. I can tell he went through the interrogation. He'll probably keep his distance from me now. All the better. I'm done fraternizing.

"Day number three!" Dominic exclaims. "Already. Can you believe it? Could someone please stop time? Anyway. Back to day number three and test number three, which will be…" *Drumroll.* "An auction! Yes, Lincoln, you were right," he says, whipping around toward us.

When? She must have mentioned it while she was being made up into some slutty librarian. The top knot on her head, her heavy eye and lip makeup, and her tweedy shift are not flattering.

"It's a natural part of the art business," she says, smiling.

"It is," Dominic says. "Now for the rules. Each one of you will have to auction off a lot. They're all worth the same, so the person with the lowest sales total loses. Now, before you go up in front of our generous crowd"—he whirls around —"you are feeling generous, right?"

The audience laughs.

Dominic grins as he turns back to us. "You will be given information on the paintings and sculptures you are selling. You'll have to present that information in a way that makes the piece attractive, and I'm not talking about fabricating stories. I'm talking about crafting factual poetry. *Ooh…*I should coin that phrase."

Clapping rises from the pit of onlookers.

When it dies down, he continues. "The bids will increase by the thousand until they've reached half the value of the object, then by five-thousand. Who knew art required math skills?" Dominic chuckles, along with a chunk of the audience. "When Brook comes around with the glass jar, you'll fish out one paper. On it, you'll find a number that determines your turn. The first contestant will not have less time to study the lots. Everyone gets the same thirty minutes."

Herrick's lips are arched high from the excitement of today's test. I don't feel excited about it.

Brook keeps his eyes trained on the jar as he waits for us to pick a paper. I'm the last one to go so there's only one paper left. I unfold it after he walks away with the empty jar. It reads *3*. At least I'm not first. I'll get to observe the others.

"Okay. Let's rearrange you by number," Dominic says.

We weave in and out of line. The order is Herrick, Maxine, me, Chase, J.J., and Lincoln. When Chase comes to stand next to me, I angle my body away from his. I don't care if it's subtle or not. Unfortunately, I can still smell him. I breathe through my mouth until Dominic dismisses us. We return to our living area to wait for the judges. They've cleared breakfast, but there's still a basket of fruit, a jug of coffee and one of hot water. I make myself tea and go sit next to Maxine who's bouncing her folded legs.

"Nervous?" J.J. asks her.

"I was a girl scout. And for three years, I never sold a single box of cookies, so yeah."

"Not even to your parents?"

"They were gluten-intolerant."

"*Ah*...the rich people's disease," Lincoln remarks.

Maxine's legs stop joggling.

"Just sayin'. No one in the shelters I grew up in ever complained of any intolerances."

For a second, Maxine doesn't answer and I wonder if she's offended, but then she says, "You're right."

Lincoln tips her head, seemingly astounded that Maxine has agreed with her. I'm intrigued in spite of my desire to stay out of these people's lives.

"You're loaded?" J.J. asks. He's leaning forward, chomping on an apple, his mouth wide open, his teeth paler than the fruit's flesh.

Chase and Herrick, who are sitting next to each other, stop discussing art to listen in.

Her cheeks get rosy. "Dad manages a fund. Mom's a homemaker even though she's never home, nor is she ever making anything." Her fingers are curled together in her lap. She seems so uncomfortable speaking about herself, yet she rambles on. "I have a brother. He's in college. We're not very close. Do you have any siblings, Lincoln?"

"Probably. Who knows?"

I toy with the bedazzled collar of my sleeveless dress as I think of my sibling. I wonder if she's following the show.

"I don't even know who my dad is, but I can bet you anything that if I win this competition, he'll seek me out pretty quick." Lincoln's face doesn't betray the bitterness of such a remark. If anything, she looks nonplussed at the prospect. "I bet I'll have tons of dads by the end of the show."

"Okay, kids." Dominic storms into the room with Josephine, Brook, and what seems like the entire film crew. "Are you ready?"

We all nod. Not that it would change anything if we weren't.

"Chase and Lincoln, you're with me. Ivy and Daisy, with Josephine. J.J. and Herrick, follow Brook." When none of us move, Dominic adds, with a smile, "Chop chop."

I get up slowly and trail after Maxine and Josephine. She leads us to the makeup room and into one of the glass cubes.

"Your *dossiers*," she says, pointing to two thick files that have been deposited on the table. She slides gracefully into one of the transparent chairs. "Sit, girls."

As Maxine lowers herself into the chair, one of her heels slips and she ends up falling hard on her butt. There's a rip in the fabric of her dress. Her face floods with color as she clumsily latches on to the edge of the table and hoists herself back up. Josephine's eyes glow, but her face remains impassive. Considering we're in a glass box, the cameras catch her fall. Everyone catches it. Including Brook whose face goes dimply, as though Maxine's wardrobe malfunction has cracked the tension in his body.

Poor Maxine covers her cheeks with her palms, but then she remembers the tear and moves them to the gaping seam.

"I'll get started with Ivy while you change," Josephine says. Her blonde-white hair is stiff with gel and slicked back as though she's just stepped out of a swimming pool.

I flip open the beige folder and balk at the first printout. Then I gulp and look up at Josephine.

It can't be…

"An *artiste* must sell themselves," she says.

I'm too rattled to say anything. I just blink.

"We were very taken with your quilt, Ivy. It's very *originale*. However, we only required pictures of your work. So I must wonder"—she leans her flawlessly pale forearms on the glass table—"why did you send it in? Especially after you were selected…" A large oval diamond graces her narrow ring finger.

I swallow. "Um…" I swallow again. "I-uh…"

"Just so we're clear, it won't help you win…if that's the reason."

The blood drains from my face. "That wasn't the reason."

"Good. Anyway, your quilt is school property now. *Tu comprends*?" I must look utterly clueless, because she adds, "You understand?"

"Yes."

"I need you to sign this form to allow the Masterpiecers to sell your work."

"What happens if I don't sign it?"

"It gets locked up in one of the vaults, which will benefit neither you nor me. It's in your best *intérêt* to sell it. Did you see the *prix* we fixed?"

"Twenty thousand." I try not to act surprised that anything I made could be worth so much. "Is the money mine after the auction?"

The corner of her mouth lifts a fraction of an inch before dropping down. "*Non.* School property. Haven't you been listening? But you get *une commission.*"

"Ten percent?"

"Five."

The topstitched seams strain over my taut shoulder blades, slicing into my skin. "For the whole lot?"

Josephine smirks, which looks as unsightly as a crack on porcelain. "*Non.* Just for your piece. We almost gave it to one of the others to sell. You should be thankful."

That's not at all how I feel. I feel confused and shocked, but definitely not thankful. I turn to the next printout before Josephine can spot my agitation.

"Sorry. I tried to be quick," Maxine says, rushing back inside. Her dress is forest-green and stretchy now.

"*C'est bon.* You still have time," Josephine says.

In silence, we study our lots while the judge circles around us like a bird of prey.

The second item I have to sell is a plaster and copper sculpture by one of the school's students. The third are two bowls molded on Marilyn Monroe's breasts, nipple and all. The fourth piece is a fluffy cotton violin encased in a Plexiglas box. The artist, Zara Mach, is a Masterpiecers' graduate. Everyone knows her name.

She's a big deal in the art world now. When I see the price tag for the violin, my lips part with a gasp. Suddenly my quilt feels like some old coverlet fit for a garage sale. Who will want to buy it when they could own a $250,000 Zara Mach?

"Two minutes left, girls," Josephine says. "*Des questions*?"

Maxine raises her hand. As Josephine walks over to her, my gaze flies over all the information on the last printout. It's a charcoal sketch by Paul Gauguin of one of his indigenous Tahitian women valued at $150,000.

"Ivy? Time's up." Josephine extends her palm.

I close the dossier and hand it to her. Once Maxine steps out of the cube, I ask her, "Is there any way I could place a phone call later today?"

"*Non*...unless it's vital. In which case, *oui*, but we'd listen in."

It's vital, but I don't want anyone besides Josh to know that. I rub the nape of my neck that is covered in goose bumps trying to come up with a better idea, but my neck isn't some magical lamp—no genie or genius thought comes out.

"Ivy, are you okay? You look pale," she says.

"I'm...I'm fine," I say, letting my hand collapse against my side.

As I walk out, I pray that Josh is watching the show. I need him to know that the quilt we've been searching for is here.

FIFTEEN

"What did I miss?" Gill asks, dropping down on the couch next to me.

"Nothing," I grumble.

"Uh-oh…" She tips her head to the side. "Does your mood have to do with the show or with the shrink?"

"Both."

"You want to tell me about it?"

"No."

Gill pouts.

"Look, I just spent the past hour talking to a shrink, so I don't want to talk anymore."

The contestants are filing in to the vacant first row of the Temple Room. Ivy sits between the aisle and that girl with the buzz cut. I study my sister, feeling like it's the first time I'm really seeing her.

I feel a hand on my thigh and I start. "Please don't do that."

Gill pulls back and burrows deeper into the couch, lips squashed together.

I focus my attention on the small monitor and pretend that everyone around me has vaporized. On the stage, they've added a golden podium that resembles a metal spider web. It's one of the pieces Maxine will sell, or so the commentator is saying.

While the contestants were studying their lots, the network was showing footage of their life off the podium. The luxury of their tents makes the correctional facility appear particularly drab. We also got to witness Maxine's dress mishap. Had I not been in a mood, it might have made me smile. It definitely tickled Cheyenne whose fat ass was already spread on one of the two couches when I stormed into the dayroom.

While Dominic goes over the rules one last time, Herrick climbs onto the stage and positions himself behind the podium. He looks confident, but appearances don't mean anything. His Elvis hair has been teased into a shiny black wave that looks like it's about to crash off his head. As I wonder how it holds, a few notes resonate, announcing the beginning of the test.

There's a flurry of activity as a scroll is brought out of the larger of the two temples. It's a religious artifact made by Tibetan monks. The bidding starts at ten thousand dollars. It ends at twenty. A flash of disappointment fires across Herrick's face. He undersold it. The scroll is rerolled and another item is brought out: a wooden chair that resembles cardboard.

"Christos Natter began wood-carving at six." Herrick's voice is trembling a little. "He began at six in his family's shed using slabs of wood his father, a carpenter, would discard. He soon entered his creations into fairs and competitions. Which brought him to the attention of Mister Delancey—"

A round of applause drowns out Herrick's voice and the camera sweeps across the room toward a seated man whose skin is shiny ebony. He gives a curt nod, which surprisingly doesn't dislodge the monocle set over his right eye that makes him look like he's snuck off the page of a nineteenth-century British novel. After another round of applause, the camera shoots back to Herrick.

"Th-the lot consists of six chairs," he stammers. The gavel in his hand trembles. "They're all one-of-a-kind pieces. The auction will begin at twenty thousand dollars." He darts a glance at the judges' bench. Brook takes an exaggerated gulp of air, probably to remind Herrick to breathe. Herrick's jaw unclenches. He guzzles in some air and begins again.

The room goes completely quiet.

Herrick's voice explodes out of his microphone. "Twenty. Do I hear twenty? Twenty-one. Twenty-two. Gentlemen's bid at twenty-three."

And up and up he goes, attaining numbers that seem downright preposterous for a bunch of chairs.

"Thirty nine, anyone? Come on, people, have a little—We've got thirty-nine in the back." Herrick's confidence is tangible. "That's more like it. Do I hear fo—forty in the corner!"

The sound of percussion vibrates across the vaulted room. It's a reminder that he's reached half the value.

"Forty-five. Fifty to the lady in the back. Fifty-five..."

One of the neon strips on the ceiling fizzles and sputters out, casting a shadow over our half of the windowless dayroom.

"He's up to eighty-five thousand now," Gill says. "*No*, ninety! Shit..." she whispers, her eyes glowing in the darkness from the reflection of the monitor.

I yank my gaze back to the screen, just in time to hear Herrick say, "Going once, going twice, sold to the lady in the back!" As he slams his gavel, the black wave of suspended hair crashes against his forehead. He rakes it back and grins.

"Who the fuck has ninety thousand dollars to spend on a buncha chairs?" a skinny woman with a hairnet asks. I think she's the cook. Seeing how skinny she is, I bet she doesn't eat her own food.

"They're sculptures," Gill says. "The buyer probably won't even sit on them."

"I bet they'd crack if I sat in them," Cheyenne says.

"Canteen benches barely hold your fat ass up," the cook says.

Cheyenne shifts around on the couch. "You got a bone to pick with my ass, because I got a bunch of bones to pick with your cookin'?"

"You don't look like you got a problem with it."

"Are you insultin' me?" Cheyenne jumps to her feet, surprisingly lithely considering the mass of cellulite she needs to haul up.

The cook springs up too. Cheyenne gets in a punch and the cook's face snaps backward. Something cracks. I pray it's not her neck. It isn't. It's her nose. Blood squirts out. She starts screeching and claws at Cheyenne's face. I look around, wondering when a guard will rush in. When nobody comes, I shoot Gill a look. She's smiling, her crooked teeth overlapping her lower lip. At some point, she moves, but it isn't to break up the fight. She scoots her legs onto the couch so they're not in the way.

The cook's on the floor and Cheyenne's on top of her now.

"She's turning blue. She can't breathe," I yell.

Still no one does anything. I race to the digital box by the door and press on the call button. Seconds later, two guards vault into the room. They each grab one of Cheyenne's flabby arms and hoist her up. The cook's coughing and choking, but her face is returning to its original color.

As they take Cheyenne out of the room, kicking and screaming, the cook yells, "I put you on a diet, bitch!" She's rubbing the red patches on her throat where Cheyenne's fingers had been only seconds earlier. She takes her seat on the couch. "Crazy fat bitch," she mutters. She stares around the room. Her deep-set eyes land on me. "You the one who called security?"

I'm not sure if I should nod or deny it. Will I be considered a rat if I admit to it?

"Yeah. She's the one," Gill says. She pats my hand.

"I owe you then. What you like to eat?"

I want to say tasty food, but obviously I don't.

"What you like? What you miss in here?" she repeats.

"Chocolate. I miss chocolate."

She nods. "Hope you're not too picky on the color."

"No. I'm not picky." My stomach rumbles at the prospect.

"I see what I can get."

Gill's still patting my hand. It's weird now, so I yank it out of her reach. "Thanks."

"The name's Miss Chacha. 'Cause I'm hot like Sriracha."

Hot as in spicy, because she's definitely not pretty. "Thanks, Miss Chacha."

"Just Chacha." Still rubbing her neck, she settles back in the couch and turns her attention to the TV.

The show. *Shit!* Maxine's on stage now. The banner on the bottom of the screen shows she's on her last lot, the spider web podium. Maxine walks around it, mic in hand, puking out detail after detail on the refined metal design and intricate netting and the polishing technique. She took Dominic way too literally on his factual poetry. Finally, she begins the auction.

As the price goes up, I ask, "How did Herrick do?" I'm hoping someone was paying attention.

"He got $405,000 in total. Apparently all the lots are valued at $500,000, so I think that's pretty good." It's a girl leaning against the back wall who answers me. She's so pale she's virtually translucent.

I turn back to the screen just as Maxine pounds her gavel. Her cheeks are all rosy and she's smiling. As she skips off the stage that is being readied for my sister, the commentators launch into a detailed discussion of her performance. "She reached the price on four pieces—the Donaski podium and the gelatin print—but had some trouble with the…"

I let their voices trail off as I read her score: $435,000. Despite my mixed feelings for Ivy, I hope she'll do better than Maxine. I see her walk up on stage. She looks so beautiful in her black satin dress. And her hair is fabulous. I can't help but run my fingers through mine that is clumpy and dry like hay. Instead of chocolate, I should have asked for conditioner, but I'm reminded that I have no one to look nice for here. Might as well eat chocolate to forget.

"She your older sister?" Chacha asks me.

"She's my twin."

"Seriously?"

"Yeah."

"You don't look alike."

I'm tempted to press down on those red spots she's still nursing, but I refrain because I don't want to end up on a "diet."

"Like real *real* twins?" she asks.

"Yeah, Chacha, like real twins," Gill says. She's turned to gaze at me. The intensity in her eyes is really disconcerting. "I see it."

"I don't," Chacha says, squinting to make out my features.

Even though she discusses my resemblance with some other inmates, I zone out. Ivy's on the screen, gavel in hand. She isn't smiling, which makes me anxious. And then I understand why when the first piece she has to auction off is brought up on stage.

SIXTEEN

Ivy

"This piece is very dear to me, because, as some of you might know, it's one of mine. What you don't know, because it's not written anywhere except in here"—I tap two fingers against my heart—"is that I created it for someone I loved right before they passed away."

I pivot toward the quilt that's twice my height and strung up to an invisible clothing line hooked between two wooden beams. It resembles *The Kiss* from Klimt—at least that was my intention when I made it. The patches of gleaming gold, burgundy velvets, emerald silks, and Indian mirror work are shaped into the interlocked bodies of lovers.

"I gave it to her in the morning, and that evening, she was gone. She didn't have long with it—just a few hours, but at least she got to see it, to touch it…" I let my voice trail off and stare into the camera poised on my face, hoping that Josh is on the other side, listening in. "It's listed as 'Untitled' but it does have a name: 'Love.'"

I stroke the fabric and my nail snags on a thread. I peer at the spot more closely and realize there's a tear in the seam. Did it get damaged in the mail?

Dominic clears his throat, so I return to the podium. "I will start the auction at fifteen hundred dollars."

From fifteen hundred to thirty-five, it's a breeze. People are bidding one after the other. Thirty-five hundred to fifty-five takes longer. And then I hit a standstill at seventy-five hundred. I try to drag out the auction a little, but no one bids. "Seventy-five hundred." I wait. Still no one raises a gold paddle. The room is oppressively silent. Even though it's a lot more money than I got for it the first time around, I'm nowhere near the price Josephine fixed. "Seventy-five hundred going once, going twice, sold." I slam the gavel against the podium. I think of the commission I just earned—three hundred and seventy-five dollars—to avoid thinking of how I undersold it.

Before it's carried off the stage, I turn back toward it, toward the gaping seam that sticks out like an ink stain on a blank page. It hits me that, if it had been damaged in transit, the tear would probably not have been along the seam where the binding is sturdiest.

The wooden beams are grabbed and lifted away. As the quilt fades through one of the arches, I still can't make sense of the tear. Dominic clears his throat again. The next piece I must auction off has already been set. I gape at the copper statue. It takes me a second to remember anything about it.

Focus, Ivy. I press the image of my quilt as far away from my mind as possible and begin. Zara Mach's work goes for $260,000. I don't feel much pride at having exceeded the set price. If anything, it brings me further down. By the last lot, my voice has become robotic and I don't even try to enchant the audience. Someone buys the Gauguin for $120,000—a bargain. I undersold it, I undersold the bowls, and I undersold my quilt.

I slam the gavel for the last time, unwrap my fingers from the wooden handle, and slowly descend the stairs. On my way to my seat, I pass Chase who I know will crush this test. His confidence vibrates off of his skin, as dense as his sickening, grassy scent. I don't look at him as he begins, don't observe how comfortable he is behind the podium. Maxine and Herrick keep praising his demeanor, his poise. It drives me insane.

"Five hundred and twenty-five thousand dollars," Herrick whispers loudly. "He got more than what he was supposed to."

"I heard," I hiss.

"What's eating you?" he asks.

"I'm tired. And I have to give a freaking press conference in a few hours. I need to get out of here." I stand up, approach Dominic who's sitting at the end of our row, and tell him that my head is spinning.

The room has gone quiet around me as everyone's desperately trying to listen in.

"Let me signal your assistant," Dominic says. "She can help—"

I shake my head. "It's a short walk. I'll be okay."

"Assistants have to accompany contestants everywhere. Show rules, sweetheart."

People stare as I stride down the aisle. I bet the cameras are getting a lens full of my inelegant escape. Chase is probably snickering, reasoning that his success vexed me. I don't care though. The only thing I care about is finding out how the hell my quilt got on the show. Even though I don't want to be disqualified, returning to Kokomo to unravel this mess would do me a lot of good.

As Cara escorts me back to the third floor, I reminisce on my one and only encounter with Troy Mann the morning he rang my doorbell not long after Aster left for her day job at the ad agency. At first, I hadn't been too keen on letting him in. I'd left the chain on the door as I spoke to him. But then he told me how he'd seen my work on TV, in that feature the Masterpiecers had run on its contestants, and I'd let him in, flattered that he'd even taken an interest in me. Little did I know he was a wanted criminal, embroiled with the mob. Had I known, I wouldn't have let him in. I wouldn't have sold him a single thing. I wouldn't have accepted his roll of hundred dollar bills that was surely tainted and illegal.

Two nights after Troy died, I phoned Josh and asked him to retrieve the quilt before the police could. I didn't want to get in trouble for having sold something to a mobster. Unfortunately, Josh hadn't found it; fortunately, neither had the police. But an anonymous tip came in on their hotline about my sister having a blanket on her lap. *Could it have been my quilt?* If it was, then that would mean she sent it to the show. But why? So that I would get in trouble? So that I would get locked up right alongside her? Could my sister be crazy enough to do such a thing?

I shiver. Yes, she could.

The second I step inside my room, I kick off my heels, drop my clothes on the floor, and turn the shower on. I make it hot and slip in, sidling along the mosaic wall until I'm sitting with my knees tucked underneath my chin.

Time goes by—a lot of time—and I'm still underneath the shower. I'm convinced it's Aster now, and my confusion and shock has turned to anger. Suddenly, the water stops and a towel is thrown on top of me.

"Get out," Leila snaps. "The press conference starts in an hour and you look like a drowned rat."

I glare up at her, but stand. Slowly, still sizzling, I settle on the bench by my bed next to a pair of beige pants and a white silk shirt—probably my press conference outfit. As she works on me, everything becomes blurry outside like everything is blurry inside.

"What's going on with you?" she asks, which is weird because Leila isn't the concerned type.

"Nothing that concerns you," I tell her.

She stops what she's doing and let her hands fall against the black apron in which she stores all of her brushes. She has a ring on each finger. On her middle finger, she has two—a simple band at the base and a more ornate piece on her knuckle.

"If I didn't value my job, I would quit on you," she says, plucking the pins out of my waterlogged hair.

"Thank goodness you're such a dedicated worker then."

"It wouldn't hurt you to be kind, you know," she says.

I let out a dark laugh. She has no idea what she's talking about. Kindness doesn't breed sympathy. I was kind to my sister, and how does she repay me? She set me up.

She played me!

SEVENTEEN

"Inmate Redd, you got a visitor," Giraffe-neck tells me.

"Not now." I'm still trying to get over the shock that the recipient of the quilt was someone on the Masterpiecers. Either Ivy isn't safe or she's involved.

"Let me reschedule." Giraffe-neck's poised next to me like some root vegetable. Her lower body doesn't shift but her lengthy neck curves and tips as she pretends to push on the walkie-talkie strapped to her shoulder.

I sigh and look up. "Who is it?"

"A police officer."

I hop off the couch. It must be Josh. Robyn kept her word.

"Never seen an outlaw so excited to meet up with a police officer," she remarks.

I don't bother explaining my relationship with Josh to Giraffe-neck. It's none of her business.

When we get to the visitation area, I realize it's pouring outside. There are no windows in the dayroom, but here there are three. The light is dull gray and the glass is sprinkled with raindrops. That's probably why they let the entire prison population stay indoors today.

When the door clicks, I go straight toward the table he's sitting at. "I need you to check my sister's bank account," I say, dropping into the chair opposite him.

"Hello to you too, Aster."

Josh's brown hair is matted with rain and his short-sleeved, navy shirt sticks to his skin. Serves him right for not wearing a coat. He says it's because coats are cut too narrow, but I know it's because he loves to put his muscular forearms on display.

"I think Ivy was paying Mom's bills."

"That's swell. Means you don't have to pay them."

"That's not swell! She lied to me, Josh."

"How?"

"She never told me about the money."

"Why are you so worked up about it?"

"Because—" *Ivy might be entangled with the mob.* Even though I've known Josh forever, I can't confess my terrible intuition.

"Aster, I came to talk to you about something really important."

God, if she is, then my present will give her quite a shock.

"How did Ivy's quilt end up on the show?" Josh asks.

I startle. "Ivy's quilt? I have no idea."

"Want to know what I think? I think you have an idea...a very good one. I believe you found it next to Troy's body and sent it there. I believe it's the one you used as a *blanket*."

The blood drains from my face.

He jolts so far forward I can see all the different shades of green around his black pupil. "You're not denying this," he whispers loudly.

I drop my gaze to my nails and the thin white crescents that are reappearing at the tips. "No. It was a blanket."

"Aster," he growls. "You're lying. Just like you lied about the pizza. Troy Mann was a vegetarian. He wouldn't order pepperoni! I have a freakishly detailed file on him. Did he even come to the pizzeria, or did you just follow him from your house?"

"I...he...maybe it wasn't pepperoni. I don't remember."

"Sure." He snorts.

"Okay fine. He didn't stop by the pizzeria. I saw him at our house. I saw him go inside, and then I followed him back to the motel."

"Finally! The truth comes out," he says, slapping the desk. "Why are you always lying to me, Aster?"

I look up. "Always lying?"

"You know what I'm referring to," he says.

"The baby?"

He nods.

"I never lied about the baby," I say.

"Your doctor told me everything."

"My doctor told you what I asked her to tell you. I was trying to protect you."

"Bullshit."

I shake my head. "I didn't make it up. I felt it move. I saw it move. I was throwing up every morning."

Josh's fingers crawl over my shaky forearm like a spider. "It was all in your head."

I swipe them off. "No, it wasn't."

"Aster..."

I can't stop shaking at the memory of the blood pouring out of me the morning I lost the baby. "It was real," I croak.

"Let's not talk about it anymore."

I push my chair back and jerk up. "I need to go."

He sighs. "Don't be like that."

"Be like what?" I say, sniffling.

"Just stay."

"And be interrogated and mocked? No, thank you. I'd rather go hang out with people who don't think I'm crazy."

"I never said you were crazy."

"You didn't have to say it." I keep my gaze leveled on his. "Don't bother coming back here anymore."

"I'm going to come back. I'm in charge of the case."

It would have been too much to hope that he come back for me. Slowly, his face fragments, and I'm left with the one of the dead man. Every night, I see it. Every day, I think of it. The chin-length dark hair muddied with sweat, the crooked nose, the olive skin tinted red with blood. I blink and he's gone, and Josh is back, still looking contrite. He claps his hand around my wrist. I let his touch warm me for a second, and then I don't.

"Before you go, can you tell the warden to inform the guards that I *am* allowed to watch the show whenever I want?"

"The warden would never listen to me."

"He did the first time around."

"What are you talking about? What first time?"

"Ivy told me you got me that privilege."

"The warden? I've never even met the man."

"If *you* didn't talk to him, then who did?"

"Are you sure someone did? Are you sure you didn't convince yourself that—"

I give him such a glacial stare that he shuts up, and then I plant both my palms on the table and lean across it. "I'm not crazy." I don't scream this, but I do make sure each word rings out loud and clear. "Got it?"

His eyes have gone wide. I whirl around and make my way back to the secure door. I expect him to call me back, maybe even apologize, but he doesn't.

"I want to see the commander," I tell the guard.

"Did you request it on your digital box?"

"No."

"No, ma'am."

Seriously? "No, *ma'am*."

"What is the nature of your request?"

"A complaint, *ma'am*."

"Against the police officer?"

"No." After a beat, I remember to add, "Ma'am."

"We can stop by his office, but if he's busy—"

"If he's busy, I'll make an appointment."

She leads me down a new corridor, her long, thick braid swinging across her podgy back. I haven't met the warden yet. I didn't think I would need to, what with my stay in this prison being transitory. I'm not sure what sort of man I'm expecting, but definitely not one who's half my size and watering a plant.

"What may I do for you?" he asks when he spots me in the doorway.

I snap my gaze to another part of the room until I think I've got my gawking under control. Then I look back at him. "It's about my sister, Ivy."

Something flashes across his face, as though the name is familiar to him. Then again, everyone in America is familiar with my sister's name now.

"You may leave," he says.

I think he's dismissing me and I'm about to lose it, because I've reached my breaking point, but then the guard steps out and closes the door.

"Take a seat." He gestures to the free chair in front of his desk.

Stunned, I sit.

"What about your sister?" he asks, setting down his watering can next to a framed picture of a little girl with a big dog posing against a colorful background. I suppose it's his daughter. I check his left hand and, sure enough, find a ring.

"She's on a show, but you must know that."

"I do."

"Ivy told me that Officer Cooper spoke to you about letting me watch it whenever it was on, but he swears he never spoke to you."

"Officer Cooper didn't ask me." His skin tone has lightened. "Your sister did."

"Ivy came to speak to you?"

Gradually, his color returns to normal. It's so gradual that I can actually see it come back in patches across his face. "Yes. She was worried about you."

Something warm replaces the chill I've carried around all day. "Well, the guards aren't letting me watch the show whenever I want."

"This is a department of corrections, not a country club." His tone is kind. "My orders only go so far. There *is* a schedule, and even though the guards can be lenient, they must still enforce it."

I want to tell him about Giraffe-neck's bribe, but ratting out a guard probably won't win me popularity points around here.

"I'm happy Ivy's doing so well," he adds.

"She didn't do well today." I chew on the inside of my cheek.

"She's not disqualified."

My teeth release my cheek. "She's not? She's still in?"

"Yes. That's what the commentators were saying, although Dominic Bacci hasn't made the official announcement."

"Who's out?"

"The graffiti artist, I think."

"J.J.?"

"Yeah, that's the one."

Happiness fills my chest like helium. I believe I'll take flight any second.

"Aster, since you're here, I'd like to discuss your medication," he says.

The balloon pops. "What about my medication?"

"A guard told me you've been refusing to take your pills."

"I don't need them. I haven't taken them in months."

"I was told you did need them."

"By whom?"

"Mental illness doesn't just go away. I had a sister—"

"And I have a crazy mother! I know what crazy is. I'm *not* crazy."

He doesn't speak, which is worse than if he did.
"Did Robyn put you up to this?" I ask.
"Robyn?"
"The shrink."
"No. Miss Pierce and I haven't discussed you yet."
"Yet?"
"You're bound to come up in our weekly debriefs."
"I'll be gone by then."
"Gone? And where will you be going?"
"Home. The DA will set my court date soon, and I'll be able to prove it was self-defense."
He blinks. Three times. "Self-defense?"
I nod as I stare at the picture of his daughter again. Our mother had a picture like that on her sewing table. One child sitting in front of one of her quilts. I wasn't the child. I know because I have a small mole next to my mouth and Ivy doesn't. The girl in her picture didn't have a mole.
"Is she yours, Commander Collins?" I point to the picture.
He does a belly-flop onto his desk to grab the frame. Is he afraid I'm going to blackmail him or something?
Frame still rattling between his fingers, he says, "Yes. She's my daughter."
"Be nice to her. That's the best thing you can do for a child."
He seems to relax when he realizes I mean her no harm, and sets the frame back down, but angles it away from me. I have to admit I'm a little offended that he would jump to that conclusion. As I stand, my gaze is drawn back to the picture. There was something about it…something familiar. I wonder if it's the little girl. Maybe I served her pizza. I have the nagging feeling that's not it.

EIGHTEEN

I'm sitting down with two lawyers, Dominic, and Josephine in one of the glass rooms we used earlier to study our lots. The crew has dismantled the other two rooms. Around us, there are no cameras and no assistants.

"So I've prepared a few words that we'd like you to learn by heart," one of the lawyers tells me. She hands me a printout, which I read over quickly.

After I set it down, they begin explaining that journalists are going to try to rile me up to get a reaction. I am not to lose my calm—like I did earlier, at the auction.

I glare at the male lawyer who's just interjected that bit. "I was feeling faint."

He doesn't respond. He just plays with his lacquered fountain pen, spinning it like a top on the glass table.

The female lawyer breaks the silence. "They're going to bring up your sister—"

"My sister? Why would they bring her up?"

All four exchange a look.

Then Dominic skews up his lips and says, "Because she's in jail. They've been trying to get a statement from you about her since the day you arrived. Anyway, they've dug up everything they could find. But not just about you. About all the contestants," he adds as though it will make me feel better. It doesn't.

"They'll bring up the murder," the woman lawyer says.

"It was self-defense."

She glances at Dominic.

"It was," I insist.

"Well, it still might come up."

"It's none of their business, right? I don't have to respond."

She shakes her oblong head. Her eyes are set so wide apart, she reminds me of a goat. "No. You don't. We'd rather you don't."

Dominic's complexion is a little ashen. "The only thing that matters today is proving you didn't doctor the images of Kevin Martin."

"Doctor images? Is that what he's saying I did?"

"He's not saying *you* did it," the male lawyer explains, "but he is claiming the images were doctored. He's even provided the originals. They've extracted the IP address from the PNG metadata and—"

"In English?" I ask.

He stops spinning his pen. "The originals date back three years and were taken in his town, but three years ago Kevin was serving in Afghanistan."

My eyes go wide. "So the images really are fake?"

"Unless his entire platoon is lying about his whereabouts, then yes," Dominic says.

"Does this mean I'm disqualified?"

Dominic gasps as though surprised I've come to that conclusion. "Of course not. But it does mean there's been some rigging, and since you're the only one who benefited from it—"

"Mister Bacci, with all due respect, *you* selected me. I couldn't have been your only runner-up. Plus, I don't know the first thing about computers or IP addresses or metadata."

"Do you know somebody who does?" Josephine asks.

"I don't think so."

"It's time," the woman lawyer announces.

I skim over my rehearsed lines, then hand the paper back. "I'm ready."

Dominic squeezes my shoulder. "It'll be quick and painless. Don't worry." That's easy for him to say.

As we file out of the room and take the elevator down to the main entrance, the lawyer with the goat face makes me repeat the lines. I recite them by heart. She's pleased, impressed even. We cross the lobby and go out the revolving glass doors. I breathe in a gust of city air, hot and humid and full of car exhaust, but at least it's fresher than the recycled air of the museum. I shade my face from the bright sun and then I dare look down. The stairs are carpeted with reporters, and beyond them, spilling out onto the street which has been closed off by blue police barricades, there is a crowd so huge that it reminds me of the computerized battle scenes Aster created for a designer launching a toga-inspired clothing line.

I've always wanted to be famous, but for my talent. No one came today to see me stitch beautiful fabrics together. They came to see me hang. I check for a pillar and a noose as I attempt to keep track of what is being said. Everything's too loud, too bright. At some point, the lawyer nudges me, and I recite my lines. I must do a good job, because she nods and turns back to the frenzied crowd. In the haze of my brain, in the fog of camera flashes, I hear my sister's name being yelled.

"Isn't Aster a Photoshop wiz?" a sweaty-faced reporter asks. Spittle flies out from his thick lips and lands on my forehead.

Mechanically, I wipe it off.

The question is repeated, distorted, distended. It's as though the entire crowd below roars it as one. The chilling truth is that my sister *is* a Photoshop wiz.

What sort of Machiavellian scheme has Aster planned? And what the hell is her endgame? To trap me in some chaotic maze to make me pay for being the sane one?

NINETEEN

I throw up when I enter my cell.

"What the hell?" mutters the guard who escorted me back. "What did you do to your pillow?"

I smell the air and heave again. And again. The third time, nothing comes out. My stomach is empty, yet the hollow contracts. The guard yells for some assistance. I slink against the cement wall and drop, forcing myself to breathe through my mouth.

"Inmate Redd, if you have a nose bleed during the night, you are asked to take your dirty linens to the laundry room. We're not your maids," Giraffe-neck bellows.

With the back of my hand pressed against my lips, I say, "It's not my blood." I hate the sight of blood. I hate the smell of it. I hate everything about it.

Blood is death.

She splays her hands on her hips. "Whose is it then?"

"I don't know."

"Well, grab your pillow. I grant you special permission to go to the laundry room."

The perspective of touching the dark stain makes the spasms flare up again.

"If you don't care to clean it, then sweet dreams."

I push my palms against the cold concrete floor and rise. Finding a stain-free spot, I pinch the pillow and avoid looking at it as I walk down the hallway. All the prisoners are in their bunks, lazing around and chatting. Their conversations stop as I traipse by. I commit those who are snickering to memory. I'll know to stay away from them. Gill, Chacha, and Translucent-girl don't smile. The really old woman with the turban also doesn't react, but then she's talking to the ceiling, so she's probably oblivious to the revolting joke that's been played on me.

I get another metallic whiff and swallow hard.

When I was eleven, I jerked awake in the middle of the night. Something warm had seeped through my pink cotton nightgown and drenched my sheets. I didn't know about periods, so my first thought was that I was bleeding out. I remember racing to my mother's room in tears and turning on her bedside lamp to show her the blood because I was too frightened to form words. She'd opened her eyes, taken one look at me, and flipped over grumbling, "If you get yourself knocked up, you're out of my house. And turn off the fucking light!"

I pass the last cell and catch Cheyenne smiling. It makes her face resemble a slab of veal loin laced in butcher twine. I don't feel shame anymore, just pure anger, and anger sharpens my senses, and I know, with perfect certainty, that she did it. I slow down when I arrive in front of her. My gaze is drawn to her hands, which rest against her side like little bloated stumps. Something's dangling from them, a half-open book, my book, the story of my ancestors. I match her syrupy smile, and then I swing the pillow into her face. The still-wet blood leaves a satisfying orangey smear on her forehead. She bellows like a wounded cow.

"Inmate Redd!" Giraffe-neck's voice is shrill. "Do you want me to take away your *privileges*?"

"I slipped," I say sweetly. "I'm so, *so* sorry, Cheyenne."

There's great silence at first, and then the dormitory erupts with laughter. The officer grabs my upper arm and drags me all the way to the laundry room where she instructs a young officer—he barely looks a day over eighteen—to pay close attention to me.

I let the water flow over the foreign stain. As the crimson turns to salmon-pink, I feel cleansed, pure again, no longer a martyr, almost a virgin. I rub the fabric together to remove the last of it. Soon, my pillow is white, but my nail beds are red, roughed up by the friction. I place the pillow in the dryer and sink to the floor to watch it spin as though it were a television monitor. It's hypnotic. I find my thoughts straying back to my sister and to her breakdown this afternoon. I wish I could syphon away her pain, but from here, with no means of communication—I'm allowed a phone call but she isn't—it's impossible.

"Did she pass?" I ask the young guard.

"Who?"

I stand up. "My sister. She's competing on the Masterpiecers."

"I don't know what that is."

"Really? Where are you from?"

He doesn't pick up on my sarcasm. "Ambia."

I'm not even sure where Ambia is on a map and I don't really care, so I go back to watching my pillow spin. But then I get an idea. "Do you have a phone by any chance?"

"Only for emergencies."

I take a step closer to him. He takes a step back. "Does it have an Internet connection?"

"Don't come any closer or I'll call for b-backup," he stutters, raising his hand to his walkie-talkie.

I stop moving. "Look, the commander gave me permission to watch TV. Because of *this*"—I tip my chin toward the rotating pillow—"I wasn't able to catch the end of the show. Could you type in Masterpiecers and just read out the results?" I add a, "Please, sir," to help my case.

He fumbles for the phone in his uniform pocket. His eyes flick from the screen to me. And then his fingers tap on the digital keyboard.

I wait with bated breath for the announcement. Finally, it comes.

"'J.J. Fails to Score,'" he reads nervously.

A breath escapes from my parted lips like a gush of steam. Ivy really is still in!

He darts his gaze to me. When he's satisfied that I haven't shifted, he looks back down. "'Ivy Not Caught Redd-Handed.'" His voice rings out in the cement laundry block. "'Jackson the Auction King.'"

"Go back," I say. "To the 'Redd-Handed' headline."

He reads out an article about how my sister swore in a press release that she had nothing to do with the doctored photos of former contestant number eight. "While police follow a new lead, Dominic Bacci and Josephine Raynoir have announced their generous offer of letting Kevin Martin enter the competition. Kevin has accepted and will arrive at the Metropolitan Museum tomorrow. The show will take a one-day break and resume on Friday." The guard glances up. "Doctored photos? Police investigation? What sort of show is this?"

The sort that will either make or break my sister.

TWENTY

Ivy

"Everyone to the prep room!" comes a voice from the concealed speaker in my tent. I still haven't located it.

I stick the pillow over my head. If only I could stay buried underneath my comforter for the rest of the evening and for our day off tomorrow. I can't stop thinking about what the reporter implied. I don't *want* to believe him, but a big part of me does.

"Everyone to the prep room!"

This time, I throw the pillow off and peel the covers away. I stop by the bathroom to splash cool water against the nape of my neck and rinse away the sour taste in my mouth. I'm still fully dressed and made up, but my clothes are wrinkled and my mascara is smudged. I carefully swipe the dark smear with my fingertips and head out.

In the hallway, I come face to face with Chase. It's the first time this has happened even though our rooms are across from each other. He clearly looks as surprised as I am from the near collision, but he gets over it quicker than I do. He steps back and tips his head in a gesture meant for me to go ahead of him. I don't want to walk in front of him—not that I believe he's going to stab me in the back—so I pretend to have forgotten something in my room. Behind the taut fabric walls, my heart bangs like thunder. I strain to hear his footsteps crush the soft grass. I count to thirty slowly, then I count back down to zero, and then I cautiously lift the tent flap. The sharp green scent of him lingers, but he's gone.

Dominic, Josephine, and Brook are waiting for us, dressed down from their usual suits and silks. Josephine sports a pair of narrow jeans and a batwing cotton sweater that makes her seem more human; Dominic, a red-checkered shirt that brings out the warm hue of his skin; and Brook, black jeans and a blue shirt.

"So, in light of these strange events, we thought we'd take you out on the town for dinner. And tomorrow"—Dominic grins—"since it's supposed to be in the nineties, Brook has graciously suggested to host you in his penthouse for a pool party. I'll organize transportation and bathing suits for noon, which will give you ample time to sleep in."

"That sounds amazing," Lincoln says, flapping her eyelashes that are so laden with mascara they look like crow wings.

"Also," Dominic continues, "as some of you might already know, we've invited Mister Martin to compete."

"But I thought—" Maxine glances at me and then back at Dominic. "I thought he wasn't *fit* for the show."

"It's come to our attention that *les photos* have been doctored," Josephine explains.

Gazes automatically land on me.

"He will arrive tomorrow," she continues. "Which is why you get a break. *Fantastique, non*?"

I'm wondering what part of it is fantastic, the break or Kevin joining us.

Dominic's lips press into a taut smile. "I'm truly sorry for all this."

"Why couldn't you have offered Kevin a spot on next year's show?" Herrick asks.

"Because there wouldn't have been a 'next year's show.' His lawyers were threatening to have it canceled altogether. You have Josephine to thank for keeping it running." His hand rises to her forearm, but instead of settling there, it continues its upward ascent toward his silver hair. Although it's rigid with gel, he rakes his fingers through it.

Maxine gives a small clap, but since she's the only one, she stops and her cheeks turn crimson.

Dominic gestures to the curtained area. "Your stylists have laid out some outfits in your dressing rooms."

Just as we're all about to head off, J.J. arrives in a pair of baggy jeans that show too much of his yellow boxers. He's rolling a small canvas case.

"Is that your doggy bag for the restaurant?" Herrick's joke is lost on J.J. In truth, it's sort of lost on me too.

"I'm not going to the restaurant." He stops in front of me as he says this; as though it were my fault that he was voted off.

Granted, I was the closest to failing, but I didn't. *He* did. I fold my arms, which doesn't prevent him from doing something totally unexpected. He hugs me. I keep my arms locked from sheer surprise, and because I don't do hugs.

"Good luck, Redd," he says.

And then he moves to Maxine and Lincoln, and repeats the hug-luck combo. He high-fives Chase and attempts to do the same with Herrick, but the latter doesn't lift his hand, so J.J. slings one arm around him and squeezes him.

"Are you sure you don't want to stay for dinner?" Dominic asks.

"Got a new paint job for a school in Harlem. Your show gives good exposure, Mister B." He's bobbing his head or pecking the air—it's hard to tell.

Dominic nods. "Glad you got something out of it. Send us a picture once you're done vandalizing public property."

"Sure thing." J.J. shakes Dominic's hand, and then Brook's. "They're documenting the whole thing for Vanity Fair so you'll definitely get an eyeful of *moi*." He winks at Josephine, who rolls her eyes. "Miss Raynoir. A pleasure."

Instead of shaking her hand, he lifts it to his mouth and gives it a languorous kiss. She surprisingly doesn't slap him, but she does wipe her hand on her jeans the minute he turns around.

"*Bonsoir*, dear friends. May the best one win!" And then his assistant walks him back to freedom.

I must watch the doorway a long time, because Brook clears his throat. "You need to get ready."

"I'm going," I murmur distractedly.

"Always hard to see someone lose," Brook continues.

"Actually, I was thinking the opposite."

Brook lifts one thick eyebrow. He probably thinks I'm cold, but that's not how I meant it. I don't care enough to explain that J.J.'s departure gives me hope, hope for doors opening in spite of losing the competition. I hadn't thought about the exposure. I hadn't thought there was any way into the art world if I didn't win this competition or attend the Masterpiecers. For the first time since I arrived, I'm not worried about losing. The treacherous tunnel I'm walking through will lead back into the light whether through a gilded doorway or a pothole in the road.

DINNER'S A BIG PRODUCTION. There are paparazzi lurking outside the museum when the gleaming black minivan emerges from the underground parking lot. Their lenses suck at the car's tinted windows like leeches. It takes nearly running them over to dislodge them. When we pull up in front of an Italian restaurant downtown, there are more of them. They swarm toward the vehicle before we're even parked.

Along with three other broad-backed, suit-clad men, Danny, my driver from the airport, fends them off to create a safe passage for us. He shoots me this strange look, the sort of look Mom would give me when my stitching was sub-par. I wonder if it's because of the press conference today. Even though I'm not a suspect, Aster is, and her actions reflect on me.

The restaurant is a hole-in-the-wall that's been reserved exclusively for us. The other tables have been pushed against the flower-papered walls and covered in overflowing baskets of fruit and dripping wax candles. The effect is lovely and romantic. I must gape around too long because when I move toward our table, the only vacant seat is between the Jackson brothers. "Fun," I mutter under my breath as I slide into the chair. Lincoln is on Brook's other side. She's lassoed him into a conversation about pasta making. And here I thought that the only thing she knew how to cook was Meth.

"So Kevin's coming on the show," Chase says.

At first I think he's talking to Maxine, who's sitting on his other side, but then I realize she's deep in conversation with Dominic.

"Apparently." I grab a breadstick from the basket in front of me and munch on it without looking at him.

He angles his torso toward me. "Why do you dislike me so much?"

I squeeze the breadstick so hard it snaps in two. One end falls right into the hand-painted presentation plate. "Let me see…you implied that I had a hand in Kevin's elimination *and* that I cheated during the riddle hunt. Are those good reasons, because they sound like pretty good ones to me?"

"I admit, I wasn't the friendliest—"

"No shit," I say sarcastically.

"But that's because I know nothing about you."

"So you assume things."

"Yes. Just like you have your own assumptions about me."

I do.

"Today, what you said during the auction, that you made the quilt for a dying friend. Was it true?"

"It wasn't for a friend."

"Who was it for? A boyfriend?"

"I don't want to talk about it."

He leans back in his chair. "This is me trying to get to know you so I can stop assuming things."

"What's the point? Soon one of us will be gone," I say.

Chase's dark eyes keep studying me.

When I can't take his scrutiny anymore, I turn toward Brook. "There was a rip in the seam of my quilt. Was it damaged in transit?"

Brook's thick lashes sweep down over his eyes, which he's trained on the platter of paper-thin cold cuts and salty chunks of Parmesan. "I wouldn't know."

"Who would?" I ask.

He shrugs.

"Didn't you see the tear?" I ask.

He finally looks away from the appetizers. "Doesn't matter, does it? It's no longer yours."

"It matters to me. I don't want the buyer to be disappointed. Could I work on it before it's sent off?"

"It's already been sent."

"What if the buyer returns it?" I ask.

"He won't."

"How can you be sure?"

"Ivy, relax." He lays his hand on my forearm. His fingers are cold. "It was a small hole. No one will see it."

"So you *did* notice it!"

"What did Brook notice?" Josephine asks.

"Nothing," Brook says, removing his hand.

"The rip in my quilt," I say.

"I thought it was intentional," Josephine says, spinning the large diamond ring around her thin finger.

"Why would I intentionally put a hole in my quilt?" I ask.

"Modern art," Maxine says, as the waiters place gold-rimmed plates topped with an assortment of pasta in front of us. "You could shred one. I'm sure it would sell well."

"That's an idea," I say.

I look down at the mounds of pasta on my plate. The raviolis are large and beet-colored; the linguine, green and deliciously fragrant; the gnocchi, ridged and glistening with a melted butter and herb mixture; and the square of lasagna, still bubbling with cheese.

Not only was Aster trying to sabotage me, but she damaged my work. The guilt that has gnawed at me since I made her sign that paper giving me power of attorney over her vanishes. Aster can no longer be left to her own devices. She is lost in the debris of her mind. I'm angry because she's my twin, and I love her more than anything, but I also hate her more than anyone. I crumple the napkin in my lap and set it on the linen tablecloth. Wordlessly, I rise and head to the bathroom before my wet eyes can expel the tears.

Lincoln walks in moments after me. She disappears into one of the stalls and emerges before I have time to escape. Over the sound of running water, she asks, "How did the press conference go?"

"Fine," I say, tossing the embroidered hand towel into the wicker basket below the sink.

"No one really believes you got him disqualified." She turns off the water and dries her hands against her eggplant suede skirt. I'm about to tell her that she shouldn't wet suede when she adds, "You didn't, right?"

"Of course not."

"And your sister?"

"What is it you heard, Lincoln?"

"That she's talented with computers."

"A lot of people are talented with computers," I counter.

She shrugs. "Chill, Ives. I wasn't accusing her of anything." She rests her hands on her flat belly. "I'm stuffed. The food was so delish, wasn't it?"

I nod and brush past her.

When I get back to the table, Josephine's gone and Dominic resembles my iced water. Tiny drops of perspiration drip down the sides of his face.

"What did I miss?" I ask Brook.

"The usual…Dom and Josephine had a disagreement."

"Over what?"

"God only knows. Josephine's been acting strange for a while now. I think she might be pregnant."

"Pregnant?"

"I know, right? Not really the maternal type—"

"Is she married?"

"Engaged."

"I didn't know."

"Not many people know."

"Is he in the art world?"

"No. He's some big shot businessman." He takes a sip of wine. "What about you? Any boyfriend back in Kokomo?"

"No."

"That's surprising," he says with a brazen smile.

Heat smears my cheeks. I grab my glass of water and take a gulp that goes down the wrong hole when Brook's hand grazes my thigh. I cross my legs to shift it off because Chase is staring. I'm the source of enough gossip already.

No need to add fuel to the fire my sister has kindled.

TWENTY-ONE

I scoop up oatmeal and let it plop back down unceremoniously into my plastic bowl. It's lumpier than usual, and settles in clumps on the filmy surface.

"You look like you didn't sleep," Gill says. Her gaze vacillates between my porridge and my face.

"I have to go do meditation. Want to come with me?"

"To meditate?"

"Yes."

"I don't know how to meditate," she says.

"I don't either, but the shrink thinks it can help me. I'm bored just thinking about it."

"Well, now *that* really makes me want to go."

I smile, and then catch sight of a black mullet. "Hey, Cheyenne," I say sweetly.

She wobbles to a dead stop.

"Got something for you." I chuck a tampon at her. Over dinner, I asked Chacha for a box of them instead of chocolate. "It's more absorbent than a pillow." I make sure my voice carries even though the cafeteria is totally quiet.

Cheyenne blushes so hard that all three hundred pounds of her turns cherry red.

Gill's face splits into a wide grin, as do many others. The only ones not partaking in the contagious glee are Cheyenne—for obvious reasons—and the ladies sitting at her table. They're all firing me vile looks, which will surely be accompanied by some form of retaliation.

"So, meditation?" I ask Gill again as though Cheyenne had never walked by and I hadn't just embarrassed the shit out of her.

"Can't believe you just did that. You have some serious balls, Aster."

I can't believe it either. "I met the warden yesterday."

Gill bites her lower lip with her buckteeth. "What did you think of him?"

"Seems nice enough." I play around with my porridge again. "He knows my sister."

"He does? How?"

"She paid him a visit when I was booked. Asked him to be nice to me."

"That's chill of her."

I nod, inspecting my nails.

"I have some cream in my room. It's real hydrating." She tips her chin toward my hands. "If you want some."

"Um…sure."

"Do you garden?"

"Garden?"

"You know, plant flowers and shit."

"No. Why?"

"Because when you got here, your nails were all torn and dirty. My aunt—she raised me—well, her nails were always ripped from growing vegetables outside our motor home."

I drop the spoon. The rounded part sticks to the porridge for a second before toppling off the side of the bowl and clattering onto the steel tabletop. "I'm just not good at taking care of my nails."

"I'd be glad to take care of them, Aster," Gill says. "If you'll let me."

I blink.

"Sorry to interrupt your moment, Inmates, but you got a visitor, Redd," the potbellied guard says.

One of Gill's tawny eyebrow lifts.

"I thought I needed to go meditate?" I tell him.

"After," he says.

"Gill will join me for the meditation."

"Does she have permission?"

"Miss Pierce suggested creating a meditation circle. Hard to create a circle with only two people. Unless you plan on joining, sir?" *Where is this cockiness coming from? The despair of lockup?*

His face colors a little. Only his scar stays white. "Get your skinny ass off the bench, Inmate. I don't like to wait."

I shoot up. "See you later, Gill."

A smile floats across her face. I wonder if giving her hope is wise. She's sort of a wacko.

Driscoll leads me to an area I haven't been to yet. There are four identical rooms with glass walls on the hallway side, and brushed cement everywhere else. Each contains one table with two iron chairs.

When I spot Josh, I swivel toward the sergeant. "I don't want to see him."

He just grunts, beeps the door open, and shoves me through. "You got fifteen minutes, Officer Cooper, then I need to take her to her shrink appointment."

Josh looks up. His expression is so grave that my mind somersaults to my twin.

The door slams shut behind me and I jump. "Wh-what's going on? Is it Ivy?"

"Sit down."

Legs trembling, I take a seat across from him.

"Aster, did you doctor the photos of Kevin Martin?"

"Who?"

"The contestant who was eliminated. Did you do it?"

"No. Why?"

"Because the media is claiming you might be behind the fake pictures."

"They're fake?"

"Are you playing dumb?"

"No!"

"Isn't Photoshopping part of your job at the ad agency?"

I snort. "Yes, but I didn't do it."

"You promise?"

"Yes! Anything else you came to accuse me of?"

He rubs his neck, or more precisely a spot that's purple and swollen.

"Is that a hickey?" I exclaim.

"What?"

"On your neck."

"Oh that…I cut myself shaving." His jaw reddens so quickly that I know he's lying.

"Are you seeing someone?"

He inhales deeply. "Do you really want to know?"

I bite my lip because it's started to wobble. "Since when?"

"Let's not talk about this—"

"Since when?"

"A month."

"Is it serious?"

"Aster," he whispers.

"Well, is it?" My voice is surprisingly steady.

"I don't know."

"Do I know her?"

He rubs the hickey again, and then he nods.

"Who is it?"

"Heidi."

"The floozy from Dairy Queen?"

"Don't call her that."

"You're the one who told me she slept around. She's going to give you HIV."

He widens his eyes. "Goddammit, Aster! You and I are no longer together."

I recoil as though he's slapped me. And then I start bobbing in my chair, forward and backward, like a reed caught in a tempest. I need Ivy. I want her to come home. She's the only one who gives a shit about me.

TWENTY-TWO

Ivy

I wake up sweating. Without windows or a watch, I have no idea what time it is. For a second, I think it's the middle of the night, but I hear noise—chatter—so I assume it's not. I throw the covers off my legs and head toward the shower. I've had the nightmare again—the one where my sister comes at me with a kitchen knife while I'm sleeping, but it's not my sister, it's my reflection, and I stab a mirror. It shatters, but then it mends back together.

Trembling, I twist my damp hair up into a bun and step into the warm spray. I let the water tumble over my forehead and drip into my open eyes, hoping it will blur the dream and wipe my mind. It doesn't, so I get out and don the khaki shorts and white tank I brought with me, then head for breakfast where they're serving pancakes and waffles topped with real maple syrup, not the imitation corn syrup that's dyed brown. It's a true feast. As I ask for a second serving, Herrick's assistant walks in and hands each one of us a fabric bag with the Masterpiecers' logo. Inside, I find a beaded turquoise bikini, a pair of silver sunglasses, and a bottle of sunscreen.

While Lincoln, Herrick, and Maxine return to their rooms to change, Chase and I remain in the living room.

"Excited to go home?" I ask.

"Home?"

"Don't you live with your brother?"

He looks like the orange juice he's chugging has turned sour. "Hell no. Whatever gave you that idea?"

"I don't know. I just assumed. Do you live with your parents?"

"At twenty-one, that would be a little sad, don't you think?"

I bristle. "*I* still live at home."

"By choice?"

I say, "Yes," even though it's not a choice. I wouldn't be able to afford paying my own rent. "Mom's not there anymore and Dad…well, he doesn't live there either."

"Where is he?"

"I don't know. He left before we were born. I don't think he ever knew Mom was pregnant."

"So you've never met him?"

I shake my head.

"And you're okay with that?"

"How could I not be okay with it? I don't know his last name. How could I find him?"

"Your mom never told you his full name? Was it a one-night stand?"

"Of course not. They dated a few months, but he was always in and out of town because of his job."

"What did he do?"

"Sold fabric. It took him all over the world." Mom told me his favorite country was India. He regaled her with stories of textile factories in which women would plunge silks and linens in vats of dye, then hand bead intricate motifs along the seams. He promised to take her there someday, but that day never dawned. "So, where *do* you live?"

"I have an apartment by Washington Square Park. Close to NYU. Still have a year left, unless I get into the Masterpiecers."

"I thought you were so sure you were going to win."

"Only idiots don't doubt themselves. But I'm still planning on crushing you, and the others." There's a glimmer in his brown eyes. In some other life, he must've been a bloodthirsty revolutionary. I can just picture him running across a field, armed with a rifle and a ferocious will to kill. "Shouldn't you go get changed?"

"I'm not planning on swimming."

"Why not?"

"Because."

"Because what?"

"I just don't feel like it, okay?" I stab the last piece of waffle and stuff it inside my mouth just as Maxine walks back in, telling us just how excited she is to get out of the museum. And then the rest of the group follows, and an assistant walks us down to the underground parking lot.

Except for the sleek black minivan, the garage is deserted. Unlike Fifth Avenue. Clouds of people and clusters of news vans swarm the street. The second our ride emerges, the paparazzi start shooting. Considering the windows are tinted, I doubt their pictures will be worth anything, but they click away nonetheless. Some even trail us all the way downtown, to what Maxine tells me is the Meatpacking District. It seems like we've left the city. The streets aren't grid-like anymore. Instead, they jut out in all directions, and the buildings are squatter and wider, like warehouses.

Brook's building is entirely covered with black glass that shimmers in the light of the midday sun. I count seven stories, which is not tall for New York, but high enough that the paparazzi won't be able to hound us. I would hope.

When we get up to the penthouse, Brook gives us a tour. His gigantic bachelor pad is filled with priceless art and sharp-edged furniture in muted colors of gray and beige. Even the satin and velvet throw pillows are sleek and puffed up, resembling something Jeff Koons would've crafted out of stainless steel.

"Can I use your bedroom to change?" I ask Brook after the others file out on the deck.

"You didn't put on your bathing suit back at the museum?"

"I didn't have time," I say.

"I would rather—You know what, go ahead." He tips his head toward his bedroom. "You can even leave your stuff in there."

"Thanks," I say, clutching my little fabric bag as I walk quickly down the hallway. Once inside, I lock the door and race to his nightstand where I spotted an electronic tablet earlier.

I press on the screen that flares to life without prompting me for a code. With shaky fingers, I pull up an Internet page, log in to my account, and write an email.

JOSH—

The quilt is here...was here. It's the one I auctioned off. There was a rip in it. I think Aster did it. Can you find out why?

AFTER PRESSING SEND, I start researching my sister's case. A knock resounds on the door, making me jump.

"Everything okay?"

"Y-yes," I say. "Almost ready."

Fingers trembling, I clear the browser history, return the tablet to the nightstand, throw off my clothes, and wriggle into my bathing suit. When I open the door, I come nose-to-chest with Brook.

"That's a nice color on you," he says.

I can smell his breath, minty and cool on the tip of my nose. "Thanks."

He peers behind me. For a second, I wonder if I turned off the tablet. Or maybe I put it in the wrong spot.

My heart thumps so loudly that I'm afraid it'll give me away. I try to sidestep him, but he claps his hands on my upper arms. "I'm going back to the museum to greet Kevin." His eyes are on me again. "Save me a swim, okay?"

"Brook? Your phone keeps—" Chase's words die off when he turns the corner and spots us.

I bounce away from Brook and mumble something about seeing them outside. I try to walk at a normal speed even though I'm tempted to run. Not so much from Brook, but from Chase. I know he's not a mind reader—I'm well aware they don't exist, unlike Mom who never took a decision without consulting the bald tarot card reader on Buckeye—but still, I worry he'll see the guilt rifling through me. I broke a show rule. I could be eliminated if anyone found out I established communication with the outside world.

Keeping my face as blank as possible, I walk past Jeb whose camera is poised in my direction, past the sliding glass doors, past Herrick and Maxine who are floating on inflatable rafts while Lincoln does laps, and straight toward the overstuffed, orange lounge chairs.

"You should come in. The water's delicious," Maxine says, readjusting the floppy brim of her hat.

"Maybe later," I lie. I'm not going in the pool. I can't.

I close my eyes against the bright heat and try to relax, but my muscles are tense and my mind is buzzing with the email I wrote Josh. I hope he replies before we're carted back to the museum because I need answers.

TWENTY-THREE

"Why did you buy it?" I ask Troy.

"Have you been following me?"

"Why did you buy it?" I repeat, this time with more authority.

Troy places his hand on my half-open car window. A large gold pinkie ring reflects the orange Vacancy sign overhead. His nails are buffed and trimmed, and his fingers are long and golden. Feminine hands. That's what they strike me as. Shouldn't a mobster have dried blood underneath his nails and bruises on his knuckles? "As a pretty investment."

"Redecorating your underground office, are you?"

He combs his fingers through his greasy, chin-length black hair. "My underground office?"

"Isn't that where the mafia conducts their business?"

"The mafia?"

"Don't play dumb. I know who you are...I know what you do."

"Really? And who am I then?"

"Troy Mann. A wanted criminal."

He straightens up, but keeps his hand on the window. "Where would you get that sort of idea?"

"I read your file. You're wanted for money laundering and arms trafficking."

His pupils pulse against the yellowish iris. "I have no clue what you're talking about," he says, but I can tell he does.

"I'm not sure why you bought the quilt, but you leave my sister out of this."

"Your sister? I don't even know your sister."

"You bought the quilt from her."

Slow...that's what he is, because he repeats, "Your sister?"

"Just give me the quilt and I'll pretend we never met."

Thick fumes from my eighties Honda drift through my open window and fill the car.

His lips lift in a wide smile. "Are you trying to con me, Ivy? Because that's not a wise idea."

"I'm not Ivy."

"Sure. And I'm part robot." He chuckles and taps on the window. "Now get out of here."

"I'm not leaving without the quilt."

"I'm starting to lose patience. You don't want me to lose patience, Ivy."

"My name's Aster."

His hand is back on the windowsill. He's squeezing it so hard that his knuckles have turned white. "Go...now," he says, his voice low and threatening.

"Not without the quilt."

As a deep growl leaks out of his mouth, his hand shoots inside the car and comes at my throat like a claw, cutting off my air supply. I eye the lever to bring up the window, but it'll take too long to wind up. Keeping my gaze on his, my fingers crawl over to the stick shift. Holding down the clutch, I back up. It rips his fingers from my throat. And then I spin the wheel and ram into him. His body hits the hood and his head smashes against the windshield, which cracks from the impact. For a second, his cheek stays glued to the glass, but then the thick blood that's oozing out of his ear and forehead makes him slide off and thump to the ground.

I yelp, my gaze darting over the two floors of motel rooms. There's no movement and no light.

"Nobody saw you, Aster," I whisper to myself. "Nobody." Yet my entire body rumbles like the Honda's crap engine. "Besides, you didn't hit him that hard. You just stunned him. That's all. He's just stunned." I grip the window's lever and wind it up, but my palm is so slick that my hand skids off three times. I abandon the third time.

I ought to drive away, but I need the quilt, so I wait two minutes, five, ten. Still Troy doesn't stand. The keys to his room will be in that messenger bag he was carrying. Breathing hard, I open my door, take my seatbelt off, and get out. His outstretched hand is the first thing I spot. I watch his slender fingers, expecting them to curl, but they remain flat against the asphalt. I creep closer, and closer, and closer until I can see all of him, as flat and lifeless as his hand. Unconscious, not lifeless, *I correct myself.*

The bag rests a few feet away from him. I hop over his outstretched arm and bend to grab it, but he grabs me first, squeezing my ankle and twisting it with his dainty hand. I catch myself on the dented hood and kick as hard as I can, just managing to dislodge his fingers. And then I run, faster than I've ever run before, and spring into the car. Without bothering to close my door, I put the car in drive. It lurches forward, then up, then down. My ears buzz like after that awful rave Ivy dragged me to a few months back.

"I killed a criminal," I reassure myself. "A bad guy. A very bad guy. Very very bad."

I peer at the bag on the passenger seat, expecting some bomb to detonate, but it isn't rigged. But what about a tracking device? Maybe there's one inside. I jam my foot on the brake pedal and the edge of the steering wheel bites into my abdomen.

With shaky fingers, I pluck the bag off the seat and set it on my lap, and then I flip it open. Inside, there's a bulky package. I take it out to search the rest of it for keys, but my fingers don't come in contact with metal...they don't come in contact with anything. No keycard, no phone, no wallet. I turn it over and shake it, but still nothing falls out.

The key must have been on him. My forehead throbs. I rub it, trying to think. If I don't go back and search his body, then his death will have been for nothing. But if I go back, and someone sees me—No, I can't go back. I spot a trashcan. I open the car door and fling the bag into the bin. I'm about to do the same with the package, but curiosity gets the better of me and I tear it open. I blink because what I see can't be real...what I see is what my mind wants to see.

Ivy's quilt.

I touch it. It feels real. I pull it out and unfold it. Gold and satin glimmers, and this fabric covered in tiny mirrored-beads speckles the drab gray interior of the Honda with tinsels. I gather it in my arms and hug it to me as though it were my own sister. She's going to be so thankful, so so thankful.

Something crunches underneath my fingers. I frown and pull the quilt back. I press down on the spot and again it crackles. I prod other parts of the quilt, but there is no noise. I go back to the spot and turn on the car light to inspect it. Something catches my eye along the seam—on about three inches, the thread is of a different color. I tug on it with my sharp pinky nail until it breaks, then carefully, I pull apart the two sides of the quilt and extricate a folded piece of wax paper.

Why in the world would Ivy place a sheet of—I don't finish my thought when I glimpse what's inside. I fold it up and stuff it back in. And then I just breathe. The empty street beyond goes in and out of focus.

I cough from sucking in too much air. I pick up the torn package and read the mailing address. It's going to New York.

"New York?"

"Yes," I say, looking at the passenger seat. It's empty. I'm talking to myself. I rub my corded neck, trying to ease my nerves.

Headlights appear from behind, blinding and bright. I yank out the wax paper and stick it in my bra just in case it's the cops, but the car is a black pickup. It sidles in next to mine.

The automated window slides down. "Having car trouble, miss?"

"Uh...no. Everything's fine."

"Redd?"

I start. I'm about to ask him how he knows my last name when he stares at my windshield, at the bloodied crack. He must be referring to the blood.

"Your ride looks pretty banged up." He's wearing a green cap with a pine tree and a deer on it.

"I hit a deer."

"Not many of those in Kokomo."

"I hit it back in Vermont."

He eyes me, then the windshield. "I got a guy who could fix that for you cheap."

"I was going to get rid of the car. It stalls half the time."

"He sells some too."

"I'm good. Thanks. My dad's waiting up for me. I should get home."

"I suppose you should."

I grip the stick shift. "You mind backing up a little?" I ask.

"You reported the deer to the police?"

My fingers tighten around the knob. "Yeah. Can you please move?"

He doesn't. Cold sweat gathers on the nape of my neck, gluing my springy curls to my skin. A hand lifts them, squeezes my shoulder blades. I jump and shiver. It's just my imagination. The guy's still in his truck, still next to me.

"What's up with the blanket?"

"My heater's broken," I lie.

"It's August."

"Well, I'm cold."

I'm about to push my car up onto the sidewalk to maneuver out of the tight spot when he taps the brim of his cap like an army salute and pulls his truck back. A swirly tattoo of barbed wire decorates his entire forearm.

The Honda springs into action so fast, it sputters and stalls. I glance into my rearview mirror. The pickup is still behind me. Praying that the guy won't follow me, I step on the clutch, then on the gas, and then I drive in the wrong direction until I'm sure I've lost him.

Even though my attention is on the dark road, my mind is on the quilt and the diamonds. If I keep the quilt here and the police find it, Ivy will get in trouble. I think of throwing it out, but I can't do that to my sister, to her beautiful work. Without braking, I grab the torn package and stuff the quilt back inside. I need something to close it. The bakery box! Bending my arm at a strange angle, I seize it from the backseat and peel the long piece of scotch tape used to keep it shut. I swerve in next to a mailbox, come to an abrupt halt, and stick the piece of tape on the tear. It doesn't quite cover it all, but enough so that the content doesn't fall out. And if it does, then so be it.

"Better lost than found," I murmur.

"Is she confessing?"

"I don't know."

I snap my lids up and blink from the harsh lighting. Large tawny eyes stare down at me. Gill's. I sit up quickly.

"What was in the package?" Driscoll is standing next to Gill.

"Wh-what?" I stutter.

"You were talking in your sleep," Gill says.

I dig the heels of my palm into my eyes, but stop when she combs a piece of hair behind my ear.

Driscoll folds his arms together and leans against my cell's open gate. "What package were you talking about?"

"Huh?"

"Can't you see she's not even awake yet?" Gill exclaims.

"She looks pretty awake to me."

Driscoll's walkie-talkie buzzes. "Sergeant, you're needed in the cafeteria."

He grumbles that he'll be right there. "Oh…Robyn wants you to go meditate again, Redd. You can go during yard time since you're no longer allowed out."

"I'm not?"

"Nope. Too many reporters out back."

"Reporters?"

"Yeah. You're real notorious."

I blanch.

"Miss Pierce said I could come back with her."

"You got yard time, Swanson."

"I think you can find it in your heart"—she taps her pelvic bone—"to allow me a free pass."

Driscoll's face turns beet red; only the diagonal piece of pink skin, on which no brow hair will ever grow back, remains pale. "Fine," he grumbles.

"What was that about?" I ask her once he's gone.

"I waxed him. Down there," she says with a smirk.

I gag.

"Yeah. Gross. I know." She plops down on my bed. "Bad dream?"

I nod even though it wasn't a dream. It was a memory.

TWENTY-FOUR

Ivy

"You're going to get a sunburn," Chase tells me.

My eyes are closed but I know his voice by heart now. "Why do you care?" I ask, looking up at him. He hovers over me, casting a shadow over the top half of my body.

"I don't. Just thought I'd mention it," he says, sitting on the fluffy orange cushions of the lounge chair next to mine.

"Thanks for your concern."

While he settles back, cradling his head on his bent arms, I peek around the deck.

"Where's the camera crew?" I ask.

"On their lunch break. I think they're waiting for Brook to return with Kevin. Stir up some drama."

I eye him, wondering if he thinks I'm going to make a scene, because I'm not. He stares right back. Even through his dark aviators, I can tell that's what he believes.

"Talking about drama, what's up between you and your brother?" I ask.

Chase's eyebrows, which look more copper than brown, draw together in a frown. "We don't get along."

"Why not?"

He flicks his gaze back up to the sky. "You get along with your sister?"

"Most of the time. But we're very different."

"I read somewhere you were Miss Popular in high school, but not her."

"That's because she never tried to make friends."

"Maybe she didn't want to compete with you."

"Huh?"

"It's hard to have an all-star sibling."

"Why would you compare yourself to your sibling?"

"You don't; the world does."

"Is that how you feel about Brook?"

His biceps tighten. I hit a nerve.

I turn over onto my side to face him. "If you feel like that, why didn't you choose another line of work?"

"Art is my passion. Life's too short to do something you're not passionate about." After a beat, he adds, "Could *you* see yourself doing something else?"

I look at the pool, at Herrick and Lincoln splashing a giggling Maxine. "I'd hope to be able to do only that."

"You sold your quilt well."

"No, I didn't."

He frowns—he probably thinks I'm conceited. "I bet your next piece will go for three times as much. You have a name now."

"That's associated with murder. Super name," I mutter.

Chase reaches over and touches my arm, which makes my breath hitch. "Ivy, you're not the one who killed a man."

I stare at my skin, so he pulls his hand back. "I know that." The spot he touched feels a few degrees warmer than the rest of my body. I lift my eyes back to his face. "What's your girlfriend up to this week?" I ask, to change the subject. And also, because I am slightly curious about the blonde who posed with him in that People Magazine shoot.

"Don't know and don't care."

"Really? I thought—I thought you were practically engaged."

"The journalist wrote that to sell more copies."

"Weren't you dating since you were toddlers?"

"Not toddlers, but yeah, we were together a long time."

"What happened?"

Chase's jaw tightens. "Brook happened."

"What do you mean?"

"He screwed my ex." I must look horrified because he snorts. "Lost some of his appeal now?"

"I'm not interested in him."

"That's not what it looked like in the hallway, or at the restaurant for that matter."

"*He* came on to me. Besides, you were so pleasant to talk with last night."

He smiles, but there are the layers of hurt behind that smile. "I was trying to be. I think I'm going to jump in. You're sure you don't want to join me?"

"Yeah. I'm sure."

After he gets up, he waits as though hoping I'll change my mind.

"I think I'll take a nap," I say. "I slept badly last night."

"You better get out of the sun then."

"I will."

Just as he leaps into the pool, I move to a shaded part of the terrace where the crew has set up a drink stand and some finger food. I pour myself a glass of icy lemonade and sit in a padded armchair with my legs curled underneath me. As I sip the chilled drink, I watch the city skyline. It's all at once mesmerizing and boring. So much so that, between the view and the lounge music playing on the deck, my lids eventually droop close.

I wake up to Chase nudging my shoulder. I uncoil my legs that prickle, and wipe the sleep out of my eyes. “How long have I been out?”

“About an hour. We have to get inside,” he says, tipping his chin toward the building next to us.

A guy with a massive camera is standing on the roof, clinging to the ledge to snap pictures of us.

“He’s going to fall off!” I say.

“Jeb phoned the police,” he says, his gaze running over my legs. “They’ll get him down.” He extends his hand. “Come on.” I must debate to take it for too long, because he pulls it back and walks away.

I rise and head inside. Maxine, Lincoln, and Herrick are all sitting on the couch, chatting about how persistent the paparazzi are and how they can’t believe the police are getting involved. As I’m about to sit next to Chase, the front door opens. It’s Brook and Kevin.

Kevin who still thinks I got him eliminated. Kevin who hates my guts. Kevin who was in the army.

Kevin’s eyes lock on mine, and I drop into the seat, hitting Chase’s thigh on my way down. When I stare back up, the sergeant is watching me. Palms moist, ears zinging, I peel myself away from Chase.

Kevin’s flip-flops flap against the stone floor as he cuts across the room toward Maxine. Trailed by one of the cameramen, he introduces himself and shakes her hand, then Lincoln’s and Herrick’s and Chase’s. He doesn’t shake mine. Probably because he thinks Aster was involved in getting him eliminated. And maybe he’s right. Maybe she did doctor those photos. But just maybe, it wasn’t to sabotage him. Maybe it was to sabotage me.

TWENTY-FIVE

Sitting on the floor of the shrink's office, I try to relax, but the memory is still raw.

"Aster, you're shaking," Robyn says. "You want a blanket?"

I nod. Gill is watching me. She's always watching me. Everyone's always watching me.

Robyn drapes a polar fleece throw over my shoulders, then takes a seat on the floor next to me. "Let's link hands," she says as she shuts her eyes and starts humming.

Gill grins.

"I want to hear you hum, girls," Robyn says, eyes still closed. "Like yesterday."

So I do, but not Gill. She's smiling too much to hum. I nearly don't see her crooked teeth anymore. Ivy and I both inherited our mother's straight teeth. It's not much of a legacy, but at least she passed on something valuable. We would have been a hell of a lot less thankful for the bump on her nose or her freckled Irish skin.

For some reason, thinking about my mother makes me think of when I was pregnant. My mind flutters to my flat stomach, which is more concave than flat now. I remember feeling the baby move, how it had filled me with purpose. I wouldn't have had much to offer, but the pregnancy proved I wasn't as messed up or weak as Ivy, my mother, and Josh all thought.

Anyway, considering all that's happened, I realize that my loss was a blessing. I wouldn't have wanted to be pregnant in jail. I do want a child someday, though. Not now. Not in the next five years. But one day. I want to love a being like I was never loved. I want to preserve that being's innocence like I was never allowed to preserve mine.

My heart is so deeply lacerated that it will never beat like a normal heart, yet it beats. This is why I don't want to keep poisoning it with medication and toxins. As I hum, as time passes, my chest vibrates and a warm current flows through my veins.

"Now open your eyes and savor the sensations in your body," Robyn says.

My lids don't snap up. They lift gradually, like motorized garage doors.

"Let's take a moment to thank our mind for the respite it has offered our body."

I don't thank my mind. There are limits I will not cross and talking to oneself is one of them. Robyn slips her hand out of mine, but not Gill. I have to release hers. She smiles at me so luminously that I become uncomfortable. I don't mind the fact that she has a crush on me. I don't even mind her company. But her touch, her attention, her intent…it's overwhelming.

"How do you feel?" Robyn asks.

"Swell," Gill says, all toothy and bright-eyed.

"And you, Aster?"

"Fine."

"Just fine?"

"It was good," I say, "for me. For my head." I tap my temple to convince her I got the point of the exercise.

She looks pleased. "Glad to hear that."

We start toward the door, but Robyn calls me back.

"Save me a seat at lunch, okay?" I tell Gill.

She nods happily, her red dreadlocks frolicking against her gray jumpsuit.

After the door closes, Robyn states the obvious, "You made a friend."

"You seem surprised."

She avoids responding. "It's healthy to have friends."

"Even if those friends are murderers?" I say, thinking of Gill's ex. Another reason I should discourage her interest in me.

"'Every saint has a past and every sinner has a future.'"

I'm astounded a prison shrink would think so quixotically. "What was it you wanted to talk to me about?"

"When he dropped you off, Sergeant Driscoll mentioned you had a vivid dream."

"Yeah. So?"

She narrows her eyes. "You want to discuss it?"

"No."

"Was it about the hit and run?"

"Maybe."

"Have you been having a lot of dreams about it?"

"Yes."

"I know something that could help. There's this new drug the FDA just approved."

I shake my head. "Drugs can make me sterile."

"Are you thinking about having children?"

"Doesn't every woman think about that?"

"You're only nineteen."

"I know, but as you said, everyone has a future."

"Do you consider yourself a sinner?"

I frown. "No."

She studies my face in silence for a bit, then walks over to her desk, grabs a pamphlet, and returns to me, brandishing it. There's a white-haired woman on the front who's smiling so widely I can see the gold fillings in her molars. "Check it out okay?"

I grumble a *yes* and shove the glossy foldout into my pocket. "Is that all?"

"I don't know. Is it?"

"Yes."

"Then you are free to leave."

If only she meant this hellhole.

JOSH RETURNS THE FOLLOWING MORNING. And not to see how I'm doing. He's back because he has questions. "Why did you send your sister's quilt to the show?" He's leaning his forearms on the metal desk of the visitation room, hands firmly clasped together. His skin is brown, but there's a thin white line visible beneath the hem of his short-sleeved police shirt.

"I didn't send it to the Masterpiecers. I—"

"You did."

"Let me finish." I shoot my gaze up to his, trying to ignore the hickey. "I left it in the package I found it in. It was already stamped and addressed."

"To the Masterpiecers?"

"To some place in New York. I didn't make the connection until I saw it on the show."

"You swear you're not making this up?" Josh asks.

"On Ivy's life."

"Why would a mobster send a quilt to the show?" Suddenly his green eyes go wide. "Ivy mentioned a tear. He was using it as a vessel!"

"You spoke to her?"

"Got an email yesterday."

I look up at the black, dome-shaped camera over the table. "Are we being recorded?"

"No. I asked them not to. Shit, Aster… Troy Mann was using it to transport something! If there was tear, then the person who received it must've taken it out. And if it's someone from the show—Shit," he adds in a low voice.

I glimpse a red dot on the black dome, but it blinks off as quickly as it appeared. I keep looking at it, just in case it returns. "I think we're being watched," I whisper.

Josh glances up. "We're not. I promise."

"I don't believe your promises anymore."

Silence hangs between us, as thick as the Indiana snowstorm that blew the night I lost the baby…the night Josh and Ivy found me curled up on a bench underneath a casing of snow. My lips were purple, or so they told me.

"What could've been inside that quilt?" Josh muses.

"Diamonds."

"Diamonds?" He's so stunned his voice squeaks. "How—You took them out?"

"Do you think Ivy was in on it?" I ask suddenly.

"Huh?"

"Isn't it a big coincidence that both she and her quilt were headed to the Masterpiecers? Do you think that's how she got on the show?"

He shakes his head.

"It would explain how she paid Mom's bills."

"What? Are you insane?" he snaps.

I bristle. "You have a better explanation as to where she found the money?"

"Yes. I do actually. She took out a loan on the apartment."

"She couldn't have. I didn't sign any paper. Unless she forged my signature…" I stare away from the camera and straight into Josh's face that has paled a little. "She forged my signature?"

"No."

"Then how—"

"Your mother put the deed in Ivy's name."

"In both our names."

He shakes his head. "Just in Ivy's."

"But Ivy told me—"

"She was trying to protect you."

My eyesight goes blurry. "Mom disowned me?"

He nods. "I'm sorry, Aster. You weren't supposed to find out."

"Of course not," I snap. "*Keep everything from Aster since she's too unstable.* I should have a T-shirt printed with that."

"That's not why we kept it from you."

"Whatever."

"Ivy didn't want to hurt you."

"I said, whatever." My tone is so shrill that Josh shifts in his seat.

"I should warn Ivy about the diamonds."

I think of the porcelain box with the gift I left her—the diamond that escaped the wax paper and landed in my bra. It had plopped on my bathroom tiles after I'd finished burying the others underneath the buttonbush shrub by our front door. "Oh…she's going to find out soon enough."

"Why? Did you leave them in the quilt?" he asks.

"Yes."

"Shit." The chair legs scrape against the cement floor as Josh pushes back from the table. "Why would you do that? How the fuck am I supposed to find them now?"

I lounge back and cross my arms. "Use your super badge power."

"This isn't a joke, Aster."

"Then you should really get going," I say.

He stands and heads toward the door. Before leaving, he glances back. I don't break. I don't tell him the truth because he doesn't deserve it, and neither does my sister. They're both liars.

Driscoll drags open the door of the cement box to let Josh out, and then holds it for me. "I don't got all day, Redd," he says, so I head out too.

My rubber soles flap over the linoleum floor like soggy fish tails.

In the dayroom, I spot Gill on one of the couches. She pats the spot next to her, and I drop down into it. Her hand crawls to mine. "Your skin's freezing."

I pull my fingers out of hers, pretending that my intention was to comb through my frizzy hair. I get a few inches off my scalp when a rope of knots hinders me. Since Gill's lips are still turned down, I pick up her hand and squeeze it. A crooked smile lights up the freckles on her face.

The show starts and I snap my attention to the TV screen. Dominic stands on top of a pyramid of trash. At least, that's what it looks like at first. He explains it's components of today's test. Each contestant will have to create a collection using ten pieces from the mound below him. And then he proceeds to explain that a collection isn't just a bunch of objects displayed next to each other, but a carefully thought-out continuum of pieces that are linked together by minute details.

He begins a countdown. The camera slides over the six contestants' faces. Kevin, whose bushy eyebrows are slanted over his high forehead, cracks his thick neck. Herrick, who's hooked the rucksack they've given each contestant on his forearm, is rubbing his hands together as though he's about to dive in. Chase looks calm whereas Maxine seems spooked by the mess. Lincoln scans the pile, eyes pinched in concentration. And then I see Ivy whose skin glows as though she's gotten a suntan.

The sound of a whistle rings out. The contestants fly off toward the pile. Some scale it, others circle it, sifting through the mess like a bunch of homeless people. Ivy comes up with a strand of pearls. She chucks them into her bag and keeps tilling the mess. Chase grabs a plastic sword. The commentators are going crazy keeping track of everyone's findings.

When the camera swings back to my sister, she's holding a bouquet of paper roses. She looks at it a second, but then pitches it back into the pile. The roses land a foot away from Maxine who grabs them like an eager bridesmaid. My sister lunges for something, as does Chase. The same thing: a gun.

One of the commentators chuckles. "A gun! Shouldn't they be fighting over that paper bouquet?" There's something about the way he says this that makes my ears prick up. What does he mean? Did something happen between Chase and Ivy?

Slowly, Chase relinquishes the weapon. A flicker of hesitation crosses Ivy's clear blue eyes, but it zips off her face as quickly as it appeared, and she shoves the pistol into her bag. As she turns away from him, her light green dress billows around her knees like an ocean wave. The camera shifts to Herrick who's collecting nails and wooden boards. He's even found a chalice-like cup. Lincoln's stockpiling tin cans and glass jars, and flattened cardboard. I can imagine her narrative: 'Containers Through the Ages,' or something of the sort. Kevin's bag bulges with large objects. He's found an old rusty pipe, which I wouldn't have touched with rubber gloves. He stuffs it into his rucksack. When the camera finally moves back to Ivy, she's studying a fur bunny attached to a magician hat.

She punches the bunny and it vanishes inside. She keeps it. The pile of crap is dwindling.

Ivy stares down at her feet, bends, and rises again clutching a broken umbrella. It goes into the bag, along with a brass trumpet. Then she runs toward an old liquor bottle tipped on its side on the outskirts of the thinning pile. Lincoln's hand is already arcing toward it, so Ivy dives to get it. Stunned, Lincoln quickens her gesture, but she's not quick enough. The bottle vanishes in the depths of my sister's bag.

"I was expecting a catfight," one of the commentators says, his deep voice rattling with excitement.

"No, you were *hoping* for one," a feminine voice answers.

The man chuckles as Ivy whirls away from a steaming Lincoln. I don't know how many items she still needs, but her bag looks like it's about to burst. She races toward one of the last three items. Only Chase, Lincoln, and Ivy are left scouring the floor. The others are all off to their mini galleries to begin arranging their loot. The camera returns to the center of the room, where my sister's unrolling a scroll. When her face lights up with a smile, and her feet carry her away to her own white box, a giddy breath puffs out of my mouth.

"Someone's excited," Gill says.

I think she's talking about Ivy, but she's watching our linked hands. I'm crushing her fingers. I let go.

"I don't mind," she says.

But *I* do, because there are other people around, and they're gawking and whispering things. I stand up and stretch. My body feels stiff. Then I pace the threadbare rug because they've gone to commercial break.

"Ladies," Sergeant Driscoll says. "Yard time."

Everyone grumbles as they stop whatever games they were playing and file out through the secure door that Giraffe-neck is holding open.

"But it's raining," Gill says.

"You won't melt, Firehead," Driscoll tells her. "Only sweet girls melt, which ain't your case."

Gill glares at him.

Giraffe-neck yells, "Hey, Redd, I'm not a door stop. Get your ass over here."

"No yard time for her. Commander's orders," Driscoll informs her.

Gill cocks an orange brow. Before she can ask why, Driscoll shoves her into the hallway.

Giraffe-neck lingers in the doorjamb. "Did you blow him?"

"Huh?"

"Kim told me the warden closed the door the other day. He usually never conducts a meeting without a guard present. Unless he's receiving special—"

"I didn't touch him," I tell her.

She eyes me a long time. "He's into that shit. Just so you know."

"Thanks for the warning."

"You still owe me."

"I know."

She lets the door swish shut behind her, leaving me with repugnant images of the warden. I think of his daughter, and how angelic she looked in that picture. If she found out about her father, it would break her heart.

The Masterpiecers' theme song erupts in the quiet room. The camera broadcasting the show lifts, as though attached to a drone—which it probably is—and films the six contestants milling around their mini-galleries from above. It looks like the Pac-Man-inspired video game I designed my first week of junior high. I'd helped Ivy out with hers—perhaps more than helped—and gotten in trouble for it: a visit to the principal's office and a low mark on my project.

Helping Ivy seems to bring me nothing but trouble.

TWENTY-SIX

Ivy

Kevin reminds me of a fairytale ogre, the sort who eats children for breakfast. Threatening and huge. We haven't talked yet. Not one word, not even hello. We avoided each other all afternoon. At some point, I even faked a headache to burrow in Brook's bedroom, which earned me a strange look from Chase. I don't know what he imagines. Even before what he told me about Brook and his ex, I wasn't interested in his brother. The only reason I wanted to go in the bedroom was to check my email. Of course, I couldn't tell him that.

When I'd stepped inside the bedroom, two things struck me. First that Brook or someone else had touched my clothes because I'd left them folded on the seat of the large armchair in the corner and they weren't folded anymore, and second, that he'd removed the tablet. I was too preoccupied with wondering if he suspected I'd used it, to worry much about him manipulating my clothes.

I feel something cold touch my lips, and realize it's the microphone. Dominic's holding it close to my mouth, waiting. "Ivy? Your collection?"

"The roaring twenties," I say.

He nods to egg me on.

"But it didn't start that way. When I found the pearl necklace and the top hat with the bunny, I thought about doing a collection around costumes. But then I realized I had more than just stage props…I had an era. The gun, the smoking pipe print—"

"For those of you who don't know, Magritte is a surrealistic painter, and surrealism started in the 1920s. This particular work—the original one—was painted in 1929," Dominic says. "So, Ivy, what would you name your collection?"

"A Time."

"Can't get more straight to the point," Dominic says. "Nicely done."

I inhale the praise. I'm lucky, really lucky, because my choice of the print was based on the popularity of pipes in the twenties. I had no clue when the surrealistic period started. Dominic has given me way more credit than I deserve.

"So, Chase, tell us about your collection," Dominic says.

"I built it around the Dutch painter, Rembrandt." He proceeds to explain how all the objects he gathered—from the horse figurine to the long brown feather—were featured in his paintings. Plus, he names each painting and explains the symbolism of the objects. Thankfully this competition isn't about knowledge. If it were, none of us would stand a chance to Chase.

The audience claps loudly for him—louder than they clapped for the rest of us. I bet they're rooting for him. When everyone falls quiet, Dominic moves to the last contestant, Kevin. His voice explodes out of the microphone and echoes through the cavernous stone lobby. His collection is about pipe dreams—illusions—thus the big rusty pipe, the paper bouquet that I thought Maxine had taken, and the magnifying glass. I hate to admit that it all makes sense. I so wish it hadn't.

After we've all defended our collections, we are dismissed until the evening show. Our assistants lead us back to the large staircase under dense waves of applause. My heart beats fast as I wonder how I did. I know that on TV, there's a running commentary, but we are not privy to it. As we reach the first-floor landing, the applause stops and a commotion erupts. It's followed by heavy footsteps on the stone stairs. Police officers dressed in plainclothes flash shiny badges as they jog up.

"Ivy Redd?" one of them barks.

The contestants and assistants part around me. I feel like I'm having that dream where I'm walking down Highway 31 in Kokomo, naked, while everyone is clothed, even the girls from the Hip-Hugger strip club.

A woman walks up to me. "I'm Detective Clancy. You need to come with us."

My mouth goes as dry as a sunbaked cornhusk. "Wh-why?"

"We need to ask you some questions."

"About what?"

"About your sister."

"What *about* my sister?" This time, my tone is a bit snappier.

"Do you really want us to discuss this in front of the cameras?" She gestures to Jeb and his crew whose devices are aimed on us.

"Just tell me if she's okay."

"Depends what you mean by okay."

"Physically?"

"Yes. Now, are you coming or do we have to cuff and drag you out of here?"

Although it's painfully embarrassing, I follow her and pretend everyone is not staring at me. As I start down the stairs, Dominic arrives. His neck is bright red, as must be the rest of his face underneath his thick layer of foundation.

"What in God's name is this about?" His usually suave voice is slightly shrill.

Detective Clancy sticks her hand on her very narrow hips. They're like man hips. "Nothing that concerns you or your show, Mister Bacci."

"With all due respect," he says, "Ivy is part of my show, so it does concern me."

"We have a few questions for your contestant regarding her sister's murder case. We'll have her back to you in no time."

I'm praying that Dominic will tell her that she has no jurisdiction here, but that would create a messier scene, so I place my hand on Dominic's forearm and put on a brave face. "It's okay, Mister Bacci. I'll get this over with quickly, in time for the announcement tonight." I turn to the detective. "I'll be back by then, right?"

She nods.

I let my hand drop and follow her across the lobby where the audience parts around me like the Red Sea. People whisper, point, gasp. It's just as shameful as the press conference. My heart is blasting against my ribcage, making my seafoam bodice vibrate. I pray no one can see it.

The early afternoon sun is blinding. I keep my eyes on it long enough to create a glare that erases the rest of the world around me. Blood gushes behind my eardrums, dimming the ambient clamor. The detective mutters something, but I don't hear her words. I doubt she's talking to me anyway. She opens the door of an unmarked vehicle and waits for me to settle in the backseat before slamming it shut and sinking into the front seat.

"Fucking move, people," yells the young guy with silver hair, slapping the steering wheel. He starts nosing the car through the crowd. Surprisingly, he doesn't roll anyone over. "I don't get this show," he adds, spinning the wheel so abruptly that I'm thrown against the door.

I gather the soft hem of my dress in my fingers and roll the material between my calloused thumb and forefinger. The softness reminds me of the rolls of cloth in Mom's locked drawer. While they dated, my father would gift her rolls of exotic fabric after each of his trips. She'd kept them all intact, never once cutting a strip to use in her quilts. Every time I'd visit her in the psychiatric hospital she'd been relocated to last spring, she'd ask me if I'd kept my promise not to tell Aster about them. She was afraid my twin would trash them out of spite for her. I don't think Aster would ever do such a thing, but what do I know? My sister's mind works in mysterious ways.

The precinct is teeming with visitors and cops and ringing phones. Detective Clancy takes the lead once inside and guides me toward an elevator. We exit on a high floor and head down a hallway of closed doors. She knocks on the one emblazoned with the number two, and then she pushes through and points me to a chair. While I sit, the silver-haired detective comes in with a folder tucked underneath his arm. He closes the door behind him and they both take a seat across the desk from me.

"So," Detective Clancy begins, clicking on a small device in the middle of the table. "This interview is being recorded. I'm Leah Clancy and this is my partner, Austin McEnvoy. Could you state your full name and date of birth?"

"Ivy Redd, born December 21st, 1996."

"Thank you. May we call you Ivy?"

I shrug.

She tips her head to the recording device on the table.

"Yes," I say.

"The date is August 25, 2016 and the time is 3:13 p.m. The interview is being conducted at the Midtown North Precinct in New York City. The purpose of your presence here today, Ivy, is to shed light on your involvement with the deceased mobster Troy Mann."

"My involvement?"

Detective Clancy holds up her finger. "One of your neighbors saw Mister Mann leave your apartment on the morning of August 17th. Could you tell us what he came to see you about?"

On cue, Austin flips open the folder. There's a picture of Troy and me standing by my open apartment door. I know exactly who took it: Mister Mancini, nosiest neighbor in all of Kokomo.

"He bought a quilt from me," I say.

"We'll give you a chance to explain yourself in a second, but first I'd like to state that this is an out-of-custody interview."

"Meaning?" I ask.

"Meaning you are not under arrest and you are free to leave anytime," she says.

"Like now?"

Austin gives me a challenging look. "We wouldn't advise you to leave now."

I narrow my eyes.

"You are entitled to free and legal representation—"

"I don't need a lawyer."

"But you are entitled to one."

"Great," I say.

"You don't have to confess to anything, but it will harm your defense if you willingly withhold or falsify information. Do you understand?"

"I do."

"Okay. So, with that in mind, if you decide not to answer a question today and that question later comes up in court, and you decide to answer the question then, you may be found liable of aiding the commission of a crime."

"I'm here of my own free will, am I not?" I snap.

Leah Clancy presses her pale lips together. They're practically the same shade as the rest of her skin, a sharp contrast to her dark brown hair and eyes. "Ivy, who is the man in the picture?"

"Troy Mann."

"So you knew him?" Austin asks, leaning back.

"*Knew* is a big word."

He taps the tip of his thick finger on the picture. "You're talking with him."

"Yeah. I am, but I didn't know him. He discovered me through the feature the Masterpiecers—"

"The Masterpiecers is the reality TV show Ivy is competing on," Leah states for the digital recorder. "Go on."

"He saw me on TV and tracked me down to purchase one of my quilts."

"Could you describe the quilt he purchased?"

"Why is that relevant?" I ask.

"Because we didn't find the quilt," Detective Clancy says.

"Maybe he sold it to someone else."

"Just describe it already," Austin says.

I glare at him. "The quilt represented two people kissing."

Thankfully, there's no flare of recognition on either detective's faces.

"How much did he pay for you for it?" Austin asks.

"That's confidential."

Detective Clancy eyes me in silence for a second, and then she says, "Then we'll have to subpoena your bank records."

"He gave me cash."

"Did you declare the sale?" Austin asks.

"I didn't have time to," I lie. Hell, I'm not going to tell the police I had no intention of paying taxes on it.

Austin snorts. "Sure."

"Ivy, did you know you were dealing with the mafia?" Detective Clancy asks.

"No."

"Yeah, right." Austin grunts and crosses his feet on the table.

"It's true. I had no idea."

"Your sister knew he was part of the mob. Said it in her testimony," Austin remarks.

"We don't tell each other everything."

"I still have trouble believing you didn't know who you were dealing with."

"Are you accusing me of something, Detective McEnvoy?"

"Not yet," he says.

Detective Clancy gives him a pointed stare. "Was your sister aware that you sold him a quilt?"

"No."

"We received an anonymous tip that your sister had a blanket on her lap the night of the murder. Could that be the quilt which you sold to Mister Mann?"

"She keeps one of my quilts with her in the car because her heater doesn't work."

"It was August!" Austin says.

"She's always cold."

"The Honda was searched and it wasn't in there," Detective Clancy says.

"Then maybe she took it out."

"You want to know what I think, Ivy?" Austin says. "I think you sold a quilt to Mister Mann, then once you found out he was part of the mob, you asked your sister to retrieve it so that you wouldn't be associated with him."

I try to suppress my increasing urge to punch him by folding my arms together. "I don't know how you treat your siblings, Mister McEnvoy, but I actually respect my sister. I wouldn't send her to do my dirty work. If I'd found out Mister Mann was part of the mafia, I would've attempted to contact him myself to cancel the transaction."

"*Attempted* to contact him?" Austin asks, tipping one of his eyebrows up.

"It's not like he left me a business card." I fix my gaze on the cigarette butt wedged in the sole of McEnvoy's work boot.

"Now, about the hit and run." Detective Clancy shuffles through the folder and takes out a picture of a dead body annotated in red pen. "Are you aware that according to the coroner, your sister hit Mister Mann, then proceeded to back up the car and roll over him?"

I swallow as a bitter taste fills my mouth. "No."

"Does your sister have a history of violence?" she asks.

"No." I shake my head. "She's not violent, but she's not always…there." I drop my voice on the last word, hoping it's so faint the recorder won't pick it up. If Aster ever hears what I think of her, it will break more than her heart. It will break *her*.

"What do you mean by that?" Detective Clancy asks.

"She suffers from mental illness," I murmur.

"What sort of mental illness?"

"Schizophrenia."

A wave of silence swells through the room. It hovers and finally comes crashing over me when McEnvoy asks, "Are you saying that your sister's actions on the night of August 17th could've been prompted by a bout of craziness?"

"No! That's not what I'm saying. Not at all."

"But you just said that your sister's not always," Austin continues, "what was the word you used? Oh, yes, *there*."

"He threatened her."

"No kidding. She tracked him all the way to where he was staying," he counters.

"Because she was trying to be a good Samaritan."

"Good Samaritans don't crush people under their car tires."

"He tried to strangle her. That must be in the police file. She had red marks on her neck."

Austin shrugs. "Could've done it to herself."

"She wouldn't do that."

"Are you sure?"

"Are we done here? Because I have to get back to the show." I make to get up.

"Whoa there, Ivy," McEnvoy says, "you didn't tell us where *you* were on the night of August 17th."

"Where *I* was?"

"What my colleague is asking is how do we know you're not the twin in the car?"

The blood drains from my face. "What?"

"You have motive. More motive than your sister."

"What?" I repeat, too stunned to think of anything else to say.

"We just want to check your alibi," Leah says.

"I was at home. Working."

"Anyone can attest to that?"

"I work alone, so no."

"So you have no alibi?" Austin states.

"I *have* an alibi. I just have no one to confirm it."

"That could prove problematic." He slips his feet off the table and plops his forearms on the metal surface.

"My sister confessed to the crime," I say.

"Perhaps she's covering for you so that you could go on that little show of yours."

My heart is pounding so loudly that it feels like it's trying to kick its way out of my ribcage. "I'd like a ride back to the museum now." When neither gets up, I repeat, "Now."

Detective Clancy holds up a finger to her lips. "In conclusion, Ivy Redd attests to not knowing Troy Mann was involved with the mafia. She also states to having sold him a quilt. And she says that Aster may not have been *herself* on the night of August 17th. Is this all correct, Ivy?"

"Yes."

"Okay. Thank you. The time is 3:25 p.m. and the day is August 25th. This was Leah Clancy and Austin McEnvoy." She presses down on a button to click off the recorder, then rises and leads me back down to the lobby and out of the police station.

The paparazzi haven't wasted a second to find out where I was taken. They probably followed the black sedan Dominic sent to fetch me. Danny, the driver with the tangled eyebrows, doesn't address me once during the ride back, but he does peek at me several times in his rearview mirror, disappointment and curiosity warring on his face. It's the same look everyone on the show gives me the second I step back into the museum, from Cara to the film crew.

As I get into the elevator, eyes cast downward to avoid the stares, a hand slides between the closing doors and presses them back open. And then Brook steps in and dismisses my assistant and the doors shut. When the elevator starts rising, he tugs the red emergency lever. It stops and the lights dim.

His Adam's apple bobs up and down, but he remains silent. Then his lips part and close, and then they part again.

"What?" I ask when I can no longer take it.

"Dominic's worried about you. He's worried you have a lot on your plate. Perhaps too much. He thinks that maybe you should…"

"Maybe I should what?"

His shadowy gaze drifts over the floor, then over the wall behind me, and finally perches on my face. "He thinks that maybe you should drop out." He speaks quickly, as if saying the words fast will dampen their sting.

"Drop out? Of the Masterpiecers? No…no way. I want to stay. I *need* to stay."

"Ivy, you're doing well, but—"

"But what?"

"But there's a lot to think about. Between the media, and Kevin, and your sister. You should see what's being written up in the newspapers."

I snort because it finally dawns on me where he's going with this. "I'm bringing the show bad press. Is that what you're getting at?"

"Well…not exactly."

I narrow my eyes.

He scrapes his hand through his perfect black hair. "Yes."

"Don't you know journalists love scandals?"

"I know that, but—"

"They don't intimidate me, Brook. And neither does Dominic. I'm sorry about the bad press, but I'm not leaving the show. This is my one chance. Maybe you don't understand because you've never had to worry about where your next meal came from, but I *can't* drop out. And I'll say this again however many times I need to, but I had *nothing* to do with Kevin's pictures." I shake my head, and my hair flutters against my bare shoulders. "You know, for a second there, when you cornered me, I thought you were going to ask me how I was doing. I thought you were worried about me. But I guess people like you, like Dominic, like Josephine, only worry about themselves."

"Don't say that," he says, stepping forward. He's close enough to touch me. Thankfully he doesn't. "I *am* worried about you. The situation sucks, Ivy. Really, it does."

"I'm still not leaving. If you want me out, you'll have to disqualify me."

From the regretful look he gives me, I realize that must be exactly what they're planning, and my mood, already soured by the precinct and the interview, spoils like bad milk.

"That wouldn't be fair," I say in a raspy voice.

Brook doesn't respond. The silence hangs heavily between us. It fills the small space like steam, thinning the breathable air.

"The public's vote counts for something," I add, mostly to reassure myself. "Now, can you please switch the elevator back on?"

His fingers hover over the lever. "Could Aster have had anything to do with Kevin's pictures?"

"I doubt it."

"But you're not sure? She's your sister—"

"If I remember correctly, you had no clue your brother entered the competition," I snap back.

He frowns, and it leaves a deep vertical groove between his dark eyebrows. "I did know. His girlfriend told me."

"The one you screwed?"

"You know about that?"

"Yeah."

After a long bout of silence, he says, "I have a great lawyer."

"Are you threatening me?"

His forehead smooths out. "I meant for your sister, Ivy."

"Oh."

"And he'd be free."

"Really?" Suspicion creeps into my brain. "Is he free even if I decide to stay on the show?"

"Yes."

"Does he work pro bono?"

"No. He's a friend."

"Why would you do that?"

"So you can forgive me for being disrespectful toward you."

"I don't know what to say."

"Just say yes, and I'll make the call."

His offer feels too good to be true, yet I find myself accepting. "Okay."

The elevator jerks to life and the lights snap back on, bright, blinding. Soon, the doors are opening. Brook brushes a strand of hair off my cheek and whispers that he's going to call his lawyer friend right away. I thank him in a muted voice before stiffly walking out, past Chase and Lincoln who are standing by the door of the makeup room, past the myriad of assistants and camera crew on their coffee break, past the tree-lined hallway, and into my tented safe haven.

TWENTY-SEVEN

I gaze at the television screen long after the afternoon test has ended, but I don't see anything.

"Male deodorant has a real fascinating effect on women," Driscoll says, tipping his head to the commercial on the television. "Want a whiff of my armpits, Redd?"

Mechanically, I look up at the guard. "I'm allergic to male stench."

His smile drops and so does his voice. "I forget. You're one of *them* now."

"One of them?" I ask.

"Lawn grazers."

"Huh?" When it dawns on me what he's inferring, I feel a sharp desire to slap him. I curl my fingers into fists against my stiff jumpsuit. "What is it you want, Sergeant?"

"What is it I want? Now let me see…a lightweight dome tent, a Harley Davidson, a set of fancy steak knives—"

"I mean with me. I doubt you came for small talk."

"You doubt right." He shifts on his spindly legs. "Turns out you're a popular girl, Redd. You got someone waiting for you in the visitation area."

I'm betting it's Josh. He probably made a U-turn on the freeway. "Officer Cooper?"

"Nope."

"It's not?"

"Just said it wasn't."

For a moment, I think it's Ivy, but she's in New York being questioned by some detectives.

"You better hurry. Fancy man like him probably has elsewhere to be."

"Fancy man? I don't know any fancy men."

"Quit stalling. I gotta go train the *yobwoc*."

I frown as I stand up and trail him to the door.

He glances back at me. "Gotta go explain that giving prisoners access to Internet on cell phones doesn't fly with me. You knew that, right, Redd? That you ain't allowed to ask guards for their phones?" As I walk past him, he adds in a low voice, "At least not for free?" He falls in stride with me. "In the future, if you ever need a phone, I got one." He pats his pant pocket, and then his hand crawls to his crotch, which he pats in turn.

Asshole, I think but don't say. My eyes must be pretty expressive though, because Driscoll's cocky grin dissolves. When he buzzes me into the attorney visitation area, a suit-clad man pushes his chair back, rises, and extends his hand. "Hi, Aster. I'm Dean Kane, your lawyer."

"My lawyer?"

"Yes."

His dark suit and pink tie held flat against his dress shirt by a gleaming gold bar makes him look too elegant to be state-appointed. His retainer alone must equal what I make in a year.

Sure enough, he adds, "You're my pro bono case of the year." Then he props his briefcase on the table and gestures toward the chair opposite him.

"So"—he takes out a folder—"I familiarized myself with your case, Aster. You're being charged with first-degree murder for running over—"

"First-degree murder?" I yelp. "It was self-defense."

"You hit a man, *then* you ran him over. You're facing forty years to life imprisonment."

"What?" I pinch the skin on my arm to make sure I'm awake. Unfortunately, I am. "But he threatened me."

"That'll be the base of our defense. But there are aggravating circumstances that aren't going to work in our favor. For one, your psych report." He takes out a paper from the file. "It says here you were diagnosed with schizophrenia at the age of twelve and that your condition has progressively worsened."

I feel like I've been punched…hard. Spasms erupt in my extremities and then move to my muscles…to my teeth…to my bones.

He shuts the file. "Also, a witness informed me that you took something from the crime scene, which gives you motive for the assault."

"A…A witness?"

"Yes."

I choke on my saliva, which makes me cough.

Dean nods. "What was worth killing a man for?"

I blanch.

He leans across the table. "I'm on your side, Aster."

"I didn't take anything."

"Did you *not* hear me say I was on your side?" When I keep quiet, he drums his fingers on the table. His large gold pinkie ring draws my attention. I try to make out the insignia. Suddenly, he stops tapping and grumbles loudly. "Look, I have several other cases I need to oversee. Either you cooperate and give me something I can work with, or I'll leave you to some newbie public defender who'll ensure that the only way you leave this place is in a casket. Now, I strongly suggest option number one as I've never lost a case in the past, and without me, judging from your file, you're not getting out of here alive."

I don't want to die. And I don't want to stay in here forever. "My sister's quilt."

It takes him a second to register that I'm speaking about the case. "What did you do with the quilt?"

"I destroyed it."

"Really?"

"Yes."

"So it's not the quilt that your sister auctioned on the Masterpiecers?"

"No."

"Did you tell anyone else about the quilt?"

"Just—No."

"Just whom?"

"Just a friend," I say.

"Which friend?"

"Why do you need to know that?"

"To make sure they don't go telling anyone else that you took a quilt from a dead man."

"He won't say anything."

"And how would you know that?"

"Because I trust him."

"From now on, you shouldn't trust anyone but me. And you shouldn't talk to anyone else. Okay?" Dean asks.

"Okay."

"Was there anything else in the bag?"

"No." I bite my lip. "Why did the cops interview my sister?"

"You're changing the subject."

"Please…I need to know."

"They wanted to make sure she wasn't the one behind the wheel of the Honda."

"Huh?"

He sighs. "That she wasn't the one who ran Troy Mann over."

"Of course she wasn't! It was me in the car."

"Don't worry, she told them that. She also told them about your affliction."

"My what?"

"The schizophrenia."

I bite down on my tongue to avoid sobbing or screaming—whichever comes first. "She told the detectives I was crazy?"

"Yes, but that'll work in our favor. It'll explain why you ran him over *after* you rammed into him. You'll get sent to an institution."

"I'm not crazy."

He eyes me in silence as he gets up and tucks the file back into his fancy leather briefcase. "Would you rather stay here?"

"No, but—"

"Then make it work, and I'll make it work."

"How am I supposed to make it work?"

He swoops down and drops his voice. "Act like your mother used to."

"You mean *does*. She's still nuts."

His lips perk into a bright smile. "You're a quick study."

I'm not sure what he means, but don't have time to ask as he's already standing and knuckling the door for the guard to open it. "Before I forget, I found out who was behind those doctored photos of the contestant."

"Who?"

"I'll tell you as soon as I inform Mister Martin," he says, before flying down the hallway, the bottom of his pink tie flapping against his shiny belt buckle.

TWENTY-EIGHT

While prepping me for the evening ceremony, Amy doesn't dare look straight into my eyes, but Leila does. Her kohl-lined gaze is blacker than usual, and tighter. She's still mad at me. When Amy leaves to gather more pins, she says, "You're throwing everything away."

"I'm not throwing anything away."

"Oh, come on, Ivy. You're all broken and hopeless. I can feel it. I can see it. And if I can see it, I know that you can too. Snap out of it."

"Snap out of it? My life outside these walls is crumbling and you're telling me to snap out of it?"

"Yes."

"You have *no* idea what it feels like to be trampled by the world, scrutinized by everyone. No idea!" My voice trembles. "So don't you dare tell me to snap out of it!"

Leila's face shutters up just as Amy returns. Her head swings from Leila to me. She can tell something has gone down, but thankfully, she doesn't get involved.

Leila undoes the black apron tied around her waist and sticks it on the counter in front of me. "My hand's cramping," she says. "I'll see you tomorrow."

"But—" Amy's mouth is gaping.

Leila's already gone.

"But—she—half your face," Amy stutters.

"Are you done with my hair?" I ask in a toneless voice.

"Almost." Her hands tremble as she sticks a bunch more pins in. "Um…do you want me to get another makeup artist? I'm sure—"

"Don't bother. I'll do it myself."

As she packs up her tools, I take the black liner and some violet powder, and finish what Leila started. One of my eyes looks smaller than the other, but I don't care. I just want to get this night over with. I toss the brushes and pencils onto the black apron and walk into the dressing room just as Maxine and Lincoln wiggle into their outfits.

"Could these be any shorter?" Maxine asks, attempting to tug the skirt on her cocktail waitress-like dress further down.

"At least we have tights on," Lincoln says, her green-gold eyes on me as I pull my outfit off the hanger.

"They're so sheer," Maxine complains. "Everyone will see my cellulite."

"Oh, stop it," Lincoln says. "You don't have any."

"I do. Look." Maxine pinches the back of her thighs.

The discussion makes me want to hit something. How can they talk about stupid butt dimples in front of me? My sister's in a correctional facility for killing a man, and I'm being accused of setting up a fucking contestant.

"Oh…well," Maxine says with a sigh. As she turns away from the mirror, she notices me. "I'm sorry about your sister."

"Sorry about what?" I ask.

Maxine's face colors. "Oh…uh…well, Kevin…he uh, told us what's going on."

"What did he say that makes you *sorry about my sister*?"

"Um…just that she…that the man…that she's being charged with first-degree murder."

"You shouldn't believe everything you hear," I tell her.

"I'm sorry, Ivy. I didn't mean—"

I pull off my bathrobe and tug on the tight satin number. "Just drop it, okay?"

She nods a great many times before finally rushing out of the dressing room.

"So…what's up between you and Brook?" Lincoln asks. They brushed her blonde hair to one side like a fifties actress and strapped a crawling diamond earring to the ridge of her exposed ear.

"Why don't you ask Kevin? He seems to know everything around here," I say as I yank on smoke-colored tights.

"Funny"—she snorts—"seriously though, you were in that elevator a long time."

"How do you know how long I was in there?"

"Because your assistant came huffing and puffing up the stairs, carping into her mouthpiece about Mister Jackson not letting her do her job. So"—she bats her eyelashes—"what happened?"

"He told me I should quit the show and I told him to go screw himself." I leave out the part about the lawyer.

"No you didn't."

"Not in those exact words, but yeah, I did."

"It would've been pretty cool if you'd forfeited."

I flip her the middle finger, which makes her laugh.

"You know, I'm pretty sure that if we weren't competing against each other, we'd get along well, you and I."

I slide my feet into a pair of pointy yellow heels, and stand up. "I guess we'll never know."

Lincoln's looking at my charcoal dress without really looking at it. "Kevin freaks me out," she says suddenly. "The way he looks at us...like we're part of the Taliban. Ever since he arrived, the atmosphere's changed. His tent is right in front of mine, and last night, I swear I could hear him pace around his room. And then outside on the grass, there was definitely noise. I don't feel safe. That's what I was telling Chase this afternoon."

"And what did Chase say?"

"He told me to come and sleep in his room if I needed to."

"How gallant of him," I say mockingly.

She cocks her head to the side. "Are you jealous?"

"Jealous? No."

"You sounded jealous."

"Well, I'm not. I don't care about Chase."

"He cares about you, you know?"

"Yeah right," I say, heading toward the curtain.

"He was pissed when he saw you in the elevator with Brook."

A little bit of warmth seeps through the armor I've wrapped around my body since the interrogation. But then I remind myself that Chase basically propositioned Lincoln. "If you do sleep in his room, keep the noise down."

She smiles. "I'll try my best."

I walk out, banishing thoughts of Lincoln and Chase together, but some still creep into my mind during the evening segment. I'm so distracted that I almost clap when Dominic announces that Maxine received the lowest score. To prevent any further mishaps, I tuck my hands together until we are released—which doesn't come soon enough.

"We need a bottle of champagne," Lincoln announces once we've been returned to our tent.

"You're underage," one of the waiters tells her.

"No shit, Sherlock. The champagne's not for me," Lincoln says.

"Are you staying for dinner or are you leaving right away?" Herrick asks.

Maxine sniffles. "I...I..."

Lincoln, who has her arm draped over Maxine's shoulder, squeezes her tightly. I strongly believe that her amiability and exuberance come from the fact that she hasn't been kicked off the show. "She'll stay for dinner."

"I don't...don't want to...to eat," Maxine sobs.

I'm not cruel. I feel bad for her. Maxine is genuinely nice...annoyingly nice. But I'm not that surprised she's leaving. To be honest, I'm more surprised she's made it this far.

"You don't look too shook up to see her go," Chase says quietly, sidling up next to me against the back of the couch.

The scent of pine needles is everywhere. "I thought I was the one who would get voted off the show, so call me selfish, but I'm relieved." With my heels on, I'm not far off from his height.

"Hey, Jackson, considering your birthday's in two days, here," Herrick says, holding out a glass of champagne.

"Considering there's a camera right there"—Chase tips his head toward the ceiling—"I'll pass."

"Give it here," Lincoln says, sticking it in Maxine's free hand.

"Bottoms up, Daisy," she says with a wink.

Maxine quits sniffling long enough to smile. Then she tips the glass up and finishes it off in four long swallows. Lincoln seizes it from her fingers and holds it out for a refill. The waiter obliges. She hands it back to Maxine, who guzzles it down. This time, swiping her mouth with the back of her hand, Maxine asks for a refill herself. Herrick and Lincoln begin chanting her name. She shoots back the glass.

"Dinner's ready," another waiter announces.

I press off the back of the couch and take a seat along with everyone else. Maxine's eyes are all shiny and her nose is tinged red. At the table, she drinks another two glasses.

"Better slow down, there, G.I. Jane," Herrick says, "or you're going to pass out before the main course."

Maxine breaks out into an uncontrollable fit of giggles.

"That's the plan," Lincoln says. "Isn't it, Maxine?"

She bobs her head and lifts her glass. "Screw you, Dominic!" She tips her head back and drinks. "Screw you, Josephine!" She takes another sip. "Screw you, Brook!" She's about to take another sip when she starts laughing hysterically. "Sorry, Chase."

"Oh. I don't mind. I'll even drink to that." He raises his glass of water. The ice cubes clink inside.

I don't cheer, because I don't want to get in trouble. The cameras might not pick up sound, but the waiters might relate our dinner chat.

At some point, the conversation switches to actual screwing. We get way too many details on Herrick and Maxine's personal lives. Kevin squirms in his chair, which looks odd for someone of his size.

"What about you, Kev?" Herrick suddenly asks.

He goes stiff as a log. "Been with one woman only."

"You never strayed while you were in Afghanistan?" Herrick continues.

"No. Never."

Herrick combs his fingers through his pompadour. "That's pretty impressive. I don't think I've ever met a monogamous person. Unless I'm in the presence of two more…Chase? Ivy?"

"Hey! You forgot me," Lincoln says, sticking out her bottom lip.

"Oh, come on, honey, you're so *not* monogamous."

Her pout turns into a smile. "Fine. You got me. Monogamy's boring." She suddenly whips her gaze toward Kevin. "To me," she adds. "Monogamy's boring to me. But maybe it's because I haven't met the right person like you have."

He stares at her, but doesn't react, which makes her feline eyes grow wide in apprehension. A stiff awkwardness ensues. Even Maxine seems sobered up by it.

"I think there's no right or wrong relationship," Chase says, which loosens the tension.

Herrick, who's had about half a bottle of champagne, asks, "What's your style, Jackson? Faithful or unfaithful?"

"Faithful," he says without hesitation.

For some reason, the rope of muscles in Kevin's shoulders loosens, as though being in the presence of a fellow monogamist is comforting.

"And you, Ivy?" Herrick asks.

"Faithful."

Chase studies me as he usually does, while Kevin snorts.

"What?" I ask him.

"You don't look the type. I know women and—"

"You know women?" I ask. "I think you stand to be corrected. You know *a* woman, Kevin. *One.* Your wife. I don't know what she's like and I don't really care. But don't go assuming you know what I'm like."

Kevin leans his beefy forearms on the white glass tabletop. "I know more about you than you think. My lawyer's connected. Did you know he's originally from Kokomo?"

"A lot of people are from Kokomo," I say, leaning my own forearms across the table. "So if you have something to say to me, say it." My voice is strong, but the rest of me isn't. Each one of my nerves feels like it's toppling over the next one, like a long line of dominoes.

"My lawyer told me not to engage with you."

"Did he tell you I bite?"

His eyes turn a forbidding shade of brown. "You'll know soon what he told me."

"It's my last night with all of you. Can we talk about something else?" Maxine asks, staring at me, pupils throbbing.

"Yes, let's," Herrick says. "I say we talk about me again."

"I say we don't," Lincoln answers.

I stand up. "I'm sorry, Maxine, but I've had a really long day. I think I'm going to try to get some sleep."

"Oh. Okay."

She looks so disappointed that for a second, I reconsider, but then I see Kevin and my resolve strengthens.

"Will you give me your phone number?" she asks.

"You want my number?"

"Yes. I want your number," she says. She stands up on wobbly legs and stumbles toward me like a newly birthed foal. "I want to throw a party for the winner after the show's over." She grabs a pen and notecard off the living room table, and gives them to me.

I write down my number, and then, before I can get away, she locks me in a big hug. I go stiff, but it doesn't bother Maxine.

"Good luck, Ivy," she says, patting my back, and then she adds in a low voice —I'm surprised she can exert that much control over her vocal cords—"You're going to win. I can feel it."

I can't, but I hope she's right.

TWENTY-NINE

"Inmate Redd, out of your bunk. It's breakfast time," Giraffe-neck yells from my doorway.

At 7 a.m. sharp, all the cell gates open and all the lights snap on.

"I don't want breakfast," I say, head buried in a new book I borrowed from the prison library.

"No breakfast, no show."

"I don't want to see the show." My sister told the cops I was crazy, so I'm snubbing her stupid show.

The guard stays quiet for a long second. "I still get my money, Redd, whether you watch it or not. Understood?"

I nod. God, will she ever stop talking about her money?

"And don't think you get to lounge around your cell, reading all day. If you don't go watch the show, I'll line up some chores for you."

"Sure."

She just stands there, with this idiotic look on her face. "I'll pick you up in an hour, then," she says, finally leaving.

I'm grateful to have another hour to mope around and dive back into my book. It's about a mother who loses her child. It's nice to know that I'm not alone. Especially these days, when I feel more alone than ever. Part of me wishes I could call Ivy, ask her why she told the cops I was crazy. I've never gone this long without hearing her voice, and I don't mean her voice on TV, I mean her voice in my ear. They're not the same voices.

After several minutes, I close the book and toss it at my feet. I can't concentrate on anything. My brain is filled with my sister, as is my heart. They say twins are two halves of a person, but that's not true. We are not two halves. She's a whole person and I am her shadow, and a shadow disappears when there's no body left to silhouette.

"There you are." Gill treads into my cell.

I sigh. "Here I am."

She frowns at my sigh, but then she gets sidetracked by the book at my feet. She picks it up and studies the cover. Before she can read the summary on the back, I roll myself up and yank it out of her hands.

"You want kids?" she asks.

Too late. "Maybe."

"You'll make a good mother."

"Doubt it. Anyway I'm stuck here indefinitely. Haven't you heard that they upgraded my charge to first-degree murder?"

"I didn't hear."

"Well, they did." Those gates I entered eight days ago feel like they're on another continent. I stick the book underneath my mattress instead of underneath my pillow so that Cheyenne doesn't find it. "What's Cheyenne up to these days?"

"I don't know. You want me to find out?"

"Can you?"

"I can do anything, Aster. Especially for you." She steps closer to me. My gaze darts around looking for something to do…anything. She takes another step and wraps her small hands around my neck and then leans in. I just manage to swing my face away. Her mouth pecks my cheek.

"I-I can't, Gill." I shrug her hands off. "I'm not stable, emotionally."

Her freckled cheeks glow red.

If I don't find a solid excuse, I'm going to have to watch my back around both her *and* Cheyenne. "I just lost a baby," I blurt out.

The flush recedes from her cheeks. "Oh. I didn't know. I'm sorry." She sits down on my bed and looks up at me. "I like children. I'd like to have one someday. Well, not me, but I'd like for my partner to carry them. But I got thirty years, Aster. I served two, and I'm thirty-seven. When I'm out, I'll be sixty-five."

"Sixty-five-year-olds can still be mothers. Especially if you don't carry the baby."

"Out there"—she points at the brick wall—"normal women…they'll be scared of me. They won't understand me like the people in here do. I'll probably end up homeless with no job. Who wants to hire a woman in her sixties who did time behind bars?"

Tears snake down her pale cheeks, so many of them that I sit on the bed next to her and drape my arm around her shoulders. She cries for a long time. When she stops, my collar is soaked.

"You're so good. You're an angel," she whispers. "That's what I thought that first day you walked in. That you had to be an angel because I'd never seen a person with such a kind, beautiful face."

"It must have been my hair. I was told the frizz makes it look like a halo."

She laughs, but then she gets up, grabs my hand, and tugs me off the bed. "I have an idea."

"I feel I'm not going to like it."

"You will! Trust me." She pulls me into the cell she shares with two other bunkmates. Underneath her bed, she has a cardboard box filled with an assortment of knickknacks, mostly hair products and creams and makeup.

"You could open a beauty parlor."

"How do you think I make a couple bucks around here?" she asks. "Here, sit on the floor."

"I don't have any money."

"Your money's no good with me."

"Gill—"

"Just sit."

Biting my lip, I lower myself to the floor and cross my legs. She takes a fine-tooth comb out of the box.

"You'll never get that through," I warn her.

"Will you please let me do my job?"

I shut up and let her work on me because after refusing her kiss, I can't refuse her offer.

An hour or so later, Giraffe-neck returns. "What do we have here? Cloning yourself, Firehead?"

Gill doesn't answer, much too preoccupied with finishing off the sections of hair she hasn't twisted and teased into dreads yet.

"Redd, get your ass up. Chacha needs you in the kitchen."

"I'll finish later," Gill says. "Don't take the rubber bands out okay? You need to keep them in until the dreads mature."

"Redd?" Giraffe-neck taps her foot. "Now."

I walk out past her.

"Firehead, yard time. It's supposed to rain again, so we're taking you out early."

It sounds like she's talking to a dog. That must not be too far from what she thinks of us.

THIRTY

Ivy

A day on the beach. That's today's competition or at least that's where it will take place.

"On Fire Island, our five remaining contestants will have to gather anything and everything they can find to create a work of art. This will test their creativity and their resourcefulness." He grins so widely that his teeth look blinding in the bright camera lights. "Although we encourage them to take their time, it would be nice if they were finished with their pieces before the evening celebrations." Dominic rubs his palms together. "We've got a wonderful, wonderful evening in store for you."

My head feels like a geyser, filled with vapor and about to blow because I had a shit night. Barely slept. And when I did manage to fall asleep, I heard the zipper of my tent lift, but when I clicked my bedside lamp on, it was shut, so I must have dreamt it.

"Without further ado, we will head out. Don't forget your hats and sunscreen. The weatherman said it will be hot. Low nineties. This ought to be good," he says, rubbing his hands together. "See all of you on the beach in two hours."

As we walk out of the lobby toward the black minivan that's parked in front of the museum, Lincoln leans in, "Sit next to me on the bus? I have something to tell you."

I nod and put on the sunglasses the show has lent me. They're big and black, with gold branches and large rims, exactly what I need to cover up the red tinge of my eyes and the dark circles Leila did a sloppy job concealing. When she showed up this morning, I was surprised, but then again, she'd be out of a job if she hadn't.

"Let's go to the back," Lincoln says, sticking her sunglasses on top of her head.

Kevin's sitting all the way in the front, right behind the driver. Chase and Herrick are on either side of the middle aisle, which leaves the backseat vacant.

As we settle down, she says, "Maxine would've loved this test. I wish she were still here." She drops her voice, "Instead of *him.*"

"So what did you have to tell me?"

Her green-gold eyes, that look more green than gold in the sunlight, glisten. "Last night…I went to sleep in Chase's room."

I stiffen, which makes a small smile cock her lips up.

"Anyway, I went to sleep there with Maxine who was drunk as shit. We were going to sleep together in her room, but she was freaking out about you-know-who"—she tips her head toward Kevin—"so we asked Chase if we could squeeze in next to him." She toys with the fringes of her see-through beach dress. "He gave us his bed and slept on the rug."

"How nice of him."

She releases the fringes. With her voice barely above a whisper, she says, "Guess who was out on a midnight stroll?"

Goose bumps scurry over my bare arms.

"He was right outside your tent," she whispers. "Chase went out and asked what he was doing. He pretended he was sleepwalking." She doesn't yell this, but it feels like she does. I can hear her words echo inside my skull, adding to the throbbing ache.

"Chase is going to talk to Brook about getting a camera installed in the hallway. One that picks up sound," she adds in a low whisper.

"Is he going to tell him why?"

She nods.

After a beat, I ask, "Do you think he was coming for me?"

She raises her shoulders. "Honestly, I have no clue. He seems nuts enough to do that. Herrick was telling me he has PTSD."

My skin feels clammy. I press the blades of the air vent overhead shut, even though, deep down, I know the A/C isn't to blame.

"Last night he said he had stuff on you. Does he?"

I think of the quilt Troy Mann bought from me. "We all have skeletons in our closet, don't we?"

"I don't."

"Really?"

"I smoked pot. Still do sometimes. But that's the worst drug I ever used 'cause I don't want to end up like the low-lives who brought me into this world. Why do you think I'm on this show?"

Perhaps I misjudged Lincoln.

Her gaze settles on the bridge we're crossing to reach Long Island.

"How did you get into chalk drawings?" I ask her.

"By accident. One of the guys I was dating—he was a teacher—decorated the wall of his kitchen with blackboard paint. One night, we smoked up a lot, and I mean a lot. So much that by the time we tried to have sex, he passed out on me. I couldn't sleep, so I got out of bed and grabbed a piece of chalk from the kitchen counter and drew…all night."

"What did you draw?"

"A landscape with swirly clouds and swirly hills and a swirly sun. A little like Van Gogh. I curled up in front of it, thinking it was the most beautiful thing in the world."

"Let me guess…when you woke up the next day, you thought it was horrible."

She shakes her head and her ponytail swishes. "No. I still thought it was beautiful, but I had no recollection of having done it. I wanted to erase everything and see if my hands could really master chalk like that, but my boyfriend forbade me to touch it. He told me to go down in the courtyard behind the apartment complex and train there."

"Under the influence?"

She smiles. "If you call coffee an influence, then yes. But no weed this time. I needed to see if I could really do it."

"And?"

"And a few of the people who lived in the building came down and sat with me while I worked. This dude practiced his saxophone and this old lady made me a sandwich."

"How did your drawing turn out?"

She grimaces. "Eh. Wasn't of the caliber of the night before. But it was good enough to make me go down and practice every morning for a month. Some of my boyfriend's students came to film me. They were working on a documentary for school. You saw some of the footage on the first night."

"Picasso's *Demoiselles d'Avignon*?"

"Yup. That was my best one. That was the day my boyfriend told me to sign up for the competition." She gets this distant gleam in her eyes.

"Are you still together?" I venture.

"Nah."

"Why'd you break up?"

"Life."

"That's vague."

Her cheek dimples. She's probably chewing on the inside of it. I do that sometimes when I'm sewing. "He wasn't ambitious like I was. It drove a wedge between us. Plus, as I said last night, I'm not really into monogamy and he was," she says with a smile. "But it ended well. We're still friends."

"You're lucky."

"Lucky?" she asks, lifting a dark brow. The contrast with her light hair makes her eyes really pop.

"To have stayed friends."

"You didn't stay friends with your exes?"

"I only had one. And no."

"I'd ask if you want to talk about it, but you don't seem like the sort of girl who likes to share."

"There's nothing worth sharing. I was fourteen; he was fifteen. All we ever did was kiss and hold hands."

"You're a virgin?" she basically shouts.

Widening my eyes, I shush her, but unfortunately it's too late. From the chuckle that escapes Herrick's mouth, I know he heard Lincoln, which surely means that everyone in the van is now aware of my…inexperience.

THIRTY-ONE

In the middle of scouring an enormous soup pot with a stainless steel scrubby, I see it! That thing in the warden's picture that called out to me. I see it so clearly that the pot, which I'd tipped to the side to conquer the burned bits, slips from my wet hands. It makes a loud banging noise against the sink.

"Hey! Watch it! I'm already half-deaf," Chacha says. She sticks her index fingers in her ears and rotates them as though trying to clear the wax. "Now my head is going to be ringing all day."

"Sorry." I tip the pot back on its side and scrub it with renewed vigor. When it's clean enough to reflect my face, I set it to dry and wash the metal prep counters. An entire layer of grease comes off. I would have found that revolting if I hadn't been so rattled by my discovery.

"Lunch is ready so I go," she says. "I like to shower after I cook. You take the ice off the shelves, okay?" She points to the steel door in the middle of the white ceramic wall.

I nod, but then ask, "Isn't shower time before dinner?"

"You're not the only one with privileges, Redd. Stick around long enough here, and you get special treatment. Been here twelve years." She takes off her apron and hangs it on a hook. "Beat that."

Before she leaves, I ask her, "Where's the ice pick?"

She smiles. She's missing her left canine. "No ice pick. That's a weapon."

"Don't you use knives?"

"Yeah, but only when a guard's around. They're locked up if not."

"Well, how am I supposed to de-ice the freezer then?"

She claws at the air between us like a rabid cat. She even hisses. "Use your nails, Redd." She laughs at my shocked face, and keeps cackling long after she's vanished from sight.

I stare down at my nails, which are soft from the warm tap water and chipped from the metal sponge. I won't have any left by the end of this chore. I'm not vain or anything, but ripped and bleeding nails hurt. I crush them into my hand at the memory of the dark closet and the wooden door I clawed at for hours. *And Ivy doesn't get why I despise our mother.*

I look around for something to use and my gaze falls on the steel scrub. I pick it up and walk to the freezer door, which I prop open with a rollaway metal island. I lock the wheels in place, turn on the lights, and step in. The coolness feels divine against my balmy skin. It must be close to ninety degrees in the kitchen, what with the stove and halogen bulbs on.

There are four rows of shelves, each coated with several inches of snow-like ice. I start by taking down all the packages and boxes from the shelves before getting around to scrubbing. After several grueling minutes, the only thing I've managed is to scrape off a few flurries. I return to the kitchen, check around for something else, anything else. When I spot the clean soup pot, I get an idea—not brilliant but worth trying.

I fill it with water and heat it on the stove. Once it simmers, I bring it into the freezer and splash the shelf. The water instantly melts the ice. It's magical. I'm so proud of my ingenuity, that I head back out and repeat the process. After thirty minutes, half of the freezer is defrosted. For a proud second, I gape at my handiwork, but then my pride vaporizes when the lights turn off and the door bangs shut. I race toward it and grope for the indoor latch—because I assume there is one. The second my fingers close over it, I expel a deep breath. I twist it and push against the door, but it doesn't budge. I do it again. Still nothing. Again. Nothing. And again. Nothing. The latch is broken.

I yell at the top of my lungs, hoping someone, anyone will hear me, but it's midmorning and everyone's still out in the yard. I slam my fists against the door out of frustration and then stick my forehead against it and focus on breathing.

I need to stay calm. Chacha will be back soon. She's only taking a shower. How long can a shower last? And then there's lunch to be served. I'll be here for an hour max, maybe two. I can't freeze to death in that amount of time...*can I?* How long was I at the park that day after I lost the baby? It was really cold too. I didn't die however deeply I wished to.

I lower my sleeves, find a spot on the floor still warmed by the boiling water and hook my arms around my knees to conserve energy. But it's a mistake, because soon the bottom of my pants is soaking wet and cold. The dampness has even penetrated my underwear, all the way to my skin.

I start humming that song Ivy hums to me. I don't know how many times I sing it, but my teeth are clattering. I clamp my mouth shut before the enamel shatters. Suddenly, I hear voices outside and I leap from my spot on the floor. I pummel the door and scream. My heart pounds in time with my fists. I'm not going to freeze to death after all.

But the door doesn't open. And no one answers me. Or rather there is an answer to my loud plea—laughter. Not the cackling sort. It's a laugh I've never heard before, yet I know exactly whom it belongs to.

Cheyenne.

Suddenly, the rage I felt the night she soiled my pillow fires through me and I shake. I'm going to kill her. I scream until my voice becomes hoarse, and still I yell. I don't tremble anymore. To say the truth, I'm so angry that I don't feel the cold. I don't feel much of anything except the thrashing in my ribcage. My heart's going to fracture one of my ribs if I don't calm down.

I hear more noise outside. I pound my fists harder and scream louder, but my voice no longer carries much sound and my arms are tired and frozen. My hope dissolves as quickly as the ice earlier. I walk to the back of the freezer, pick up the soup pot, and throw it against the door. It makes a loud clatter. Someone must have heard that. Still no one comes.

The noise beyond the door is deafening. It's lunchtime, which means that I've been in here for at least two hours. I pick up the soup pot and throw it again. Uselessly, it clangs to the floor. I try to do it a third time, but my arms are too stiff and it crashes before reaching the door. It still makes noise though. So I do it again. I lift it, drop it, lift it, drop it. Over and over, until my arms feel like they're about to rip from their sockets.

I sink down and tug my arms through my sleeves to rest them against my bare skin. I need to keep my extremities warm. For the first time in my life, I'm thankful for the amount of hair on my head. I curl my toes, in and out. At some point they stop moving. I try to jiggle my legs, but they feel heavy…so heavy.

Maybe I should get up and walk to keep my body temperature up, but then I'll breathe a lot and might deplete the air of oxygen. I try to get up anyway, but I stumble. I can't lift my heavy, rigid body off the cold, steel floor…and I'm so tired…my lids feel like iron shutters…my forehead tingles…everything's very black…black like molasses…thick like molasses…shiny like molasses…sticky like…

THIRTY-TWO

Ivy

The beach is a wide strip of creamy sand bordered on one side by the Atlantic Ocean and on the other by tufts of long, wild grass. Even though the sky is light, the sea is deep cobalt, the same shade as one of the fabric rolls in Mom's secret drawer. Small waves lap the shore, dragging along broken shells, slimy algae, pale rocks, and sticks of all sizes. It's wild and briny—not the sort of beach I dream about with turquoise water and white sand—but it's a beach nonetheless. As I watch the landscape with its swooping, loud gulls, an idea for a quilt flourishes in my mind. I snap my lids to store the image in the depth of my imagination.

The show has set up a row of striped tents that resemble vintage popcorn boxes to house port-o-potties and changing rooms. Further down the beach, there is a pleated organza big top underneath which several long wooden tables are being decorated with copper pots overflowing with rosemary and lavender, and ceramic bowls piled high with yellow lemons. Acoustic music trickles out of speakers. It mirrors the landscape, sounding like breaking waves and the balmy breeze.

Our assistants come toward us to take our shoes and spray us with sunscreen. Then they hand us the mesh bags we used yesterday and lead us to the cleared spaces on the sand destined for our works of art.

The camera crew is in place. They wait for Dominic's signal to begin taping. In front of Dominic, amidst the packed crowd, I spot the star-maker, Delancey. In spite of the sweltering heat, he's wearing a white pin-stripe suit with shortened pant legs. I haven't seen him since the first day, but I bet he's been here all along, meandering around us like the rest of the audience. To say the truth, I've been so focused on competing that I've barely looked at anyone. I scan the faces surrounding us. Some look vaguely familiar—either from the silver screen or from the tabloids.

A photographer has his camera ready on a tripod. It takes me a second to recognize Patrick Veingarten. He waits for Dominic's signal like everyone else. It comes in the form of a launching of white helium balloons. There are five of them just like there are five of us. I tip my face up and watch them sail away, chalky dots against the bright blue.

I hoist my bag onto my shoulder and set out. I'm still not sure what I'm going to make, but I know something will catch my eye and jumpstart my creative juices. I tug my fingers through the swaying tall grass that looks bluish-lilac up close. I break off a piece and inspect its elasticity and strength by tying a knot. It's sturdy, so I grab a bunch and place them into my bag. I spot Kevin not far from me. He's pulling out bundles of the grass, so many handfuls that his piece will surely consist of only that, which spurs me to find some other material to use.

I walk further away from the water line, kicking branches and twigs off my route. A broken slab of wood calls out to me. I bend over and pick it up. When I stand up, I find myself nose-to-nose with Patrick. Well, maybe not nose-to-nose, but nose-to-camera. His index finger is poised on the shutter release.

"Hi," he says. His bald head shines in the sun.

"You shaved your mustache."

He smiles. "I shaved my mustache." He snaps another picture of my face, then one of my hands wrapped around the piece of wood.

"Wasn't it your trademark?" I ask.

"It was, but I turned a page in my life, and in this new chapter, I don't have a mustache."

I raise a skeptic eyebrow, which he captures on camera. Still smiling, he winks and walks toward the other contestants. If I cut off my hair, would I be starting a new chapter also? At least, I would no longer be mistaken for Aster. No one would ask if I was the twin at the wheel of the Honda.

I stick the plank in my bag and meander back down to the beach, fingering the curled tip of my ponytail. I'm not careful and trample a twig. A sharp, stabbing pain makes me curse and sink to the ground to inspect my sole. Sure enough, it's punctured, and blood beads over the surface. I look for Cara, and see her chatting with another assistant. I wave. She doesn't see me, but a middle-aged man in a pink polo shirt and checkered shorts does, and waves back.

Idiot, I grumble. Since he's the only person whose attention I've managed to grab, I gesture him over. He races toward me.

"I don't think I'm supposed to talk to you," he says, swiveling his face around like an alarmed puppy.

"Can you just get my assistant? I need a Band-Aid."

He catches sight of the trickling flow on my foot. "Right away." He jogs back toward the shore, but does a U-turn. "Which one is she?" He runs in place, which just looks odd.

"The peroxide blonde with the short hair," I say, pointing her out.

"Righty-o," he pants, and runs toward her. Still running in place, he taps her shoulder and aims his entire right arm toward me.

Cara disappears into one of the popcorn tents, reappears, and trots toward me. The first aid box in her hands reassures me that the guy wasn't a total idiot.

She kneels beside me and takes my feet in her hands. "It's not too bad."

"It hurts like a bitch," I say.

When she sprays antiseptic on my skin, a shrill scream jerks out of my throat. She eyes my sole more carefully. "Actually, the shard is pretty big."

"No kidding," I mutter.

She grabs a pair of tweezers from the medical kit and proceeds to dig through my skin for the sharp piece of wood. I clamp my teeth shut to avoid yelling again.

There's sweat on her brow. "I don't know if I can get it out. Maybe—"

"Give me that," I say, wrenching the tweezers out of her hands.

Trying not to flinch, I press my thumbnail against the butt of the shard to coax it out. Slowly, it moves back the way it came, and soon, the end of it appears like a baby squeezing out of its mother. I snap the tweezers around the shard and pull it out. It's no longer than my smallest nail, but it's sharp as a stake.

Cara, who's turned a little pale, soaks a fresh piece of cotton with antiseptic and applies it to my small wound, then she dabs some cream and covers the area with a large waterproof bandage. My foot throbs, but I stand up and walk on it. That's when inspiration hits. I pick up every piece of wood I can find, from twigs to branches.

When the mesh bag is about to burst, I return to the beach and dump out the contents in the space I was allotted. Lincoln is kneeling, a small piece of wood clasped in her hand. She's drawing or writing. Herrick is building a wall out of seashells. It's intricate, but doesn't look stable. Chase has been digging: inside an enormous hole, he's sculpted hills and towers. He's building a sand castle. I smile to myself. Good dealers don't make great artists. But my amusement fades when I see the beginnings of Kevin's work. He's weaving the tall grass together and it's starting to pool at his feet like a rope.

Forgetting all about my foot, I commence, praying that the structured piece I'm planning will hold. I take two twigs and weave a stalk of grass around the ends to keep them together at an angle. Surprisingly, it works. I take another stick and then another, positioning them this way and that until I have something that resembles a small web. I keep at it until I run out of wood. I lay my piece down and pick up my bag. Fueled with excitement, I race back toward the long grass and tear more stalks and replenish my stock of wood. I step on a small seashell on my way back, and my foot pulses with pain, but I push on. The sun is no longer high in the sky and Lincoln and Chase are no longer crouched on the sand. Both are finished, and are being interviewed by Josephine in front of one of the cameras.

I kneel down, flip my bag over, and start again on my wooden spider web. I use longer sticks, which airs out the piece and makes it grow quicker. I can feel a crowd building around me, curious, but I don't waste time looking up. Spinning the web, I tie and angle, tie and angle, until the disk is larger than I am. Then I get up and study it. Against the pale sand, it resembles a trap.

My gaze lands on the large plank. I decide to strap my piece to it so that I can stand it up. I don't know if the long grass will suffice in maintaining it upright, but it's worth a shot. Inspired by Kevin's rope, I create a large plait with the grass, which I then wrap through the bottom rung of my web and tie around the plank. I craft five more fat braids to hold the plank base in place.

And then I pull my piece up. If it holds, it will be the most magnificent and complex work achieved today. If it collapses, it will very possibly get me eliminated.

THIRTY-THREE

"What the hell, Redd?"

I try to tip my head up, but it's as heavy as a bowling ball. It lolls right back to the floor where I've collapsed. I'm hoisted up. I try to pry my lids open, but they're glued shut.

"What the hell?" Chacha mutters again. "Get her some blankets. Anything in wool. Socks."

Light burns my lids. Warm hands rub my skin. I'm being moved from one side to the other. They're going to hurt the baby, but then I remember the baby's gone.

My clothes come off, or is it my skin? There's more rubbing. It feels like they're massaging bruises. It hurts. I want to tell them to stop, but my lips can't shape words. Besides, my mouth is too weak to expel them.

"I'm here, Aster," I hear.

Ivy...Ivy came back.

Sluggishly, painfully, I crack open my lids; it feels like cracking thick ice. I look for my sister, but can only see blurred shapes and blobs of color. I blink, but still, nothing is sharp, which pains my eyes, so I close them.

"Stay with me, Aster."

You *stay with me.* My heart moves delicately, like an eyelash flutter. *Choose* me *this time, not the show.*

"Don't cry. You're going to be all right." The voice is clearer, clear enough for me to realize that it doesn't belong to !vy, but to Gill. "They sounded the air horn an hour ago. They thought you'd broken out. Didn't you hear it?"

I try to shake my head, but my neck is frozen.

Chacha grumbles, "Said she would take my shift so I could rest. Shoulda known. Shoulda known. Going to tell Driscoll. Stay with her."

I grab her arm but can't hold on. "On't," I whisper, unable to sound out the *D*.

"What did she say?" Chacha asks.

"I didn't hear anything."

The light goes gray behind my clasped lids.

Something soft touches my lips, like peach fuzz. "Say it again, Aster." Gill's voice is so close that it sounds like it's inside my head.

"On't," I whisper faintly. My throat is scratchy, like the fabric bunched around my hand.

The light turns gold again.

"She says *don't*. I don't think she wants you to tell Driscoll."

I part my lips and swallow a long sip of hot air. It stings my throat. And then I try to talk again, but my teeth keep clattering. Still, I manage, "Acci…acci…ent."

"Accident my ass," Chacha says.

"P-pease," I murmur.

"Maybe she's right. Maybe don't say anything."

"Cheyenne is a mean bitch. She—"

"It's Aster's choice."

"My kitchen. My rules."

"Then talk to Cheyenne, but don't involve the guards. Would that be okay, Aster?"

I manage a minuscule nod.

"What the—" It's a man's voice. "Where was she?"

"In the freezer," Chacha says. "It was an *accident*." I can tell from her intonation that she's pissed I've chosen to lie.

"I've got two patrols canvasing the area and she's in a fucking freezer? You got to be kidding me," Driscoll says. I hear him yap orders—probably calling the cavalry back. "Can she walk?"

"Keep her horizontal!" Chacha says. "Don't you know nothin'?" She grumbles something in a language I don't understand.

"*Yobwoc,* get in here! Carry her to the infirmary," the sergeant snaps.

Hands lift me. They're not very big, but I can tell they're not Gill's. They're calloused. How can I feel callouses through wool? Am I naked?

"I'll get her feet," Gill says.

"Keep her wrapped. Like a burrito. She needs to stay warm."

As I'm carried down the bright hallway, I squeeze my lids tighter, trying to block out the glare. I don't know where the infirmary is, but the trip there seems endless. Once we arrive, I'm deposited on a sheet of paper that crinkles underneath my weight.

Gill's explaining that I was locked inside the walk-in freezer for close to five hours. Fingers probe the vein on my neck. The blanket is removed. My hands are inspected. My toes, which feel like they are being pricked by a million needles, are probed. Something goes in my ear. It beeps.

"Ninety-one point five," the nurse reads out. "Mild hypothermia."

My lids are pressed up. A flashlight blinds me. I blink them back shut.

"Responsive eyes. Good. What's your name?"

"She's conscious," I hear Gill say.

"Did I ask you something?" the nurse snaps. She has a sturdy and authoritative voice. "What's your name?"

"Aaas…ssser," I murmur. My teeth are still chattering.

"Last name?"

"Rehh…"

"Inmate Swanson, can you get a bowl of broth from the kitchen?" she orders.

"Right away," Gill says.

Drawers open and close. Paper crinkles.

"Officer Landry, help me roll this under her," the nurse says.

I'm unwrapped, exposed again, and then squashed between something brittle and cool that turns hot in seconds. It crunches like paper, but it's not. *Foil.* That's what it must be.

"You can leave. I got it from here," the nurse says.

Silence.

"She'll be awhile."

"The sergeant will want to know how long," the young guard says.

"I don't know," she huffs. "First I need to stabilize her temperature, and then I need to get her to stop shivering."

"What should I tell him? He's going to want to know when he should pick her up."

"*When he should pick her up*?" she says. "Tell the sergeant he should *not* pick her up, because if he puts even a single toe in my infirmary, I'll cut off his tiny testicles and string them around my neck. Tell him that, will you?"

I wonder if my muddled mind has just made that up.

After a very long minute of silence, he says, "I-I can't tell him th—"

"Just tell him I'm keeping her overnight," she says. "Got it?"

"Yes."

"Now get."

After he's gone, she bustles around her infirmary. Gill returns. Together, they try to tilt my head up and slide some broth down my throat. I cough and gag. After another failed attempt, they release me. My head rolls to the side, and my cheek meets the pillow. The skin on my face has thawed out enough to feel the soft firmness. It reminds me of my pillow, the one I don't have to prop up with a book.

God, I miss my pillow. I miss my home.

I'M startled awake by the clicking sound of a keyboard.

"Good. You're up."

I jerk up on my elbows. Sweat coats my brow as my eyes dart from the white room to the middle-aged blonde shutting her laptop screen and coming toward me. I don't know who she is. Nothing looks familiar. Paper crunches beneath me and foil crackles. Why am I wrapped like the garlic bread we serve at the pizzeria?

The woman gently coaxes me back into a horizontal position and takes my pulse. It's late. I'm not sure how late, but there's barely any light outside.

"Do you remember what happened to you?" she asks, fastening a blood pressure monitor around my bicep.

I blink. Like feathers, fragmented memories drift into my mind. *Chacha. The basin of boiling water. The walk-in freezer. The cold.* Slowly, I nod.

"Being disoriented is a normal symptom. It's also a side effect of shock. But you'll be pleased to know your vitals are back to normal and your temperature's up. You're good as new."

She begins peeling the foil off my body. My skin is slick with perspiration, yet I don't feel particularly warm. I shiver when the air hits the sweat. The nurse catches my tremor, stops what she's doing, opens a cabinet, and extricates a folded towel. She lays it on top of me, and then proceeds to remove the rest of the foil.

"I heard talk it wasn't an accident," she says, peering at my face through a pair of canary-yellow bifocals.

I don't answer. I just stare at her boy-cut hair as it swishes around her face.

"You missed a good show today."

I raise an eyebrow.

"The Masterpiecers," she says, balling the foil and chucking it into the bin at the foot of the exam table. "It's my guilty pleasure, but don't tell anyone, okay?"

The pillow is soft and takes the shape of my cheek. "I won't," I whisper. But I don't want to talk about Ivy because, even though she didn't lock me up in the freezer, she told the cops I was crazy.

"You okay, hun?"

"Yeah," I croak, even though I'm not okay.

"Your sister's real talented."

Don't talk about her, I scream inside my head.

Unfortunately, she forges on. "I wish I could've bought something of hers before she got on the show, but it was already too expensive then. I got a stack of bills this high." She holds her palms apart as though there was an invisible accordion in between them. "And a mortgage and—"

I'm startled she knows the price of my sister's quilts.

"What?" She glances at the door. When she sees no movement behind the frosted glass, she peers back down at me. "Are you okay?"

I'm about to nod, but I find myself asking instead, "How do you know how much her quilts are worth?"

"Oh. Harry told me…I mean Commander Collins. He has one."

My brain catapults the picture on his desk to the forefront of my mind. That was what I'd realized when I was scouring Chacha's soup pot! His daughter was posing in front of one of Ivy's quilts. "The warden owns one of my sister's quilts."

It's not a question, yet the nurse treats it as such. "Yes. And it's *gor*-geous."

She smiles because she attributes my astonishment to sibling pride or awe when in fact, it stems from confusion. Did he buy it, or did she bribe him with it?

The nurse tucks me under the towel. "You can be really proud of your sister."

I don't answer.

"You want to watch some reruns of today's show on my laptop?"

"Do I have time?"

"Time? Hun, you're not going back to your cell tonight, and it's only seven thirty. Before they announce the winners, they'll show a recap of the day's highlights. I missed a bit when you came in." Since I'm not very enthusiastic, she adds, "But if you're too tired, I'll just listen to it on my headphones and let you rest."

"No. I want to see it."

"Great. Here, let me raise the backrest up a notch." She adjusts it so that I'm propped up. Then she sits on her wheelie chair, places her computer on her lap, and drags herself back over to my cot. She logs in to the TV network's website and pulls up the first and most popular tab: *The Masterpiecers*.

Her screen goes momentarily dark and then the image of a bright shore fills the blackness. How ironic that while I was freezing, Ivy was on a warm beach. The commentators launch into vivid descriptions of the day's test, from Lincoln's intricate drawing, to Chase's sand city, to Kevin's wild grass rope, to Ivy's magnificent stick spider web, to Herrick's transitory seashell wall. They're making prognostics as to who will get eliminated tonight. After seeing my sister's piece, I'm a hundred percent sure it won't be her. Nevertheless, I'm not enthusiastic because her talent has brought me nothing but pain.

As the recaps stop and the show goes live, I look for my sister. I find her sandwiched between Lincoln and Herrick, dressed in a flowy, Grecian gown that billows around her ankles. All the competitors are in white tonight. They're standing a few feet away from a massive bonfire like warlocks and witches about to leap into the pyre to burn for their sins. The flames dance across their tense faces. I search my sister's expression for emotion and spot nervousness. I wonder if she knows what happened to me today.

"I don't see how she would," the nurse tells me, her gaze taped to the screen.

"What?"

She swings her gaze toward me. "You asked if she knew what happened to you today."

I said it out loud. *Wow*, my brain must not have thawed out completely. "Right."

The video montage people have divided the screen into six equal parts. Five of them show the artworks, and the last show Dominic raising the microphone to his lips to announce the loser.

"This is my least favorite part of the show," he begins by saying. "Especially now that we—Josephine, Brook, and I—have discovered how talented you all are. Please remember that disqualification doesn't mean you lack talent or intelligence. Disqualification just means you didn't score well on this particular test."

He studies them, offering each a pearly smile. But then his smile fades as his gaze settles on one particular contestant. I can't tell if he's looking at Ivy or Herrick.

"Herrick Hawk, your piece was inspired, but not thought out enough. One puff of wind, and it buckled. Even though some art is as transient as a butterfly, at the Masterpiecers, we believe in creating something perennial." Dominic walks toward him and puts his hand on the twenty-three-year-old's shoulder. "We will miss you deeply. And on behalf of everyone here on the show, I wish you the best of luck with all of your future endeavors."

As Herrick's face decomposes, the image switches to flashbacks of his journey on the show: snippets of interviews and slow motion highlights of Herrick competing, laced with pretty music. The nurse sniffs next to me, lifting her glasses to blot the tears from her eyes. I don't feel particularly sad for him. It's just a stupid show. He's not going to rot away in a cell for having rid the Earth of a bad person.

THIRTY-FOUR

Ivy

"I really didn't think I'd be sticking around after my sand castle exploit," Chase tells me as we are led to the banquet underneath the white big top.

I laugh because I'm in a good mood. Not only am I still on the show, but my work has been touted as the most magnificent piece of the day. I felt it would be, but a gut feeling isn't worth as much as spoken compliments. I spy Herrick in my peripheral vision. His cheeks are blotchy red and his nose is running, and his big hair, which is usually so perfectly slick, is standing on end. He's a mess. If I lose, I won't make such a miserable display of myself in front of the cameras. I'll keep it together.

"By the way, Chase, thank you for last night."

"Last night?" Brook says, appearing beside us. "What happened last night?" Brook eyes his brother, then me, but thankfully doesn't insinuate anything.

"Kevin was out late," I tell him. "And since we don't have locks on our tents—"

"You have nothing to worry about," Chase says.

I frown. "Have you seen the size of him? Plus he hates my guts. Brook, would it be possible to get an extra camera to monitor our hallway?"

"I'll see what I can do. Anyway, congratulations, you two."

"It's Ivy you should congratulate. My work was pretty pathetic," Chase says.

"Maybe, but you're still here," he says.

The vein in Chase's temple throbs. I don't think he wanted Brook to validate his comment, I'm pretty sure he wanted him to tell him how crafty it was. Brook's gaze is focused on me, so he's oblivious to his brother's soured mood.

"I'm going to grab something to drink," Chase mutters. "You want anything, Ivy?"

"I'm fine, thanks."

"Nothing alcoholic," Brook says with a grin. "At least not for the next"—he checks his expensive wristwatch—"three hours and forty seven minutes."

Chase doesn't return his smile. He just leaves.

"What happens in three hours and forty seven minutes?" I ask.

"He's going to be legal."

"Oh, right." I glance at Chase. The white linen shirt is stretched tight across his shoulder blades and his dark copper hair gleams in the firelight. "He doesn't seem very excited about it."

"Oh, he will be. I've organized fireworks and s'mores and a champagne fountain."

I don't think a big celebration will thrill Chase.

"I wanted to tell you something." Brook's voice has dropped so much that I think he's going to bring up the elevator conversation again. "Kevin's lawyer is here."

"Really?" I squeak.

"He scored an invite without us knowing. Jeb was reviewing the raw footage earlier and recognized him. Anyway, I've told Dominic, who's asked him to leave, but he says he didn't come here as Kevin's lawyer, but as Madame Babanina's guest."

"Madame who?"

"Madame Babanina. One of the show's biggest sponsors. Cleaned her husband out in a divorce, and then donated half his money to the school to annoy him. Anyway, Kevin's lawyer was her lawyer and—"

"Can you point him out?" I ask.

Brook turns and inspects the beach. After a few seconds, he tips his chin toward a man sitting to the right of a woman sporting tight black lace and exaggeratedly curved bangs—Madame Babanina. "If he talks to you, you come straight to me, okay?"

I nod.

"On another note…"

"Yes?"

"Would you consider selling me your web?"

"You want to buy my web?"

"Yes. I'd like to buy it."

"Can you?"

"I have money." He gives me a big smile.

"No, I mean, doesn't that break some show rule?"

"There's no rule against purchasing art from an artist. Didn't you see the Zara Mach accordion over my bed?"

My heart's vaulting against the walls of my chest at being called an artist by a real connoisseur. I take a deep breath and try to think of something to say besides yelling, *hell, yes*. "I wasn't going to sell it…" My voice shakes. I suddenly wish Chase were here. He'd get me a hell of a price.

"Okay, but now that I'm offering, how much would you find fair?"

I pretend to think about it. When enough time has passed, I say, "Thirty thousand."

"That's reasonable," he says.

Reasonable? It's outrageous! I made the piece out of twigs and grass. I keep my cool and fold my arms. "Cash."

"No. I need to write you a check. For tax and insurance reasons."

"Oh. Right."

"Trust me, you don't want to get acquainted with the IRS."

I run through mental calculations of how much I'll be left with.

"Don't worry, you're still going to make a bunch of money, Ivy."

He's right, but it probably won't be enough to cover the amount of Aster's bail now that she's being charged with first-degree murder. If she can even make bail. I shiver and look down at my bare feet. They replaced the Band-Aid with a sturdier one, so that I can go into the sea, but the inky darkness doesn't inspire me.

"So do we have a deal?" he asks.

I crane my neck to look at Brook. "Yes."

He extends his hand. I lift mine and feed my fingers around his.

"What are we shaking hands to?" the photographer asks.

I yank my hand away.

"I've just bought my first Ivy Redd piece," Brook says with a smile.

Patrick's brown eyes grow rounder. He snaps a picture of my face, and then finally lowers his camera. "The web?"

"The Web," Brook says, grinning. He glances at me, the smile growing on his lips. "Shall we call it that?"

"Sure."

I spot Kevin a few feet away, hard to miss considering how sunburnt his large forehead has become. He's talking with his lawyer and another man sporting a wool suit and a cherry-red tie. Something about him strikes me as familiar. I'm sure I've seen him before, but where?

"I might not be the first owner of a Redd original, but I'm certainly the luckiest because I saw it come to life under my very own eyes. How many collectors can claim that?" Brook is telling the photographer. Suddenly, his hand closes over my arm. "Excuse us, Patrick. I have someone I'd like to introduce to my contestant." We walk straight toward Kevin and the two men. "Ivy, I'd like you to meet Dean Kane, my dear friend and the lawyer who will be defending your sister."

Frowning, I shake hands with the man with the bright tie. And then it hits me where I saw him. After the performance art test.

"And this is Mister Kelley," Brook says, gesturing to Kevin's lawyer.

I shake his hand too, even though I really don't want to.

"I should get back to Madame Babanina. She doesn't like to be left alone," he says. "Mister Martin, I am deeply sor—"

Kevin, whose chin is tucked into his neck, doesn't wait for him to finish his sentence before traipsing away.

"Brook, may I speak to Ivy privately? I'd like to discuss her sister's case," Dean says.

"Sure, but don't bore her with too many details."

He nods and we set out along the beach, toward the obscurity beyond the big top.

Once we cross over into the darkness, I ask, "What were you talking about with Kevin and his lawyer?"

"His press release. I told him to cancel it."

"Did he agree?"

"He did."

"Really?"

Dean nods.

"How? Why?"

"I have proof that your sister didn't doctor those photos."

"Who did, then?"

"I can't disclose that information."

"I won't tell anyone."

He shakes his head. "Sorry, Ivy, but you'll find out if Kevin decides to go public with it. Now, about your sister's case. I'm unclear about something. How well did *you* know Troy Mann?"

"Me?"

He nods.

"I sold him a quilt, but that's it."

"Your sister told me you spent a long time in the apartment with him."

"What? How would she know? She was at work."

"No. She was leaving for work. Got in late. I checked with the receptionist at the ad agency."

"She was spying on me?"

"What did you talk about with Mister Mann when he came to your place?"

"I just showed him the different quilts I'd made, and then we discussed prices."

"Which one did he purchase?"

"A quilt depicting a city skyline."

"I'd appreciate if you told me the truth, Ivy. I might be your sister's lawyer, but I'm also working on your behalf."

"I-I am."

He cocks his head to the side. His hair is so slick with gel that it reflects the moonlight. "Aster sent the quilt he bought to the show, so I assume it's the one you auctioned off."

I freeze and look beyond him, at the lavish, prattling crowd. "Fine…yes… that's the one. Did she tell you why she sent it?"

"No."

"Could you ask her?"

My gaze drifts to the red tie hooked around Dean's collar that's held tight against his dress shirt by a large gold bar. He fingers it. "Sure, but that wouldn't do much for her case."

"It would do a lot for my state of mind."

"Apparently, the quilt was torn," he says, obviously not caring much about my morale.

"Did *she* tell you that?"

"No. Brook did. Would you know why?"

"Either Aster ripped it because she was angry with me or it was damaged in transit," I mutter.

He narrows his eyes, and I bristle. I don't like him. I bet Aster doesn't either.

"What? You have another theory?" I ask.

"We're dealing with a mobster, so yes, I do have another theory. I think he was using the quilt to transport something."

I blink.

"Any thoughts as to what that might be?" he asks.

"No," I whisper.

"Well, if you think of anything, let Brook know and he'll convey your message to me. Now, about your sister's case. The DA upgraded it to first-degree murder, which means that she's facing forty years to life."

"I heard, but it was self-defense."

"Your sister followed Troy Mann back to the motel he was staying in, thus instigating the threatening situation, so pleading self-defense would work as well as an apology."

"But she didn't mean to."

"I beg to differ. From the coroner's transcript, she hit him a first time, then backed up and rolled over him. I'm building my defense upon the fact that she's schizophrenic."

"She what?"

He repeats what he's just said, padding the account with such vivid details that I think I'm going to throw up.

"So I'll have her plead insanity," he tells me.

"She's going to hate that," I say in a small voice that's almost swallowed by the sound of the waves lapping at my feet.

"It's her only hope of getting out."

After a long moment, I nod.

"You'll have to testify—"

"No."

"Do you want to save your sister or not?"

"I do."

"Then you'll have to give a testimony."

"I have a paper."

"What sort of paper?"

"One she signed to give me power of attorney over her. If you show it to the judge, then I won't need to testify, right?"

The ocean fills the night with its briny, wild scent.

"I'll need that paper."

"You won't tell her about it, will you?"

"She signed it, didn't she?" he asks.

"She didn't read it."

"Oh." Dean tips his head to the side and observes me. "To use it in court, she'll have to swear she signed it of her own free will."

I dig my feet into the cold, wet sand. "There's no way around Aster finding out what I think about her?"

"If I were you, I'd be less worried about offending your sister and more worried about convincing a judge that her actions stemmed solely from her…how should I put it? *Bewildered* mind."

"Where else would they stem from?"

"Did you ever think that perhaps your sister knew there was something in the quilt…something extremely valuable? And that's why she killed Troy Mann."

My jaw slackens because I hadn't considered that. And suddenly it all makes sense. And I understand how my sister—who barely can afford food and gas—managed to give me a diamond as big as one of my nails. She found it inside the quilt.

THIRTY-FIVE

When my burger arrives, my appetite vanishes. Or maybe it vanished when the nurse confirmed the warden owned one of my sister's works. It's not so much the fact that he possesses one that bothers me, but the fact that he hid it from me. I've been trying to come up with reasons. I have two. My sister sold it to him, and then asked him to keep quiet about it so that I wouldn't know she'd made money and ask her for some. Not that I would ever grovel. Or, she gave it to him so that he would treat me well.

If she gave it to him, then I should be ashamed of all the bad thoughts I've been harboring about my sister. If she sold it to him, then my bad thoughts are founded.

"I have some fresh clothes for you to change into," the nurse says, handing me a folded gray jumpsuit, a white T-shirt, a white bra, and a pair of cotton panties.

I loosen the towel, but keep it over me as I pull on the underwear. The nurse surely has seen me naked, but that was when I was unconscious.

"I'm going to head home, but I'll be back first thing tomorrow morning. I've organized for Officer Landry to move you to a cell in the medical unit. Another nurse will come in for the night shift. If you feel ill or anything, just let her know."

"Okay."

She slings her roomy handbag over her shoulder. Her laptop peeps out of it. "I hope you have a good night."

"Nurse—"

"Celia," she finishes.

"Nurse Celia, thank you."

"Just doing my job." She smiles and draws open the door, and her yellow bifocals that hang on a chain around her neck bounce against her double Ds. "Sweet dreams, Miss Redd." *Miss Redd*…not Inmate Redd or Redd…*Miss*. Never thought I'd appreciate the title as much.

The young officer—the one Driscoll bosses around—is standing right outside. She clicks off the light and leaves me with him.

"Can you walk?" he asks.

"I think so. Is it far?"

"No."

I lower myself off the exam table and take wobbly steps to the open doorway and past the guard. He leads me to a cell two doors down and unlocks a gate. The windowless room is entirely padded and contains a single iron bed. No toilet. No sink. A chill races over my skin because it looks fit for a crazy person. He waits until I'm inside, then bolts the gate shut behind me. I sit on the bed. The springs creak and the mattress feels like a slab of wood.

"You sleep now," he says, settling on a chair outside.

"I'm not tired."

"Well, you have to sleep. The nurse—"

"Okay. Okay." I lean back and close my eyes just to please him.

I hear paper rustle. I crack one lid up. He's pulled out a small paperback from his jacket pocket. From the cover, I can tell it's a spy novel. Spy novels always look the same: dark woods with just a faint source of light. His gaze lifts toward me and I snap my lids shut again.

I try to sleep, but I just can't. "Actually, I'm hungry," I say, sitting up. "My dinner's on Nurse Celia's desk. You mind bringing it over?"

He looks perplexed, as though I've asked him to fetch me the moon.

"I promise I'll sleep right after."

"Fine." He stuffs the book back into his pocket, leaves and returns seconds later with my tray. He unbolts the gate, slides the tray in, and locks it up again. Then he just stands there, arms crossed.

I hope he's not planning on staring at me while I eat. "You mind?"

"Unwrap the foil and open the bun."

"Are you serious?"

"Very. I need to check for weapons."

I grumble, but do as I'm told. The beef patty is squashed and overcooked, the single leaf of salad wilted and wet with ketchup, and the bun mushy from having stayed wrapped in the foil. "No razorblade. Happy?"

He nods and sits back down while I reassemble my burger and take a bite. It turns out to be the best thing I've eaten since getting sent to prison. My mouth literally waters as I shove bite after bite down my throat. Too soon, not a crumb remains, yet my stomach rumbles for more.

I ball up the foil and place it on the tray. "How old are you?" I ask him.

"Why do you want to know?"

"Geez, it's just a question."

"Nineteen," he says.

"Shouldn't you be in college?"

"I'm trying to earn some money to pay for college."

"And then what?"

"I'd like to become a lawyer."

"A lawyer?"

"I'm studying already."

"Let me guess...you're going to specialize in criminal law."

"Maybe. I don't know yet."

"What does *yobwoc* mean?" I ask him.

"It's cowboy spelled backwards. That's what Driscoll calls the new officers."

I stretch out on the hard mattress and turn on my side, but I can't get comfortable, so I turn on the other. I stare at the cream-colored padding that's ochre in places and try to even out my breathing. There's a particularly gross spot on one of the seams that's more brown than orange. I stare at it until my vision blurs and I see double, and then triple. But still, I don't sleep.

"Can you read the story out loud?" I ask the nineteen-year-old officer.

Surprisingly, he does. And even more surprising, the story's enthralling. It's about a detective who unscrambles a prostitution ring. And, lo and behold, discovers his wife belongs to it. At some point, the brown stain fades, and the officer's voice lulls, and I finally fall asleep. And I dream.

THIRTY-SIX

Ivy

"Who was that?" Lincoln asks me after I've returned from my stroll down the beach with Dean.

"My sister's lawyer," I say.

"He's hot."

I shrug as I roam around the buffet, my plate still empty.

"Is he single?"

"Don't know. He's Brook's friend. Ask *him*," I say, just as I spot the two of them in conversation.

"Are you going to eat anything?"

"Yeah. But I don't know what."

"The smoked salmon's really good."

"Okay." I scoop some onto my plate, ladle a dollop of cream, and select some bread that looks like a pancake, which I assume goes with it since it's on the same platter. "Where are we sitting?"

"Over there." She pokes her chin to the table closest to the water. "I'm going to get a refill and be right over. I got the bartender to add some rum inside. Want one?"

I'm about to say no, but end up saying yes. I want alcohol. I want to cloud my brain so I can stop thinking about Aster deliberately flattening a man's skull with her car to steal his diamonds. There are two empty seats: one next to Kevin and one next to Chase. It's a no-brainer. I'm sitting next to Kevin. I want to know why he canceled his press release.

"Can I get an apology?" I ask, sliding in next to him.

He's staring at the bouquet of lavender in front of him. His neck is larger than my thigh and marked with thin white lines as though he repeatedly cut himself with his razor blade. "For what?"

"For wrongfully accusing my sister."

He turns toward me and I notice that his eyes are red-rimmed.

"Have you been crying?"

"It's none of your business," he mumbles.

"I didn't know sergeants were such sensitive beings."

His eyes taper dangerously close to his crooked nose. "Shut up," he murmurs.

"I'll shut up if you stop lurking in the hallway at night."

"What are you talking about?"

"Lincoln told me all about it."

"All about what?" he asks.

"About Chase finding you just outside my tent," I say.

"What?"

"Are you going to deny it?"

He shakes his head and gives a mean laugh. "I wasn't stalking you."

"I heard you! Just outside—"

He presses his chair back and shoots up.

"Is the big, mean soldier angry?" I tease as he hurries away.

I must have said it louder than I intended because both Herrick and Chase glare at me like I'm the callous one.

"What?" I say.

"You're a bitch, Ivy," Herrick says.

I frown. Lincoln's on her way back from the bar. When she walks, her hips roll from side to side. "Hey, kiddies," she says, and swoops down next to Chase. She places a glass in front of me and winks. "What did I miss?"

Herrick pushes out of his chair and heads in the direction Kevin disappeared in.

"*O-kay*? Did I say something?" she asks, taking a huge gulp of her drink. Some of it dribbles down her chin.

"Chase, can I talk to you a sec?" I ask.

Lincoln waggles her dark brows.

"I'm good here," he says.

"Ouch," Lincoln says.

I try to catch his attention, but he's purposely looking away.

"By the way"—Lincoln raises her glass—"I heard we have something to celebrate." I think she's about to mention Chase's birthday, which I'm not in the mood to celebrate, when she says, "To your big sale!"

"What big sale?" Chase asks.

"Oh…you didn't hear? Your brother bought the piece she made today. For a *lot* of money," she adds, with a sly grin. She knocks back her drink. "Ivy, why aren't you drinking?" Her voice is really loud, and in spite of the music blasting out of the loudspeakers dotting the beach, some people have turned to stare. "One teeny sip. Come on, Redd. Don't leave me hanging."

I pick up the glass. Instead of taking a sip, I down the entire thing. Just to get her off my case.

"Good girl," she says.

The second the alcohol hits my empty stomach, I feel it bubble in my veins, irrigate my organs, and froth upward. I grab the salty pancake and stuff it inside my mouth, barely chewing it. My head spins a little and my face feels bloated. I touch it to make sure it isn't. Maybe I'm having an allergic reaction. Maybe—

The drink rises. I fling myself away from the table and cross the beach toward the port-o-potties. I'm going to throw up any second. I focus on keeping my lips sealed so I don't spout vomit. I try the first door but it's locked. The second door opens. I just have time to kneel before my stomach drains itself. Tears surge up and drip down my cheeks, plopping inside the toilet bowl. I'm not sure if I'm crying because I threw up or because of my sister's crime.

When I feel steady enough, I get up and wobble over to the glass sink. I rinse my mouth and splash cool water over my face. I take one last gulp of tap water, spit it out, then leave. I don't want to return to the table, so I wander away from the festivities. I hear hushed voices nearby belonging to two dark bodies pressed against each other. One is unmistakable—Brook—the other is a woman in black lace. Madame Babanina, the notorious divorcée. I scurry away before either of them can spot me and run smack into Chase, who steadies me. Before he can talk and have us discovered, I place my finger against my lips, point to the couple behind me, and walk to the water's edge, my footsteps muffled by the soft sand.

"Ivy?"

I turn around, surprised that Chase followed me.

"Why are you talking to me?" A gust of wind kicks up my hair and swirls it. "I thought I was a bitch."

"I didn't say that."

"But you were thinking it."

"You have no idea what I was thinking."

I take a small step into the water, not bothering to lift my flowy skirt. It's cool and prickles my ankles. "Kevin was outside my tent last night. Apparently, you saw him."

"I did."

"Then why am I the bad one?" I ask him.

Chase's eyes gleam, dark and shiny like the ocean. "He didn't come to see you. He came to see me."

"You? Why?"

Chase stares at me long and hard, as though trying to decide whether to confide in me. "He's…confused."

"About how to kill me?" I say with a snort.

"About how he feels about men."

My stomach, which is still unsettled, now feels as though it's been sucker-punched. "Oh." As I attempt to link the beefy sergeant to his sexuality, I ask, "Why didn't he go see Herrick then?"

"Were you attracted to J.J.?"

"No."

"Well, he's not attracted to every man either."

"He has feelings for *you*?"

"I know, right? Unbelievable…someone actually has feelings for me."

"That's not what I meant."

"It's fine," he says. "But we're unfortunately not wired to automatically return an admirer's affection, so I had to turn him down. I promised to keep his secret, though."

"Yet you told me…"

"So you'd stop hating him. He's not a bad guy, Ivy."

"He hasn't been very nice to me," I say.

"And you haven't been very nice to him. Now, you can start being nicer."

"But Lincoln told me—"

"Don't listen to her. Listen to *me*."

I'm not sure whether I should listen to anyone. "Why was he crying?"

"I think it has to do with those pictures."

A high-pitch screech makes my heart pitch. I spin around and notice that people have jumped into the water and are squealing with delight. I feel a hand close over mine and tug on my fingers.

"Swim with me?" Chase says.

"I—I, uh…don't know how to swim."

"You don't?" When I stay mute, he adds, "Is that why you didn't want to go inside Brook's pool?"

I nod.

He smiles. He's very handsome when he smiles.

"I can teach you."

I swallow. "I don't feel like learning tonight."

"Then let's not swim. But let's go in a little deeper."

"What if a wave knocks me over?"

"I'll catch you," he says softly.

Perhaps it would help me get over what happened to Mom. "Okay." When my skirt floats up around me, I stop. "That's far enough."

His eyebrows quirk up.

"Don't swim away, okay?"

"I won't," he says, inspecting my face. He must notice the tension thrashing inside of me, because he adds, "There's a simple way of keeping me close."

Even though the water's cold, I can't feel it. The only thing I can feel is an increasing amount of blood pumping through my body. "Promising to let you win?"

"Not everything is about this competition." With his free hand, he touches my jaw, brushes his palm over my cheek, runs a finger along the ridge of my creased brow, and then he inches closer to me and moves his mouth over mine. His lips are soft and warm, as soft and warm as his hands that he's wrapped around my waist. As he nudges my mouth open, one of his hands travels up my spine, while the other pulls me closer. When his tongue touches mine, tremors and tingles explode everywhere in my body.

"We shouldn't," I whisper into his mouth, before pulling away.

"Why?"

"Because. There are a lot of people around. And cameras. And—"

He kisses me again.

I press him back. "Chase, I'm serious."

He frowns this time.

"People will gossip," I say.

"Let them."

"But—"

"Ivy, in four days, all of these people"—he motions to the big top—"will be gone."

"And so will one of us." My voice is muffled by an explosion overhead.

The fireworks have started. Is it already midnight? The sky glistens white and blue and gold.

"It's your birthday. You should go celebrate," I say, stroking the foamy surface of the water.

"I am celebrating. By being with you," he whispers. His breath is warm and makes goose bumps appear along my lobe and jaw.

"I thought you didn't like me."

"Well, you thought wrong."

My pulse pounds in my ears, rivaling the multicolored thunder overhead.

Suddenly a loud "Happy Birthday" chant erupts from the speakers and a spotlight falls over us. I spring away from him, but he reins me in.

"Stay with me," he whispers.

So I do. Because it's his birthday, and because I like the feel of his arm wrapped around my waist. But then I spot something behind him, a shape floating on the inky surface, a human shape, face down, moonlit and motionless. I tear my hand out of Chase's and fling myself into the cold surf, my arms cutting through the water.

I'm the first to reach the body.

THIRTY-SEVEN

I gasp awake and press a clammy palm against my lungs. It was just a nightmare…just a nightmare. As I spot Celia trundling inside the padded cell, I recall the horrid dream. I was in a water tank with no air, and this dead body was floating next to me with shimmery straight teeth and long blonde hair twisting like seaweed. At first, I thought it was Ivy, but then I saw my sister standing just outside the tank, sad but resigned, mouth opening and closing as though trying to tell me something. Something I couldn't make out. I force the nightmare into a dusky recess of my mind, but it clings to me like an insect trapped in jam.

"I'm taking Miss Redd back to the infirmary." Celia hoists me up. She's breathless, and a rivulet of sweat snakes down her neck between her large breasts.

Officer Landry rubs his eyes, which makes me think he was on duty all night.

"You'll never believe what happened," she whispers as we walk past him.

"Has there been a breakout?" Officer Landry blinks rapidly and repeatedly, like a caffeine addict before their first morning cup.

Nurse Celia flaps her hand at him. "No, no. Settle down. There's a world outside prison, you know?"

He stops blinking.

It takes me a second to get my bearings. As she leads me back to her blindingly white office, yesterday dribbles back into my muddled brain.

She orders me to lie down on the exam table. "Last night, during the fireworks, Martin was found dead."

"Who?" I ask.

"Kevin. You know, on the Masterpiecers! He drowned! Can you believe it? I can't. It's chaos in New York, and it's all over the news, and when I stopped by Starbucks this morning, everyone was talking about it. It's crazy. Pure insanity." She has her hand over her heart as though trying to squish her excitement.

My own heart is bouncing inside its cavity, not from excitement, but from dread. And from the nightmare that still feels too real. "Was he killed?" I think of those forms my sister made me sign before leaving. Perhaps the show *is* dangerous.

"Oh, no. No foul play. He committed suicide. Apparently he was crying most of the night. Can you believe it?" she asks me again.

I shiver, which makes my dreadlocks tickle my shoulder blades.

"That photographer on the show...what's his name...you know, the famous one? Anyway he snapped some pictures of the evening and he caught one of Kevin running into the water."

"Didn't he know how to swim?" I ask.

"Are there soldiers who don't know how to swim?"

"I don't know."

"Landry?" she says loudly, spinning around. "Are there soldiers who don't know how to swim?"

"It's not a requirement to join the army, ma'am, but usually people are taught during training."

Then she asks, "What are you still doing here?"

"Uh...I'm waiting to take Inmate Redd back."

"That won't be for a while. I need to run some blood pressure tests and monitor her temperature. And then Robyn wants to see her."

"I'll wait outside then."

"No, no. Just go. I'm sure you have better things to do. Wouldn't want Driscoll to get his panties in a twist, now would we?" She flashes him a brazen smile, which deepens the small lines on the outer corner of her eyes.

After he nods, she shuts the door and locks it. Then she goes to her desk, yanks her laptop out of her slouchy bag.

"I'll show you," she whispers, putting on her yellow glasses.

As she clicks here and there, she rambles on, "Barely slept all night I was so darn agitated. I think it's because it feels like I know one of the contestants personally this year. What with Ivy being your identical twin and all."

Just as she mentions Ivy, a picture of her appears: she's standing alone, on the beach, her profile illuminated by a burst of firework. Her dress is entirely transparent, and her blonde hair is pasted to her forehead and breasts.

Nurse Celia clicks through the rest of the pictures available on the website. One of them makes me grip her wrist to stop her from snapping to the next. I let go right away.

"Could you zoom in?" I ask.

She does. Two darkened figures stand by the water line.

"Who's that?" she asks.

"My new lawyer."

"He's dreamy. Is he single?"

"I don't know." *But he's a good two decades younger than you.*

Someone knuckles the door. It makes us both jump. Nurse Celia shuts her laptop and leaps off the exam table. "One second," she yells, grabbing some keys from her bag and unlocking one of the closets. She grabs her lab coat off a hanger and throws it on before opening up. "Oh. It's you. You don't take orders real well, now do you?" She snaps the press-studs of her white coat closed. "Aster's not ready."

She's about to shut the door in Driscoll's red face, but he presses it open and barges in. "She has a visitor."

"Who?"

"Her lawyer."

"Why?"

"I don't think that concerns you, Celia."

Celia folds her arms in front of her chest.

The sergeant's gaze travels to the crest of her bosom and lingers there. "Is she well enough to see him?"

She turns toward me. "Aster, you well enough to see your lawyer?"

"Yes," I say, hopping off the exam table.

"Okay then." She snatches the keys off her desk and walks over to me, extending her arm. "Lean on me, okay?" Even though I don't feel the need for a crutch, I hang on.

"Where are *you* going?" Driscoll asks Celia, as we step out of the office.

"I'm walking her to the attorney visitation area," she says, locking her door.

"That's my job."

"She's *my* patient," Celia counters, even though I doubt that's the reason she's accompanying me.

"You are impossible," he grumbles, tailing us down the hallway.

"Don't you have some young guard to annoy?"

"I'm training him."

"He's not a dog," she says. "Then again, that's how you treat everyone."

Ouch.

"Don't you go pretending you're some saint, 'cause you're not, Cee! Saints don't sock their boyfriends with their keys." He's pointing to the scar on his eyebrow.

She whirls around, jerking me with her. "You got blown by a fucking convict while we were dating," she hisses. "You deserved it!" Then she spins back and marches me down the hallway. "Sorry, Aster. Didn't mean to stick you in the middle. Men are such a-holes."

Dean's already inside the visitation room. He's looking over some papers and drumming his fingers against the desk. When the door clicks open, he looks up. His eyes travel first to me, then to the nurse's flushed face. He stands up, extends his hand, and introduces himself. Celia does the same.

"*Nurse*?" He raises an eyebrow. "What happened?"

"An incident. Terrible what these girls do to each other in here. Just terrible." Obviously, she's decided not to believe in the accident theory.

"What did they do?" he asks.

Celia's shaking her head; her short hair wisps around her heart-shaped face. "Locked her in the freezer for hours."

I shrug away from Celia. "Why did you go to New York?" I ask, redirecting the conversation.

He gestures to the table. "Let's sit. Celia"—he fishes a business card from his pebbled black wallet and gives it to her—"it was a pleasure meeting you. Can you keep me informed of any more incidents?"

Celia smiles widely, takes the card, and slips it into her lab coat's breast pocket. He's going to regret giving it to her. "Of course. You can count on me. I'll leave you two to it. Aster, come see me after your appointment with Robyn…to run all your tests."

When she leaves, Dean and I both sit. I knot my fingers together on the table. "What were you doing in New York?"

"I went to see Kevin and his lawyer."

"He's dead."

"I heard. Suicide." There's no emotion in his voice.

"Why?"

"His wife claims it resulted from his PTSD."

"It's crazy. Just yesterday he was threatening Ivy and now…now he's gone. Is she okay?"

"Who? His wife?"

"No. My sister."

He shrugs. "She seemed all right. Maybe a little shaken, but considering she's the one who fished him out, it's understandable."

My water nightmare. I dreamt of drowning because of Ivy. They say that one twin is the receiver and the other, the transmitter. I've always felt Ivy's fears, joys, melancholy, but she's never sensed mine.

"I updated her about your case," Dean's saying. He plays with his tie. Today, it's sky blue with geometric motifs. "What was inside the quilt, Aster?"

"Inside?" I whisper, my voice catching. "Inside what quilt?"

"Don't play dumb with me. Your sister told me the quilt you stole from Troy Mann is the one that ended up on the show. I know you didn't destroy it."

"I-I…"

"She also told me there was a tear in it, which I assume was used as a makeshift pocket to transport something. Now the question is, what?"

I look down at my overlapping fingers. I'm squeezing them so hard, the tips are red and the knuckles are white.

"Any ideas?"

I shake my head.

"You were the first person to handle it after Troy Mann," he says.

"There was no tear when I had it."

Dean watches me for so long that I shift in my seat.

"I have to go meet with the prison psychologist now," I tell him.

He sighs. "Fine. Don't answer. You're the one losing out. Not me."

As I get up and walk toward the door, he slaps his papers back into his briefcase.

"I have an appointment with Officer Cooper this afternoon," Dean says.

I whirl around. "You do? Why?"

"As a character witness. I heard he was a friend. A close friend."

My palms become moist. "He doesn't know anything."

"He doesn't know anything about you, or about the quilt?"

"About nothing." I wipe my hands against my jumpsuit. "I'd like to see him. Can you tell him I'd like to see him?"

"Didn't I make it clear that the only person you should be in contact with is me from now on?"

"I won't discuss the case."

He fixes me for a long moment, as though attempting to decide whether to believe me.

"He's my only friend."

"I'm not surprised."

I frown. "Why would you say that?"

"I'm good at reading people, and you don't strike me as a social butterfly."

"Well, it's not true. I made friends here. Gill's my friend."

"Gill who?"

"Swanson. You can use her as a character witness."

"Noted."

I press on the buzzer to signal the guard I want out.

"Oh...before you go, Ivy entrusted me with this." He digs something from the front pocket of his briefcase and plops it onto the table so indelicately that the porcelain practically shatters.

I stare at it without moving for so long that Dean picks it up and walks it over to me. He yanks my limp hand open, places the box on my palm, and rolls my fingers over it.

And then he gives me an oily smile. "She also told me to tell you that she's terribly angry with you. Disappointed were her exact words. She said you would know why."

I blanch.

He glances down at his gold wristwatch. "Shouldn't you be going? I wouldn't want you to be late."

THIRTY-EIGHT

Ivy

The ride back from Fire Island to the Metropolitan Museum was quiet and the night even quieter. We all retreated to our rooms, stunned into silence at Kevin's fate. I didn't sleep, and after close inspection of the faces around the breakfast table, I'm pretty sure no one else did either. We weren't woken up this morning, yet we all converged in the dining room at approximately the same time. It's Herrick's last meal with us. I can't bring myself to say anything to him after he called me a bitch. I know it's petty of me to hold on to that after what happened, but I can't help it.

"It'll be weird being just the three of us," Lincoln says.

"I have to admit, I'm sort of glad I'm leaving. It's going to be such a fiasco around here," Herrick says, spooning scrambled eggs into his mouth.

Lincoln smirks. "More than it was already?"

Chase picks at his blueberry muffin, turning it into crumbs. He doesn't eat the crumbs. He just stares at them as though trying to divine his future from their pattern. He hasn't spoken a word to me since I dragged Kevin's body back to the beach. I don't know if he blames me for his death or if he's angry I lied to him about not knowing how to swim.

"That was the first dead body I ever saw," Lincoln says. "It's weird how colorless we become in death."

"Please stop. I'm trying to eat," Chase says.

Lincoln checks his plate. "No, you're not."

He shakes his head. He hasn't combed his hair, and it's spiky in places.

"Morning." It's Brook and Josephine. "Herrick, Dominic apologizes for not being here to see you off. He's in negotiations with the network. They want a guarantee that the show will wrap up and not be abandoned mid-competition."

"So it really will go on?" Lincoln says. There's a hopeful undertone to her voice.

Brook gives a grave nod.

"*Demain*," Josephine says. "Tomorrow. We start again tomorrow."

"Chase, Mom and Dad would like to spend the day with you. To celebrate your birthday. I'll try to meet you for lunch. Lincoln, Ivy, I would suggest you girls take it easy today, but I'd understand if you want to go out. Is there any attraction you'd like to see? A Broadway show maybe?"

"I wouldn't mind doing some sightseeing," I say, thinking about the diamond in my bag. I need to get rid of it. I'm tempted to pawn it off, but what if the salesman recognizes that it's stolen? I'd get arrested. *No,* I'll have to toss it out somewhere.

"I'll take you," Lincoln offers.

He nods. "I'll get one of the drivers to accompany you. Just in case."

"In case what?" I ask.

"In case journalists spot you. They know the show's been canceled for the day, so they'll be on the lookout. If you meet any, *please* refrain from saying anything. Herrick, the same goes to you. You are off the show, but it would mean a lot to the rest of us if you don't talk about Kevin."

"It was written in his *contrat*," Josephine says. "In all of their contracts."

Herrick mimics zipping his lips anyway.

"It was really great to have you with us," Brook says, hugging Herrick. "Really. You have a lot of talent." He pats his back and then lets go.

Josephine extends her hand and Herrick shakes it.

"Thank you. All of you. You've made this competition challenging and memorable." Herrick smiles.

"Ivy, Lincoln, someone will fetch you when the car's downstairs. We'll all reconvene at my place tonight for a quiet dinner. Have a nice day, guys." Our faces must be grim, because he adds, "At least, try to."

Along with Lincoln and Chase, I withdraw down the grassy hallway. I wait until she's in her room before following Chase into his.

"You've got the wrong tent," he says.

"No. I got the right one. Why are you angry with me?"

"You lied. I don't like liars."

"I lied because—"

He doesn't let me finish my sentence. "My ex was a liar."

"If you'll just let me explain."

"Don't bother."

"Chase—"

"Really, Ivy. You don't owe me an explanation."

"So that's it? You're just going to push me away because I pretended not to know how to swim?"

"I wasn't thinking straight last night. As you said, one of us will be gone soon, so there's no point in starting anything."

For some reason, even though he's throwing my words back at me, it stings.

When I don't move, he adds, "Is that all?"

Swallowing hard, I turn around and escape through the zippered opening, running right into Lincoln. Her eyes glow like a cat's among the twinkling tree lights.

"I was looking for you. The car's downstairs," she says. "Oh. You're not dressed."

My cheeks flame. "I will be in a minute."

"I'll wait in the living room," she says.

I walk into my room and yank on the outfit laid out on the bed. I should have stuck to my gut feeling about Chase instead of getting whisked away in the heat of the moment. I trace my steps to the red duffel bag to fish out the diamond and the paper I made Aster sign, the paper that will destroy her trust in me. For a moment, I'm tempted to throw it away, but Dean said it was her only way out, so instead, I stuff it inside the back pocket of my shorts. And then I reach further down, prepared to rip the seam. But it's already been ripped. And the box is gone!

A chill discharges up my spine. I check the zippered compartment for my money. It's all there. All three hundred dollars, but the porcelain box is definitely gone. Someone knew about the diamond. I drop down on the bed. What am I supposed to do now? Signal the theft of a diamond that most probably was already stolen? *Ugh!*

I think about going into Kevin's room and turning it upside down. He must have taken it. What if he gave it to his lawyer last night though? I pound my palms against the duvet and groan.

"Are you ready yet?" Lincoln asks, sticking her head inside my tent.

I roll up.

"What's eating you?" she asks. "Trouble in paradise?"

"Yeah," I say, because it beats explaining the whole diamond debacle. I stand up, stick the cash in my pocket, and join her in the hallway where her assistant is waiting to escort us to the underground parking lot.

"Hi, Miss Redd, Miss Vega," Danny says, holding the door of a sedan open. He seems shy—or repentant.

I don't answer him. He doesn't deserve an answer after the aversion he showed me when he believed I'd doctored Kevin's pictures. I slide in next to Lincoln, who takes out a huge pair of leopard sunglasses from her tiny purse. I didn't look for sunglasses and regret it because it's bright out.

"You like bargains?" Lincoln asks me.

"Sure," I mumble, even though I'm in no mood to shop.

She leans forward. "Century 21," she says, then lounges back and crosses her legs. "You'll see Times Square on the way downtown. And the store isn't far from the Brooklyn Bridge. We can have lunch in Brooklyn Heights. There's a little organic restaurant I used to work in. They still give me free meals."

She's extra chatty during the drive, telling me all about her city. She shows me the school where her ex taught, and the subway station where she recreated the Picasso painting in chalk. She points out the club where she waitressed to pay for her sixth-floor attic studio.

Hordes of shoppers are out, dappling the sidewalks with their colorful plastic and paper bags. Cars honk, people shout into their cell phones, garbage trucks beep, drills shatter asphalt, and kids squeal. It makes for a deafening, lovely cacophony.

"I would've liked to live here," I say.

Her elbow is bent against the built-in armrest in the door, and her fist cushions her head that's angled toward me. "Kokomo was no fun?"

"It was okay. It's a small town, though, so everyone knew everyone else's business, which can be suffocating," I whisper, watching the billboards stretching several stories high, the enormous, wrap-around screens displaying bright ads, and the cowboy in tighty-whities and lizard boots playing the guitar in the middle of all that. New York looks like some futuristic civilization.

"Why do you think Kevin took his life?" she asks. "Because he was"—she mouths the word *gay*.

"I think it's because of the doctored photos."

"Do you know who doctored them?"

I shake my head.

"So much intrigue," she whispers. "Do you remember how I joked my parents would probably come out of the woodwork if I won? Well, guess what? I got a letter."

"You did?"

"The person sent it to the show. This guy claiming to be my long-lost father. He seems way too young, though, so I don't know."

"How old is he?"

"Thirty-six. Which would have made him sixteen when I was born. Then again, teen pregnancies happen, right?"

"Did he send a picture?"

"Yeah."

"And? Do you look like him?"

"You tell me." She digs a picture out of her bag.

The man is quite handsome, with large green eyes like Lincoln's, and the same mouth with the plumper upper lip.

"I see a resemblance," I say.

She studies it too. "What if we don't have anything in common?"

"I have a twin sister, and we couldn't be more different."

"Like how?"

She's a thief and a liar. "She's a loner," I finally say.

"How's she coping behind bars?"

"I'm sure she's fine."

"You don't know?"

"No communication, remember?"

"Wasn't her lawyer there last night?"

I bite my lip, ashamed I didn't ask Dean how Aster was doing. "She's fine, apparently," I lie.

Danny clears his throat.

"Sick of being locked up, but fine," I repeat.

He does it again.

"What?" I snap.

"I read on the Internet that she was almost killed. Locked in a freezer by another inmate."

All the blood flows out of my face.

"Jail's harsh," he adds.

I'm so perplexed by the news that I let the city go in and out of focus. I do the same for Lincoln's ensuing conversation with the driver about the atrocities in prisons. Sickened by the news, I lower the window.

"We're here," Lincoln says.

We've finally stopped in front of a block-long store.

"I don't feel like shopping anymore," I tell her.

"Why not?"

"I just don't. But go ahead. I'll wait in the car." As Lincoln clicks off her seat belt, I ask the driver, "Could I use your phone?"

"No can do. Show rules."

"Please. It's to call my sister. Please."

His eyes travel over my face, then dart to Lincoln's. Maybe if I'd asked once she was gone, he would've accepted. Stupid me. "I'm real sorry."

"On second thought"—she straps herself back in—"I don't need to buy anything. Let's go to the bridge."

By the time we park next to an overhanging walkway that rises above the murky waters of the East River, I feel so sullen that I want to yell and cry. I do neither. I get out and slam my door. Danny tails us, conspicuous in his black suit and aviators. If anything, he makes people gawk and whisper.

When we're halfway across the bridge, he says, "We should head back to the car. You've been made."

Lincoln flaps her hand in the air. "Relax."

"Mister Bacci made it clear to keep you away from crowds."

"I'm not agoraphobic." Lincoln's smiling for the raised smartphones. She even waves.

I keep my face angled down. "He's right. We should head back."

"Oh, stop it, you two. They're harmless. They just want some pictures," Lincoln says. "They love us."

They love us so much that they close in on us, asking for autographs on their water bottles, their bags, even on an unused diaper. At first, Danny fends them off, but the crowd grows so deep that he is rendered powerless. He takes out his cell phone and calls for backup.

A large video camera pushes past the crowd, along with a woman holding a microphone. The reporters have found us. My breathing becomes shallow and my heart pounds harder. I look around like a crazed animal, trying to locate an escape hatch, but I can't even see the bridge railing.

I feel hands stroke my back, my bottom, my chest, and my stomach. Fabric and skin brush my bare legs and arms. The stench of armpits, of un-brushed teeth, and pungent perfumes slap me. I scramble backward, taking shelter between Danny and Lincoln, using their bodies to shield my own. An arm drapes around my stiff shoulders. Lincoln's. She's chatting with the reporter.

"Ivy was the first to find him," she says.

My breath hitches.

"Did you have anything to do with Mister Martin's death, Miss Redd?" the reporter asks.

"I said she was the first on the scene. I didn't say she killed him. Right, Ivy? You didn't kill Kevin?" Lincoln asks sweetly.

I gape at her bright teeth as she squeezes my shoulder. And then I step away, because I finally see her for the viper she is. She wants me out of the running, and by implying I could have had a hand in Kevin's death, she just might get her way.

THIRTY-NINE

"If you were to commit suicide in here, how would you do it?" I ask the women sitting at my table in the middle of our breaded chicken and mushy corn dinner.

"I'd hang myself," Gill says.

"With what?" Chacha asks, readjusting her hairnet.

"I'd roll up my bed sheets," Gill says. "Tie a noose."

"Okay. And where would you attach them? It's not like there's a hook on the ceiling of our cells." The woman who speaks is one of Chacha's relatives apparently—a distant cousin. She sort of looks like her even though her eyes are much lighter, almost honey-colored, and her hair's dyed blonde. Her name's Gracie.

"I dunno. Maybe on the upper railing of our bunk beds. And then I'd have to keep my knees bent until my neck broke," Gill says.

"I would use a knife," Chacha says.

"Yeah, but you have access to knives. That's too easy," Gill says.

"Then I'd drink a cleaning product. A toxic one."

"What about you?" I ask the translucent-skinned girl sitting alone a few spaces down. She's been listening to our conversation. I can tell by the way her clear eyes keep darting our way.

She sits up straighter. "I'd cut my wrists with a shiv."

"A shiv? What's that?" I ask.

"Homemade blade, dumb-dumb," Chacha says.

"You can make it out of a toothbrush," Gracie adds. "I even heard of a prisoner making a shiv in papier-mâché out of a toilet paper roll."

"How would *you* do it, Gracie?" I ask her, pushing the corn kernels around with my fork. Chacha looks at my plate, so I scoop some up and shovel them inside my mouth.

Gracie spins a small container of creamer between her index and middle fingers. "I'd light this baby up. It becomes a flamethrower." She drops her voice. "But don't tell anyone or we'll be forced to drink our coffees black." She sets it back down and fixes me with her yellow eyes. "How 'bout you? How would you do it, Aster?"

"I think I'd just lock myself in the freezer again. At least you pass out before you die."

Chacha wrinkles her wide nose. "You're morbid."

"Why are we talking about suicide?" Gill asks, her red dreads swinging past her shoulder blades. "You aren't planning on killing yourself now, are you?"

"No," I say, even though the thought crossed my mind after Dean left. I spear a piece of soggy, breaded chicken and eat it.

Gill's brown eyes stay narrowed; she doesn't believe me. Suddenly another tray slides in next to mine. It's Translucent-girl. I wasn't sure what part of my question was an invitation for her to sit closer.

"Was that what happened yesterday? You tried to off yourself?" the girl asks. She smells like water, mineral and tinny.

"Yesterday was an accident," I say.

Chacha leans over the table to see past me. "What you in for, Sofia?"

"I killed my professor," Sofia says. "He gave me bad grades. He would've ruined my future."

Gracie snorts. "And killing him didn't fuck it up?"

Sofia shrugs. "At least I was in control of my fate."

"Ever killed anyone else?" Gill asks.

"No, but I did kill an animal once. My grandma's parakeet. I plucked it, hoping it would shut up. It just screeched louder, so I had to snap its neck." She forks another big bite of chicken into her mouth.

"Ouch," Chacha says. She scoots back, probably to put some space between herself and the pallid nutcase next to me.

"If I hadn't killed him, someone else would've. The man had it coming," Sofia says.

"How did you kill him?" I find myself asking.

"Followed one of his recipes to make acid, and then splashed it all over his body. Worked really well."

"You're real fucked up." Chacha readjusts her hairnet and then swings her bony bowlegs off the bench. "I need to get back to the kitchen. Gracie, you coming?"

Her cousin stands and follows her out. No longer under the cook's scrutiny, I push my tray away.

"Can I have the rest?" Sofia asks. "I love chicken."

I nod.

"Parakeet tastes a little the same."

"You ate the fucking bird?" Gill asks.

"I wasn't going to let it rot."

"Did you eat your teacher too?" Gill asks.

"That's sick. I'm not some cannibal. Yuck." After sticking my chicken on her plate, she asks, "Have *you* ever eaten human flesh?"

"Hell no," Gill and I say at the same time.

"Did you hear about your sister, Aster?" Sofia asks out of the blue.

"Hear about what?"

"That she might be connected to Kevin's death."

Every muscle in my body coils. "She had nothing to do with it."

"Apparently she was in the water, next to his body and—"

"What?" I say.

"Apparently she was in—"

"I heard you!" I've raised my voice. "A lot of people were in the water."

"It's Lincoln who suggested it. She said your sister was trashed last night. She could've lost control—"

"Ivy doesn't lose control."

"Are you sure about that?"

"Yes."

"But—"

Gill wraps her hands around her freckled elbows. "Drop it, Sofia."

Sofia's talc-pink lips open, but close immediately. She scrapes the remainder of my plate onto hers, and then moves back to her original seat. I get another strong whiff of her boggy scent.

Neither Gill nor I say anything for a while. After several long minutes of me staring daggers at the cup of green Jell-O on my tray, Gill speaks up, "Why were you asking about suicide?"

"It was just a topic of conversation."

"My ass. You're not the sort of person who comes up with *just a topic* of conversation. Everything you say and do, you think about…a lot."

I hoist up my shoulders, then let them slump. "Maybe I've been feeling down."

"Well let's bring you back up then," she says. "What makes you happy?"

"Popcorn and a movie."

Gill jumps off the bench. "Consider it done."

"Really?"

"Yes. I hope you're not too picky about the movie," she says. "We'll have to see what's on cable."

"I'll watch anything."

"Good."

She walks over to Officer Landry and, after a brief conversation, she's granted access to the kitchen.

A movie and popcorn sound surreal.

"She your girlfriend?" Sofia asks mid-bite.

"She's my friend."

"You sure she's clear on that?"

"I'm sure."

"Can I have your Jell-O?"

"You can have my Jell-O." I slide it over so she doesn't come near me again.

"Thanks." As I make to get up, she adds, "Another good way to get killed is messing with the wrong person." She tips her head toward Cheyenne. "But it could backfire. You could become that person's bitch, although I don't think she swings that way." After a spoonful of the wobbly green stuff, she adds, "She's probably your best bet. That is, if you're serious about leaving the DOC in a body bag."

"I'm not suicidal."

"I thought you were down."

"Eavesdrop much," I grumble.

"I don't eavesdrop. I'm just aware. Some friendly advice: no one can hurt you if you're aware 'cause you can figure their next move before they make it. I was a grandmaster when I was a kid."

"A what?"

"A professional chess player." She winks at me, her see-through eyelashes grazing her diaphanous cheek.

I've never seen anything coming. In the past, it was because I was so focused on Ivy. Now, it's because I'm so focused on my predicament. Or perhaps those are excuses. Perhaps I don't want to see things coming. Who wants to keep their eyes on the headlights of a truck that's barreling straight for you?

"We're all set," Gill says.

She's crept up so quietly that I jump.

"Already?" I ask.

She nods and extends her hand to help me up. I pretend not to see it and rise on my own. Underneath her arm, I spot a brown bag with grease smudges that make the air smell divine. Together, we walk over to Landry, who signals the squat guard in the opposite corner, the one who always sports her hair in a thick braid.

"Kim, could you take Inmates Redd and Swanson to the dayroom and stay with them. Sergeant Driscoll granted them one hour of television."

Kim frowns, but leads the way.

"How did you swing that?" I whisper to Gill. "Another free wax?"

She smiles. "Yup."

"Thanks," I say.

"Anything for you."

Her eyes sparkle like the diamond in the porcelain box. The one that's no longer there.

FORTY

Ivy

"Do not come near me!" I yell at Lincoln, grabbing fistfuls of the dove-gray sham.

After the bridge incident, Danny and two cops escorted us back to Brook's apartment where I burrowed in his guest bedroom. I haven't spoken a word to anyone since the revolting accusation. I've just lain on my side, facing the cloudless sky and wondering how I could have been so shortsighted.

"I never meant to accuse you of anything."

"Leave me alone, Lincoln."

She sticks one hand on her hip. "You think the world is out to get you, don't you? Well, you're wrong. And the only reason I mentioned you were in the water was because you were."

"And the alcohol? My vomiting? Why did you mention that?"

"The reporter brought it up. I didn't. Besides, it works to your advantage. If you were buzzed, then it looks less suspicious."

"*Suspicious*? Are you hearing yourself, Lincoln? Just get out," I growl.

I turn my gaze back to the dazzling slice of city visible through the panoramic window. The building across the street is entirely made of glass. It reflects Brook's penthouse, down to the bodies stirring around the pool deck, setting up dinner. A hubbub erupts in the hallway.

"She's in here," Lincoln calls out.

"Ivy, we tried to come as quickly as possible but the negotiations with the network took longer than expected," Dominic says. He steps around the bed. His perma-tanned skin looks a little orange and wrinkled. "I don't like these new accusations. *And* I don't believe them." He shifts my feet to the side to sit. "Tell me what happened, sweetheart." When I don't, he looks toward the door. "Lincoln, go get ready. Your stylists are in the living room. Brook, shut the door, please." Once it's closed, he says, "It's just us now. Tell me what happened."

"Haven't you seen the news, Mister Bacci? I was accused of murdering Kevin," I say bluntly.

"And did you?"

I sit up so quickly that my head spins. "Of course not."

"Then why are you so worked up?"

"Because it's all lies." I gather my knees against me. "Just like the doctored photos."

"Then you have nothing to worry about. When the detectives get here, just—"

"The detectives?" I yelp.

He nods. "The show's lawyer—the one you met—she'll be here too. You have our total support, Ivy." He pats my knee. "You know," he adds, "last night, on the beach, I spoke to Kevin's lawyer. He told me about the sergeant's wife. About what she did…I even have a copy of her letter." He pats the breast pocket of his beige linen jacket.

"What did she do?"

"You don't know?"

"No."

His pupils pulse.

"Did *she* doctor the photos?" I ask.

"I shouldn't—"

"I was wrongfully accused—twice now. I think I deserve to get some answers."

He fixes me for a long time. "Kevin was going to leave her. So she destroyed his dream of getting on our show."

"By doctoring those photos," I say in a shocked whisper.

Winded by this discovery, I barely react when Brook, the female lawyer with the goat face, and the two detectives file into the room. McEnvoy, without asking the ladies if they'd like a seat, sinks into the leather desk chair. Combing his fingers through his prematurely graying hair, he crosses an ankle over his knee. He's wearing his black work boots again—in ninety-degree weather. They must stink.

"Good evening, everyone. I will be acting as Miss Ivy Redd's council this evening," the lawyer says, taking out a massive number of files. She thumbs through them until she finds a particular sheet of paper. "I believe this meeting will only take a minute. Here." She gives the paper to the female detective who glances down at it. I can't see what it says, but it looks like a photocopy of a ripped note.

"This only proves that Miss Redd didn't tamper with Mister Martin's pictures," Clancy says, wetting her ultra-pale lower lip. I'd forgotten how her mouth blended right into her face. "It doesn't prove she didn't kill him."

"Nor that she wasn't under the influence," McEnvoy adds.

"Oh, come on!" Dominic throws his arms in the air. "What is your obsession with our contestant?"

The lawyer holds out her hand to calm him down. "I've spoken to the bartenders catering the event and to each waiter working last night. They've all testified to never having come in contact with Miss Redd. Underage drinking might be punishable by law, but I do believe it's below your pay grade to worry about Miss Redd's alcoholic intake."

"Maybe someone gave it to her," McEnvoy says. "The gift of alcohol is illegal."

"Could we return to the matter at hand? Miss Redd's alleged involvement in Mister Martin's death."

McEnvoy's mouth opens, but Clancy speaks before he can. "Ivy, a source tells us you got in a fight with Mister Martin shortly before his death. Is that true?"

"You don't need to answer that," the lawyer tells me. She glances at the door, then at her watch.

"I have nothing to hide," I say. "Yes. We had a fight."

"What about?" McEnvoy asks, bobbing in the chair.

I don't tell them I made fun of his sensitivity; I don't think it would look too good for me. "He stole something from my room."

Dominic blinks. "Are you sure?"

I nod.

"What was it?" he asks.

"A piece of jewelry." I don't clarify it was a diamond, because if it surfaces, and it really is *dirty*, I can always say that I was talking about a ring or a necklace.

"Why didn't you come to me with that? Or to Brook?"

Brook's eye twitches.

"Can you pull the camera footage?" Dominic asks him.

"There's no camera in the hallway."

"The angle of the one in the living room should be wide enough to see if anyone went into her room." Dominic's forehead glistens with a thin layer of sweat. "This is just absurd! I swear, the show's cursed this year."

"Can we get back—" Leah begins, but Dominic interrupts her.

"When did you notice the theft, Ivy?"

"The night Kevin arrived," I lie.

"And you're sure it couldn't have happened before he got there."

"I'm sure. It was still in my bag when I left for the pool party."

Dominic slaps his thigh. "Absurd, I tell you. Brook, pull the footage of that day."

Brook's Adam's apple bobs up and down in his throat. "I'll phone Jeb."

"What were you doing in the ocean last night?" Leah asks me, her voice sharp.

"In case you didn't notice, there were a lot of people in the water," I say.

"Yes, but what were *you* doing?" McEnvoy asks.

I'm about to tell him I was swimming when a knock echoes on the door.

"Come in," Dominic says.

The door opens, and Chase comes in.

Detective Clancy frowns. "Why is this boy here?"

"Mister Jackson is here because he's Miss Redd's alibi," Dominic says. "And since you don't seem to believe a word that comes out of my contestant's mouth, I asked him to testify. Chase?"

He heaves a deep breath. "Ivy was in the water last night because I asked her to come in with me."

"And why should we believe you?" McEnvoy asks.

"Because I brought proof." Chase fishes a picture from the back pocket of his khakis. "Here." He gives it to the female detective first.

She studies it.

"Will that do, Detective? Can I be dismissed?" he asks.

She lifts her gaze back up to his face. Her eyes are as round as billiard balls.

McEnvoy rips the picture out of her hand and ogles it. Then he repeatedly flicks his index finger against it. "How do we know this hasn't been doctored?"

The vein in Chase's forehead throbs.

"Shut up, Austin," Detective Clancy mumbles, eyes flashing over the room. "Thank you for your time, Council, Mister Bacci, Mister Jackson. Miss Redd, I'm sure we'll see each other again soon."

"Why would we?" I ask.

"Just a hunch," she says.

Goose bumps scatter over my skin, because I can tell it isn't "just a hunch."

"Let me walk you out," Dominic suggests, ushering the lawyer and the two detectives out of the bedroom.

Chase leaves right after them. Before Brook can follow them out, I call him back. He seems reluctant to stay behind.

"I have a paper to give to Dean. It's for Aster's trial." I fish the signed form from my pocket and hand it over.

"Okay," he says, stuffing it in his pocket. "So you and my brother, huh?"

"There is no *me and your brother*."

"But the picture—"

"Pictures lie." I think of Kevin and the picture that got him disqualified.

"Kevin's personal effects are being packed up as we speak. I'll have the cleaners check for jewelry. What was it exactly that was stolen?"

"A necklace," I finally say.

"Can you describe it for me?"

"It was a diamond pendant. I kept it in a porcelain box."

"Why weren't you wearing it?"

"Because the show lends the jewelry. I thought my stylist would make me take it off."

"You should've left it at home then."

"I don't have a safe at home."

Brook stares at me, but then his eye twitches again, and he lowers his gaze.

"Sorry to interrupt, Mister Jackson, but we need to get Ivy ready for dinner," Leila says.

"Already?" Sure enough, the light has softened outside.

Brook gives a jerky nod.

After he leaves, Leila shuts the door and points to the chair McEnvoy occupied just minutes ago. "Sit."

Even though she makes up my face, her kohl-lined gaze never once grazes mine. Perhaps I owe her an apology—or rather I owed her an apology. Now, it's too late. Amy feels like she needs to fill the silence with chatter. She talks about everything, from the latest clothing trends to the newest weight loss cleanse. She switches from one topic to the next so swiftly that her skin purples from lack of oxygen. Strangely, I find her babbling soothing.

Leila puts the final coat of gloss on my lips and repacks her stuff. Once she's left the room, Amy unhooks the rollers from my hair and brushes them out to soften the rich curls. The effect is beautiful. I pull off my T-shirt and shorts, and yank on the electric blue frock laid out on the bed. The top is loose and gauzy, unlike the bottom, which is made of tight, overlapping bands of fabric.

"If I could keep one outfit, it would be this one," I tell Amy as she folds the garment bag.

"I'm sure Mister Bacci would allow it. You should ask him," she says. "It looks really pretty on you. Then again, is there anything that doesn't?"

"That zombie get-up," I say. It feels like it was a lifetime ago that I wore it.

"Even *that* you pulled off."

"You're way too kind, Amy. And very talented," I tell her. "You'll have to leave me your card."

Her cheeks turn as pink as her hair. "Of course! Here."

She fishes a business card from her box of pins and elastics. It's totally tacky: gold with swirly pink lettering. "Can you leave it in my room?"

She nods so many times that it looks as though she's pecking the air.

As I walk out of the bedroom, I feel lightheaded—perhaps because my stomach is near empty, or perhaps because of how resilient I've grown since arriving in New York. The Masterpiecers has transformed me. I think of Aster and wonder if prison has changed her too. I hope it's hardened her, made her more able to cope with life in society, to deal with her insecurities without having to fabricate stories about aborted pregnancies. And then, I think about the dead man and the tear in my quilt, and my sympathy for her dries up.

When I step out onto the terrace, the sky is streaked peach and pink and gold, like a Monet painting.

"Ivy, you're here, next to me," Dominic says, pulling out my chair.

To my right, I have Brook and in front of me, Chase. Lincoln and Josephine are on either side of him. I glance at Lincoln, pleased that I foiled her plan. Her face is blank, like a child who's been reprimanded.

Dominic starts dinner off with a toast. He closes his eyes and lifts his glass. "To Kevin, who we hope has finally found peace."

"Amen," Josephine and Brook say.

"*And*, to the most eventful, and surely the most memorable, competition." He says this with a soft smile. "And to the last two tests! We're raising the stakes."

"Sh…Dom," Josephine says, setting her glass of white wine down. "Don't give it away."

"And to Chase's birthday…a happy one this time," Dominic adds as servers bring out little glass bowls of chilled tomato soup topped with teeny, golden croutons.

"I'd also like to propose a toast. *Plus de drame*. No more drama. Okay, Brook?" Josephine asks, giving him an oblique smile that doesn't create a single crease on her face. Even her forehead stays perfectly smooth.

Brook's smile washes off his lips, and as dinner progresses, he becomes more and more restless, jostling his knees, toying with his fork, drinking more than he should. I count five refills. When Josephine excuses herself, telling us she needs an early night, Dominic pulls Brook aside. They talk quietly and then Dominic leaves and Brook returns. He sits down even though the table has been cleared and the camera crew is packing up.

"Dom has agreed to let all of you hang out a while longer. To decompress," Brook says.

Chase eyes his brother. "Is that what *you're* doing?"

"If you were under the stress I was under, little brother, you'd—"

"I just think you should quit while you're ahead."

"Why don't you mind your own business?" Brook answers dryly.

Chase presses away from the table and walks over to the opposite side of the terrace to lie on one of the lounge chairs.

"Well, this isn't awkward," Lincoln says. "I'm going to go powder my nose." She rises and heads inside Brook's bachelor pad.

"I feel like I'm missing something," I tell Brook once it's just the two of us.

He twirls his glass of wine between his long fingers. "Josephine doesn't like me."

"I don't think she likes anyone."

"Yeah, but she really has it in for me."

"Why?"

He glances at his brother who's staring up at the starless night sky. "Because she's afraid Dominic's going to promote me."

"So what if he does?"

"I'd be taking her place."

"Ah. I can see how that would be a problem."

"Remember that day at the airport, when you arrived at the same time I did?"

"Hard to forget when someone treats you like dirt," I say.

He doesn't react to my comment. "Josephine orchestrated that."

"If you have proof, then she can't use it against you."

He leans in closer. "Exactly."

Plumes of stale alcohol hit my nose. Before leaning back, he tucks a strand of hair behind my ear.

"You shouldn't do that," I say.

"Do what?"

"Touch me. I'm a contestant."

He drops his hand back to his lap. "Right."

In the corner of my eye, I spot Lincoln. She smiles her dark, bright smile.

"Crap. Now she's going to tell the press that you and I are hooking up," I whisper in his ear.

His dimples appear as a grin spreads across his face. "Watch me take care of that." He stands, walks over to her, and tells her something. At first, she looks startled, but then she nods. "Anyone else up for a midnight dip?" Brook asks loudly, so that his words reach his brother, the only other person on the terrace.

"I think I'm over midnight dips," I say, thinking of Kevin.

Brook winks at me before tugging Lincoln into the apartment to change into swimsuits.

I stroll over toward Chase, shake off my shoes, and lay down on the lounge chair next to his. His cologne is faint tonight, yet I can still smell the pine needles and the grass in the dark air. "At some point, you're going to have to talk to me," I say.

"Why?"

"Because we're on the same show. Anyway, I just came over to say thank you," I tell him.

"For what?"

"For stepping up for me earlier with the detectives."

The ligaments in his neck stretch and tauten. "I didn't have a choice. Dominic was going to show them the picture." His words sting. I'm about to leave, when he adds, "I've been meaning to ask how you knew Dean Kane."

"Your brother introduced us last night on the beach."

"Why?"

"For my sister. Brook offered to have him defend her."

"You should pass up on his offer."

"Why?"

"He's famous for getting some of the worst people off death row."

"That'll work in my sister's favor."

"I wouldn't trust him, Ivy."

"You don't trust anyone."

He turns to look at me. His eyes are dark, yet I can detect emotion in them, grief, disappointment, anguish. I feel the urge to stroke his cheek and comfort him, and begin lifting my hand when he turns away.

"Don't look at me like that," he says.

"Like what?"

"Like I'm some hurt little kid."

I let my arm drop back to my side just as Lincoln and Brook cannonball inside the pool.

"Are you going to join them?" he asks. "Or are you going to pretend you don't know how to swim?"

Tears laminate my eyes and blur his pale profile. "You're a dick," I murmur, turning my face upward, toward the blackness, to guide the stupid, wasted emotion back into my eyes. I'm about to ask Brook if I can return to the museum when I see him locking lips with Lincoln. As I walk by, he catches me staring and winks.

Inside the dark and deserted apartment, I find the house phone on the marble kitchen counter. I swipe it from its base and carry it into the bathroom. I lock the door and dial a number I know by heart.

When I hear a click, I whisper, "Josh?" but it goes straight to voicemail. I'm tempted to empty my heart, tell him that I think Aster didn't kill Troy for my quilt, that I think she killed him for what was inside, but I don't want there to be yet another trace of my suspicion.

Especially if I'm wrong.

FORTY-ONE

I was sick all night. When I spot Sofia scarfing down her bowl of porridge the next morning, I deduce it's not salmonella poisoning.

"Hi," Gill says, a smile stretching from one side of her face to the other. All of her teeth point in different directions like those strings of square, paper lanterns people loop around their porches in the summer.

She swoops down to plant a kiss on my cheek, but I hold her back. "I'm sick. I don't want to infect you."

Grin still intact, she says, "I'm probably already infected." She tries to peck my face again when I slap my hand over my mouth and jump off the bench to run toward the bin. I just make it.

Cool fingers stroke my neck, gather my dreads. *God, she's everywhere*. What have I gotten myself into?

"Sergeant Driscoll, can I go to the infirmary? I'm not feeling too well."

"Morning sickness?" he asks. His potbelly shakes with a chuckle while my cheeks flame.

"I'll walk her over. To spare you an uncomfortable run-in with Nurse Celia," Gill says, repaying his snarky comment.

The laughter dries in his throat. "*Yobwoc*," he yells. "Get your ass over here."

"Inmate Redd needs some medical attention," he says, glaring at Gill. "Walk her to the infirmary."

He nods. Gill hooks her arm through mine and begins to follow him, but Driscoll stops her. "Swanson, you're needed in the laundry room. Got some linens to press."

Gill sucks in a breath and releases my arm. "Asshole," she murmurs. "I'll try to stop by later, okay?"

I nod, and the movement angers my throbbing head. I hold on to the walls as I trail Officer Landry. He turns around a few times, and although he seems concerned, he doesn't offer me support. He's probably worried that touching an inmate will look bad. Or that I'll give him what I have.

The hallway floor shifts like in a funhouse. The ground goes forward and back and side to side. I trip at some point and one of my flip-flops flies off, but I catch myself before I hit the floor. Landry stops, casts another worried glance my way, but still doesn't help. My fingers tremble as they slip the flip-flop back on. My feet are white and as stiff as when Chacha extracted me from the freezer. The world spins again and suddenly I'm flat on my back and Officer Landry is upside down. Nurse Celia's face pops into my line of sight. I think I hear her call out my name but I'm not sure.

She hoists me up with the help of Landry, and together, they carry me to the cot in her office. Drawers slam, metal clangs, wheels spin. A sharp pain explodes in my wrist. I peer down and see she's stuck a catheter inside my vein and is hooking it up to an IV bag.

"When was the last time you ate something, Aster?" she asks. It sounds like she's at the bottom of a well.

"Last night."

"I mean really ate?" she repeats. "Like a proper meal."

"The burger," I croak.

"That was two days ago! Landry, get me a bottle of Coke."

While he's gone, she takes my blood pressure, inspects my eyes with a small flashlight, and prods my abdomen.

"I'm going to keep you a few hours. You're completely dehydrated."

"Sure," I say, as my head lolls to the side and my lids slam shut like magnets. "Nowhere else to go."

WHEN I WAKE UP, the nausea has receded and my vein, the one with the catheter in it, is cold from the drip. Slowly, I drum my fingers and shift my legs. The paper crinkles under me, alerting Nurse Celia of my wakefulness.

She simultaneously prods my free wrist for a pulse and keeps an eye on her watch. "That's a better rhythm," she says, and proceeds to remove the needle taped to my opposite arm. The IV bag hangs limply on a pole, near empty. "Can you sit up?"

I nod and do as I'm asked.

"I've requested they add two granola bars to your diet every day. Please eat them." She returns to her desk and grabs a glass filled with brown liquid. "Now, drink this. It'll get your blood sugar zinging."

I take a sip. When I realize it's Coke—even though it's room temperature and most of the bubbles have fizzed out—I gulp it down. "What time is it?"

"It's ten."

"My sister's show must be starting."

The nurse's eyes light up. "Want to watch it?"

"Yes," I say, because I need to see my sister's face. I need to know if she's truly angry with me. "But I can go to the dayroom if you've got other patients to see."

"No other patients. Just you." Her door is already shut, but she moves toward it to test the handle. "Don't want to be disturbed."

More like caught.

Keeping her laptop on the desk, she turns it toward the exam table. It's already broadcasting the show. She wheels over her chair and plops down. Her gaze glued to the monitor, she says, "I called Dean"—a faint linear flush extends from the bridge of her nose to her hairline—"to tell him that you fainted, but that you were okay now."

I doubt he'd care much.

Dominic's on the screen, microphone in hand. He's not smiling today. "Ladies and gentlemen, after a strange few days, and after hours of discussions, Josephine, Brook, and I feel we cannot disappoint our faithful audience, nor can we rob our remaining contestants of the chance of a lifetime. We offer our deepest condolences to Mrs. Martin and Kevin's parents and siblings, and hope that the magnificent rope Kevin wove on his last day has reached them. Also, I wish to take a moment to clear up certain assumptions that seem to have sprouted since my contestants' run-in with the press yesterday on the Brooklyn Bridge. Miss Ivy Redd had nothing to do with Mister Martin's death. Miss Lincoln Vega would like to say a few words to that effect."

The camera perches on Lincoln's face. She is sitting behind Dominic, legs folded and back rigid. When he approaches her with the microphone, her green gaze turns to Ivy whose face is impassible.

"Ivy, I regret the terrible confusion my words created. I didn't mean you any harm," she says.

Her apology sounds rehearsed.

My sister nods and her straightened hair ripples. I wonder if she's gotten highlights. It's more golden than I remember. Perhaps it's because she's tanned so her eyes and hair look paler. I touch my own hair, coarse with dreads that, according to Gill, are maturing nicely. Ivy will hate them and tell me they're ugly and I'll get them raked out.

"Now, for today's test. We are going to attach a small camera and recording device to our contestants' chests and give them a list. That list will be for their eyes only and will contain the instructions of today's tournament. And that is all I will reveal to you, dear audience." He shoots the crowd a white smile. "No camera crew will follow them. The only footage you will be privy to will be the one that will be recorded by their personal devices. However, it will only be broadcasted once they've safely returned to the museum. We do have to keep you guessing." His smile stretches all the way to his silver sideburns.

"What?" Nurse Celia's voice is so strident that I jump. "They're horrible! They can't do that to us!"

"Lincoln, Ivy, Chase," Dominic continues, "are you ready?"

Lincoln's knee shakes; she's the only one who seems anxious.

"Brook, you may hand them their instructions," Dominic says.

The camera shifts over to him. He stands, walks to the contenders, and distributes three scrolls, each tied with a shimmery bow. They tug off the binding and unroll the thick, crackling paper.

My sister's knuckles turn white as she reads. Without even realizing it, I've jumped off the exam table and approached the computer. Ivy's expression quickly turns cool again, but the surprise and—*distress?*—are still there, etched deep into the blueness of her irises. To the world, she may seem confident, but I know she's frightened.

FORTY-TWO

Ivy

I read over the paper again. And again. The instructions are succinct and easy, but the task…God, the task sucks! I try to take a calming breath, but the air in the Temple room is stale and doesn't do crap to calm down my riled nerves. And Dominic's beaming teeth make me want to slap him. If he's so excited, why doesn't he do it himself? What he's asking of us is insane, impossible…illegal!

I go over the list one more time.

1. Corinne Bally's wooden *Babylonian Idol* at the Guggenheim Museum.
2. Otto Milo's *Painted Tissues* installation at the Museum of Modern Art.
3. Zara Mach's *Fuzzy Castanets* at Christie's Auction House.
4. Annabelle Wyatt's lithograph, *Life Dream,* at the Whitney Museum of American Art.
5. Sue Ling's turquoise and bone, *Tusk Goddess,* at the Rubin Museum of Art.
6. Christos Natter's *Miniature Barrel Chair* at the Wilde Gallery of Modern Art.

"CONTESTANTS, you must choose a number and say it out loud. Just the number. Obviously, don't choose the same one." Dominic guffaws, which elicits chuckles from the audience.

I swallow as Chase rolls up his paper and says, without hesitation, "Three."

I stare at the list. Of course…*Christie's*. He must know the auction house inside and out, having worked there. He probably still has an employee key card.

Just the thought slices the threads of hope I'm clinging to as I dangle over the bottomless precipice Dominic has excavated beneath me.

"Six," Lincoln says. Her voice is steady even though she's bouncing her knee.

I go over the remaining four objects. They've left me with only museums. There's so much security in a museum I'm going to fail.

"Ivy? Have you made your choice?"

My lips have gone dry. I swipe my tongue over them and blink into the camera. *Shit, shit, shit.*

"Ivy?"

"Two," I say, just like I could have said any other number.

"Have you memorized your choices?"

My gaze flits over the words again. *Milo, painted tissues, Museum of Modern Art*. I'm the last to nod.

"Okay. You may leave to get outfitted with your recording devices and *other* equipment." Dominic winks, as gleeful as a kid on a merry-freaking-go-round. "Good luck."

Even though I've never believed in luck, today I want to. I also want to bang my head against one of the Met's wainscoted walls and shout, but I iron out my composure. As I stand up to leave under the audience's applause, I wave and flash a fake smile. Quietly, we take the elevator back up to our quarters. Neither Lincoln nor Chase speaks to me—or to each other for that matter. Everyone is focused on the task at hand.

As someone from the film crew hooks the audiovisual recording devices into our clothes, our assistants hand us nondescript black backpacks.

Milo, tissues, MoMA.

"How are we getting there?" Lincoln asks her assistant.

"On motorbikes. We have three waiting for you downstairs."

"I've never driven one," I say.

Cara smiles. "Good thing you won't have to, then," she says, finger-combing her peroxide-blonde hair. "Riders have been assigned to each one of you. They know where to take you so don't speak your locations." She taps the miniature gadget peeping through the ruffles of my wisteria-colored shirt.

"Why not cars?" Lincoln asks.

"So you can go faster…that's what I heard at least," Cara continues, her eyes drifting over our faces.

"They're all set. Run the test!" the person from the film crew yells.

"Ivy's a go. Chase is a go too. Got audio for Lincoln, but not visual. Bring her over."

"Turning off all mics!" someone else shouts as Lincoln is led over to the tech person.

The assistants disperse, leaving me to stand awkwardly next to Chase. Even though my mic is off, I cover it with my palm and drop my voice to a whisper, "Can't the show get in trouble?"

Chase doesn't bother covering up his device. "They have insurance. Plus it's all former students of theirs."

"Yeah, but still…"

"Just don't blow your nose in the tissues," he says. His lips don't quiver, yet there's a tangible hint of humor in his voice.

"Funny," I mutter. After a beat, I add, "This is going to be so easy for you, isn't it? You'll just strut in there with your keycard and—"

"Easy?" he says. "Don't delude yourself, Ivy. It's not going to be easy…for any of us."

"Why did you choose Christie's then?"

"Because it's small, so I'm not going to be hounded by hundreds of curious people like in a museum. I'm not a big fan of crowds." He stares down at me, his gaze devoid of yesterday's animosity. If anything he looks drained, even underneath the thin coat of foundation they've brushed over his skin. "How's your sister?"

"Aster?" I ask.

"Do you have another sister?"

I shake my head dumbly.

"My parents told me yesterday that she'd been hurt in prison."

"I haven't heard from her. No communication, remember?"

"Right." He studies me. "You must miss her."

I feel freer without her, but I can't admit that to anyone. I'd sound cruel. As Lincoln and the two other assistants walk back toward us, I say, "Yeah."

Cara readjusts my device, tests it again, and then leads us down to the underground parking entrance where three gleaming motorbikes are waiting for us. The drivers hand us bulky black helmets, which we strap on.

"Ready?" mine asks, his question muffled by his impressive handlebar mustache.

I nod and hop on, black backpack in place. And then we're off, and warm air blows into my face and blends into my hair and makes my shirt frills flutter and tickle my collarbone. I close my eyes, not from fear but from delight. The ride is exactly what I need, albeit too short.

As soon as we're parked, I take off the helmet and shake out my hair. Amy must have drenched it in leave-in conditioner because it hasn't tangled.

"I was told to give you this," he says.

It's a ticket for the museum. Dominic has thought of everything.

"I'll wait right here for you," he adds.

Gripping the tiny piece of paper, I step through the revolving doors of the Museum of Modern Art, as prepared as I'll get for the outrageous task. *Steal a work of art. Don't get caught. Don't damage it.*

FORTY-THREE

"What do you think they're going to do?" the nurse asks me for the tenth time as though I could somehow have divined it from Ivy's facial expression.

"I don't know," I tell her again. "But it's something she's not looking forward to."

The nurse heaves a sharp sigh. "Man oh man, my blood pressure must be through the roof."

There's a knock on her door. She springs out of her wheelie chair and shuts her laptop. "Lay down," she mouths.

I return to the exam table just as another knock resounds.

She flings the door open and adopts a disgruntled look to mask the flush brightening her cheeks. "This better be important," she grumbles, "because you woke up my patient."

Landry shifts on his work boots and his skin colors. "I'm sorry, Nurse Celia, but I was told to check up on Inmate Redd."

"By whom?"

"Um…by—"

"Let me guess. Driscoll?" she hisses.

"No. Actually by Mrs. Pierce. She wants to see Aster. Something about her trial."

I perk up at those last words, not mood wise, but physically. I lift myself up on my elbows. "My trial?"

Landry nods.

"Am I okay to leave?" I ask Celia.

"I suppose."

"Thank you."

"For what?"

"For treating me like a human being."

Her eyes get this sheen about them. "You *are* a human being. Don't ever forget that."

I follow the young guard down the maze of hallways. The shrink's door is already open.

"Come right in," Robyn says, before exchanging a few quiet words with Landry and shutting the door.

"I've heard you've had a strenuous day," she says, lowering herself into her big armchair and folding one leg over the other. "I also heard that you've been asking about suicide."

"Who told you?"

"It doesn't matter. Is it true?"

"I've been discussing it, not asking about it."

"Are you thinking about killing yourself?" She holds her pen over her paper, waiting for my answer.

"No."

She sets the meaty part of her hand against the paper.

"You wanted to discuss my trial?" I ask.

"I did." A long pause. "But before we get to that, I have a question for you. Are you aware that your mother is dead?"

"Excuse me?"

"Your mother. She's dead. She drowned in the pond by the psychiatric home this spring."

"On purpose?" I've scooted so far forward that I'm teetering on the edge of the cushion.

"It says she slipped."

I snort. "She probably did it on purpose. To get some attention."

"Did you know?"

My eyes burn from the bright sun streaming in. "She's really gone?"

"In your file, it says you didn't attend her funeral."

I stare at her face unseeingly. "Why would I attend her funeral?"

"To say good-bye."

"I said good-bye when she was committed. Besides, she wanted to be cremated. Not buried. Ivy had her buried," I find myself telling her.

Robyn rises and moves around her office, then returns with a tissue. She dangles it in the air between us. I stare at it. She brings it closer to me. I still don't take it. "It's okay to grieve, Aster."

"I'm not grieving."

She cocks her head to the side and studies my face.

"Why would I cry for a woman who made me think I was worthless?" I ask her. My eyes are really hot. I shade them with my hand. "Can you draw the blinds? The sun's in my face."

Robyn doesn't budge for a while.

"Can you please close the blinds?" I repeat.

Carefully, she lays the tissue on the couch, shuts the blinds, and switches on her desk lamp. "Better?"

There's a lump in my throat. I must be coming down with a cold. I massage the back of my neck. My tendons feel like they've been swapped for metal cords.

Robyn returns to her chair and flips through my folder. "This arrived on my email this morning." She holds up a printout. "Is this your signature?"

"I can't see from here."

She comes to sit next to me, places the paper on her lap, and points to the bottom of the page.

My eyesight is still blurry, so I have to squint to make it out. "Yes."

"Why did you sign it?"

"Why wouldn't I sign it?"

"Did you read it?"

"Why?"

"It's a yes or no answer, Aster. Did you read it?"

"No."

"So you don't know what you signed?"

I bristle. "I do. Ivy explained everything. It's a waiver form. In case anything happened to her while she was on the show."

"It's not a waiver." She clears her throat. "Let's read it together, shall we?"

As she begins, my knees and elbows lock. Then my fingers clench into fists and my lungs close and my veins constrict and my throat clogs up. The only part of me that doesn't shut down is the only part I wish would: my heart. Instead, each word cleaves it open a little wider. When I start crying, Robyn hands me the tissue.

Ivy doesn't care about me.

Just like my mother never cared about me.

FORTY-FOUR

Ivy

Unlike the Metropolitan, the Museum of Modern Art is a temple of sleekness and design, all white and glass. For a moment, I forget my mission and stare up and around while hordes of people enter and exit beside me at dizzying speed. No one notices me. They just walk by, their conversations contributing to the din that already resonates against the sharp, smooth surfaces.

When some teenager bumps into me, I get moving. Keeping my head bowed, I grab a museum map and head over to the ticket entrance. The woman scanning the tickets asks me to unzip my bag. She hooks one long vinyl nail inside and angles a small flashlight to view the contents. Only then does it hit me that I should have stuck something in there…anything. Walking around with an empty backpack is sure to arouse suspicion. Sweat beads on my upper lip. I don't dare swipe it off. I just hold my breath until she lets go.

As I start walking away, she says, "Hey, you."

Surely she doesn't mean me. I take a few more steps.

"Hey, I'm talking to you."

She *does* mean me. I freeze and close my eyes. I'm going to get disqualified because of an empty backpack. I don't know whether to be embarrassed or depressed. In slow motion, I turn around.

"Wear the bag on your stomach." She pats her belly. Maybe she thinks I'm foreign…or stupid. I do feel stupid.

I switch the straps to the front as she moves on to the next person. The absurdity of the whole situation exacerbates the anxiety rising within me, to the point where I let out a bark of laughter. I slap my palm in front my mouth to stifle the giggling that ensues while I check my museum map.

The second floor is the one allocated to temporary exhibitions, so I head up the escalators, still smiling like an idiot. I walk through three galleries before I find the one with the painted silk tissues. They're larger than I thought, but also wispier, practically transparent in spite of the splashes of paint. When I see that they're just lying there, haphazardly on the floor with no barriers around them, I am filled with renewed hope. This is going to be a breeze. I walk around them first, scanning the room to locate the security guards. There's only one in this gallery, and he's sitting in a folding chair by the entrance, looking bored out of his mind. I turn sideways and pretend to be captivated by a painting on the wall.

Still facing the painting, I pull one arm out of my backpack so that it hangs off one of my shoulders, then I pivot around and approach the silk tissues. Earlier, I counted five, but there are only four on the ground. I find the fifth wedged in some man's hand. I'm expecting an alarm to resound or the guard to yell, but nothing happens. When I glimpse a second person doing the exact same thing, I realize that handling them is permitted. So I bend over and pick one up too. As I twirl it around in false admiration, a man snaps a picture of me.

"You're that girl," he says way too loudly.

A woman jumps in front of him and screams, "It's Ivy Redd! In the flesh! Oh…my…God!" She fans her face, which is flushed all the way to her hairline.

Her exclamation and hyperventilation attract more attention. Soon the entire room gapes at me, while more people pour in from adjacent galleries. The security guard jolts out of his chair and begins weaving himself through the gathering crowd.

"Back off," he says, arms fanned out wide as though the rubberneckers were dry leaves he could just rake away.

Arms shoot up with cell phones. Everyone is trying to snap a picture of me.

"Let me get you out of here," the guard tells me, after warning onlookers to step back…again.

I can't leave with him. "I'm okay," I say, as my hand drops to my side and gathers the tissue in a ball. I discreetly coax the zipper up with my thumbnail to create a small opening and stuff my fist inside. Trembling, I release the fabric along with the breath I'm holding. No one has noticed anything since I'm standing behind the guard. I strap on a wide smile and raise my voice, "Who wants an autograph?"

A chorus of *me* rings through the small gallery.

"I don't think that's a good idea," the guard says, but I brush past him and grab an outstretched pen and notebook.

I hadn't planned on a mob, but now that there is one, I'll use it to my advantage. As I sign my name, I scan the ground. I spot bright silk just a foot away. I make the pen slide out of my clammy hand. Before anyone else can retrieve it, I squat to grab it and seize the tissue.

"Who's next?" I ask, making sure my grin stays intact in spite of my galloping heartbeat.

While I sign my name, the fingers of my other hand gather the silk in a tight ball. A woman approaches me with her phone.

"So what's the test?" she asks me. I guess she must be filming.

"Aha," I say, with a giant smile. I approach the camera so it won't pick up on my hand snaking into my bag. "It's a secret." I raise a steady finger to my lips and add a theatrical wink.

The crowd goes absolutely wild.

Amid the anarchy, a little girl pulls on the frayed hem of my shorts, large eyes raised toward me. "Can I get your autograph, ma'am?" she asks, extending a Barbie diary.

"Of course," I say.

I glimpse another square of blue-green sticking out from underneath a teenager's sneakers. Praying it isn't damaged, I make my way toward it. Sandwiched between so many people, bending over is impossible, so I pretend to stumble. I catch my balance on the teenager, making her shift off the silk.

"Sorry," I say as I pull one foot out of my crystallized loafer and hook my toes around the silk. I deposit it in my shoe, then jam my foot back inside.

"That's fine," she says, flushed with excitement. "More than fine. I don't think I'll ever wash again."

As she gushes to all of her friends about our run-in, I locate my fourth target. I repeat my circus act with the right foot. When it's safely stuffed inside my shoe, I exhale again.

One to go.

More security guards have arrived and are pushing their way through the crowd toward me. My heart pumps so frenziedly that my veins bulge with blood. The one zigzagging down my arm sticks out abnormally. I snap my gaze away from my skin and desperately search the ground for the last tissue. My luck is going to run out. I can feel it like you can feel ants crawling over your skin. Sweat bleeds down my neck into my shirt collar, gluing it to my rapidly rising chest.

"Move," one of the guards orders.

Thankfully, no one listens to him. He begins to shove people backward. That's when I see it…the last tissue. It's still clutched in the man's fist—the one who sighted me—and rests limply against his thigh. I lunge over to him. With one hand, I wheedle the tissue out; with the other, I pry his fingers open and move the pen over his palm to draw my name in loopy letters. He's so stunned, he doesn't notice the handkerchief is gone, just like he didn't notice he was still holding it.

I raise the pen in the air real high. "Whose is this?" I exclaim.

Three people shout, "Mine!"

The silk bunched in my shoes makes it hard to walk normally, so I choose the person closest to me, a pimply-faced middle-schooler surrounded by two other nerdy boys. As I stick the pen behind his ear, I drop a kiss on his suppurating cheek. Our two bodies' proximity hides my fist rocketing into the backpack. I don't bother tugging the zipper closed because the opening isn't gaping and the bag is black—no one can see the colorful installation nestled inside.

One of the guards grips my upper arm. His expression is so stern that I think I've been made. I'm sure of it, actually.

"That's it. You're a security risk. I can't even believe you were allowed to come here! The museum director is going to give Mister Bacci hell!" He's livid now. "You're going to go back to your little competition and tell him he's to expect a phone call. And if any artwork has been damaged, he should expect a bill along with that call."

As he drags me back to the escalator, I realize he has no clue what I was sent here to do and find myself grinning.

"You think it's funny?" he growls.

"No. Of course not. I'm sorry it got out of hand."

"Sorry?" He snorts while shaking his big head.

He hauls me across the lobby. At one point, my foot begins to slip out of my shoe, so I shove the rubber toecap into the ground. I nearly trip, but at least my foot shoots back into place.

When we're out on the pavement, the guard stares around. "What the—?" he mutters, releasing me. The crowd is denser out here than it was inside, as though the whole city was alerted to my whereabouts.

"Back inside," the security guard says. "We'll go out another entrance."

He grabs my arm again, but I shrug him off, scanning the crowd more intently. If only I knew my driver's name. Like a mirage, he materializes in front of me, elbowing his way through the mass of bodies.

"Grab on to my waist," he says, and I do, and I don't let go until we've reached his gleaming black bike.

I plop the helmet on my head and straddle the motorcycle, the backpack flush against my stomach.

"Hang on," he says, revving up the engine.

The euphoria swirling through me is so great that I squeeze the roaring, sun-warmed frame between my thighs and experience the high of a lifetime. That's not to say I'm changing profession to become a world-class crook, but I understand the thrill. It feels as though I've cheated death.

Is that why Aster stole the diamond? The thought unfortunately sobers me up.

FORTY-FIVE

After

After she finishes reading the document I signed giving my sister power of attorney over my life, Robyn accompanies me back to my cell and instructs the guard on duty to let me rest unperturbed. Although I would never have expected to sleep, the second my head touches the pillow, all of me shuts down. When I wake up some time later, my forehead throbs. Since I can't stop visualizing my hand signing the destructive paper, I force my eyes open. I stare at the ceiling for a long while, and then I roll onto my side and study the closed door and the quiet hallway.

I spot a cardboard box inside my cell. I sit up and plod toward it. It's already sliced open, so I lift the flaps. Inside are rows and rows of granola bars. My stomach growls so I reach in and rip one open, then another. As I chew, my mind returns to the form and my throat tightens. A clump of oat flakes goes down the wrong hole and I cough so many times and so hard that I think blood will sputter out. It doesn't. I keep coughing; I'm going to choke. I suddenly clamp my lips shut and will that death-by-granola be quick, but it doesn't happen.

It reminds me of one of my mother's exes who choked on a piece of steak. He was standing by the kitchen counter, picking large pieces of meat from a Tupperware container with his grubby fingers and shoving them inside his mouth. I was doing my homework on the kitchen table. Although I knew what to do to clear his airway, I couldn't get myself to move and hug his torso. I feared it would make him hug me back and I didn't want him to touch me. The man survived by heaving himself against the back of a chair. The meat rocketed out of his mouth and onto my calculus notebook. It looked like a piece of his own flesh. He broke up with my mother soon after, telling her how insensitive I was. Mom, who already blamed me for everything that went wrong in her life, hated me even more after that.

"Aster," a soft voice calls out through the bars of my gate. It's Gill. Her forehead is creased with worry lines. "How are you?"

"Better. Much better."

"I've been going crazy. No one wanted to tell me what was going on."

I don't approach the door for fear she will try to kiss me. "I've been sleeping."

"Good. That must have been what you needed. You look better. Not that you ever looked bad, but you have color in your cheeks again."

I'm tempted to snort, because deep down, I feel more awful now than I did this morning.

"I saw a bit of the show. It was crazy," she says.

I don't want to talk about the show, but I can't tell her that without explaining, so I listen quietly.

"The test was stealing art! Crazy, huh? I'm not sure what sort of message that sends out to the world."

"Did Ivy make it?"

Her eyes glow like two pieces of amber. "Yes! She was in the MoMA and this mob of people…" As Gill rambles on about my sister's prowess, I swallow thickly. "She's really resourceful," she concludes.

I sigh. "That she is."

"I don't know if she's a finalist, though. I just caught her bit and a few minutes of Chase's. I don't know how Lincoln did. Do you want me to go find out? Or we could go together…I'm sure they'll grant you permission to go to the dayroom—"

"I can't. Robyn wants me to meditate in her office."

"Can I come? I really enjoyed it last time."

"I should go alone."

The enthusiasm, which made her eyes sparkle, wilts off her face. "Oh."

"I can't concentrate when you're around," I add, attempting to cheer Gill up.

"I have that effect on women." She winks at me.

"I should get going."

"Do you want me to call a guard?"

"No, I'll do it," I say, before realizing that to do so, I must walk over to the gate to enter my request on the digital box.

Gill moistens her lips with her tongue. Taking a breath, I move forward, like a criminal headed for the gallows. After I've pressed on the call button, she grips my wrist and spreads my fingers with hers, and then she tugs me close. Her lips come at me like a freight train. I don't move. I don't breathe. She cares about me, unlike Ivy. I let her kiss me even though I feel the granola bar rise. Her mouth opens a little and her tongue prods mine. For a second, I'm disgusted. But then, I get this overwhelming urge to feel something other than misery.

In my peripheral vision, I spot black boots. I jolt away from Gill.

"You called, Inmate?" Officer Landry says. His face is stoplight-red.

"Miss Pierce is waiting for me."

Gill backs up so he can open my gate. As soon as I step out of the cell, she skims my ear with her lips. "I'll catch you later," she murmurs. "I'm not done with you."

Swallowing hard, I tread past the rigid officer. Gill doesn't know this was our one and only kiss, but she'll figure it out before the day ends.

WHEN I LEAVE Robyn's office later that evening, I know exactly what I must do to crush Gill's interest in me.

"I'd like to go to the dayroom, please," I tell Kim.

"I need to run this past the warden," she says, her long fishtail braid swishing from one side of her back to the other.

"He's on board."

She turns and bunches up her eyebrows that are in dire need of plucking. "I need to run this past the warden," she repeats.

"Fine. Let's go to his office now, so that he can confirm what I've just told you."

"Don't be snarky with me, Inmate, or we won't pass by his office."

I don't apologize, but I also don't speak the rest of the way.

When we arrive in front of his door, Kim knocks. "Commander Collins?"

"Come in."

She cracks the door open, but doesn't step in. Neither do I, but I make sure he can see me.

"Inmate Redd is asking for permission to go to the dayroom," she says.

His gaze meets mine. "Okay."

Kim blinks back in surprise. Even though I warned her he would accept, she clearly thought I was bluffing. "How long, sir, may she stay?"

"'Till her sister's show's over. Right? That's why you want to go, Aster, correct?"

I nod.

"Really?" Kim asks.

"Yes, Officer, really." His tone is sharp. "Anything else?"

"No," she says quietly.

Right before she closes the door, I say, "I've been meaning to tell you what great taste you have in art."

From the way his eyes jut out, I fathom he's realized that my compliment isn't directed at the print in the plastic frame hanging by his window.

FORTY-SIX

Ivy

Leila is jubilant tonight, probably because I accomplished the heist. She smiles as she brushes shimmery powder onto my cheeks and lines my eyes with black kohl. She doesn't lay it on as thick as on herself, but she does use quite a bit more than usual. She keeps the rest of my face neutral, down to my lips and nails that she paints a nude color.

Amy twists my silky hair into a sleek knot that suits the simple black sheath I am to wear to the ceremony tonight. I'm no longer as confident as I was on my way back to the Met, because we all succeeded. Who passes to the next round is a mystery. Possibly, it will depend on how long it took us to accomplish the theft—which would not work in my favor considering I was the last to return—or possibly they will base their assessment on our creativity. I'm hoping for the latter.

Lincoln and Chase look like they've walked off some glamorous fifties movie set, what with her pinned curls and his open collared tux. When his eyes touch mine, I look down at the crosshatched floorboards and will my pulse to decelerate. No point in wasting heartbeats on someone who doesn't care about me.

Cara leads the way down to the Temple room. Tonight, burgundy candles rise from massive bronze candelabrums and red roses, in various stages of bloom, dangle from transparent threads attached to the glass ceiling. The effect is sumptuous.

"Don't you feel like we should be wearing masks and nothing else?" Lincoln tells both Chase and me with a brazen smile.

Chase's facial expression tightens. "It's an art show, Lincoln, not an orgy."

"Geez, Jackson, lighten up. It was just a joke," she says. When she spots Brook a few paces ahead of us, she scampers off to join him.

Although smiling, he shifts away from her when she tries to touch him. I wonder if it's because there are cameras around, or if it's because, last night, he kissed her to get her off my case.

"You look very pretty tonight," Chase says, drawing my attention away from them.

"As opposed to all the other nights?" I ask, attempting humor.

"Why would you say that?"

"I'm weird about personal compliments."

Chase smiles.

For a second, I forget how rude he was to me last night. But only for a second. "I'm not into games, Chase. Maybe you get off on toying with women, and good for you if that's your thing, but it isn't mine."

The smile drops off his lips.

"We should get on stage," I say and walk away, toward the Egyptian stone temples to take my place on one of the three chairs.

Lincoln sashays up the steps to sit next to me. Her cheeks are flushed and her eyes sparkle with excitement. Has Brook told her she was still in the running or did he promise her a repeat of last night's performance?

Chase arrives and takes his seat just as Dominic hops onto the platform in a great flourish that reminds me of the first night. Brook joins him, debonair in his burgundy tuxedo that matches the silk scarf wrapped around Dominic's neck. I don't see Josephine, but can only imagine she's still working the crowd. The audience quiets down and settles around the tables as the anthem resounds.

Dominic raises the microphone to his mouth. "Lift up your hands if you guessed today's challenge?"

Arms shoot up left and right. Dominic leaps off the platform and walks over to the first table. He holds the microphone in front of a set of heavily botoxed lips.

"I'm listening, Arabella," he says.

Smiling, the woman says, "An art heist."

"Yes! However did you guess?" He moves away before she can answer and dashes back onto his stage. "They were given some rules though: don't get caught *and* don't damage the pieces. Without further ado, our first winner is…"

There's a drumroll from the orchestra along the far wall. I bite my lip, but quickly release it so I don't spoil my lipstick.

"Jeb, shoot us the image," Dominic says.

The lights dim and the surrounding screens light up with Chase's face. It's the portrait of him they used the night they announced the contestants on national television. Aster had made popcorn, which I'd nervously noshed on as Dominic revealed the eight winners. When my name failed to appear on the screen, I'd gone to get a tub of pistachio ice cream from the freezer.

"Don't be sad," she'd said.

"Sad? Why would I be sad?"

Aster had seemed pleased I hadn't won. I tried not to let it get to me. A few weeks later, there had been this news brief about Kevin's disqualification, followed by the judges' new pick—*me.*

As Chase's face fades off the screen, so does the memory of that fateful day. Jeb has assembled scenes from his hidden camera. They've even added some spy movie soundtrack that makes the wobbly, amateurish images resemble a Hollywood feature. His performance is excellent. He banters with a young, overly made-up intern and swipes her keycard without her noticing. Then he makes his way toward the vault, greeting people left and right, stopping to ask them about their children, dogs, girlfriends. Everyone—and I'm not blowing this out of proportion—is thrilled to see him. He gets smiles and hugs and pats on the back and flirtatious winks. It's insane how much people are drawn to him. Either he's a great actor, or he's nice to everyone but me.

Finally, Chase enters the safe and searches for the Zara Mach piece. It takes him a few minutes to locate the Plexiglas box. When he does, he seizes it and strolls through the auction house with it in the crook of his arm. Once outside, he places it inside his backpack. The screen goes dark.

"You just walked out with it?" Lincoln whispers, voicing my own thoughts.

He nods, just as Dominic says, "How come no one stopped you?"

"I told them my mother wanted to see what the cotton castanets would look like on her chimney mantle before she went ahead and bid on them."

"Was it true?" Dominic asks.

A corner of his lips curves up. "No. I just thought that hiding in plain sight would work best."

Dominic grins so widely it slants his eyes. "And work best it did," he exclaims. "Your brother's a genius, Brook."

Brook nods stiffly.

"Before we announce the second, and last, finalist, we will show you the footage. Girls, are you ready?"

Lincoln smiles while I clasp my hands on my lap to keep them from shaking.

Jeb has split the screens in half: on the right side, I'm entering the MoMA; on the left, Lincoln is entering a private gallery. Since I know what I did, I watch Lincoln's footage. I watch her flirt with the young salesperson, introduce herself as a contestant on *The Masterpiecers*, explain how she's gathering inspiration for today's test. So he shows her around, unlocking the basement in which there's a special room designed for viewing art pieces. She asks him to see the miniature chair collection and he obliges. He sets everything on the Corian table and adjusts the lighting. She handles each piece with great care, oohing and aahing profusely, while he launches into painstaking details on the manufacturing process of each piece.

The camera angle shifts to an empty white wall and the man stops talking. It takes me a second to understand what's happening, but when the screen goes dark, I can only imagine she's undone the buttons on her blouse and has pressed herself against him. I look at Dominic and Brook for condemnation, but both seem amused by Lincoln's audacity.

Suddenly, the camera angle changes again—probably from her blouse flopping open. Her hands grope the brushed white surface, closing around the barrel chair. Once she's swiped it, she presses the guy back and the camera shakes as she buttons up her blouse, her hands empty. She must have already placed it in her backpack.

The man is flushed. She asks him for a pen, rolls up his sleeve, and etches her phone number on his forearm. She ends the interlude with a flirtatious, "Don't wash that arm until you call me." And then she just climbs back up the stairs and strolls out of the gallery.

The dim room becomes darker now that all of the screens are black, and two spotlights fall on Lincoln and me.

"Girls, you were both great, and your performances deserve a round of applause," Dominic says.

The room breaks out into loud clapping and shrill whistles.

"But only one of you managed to bring back your plunder undamaged."

I play the relinquishment of the five tissues over in my mind, attempting to remember their state. Maybe I irreparably wrinkled one. Or maybe one had a tread mark on it. My pulse thrashes so wildly that I think I'm going to be sick. The only thing that's keeping me from hurling is the fact that Lincoln's grin has vanished.

"Ladies and gentlemen, this year's second finalist is…" Dominic begins.

A drumroll resounds. I feel it echo inside my body, reverberate against my organs, resonate inside my skull. I don't breathe until the black screens flash back to life.

FORTY-SEVEN

Of course my sister wins. She always wins. She's draped this surprised look over her face, but I know it's just for show. Ivy never doubts herself.

Chacha's slow-clapping, having paused her card game against Gracie to marvel at my sister's achievement. "Your sister, she's a finalist now. You gonna be rich soon."

"*She*'s going to be rich," I correct her.

The door of the dayroom flies open and in file a bunch of the inmates. Gill isn't among them.

"Hey," Sofia says, coming to sit next to me. "How was your day?"

I shrug. "Does any day in here not suck?"

"Some are better than others. Heard you and Gill are a couple now."

"Where did you hear that?"

"From her. She was telling everyone during yard time."

"Everyone?"

"Whoever would listen."

"We're not."

Chacha raises one of her over-plucked eyebrows.

"Me and Gill are *not* together," I exclaim.

"Told you, Gracie," Chacha says. "Pay up."

"I saw them making out," Gracie says.

"It wasn't real," I say.

"Looked real to me."

"She forced herself on me."

Sofia's see-through eyes grow wide.

"What? You don't believe me?" I say.

She tips her head to the side.

I frown. "What?"

"I forced myself on you?" a voice thunders. Gill is standing by the door, hands on her hips.

"Shit's about to hit the fan," Chacha says, slinging one skinny arm over the back of her chair to better take in the room.

"Yeah. You did," I say. I can't back down now.

A deep blush crawls up Gill's collarbone, her neck, her jaw. It floods her face and darkens her freckles. It even seems to stain her eyes. "How dare you," she hisses. "After everything I did for you."

I point to the dreads. "You mean this?"

She tramples over the scratchy rug that's threadbare in spots and slaps me so hard my neck snaps to the side.

"What the hell?" I screech, nursing my stinging cheek. I haven't been slapped since Mom.

Mom who's gone. For a second, when I look into Gill's face, I see Mom. I see the hatred and the disappointment and the disgust.

"You really are insane," she whispers.

"I am *not* crazy."

"You fucking think everyone's always watching you. That everyone's always after you!"

"Everyone *is* always watching me!"

"I bet you locked yourself in the freezer to get us to pity you."

"I did not!"

"What's that?" Cheyenne asks, looking up from a magazine she's been flipping through.

"Nothing," I mumble.

She cracks her knuckles. "I didn't hear real well from where I was sittin'."

"Aster told us it was you," Gill says.

I glare at her. She glares right back.

"She heard your voice, but it was probably in her head. I bet she hears a lot of voices in her head."

"Shut up," I yell.

Gill smirks. "Are you talking to your head or to me, Aster?"

I bound off the couch. "Shut up," I yell again. Tears run into my mouth. They taste like salt water.

"Aw…did I hit a nerve?"

I'm shaking. "You don't know anything about me."

"I know you're not as innocent as you claim. I saw the news. After slamming that dude with your car, you backed up and ran him over. That takes a special kind of crazy to crush someone's bones."

"You shot your girlfriend," I counter.

"Because she hurt me. What did he do to you, huh? Nothing. You killed someone for no reason."

"He was a criminal!"

From the corner of my eye, I see Chacha rising, and Gracie too. They're creeping closer to me, as is Giraffe-neck. I back up and my calves knock into Sofia's kneecaps.

"He was a mean man," I say.

"A mean man," Gill mimics in a high-pitched voice that doesn't sound a bit like me. "And you're a mean girl."

"Am I going to need to stick you in a strait jacket, Redd?" Giraffe-neck hisses, collecting my hands against my back.

Josh is standing next to Chacha. I don't know how or when he arrived, but I don't care…I'm so relieved to see him. "Help me, Josh."

Chacha looks from me to Josh and then back to me.

"Please," I whisper.

"Who's Josh?" Chacha asks.

"My boyfriend," I tell her, staring at Gill. "He's my boyfriend."

"Josh, can you please leave?" Giraffe-neck asks, eliciting chuckles from the rapt assembly.

"No! Don't."

Josh gives me a pained look.

"What is it? Is Ivy okay?" I ask, trying to elbow my way out of the guard's grip.

She just squeezes harder. "I need another officer in the dayroom. Prisoner not cooperating."

"Josh? What's going on?"

Chacha's staring at Josh. "What's happening to her?"

"Oh, God. Something *is* happening to Ivy." My pulse skyrockets. I whip my face toward the television screen. Brook is standing next to my sister, guiding her off the stage. And that's when it hits me. "It was *his* name on the package! I remember!"

Josh's green eyes glow like alien spaceships.

"He's going to hurt her, Josh! You need to—"

The door of the dayroom swings shut. He probably ran out to warn her.

Ponytail swishing, Kim jogs through the space Josh's body occupied only moments earlier.

"Brook Jackson is mixed up with the mafia," I tell Chacha who's gaping at me.

"Mafia?" Chacha asks.

Gracie shrugs.

Kim hands Giraffe-neck a pair of cuffs, which the latter proceeds to snap around my wrists.

"Told you she was nuts," Gill says.

"I'm not nuts," I yell.

"Take her to the pink tank," Giraffe-neck tells Kim.

"What's the pink tank?" I ask.

"A place for people like you," she says, long neck curving to the side.

Cheyenne grins, as do several other inmates. Gill doesn't, but I'm sure she's pleased to see me leave in handcuffs. I bet she would have been even more pleased to see me leave in a body bag.

"People like me? What's that supposed to mean?"

Cheyenne twirls a fat finger over her temple just as I'm shoved out of the room.

FORTY-EIGHT

Ivy

I still can't believe it was my face up there.

My neighbor at the dinner table has angled his body toward me and his mouth is moving like a fish sucking in plankton. "You can imagine how difficult it was not to inform my staff about Dominic's test," the man, who happens to be the curator of the museum I robbed earlier, tells me.

I smile politely. "I didn't know you were in on it."

"Can you imagine the scandal if I weren't?" He chuckles.

"Am I blacklisted from the MoMA or will I be able to come back for a visit?"

"You may return, but only in flip-flops."

"Deal," I say with a smile.

I spot Lincoln halfway across the room. I can tell she's pissed all the way from here. And I understand. One of the toothpick-like pieces from the miniature chair splintered in her backpack. When she catches me staring, I look toward Chase, my last adversary. He's deep in conversation with Delancey, who's wearing his usual monocle and pinstripe suit—brown tonight.

Hands settle on my shoulders. I tip my face up to find Brook grinning down at me. "How many special orders have you received already?"

"None yet," I say.

"What?" He seems genuinely astonished. "What's wrong with you people? Grab her while you still can."

"We were waiting until dessert to ask such forward questions," the curator says with a chuckle.

The man sitting across the table from me—a thirty-something blond art dealer and Masterpiecers alumni—leans back in his chair and folds his arms over his chest. "I'd like to buy your entire collection, Ivy."

Brook laughs. He probably thinks it's a joke. I sort of think it's a joke too. I smile so as not to appear stupid.

"I'm serious. All of the pieces you've made."

My smile falters and Brook stops laughing. His fingers tighten around my skin.

"Have you signed with anyone yet?" the man asks.

"Signed? You mean with a gallery?"

"Yes."

I shake my head.

"But if she wins tomorrow, she'll automatically be represented by the school," Brook says.

"And if she loses?" the guys asks.

"She'll be represented by me."

I start at Brook's avowal.

"Are you allowed to take on private clients, Brook?"

Brook's fingers are so tight now that they're probably going to leave red imprints on my skin. "Why don't you call me tomorrow and we can discuss this matter in private?"

"With pleasure. You have my number. Call me at your convenience."

The conversation has created tension, which doesn't disappear when Brook leaves to work the other tables. When dessert is cleared away, I thank the people around me for the pleasure of their company, then thread myself through the room, determined to reach the exit quickly. I don't. I can see the glass door that will lead me out. I can even see Cara, and yet I can't get to either because so many people stop me.

"Excuse me." Brook interrupts one of my fans who smells so strongly of musk, it's making my head spin. "I need a word with my contestant." He waits for her to leave before saying, "Don't sign with that guy, okay?"

"Are you really going to offer me representation?"

"I've been considering it."

"Are you allowed?"

"It's one of the clauses I've asked the show's lawyer to implement in my contract. I just need to get it past Dom."

"And past Josephine."

"Josephine's opinion won't matter."

"It won't?"

"No. Soon it won't."

"Is she leaving the show?"

"I wouldn't use the word *leaving*, but yes. Something like that."

"Was she fired?"

His eyes grow wide with a silent warning. "The heist was all Dom's idea," he says, his eyes darting to a space behind me. I imagine that either someone is coming or that we're being filmed.

"What an idea," I say, playing along. "Anyway, I should get to bed. Larceny is exhausting, isn't it?"

Brook stares at me with this bizarre expression on his face.

"Goodnight," I say since he's still just gaping.

As I join Cara, I wonder if I said something wrong, but by the time we exit the Egyptian wing, I decide that it doesn't matter if I did. The only thing that matters now is getting through the next twenty-four hours and emerging victorious.

Once I'm alone in my tented room, I untie my hair, clean off my makeup, and slip out of my dress. As I brush my teeth, I catch movement behind me. I grab a towel and wrap it around my bare chest, then turn around, half-expecting Cara to have forgotten to tell me something.

It's not Cara.

"What do you want?" I ask Chase, narrowing my eyes.

"I came to tell you I was sorry."

"For being an asshole?"

"Yes."

At first, I bite my lip, but then I raise an eyebrow. "You admit you were an asshole yesterday?"

"I do."

"Why?"

"Because I was."

"I mean why did you say those things to me?"

"Because I was angry."

"Angry at me? Because of the whole swimming thing?"

"Because I like you…a lot…and when you lied to me, it reminded me of my ex. And I panicked." He tucks his hands inside the pockets of his tuxedo pants and looks at my red bag that sticks out in the beige-colored room like a bloodstain on a rug. "Ivy, tonight, during dinner, they were discussing your family. I heard how your mother died." He studies his feet, which he's shuffling. "That's why you told me you didn't know how to swim, isn't it?"

"I haven't been in the water since. At least not until the other night." I shiver at the memory of Kevin's body. "I don't think I'll ever be able to go in the water again now."

Chase lays a warm hand on my arm. When he sees me glance at it, he lets it fall back alongside his body. "I'm really sorry I called you a liar."

"I did lie."

"But you didn't do it to hurt me," he says.

I toy with the herringbone pattern on the hem of the towel. "Why did you help me, that day with the riddle?"

His lips perk up in a smile. "Because you're an intimidating girl, and I've never felt intimidated before." His eyes grind into mine. "I thought that if I helped you, somehow I'd stop feeling threatened."

"Did it work?"

"It did. But it wasn't until our conversation at Brook's place that I managed to humanize you."

"Humanize me? What did I say that made me so *human*?"

"You told me about your dream of living off your quilts, about your imperfect relationship with your sister, and I understood that you had all these insecurities, and for some reason, that reassured me."

"And it made you like me?"

A corner of his mouth lifts. "Oh, I already liked you. It just made me think I stood a chance."

I tilt my head to the side to observe him. "This isn't some ploy to distract me so that I lose tomorrow?"

Laughter ripples out of his mouth. "No. No ploy."

"Oopsy"—Lincoln hiccups—"did I interrupt something?" She's standing by the opening of my tent, clutching a bottle of champagne.

"Please go away, Lincoln, and take your bottle of champagne with you," I tell her.

She sticks out her lower lip. "I'll be leaving tomorrow. I didn't want to spend my last night in here alone."

"Why don't you go find my brother?"

"Your brother's the reason it's my last night."

"Huh?"

"Someone caught us making out on camera and leaked it on the Internet. Probably someone from the film crew."

"But your chair broke," I say.

"No it didn't. They just said it did to eliminate me."

I blink.

"Yeah, Ivy, you didn't win tonight because you were better than me—because you're not—you won because Dom said it was conflictual or conflicting or something like that." She takes a swig of the champagne.

Chase walks toward her. I think he's about to leave, but instead he stops in front of her and squares his shoulders. "You should go back to your room, Lincoln."

She pokes his chest. "You're not my mommy, Chase."

He swipes her finger off. "And give me the bottle before you get yourself sick."

She swings her hand out of his reach. "Okay, Mommy," she teases.

He tries to grab it from her, but she lifts her arm higher. The bottle slips and falls on the floor, but doesn't shatter. Instead, it spills champagne everywhere. She bends over and grabs it.

"Goodnight, you two," she singsongs as she finally turns to leave. "And congratulations in advance, Chase, for your win tomorrow."

Once my tent flap settles, I ask, "Is it true?"

"You deserved to win. Your performance was—"

"But is it true?"

"Is anything she says true?" he asks, grabbing some tissues from the nightstand to clean up the spilled champagne.

"Don't worry. I'll do it," I say, crouching down beside him. The towel begins unraveling, but I catch it.

Chase sits back on his heels, his eyes stuck to the flash of thigh he's just gotten. "I never thought I'd be thankful toward Lincoln for anything," he says, his tone light.

I shove him and the towel comes undone again. This time, *he* catches it. Instead of peeling it off my body, he tucks the hem back between my breasts, letting his fingers linger there. Then he leans forward and deposits the sweetest kiss on my lips. And I forget about the bad blood between us, but I don't forget that he's still my opponent, and that tomorrow—like Lincoln said—he'll most probably defeat me and that'll be the end of us…

Of this…

Of me.

FORTY-NINE

The pink tank is a padded cell painted bright pink. It's supposed to be soothing. It's not. I hate pink. The color gives me hives and I begin scratching my skin. Soon, it glows brighter than the walls. And not long after, I manage to draw blood.

I pace the cell and think of my sister and Brook and Josh and Troy and the package. Why couldn't I remember the name sooner?

"What happened to your arms?" I hear someone ask. It's Landry.

I rush to the gate and wrap my fingers around the bars. "I need to get out of here. Please."

"I, uh…I'll go get the nurse."

I nod enthusiastically. Celia will help me. She'll take pity on me. After he leaves, I strain to hear footsteps resound through the narrow hallways, but the minutes tick by and still no one shows.

I begin pacing again. And scratching. The blood under my jagged nails has turned a rusty shade of brown by the time the nurse arrives. Instead of flashing me a kind smile, Celia's face contorts into a grimace.

"Landry, walk her to my office," she says. "I need to bandage her arms."

Landry cuffs me.

"Why—I don't need these. Nurse Celia, can you please tell him I don't need to be restrained?"

She doesn't.

In silence, we make our way to her office. There's a spot of blood on the paper covering her exam table. That's why she was late. She was treating another patient. She gathers the soiled sheet, balls it up, and chucks it into the bin, then rolls out a fresh one. Landry removes the cuffs so I can climb onto the exam table. I'm half-expecting Celia to kick him out, but she doesn't. She brings over a metal kidney tray filled with cotton swabs, antiseptic, and a roll of gauze.

"Right arm," she says.

I give it to her. Gaze cast downward, she cleans it and assesses the damage, trades the gauze for a few Band-Aids, and pastes them on.

"Left arm."

"Are you mad at me?" I ask her.

She peers up at me through her yellow bifocals, but still doesn't speak.

My breath hitches. "You are."

Landry stares out the window, but I know he's listening.

"Why?" I ask.

Still she doesn't say anything. At least not to me. "Landry, you may bring her back wherever she needs to go."

"Not to the pink tank…please." My voice comes out as a hoarse whisper as the officer approaches the exam table. "Can I go to the dayroom? It's my sister's last day."

"I'm not sure you deserve to go watch TV right now," Celia says.

I gasp. "Why are you being so mean to me?"

"Me? Mean? I'm not the one blaming some poor girl of forcing herself on me. Gill tried to take her life. She was so embarrassed by your accusations that she cut her wrist on the prison fence," she says. "I tried to see the good in you, Aster, but in here"—she pounds her fist against her heart—"there's too much bad."

I squash my lips together to stop them from quivering.

"Take Inmate Redd away. I have work to do."

The handcuffs dangle from his hands.

"I'll cooperate, but no cuffs," I say.

Landry glances at Celia who's wheeled herself behind her desk and is typing something on her laptop. "Okay," he says softly. "But don't try anything."

I lower myself to the ground, and, hunched over, walk docilely out of the infirmary and away from the only person who didn't hate me in this prison.

"Where are you taking me?"

"Back to your cell."

I stop in my tracks. "No. To the dayroom…I need to see my sister."

He freezes and turns sideways. "I-I don't think that's a good idea."

"Please. Everybody hates me around here. Everybody thinks I'm crazy, and that I'm a liar. The only thing keeping my head above water is watching my sister." I take a breath. "In some ways, it feels like I'm watching myself, like I'm getting a chance to live again, and be someone…someone people respect and admire. I've never had that."

Landry rubs the back of his neck.

"Do you know what it feels like when your future contains no pigment, no sparkle? Because that's what mine looks like. I have nothing…no one besides my sister."

I think he's about to say yes when the radio strapped to his shoulder buzzes. "*Yobwoc*, you copy?"

"Copy," Landry says.

"What's the status on Inmate Redd? Is she stable?"

Landry's round face colors.

"*Yobwoc*?" Driscoll barks again when Landry remains quiet for too long. I don't like what his silence implies.

"She's okay, sir," he finally says.

"Well, she got a caller in visitation room two. Escort her there, will ya?"

"On it, sir."

As we walk down the string of hallways toward the visitation area, I take mental bets as to whether it's Josh or Dean. I'm hoping for the first, because I need to know why he didn't defend me back in the dayroom.

Unfortunately, it's Dean.

"Inmate Redd's just been released from the pink tank," Landry tells him.

Dean doesn't ask what it is. He must know. "What happened to your arms?"

I flop down in the chair across the table from him.

"Were you attacked?" he asks.

"She scratched her arms."

"Because I had a rash," I add.

Dean raises an eyebrow, but drops the topic. "I can take it from here, Officer Landry."

As soon as the young guard shuts the glass door, I say, "Thanks for sending Josh over."

The gray in his eyes looks silver in the bright concrete room, like the reflective tape on running shoes. "Officer Cooper stopped by to see you?"

"Yes. This morning. He left quickly though."

"Where did he go?" Dean's frowning.

"New York."

"He left for New York?"

I nod. "Yeah."

"That's odd."

"Why?"

"I met with his chief the other day who told me that your boyfriend was never authorized to investigate your case because of your relationship. Last I heard, he was on probation for disregarding direct orders."

"You must have heard wrong, because the chief okayed it. Josh told me so."

"I'm going to have to report him then."

My eyes widen. "No!" I shake my head. The dreads whip my collarbone. "You can't report him! He needs to save Ivy."

"Save Ivy? From what?"

"From Brook."

"Excuse me."

"Brook's name was on the package. The one that was addressed to the show with my sister's quilt in it. I remembered it when I was watching the show."

He drums his fingers against the metal table. My gaze sticks to his pinky, the one with the heavy gold ring. I've seen it before, on someone else's hand…I'm certain of it. But whose? The person had long fingers with buffed nails, feminine fingers. Was it a woman? Dean stops tapping the table. Instead, he flattens both his palms on the table and stands up. And that's when it hits me. Where I've seen it before. I jump away from him, knocking over my chair that crashes against the cement floor. As I cower against the wall, Landry races into the room.

"What? What's going on?" he yells, hand on his Taser gun.

"He knew Troy Mann! He knew Troy," I exclaim, pointing to Dean. "They have the same ring!"

Landry's face swings between me and Dean.

"You have to arrest him. He's in on it," I yelp.

"On what?" Landry asks, head still swinging back and forth. "What is she talking about?"

"I think she needs to return to the pink tank. She's obviously not stable yet," Dean says.

"The hell I'm not stable!"

More voices buzz around me. "What the fuck is the matter in here?" Giraffe-neck asks, face flushed. She must have run.

"Your prisoner is making baseless accusations," Dean says with a snort. He's so calm—too calm.

"They're not baseless. They have the same ring. Take his ring. Compare it to Troy Mann's! They're the same!"

"A lot of men have rings." He snorts again.

"I know what I saw," I say, trying to catch my breath. "You have to believe me."

For a second, I think she does, but then her mouth contorts into a smirk when someone behind her says, "Just like you saw Officer Cooper this morning?" Gill is leaning against the glass wall of the room, arms folded.

"What's she doing here?" I ask, eyeing the gauze wrapped around her wrist.

"You told me I should interview her for a character witness," Dean says, stroking the gold bar hooked into his yellow tie.

"No," I yell. "She's not my friend anymore."

"You don't have any more friends around here, Aster," Gill says. "But that's your own fault."

"I'm sorry, Mister Kane. We shouldn't have been so hasty to release her from the tank." There is no more smile on Giraffe-neck's face. "Landry, cuff her."

"What?" I roar. "No! No! I'm telling the truth—"

"Shut it, Redd," she snaps. "Or we'll have to Taser you."

"No! Don't let him get away! Don't—" Two copper wires latch on to the skin below my collarbone, delivering a jolt of electricity so great it sets my organs on fire, paralyzes my muscles, and darkens my mind.

FIFTY

Ivy

"Authenticity!" Dominic's voice booms out of his microphone. "You will be shown to a gallery in which we have arranged six of the Met's most celebrated treasures. Amidst those six, one is fake. Ivy, Chase, to win, not only must you uncover the fake, but you must also explain how you've arrived at this conclusion, because, although luck exists in the art business, expertise is still key."

The screens around the Temple room switch to visuals of the nominated pieces. The first one is a Monet representing a bridge overhanging a pastel water lily pond. The second is a swirly Van Gogh landscape with a tall cypress tree and a tumultuous summer sky. A bronze Degas statue of a fourteen-year-old ballerina is object three. Then an epic-looking painting of Washington crossing the Delaware River is number four. The fifth piece is a terracotta-hued bust of a man by Pablo Picasso. And the last is a marble statue of a mythological hero holding Medusa's severed head.

The slideshow of works dissolves back to the Masterpiecers' logo.

"Contestants, you will be given all the tools afforded to professional appraisers and you will be shown how to use them. As always, have fun, and good luck."

Bodies parallel but not touching, Chase and I descend the stairs and ford across the standing audience. I don't glance at him, afraid to spot the confidence I'm lacking...and afraid that my glance will give away my growing feelings for him. His pinkie grazes the side of my hand and I shiver. I stare into the cameras that are being wheeled in front of us, then over my shoulder at the audience marching like a disciplined army behind us.

This is it. The last day. The last contest. The last chance to win a hundred thousand dollars and an entry into the school.

Too soon, we're in the herringbone-planked gallery with the masterpieces. Dominic is standing before us and the cameras are circling us, while the audience presses up against the velvet ropes erected at each entrance. Only Josephine and the orchestra are missing.

"And now, I'd like you to meet our wonderful experts," Dominic says, gesturing to two women. Both wear simple black pantsuits. The younger one sports a pair of glasses with thick purple frames and has her hair up in a bun, while the other wears it down to her shoulders. "Chase and Ivy, meet Genevieve and Larissa. Both have trained at the Masterpiecers and still consult for us. However, Genevieve now works for the Metropolitan as their art specialist and Larissa is the woman the auction houses call upon in case of doubt."

Both women nod. Neither smiles.

"They will be assisting you today with each tool. They will, however, not be answering any questions. It will be up to you to figure out the results." Dominic pauses to make the moment more dramatic. "Finalists, it is time to begin. Ready…set…go!"

Chase pounces toward the woman who works at the Metropolitan. Smart. As I watch him move to the table covered in appraisal tools, the other woman comes up to me and sticks out a manicured hand.

"Hi, Ivy," she says as I shake it. "Shall we get started?"

When I release her hand, my fingers fall back against my thighs, cold and stiff. I nod.

"Let's go to this side of the room." She indicates the Washington painting since Chase is studying the Monet.

I walk on autopilot alongside her and stop in front of the monstrous oil painting. I read the small plaque on the wall, take in the year and the dimensions. The painting has been presented without its frame.

"Is there a measuring tape?" I ask.

Larissa smiles, which convinces me that my approach is smart. "I will get one right away."

She returns with a coiled ruler, which she holds in place while I pull it the length of the canvas, then the width. All the dimensions check out, to the fraction of an inch. I decide it must be real.

"Let's go to the next," I say, clutching the measuring tape.

Her wide, bright red lips curve up. Does she smile because I'm right? Or is it mocking? Chase is still studying the Monet, using some tool that resembles a supermarket scanner. Maybe my assessment was too rushed.

"Can I touch the paintings?" I ask.

She nods. "Lightly, though."

So I run the tips of my fingers over the subtle, sloping oil reliefs and close my eyes. If only paint could talk, tell me who brushed it atop the canvas.

"Is there another tool you'd like to use?" she asks me.

My lids snap up, and I find Chase handing back the scanner. "That," I say, pointing to it.

"Let me get it."

She crosses the room and takes it from Genevieve. Chase's gaze lifts to mine, all at once intense and gentle, and my brain becomes fuzzy. I shake my head. I need to concentrate.

Larissa's on her way back. "Here's the Proscope," she says, handing it to me.

"How…um…does it work?"

"You hold it up to the signature and it acts as a microscope. It'll show you each pixel with a clarity the human eye cannot discern. Let me just plug it into this tablet for a visual."

She holds the screen up to me as I take the small apparatus and hover it over the signature. I'm not sure what I'm looking for, but I move it over the word *Leutze* slowly. There's a feathery quality to the second letter and a sort of break in the *t* that makes me study the letter more closely. I look up from the tablet screen. As Larissa said, I don't spot any discrepancy with my naked eye. But I didn't imagine it. On the screen, it's there, unmistakable.

"Can I get a pen and paper?"

She frowns, but obliges.

I hand her the tablet and handheld microscope and take the pen and paper. I sign my name, and then take the device and run it over my autograph. I watch the screen, satisfied. There isn't a single crack in my writing, which leads me to believe that whoever signed the Delaware River painting is not Leutze.

Excitement bubbles through me, but I squelch it down as I walk over to the table laid out with all the tools. There's some handheld electric torch that dispenses black light.

"What's that used for?" I ask Larissa.

"Detecting lead in pigments."

I can't see the use of analyzing lead content.

"There was more lead in paints before the turn of the twentieth century," she explains.

I seize the tool and bring it over to the Monet. I shine the black light inches away from the pretty paint smudges. I don't see any variations and am about to let the torch fall to my side when the light touches a smear of white. The white turns blue and gray.

"Does that mean a high lead concentration?" I ask Larissa.

Her lips press together. "Yes."

So it must be real. Dominic mentioned spotting the fake. The Leutze is fake. On second thought, maybe it's just hard to sign in paint. "Can you still buy lead-heavy paint today?" I find myself wondering out loud.

Her bottom lip drops in surprise. "Yes."

So lead content isn't going to help me age the painting. I check the dimensions on the plaque and pull out the measuring tape to size up the water lily canvas. They match. I'm racking my mind for other ways of telling if something is old. On humans, wrinkles or gray hair are a good sign. Billboards fade and book pages turn yellow. "Can we pull it off the wall?"

"We can't," Larissa says, and my hope plummets. "But *they* can." She points to the guards stationed on either side of the wall. "We need help here," she calls out.

As I turn, my forehead knocks into the large camera that's been filming my every move since the day I arrived at the Metropolitan. Improbably, it's become part of my landscape, and I usually don't even notice it anymore, but I also usually don't collide into it.

"Sorry," the woman filming says. She gets a stern look from Jeb who's handling the camera aimed on Chase.

The guards flip the canvas over. I look for a yellowing of the fibers. There is none. "Can canvas be bleached without it affecting the paint?" I ask Larissa.

She tips her head to the side and her shiny black hair brushes the sharp shoulders of her suit. "No."

I catch Chase's eyes, but too briefly to read anything. He shifts back to the ballerina, leaving me to ponder the Monet. Why in the world would someone spend time cleaning the back of a painting anyway?

Could the Leutze be real and the Monet be fake? I move on to the Van Gogh. I shine the black light on the swirly clouds. Like on the pale water lily pads, the white takes on hues of blue and gray indicating that the paint is from Van Gogh's era.

I switch off the torch. "What other tools are available?"

"The Oculus Aperture. They're x-ray binoculars that reveal the different layers of paint so you can see if the artist intended to put a mouse in the corner of his creation or if he changed the angle of a limb."

That's exactly what I need. I walk to the table in the middle of the room, where Chase is perusing what's available. As I reach out for the pair of silver binoculars, our hands collide. I snap my fingers back to my side, while his continue their trajectory. He seizes the binoculars and I think I'll have to wait, but he says, "Ladies first."

Startled, I don't take them from him, so he grasps my hand and unbolts my fingers, then places the instrument in my palm and presses my fingers closed.

"Bring them back to me when you're done."

I stare up at him, forgetting there's anyone else in the room. As the deep brown of his irises eddy around his pupils, his hand slowly releases mine. I should swim against the tide sweeping me toward Chase. It's too strong and too quick, flooding me with too many emotions.

I will drown if I'm not careful.

FIFTY-ONE

Ivy is so beautiful in her red dress and sleek hairdo, whereas I'm so ugly. I long to yank out the dreads, but they're as resilient as the rope Ivy and I tied to a tree branch one summer, to attach a castoff tire. How we would swing on that old piece of rubber!

The memory tugs on my fraying heartstrings. *Ivy and me*. There should have been a song written about us, one with a sweet, plucky melody. Two stick-thin girls with bushy curls swinging on a craggy tire, making forts out of branches and blue Ikea bags, and rolling in tall, tickling grass until their bellies hurt from laughing. But no one will ever write a song about us. They might compose one about Ivy, though, now that she's a celebrity.

I'm propelled into the dayroom, staring at myself pulling on my ratty tresses. From inside the TV, Ivy sees me too. Her eyes are wide and expectant and scared. She needs me, but I can't help her, I can't leap through the screen. The dyed fibers of her dress tremble as her heart beats quicker. My pulse hastens in turn, making the stiff gray shroud that ensconces me vibrate too.

"Aster," she whispers. "Aster…"

"I'm here, Ivy! Right here." My voice sounds foreign to my ears, yet it's my voice. It vibrates in my chest, making it ache. "Ouch," I murmur as I shift. Paper crackles. I try to lift my wrists, but I can't. "I can't get to you. I can't move."

"No shit. You're attached to a gurney, you fucking bitch."

My lids snap up and light bounces into my eyes. Too much light and too much red. So much red, I squeeze them shut again. I pretend that I'm unconscious.

"Wakey, wakey," Gill says, digging something into my palm.

I scream out in pain, but she stifles my scream with her hand.

FIFTY-TWO

Ivy

Larissa plucks the Oculus Aperture from my hand like a child reaching into a bucket of popcorn for their first handful. "It's brand new technology," she explains. "Before, you had to take x-rays like in the dentist's office. But now, we have these! They're amazing, aren't they?" Her dark eyes glitter with excitement as she finally hands them back.

There are a few straps that go around the top of the head to stabilize them. Once they're in place, all I have to do is press a button and the binoculars flood to life and self-adjust to my vision. I focus them on the Van Gogh.

After a long surveillance, I say, "I don't see anything."

"What do you mean?" Larissa asks. "Did you turn them on?"

"Of course I turned them on," I tell her. "I just don't see any layers. Is there something I'm not pressing on?"

Without glancing away from me, she says, "Don't look for something that isn't there."

I make mistakes when I create quilts and often have to unstitch what I've sewn. But maybe Van Gogh doesn't. Maybe he's some genius who gets it right from the beginning.

With the Oculus still on, I walk to the Monet and scrutinize it through the computerized lenses. No layers. I stride over to the Leutze, stumbling into one of the guards. Large hands steady me and then I'm on my way again. I study the scene from top to bottom and side to side. There isn't a single hesitation, no soldier out of place, no fishtail sticking out from the icy river, no musket covered by a new layer of paint. Could all three be fakes? With the interactive glasses still on, I circle the room, stopping in front of the small terracotta-hued Picasso. I almost zip past it when I spot something that makes me stop and stare: the shadow of another face, a woman's face. I lift the binoculars. The woman's face vanishes. I place them back on, and the rough sketch returns.

What the hell does it mean? That it's real and the rest are fakes? I pull the Oculus off and cross the room toward Chase who's studying the Van Gogh with the black light.

"Here," I say.

He takes the binoculars from me. "You okay?"

"Just confused."

He frowns.

Dominic's arms are folded against his double-breasted navy suit, head tipped toward Brook in a quiet exchange. When they see me watching them, they fall silent. I return to Larissa who's rearranging the gauging instruments on the table. Without a word, I grab the measuring tape and head to the Picasso. The width and length match up. I'm still convinced it's real. I check the signature with the Proscope. I'm expecting solid letters, but most resemble thread ends unraveling. I turn the device off, my earlier conviction smashed to pulp. I add the Picasso to the list of fakes and move to the statues.

I start with the bronze and measure it. The dimensions check out. Degas's signature is etched in the square base by the dancer's feet. I wouldn't know if it was real or fake though. The plaque says the skirt is made of cotton and satin hair ribbons. Delicately, I run the tips of my fingers through them. Although browned with age, I don't feel the cool, filmy texture of satin.

Frowning, I move to the other statue—the white marble one. I need a chair to measure it and ask a guard for one. He returns with a stool and insists on helping me up and holding me as I reach past Medusa's severed head to Perseus's winged helmet. Just shy of eight feet tall, as it says on the plaque. As I descend from the stool, I lose my balance. Although the guard bares most of my weight, my hand flails out toward the statue. The second I touch it, I know it's fake. Although veined like marble, it isn't cold and silken like stone. It feels like plaster. I scramble back onto the stool and swipe my index finger in the hollow of Medusa's head. A dusty white residue remains on my skin.

I take in the room from my vantage point and feel a sense of smugness and pleasure at not having been outsmarted by Dominic and Brook. I spot Chase in front of the Picasso, running his last tests. Has he come to the same conclusion?

Could we both win?

I hop down from the stool and amble toward Dominic. "I'm done."

"Are you now? You still have plenty of time—"

"I don't need more time."

"Are you certain? There's no revising your answer once you give it to us."

My certainty momentarily flounders. I feel a presence behind me and don't need to whirl around to know it's Chase. I can smell the pine needles in the small space separating our bodies.

"You have your answer too, Chase?" Brook asks.

"Yes."

"Okay, then. Ivy, you come with me, Chase, you go with…" Brook's voice dies off as his eyes settle on the entryway behind us.

"Hello, *finalistes*," comes a sharp, accented voice. "I hope I did not miss the big reveal."

FIFTY-THREE

"I don't like spending hours on people who screw me over." Gill's twirling something shiny between her fingers. She sees me looking at it and smirks. "Makes me discontent."

"What is that?"

"Oh, this? Something I was offered for my flowery character assessment. Something I sharpened."

My palm throbs. I shift my head to the side to glance at it. Blood trickles down my shackled wrist and along the pale skin of my forearm.

"It's worth a lot apparently. It's real gold," she says. "Slices real well too." She juts her chin toward my palm. "Now, Aster, *I'd* like my dreads back, and *Mister Kane* would like to know what you did with the *rest of them*."

"The rest of what?"

"He said you would play dumb."

How I ever felt anything but alarm toward Gill is beyond me. As her hands move toward my head, I eye the door of the infirmary. It's sealed shut.

"Nurse Cee—"

Gill stuffs a wad of gauze inside my mouth. For some reason I think of Sofia and her prowess for chess, wishing I possessed even an ounce of it. Then I'd be two moves ahead of Gill instead of strapped down and defenseless.

"While you think, I'm taking my hard work back." Her breath whistles in my ear as the shiv saws through my hair. At some point, the serrated metal bites into my skin. "Oopsy," she says, delight lilting her tone.

She hacks through more dreads. My scalp throbs as something warm oozes down my neck. I'm not sure if it's blood or perspiration. My lashes become wet.

"You've been a bad girl, Aster. Very bad."

The right side of my head feels light and cold now.

"You've hurt a lot of people. Especially me. I should've known you would screw me over, but I was hoping…hoping we could become something. But we couldn't, could we? You were just using me. You never liked me. And I liked you so"—her tongue glides across my jaw—"so much."

I gag and spin my head so abruptly that the sharp blade saws into my neck, tearing my flesh. I whimper.

"Shit," she says as a cascade of heat gushes down my collarbone. "I think I hit your artery…*shit*."

Instinctively, I lift my hand but the metal cuff holds it back. Gill jumps up and looks around, eyes wide, spooked. She grabs on to stuff then scrambles back toward me.

"I'm going to get it under control! Don't worry."

She presses a wad of cotton against the gash in my neck. Since I can't see or touch it, I gauge the state of my wound from the roundness of her eyes. It must be bad because the amber irises float on the white.

"Shit!" She throws the cotton on the floor. It's so full of blood it doesn't even arc through the air. It just drops like a rock. She rips one of her sleeves and wraps the fabric around my neck. "Stay with me! Nurse! Guards! Someone!" Her voice sounds like it's coming from inside a seashell, yet I know she's yelling from the way her lips contort over her buckteeth.

"What the hell, Swanson? You said you wanted to make up," Nurse Celia's voice trills.

My ears ring, my palm throbs, and my neck aches, but what I feel most is the temperature warring within and outside of me: cold floods my veins while warmth streams over my skin.

"Aster! Aster!" Gill's freckles glow like the cinnamon sprinkles atop Ivy's favorite donuts. "Stay with me!"

I become fluffier, my body weightless, my mind empty like a helium balloon drifting toward the sky. The white room grows brighter, louder. Gill's eyes spin like those pinwheels I loved to blow on when I was a child.

Her eyes are red now. She's entirely red, from her thick ropes of hair, to her pale skin that glows as though it were on fire, to her hands that are wet with my blood. She's red like the dress Ivy wore in my dream. Like the sticky, soiled fabric of my gray jumpsuit. Like our last name.

Redd.

Ivy's suddenly there, small and distant, sitting on Celia's desk, swinging her legs like she used to on those tire swings. She watches as death heaves me away. She doesn't move. She just stares, her expression blank, emotionless, like the last time I saw her and tried to hold her hand.

"I gave up my future so that you could have one," I tell her, but she doesn't hear me because the blood makes me sound like I'm gurgling.

Perhaps my life ending will allow hers to truly begin. One less person to make plans for, one less hospital bill to pay with the loan she took out on *her* apartment and with the money she made from the sales of her quilts. I hope she's forgiven me for sending one to *The Masterpiecers*. I hope she knows it was a coincidence. A sad coincidence.

The shadow fades as the body steps into the sun.

FIFTY-FOUR

Ivy

"How much longer do we have to wait?" I ask Cara, who's sitting in my tent, bouncing her sneakered feet.

"Until I get orders to get you to the reception room," she says.

"Can you at least get me a magazine?"

She shakes her head.

"A book?"

Again she shakes her head.

"*Ugh*," I grumble, flopping onto my back in the silver gown Amy has laboriously buttoned me into. "This is so boring!"

"You're going to mess up your hair," Cara says.

"Like I care."

"*I* care. If I bring you down with a lopsided hairdo, I lose my job. I don't want to lose my job."

"It's your last day," I say. "And possibly the last year of this show with all that's happened."

Josephine arrived with a lawyer this afternoon. When our assistants took us back to our quarters, making sure there was absolutely no contact between Chase and me, a grim-faced Dominic and a nervous Brook exited the gallery with her. As if this show hasn't been splashed across the media enough! But more troubling—at least in my opinion—is the fact that Josephine's new right-hand woman is Lincoln. Should have known those two were kindred spirits. I'm dying to speak to Chase about it, hear what he thinks.

I drum my fingers, perplexed about the upcoming evening. The anticipation contracts my muscles and spouts blood through my veins at such speed that my heart feels like it's about to detonate. I roll up and start pacing the room.

Cara watches me. "I didn't think Ivy Redd ever got nervous."

"I'm anxious, not nervous."

"Chase didn't seem particularly anxious," she continues.

Is she trying to get a rise out of me? "Good for him." I look in the direction of his room. I wonder if his assistant has him locked in there with nothing to do as well. For a second, I think I see the outline of his body through the fabric walls, moving around the room, but it's just my shadow. Cara's right, though—Chase was totally self-assured when he left the gallery.

"We're a go," Cara says, readjusting her head mic.

I inhale so quickly that the air tears through my lungs, making me sputter. Cara unzips my tent and gestures for me to go ahead of her. Instead of walking, I freeze.

"You wanted out. You got out. Now let's go," Cara says, holding up the flap.

I quickly pat my hair down to make sure the braid swinging between my bare shoulder blades is as sleek as Amy intended it to be and that the gold chain she wove into it is in place. Finally, I step past Cara, into the empty grass hallway lined with the twinkling potted trees. I take them in—I take in everything around me, the makeup stations, the stone stairs, the vertiginous main hall, the Egyptian artifacts—because, whether I win or lose, this is my last night on the show, and probably my last time ever sleeping inside a museum.

Chase is waiting by the entrance of the Temple room. Sensing my presence, he turns to stare at me. Warmth battles the chill that's enveloped my body.

"Any day," Cara says, tapping her foot again. "There's only a couple million people waiting."

Chase rolls his eyes. I'm tempted to smile, but my lips just quiver limply. As I arrive at his side, he grabs my hand and laces his fingers through mine.

"Whatever happens, you were great," he says.

"Thanks." My voice is hoarse.

"And you're not a phony, Ivy. Your beauty and intelligence might be enhanced by all the makeup and nice clothes, but you weren't fabricated like some forgery."

My brows draw together. "Have you been drinking? Because if you have, then you've had way more fun than me."

Cara clears her throat. "That's enough talking," she says.

His black pupils throb. "I just hope you know the difference."

Surprisingly, all three judges are standing together on the raised platform between the temples, all in glimmering outfits. The guests also have selected glitzier attire for the occasion.

"Ready?" Chase asks just before we enter the room.

I glance at him and attempt to smile. I even try to answer, but no words come out of my mouth. He tugs me through the cavernous room underneath a shower of applause and music. Although Dominic is smiling, there is no cheer in his eyes. Josephine, on the other hand, appears truly content, her smile as sharp as the conical studs adorning the collar of her gold lamé dress.

I pull my hand out of Chase's the second we're on the platform. The spotlights trained on us are blinding, yet I can see Lincoln on the outskirts of the circle, her eyes as shiny as her sequin-heavy dress. I look beyond her at the sea of people staring. A wave of nausea arcs through me, so powerful that cold sweat begins trickling down my spine. I curl my fingers and dig my lacquered nails into my palms. Voices hum louder as the clapping dies out, and then the voices evaporate in turn, supplanted by the theme song.

When the final notes fade, Dominic takes the microphone. "We've made it," he exclaims, pumping his fist in the air victoriously. "After the most tumultuous show, we've made it! Through tears brought on by a great human loss, and through the strain of false rumors and bad publicity, we did it."

I pull my shoulders back. Chase's shoulders are also stiff, straining the shiny fabric of his tuxedo.

"I was afraid of letting down our final contestants, our sponsors who have so graciously funded us, and the network, which has been so very tolerant of our erratic schedule. I thank you...all of you...for your patience and support. I thank our viewers who have spent hours with us on the other side of their television screens, cheering and voting for our contestants. And last but not least, I want to thank the amazing team of people, the assistants, the camera and lighting crew, the museum, the insurance company and their guards, and the stylists without whom none of the magic of these past nine days could've been possible."

The crowd is still standing, stitched together like the pieces of my quilts, basking us in applause.

Dominic raises his palm in the air to ask for silence, which comes so swiftly it's as deafening as the uproar. "And now, for the moment of reckoning...Chase and Ivy have had no contact with each other, or anyone besides their assistants since the last time you've seen them."

Perhaps I'm imagining this, but his eyes seem to mist over as he looks at me. After what feels like an eternity, he turns back to his adoring audience.

"So, the way we're going to do this—so that their answers don't overlap—is have the finalists write down their responses. Jeb will transcribe them onto the monitors displaying their faces."

Just as he says this, every screen lights up, alternately with my face and Chase's. Keeping his eyes averted from mine, Brook hands me a small tablet and an electronic pen.

"Go ahead," Dominic says.

Fingers shaking, I write my answer:

They are all fakes.

CHASE IS STILL WRITING which either means that he's very slow or that his answer is more elaborate. I tip my head toward one of the screens that is reflecting my own face back to me. My answer hasn't magically appeared yet, so I drop my gaze back down to the tablet and think so hard my brain begins to hurt. Suddenly, the conversation I had with Chase before entering the Temple room wallops me upside the head. I try smudging my writing with my thumb, but the tablet doesn't work like that. Too soon, Chase is handing his tablet over to his brother.

I got what Chase wanted me to get: that there's a difference between fake and forgery. I glance back down at the short line I wrote, and then back up at Chase's sharp profile. I can still win. All I need to do is add a few more words, a sentence. Dominic's instructions were to find the fake, and that's the Picasso—the only one that was tampered with to give the illusion it was real. The other paintings and statues were all counterfeited: erroneous sizes, too flawless, wrong materials.

But would I have come to this realization without Chase?

"Time's up," Brook says.

I'm still clutching the stylus. I place the tip on the tablet, the temptation so great it makes my fingers shake harder. But then I think of Brook and of his offer to represent me. And I think of the man at my table last night and his proposition to buy all of my pieces. And of how art dealing is Chase's calling and he won't be able to do it if he doesn't get into the school. And then I think of Aster and realize that it's time for me to go home and take care of her.

Without adding a single word, I transfer the tablet to Brook's empty right hand. He clicks on both tablets, and our answers materialize on the surrounding screens.

Mine will be wrong, but it's okay. These last few days were a dream. And like all dreams, there comes a moment when you must wake up.

FIFTY-FIVE

FIFTY-SIX

Ivy

When Dominic announces Chase is the winner of the third annual Masterpiecers' competition, I hoist up my brightest smile. Once Brook has patted his back, once Dominic and Josephine have shaken his hand, I walk over to congratulate him, but the crowd moves in, climbing onto the platform, crushing me, and Chase disappears in the sea of tuxedos and rainbow silks. People touch my arms, grab my hands, tell me how impressed they were with my performance. Some even give me their business cards. My breathing becomes shallower, like on the Brooklyn Bridge, and I hasten my search for Chase. He spots me, yet it's as though a wall separates us because we still can't reach each other.

"Even though you didn't win, I'm very proud of you, Ivy," Dominic says.

The somberness I noticed earlier is still there. Did he know I was going to fail? Or does it have to do with his meeting with the lawyer and Josephine?

I touch his sleeve as I thank him. He nods, then retreats into the crowd. In the mayhem, someone bumps into me. Lincoln.

"Losing sucks, doesn't it?" she says.

"Chase deserved to win."

She smirks. "Tell yourself that if it makes you feel better."

She once said we'd probably be friends if we weren't adversaries, but she's wrong. "So, you're working for Josephine now?"

"Yep. I reached out to her this morning before leaving. I offered to become her personal assistant against housing at the Masterpiecers and use of the facilities."

"And she accepted?"

"You know many people who turn down free labor? Besides, I had some information she wanted."

"You always have an angle, don't you?"

"It's not an angle, Ivy; it's an extra ace. I learned at a young age that the world is far from fair." Her eyes gleam like the coins in the basin girdling the temples.

"What's going on with Dominic?" I ask.

"I can't tell you, but you'll know very soon."

"Does it have to do with me?"

Her gaze skims mine, but settles on the person next to me.

"So you're working for the devil, now?" Brook says.

"If Josephine's the devil, what does that make you, Brook?" She gives him a strange smile. "Enjoy your evening. I know I will." She winks and leaves.

Neither of us speaks. Then I feel an overwhelming need to ask, "Did she really get eliminated yesterday because of…of what happened in your pool?"

He snorts. "Is that what she told you?" he asks, watching Lincoln cross the room toward Josephine.

I nod.

"She was eliminated because she was careless," he says, just as a fuchsia-clad Madame Babanina accosts him.

"Brook, dear, you look so handsome tonight," she says, not bothering to address me. Perhaps if I'd won, I would have been of interest to her.

"So this is good-bye?" I ask Brook, hoping he'll mention his offer to represent me. He doesn't. Maybe he never meant to.

"I suppose it is," he says.

The notorious divorcee swings her head toward me, and her curvy bangs bob against her forehead. "Sorry for your loss," she tells me, snaking her arms around Brook's like vines. "Brook, dear, I have someone I'd like you to meet." She begins tugging him away. "He'd like to start a collection and I was thinking who better to advise him than—"

She stops chattering suddenly. Many people have gone quiet and are shifting, creating an aisle down which march a squadron of men and women in navy uniforms with yellow FBI insignias. Spearheading the cortege is Detective Clancy and Detective McEnvoy—in navy and yellow also.

"FBI," McEnvoy yells. The lights in the room flare up, making his silver hair look metallic. "Nobody move!"

When his gaze lands on mine, I take a step back and bump into another body. A pair of hands shoots out to steady me. "It's me, Ivy," Chase whispers. "Just me."

Clancy said she would see me again—is this what she meant? Did she come here to arrest me?

Suddenly, she stops. And it's not in front of me. "Brook Jackson, put your hands where I can see them."

Brook doesn't react.

"Hands up, Jackson, now," she repeats.

As a collective gasp echoes through the room, Chase's fingers harden, crushing my skin.

Slowly, Brook raises his arms.

"Austin, frisk him," Leah says.

"Is this a joke?" Brook asks, as McEnvoy pats him down.

"Do I look like I'm laughing?" Leah says.

"He's clean," Austin announces.

"Brook Jackson, you are under arrest for colluding with wanted criminals, trafficking stolen goods, and laundering money for the mafia."

"What?" he yelps.

Chase's hands slip off my arms and plummet limply against his sides. I catch one and squeeze it.

"Did you know?" I whisper.

"I knew he was up to something, but I didn't—I—" His voice cracks. He stares down at me, then at our hands, then squeezes back. "I didn't know he was working for the mob."

"This is fucking ridiculous," Brook thunders.

"Is it?" Josephine lunges out of the crowd toward him. She has something in her hands. An empty package. She waves it around. "You were using the Masterpiecers as a front! Using art for terrible things."

"What the hell is that?" he asks.

"It's *un paquet*. The package that your friend Troy Mann sent you. We had the handwriting analyzed and the paper dusted for prints. At first, I thought Ivy was trying to earn brownie points, sending us a quilt after she got in"—she looks my way—"but she didn't send the package. She didn't write your name on it. *Troy* did. And it's not the first you've received from him. What did he send you this time? Money? Drugs?"

Brook's left eye twitches as he glares back at Josephine.

"Ma'am, please step back," an agent tells her. When she doesn't, they pull her back.

"*Tu devrais avoir honte*!"

Jeb, who's handling one of the cameras, angles it toward Brook before whirling it back toward Josephine.

Her icy blue eyes glow like the flames atop candlewicks. "You are a disgrace, Brook."

"Ma'am," Clancy says, "calm down or we'll have to ask you to step out."

Jeb zooms in on Josephine's face. On the overhanging screens, I can see her skinny nostrils flare.

"Turn those goddamn things off before I arrest you for interfering with criminal proceedings!" Austin presses his palm over the lens. "This is a federal arrest people, not some episode on your fuckin' game show."

In seconds, all the video equipment is shut off, and the screens go dark.

"Read him his Miranda rights, Austin," Clancy tells her partner.

"Brook Jackson, you have the right to remain silent. Anything you say can and will be used against you in a court of law. You have the right to an attorney. If you cannot afford an attorney, one will be provided for you. Do you understand the rights I have just read to you?"

"Dominic, tell them this is a misunderstanding."

Slowly, hunched over like a very old man, Dominic walks away.

"With these rights in mind, do you wish to speak to me?" Leah asks Brook.

"I'm not speaking to you, or to anyone else here." Brook's jaw is ruddy and his hair, which is usually so well brushed, sticks out in places. "I want a lawyer. Chase, call Dean right away!"

"Dean Kane?" Austin asks.

"Yes!"

"Doubt Mister Kane can represent you as he'll be needing his own defense." Austin glances my way when he says this. "Once we catch him."

"What are you talking about?" Brook asks in a shrill voice.

Clancy comes toward me. "Ivy, why don't you come with me?" she says, her voice low.

"Wh-why?" I stutter.

She looks around. Agents are escorting the agitated audience outside.

"What happened?" I ask, trying to make myself heard over the din.

Her large brown eyes settle back on mine. "Your sister was attacked."

Is it possible to flatline when you're still alive? "Attacked?" I repeat stupidly.

Clancy nods.

"Is she…" I swallow thickly. "Is she alive?" I ask, as Chase winds one arm around my waist.

"She's in a coma," she says, before telling me how it happened.

At some point, I interrupt her. "I don't understand."

"What don't you understand?"

"Why did Dean order the hit?"

"To retrieve the diamonds Troy Mann hid inside your quilt."

"Diamonds?" *There was more than one?*

"Dean and Troy were working together. It's your sister who made the connection."

"But then that would mean—" I shoot my gaze toward Brook, the shock of my realization so violent that I'm unable to finish my sentence. "You didn't send Dean to help her," I yell at him. "You sent him to execute her!"

I launch myself toward him, but Chase holds me back.

"Let go of me," I scream.

"No."

"Let go of me right now or help me God—"

He still doesn't.

"Chase, please," I beg, my voice breaking.

"Did your sister take the diamonds, Ivy?" Leah asks.

"I don't know," I say.

Brook laughs, a dark, mean laugh. When I glower at him, he winks.

Leah turns toward her partner. "Take him away," she says, at the same time as Chase whispers inside my ear, "What do you want to do? Punch him? Then *you'll* get arrested." His fingers dig deeper into my waist. "He's not worth it, Ivy."

I'm trembling so hard that my teeth rattle.

"Ivy, our liaison back in Indiana, Officer Joshua Cooper—he's a friend of yours, isn't he?" I don't think I nod, but I must, because Clancy continues, "He's with your sister. He asked me to tell you that he'll stay by her side until you get back."

Her mouth moves some more, but my ears are buzzing so loudly I can't make out much of what she's saying. I do pick up four words, though.

"Might never wake up."

She insists on the *might,* but all I hear is the *never.*

EPILOGUE

Ivy

It's been three weeks, and still Aster is asleep. Every day I visit her, and every day, it tears me apart a bit more.

When I arrived at the hospital, I asked the nurse to shave my sister's hair off. The woman who attacked her hacked off strands, leaving half of her head bare and the other half covered with ugly dreadlocks. I heard her name was Gill Swanson. I've been tempted to pay her a visit, but I think I would strangle her if I were to meet her.

The heart monitor beeps, reminding me that Aster's still alive. I don't know if she can hear me, but I talk to her all the time. I tell her about my new project, making a quilt just for her. I tell her I'm using Mom's prized fabrics. I even tell her about the history of the cloth rolls. Her heart spiked when I mentioned they were gifts from our father, so I embellish the few stories Mom shared with me about our dad.

Her heart hasn't spiked since.

"Hey," a gentle voice calls out from the doorway of the hospital room.

I put down my needle and the strips of ochre satin I've just cut, and stare at the one person who's made the past weeks bearable. "Hey back. I missed you."

Chase crosses the room in four quick strides and deposits a kiss on my mouth.

"One week in, and you're already skipping school," I tease him.

He chuckles, but then he stares at Aster, and his laughter dies out. "Anything new?"

I shake my head sadly.

"She'll wake up. I can feel it," he says.

"Just like you felt I would win?"

"I never thought you would win."

"Aha! You finally admit it." I wink when I spot his jaw darkening with a blush. "You even tried to help me at the end, and I still didn't give the right answer."

"I wanted you to win. I really did. I knew my brother was going to be kicked off, which would've made room for me."

"How is he?"

"He keeps claiming how innocent he is, but I know he's not."

"I hope he'll survive prison better than Aster."

"You're too nice."

"He's not entirely evil, Chase. No one is."

He stares at me with that penetrating gaze of his that makes me feel as though no one else exists in the world, and then he digs into his jacket pocket for something. "This arrived for you. The nurse asked me to bring it up." He extricates a lumpy envelope with no return address and places it on top of the shimmery satin strips.

My name is printed on the front, along with the hospital's address. Cautiously, I slice the paper with my sewing scissors. When I spot a black velvet jewelry box inside, a chill shoots up my spine.

"Someone sent you jewelry?" Chase's voice is so loud that I fear the cop stationed outside the hospital room will overhear him. Thankfully, the door doesn't open. "Should I be jealous?"

I lift my eyes to his face. The vein on his temple lobe is pulsing. He's not just jealous; he's angry.

"It's probably the family heirloom Kevin stole from me," I say in a low voice. I know now that it wasn't Kevin. It was Brook. I figured it out when he winked at me the day he was arrested. I'm surprised he hasn't told the police about the diamond yet.

"He stole something from you?"

I inhale a slow breath and nod. I hate that I'm lying to Chase, but what choice do I have?

"Did he send it from his grave?"

I lower my gaze to the velvet box. "His wife must've found it in his personal effects."

"Wouldn't she have assumed it was a gift he got her?"

Why must Chase be so smart? "Maybe Dominic told her they were looking for it, and she felt obliged to return it, what with all that's happened."

I stare at the box. It shimmies in and out of focus.

"Well, aren't you going to open it?" His usually calm voice sounds somewhat sharp.

I swallow. And then I click on the latch. And it's as excruciating as if I were pulling the trigger during a game of Russian roulette. The box unbolts and the lid rises. Silence hangs, thick and heavy like the rainclouds outside. Not only is the stolen diamond back, but it's been woven into an intricate setting that spells my name.

"I understand why she couldn't keep it," Chase says. "Although she could've removed the stone from its setting."

The brilliant rock winks at me, a scornful reminder of why I'm sitting in a guarded hospital room next to my sister's lifeless body.

"Here. Let me put it on you," Chase says, reaching for the box.

"No," I say quickly, snapping it closed.

He frowns.

I want to tell him the truth, but how can I explain it now that my name is linked to the diamond? "If Aster wakes up and sees it, she'll be sad. Mom never made her one."

I was wrong.

Brook *is* entirely evil.

COLD LITTLE HEARTS

BOOK 3

USA TODAY BESTSELLING AUTHOR

OLIVIA WILDENSTEIN

PART 1
BEFORE

ONE

Brook

A girl who stitches quilts.

This is the first thing I learn about Ivy Redd. After skimming through her *Masterpiecers* application, I toss it aside because quilt making is not really art. I admire people who stitch stuff. My grandmother was one of them. Up until the day she died, she met with her quilting club each week. They'd cut and sew squares of gaudy-patterned fabric with fervor, as though their lives would fall apart if they paused.

Dominic, the president and founder of the Masterpiecers School, picks up the application and thumbs through it.

"Don't bother. It's quilts," I say, grabbing the next file.

He studies the picture stapled to the last page. "You are too rash in judging this girl. She has something. What do you think, Josephine?"

He hands it over to the vice-president of the school.

"*Pas mal*. But we only have one more slot. And I found the perfect *candidat*."

"Really?" Dominic leans back against the silk upholstery of his wooden chair. One of the school's graduates, Christos Natter, carved it. One side is curved and smooth, while the other looks windblown, stretching irregularly toward Dominic's bulky chestnut bookcase. "Who struck your fancy?"

Josephine flings a file onto the eighteenth-century French desk. It lands next to the industrial steel lamp.

Dominic glances at it. "No."

"*Pourquoi pas*?"

He flaps his hand in the air. "He's a former soldier, not an artist."

She folds one leg over the other and rests her hands on her bony white knee. "That is not a reason, Dom. He is skilled. Look at that rope he wove while he was on tour."

"Come on, Jo. It's a rope," Dom says.

"And this"—she nods toward Ivy Redd's file—"is a quilt. Why does quilt trump rope?"

"Because!" The way he looks away from Josephine says there's more to his staunch refusal than the medium of the pieces.

"You both have a special person, who you did not pick on merit," she says. "I am certain Chase is a talented boy, Brook, and Maria—actually, I am not certain Maria has anything to offer besides her body, Dom—but I accepted. Now consent to my choice."

Dominic reddens at the mention of his ex-girlfriend, a former beauty queen and ham-fisted artist whose claim to fame are crude renditions of overly made-up pageant contestants. I heard he impregnated her, and the only way to get rid of the baby was accepting her onto the show.

Josephine rises, and her tailored pearl-gray dress slips right into place over her skeletal body. "I will alert Mr. Kevin Martin that he has been selected. Oh, wait. That is why we have Brook now, *n'est-ce pas*? To do all the menial jobs."

I glare at her, although she's right. That is why I'm here. "I'll notify the contestants this afternoon."

She gives me a crooked smile before stepping out of Dominic's office.

"She hates me," I tell Dom some time after she shuts the door.

"She hates everyone."

"Except her fiancé."

"I doubt she even likes him."

As I straighten out the files of applicants who didn't make the cut, Dominic tut-tuts.

"What?"

"The girl who sews quilts; keep her application aside. We'll be needing it."

I slip it out of the pile and put it on top. "Why?"

"Because." He shifts his eyes toward his cell phone. Dominic is certain we are being listened to. "She's a sound runner-up." As he talks, he grabs a piece of paper embossed with his name and scribbles something.

I scratch the stubble on my cheek as I read it. When my jaw unhinges, Dominic picks up his message and shreds it into a dozen tiny pieces that he drops into his leather bin. They flutter down like confetti, settling in the dusky emptiness. I doubt anyone will collect them and glue them back together, but just in case, I crouch down, swipe some into my palm, and stick them inside my blazer pocket.

I have as much to lose as Dominic. No, that's a lie. I have more to lose because it's my name that's being used, not his. Mine.

"It's a beautiful day, isn't it?" he says, all cheery again. "I love spring. Don't you?"

I'm tongue-tied.

"I'm heading out for lunch. I'll see you tonight," he says.

"Tonight?"

"Didn't your father tell you? We're having dinner all together at his house. To celebrate the sale. It went well, didn't it?"

I make a jerky head movement that's supposed to be a nod.

"Did it pay the bills?"

"Not all of them."

He pats my shoulder. "I'm sure they'll get paid soon. I have an idea." His fingers clamp down around my shoulder like a metal claw. I'm starting not to like his ideas. "I'll tell you later." He squeezes once, then lets go and walks out, whistling a tune that sounds like something from *Les Misérables*.

Clutching the pile of applications against me, I stop by my office, which is more of a glass cubicle than an office. I don't even have screens or blinds. As I heave the folders onto my desk, I notice one of the secretaries fanning a leaflet out in front of a young boy. It throws me back in time. Four years to be exact. I stood at his exact spot, overwhelmingly excited at the prospect of starting at the Masterpiecers. Four years ago, when everything was still so peachy. When my family was still rich. When my little brother didn't despise me for having usurped "his life." The school has strict laws forbidding siblings from attending. Supposedly, it's to discourage family feuds. Didn't discourage Chase from hating my guts.

Movement behind the secretary catches my attention. Josephine stands next to her triangular-shaped desk, where a lone potted orchid holds court over an ultra-flat computer screen and a pencil cup made of cerulean blue clay. It looks as though a kindergartener crafted it, when in fact, it was an alumni from this school.

Josephine sees me staring. There's something unsettling about the way she gazes back, eyes sort of slanted. My shirt collar suddenly feels tight, so I pop the top button open. She smiles that glacial smile of hers, then gazes down at my jacket pocket. I stick my hand inside protectively before reassuring myself that Josephine Raynoir does not have X-ray vision. I rub the pieces between the pads of my fingers, feeling the raised edges in the vellum where Dominic inked his command: *Find out who Kevin Martin really is.*

Josephine flicks a switch and her glass walls blur. I am left with the shadow of her body moving about like the giant stick insect I won at a fair when I was twelve. I kept it in a terrarium, which I couldn't be bothered to clean. Our housekeeper, Carmelina, was too frightened of the bug to touch the thing, so the sides became filthier and filthier until my mother got so sick of it, she seized the glass case and dumped it on the curb for some other little boy, or some garbage collector, to find.

I eye my trashcan, but decide against putting anything inside. It's lunchtime, and even though I'm not hungry, I walk out of Delancey Hall, a two-story building with glossy green ivy scuttling over the brick walls. It was named after Dominic's favorite adviser, Robert Delancey. A few years back, when I was starting on college applications, *The New York Times* dedicated its entire art section to the man. It was titled *The Monocled Star-Maker*. My father read it out loud to us over breakfast.

"Art is Chase's dream, Dad. Not mine," I remember telling him, mostly to get him off my case.

Chase looked up from his big bowl of cornflakes, milk dribbling down his chin. He was fourteen then. His upper lip had finally grown some fuzz.

"*I* wasn't given a choice," Dad said.

"Well I'd like a choice," my seventeen-year-old self demanded.

"And you'll get one," Mom chimed in, clicking into the dining room for breakfast. She dropped a kiss on my forehead, and then tried to peck Chase's, but he ducked away from her. "Right, Henry? We always said we would let the kids choose."

In the end, after two years spent at Duke University, I asked to transfer into the art school to my father's delight. It was the same year Chase sent in his college applications. His top choice was the Masterpiecers, but I beat him to it, something he never forgave me for. Just like he never forgave me for consoling his ex after their messy breakup.

As I walk toward Riverside Drive, I grab the slivers of paper from my pocket and dump them inside the nearest trashcan. Then I slip my phone out and open a search window in which I type Kevin Martin's name. There are several pages of results. I add the words 'retired sergeant.'

There is only one result: *Kevin Martin, Private Investigator.*

Dominic was right. Josephine is investigating him.

TWO

1 MONTH PRIOR TO THE SHOW

JOSH

It's strange keeping a secret from your best friend. In my case, from my two best friends. The girls who, in spite of being two years younger than me, and somewhat cool—especially Ivy—ate their lunches with the fat kid every day.

Yes, once upon a time, I was that kid whose belly plopped out of elastic-waisted pants and whose cheeks earned him the nickname of Hamster. Ivy would smack anyone who dared call me by my furry moniker, while Aster reassured me I was the handsomest boy she'd ever laid eyes on. Said she'd had a crush on me since the age of five when we met in the McDonald's jungle gym, where I rescued her from the ball pool.

I drop on the couch, draping one arm around the back cushion. "What time are they broadcasting the selection?" I ask Ivy, who's sewing something red. Her fingers move so fast, tucking the needle in, gliding it out, in, out, it's hypnotic.

"At nine. Hopefully, Aster will be home by then."

"They work her too hard at that pizzeria."

"It's good for her."

"Is it?"

"It gives her purpose."

"The ad agency gives her purpose," I say.

"Yes, but it's an internship. She doesn't make any money."

"She would've been better off working at Mom's bakery."

"Possibly. But she would have seen it as charity, and you know as well as I do, that she hates charity." Ivy sets the red thing down next to her. "Joshy, if I get picked—"

"*When* you get picked."

Ivy wrinkles her nose. For as long as I've known her, she's made that face when she's nervous. "*If* I get picked, will you stay with her while I'm gone? I know it's a lot to ask, what with you guys being broken up and everything, but I don't like the idea of leaving her on her own."

"Why are you even asking, Ives?"

"Because you have a new girlfriend now."

Heat crawls up the sides of my face. It prickles, like when I slap on aftershave after nicking my skin. "How do you know about Heidi?" I half-whisper, gaze darting toward the door.

"Don't worry. I haven't told Aster," she says, tucking a strand of blonde hair behind her ear. It's flat and shiny, unlike her sister's springy corkscrews. "Is it serious?"

"I don't know."

"Promise me you won't tell Asty until it is?"

I nod, ogling the threadbare carpet because Ivy has a way of looking at you that's really unsettling. Maybe it's because her eyes are so light. *Nah.* Aster has light blue eyes too. That's not it. "How did *you* find out?"

"I saw a picture of you two on her Facebook feed, and guessed."

I lift my gaze back up to hers. "Crap. What if Aster saw the same picture?"

"She's not friends with Heidi." Ivy leans forward and pokes my chest. "You can't keep secrets from me for long, Joshy."

Actually, I can.

And I have.

Twice now.

I never told the twins I met their father two years ago. He's a man they're better off not knowing.

Like I haven't told them the FBI put my chief on a huge case a couple days ago, and I'm part of the task force.

I so wish I could tell someone about my latest assignment. Anyone. But especially Aster and Ivy. They're like my sisters. Well, Ivy is; not Aster. Aster is something else to me, something pure and painful and complicated.

Our relationship was bittersweet and intense. We loved deeply, but not well… because she wasn't well. Her mental health pierced the fragile bubble that had formed around us. I still remember the exact moment it happened. It was the morning the gynecologist phoned Ivy to tell her that her twin left her office upset, convinced she had just endured a miscarriage although she hadn't. It took us hours to locate Aster.

She was covered in snow on a bench, in the middle of Highland Park, clutching her empty abdomen. Cradling her in my arms, I carried her home. She believed her jeans were soaked in blood when in fact it was a mixture of snow and urine. I ran her a warm bath, sponged away the imaginary blood, and let her fall asleep in my arms one last time.

"Joshy?" Ivy says, flapping her hand in front of my face. "I lost you there."

I fire up a smile to raze my brain of that chilling, snowy morning. "What are you making?"

Ivy bites her lip. "A bag."

"That's cool."

"It's Mom's last quilt. Maybe I shouldn't turn it into a bag."

"At least it's practical now."

She smirks. "I can't believe how dense you still are about art."

"Dense? Really?" I chuckle. "It must be so hard to be an artist around all of us *dense* Kokomoans."

"You're not *all* dense," she says, still smiling that brazen, brilliant smile of hers.

"Just me?"

She winks.

I fling the remote control at her, making sure it arches up in the air and falls a foot away.

"Using force to retaliate, Joshy? How very masculine of you."

I laugh. She laughs. It's always been like that between us. Easy.

"Turn the damn TV on so I don't have to listen to you assault me verbally anymore," I tell her.

"*Assault you verbally*? Learn those big words in cop school, Officer Cooper?"

"I know you underestimate me because I have all this awesome muscle"—I flex my arm and my bicep bulges—"and you're into nerdy, little artists."

She snorts. "I'm not into anyone."

"Luke's still pining for you."

Ivy went out with him briefly when she was thirteen. Five years later, they attended prom together. But that was it.

"Luke's a bit boring," she says.

"Because he doesn't know who Monette is?"

"Monet, not Monette. And no. There was just no chemistry between us. I tried *twice*."

"You want a medal?"

"No." She purses her lips as she says the word, which makes me grin.

I stretch my arm out to grab the remote control and surf the channels, while Ivy resumes transforming the quilt. We sit in comfortable silence until Aster arrives, right in time for the announcement.

Ivy tenses, fingers curling like claws, and her skin, which is usually this gold-copper shade, even in the winter, has turned as pasty as the balls of fondant my mother kneads at the bakery. Heidi's dying to work there instead of at the Dairy Queen where she picks up a few hours here and there, but I don't know how I feel about introducing her to Mom. I mean, Mom knows her, but not as my girlfriend.

Aster surprises me with a hug, which makes me forget all about Heidi and my mother.

"Did I miss it?" she asks, plopping a bowl of popcorn on the coffee table and taking a seat between us on the lumpy, L-shaped couch.

"No," Ivy says. She sounds croaky, like someone who's coughed a lot. She grabs a fistful of popcorn and tosses it inside her mouth.

I shoot my gaze to her face, and sure enough, she's wrinkling her nose. "Relax. They cannot *not* pick you."

Aster squeezes Ivy's hand. "You're the best."

"I'm not the best, and yes, they could *not* pick me. They probably didn't pick me. I make quilts."

"Works of art," Aster chimes in.

Ivy yanks her hand out of her twin's and reaches for more popcorn.

"The most beautiful works of art," Aster continues.

Ivy sighs. "Please stop."

Aster's lips wobble, so I circle an arm around her shoulder. Her rough curls tickle my jaw.

Dominic Bacci's face materializes on the television. He smiles. The dude's always smiling. And he's always tanned. He's so rich he probably spends his life vacationing on yachts. He's sitting across from a heavily made-up anchorwoman with feathery blonde hair like Faye Dunaway's. Dad's a big fan of hers. Or was. Can't recall if she's dead.

"You've made us wait a whole year, Dominic! Do you have any idea how excited we all are? And I'm speaking for the seven million viewers watching us tonight," she says, her voice reflecting the enthusiasm animating her plastic features.

"These contests take meticulous planning. We pour our hearts, and our sponsors' money"—he winks at the camera—"into these competitions. You should see what we came up with this year."

"For those of you unfamiliar with the show," the anchorwoman says, "the third *Masterpiecers'* contest will begin on August 21st. The top contestant will win not only admission but a full tuition scholarship to the exclusive Masterpiecers art school, as well as a hundred-thousand dollar check." She smiles, lips as plump as whoopee cushions. "So, Dominic, who are the talented eight who made it onto this year's show?"

Dominic, still grinning, extricates something from the inside pocket of his velvet blazer. "Let's see." He gazes down at the paper. "Number one." He raises his eyes to the screen, which has been split to display the contestants' images alongside his face. "Miss Lincoln Vega."

A picture of a pretty blonde girl brightens the black square.

"Number two…Mr. Herrick Hawk."

The picture of the blonde transforms into a picture of a guy with poufy black hair and a neck scarf.

"Number three, Miss Maria Axela."

A super smiley, Hispanic-looking woman replaces the scarf dude. She has on red lipstick.

"Number four—" Dominic takes a dramatic pause. It's probably to give viewers a chance to quit hyperventilating. "Jared J."

Another toothy person fills the split screen. This time, it's a guy with a grown-out buzz cut, kind of like mine.

Aster sits up straighter. She chances a glance at her sister, who's hovering on the edge of her seat, no longer munching on popcorn.

"Number five, Maxine Specter."

Maxine's hot, even though she has a proper buzz cut.

"Number six…" Dominic's grin widens. "Chase Jackson."

Unfortunately, the hot chick is replaced by this somber-faced dude who looks like he's just gotten dumped.

"That's Brook Jackson's little brother," Ivy says, sounding spellbound.

"Who's Brook Jackson?" I venture.

"One of the judges. He graduated from the school two months ago," she explains, eyes stuck to the picture of the brother.

"I wonder how *he* made it onto the show," I mumble.

Obviously, it's not a question, but Aster answers anyway. "It's because he's the judge's brother."

I wince.

"Number seven, Mr. Nathan Stein," Dominic says.

A picture of an old dude with greasy hair pops onto the screen.

"The last spot will be yours. I can feel it," Aster tells Ivy.

Ivy bounces her legs so fast it makes the couch vibrate.

"And finally…" Dominic pauses theatrically again. "Number eight..." Another long stretch of overwrought silence. "Mr. Kevin Martin."

Ivy leaps off the couch just as Aster reaches out for her.

"They're stupid," Aster says, following her sister into the kitchen.

Ivy bangs things around before trotting back out with a spoon and a tub of pistachio ice cream. I'm torn between trying to comfort her and pumping my fist in the air. If Ivy had made it onto the show, she would've left Kokomo…and probably forever.

THREE

1 WEEK LATER

Brook

The doorbell of Dominic's townhouse chimes, ricocheting against the marble floor and the Plexiglas frames encasing the dyed sand creations of a Masterpiecers' graduate.

His housekeeper scuttles to open the door while I pace his octagonal living room with the stiff, purposely mismatched furniture and the loud turquoise rug.

"What's the emergency?" Josephine asks, breezing past the housekeeper into the living room. Her cheeks are flushed, and not from make-up.

"Sit down, Jo," Dominic says, gesturing to a peacock-green loveseat.

Josephine sits, straight as a board. "*Que se passe-t-il*?"

"Pictures surfaced. Pictures of Kevin Martin. They're going to be aired on the evening news edition," Dominic says, making sure his voice sounds dismal.

She cocks an eyebrow. "What sort of pictures?"

"You tell her, Brook."

I freeze.

"Brook?" Dom says, peering at me.

"Kevin was photographed at a white supremacist rally," I blurt out.

"You don't say." Josephine doesn't sound convinced. "Can I see?"

Dominic's jaw pulses. "It's not pretty."

"I am not faint of heart. *Montrez-moi*."

So I prop my cell phone in front of her face. She grabs it and flicks her fingers against the screen to blow up the shot.

"Where did you get these?" she asks.

"They were sent to me by an anonymous source."

"Belonging to a religious group is not against school regulations."

"A religious group?" I say incredulously. "This is not a religious group, Josephine."

"Miss Raynoir." Her upper lip twitches. "I am not your *copine*, Brook." She shoves the phone into my hands. "So you have disqualified him, I suppose?"

"Of course. We can't encourage racism. Our school stands for tolerance and morality," Dom says.

"Morality? Is that what the school stands for?"

"What are you implying, Jo?"

"*Rien*. I misspoke." She rises and her silky, oyster-colored pants billow around her legs, tenting over her protruding hipbones. "So who is the lucky runner-up?"

"The girl who makes quilts," Dominic says.

She tilts her head. For a second, she doesn't say anything, and then she nods. "She is a sound choice."

I'm surprised by her approval.

She seizes her Hermès bag and walks toward the door. She stops midway and turns. "Have you asked Mr. Martin about the pictures? Maybe he can explain himself."

"We've informed him," Dominic says.

Or rather I've informed him. I called him up last night and told him we'd found unsettling evidence that compromised his selection. When he asked what it was, I told him to turn on his TV tonight. Fun phone call.

The front door slams shut, making the plastic frames shudder. Warm street air gusts inside the house. I must stare at the armored front door for a long time, because Dominic has walked over to me, holding out a cup of tea from a platter that wasn't in the room when Josephine was still there.

I take the tea from him, but don't drink it.

"Let's go over the contest ideas," he suggests.

Applying pressure to the spot between my shoulder blades, he guides me into his adjacent study, and presses me into one of the four big leather and velvet chairs. The thick, wine-colored drapes are closed, which makes the small room feel tighter and darker. The only sources of light in the room, besides the faint trickle of afternoon sun around the curtain edges, come from the shelf lighting of his bookcase and from the elephant-tusk desk lamp built into the copper coffee table.

"Did I mention the *Times* is doing a big spread on the competition next week?"

He pulls a file from the bookcase and places it on the table, then scratches his pencil against the top. *A package will arrive for Dean.*

I blink up at him. I received my Duke University friend's last package, an articulated pewter statue full of rolls of cash, barely ten days ago. Scheduling deliveries so close together isn't smart.

Dom tips his head toward the file. "And I booked Patrick Veingarten for the group photograph. He has some magnificent ideas."

All you need to do is sign for it, he writes.

Beads of sweat slide down my neck. *All I need to do?* It will be my name on the package again. Not his. Not Dean's.

"How fun is it that Chase is coming to compete?" Dom asks.

I choke on my saliva and cough. Is he threatening me or reminding me of his generosity?

While he resumes his monologue about the upcoming photoshoot, he scribbles some more. My attention is glued to the lead tip of his pencil. *You'll get a commission for this one as well.*

If only my family hadn't needed the money...didn't still need it. My pulse pounds against my eardrums, harder than it used to during workouts with my personal trainer. I can't afford a personal trainer anymore; not that I'd want to take orders from yet another person. I jiggle my leg. Dominic claps his hand against my kneecap to steady it, then he turns to the next page.

"Patrick's ideas are genius. He wants to use frames and..." His voice vanishes in the fog of my brain as I take in the headshot of a girl with long blonde curls and an uneasy smile. Her face isn't unfamiliar to me, but I can't quite place it.

"Who's that?"

Dominic places his index finger against his lips. "Sistina."

It's not Sistina. Sistina was in my graduating class.

As he says, "I've commissioned her to build structures reminiscent of French Renaissance frames," he writes, *Package is coming from Indiana. Like Ivy Redd.*

I rack my brain. Ivy Redd? Ivy Re— The girl who stitches quilts!

He flips to the next page.

It's the picture of the quilt she'd attached to her application. The one that looks like a Klimt. The one I dismissed. Dom taps his finger against it, then draws little circles inside.

"You understand?"

"Yes." Her quilt will be the package.

"Good." He lowers the pencil tip to the paper again. *Troy will mail it.* He must sense my nervousness, because he adds, *Your share will be 10%. Of 4 million dollars. That should help your family.*

I grab his pencil and write. *And Chase will win?*

"That's not up to me," he says, disturbing the slick silence that has settled over the small, airless room.

He snatches the pencil from my stiff fingers and removes the words he wrote, blowing the eraser crumbs onto my lap. "I have a feeling this year's show is going to be stupendous," he says, fostering a smile that takes over his entire face.

He looks like the Joker in Batman. I was terrified of the Joker as a kid. Still am, although I've never shared this with anyone. Only Chase knows. He found out one night when I woke Carmelina up to change my bed sheets because I had a nightmare about the Joker. I was eight. Chase was five. He'd heard me cry through our shared wall. I didn't think anyone kept memories from that early, but my little brother isn't anyone. He's wired differently. He listens and stores information like a human pressure cooker. That's why I forbade my father from breathing a word to him about our colossal debts. I was afraid that if Chase blew, we'd make *Page Six* of the *Post.*

FOUR

JOSH

In the middle of a briefing, my chief gets called out of the assembly room. I'm supposed to pick up Heidi in twenty minutes for a movie date. As I wait for him to return, I text her that I'll be late. The dot dot dots light up, so I know she's typing back, but nothing appears. The dots blink again. And then they stop again. No answer. Is she mad?

I don't have time to ponder this as the chief is back, jaw flushed.

"What happened?" asks Fred, my hefty, thirty-seven-year-old partner.

"The tip we got was a bust. There was no meeting between Mann and the Discolis," Guarda says. He pinches the tip of his handlebar mustache and rolls it between his fingers. He always plays with his mustache when he's stressed out. "The Feds want us to stand down. They think Mann is getting spooked."

Behind the chief, on the screen always displaying the news channel on mute, I catch the words *Breaking News* and *Masterpiecers*. I push away from the long desk and approach the monitor. A black-and-white picture of a heated rally appears. I frown as I attempt to understand its connection to the art school. A sentence scrolls along the banner at the bottom of the image, right underneath the reporter's lively face.

Contestant number 8, Kevin Martin gets eliminated for ties to the racist group.

This is huge news. So huge that the chief is standing beside me, silent for once. I'm about to turn away when a new picture flashes on the screen. It's a head-shot of Ivy. I step in closer.

"Isn't that your girlfriend?" Fred asks. He's halfway through a bag of Werther's Originals. How he can fill his body with that much fat and sugar is beyond me.

"No. It's her twin." I should have added that Aster isn't my girlfriend anymore.

"How can you tell?"

"She doesn't have a beauty mark over her lip."

"And here I thought Dominic Bacci had no values," the chief says.

I gape at him. "You follow the competition?"

"My wife does. She's obsessed with him." His eyes dart around the room. "They were probably forced to pull him off the show. Imagine all the viewers they would've lost if they hadn't."

"I hope he loses more than just his spot on this reality TV show," Fred adds.

We watch the TV a while longer.

"Are we still going to investigate Troy Mann, Chief?"

"How long have we known each other, Fred?"

"Going on ten years now."

"Have I ever closed an unresolved case?"

"No, Chief."

"There's your answer."

"Can't we get in trouble?" I ask.

Guarda smirks. "You're so young, Cooper, so idealistic." His expression grows serious. "If you want to work for some halfwit who plays by the rules, then I'm not your man. If you want to learn the ropes from someone who cares about justice, then you've come to the right place."

Fred twists his lips as though he were trying to dislodge a piece of sticky caramel.

"Before Jackie died, she asked me to train you, to give you a spot on my team. But I won't uphold my promise if I don't feel like your heart and mind are invested. So what'll it be?" the chief asks.

The mention of Jackie makes my eyes sting as though the chief squirted pepper spray into them.

Jackie was the cop who made me want to become a cop. I met her the same day I met the twins in the McDonald's jungle gym. She was the responding officer. I still remember how she'd knelt down beside the twins and me, and showed us her badge, then told us the story of a man she'd just arrested for stealing a gumball machine. To this day, I'm not sure if her story was made-up or real.

And now I'll never know.

Stupid liver cancer took her from us a year ago.

"I'm not letting a crook from my hometown get away with multiple counts of fraud," I finally say. There is no way I'm letting Jackie down.

Both my partner and my boss nod. "Good boy. We'll meet back here tomorrow at fourteen hundred hours," he says, leaving before us.

Guarda is ex-military. He diffused a bomb once, saving his entire regiment. It won him a big medal, which he keeps displayed on his work desk in place of his nameplate.

"Could I lose my badge?" I ask Fred when it's just the two of us.

"You might. Or you might get an honorific award."

"I don't care about awards."

"Doing the right thing always pays off. And getting a prick off the streets is the right thing."

"Look who's idealistic now?"

"It's not idealism, Coop, it's integrity." He checks his wristwatch that's so tight it looks embedded into his pudgy wrist. "I gotta hurry. The wife hates it when I'm late for dinner." On our way to the locker room, he asks, "What you up to tonight? Victory drinks with the new contestant?"

"I have a date."

"With her sister?"

"With another girl. Aster and I aren't together anymore." I glance down at my phone. Heidi finally answered me.

I must look disappointed because Fred asks, "Got stood up?"

"She's going to hang out with her mom. Her parents are divorcing."

"Must be tough on the kid."

"She's doing a summer semester at Ivy Tech to stay out of the house."

"What she studying?" he asks, banging his locker shut.

"Culinary Arts. She wants to be a chef." I grab my windbreaker and put it on.

"Seriously? I thought programming was the 'in thing' these days. All I hear around the dinner table is Facebook this and Twitter that. Apparently someone's even coming out with flying cars soon. If that's true, I hope the precinct will replace ours."

As Fred goes on about futuristic automobiles, I zone out. I have to pick up flowers for Ivy. To congratulate her. She needs to know I'm proud of her since her mom is no longer there to tell her. Not that her mother ever expressed much pride in her daughters.

I drop Fred by his car and then get into mine. All the nice florists are closed at this hour, so I drive over to Kroger on the corner of South Washington and pluck a bouquet of red roses from the gray plastic buckets that line the shop window.

I dump it back into the water. I can't give Ivy red roses. Red roses are romantic. I eye the white ones. What does white mean? I look it up on my phone. *Traditional wedding flowers.* Hell no. I check what baby pink represents. When I read some stuff about poetic romance, I grab a bouquet of multicolored tulips.

On my way over to the twins' apartment, I drive by the pizzeria where Aster works. I watch her ring up a customer. She's smiling. She must have heard the news of Ivy's acceptance. It's good to see her happy. After the past year, Aster deserves a break. Plus her grin reassures me she's taking her meds. When she's off them, she doesn't smile much.

As I glide away from the curb and drive in the direction of Ivy's apartment, I glance at the tulips. I should've bought a bouquet for Aster. I count the flowers when I stop at a traffic light. *Twelve.* I can make two bouquets. I start unwrapping the plastic when the light turns green. While driving, I reassemble the flowers. The car swerves, and I jam my foot against the brake. Pulse hammering, I pull up by the curb to rearrange my flowers.

Six and six.

Both bouquets look puny. I squash all the flowers together again.

Today's Ivy's day. Aster won't be jealous.

One of the tulip heads lolls from its tubular stalk. Another falls off. The bouquet looks scruffy, as though I picked the flowers from someone's backyard. Groaning, I toss the whole thing out the window. Ivy's not a flower person anyway.

FIVE

2 WEEKS PRIOR TO THE SHOW

Brook

In the basement of Delancey Hall, there is an amphitheater complete with a drop-down screen that spans the length of the enormous stage. It took two years to dig up the equivalent of four floors to accommodate the hundred rows of seats that curve around the stage in a semi-circle. It's in this theater that Dominic will project the features of the eight contestants. He's invited the entire student body, and from the sight of the packed auditorium, it seems like they all cut their vacation short to attend.

As Josephine and Dominic come on stage, everyone stands.

"Hello, my masterpiecers!" Dominic's brown eyes crinkle with the delight of being on stage. "I am so touched that you—all of you—have returned early from your holidays to watch the marvelous feature we have put together for you. Soon, you will be greeting a new, freshman masterpiecer. Am I wrong in assuming some of you have bets going as to who will win?"

Laughter warbles all around.

"To a great show, great talent, and a great forthcoming year! I cannot wait for the end of the summer to discover what you all have in store for me."

Everyone applauds as Dominic passes the microphone over to Josephine. She steps away from Dominic, holding the mic with two hands as though afraid he might snatch it back. She utters lots of niceties in a tone that doesn't sound especially kind. I asked Dominic once why he'd selected her as his VP. "What would happen if kids raised kids?" he'd said. "Josephine's the responsible one, Brook. The parent. Because she's here, I'm allowed to remain a little reckless."

Recently, Josephine was proving to be too responsible in Dominic's eyes. Before she'd even hired a PI to sniff around Dom, he was already looking for a replacement, or so he'd told me the night of our school's graduation ceremony back in May, the night Dominic offered me the job of personal assistant, the night he asked me to run the first "errand."

A round of applause fills the amphitheater, not as loud as that proffered to Dominic. He takes Josephine's arm and escorts her off the stage. White feathers line the bottom of her floor-length dress, creating the impression that she's walking on a cloud.

The lights dim and the colossal curved screen brightens with the first feature on Lincoln Vega, an attractive girl who spent most of her childhood sleeping on a street in Alphabet City, begging for money.

She shows the interviewer the subway station in which she reproduced Picasso's *Demoiselles d'Avignon* in chalk. And then she explains how her passion for chalk art began. "The city streets were my canvas. The city streets were my everything." With no shame, she speaks of her drug-addicted parents and recounts her childhood on the asphalt, stealing day-old Wonder bread from the convenience store and digging through trashcans for leftover treasures. She survived poverty. This is what I silently repeat to myself as I watch the rest of her feature. If she survived it, I can too.

If it comes to that.

Which it won't.

I shift in my seat as the second feature begins. A close-up of Herrick Hawk fills the screen. It's so close that most of the pompadour he sports doesn't make it into the frame. Grinning, he fingers the blue paisley scarf knotted around his clean-shaven throat and walks the camera crew through his outrageously ornate house, making them zoom in on the trompe-l'oeil details of his Michelangelo fresco. Standing in front of a wall decorated with exotic blue mountains, his parents are stiff and broad-eyed. They take a step back when Herrick introduces them to the camera, but still offer shy smiles.

I lean in toward Dominic and whisper, "They make me think of that *American Gothic* couple, you know the farmer and his wife."

Dominic smiles and whispers back, "Yes, but silk-screened into an Italian Renaissance painting."

I chuckle.

Josephine gives me a pointed stare that reminds me of my seventy-year old professor back at Duke, Miss Hendrix. She was so frigid and unpleasant that Dean started a bet about whether she was a virgin or not. It had reached such astonishing proportions that by the end of freshman year, the wager pool was in the tens of thousands of dollars.

Feature number three has started. Nathan Stein. This one makes me uncomfortable, for he speaks of the art the Nazis stole from his family during the Second World War, art he is still trying to locate, but that hasn't surfaced. I glance over at

Dominic, who doesn't look uneasy like me, but who also isn't smiling anymore. Nathan shoots the camera a painful smile.

When the next feature begins, I lean in toward the screen so I don't miss a single beat. It's Chase's feature. Dominic promised it was fine, but until I see it, I will not be appeased. My brother speaks of his passion for collecting art. When the interviewer asks him about his talent as an auctioneer, Chase dismisses the compliment. It's not false humility, although it comes across that way. Even though Chase thinks the worst of me, I think the best of him. He's my little brother, the tiny baby my mother made just for me. I'm hoping this competition will heal the bond of brotherhood severed over a school and a misinterpreted night with a girl.

When my brother vanishes off the screen, a woman with a buzz cut and long feather earrings replaces him. Maxine Specter. Although Dominic doesn't know her, he knows her parents. They're avid art collectors, which she exhibits by walking us through their Hamptons home that makes my parents' former beach house look like a surfer shack.

The next feature is on a guy who's already sort of famous. Jared J. is a graffiti artist who's made a name for himself with cans of spray-paint and public walls. His application was a unanimous favorite for both Josephine and Dominic. Although they love growing new artists, having someone with a social following looks good for the show.

Dominic's former beauty queen, Maria Axela, is next. Her portraits of pageant friends are kitsch. It's painful to watch her speak with such pride of her art. She's like those contestants on singing competitions who think they possess a golden voice, but who sound like farrowing pigs.

Contestant number eight's face materializes on screen. I blink as my gaze meets clear blue eyes. Ivy stares into the camera lens with such disconcerting intensity that I find myself sitting up straighter. I've spoken to her like I spoke to the others, so I know her voice, yet it sounds nothing like the voice I remember. Can overwhelming guilt distort the senses?

SIX

JOSH

I first heard Troy Mann's name three months ago. He grew up on the wrong side of Kokomo with an alcoholic father on welfare and a too-soft mother who ended up running out on them. His one saving attribute was his brain. By junior year of high school, one of his teachers managed to convince the dean that he was too advanced for the school. He was offered a scholarship into a private establishment, before scoring a full ride to Duke University.

Troy chose drug trafficking as an extra-curricular activity. Stupid choice for a smart boy. Not only did he get jail time, but he lost his scholarship and was kicked out of Duke during his junior year. My mother would have slapped me silly if I'd gone and ruined my chances, but Troy didn't have a mom, and his dad just didn't care.

A snitch for the FBI informed them of other sorts of trafficking. Troy must have realized he was being monitored because he stopped all illegal activity. He moved back in with his father and started working for a construction company as a legit metal welder. And then Troy's life changed again. He met a girl called Stephanie and settled down. Apparently she got pregnant, but it didn't work out, or so Heidi told me—Stephanie is one of my girlfriend's thirty-two cousins.

I tap out the Maroon 5 song playing on my phone against the steering wheel. If I hadn't made trooper, I would have moved to Nashville and become a drummer. Instead of pounding drums, though, I pound pavement in search of criminals, which has made both my parents super proud. My mother tells everyone in her book club what a good son I am, and how eligible I am. That part, I wished she'd quiet down about. When she heard I was dating Aster, she cautiously reminded me it would be a complex relationship because of her "affliction." She'd asked me why not Ivy, to which I'd responded: "Just because they're twins, it doesn't make them interchangeable."

A bird chirps on a nearby red maple. It's such a nice day, yet I'm stuck in a car with no air conditioning. I've been staking out Troy's newest construction site for the past week, and like every day, nothing happens. He goes in at eight, has a sandwich with the guys around noon, leaves at five, and drives straight home to Stephanie. I'm waiting for him to make some mistake to link him to the Discolis, the big Indiana mob family he's apparently running errands for again.

I check the clock on the dashboard: 4:57 p.m. On cue, Troy Mann emerges from the building's foundations with his black messenger bag slung across his shoulders. I wait until he's inside his metallic blue Cadillac Eldorado before revving up my car. I count to five slowly and follow him. He goes left—like every day this week. And then he goes right—like every day this week.

My cell phone lights up with a call from the chief. I pick up and put him on speakerphone.

"Just got news that Troy received a call from New York yesterday."

I wait for my chief to elaborate because getting a call from another state isn't illegal.

"The Feds tracked it to a burner cell. Something's about to go down. Any activity in the work place?"

"Nope." I spin my wheel right at the intersection. He's four cars ahead of me. "And it looks like it's going to be another quiet evening. He's driving home."

"Phone back once he gets there."

I hang up and tap my fingers against the wheel until the light switches to green. I'm so absorbed by my finger drumming that I nearly miss the slight left Troy makes at the junction. Hoping my tires don't squeal, I spin the wheel.

"That's not the way home," I mumble out loud. "Where are you going?"

We must drive for a good twenty minutes off course. Finally, the Cadillac turns into the parking lot of a motel off Route 9. I pull up against the curb some fifty feet away. I can still see him from my vantage point, but not well. I hop over the crooked fence and move into the shadows of the thick palm trees planted next to a kidney-shaped pool.

Troy's head swivels back and forth as he enters the motel, like a spectator at a tennis match. I crouch down lower. When he's out of sight, I straighten up but don't come closer. Five minutes later, he's back out. I duck again. He climbs inside his car and swerves out of the lot in my direction. I scramble around the tree trunks and fling myself onto one of the lounge chairs. It creaks and the backrest, which must have been poorly hooked into the base, slams down. Reeling from the impact, I pull my hands behind my neck and try to act like I'm tanning.

The Cadillac doesn't slow, and soon it glides around a street corner. I drag myself off the lounge chair and phone Guarda. "Hey, Chief, I think you're right."

"What happened?"

"He took a detour. Stopped by a motel. I'm going to go check it out."

"Good, Coop."

After he disconnects, I walk past the flashing orange sign advertising vacant rooms. A scrawny middle-aged man sits behind the desk. He looks up from the television he's watching.

"Can I help you?" he asks.

I tap the badge hooked onto my belt. The clerk's eyes roam over it before returning to my face.

"Is there a problem, Officer?"

"The guy who just came in, chin-length black hair, denim shirt."

"Yeah?"

"What did he want?"

"He wanted a room."

"A room?"

He nods.

"Just any room?" Sweat trickles down my neck and soaks into the collar of my navy shirt. It must be close to a hundred degrees inside.

"He asked for 2B."

"What's in 2B?"

"Same thing that's in all the other rooms around here. A bed, a TV, a—"

"No, I mean who's inside 2B?"

"He is," the scarecrow clerk says.

"I saw him drive off."

"Then I guess no one's in there."

"Do you have an extra key?" I ask.

His blond eyebrows mash together on his forehead. "Yeah. But I gotta go inside with you."

"Fine. Take me."

He comes around the reception desk. He's even skinnier standing than he is sitting. At least if he tries anything funny, I can take him out with my right hook. Actually, I could probably flick my fingers to knock him out.

As we walk to room 2B, I scan the quiet lot. Once he unlocks the door, I kick it open and flick the lights on. Nothing seems out of place. I'm not sure what I was expecting. Duffel bags of cash on the bed? Bricks of white powder?

"Was this room rented out recently?" I ask the clerk.

He shrugs. "Not that I know. I'd have to check the books."

I step inside the room. Careful not to disrupt anything, I look under the bed, behind the TV, in the nightstand drawers, and walk through the bathroom. I even peer into the toilet tank. Nothing. The room is clean.

Annoyed, I trek back out. The clerk locks up and walks me back to the front desk. He takes out a large appointment book and runs his long finger over the 2B column.

"No one's used it since late June."

I sigh. "Well, if he comes back, or if anyone else asks for 2B, phone me," I say, sliding my card across the desk.

"Yes, Officer—" He reads the card, "Joshua Cooper."

Don't know why he feels the need to say my full name.

"Are you Moses's son?"

"Yeah. You know my dad?"

"We went to high school together! He tutored me. Did he become a teacher in the end?"

"Yeah."

"Well, good for him. Good for him. Say Dennis says hi, okay?"

"I will."

"And I'll call you if that man returns."

"Or if anyone else asks for 2B."

"Aye-aye." He salutes me, then smiles. He's missing a couple teeth.

Once I'm back in the car, I call the chief and tell him what I found, or rather, didn't find. On autopilot, I drive home, park, and take the elevator to the third floor. The heat in the hallway makes me fear the heat inside my apartment. My AC is broken, so sure enough, it's stifling. I turn on my desk fan, then stick my face close to it and shut my eyes.

When two hands slink around my waist, I spin around and trap the person's wrists. Breathing hard, I loosen my grip and frown. "What are you doing here?"

"I wanted to see you," Aster says.

"How did you get in?"

She blinks, and her blue eyes look shiny, almost glittery, like bouncy balls from 25-cent dispenser machines. "With the emergency key."

"Is this an emergency?"

"No." She looks down. "It's not."

I sigh, hook an arm around her shoulders, and pull her against me. But then I think of my sweaty shirt and push her away. "Didn't mean for it to come out like that, Asty. I've just had a long day. What do you need?"

"I—I—" She bites her lip. "I just wanted to see you." She tries to hug me but I press her away again.

"I need a shower."

"Okay. I'll wait."

I take a quick, cold shower, after which I don't bother drying off, considering the heat. I tie my towel around my waist and walk back out.

"What do you think you're doing?" I snap.

Aster jumps away from my desk.

I cross the room and shut Troy Mann's file. "You're not supposed to see this!"

"I'm sorry. It was just there."

"I could get in real trouble for this. Forget you saw him, okay?" I say, stuffing it inside a drawer.

She nods, then moves closer to me and lifts her hands, settling them against my pecs. "I miss you," she whispers, pushing up on her toes.

When I realize what she's planning, I jerk backward. "We can't. I can't."

"Why not?"

"I just—We're not together anymore."

She curls her fingers over the top of my towel.

"Aster, I said no."

"One last time, Josh. Please. Just one last time. And then I'll leave."

I grab both her hands in one of mine. "What's gotten into you?"

A sob catches in her throat. "I feel so empty, Josh."

"I have some leftover lemon cake from the bakery."

"Not that sort of empty." She touches her abdomen. "In here." She touches her heart. "And in here. I feel empty."

I don't say, "You were always empty," but I think it really hard hoping she'll get my silent message.

"I need you," she whispers.

"Are you taking your meds?"

Her eyes widen in shock.

"Aster?"

"Yes." She grits her teeth. "I'm taking them."

"I don't mean to upset you. I just care."

"If you cared…if you cared you wouldn't treat me like a baby. You'd treat me like a woman. You'd love me. You'd give me a—"

"Don't even say it." I've lowered my voice to sound soothing instead of harsh. "You're nineteen and I'm twenty-one. This is not the right time for a baby."

"Will it ever be the right time?"

"Babies are a lot of work."

"But they bring so much joy."

"Can we find other ways of bringing you joy? You always liked flowers. Maybe we can go to Home Depot to pick up some new plants. I'm sure the buttonbush would like some company."

"Mom hates the buttonbush."

"Hated," I whisper gently. "She's not here anymore. Besides, this is for you. Not for your mother."

Her eyes shimmer. "I love you, Josh. I loved you since the day you rescued me from the ball pool."

"I didn't really rescue you," I say, flushing.

"All the other kids kept jumping on top of me. You pulled me out. That's called rescuing." She cradles my jaw with her hands. "You love me too, don't you?"

"I do, just"—I look away—"not like that anymore."

I think all she hears is the last part of my sentence because she bounces away from me and sprints out of the apartment. I don't run after her, because running after her would mean something—something I don't have the heart or the energy to rekindle.

SEVEN

1 WEEK PRIOR TO THE SHOW

Brook

After an endless day of helping set everything up in the Metropolitan Museum, I feel like I deserve a drink. Or two. I drive over to Humi, the newest fusion restaurant on the Manhattan dining scene.

Sure enough, the restaurant is packed and the noise level is deafening. I came here to avoid thinking, and that's exactly what I intend to do once I sit in front of the backlit bar and order a martini. By the second one, I start to unwind.

When a blonde girl tips some of her drink on my jacket sleeve, I don't even care. She pats it dry with some paper napkins, even though I tell her it's fine.

"I'm so so sorry," she keeps repeating.

I place my hand over hers and glance up at her face. Her eyes are unnaturally large, enormous really, straight out of a Margaret Keane painting. "It's okay."

The girl tries to engage me in a conversation, but talking feels like an effort and I don't want to make an effort. I just want to drink, perhaps even get drunk. After two more martinis and two spicy tuna rolls, I get the check. The restaurant is more crowded now, and moving toward the exit reminds me of kayaking in a blustery sea.

I did that once with Troy and Dean in Florida right before a storm hit. I thought we would never make it back to shore. Troy tied the three kayaks together so that no man was left behind, then all three of us plunged our oars over and over, arms pumping fiercely, shoulders burning with exertion, eyes stinging with salt.

Drenched in rain and sweat, we'd made it back to the beach, feeling like victors after a grueling fight.

As I hail a taxi, a silver Ferrari zips up to the curb. Before the tinted window rolls down, I let out a sigh.

"Brooky," Dean exclaims. From the way his eyes glow in the obscurity of his car, I can tell he's high. I used to find it exhilarating to hang out with a guy who didn't have a care in the world. I don't anymore. "Get in."

"I'm going home. I seriously need to unwind, Dean."

"Just get in."

Sighing, I drag the passenger side door open and climb in. "What do you want?"

"Good to see you too, brother."

"How did you even find me?"

"Lucky guess."

I tilt my head to the side. "I'm not buying that."

"Okay, fine. I know the hostess. And she knows you. She's obsessed with Dom's little show, and she called to ask if it would be too forward of her to ask for an autograph. I told her to leave you the fuck alone. Anyway"—he fires up the engine, swerving in and out of car lanes more perilously than yellow cabs—"I just finished dinner with the D.A. He'll suspend Diego Discoli's sentence as soon as you pop over to meet him."

I nod even though I feel like shuddering.

"You have a meeting with him at his home the day before the show begins. The package should arrive by then. Troy confirmed he's expediting it," Dean says, turning left after Union Square Park.

"Where the hell are you taking me?"

"It's Friday night. We're going out to celebrate!"

"Celebrate what?"

Dean's already incandescent eyes blaze brighter. "My little deal. Your incoming commission. Chase's acceptance. Getting rid of Josephine's PI. The start of the show. There are so many things to celebrate."

"I don't feel like celebrating until it's all done."

Dean places his hand on my arm. "The Masterminds never fail."

I sit up so abruptly I fling his hand off me. "Never *failed*. Past tense. Troy got kicked out of Duke, remember? He's now a construction worker. He could've been so much more."

"He's content with his life."

"If he's so content, why did he agree to run an errand for you?"

"To help you. I told him your situation was serious."

I rub my hand over my forehead. "Well now, I feel awful. I didn't want to drag anyone else into this."

"That's what friends do for each other, Brook. Remember when you and Troy hauled my ass out of the ocean and trussed me up like a turkey after I od'd? I would've drowned if it hadn't been for you guys."

I picture the horrific night, remembering the shouting, the crying, and the vomiting. It still gives me chills.

"Troy said you could have his share, too, by the way."

"I couldn't accept."

"Well, you talk to him about it, okay?"

"Okay."

"I heard you sold your Hamptons house. I loved that house! Did you get a good price?"

"Where did you hear about it?" I ask.

"Dom told me."

"Did he also tell you how badly my family's art collection sold? The fire-sale he organized—"

"Don't you dare put the blame on him. He could've refused to help you."

"Could he? Could he truly refuse to help me? I know too much."

"He treats you like a son, and this is how you repay him? By saying how calculating he is?"

"That's not what I said."

"That's what you meant."

I growl. "Shit, Dean! Running errands for the mob…that's not the life I want."

I expect him to go off on me again, or to kick me out of his car while it's still running. Instead, he says, "This is the last time. We won't involve you again. You can go and live your life. Maybe you can even buy that ranch in Montana you always dreamed about and start your eco-farm."

"My eco-farm?"

"Isn't that what you wanted to do?"

"I made that up when we had to come up with an innovative business plan freshman year. Can't believe you still remember."

"You and Troy are the biological brothers I never had." His eyes flash to my hand, to the pinkie ring he commissioned for the three of us at the end of our freshman year, the shiny tie that binds us. "Even though you speak of us in the past tense, we will always be the Masterminds. The trio who ruled the school. Who threw the best parties. Who came up with the most lucrative bets."

I stay quiet.

"You know what? I'm not giving you a choice. We're going out. You need to let out some steam."

He goes through a red light, not because he doesn't see it, but because he doesn't care. Cars screech to a halt around us. Some honk. Dean lowers his window and gives them the finger. As I watch the joy he gets out of being reckless and rude, the ring tightens around my finger.

EIGHT

AUGUST 16TH

JOSH

Something rings. It takes me a second to realize that it's my cell phone. I peel my eyes open, expecting sunlight, but my bedroom is dark. Who could be calling me at this hour?

Aster?

I sit up so quickly my head spins. I grip my lit phone and fumble to answer it, heart blasting inside my ribcage.

"Joshua Cooper?" a male voice says. *Not Aster*. I can't decide whether to feel relieved or alarmed.

"Who's this?" I say, walking to the bathroom and shutting the door.

"Dennis. From the motel."

I'm fully awake now, even though it's…I check the time on my phone's digital clock…4:13 a.m.

"You told me to call you if someone stopped by." He's whispering. "Mr. Mann just arrived with some lady. They're in the room together now."

I frown. Some woman? I massage my brow. "I'll be right over."

I pull on some clothes, stick my feet in a pair of sneakers, and grab my handcuffs, my badge, and my gun. "I'll be right back," I whisper, but Heidi has plopped a pillow over her head, so she doesn't hear me. I kiss her bare shoulder that smells like apricot, and, rubbing the sleep out of my eyes, I drive back to the motel. When I pull up in front of the reception, Dennis is waiting, shifting around like a tweaker.

"You might want to go back to the front desk. This might get messy," I tell him, pulling out my gun.

"I got your back."

"I don't—"

"Please. This is the most exciting thing that's happened around here in years."

"Okay, but stay out of the room."

"Deal."

We trot over to room 2B. I press my ear against the door, but don't hear anything.

"You heard her scream, right?" I ask.

"No."

"I need probable cause, Dennis. You heard her scream, *right*?"

"Yeah. Lots of screaming."

"Let's go."

Dennis unlocks the door. I push it open.

"KPD, put your hands where I can see them," I yell, aiming my gun at the shape on the bed.

Dennis flicks on the light, then skips back out of the room.

Troy rolls off the woman, and without covering his bare chest, he lifts his hands. I want to look away, but the damage is done. I'll never be able to get rid of the image of his bushy torso.

The woman sits up and raises one hand. She readjusts her thin tank top straps with the other. "What's the problem, Officer?"

Troy rented a motel room to cheat on Stephanie. "I um…got a call about a disturbance."

"We must have been too loud," the girl says, grinning. "We'll keep it down. At least we'll try to."

My gaze flashes to Troy's face. His thick eyebrows are scrunched up as though he's trying to figure something out.

At the foot of the bed, I spot a navy T-shirt, but nothing else. At least I arrived before they got down and dirty.

"If you can hit the light on your way out," the girl says, "it'd be much appreciated."

With stiff fingers, I flip the switch down and start dragging the door closed when Troy says, "If Stephanie finds out, I'll know who she heard it from."

I'm tempted to let out a relieved breath, but instead I say, "What you do behind her back is none of my business."

That's what Troy Mann was figuring out! How we knew each other.

I get back in the car and drive home, debating whether to inform the chief about my nocturnal intervention. I decide against it. It's not like I discovered anything groundbreaking besides the fact that Troy is a two-timing creep.

NINE

AUGUST 19TH

Brook

Twenty-four hours left until chaos descends upon me.

I've been eating and sleeping and living at the Met for the past two days to make sure everything is ready for the arrival of the eight contestants. While Dominic and Josephine review the "props" needed for each test, I go over the equipment with Jeb, our videographer.

"We need a camera in here too," I tell him, pointing to a corner in the makeshift tent, right above a white glass dining table.

"Are we picking up sound or just image in here?" he asks, putting an x on his technical floor plan.

"Dominic wants both. He also wants two speakers in this corridor." I walk down the hallway separating the eight bedrooms. The event planning crew just unrolled real grass and it fills the enormous tent with the scent of the outdoors.

I glance inside the rooms separated by fabric walls. Housekeepers are fluffing pillows and tucking in comforters.

"Coming through," says a guy lugging a potted tree. From the bulge of his biceps, I assume the tree is heavy and dart out of his way.

I carry out my inspection of the contestants' private quarters. An electrician sets up a projector over the table to display video art and the recap of the days' trials on the white glass surface, while four more trees are carried into the hallway. Garlands of lights spiral around the slender branches. When they're plugged in, the dim hallway twinkles. As I stand there, admiring my dazzling surroundings, I reconsider my decision to leave the Masterpiecers after the competition is over, but then a short circuit fizzes out all the lights, and I'm left peering into the obscurity at dark shapes and shifting shadows.

The lights come back on, but they no longer enchant me. "You need anything else?" I ask our squat videographer.

He looks up at me. "Nah. I'm all set."

"You'll be done by tonight?"

"I'll be done by this afternoon. Come on, people," he calls out, "let's get a move on."

I'm dying to take a shower in my own bathroom and unwind on my own couch in front of some thoughtless TV, so I phone Dominic. "They're all set here. Do you need me to do anything else?"

"My secretary informed me there was a delivery for you at Delancey Hall."

Goose bumps cover my skin. "A-a delivery?"

"Considering how hectic tomorrow will be, I suggest going to retrieve it today."

I tug on the collar of my button-down. It's already unbuttoned, yet feels as though it's choking me. "Okay."

"And then you're free." I hear a smile in Dominic's voice. "Until tomorrow that is. I need you to fly up to Montréal for the opening of Zara Mach's new exhibit. And schedule a flower delivery to congratulate her. We have to take care of our rising stars."

Zara Mach uses cotton flowers to create poetic musical instruments. I own a piece myself, a fluffy accordion sheathed in a Plexiglas box that I've hung over my bed. It's worth quite a bit already, but unfortunately, not enough to cover the remainder of my family's debts. Still, I should sell it.

In the museum's underground parking lot, a company car is waiting for me. I ask the driver to take me back to the campus. Although he attempts to make small talk, curious as to how the preparations are unfolding, all I can think about is the package. I watch the sun glint off the polished glass towers and large shop windows full of superfluous and colorful merchandise. I never thought I'd think this, but I'm ready to leave this city.

A half hour later, we pull up in front of the brick hall crawling with ivy. I pounce out of the sedan.

"Last errand," I say under my breath. I take the steps two at a time. When I arrive on the second floor, I'm winded, and not from exertion. "Something arrived for me?" My voice rings inside my ears.

The secretary smiles and hands me a thick orangey envelope. She speaks, but the zinging has intensified, so I can't make out her words. Rigidly, I walk away and lock myself in the bathroom. I set the package on the black marble sink top and stare at it. With clammy hands, I pick it up. One of my fingers drills through the paper casing and touches something soft. I flip it over. A piece of greasy scotch tape dangles off a long tear.

Did Troy do this? Make it look tattered so no one would snoop inside?

I yank off the rest of the tape and tug the quilt through the large slit. The heavy fabric spills out. Ivy's creation is incredibly exquisite, thick in parts, thin in others, soft and jagged. I am so subjugated I momentarily forget why I'm locked inside the bathroom, but soon, I snap into action and inspect the edges. I find a small gap, in which I slide my hand. When the only thing I retrieve is a frayed piece of black thread, the sweat running down my neck turns frosty.

"Where the hell did you hide them, Troy?" I mutter, flicking the thread in the wastebasket, along with the package.

I take out my keys to hack through the seam. My phone rings. No caller ID. "Yes?"

"He's dead," Dean says.

"What?" My heart levitates. "Who?"

"Troy...he's dead."

"What?"

"I found out a few hours ago."

"What?" I repeat, like an idiot.

"Aster Redd—Ivy's twin—she ran him over. Little bitch. She ran him over!"

"What?" I have to stop saying *what.*

Dean sobs. "Troy's gone."

Troy can't be gone. "The quilt's here. How'd it get here if he's...*gone*?"

"It is?"

"Yes."

"He must've sent it before—Right before...*fuck*..." All I hear for a moment is choppy breathing.

I don't think *I'm* even breathing. My lungs, my chest, they feel as though I were a hundred feet underwater with an empty diving tank.

"He told me he placed them in one of the sides," Dean murmurs, "and sewed it back with black thread."

With trembling hands, I scan the quilt's seams, on the lookout for more black thread. I have to rub my eyes repeatedly to clear them. I don't cry. I never cry. Yet tears are dribbling off my chin and onto the quilt, dispersing into the fabric. I watch them fall, perplexed and numb.

"So?"

I shut my eyes hoping it will be like sealing a leak, but my body's not a pipe. "I found...a piece."

"What do you mean a piece?"

I turn on the tap to rub water over my face and to drown out my voice. "There's a tear in it, but nothing else. The envelope it came in was ripped, too."

"Then that would mean...that would mean that little tramp went through it." He stays silent for so long I wonder if he hung up. "That's why she killed him. She knew about the diamonds."

I gulp down a mouthful of water, then dry my face with a hand towel. "How?"

"I don't know how, but I'm going to find out. Maybe her sister knows. Maybe she's in on it."

"What if Troy never put them in?"

"If you found a piece of black thread, then he did, Brook."

I inhale a long breath. "Hold off on cornering the girl." Dean showing up at Aster's jail would expose him, and in turn, me. "We'll find them."

He snorts. "If we don't, I'll end up like Troy."

The quilt slips through my fingers, pooling on the mosaic floor. "They won't kill you."

"You don't know this family."

Truth is, I don't. "I'll bring the quilt home with me. Maybe they *are* there."

"Maybe."

"And if we don't find them, I'm sure Dom can bail you out. He has that sort of money."

"No. And don't tell him anything. This stays between us. He needs to stay focused on the show."

"But he's going to ask. He worries."

"Tell him you delivered them."

More lies. "Are you going to Troy's funeral?"

"And risk running into one of the Discolis? No way. You?"

"If it's after the show." A heaviness settles over me. "He's really dead, Dean?" I murmur.

"Yeah."

We stay on the phone, both of us silent and thoughtful. And then Dean hangs up, or maybe I do. I don't know anymore. All I know is that one of my friends died, and his death is partly my fault.

I punch the sink top again and again, until my knuckles crack and bleed, until the pain in my hand matches the one in my chest. I run lukewarm water over the gashes and watch the pink stream disappear down the tap. After wrapping a tissue around my battered knuckles, I pick up the quilt and leave the restroom. Since my day hasn't been awful enough, I run straight into Josephine. And I don't mean we pass each other in the hallway and our elbows brush, I mean I collide right into her.

"*Tu es encore là*? I thought you went home," she says.

"I was on my way."

"What is that?" She tips her pointy chin toward the quilt.

"Oh, that's…um…that's one of Ivy Redd's quilts. She just sent it over."

"Why did you bring it into the bathroom?"

"Because my hand was bleeding, and I got some on the fabric."

"Were you in some bar brawl?"

"No. I tripped and fell."

She arches her eyebrow. "Can you show me the quilt now?"

I grab two edges and pull on them. The fabric unfurls and flops to the floor. I take a few steps back, so that Josephine can get the whole picture.

She rubs her thin, pale thumb against her lips as she takes it in. "*Magnifique*," she whispers. "Don't you think?"

"It's something else."

She steps in and runs her fingers over the gold portrait. "I have to wonder why she sent it *after* she was accepted, though," she adds, leaning in closer. Her gaze snags on the seam. "Did you notice the tear?"

"A tear?" My stomach feels as though it's filled with ice cubes.

"Right here." She jabs the edge of the quilt with her index finger.

"Must be intentional."

"Perhaps," she finally says. And then her eyes light up like the blue flashers atop police cars. "I have just had a fabulous idea."

"What is it?" I shift away from her.

"We will include it in the auction test!"

I gulp. "She'll take it badly."

"To be sold by the Masterpiecers?" Josephine snorts, which makes her nose wrinkle. It's the only part of her face that creases since everything else is stretched tight, thanks to plastic surgery or Botox-infused night cream. "It will be *un honneur*." She crouches down and picks up the two corners resting on the floor and brings them back up toward the ones I'm holding. When she pinches the edges and tugs on them, they slip right out of my grasp.

I watch her fold the quilt like one watches a car cut across several lanes on a teeming highway. I need to get it back before the truth comes crashing out.

TEN

JOSH

It's been almost two days since my life spun out of control, yet it feels like minutes since Ivy phoned me…since I rushed over to her apartment and saw the crack in the windshield of Aster's car…since I spotted the blood and black hair stuck to the dark red substance…since I flung their front door open to find them huddled on the couch.

Aster's hair dripped from a shower. Her eyes were bloodshot. Her skin was white, paler than Heidi's. She barely reacted when I stepped in. She was still in shock. Ivy, though, hopped off the couch to hug me.

I never want to relive that night, but like a curse, it plays in a loop in my mind.

"If we get rid of the car, then—"

"Don't ask me to do this. I can't, Ives. I'm a cop."

"You're our friend. Before you were a cop, you were our friend," she said, tearing my heart in two. "Please."

"I can't."

"Then I'll do it." She untangled herself from me and walked toward the door but I captured her wrist.

"No. If you get involved, and the guy truly is dead, then you become an accessory to murder."

"But she's going to go to prison if…if he's dead."

"It was an accident," Aster said mechanically.

"I'm sure it was, Asty, but if he's dead, then he's dead. There will be charges and consequences."

"But he threatened her!" Ivy threw her arms in the air. Maybe for emphasis, or maybe to get away from me. "It was self-defense."

"Where did you hit him?"

Aster clasped her hands tightly in her lap, the tips of her nails ragged and brown, as though she'd tried scrubbing the blood off the windshield with her bare hands. "In the stomach."

"I didn't mean where on his body, I meant in what part of town? On what street? I need to call it in."

"Why?" Ivy asked.

*"*Because, *there's a dead body in the middle of the road, one your sister put there, and if I don't call it in, and someone notices I stopped by your place after the crime—"*

"The accident," Ivy corrected me.

I flinched. "After the accident, then that makes me an accomplice."

"The body's not in the middle of the road," Aster whispered.

"You moved it?"

"No. It's in a parking lot."

I slapped my forehead. "That's still the middle of the road." I took my cell phone out of my pocket. "What parking lot?"

"The motel off route 9."

I shut my eyes, and then opened them super wide. "Tell me it's not Troy Mann."

Aster looked up then. "He stopped by the pizzeria. I recognized him."

"Who's Troy Mann?" Ivy asked.

My phone rang. It was Dennis. After I picked up, he confirmed my worst fear. "Should I call the cops, Joshua?"

"I'll do it."

My hands shook as I spoke to dispatch. My voice too. The patrol car arrived minutes later. As old Mr. Mancini, along with the rest of the neighbors, watched on, a cop from the precinct ripped Aster out of Ivy's arms.

I didn't want to leave Ivy alone, but she forced me to go, so I trailed the cruiser. Shaking, I nearly rammed into its bumper. I drove too fast. Recklessly. Because I was a wreck.

From the car, I called Dennis back to ask what he'd seen. "I was fixing the ice machine in the back when I heard glass break. And then Troy Mann...he was just laying there, in the middle of the road."

"Is he dead?"

"As a doorknob."

"Doorknobs don't live, so they can't die!"

"I, uh...I meant he's dead."

"I got it." It wasn't fair to yell at poor Dennis, but nothing at that moment felt fair.

"They're taping off the crime scene now."

"Okay."

"And, Joshua...that lady friend of his was here again tonight, but I don't think they um...did anything. They only spent five minutes in the room. I checked my watch. Although maybe they had time."

"Did you give the cops access to 2B?"

"Yes. Was that the right thing to do?"

"Yes," I reassured him. "Did they find anything?"

"If they did, they didn't tell me, but I can go ask."

"No, no, don't. I'll call my partner to find out." Before I disconnected, I remembered to say thank you.

"You're welcome, Joshua."

I tossed the phone on the seat next to me and squeezed my steering wheel. The street blurred. I blinked. The road was sharp again. Too sharp. Like the pain inside my skull. Like the sirens outside. Like the red taillights of the cruiser. Like the fear in Aster's eyes when they hauled her away from Ivy.

FORTY HOURS LATER, the pain is still raw. Not only has Aster been placed in custody of the Department of Corrections, but also, Guarda put me on probation when I admitted that Aster saw Mann's file at my place. I'm too honest for my own good. At least, that's what Fred told me when he heard about it all.

My phone pings with a text from Ivy. *Are you coming?*

On my way now, I write back. At the same time I press send, my phone rings.

"Hey, Fred," I say. "Has the chief—"

"This isn't about your reinstatement, although I'm working on it." He's whispering. A door squeaks shut. His voice doesn't get any louder, though. "I just wanted to pass on something I overheard by the water cooler about your girl."

"What?"

"We got something from the tip line. The night of the incident, Aster was seen with a blanket on her lap."

"Okay…why is that important?"

"I'm not sure yet, but it wasn't found in the car. I just wanted to keep you in the loop."

"I appreciate it, Fred."

"Don't beat yourself up over this. I'm sure it's going to be resolved fast."

"I hope. Did they find anything at the motel?"

"Nope."

"Nothing in room 2B?"

"Nothing. How's her sister?" He's chewing something crunchy.

"Not great. I'm on my way to her now."

"Wish her luck for tomorrow. She's still going, right?"

"I think so."

More chomping. "I'll call you if I hear anything else."

I park in front of Ivy's apartment, then let myself in with my key. "Ivy," I holler.

She walks out of her veranda studio, limbs rigid. "We have a problem." The skin underneath her eyes is violet. "*I* have a problem."

"Related to Aster?" I'm praying she's going to say no. At this point, I'd rather discuss genital warts than the crime that went down in the motel.

She picks up the newspaper and shoves it in my arms, and then she wraps her long red wool sweater tighter around her.

"You knew there'd be some buzz around the murder," I say softly.

She unties her arms and jabs her finger at the mug shot of Troy Mann taken a year ago. "He's the guy who bought my quilt."

"Rewind."

Ivy paces the threadbare rug. "Remember when I told you I sold a quilt? He's the guy I sold it to."

"Shit. Why didn't you mention this before?"

"Because that's not the name he used when he introduced himself, Josh! He said he saw me on that *Masterpiecers'* feature and wanted to own something of mine before I became too big. If my quilt is found on him, then I'm as good as convicted too, right? Selling art to mob runners—or whatever he is—it can't be a good thing."

My saliva turns to cement.

"Do the cops have it?" She's standing right in front of me now, arms folded tight.

I shake my head. "No. Nothing was found on him."

"Fuck," she whispers. The word sounds ugly coming out of her mouth.

I wrap my arms around her shoulders and pull her in tight. "This is all my fault. If I hadn't left that file out, Aster wouldn't have gone after him."

"This is nobody's fault."

Her vertebrae jut out under my palms, even through her sweater.

"Should I still go to New York tomorrow?"

I want to say no; I want her to stay. For Aster…and for me. "Yes, dummy. You have to go. You have to kick ass and come back super rich so the three of us can retire somewhere tropical."

She snorts a laugh. "How very Mormon of you, Josh. Suggesting a *ménage à trois*."

I pull away fast. "I didn't mean it like that." My face is hot. "It was a joke."

Ivy smiles. "I know." She places her palm over my cheek. It's cold and soft and familiar. "I'm going to kick ass. I have to. I need to bail Asty out. And then I have to repay the loan I took out on this place." She sighs and lets her hand fall to her sweater.

She grips the hem and rolls it between her fingers like she used to roll the tiny quilt her mom made her eons ago. She took that thing everywhere with her.

"How's she going to survive in there, Josh? She's so fragile."

"I'll go see her. Every day. I promise."

She nods. After a long stretch of silence, she says, "I went to visit her today."

"And?"

"She looks like a ghost. I don't think she *was* taking her medication. I think she flushed it down the toilet. I went to speak to her warden. I asked him to put her back on it. He had a sister who was schizophrenic too. She ended up committing suicide." Her voice is barely above a murmur. "Like Mom." Her beautiful blue eyes blur with emotion. "I'm so afraid that's what Aster's going to do, Josh. So afraid. Especially now that she's in—"

I press her against me and rock her. "Shh…Don't think like that. Aster's not weak. She wants to live."

"Suicide is not weakness. It's despair."

"Let *me* worry about her, you hear? I'll be there for her every step of the way."

"But you have a life, a girlfriend, a job."

"You girls are my life." I don't add that I'm currently out of a job. As for Heidi, she detests Aster so fiercely that I worry it will impact our already brittle relationship.

As I hug my friend, my gaze wanders over the small room. How empty it will feel once she's gone. The red quilt Ivy turned into a bag is propped on the couch, full of clothes.

"What did the quilt look like? The one you sold Troy?"

"It was gold, lots of gold. Two people kissing. I made it for Mom. Right before she…right before she left us."

A thought knocks into me. The blanket Aster had on her lap…could it be the quilt Ivy asked me to locate?

PART 2

DURING

ELEVEN

Brook

Zara Mach's show was a success. And a pleasant distraction from the nightmarish quilt episode.

The second I step off my flight, my phone rings. No caller ID, so I assume it's Dean.

"I thought about it all night," he says. "I want to go search the twins' place. The stones *have* to be there."

"What if they're in her car?"

"It's been impounded, so if they are, we'll never get them back." He pauses. "But she wouldn't have left them in there. Right?"

"Right," I say, even though I have no idea. "Don't go yet. Let's wait until we get the quilt back. You know, to make sure we didn't miss them."

"I can go inside the vault tonight—"

"And set off the alarm?"

"I have Dom's code."

"Every time you input the code, it adds it to a log book. Dominic is supposed to be on the show all week. Visiting the vault is *not* a good idea, you hear me?"

"The D.A. warned me that either I get him the stones by next week or my client goes to jail for an extremely long time."

"Next week is plenty of time, Dean."

"Next week is tomorrow."

As I walk out of the terminal, someone calls my name. It's Dominic's driver, Carl. I nod hello and follow him to the parking lot.

"That PI Jo hired…I heard he lawyered up," Dean says. "I should've offered him my services."

"And become a public figure? Dominic wouldn't have approved."

"That's why I didn't do it. Wait. I got to take this call. It's Mom."

"Send Alaina my love." I hand my carry-on to Carl who sets it in the trunk of the Denali.

When I hear him ask this blonde girl if she wants to put hers in the back too, I slip my phone into the breast pocket of my jacket. My gaze jets over to the sign wedged in Carl's hand.

I read it out loud, "Ivy." Once her name reaches my eardrums, I snap my eyes up to her face. "Carl," I yell. I was just talking about her. What if she heard Dean say her name? "Get the girl another ride. Judges and contestants can't be seen together! Who was in charge of this planning?"

"Miss Raynoir, sir. She told me to pick you up since I was already at the airport."

She's trying to get me in trouble.

"This could've been a disaster. If the paparazzi—"

"You better get in the car, sir." Carl tips his head toward two men with large cameras. "They're here."

I lunge into the Denali. In the rearview mirror, I see Carl push Ivy into the backseat of a black town car that has just pulled up.

How did I not recognize her when I walked out? I watched an entire feature about her. I let out a breath that sounds like a growl. Everything will be okay, I whisper to myself. A picture taken of me with a contestant pales in comparison to the shit Dean is going through.

That's all I can think about as Carl drives me back to my place. I shower and change and then return to the car to be driven uptown to the Met. When I arrive, I try to tell Dominic about the airport fiasco, but he's too preoccupied to listen. I eye Josephine, debating whether to confront her, but I'm not sure that would work in my favor, so I let it slide. Then the first guests walk in, and I slip back into the role of Dominic's assistant *extraordinaire*.

Between greeting people and leading them to the decked-out Temple room, I momentarily forget about Dean and his missing diamonds. Music and champagne and the aroma of the white roses gracing the round dinner tables smooth the ragged edges of my nagging thoughts until I am almost blissful. Almost because I haven't seen Chase yet.

A half hour of schmoozing later, Dominic asks me to take my place on the stage between the two floor-lit Egyptian arches. As I walk up, Lincoln Vega, the pretty blonde chalk artist struts in, her beaded dress glimmering under the strobe lights Jeb has trained on her. Behind her, Herrick Hawk enters, black hair teased and floral scarf knotted neatly around his neck. Nathan Stein walks in next, longish hair framing his face that looks drawn and tired, in spite of the make-up. And then I spot my brother, and my stomach does a backflip because he spots me too, but looks away almost instantly. Maxine Specter, the girl with the buzz cut and the massive Hamptons house walks in next. Jared J., the graffiti artist files in behind her, grinning to the crowd whose applause rise in tempo. And then Dominic's former beauty queen, no-talent-Maria, sashays inside the room, waving hello with a cupped hand.

They snake around the tables and climb onto the stage to take their assigned seats. Ivy Redd's chair remains empty. For the flimsiest second, I hope she changed her mind about competing, that she commanded the driver to do a U-turn on the highway, because having her on the show complicates everything.

But then Dominic's strident announcement rips my wishes to shreds. "Eight! Lucky number eight, you made it!"

I almost snort when he says *lucky*, but that's before I lay my eyes on her. As she carves a path toward us, I am mesmerized. She is stunning in her floor-length, blue silk dress, which makes me wonder if this is the same Ivy Redd I watched on the feature, the same girl I ran into at the airport.

When I feel Josephine's gaze on me, I throw my attention on a random table below. I keep my eyes averted throughout most of the introductions. When Dominic presents my brother, though, I jump to attention. Literally. I smile and sling an arm around Chase's shoulders but he shrugs it off. Selfishly, I want to grab the microphone out of Dominic's hands and tell the crowd that Chase is here thanks to me, but no one can know what I traded to get him on the set of this game show. No one besides Dominic, Dean, and my father. It shouldn't matter anyway. I didn't do it for recognition; I did it because it was his dream, and that's what brothers do.

I lift my chin and keep smiling as Dominic bombards him with questions. When it's over, I return to the gold bench where sitting next to Josephine suddenly feels more comfortable than standing next to Chase.

While Dominic introduces his beauty queen contestant, my gaze wanders off the screen displaying her hideous paintings and onto Ivy, on her sloping nose, her full lips, her startling pale eyes. Her wild hair has been tamed and drapes glossily over her sculpted shoulders. I've met many beautiful women, but Ivy is something else. She turns her head and catches me staring. Like a fifteen-year-old boy, I jerk my gaze away.

When she stands up to be introduced, I listen to her speak, and her voice echoes in my chest. It's calm and smooth, the sort of voice you want to listen to at night, in the silence of your bedroom.

After the presentations, I breathe a little easier, until Dominic informs me it's picture time. A group photograph means I need to spend more excruciating minutes trying to act like the poised judge the contestants must respect and fear. I don't think I could inspire fear in a mosquito.

When Patrick Veingarten claps a big hand against my back while saying, "If it isn't the Masterpiecers' most beloved graduate," I kick the awkward teenage boy out of me.

I smile. "You mean, the one who stuck around?"

Patrick chuckles.

"So what are you thinking?" Dominic asks, gesturing to the eight ornate golden frames.

"You'll see." Patrick's gaze perches on Ivy. He strides toward her and takes her elbow. "Let's start with you." I lower my gaze and try to stay calm when Patrick adds, "I hope my camera will do you justice."

I look up and see the sleazy fashion photographer whisper something else in her ear. When she laughs, I fold my arms in front of my chest.

"Let yourself go. Think languid, just pleased, but still ravenous. I'm sure you know how to do that," he tells her.

Asshole.

"Perfect...a true work of art," he adds a moment later.

Even though I have to agree with him, my blood warms at the way he's staring. As I wait to be directed, I concentrate on cooling down, but it backfires once Patrick puts me in front of Ivy, instructing me to watch her as though I'm appraising her value. Is he toying with me? Trying to make me look like the blubbering fool I've become around this nineteen-year-old girl?

"Brook, I'm sure your shoes are valuable, but eyes on Ivy please," he says.

Fine.

Slowly, my gaze climbs to her face. I take my time absorbing each detail, from her almond-shaped eyes to her bee-stung lips. If I were an artist, I would choose this girl as my muse. But even an artist could never do justice to such a face.

She flicks her gaze to mine. As I grind my eyes deeper into hers, my breathing turns raspier, heavier. Patrick gave me permission to admire her, so that's what I'm doing...admiring her.

TWELVE

JOSH

I rush through the mall toward the food court where I was supposed to meet Heidi almost an hour ago. I pray she's still there. My cell phone ran out of battery after my stopover at the prison, where I spoke with Aster and with the woman who's going to conduct her psychiatric evaluation. The shrink pummeled me with questions about the relationship between the two sisters. She sounded skeptical as to whether they were as close as I "made them out to be." And then she asked me about their mother, and I explained that she drowned back in March, and was never kind to Aster.

"Sorry I'm late," I tell Heidi, as I swoop down in the plastic chair next to hers, and peck her lips.

She places her forearms over a magazine. Her skin is creamy and sprinkled with freckles that darken in the sun. The first time I saw Heidi was at a pool party. She was lying on an inflatable raft shaped like a doughnut, with her legs draped over the plastic frosting decal. She has beautiful legs, but it was her floppy sunhat that drew me in. She seemed so much classier than all the other girls in their teeny bikinis and oversized sunglasses.

"It's okay. I was busy." She tips her chin toward the magazine, which makes her purple-framed glasses slide down. She pushes them back up.

We're trying to make our relationship work, even though she was pretty reluctant to meet me. I try to grab her hand but she pulls it away.

"What's going on in"—I glance down at the cover of the glossy tabloid—

"Angela Discoli's life?" I peel the magazine off the sticky table and stare at it, feeling suddenly lightheaded. "That's Angela Discoli?" I ask out loud even though I know the answer.

"Uh-huh. You know her?"

Does seeing her in bed with a man count as knowing someone? "Can I borrow your phone?"

"Sure."

"I'll be right back," I say, squeezing her sparkly Hello Kitty rubber case between tense fingers. When I'm far enough away from her, I dial Fred's number. "Fred?" I say, but he hasn't picked up yet. I carve my hand through my hair and start pacing. Suddenly a voice says *hello*. "Fred! It's me. Josh."

"Oh. Hey, buddy. What's up?" I hear his wife chattering in the background and a cartoon running.

"Fred, I've just discovered something big."

"What?"

"The night before Troy Mann died, I found him at the motel with someone."

"You didn't mention that."

"Because I thought he was having an affair, but I don't think that's it. The woman I saw him with, guess who she was?"

"Who?"

"Angela Discoli!" I must say it way too loudly because Heidi perks up at the name, even from the distance.

Fred doesn't say anything.

"Fred?"

Still nothing, so I move over a few feet, bumping into a potted plant. The connection must be bad.

"Fred, can you hear me?"

"Yeah, yeah, I heard. I was peeing and thought I'd spare you the sound. Forgot to take my phone off mute. So Troy was screwing Trashy Discoli?" He doesn't mean trashy as in bimbo-y; he means it as trashy. The Discolis are the largest waste collectors in Indiana. That's their official business. Their unofficial business is laundering money.

"Her engagement just made the cover of a magazine, so I don't think that's it."

"Women cheat. It happens."

"My gut tells me there's more. She wasn't even undressed when I came in." I pace the shiny floor. "What if the affair was a cover-up? What if she was giving him stuff to move?"

"*Oh.*" Silence, then Fred says, "I should call the chief."

"Okay. Will you tell him it was my theory?" I hold my breath and cross my fingers until he speaks.

"Yes, Coop. I'll tell him. This could be huge."

I get goose bumps, because if I'm right and Troy was moving stuff for the Discolis, life in prison is the least of Aster's worries.

THIRTEEN

DAY 1

I negotiated with Dominic about using my own clothes for the show. I have a wardrobe full of fitted dress shirts and tailored suits I bought to complement my status in the art world, a wardrobe that will soon go to waste.

I would gift some suits to Chase, but my little brother is a few inches shorter than I am, and broader in the chest and shoulders. Plus, he would never accept a gift from me. It would be like accepting a gift from your wicked stepmother.

When I arrive at the Met, I climb up the three flights of stairs to the contestant quarters. The first person I run into is Ivy. I see her from behind, but I know it's her from the perfect curves on display in her white outfit. The irony that I'm dressed all in black while she wears only white isn't lost on me: the devil and the angel. Sadly, that's not far from the truth.

"Hey, Ivy," I say, catching up to her.

She spins around. She seems hesitant to engage with me, and almost fearful, so I smile, hoping it will ease her tension. She studies my face for a moment, then returns my smile.

"And here I was afraid I wasn't recognizable like this." She points to the thick white make-up smeared over her face.

I chuckle.

"So what are we doing today?" she asks.

"Can't tell you."

Her eyes spark. "Really? Not even a hint?"

"Not even a hint." Time stills as I take her features in one by one.

She tips her chin down, and the faintest blush stains her cheeks under the heavy white grease paint. "I should go eat something."

I swallow hard, then gesture to the enclosure in the fabric wall. "After you."

Ducking, she walks ahead of me and straight toward the buffet.

"Morning, everyone," I say. I'm cheerful until I notice my brother's face is painted white like Ivy's, and he's wearing the same outfit as she is. And I suddenly remember why. I don't feel chirpy any longer, yet I keep up the smile and friendly banter until the make-up artists barge in for last-minute touchups. My cue to go find my spot next to Dominic in the grand hall where the row of vaulted ceiling windows have been obscured.

"They're on their way," I tell him.

Dominic beams at me, and then he grins at the crowd below. "Lights out," he orders.

Whispers and sharp intakes of breath arise from the dark pit of onlookers filling the titanic stone hall. And then the click of shoes on the winding staircase behind me replaces the noise from below. Like everyone else, I watch the eight hopeful contestants descend into the darkness. As Dominic introduces the first test —performance art—Ivy gasps. I want to reassure her that the next eight hours should be easy.

For her.

Not for me.

Watching her in a soundproof box staring only at my brother—her mission for the next eight hours—will be some version of hell. When Dominic describes how intimate it is to make eye contact for so long, my dread increases.

"Can I get a countdown?" he asks as the contestants find their stages.

Neither Ivy nor Chase seem eager about their task. As they take their seats, I step up to the large glass box, along with a couple dozen spectators. A drone camera buzzes over the box, capturing footage from above.

Ivy shifts in her transparent plastic seat. She's uncomfortable. I'm not sure if it's from being watched or the proximity with my brother. I suspect it's Chase's presence. Or perhaps I hope it's Chase. Her gaze travels over the miles of faces surrounding her. When it glides over mine, my heart holds still. I'm expecting her eyes to drift right off, but they don't. She looks at me, and I look at her, and even though there are hundreds of people around us, it feels as though we are alone.

"Three..." The chanting startles me. *"Two..."* Still, she watches me. *"One..."* I fold my arms in front of my chest. *"Showtime!"*

Her eyes settle on Chase.

My brother scowls. He enjoys challenges, and being locked in a box staring at a girl is not challenging. I bet he finds it terribly boring. I observe his face. Every feature is pinched, down to his lips, which are pressed together as tightly as a Ziploc baggie.

"So that's her?" someone breathes in my ear.

I jump. "You came."

"Wouldn't miss the first test," Dean says, staring at Chase, then at Ivy.

Placing my hand on his shoulder, I guide him away from the girl inside. We thread ourselves through the swarming crowd who gobble down buttery pastries and sip coffee from fancy porcelain cups, discussing the fabulousness of Dominic's imagination.

"Did you tell Dom about the…*doughnuts*?" I ask.

Dean snorts, but I can tell he's not amused by the way he fingers the gold tie bar his father bought him when he graduated high school, along with a hundred Hermès ties. He readjusts the perfect silk knot. "They called me," he says as we approach Lincoln's stage. His gray eyes gleam silver in the overhead lights, then flicker as one of the soap bubbles Lincoln blows pops right in front of his face. As she brings her outsized bubble wand back up to her mouth, she grins at me, her Lolita-pink lips stretching wide. "I told them we didn't receive the package yet."

We both stay silent for a minute.

"They're probably still in the quilt, right?" he asks.

"Probably." *Hopefully…*

Madame Babanina, who hadn't spotted me yet, trundles toward me, shoving people out of her way.

"Crap," I mutter.

"You can say that again," Dean says, but he's not talking about the crazy divorcée in the leather pants and see-through blouse who's obsessed with me; he's talking about his missing package.

"Brook, my love, I looked everywhere for you." She pounces on me, kissing both my cheeks, hopefully not leaving lurid pink stains behind. I wipe my skin when she turns toward Dean. "And who's this handsome boy?"

Dean slaps a smile on his face, picks Madame Babanina's hand up, and pulls it to his lips. He grazes her knuckles with his mouth, which fills her face—or what's visible of it underneath her long, thick bangs—with a blush. "Dean Kane, Brook's closest friend from Duke University," he tells her. Although he releases her hand, he doesn't release her gaze. "And I'd like to assure you that I'm very much a man, not a boy."

She throws her head back in laughter.

Dominic notices and makes a beeline straight for us. "Madame Babanina, you made it!"

"Of course I made it. I wouldn't miss the show I'm sponsoring," she says, with an upward twist to her lips.

"Of course not," Dominic says with a tense smile. "Dean, may I have a word with you?"

As the two of them walk away, Madame Babanina laces one hand around my bicep and brings her plump mouth toward my ear. "He's cute, your friend." With any luck she'll find him cuter than me. "He looks like a young Dominic."

"Did you hang your new—"

"He has the same round eyes."

"A lot of people have that eye shape." I drag her toward Herrick, who's buried in dirt up to his neck.

"Are they related?" she asks, trying to catch a last glimpse of them.

"No."

Finally, she stops prying and moves her pink lips closer to my ear. "I heard Dominic and Maria"—she tips her chin toward the beauty queen who's attempting to knit—"I heard they had a thing…is that true? Is that why she's here?"

"Well, I don't think she's here because of her talent."

Madame Babanina cackles again. Many people turn to stare. Thankfully, Ivy doesn't turn. I don't want her to get disqualified.

FOURTEEN

JOSH

I read Heidi's tabloid and find out that Angela Discoli's engagement party is taking place at three o'clock this afternoon at her parents' estate.

So here I am, dressed like one of the wait staff thanks to a bill with Benjamin Franklin's face on it. It's expensive, risky, and uncomfortable, thanks to a jacket two sizes too small, but I want to know her reasons for meeting up with Troy Mann at a motel. Since I think she won't want her fiancé to find out about her rendezvous, I'm planning on blackmailing her into a confession. I used to be a good cop, one who played by the rules, but that was before I lost my badge and found out that my friends had tangled with the mob.

I've seen satellite pictures of the estate on the Internet and photos of it in the magazine, so I know it's huge, but I was not expecting rolling hills, a car path edged with cypress trees, and a house modeled on some French chateau. It's preposterous, but I could totally picture myself living there. I'd add waterslides to the winding outdoor stairways and a moat-style pool around the house.

A woman with a head mic, a pink floral dress, and an armful of white helium balloons steps in front of me. "Where do you think you're going?"

I hope she's talking into her mouthpiece, or to the six other people around her, but I doubt it, since she's glaring at me.

"Wait staff goes through the back of the house," she says. "They don't come up the main hill."

My shoulders tense, stretching the already tight fabric. A tiny ripping noise reaches my ears. I try to relax before the jacket snaps off me like some two-cent Chippendale suit. "I was looking for the way to the back."

She sighs, annoyed. "You were briefed during the rehearsal engagement party."

"I couldn't make that one," I say. "My hamster died." *I couldn't think of another animal, could I?*

She scrutinizes me from top to bottom, then, handing her balloons to her assistant, she flips a few pages on the clipboard wedged underneath her arm. "What's your name?"

"Stuart Mason." I hope the guy I paid gave me his real identity.

She studies her list. When she nods, I can almost hear my muscles loosening. After pointing out the correct path, she grabs her balloons and starts tying them to the tree branches. "One hour till the guests arrive! Hurry up, people," she yells as I scurry away.

I walk back down the hill and find the narrow road bordered by the property's wrap-around wall. Moss and clumps of purple flowers sprout out of small cracks, making the high gray boundary less forbidding. I cross paths with other waiters. Most are jogging, lugging trolleys of food and decoration. I latch on to a trolley to melt into the workforce. After rolling it into the house, I stare around. When I see waiters collecting trays of drinks, I fall in line and grab one myself. Thankfully, I worked a couple weddings back in college, so I can balance a tray.

Fingers spread wide underneath the center, I rest some of the weight on my shoulder and walk up the stairs to the main hall where both families are posing for pictures. I look for the bride, but she's not there. I find a teenage girl playing with her cell phone and ask her where I can find Angela.

Barely looking away from her screen, she points to the huge staircase covered in a yellow carpet with blue flowers. "Second door on your left."

I trot up the stairs, nearly crashing into Angela's mother. Only one glass tips over, but thankfully, it doesn't spill on the mom's pink rhinestone dress that makes her look like an overgrown disco ball.

"Sorry, ma'am, I was told to bring refreshments up to the bride," I say, righting the glass.

She pats her puffy peroxide 'do. "Who told you to bring some up?"

"The planner, ma'am."

She inspects me through narrowed eyes ringed in black makeup. It's not flattering. "Well, don't spill any on her."

"Yes, ma'am."

As she starts down the stairs, I walk to the door the girl indicated. I would've barged inside if I wasn't a hundred percent sure Angela would call one of her bodyguards and have me shot on the spot. I want an explanation, not an early death.

A woman is working on the bride's light blonde hair, something I had stupidly not anticipated. Since asking her to leave would alert the household, I walk over to Angela and slide my tray too close to her stylist's arm. Sure enough, the woman's wrist collides with one of the glasses. I pretend-catch it, but make sure she still gets a hefty dose of orange juice on her.

"What the hell? Are you an idiot?" Mumbling angrily, she walks toward the adjoining bathroom to wash her hands.

Angela looks away from the flat-screen TV on the wall in front of her. "I know you." Her dark eyebrows slant toward her perfect nose.

"I just met your fiancé. Nice guy. Nicer than Troy."

Her eyes spring wide open. She remembers me. "What do you want?" She toys with the diamond necklace around her neck. The stones are so huge they seem fake, but she's a Discoli, so they probably aren't.

"Why were you meeting with Troy?" I don't add *in the motel*, because her stylist is walking back over. I'm allowing Angela to retain a bit of dignity. If she doesn't cooperate though, no more Mister Nice Guy.

"Angela, you want me to call security?" the stylist asks, backing up toward the bedroom door. She bumps into the bed and falls on the red satin cover.

"She calls security and I signal the team I have waiting just outside the property wall."

Angela snorts. "Do you even have a warrant?" Her voice isn't loud, but it's sharp.

"I do. I can go get it if you want, but that would mean going downstairs and alerting your family—"

"Wait outside," Angela tells her stylist.

"No way." I nod toward the far wall. "Wait in the bathroom and close the door."

She scampers back into the adjacent pink marble room, shuts the door, and spins the lock.

I'm still balancing the tray, so I set it down on the desk next to a bunch of eye powders and sparkly goo.

"Troy and I were in love." Her voice is as strained as my squashed shoulder blades.

"Seriously?"

A tear rolls out of her eye and curves down her pink cheek. She takes a tissue and blots it. No other tear slips out. When Aster cries, she has tons of tears. A single tear seems calculated.

"I met him when he worked for Dad."

I'm letting her think I believe her pathetic lie. "What did he do for your father?"

"He got us contracts with private companies."

"Is that what laundering money is called nowadays? Getting contracts?"

Angela's now perfectly dry eyes narrow. "You have some nerve, Officer. I'm cooperating, and you accuse me and a dead man of corrupt dealings."

"Why did you meet him at a shitty motel? You obviously have money."

"Because I didn't want anyone to find out about the affair. If I went to a nice place, I'd be on the front page of some trashy tabloid right now."

I don't remind her that she's already on the front page of a tabloid. "If he hadn't died, were you going to call off your engagement?"

"It's arranged, so no. I don't have a choice."

I startle. *An arranged marriage?* I didn't even know modern Americans organized those anymore.

"Are we done?" she asks.

"Troy Mann bought a quilt from an artist called Ivy Redd. Do you know anything about it?"

Her pupils pulse as though two tiny grenades exploded inside.

"You do know about it…"

Her features contract into that sophisticated, impenetrable mask again. "You mean"—she raises a pointed finger to something behind me—"one of *her* creations?"

I turn around to find Ivy on TV looking pale and electrocuted. On the bottom of the screen, I read the words, *5th hour of Performance Art Test*. "Yes."

"He was going to buy me one as a wedding gift, but I didn't think he got around to it."

I study her face, but can't tell if she's bluffing.

"Why did that psycho sister of hers run him over?"

I squash my impulse of defending Aster by muttering, "He threatened her."

"What was she doing in the parking lot of the motel?"

"She was—I'm the one who's asking the questions. Not you."

The door of the room flies open. Two large men with earpieces march in. I check the bathroom door, but it's still closed.

"This is my grandma's room. She has an emergency buzzer near her bathtub," Angela says, smiling brazenly at me. "Ray, any police activity outside the property walls?"

Keeping his eyes glued to me, he dials a number, raises his cell phone to his ear, then shakes his head.

Angela's grin broadens. "Look who's lying now," she says sweetly. "Take him away."

The two piles of muscles stalk over to me and grab me under my armpits. The waiter uniform that feels like a straitjacket finally rips, which is a relief, but it's short-lived. As they haul me toward the door, I wonder if they're going to dump me in some landfill next to a bunch of other corpses.

"Ray, I'm feeling generous today," Angela says, stroking her necklace. "I might not be in such a generous mood next time, Officer, so make sure there is no next time."

I have zero desire to see her again, yet somehow, I sense I will.

FIFTEEN

DAY 2

Brook

While I meander through the maze of galleries, the camera crew rushes past me, almost knocking me over. Maxine Specter, aka Daisy after the alcoholic shots that gave her the courage to enter the art competition, solved her riddle with impressive celerity. It was almost as though she knew exactly which piece she was searching for. Growing up with an art background probably helped. It hasn't helped my brother; at least, not yet.

As I penetrate one of the galleries, I freeze. Ivy is sitting on a bench, alone, eyes closed. I watch her. Her lips move and her head bobs.

I walk over to her and sit. "Think synonyms," I whisper, because I sense she needs help.

Her eyes fly open. "Trying to get me eliminated?"

"No. Synonyms are the foundation of a riddle. It's a fact, not a clue."

She studies me. I suppose she's debating whether to trust me. "Who solved theirs?"

"Believe it or not…Daisy."

"Daisy?"

"I mean Maxine."

"No, I know who Daisy is. I'm just surprised—I thought it would be your brother."

"He's still searching."

"He'll get it soon enough."

"He *is* pretty obstinate."

"I can tell," she says.

"This is his chance to get what he wants."

One side of her mouth lifts. "If he wins, will he be allowed to attend the Masterpiecers, or does he just get the hundred grand?"

"He'll be allowed to attend."

"Won't that destroy the school's policy?"

"It will complicate it," I say as Ivy stares at the Jackson Pollock in front of us. "Is your sister also artistic?"

"No. Not in the least."

"You don't talk about her." I keep my gaze on the painting.

"I came to compete in an art show, not to discuss my family."

"Fair enough."

"Now can you please leave so I can concentrate?"

My insides harden from her dismissal. "I'll be quiet." It's lame, but I want to stay next to her a moment longer.

Suddenly, she jolts to her feet and runs a shaky hand through her long, blonde hair. I peer behind her. My brother is standing in the doorway.

"How are you holding up?" I ask, rising and walking over to him.

"I thought the contestants weren't supposed to speak with judges or people from the audience." The vein on Chase's temple throbs.

"I can ask how you're doing."

"Is that what you were asking Ivy? How she was *doing*?"

I grind my teeth. "Yes. I wasn't giving her any clues, if that's what you're worried about."

We eye each other for a long moment. There are so many things I'd like to tell him but can't, because of rules and because of pride. Mine and his.

Loud applause cuts through the quiet gallery.

"Another winner. You two better hurry up," I tell them, brushing past Chase.

I don't turn around, although I think I hear Ivy leave. Lincoln is being interviewed when I reach the gallery. She found her riddle. J.J. runs in to announce he's uncovered his too. As I stand next to him in front of the Persian rug he needed to find, Ivy waltzes in.

"Ivy? Did you solve yours?" Dominic asks.

She starts from the sudden attention, but then she smiles. It doesn't reach her eyes.

"Almost." The smile falters once the audience turns away.

She glances at me, and adrenaline spikes through my veins. She needs help, but I can't give her any. I'm useless. I trail her with my eyes as she leaves.

My brother solves his riddle next.

Come on, Ivy.

When the camera crew angles their cameras toward one of the entrances, I hold my breath. It has to be her.

It's not.

It's Nathan.

But then she appears next to him, cheeks bright. "I got it!" she yells, but it's too late.

It's fucking too late!

I despise Nathan in that moment. Until he gives his answer and it's the wrong one. Then I could just kiss him.

"I'm sorry." Dominic pats him on the back, then turns toward Ivy whom he gestures forward. "What do *you* have for us, sweetheart?"

She walks over to us, shoulders held stiffly back. She comes to stand between Dominic and me, and I swear I can sense her heart thundering inside her chest. Our hands are inches apart. If I shift mine, I'd touch hers, but I stay immobile and hold my breath.

"*White Flag* by Jasper Johns," she says, her voice steady.

Yes. Yes!

But then Dominic hisses, and asks her if it's her final answer, and I think she got it wrong. But she couldn't have gotten it wrong for Jasper Johns's *White Flag* was one of the riddle answers, and it wasn't given yet. Could it have been Nathan's riddle? Was she supposed to find the—

Clapping erupts.

Dominic was toying with her.

I take Ivy's hand and pump it into the air victoriously. She turns to smile at me, and her eyes glisten.

"Good job, Redd," I whisper.

"Thank you."

I hold her gaze a while longer, and I clutch her hand until it becomes inappropriate for me to keep it nestled in mine.

THAT EVENING, after the dinner festivities, Dom asks me to accompany him to the post-production area to review the footage of the contestants' private dinner. They're aware cameras are recording them, but they don't know those cameras pick up sound.

"What are you doing, Brook?" Dominic asks in a quiet voice.

"What do you mean?"

"With Ivy. What are you doing with Ivy?"

"I'm being nice."

"This isn't you being nice; this is you flirting with a contestant. It's unprofessional, and it's not acceptable."

I bristle and turn defensive. "It's because I feel guilty, all right?"

Dominic sighs and plays the segment Jeb has kept for him to watch before running it on live TV.

Ivy's leaning back into her chair, arms folded tightly. She's glaring at someone. When I discover that someone is my brother, I smile smugly.

"I didn't rig the competition. I was chosen," she says. *"Based on my application. On my skill. But perhaps you did, Chase. After all, your brother's a judge.*

How difficult could it have been for him to get Josephine and Dominic to endorse your application?"

"You don't know the first thing about me and my brother," he says.

"I know he got into the school, and you didn't."

"Because he was older. He applied first."

She leans forward. *"Is that the reason, or is he just better than you?"*

"Is that what Brook was telling you during the riddle hunt? That he's better than me?"

Dominic glances at me, but doesn't speak. He doesn't have to. I know what he's thinking. "I didn't help her, Dom."

"You swear?"

"Yes."

"Cheating, Redd?" Lincoln asks, dragging my attention back to the flickering screen.

"Of course not!" she says.

"Then why were you talking with my brother?" Chase asks.

"We were talking about you, *"* she says.

"We were," I tell Dominic.

"Brook was telling me how badly you wanted to get into his school. Basically, he pleaded with me to let you win," she says. *"How's that for fraternal love?"*

I frown. "No. We spoke about school policy."

"Wouldn't be surprised if he came to all of you at some point to ask you to go easy on Chase," she adds.

Chase is going to detest me now.

Dominic places his hand on my forearm. "Will you still feel guilty when she destroys your relationship with Chase?"

"It's already ruined."

"This show can salvage it, but only if you stay away from her. He's the one you're cheering for, not some girl from the Midwest."

A hush falls over the contestants' table and over the small, dark room.

"If you forget again, I'll remind you," Dominic says.

I nod stiffly.

"We're getting the piece back tomorrow," he tells me, and it takes me a second to realize he's talking about Ivy's quilt.

"During the auction?"

He nods.

"Dean shouldn't—"

"It won't be him. I don't want Jo sniffing around him."

"I wonder what they'll have us do tomorrow," Lincoln says.

Dominic stares at her. "They proved the white supremacist rally pictures were fakes."

My eyes grow wide. "How?"

"Apparently Kevin was deployed at the time the pictures were taken. Did you know that digital pictures have a date stamp in the metadata?"

"It was Dean's idea."

"If you delegate a job to someone, and the job is poorly executed, don't blame the emissary." His voice is low, but far from soft.

Of course. Dean can do no harm. But according to his logic, Dominic shouldn't be blaming me. After all, he's the one who told me to get Kevin Martin eliminated after I confirmed that he wasn't just a retired sergeant.

"What do you want me to do about it?" I ask.

"Nothing. I'm taking care of it this time," Dom says, as Jeb penetrates the post-prod area.

"Should we air the segment, Mr. Bacci?"

"No." Dominic pats my arm on his way out. "I got to the bottom of the story, and it's not at all what it sounds like."

I tense up.

"But the audience would love it. Our ratings would go through the roof."

"No," Dominic says, blunting Jeb's enthusiasm. "It's too personal."

Sometimes, I can't tell if Dominic is my protector or my executioner, since he's capable of both.

SIXTEEN

DAY 3

JOSH

On one of the gym's wall-mounted TVs, Ivy has just walked onto the podium to present the first piece she has to sell. The quilt she described to me, the one with the gold fabric representing two people embracing. The water I'm drinking spurts out of my nose. I sponge it off with the towel hung around my neck. Fortunately, there aren't many people around the gym at this time of day. Most people are at work, which is where I would rather be, but lifting weights takes my mind off my dire situation.

"Shit," I say, wiping my forehead with the damp towel. How did Troy Mann's quilt end up in New York, on the set of *The Masterpiecers*?

I rush to the locker room to shower and change. I don't bother drying my hair since it's pouring outside. Taking cover under my gym bag, I jog to my car and drive toward the prison. I don't think to call ahead to get a meeting. I don't think about anything besides the quilt. By the time I reach the gates, I'm convinced Aster sent it there.

At the front desk, I ask to see her.

"What's your relationship to the prisoner?"

"I'm the investigating officer," I say, squeezing my car key into my palm. "I came to visit Miss Redd on August 20th. You probably have it in your records," I add, pushing myself on my tiptoes to see past the glass wall surrounding the desk.

The woman is slow to check, but the inspection pays off. She nods and radios in one of her colleagues to lead me into the visitation area. Dread pulses through me as I enter the bleak room with the barred windows overlooking the barbed wire fence and the purple-gray sky. Raindrops splatter against the glass, making the atmosphere sort of relaxing, although relaxing is a big word to use for this place.

The door buzzes and Aster barrels through, cheeks flushed. "I need you to check my sister's bank account," she says, dropping into the chair opposite me.

"Hello to you too, Aster."

The bones in her face press against her skin. "I think Ivy was paying Mom's bills."

"Swell. Means you don't have to pay them."

"That's not swell! She lied to me, Josh."

"How?"

"She never told me about the money."

"Why are you so worked up about it?"

"Because—"

I cut her off because right now, her mom's institution bills and the apartment deed are at the very bottom of my worry list. "How did Ivy's quilt end up on the show?"

Aster's pin-sized pupils throb against their sky-colored background. "Ivy's quilt? I have no idea."

"Want to know what I think? I believe you found it next to Troy's body and sent it there. I believe it's the one you used as a *blanket*."

She turns pale, like the time she ate bad chicken and threw up in my car.

"You're not denying this?"

She studies her lap or her socks. "No. It was a blanket."

"Aster, you're lying. Did you follow him from your house? Is that it?"

"I…he…"

"Asty, please tell me the truth," I ask in a soft voice. I can tell she's worked up and on edge.

"Okay, fine. I saw him at our house. I saw him go inside, and then I followed him back to the motel."

"Thank you for trusting me."

She looks up. "You mean, for always lying?"

My forehead furrows. "What? No. I never said that."

"The baby was real."

"I know."

"I never lied about the baby."

"I know."

"My doctor told you what I asked her to tell you. I was trying to protect you."

I play along. "I know you were, Asty."

"I didn't make it up. I felt it move. I saw it move. I was throwing up every morning."

"Are you taking your meds?" I ask her.

"No, it wasn't."

I'm not getting through to her. I squeeze her arm. She flings my hand off. "What wasn't?"

She's trembling. "It was real."

"Let's not talk about the baby anymore. It always makes you sad."

She stands up. "I need to go." Tears cling to her lashes, then tumble down her caved-in cheeks.

"Don't be sad."

"Be like what?"

I sigh. She's hearing another conversation in her head. "Just stay."

"And be interrogated and mocked? No, thank you. I'd rather go hang out with people who don't think I'm crazy."

"I never said you were crazy."

"You didn't have to say it." She stares at me with wild eyes. "Don't bother coming back here anymore."

"I'm going to come back. I'm in charge of the case."

She blinks, and more tears slide out. This time, I capture her hand. As I look at her face, her features soften. She's back.

"Before you go, can you tell the warden to inform the guards that I *am* allowed to watch the show whenever I want?"

"The warden would never listen to me."

"He did the first time around."

Maybe she's not back. "What are you talking about? What first time?"

"Ivy told me you got me that privilege."

"The warden? I've never even met the man."

"If *you* didn't talk to him, then who did?"

"Ivy went to see him. She probably—"

"I'm not crazy," she shrieks.

My heart jumps. I long to hug her to me until my Aster comes back, but this Aster...she'll fight me. Causing a scene will attract unwanted attention. What if I'm asked for my badge? What if they never allow me to return? I can't take the risk.

"Got it?" she asks, before returning into the entrails of the prison.

I stay sitting for a long time, staring at the space she occupied. Finally, hunching over, I cradle my forehead in my hands. Her condition is worsening. After her mother's death, her shrink told me trauma could aggravate the schizophrenia. I didn't want to believe it at the time. I wanted to believe she would overcome it and turn back into the girl with pigtails I plucked from the sea of multicolored plastic balls, the girl I spent my weekends chasing through the vast sunflower field bordering my grandparents' home, the girl whose laughter bubbled out of her mouth and spilled into her eyes.

I pray she's still somewhere in there.

Sighing, I realize I didn't get a straight answer from her. I still don't know if she sent the quilt or if it was Troy. Deep down, I think she shipped it, but when? She hit him around 10 p.m., and I got to their house an hour later. No post office would be open at that time. Unless she already had a stamped package, but why would she?

I slap the table because nothing makes sense. I feel like it should.

SEVENTEEN

Brook

I watch the slow drizzle of coffee, and slender threads of steam drift out of the espresso machine. The smell is intoxicating. If I close my eyes, I'm back in Durham, drinking iced Americanos and shoveling omelets with hash browns after a night of too much everything. Troy and Dean are there, sitting in front of me in the Union, planning out the next campus-shattering party.

The machine clicks. I'm no longer in North Carolina, no longer planning parties, no longer with Troy and Dean. I'm in New York, in my parent's apartment where I grew up, about to watch the press conference during which Ivy must deny her involvement with Kevin's doctored pictures.

And Troy is dead.

"Brook, honey, let me take care of the coffees," Carmelina, my parents' live-in housekeeper, says, bustling into the kitchen.

"I've got it."

She stares at me through bifocals that make her eyes look like vast, grassy plains. "You work too much. You need to rest."

If I rest, her salary won't get paid. Knowing Carmelina, who's been with us for over two decades, she'd probably insist on staying, but one of her kids just lost his job. She can't afford to work for free.

"Are you staying for dinner tonight? I'm making your favorite tamales."

"I have to get back to the museum, but as soon as the show's done, I want tamales."

She strokes my cheek like she did when I was small, when she helped me fall back asleep after bad dreams.

"Your mother told me about Troy. It made me so sad." Her thick lenses magnify her tears.

I swallow.

"The young should not die young." She lowers her hand. "Now, go sit. I'll bring your coffee." She all but shoves me out of her kitchen.

Snatching a tissue from the shiny metal box by the home phone, I return to Dad. He glances at me, and his face, already contorted with stress, warps even more.

"Pollen allergies," I lie. I'm not sure why I do. Perhaps I don't want to burden him with *my* grief.

We listen to the reporter who's summarizing the Kevin fiasco before Ivy's arrival.

"Did she alter those photos?" Dad asks me.

"No."

"You know who did?"

"No."

His eyes linger on my face, but he doesn't ask again. "How's Chase?"

"He's doing well. He floored Dominic at the auction."

"I saw," Dad says, smiling, but the smile doesn't smooth out his worry lines. "Every day, I fear an *artistic* test. He'd be eliminated for sure. He has as much talent as I do."

"There'll only be one, and it should be pretty easy." With Dominic, we designed this year's tests according to Chase's strengths.

"Thank you," Dad says.

"For what?" I stare at the crosshatched silver pattern on the pastel rug instead of at Dad.

"You know for what," he says. "I had a box of cigars sent to Dominic. Did he get them?"

"I'll ask."

Suddenly, the reporter whirls around, along with the crowd assembled on the Metropolitan Museum steps. I lean forward in my seat. Ivy steps out of the museum, flanked by Dominic, Josephine, and two lawyers. Her blonde hair seems lighter in natural sunlight.

Carmelina walks in front of the TV, sets down the platter, then moves to the side to watch the news with us. "I don't like her," she says after a bit.

"You don't know her, Carmelina."

"Her sister killed Troy."

"*Her sister*. Not her."

Both Carmelina and Dad eye me.

"She looks sad," he says, perhaps to deflect the strain in the room.

"She lost her mom recently, and her twin's clinically insane."

"Poor girl," Dad says.

Carmelina folds her arms in front of her. "You should be even more careful, then."

"She's just a contestant, Carmelina."

"Is she?" she asks.

Dad is busy tweaking the volume with the remote control, so I don't think he picks up on Carmelina's insinuation.

"I watch the show, Brook," she adds in a hushed voice. "I see."

My palms turn clammy. I grab my cup of milky coffee and it almost slips out of my hands.

Ivy's rehearsed speech echoes in my mind. Her voice gives me shivers. I'm afraid that Carmelina, who keeps swaying her gaze between Ivy and me, will spot the goose bumps on my forearms.

"Isn't Aster a Photoshop whiz?" a reporter asks Ivy.

Ivy wipes her forehead. Her hand doesn't shake, but she doesn't answer him for so long I can tell she's shocked. Her silence grows, becomes deafening. It's Dominic, of all people, who jumps to her rescue, defending Aster Redd. As he stares into the camera, I flinch.

Maybe he'll blame me. What's stopping him, after all? And technically, it would be true. But he simply apologizes to Kevin Martin for the injustice that was caused to him and publicly invites him to compete on the show.

My tepid coffee goes down the wrong pipe. I cough, then try to wipe the brownish spray from my white shirt with the used tissue I tucked into my jeans.

Carmelina leaves, returning a moment later with a clean shirt. "Here. Give me your shirt. You shouldn't let coffee stains set in."

I unbutton it and hand it over.

"You weren't aware he was going to be invited to compete?" Dad asks once she's gone.

I shake my head, too stunned to speak. Dominic has just invited a private investigator on the show. He'll get caught. *We'll* get caught. My boss puts his arm around Ivy's rigid shoulders and steers her back into the museum.

"The bank is going to repossess the apartment."

"What?" I snap out of my dazed state. "But they already pocketed the Hamptons sale." I stare at the empty walls on which used to hang masterpieces. "I thought we didn't owe them that much anymore."

Dad places his elbows on his knees and cradles his forehead.

"How much do we still owe, Dad?"

"Seven million."

"Seven?" I gasp. "I thought it was just one. When did one become seven? *How* did one become seven?"

He lifts his head up to look at me. "Back taxes. I...forgot...to declare a few sales."

"Forgot?" I yell.

His Adam's apple jostles up and down in his scruffy throat. "The apartment is worth seven million dollars. So that should settle it." Dad runs a hand over his nascent beard. In the past, he was always impeccably dressed and groomed. Now he wears high-waisted jeans and forgoes shaving. "What am I supposed to tell your mother?"

"How about the truth?"

His brown eyes are red and swollen with dread. "She'll leave me."

"She won't leave you."

"She will. She's already threatened to leave. She says I've changed."

"Stop letting yourself go, then. Woo her back."

"With what? I have no more money. I've bankrupted our business. I've left you and Chase with nothing. What sort of father am I? What sort of man am I?"

I touch my Dad's hand. "What about selling Mom's jewelry? Her engagement ring—"

"I will *not* sell your mother's things." He shakes his head, and his still-dark hair flutters around his ears. "She's already lost one house, soon two."

"So what are you planning to do? You can't borrow money to keep up appearances. And I don't have enough to lend you, not even if I sold my Zara Mach piece."

He digs his knuckles into the inner corners of his eyes. "My life insurance policy. There should be enough in there to keep her—"

"Shut up, Dad."

He jerks. How could he not? I've never spoken disrespectfully to him. Then again, he's never suggested suicide to finance our family's lifestyle.

I stand up. "I have to get back to work. I'll find a way. In the meantime, talk to Mom. You can both move in with me until we can figure something else out, okay?"

I dash past Carmelina who stands in the doorway of the kitchen, rigid with terror.

When I get home, I dive into the pool of the apartment Dominic lends me as part of the package of working for him. Lap after lap, I think of ways to right my father's wrongs.

Ideas, all terrible ones, coil through my brain like a cloying song on repeat. The only way for me to help my parents is to continue laundering money through art for Dominic and Dean. The ties I'd felt loosening snap back into place. When I reach the point of physical and mental exhaustion, I climb out of the pool and grab a towel.

My cell phone rings. No caller ID.

"I shredded the whole fucking thing. They're not in there!" Dean yells, and I realize he means the quilt he bought at the auction, and it makes my stomach sour that he destroyed it. "She fucking stole them. The crazy bitch stole them! Or her fucking sister. Have you searched her yet?"

"Not yet."

"What are you waiting for?" he hollers.

I pull the phone away from my ear. "I was waiting for you to look through the quilt," I say calmly, "but I really doubt—"

"I heard about your little crush."

I freeze, and the towel slips out of my hands. "I don't have a *crush*."

"Whatever, Brook. I personally don't give a fuck if you do. All I care about is getting my diamonds back. If I don't get them to the D.A., he's going to convict my client. So go through her room and fucking help me, man. Fucking help me before they off me."

"Don't talk like that."

"I'm not exaggerating, Brook."

"I know I mentioned this already, but, now that he knows, ask Dom to cover what they're worth until we can find them."

"He doesn't have that sort of cash on hand. And taking a sum like that out of the bank…it'll raise eyebrows. He's already being monitored. He doesn't need to arouse more suspicion."

I step inside the penthouse and slide the door closed.

"Tomorrow, there's a pool party at your place," Dean says.

"There is?"

"Yeah. So everyone can blow off some steam. Anyway, when the contestants show up, go back to the museum and comb through her room. And if you don't find anything there, you get your ass home and frisk her. I want those fucking stones."

When he hangs up, I realize his problems are bigger than mine. Dominic phones me soon after to inform me I'm going to be hosting a pool party the next day.

"I heard," I say.

Dominic doesn't say anything for a long time, but he's still on the phone. I can hear him breathe. "We're taking the contestants out to the restaurant tonight. Dress casually."

"Okay."

"I'll see you later."

WHEN I ARRIVE at the museum dressed in black jeans and a blue shirt, Dominic and Josephine are informing the contestants about Kevin Martin's imminent arrival at the same time as J.J. is wishing everyone goodbye. He scored the lowest on the auction test. When he hugs Ivy, she tenses up in his arms. I wonder if she would tense up in mine.

I'm standing next to her when he walks off. She watches him for a long time.

"You need to get ready," I tell her.

"I'm going."

"Always hard to see someone lose," I say, because she's still surveying the doorway.

Her gaze shifts to me. "Actually, I was thinking the opposite."

When she walks away to get dressed, I find myself frowning at her frostiness. But then I remind myself of what winning this competition would mean for her.

"Brook, who is this Elise Frothington?" Josephine asks, sidling in next to me.

"Huh?"

"The woman who bought Ivy's quilt. I feel like I have seen her before, but cannot put my finger on where." She studies my face with her hawk-like eyes. "Who is she?"

"Probably a collector," I say, to lead her astray. "Or a sponsor."

"This is the first event she attends."

"Maybe the others bored her."

"*Peut-être*."

Lincoln plants herself right next Josephine. "The clothes on this show are so gorge." She palms her purple suede skirt. "I want your life, Miss Raynoir."

"I am certain you do," Josephine says, as the rest of the contestants arrive.

There is no seating arrangement at the Italian restaurant, yet I find myself next to Ivy. Dinner starts out nicely, especially when she snaps at my brother a few times. I shouldn't enjoy it, but I do. However, she suddenly asks me about the tear in her quilt, and the anxiety I thought I'd gotten rid of in the pool is back with a vengeance. Even Dominic grows fretful. His unease increases when Josephine asks if he's found out the source of the slanderous e-mail.

"It was sent to Brook." Perspiration beads on his forehead.

"It was encrypted," I say, when her attention lands on me.

"Can you forward it to me, Brook?"

"Sure. Remind me tomorrow," I say. The hacker Dean used was smart enough to encrypt it since we guessed the police—or Josephine—would eventually subpoena the e-mail. If only the Photoshop guy had been as smart.

"I do hope we find who sent it." She folds her napkin neatly next to her plate and rises. "*Bonne nuit*," she tells everyone, and then leaves just as Ivy returns from the bathroom.

Even though Dominic put the blame on me, he's acting more nervous than I am. Then again, I'm drowning my anxiety in wine. I've clearly had too much when I dare ask Ivy if she has a boyfriend. When she says no, I think it's a good idea to slip my palm over her lap. Not only does she cross her legs to shift my hand off, but Chase, who's seated on her other side, observes the whole thing. I glare at my empty glass of wine, wishing I could blame it for my lack of judgment, but alcohol only enhanced my stupidity.

EIGHTEEN

JOSH

I watch Ivy's press conference from my parents' couch. Mom kneads my hand throughout. I'm too nervous to tell her to stop. The implications reporters raise unsettle me so much that I don't eat a bite of the roast she's prepared.

When Heidi meets me at my place later that night, she's in a good mood, but I'm not, and my bad mood ends up spoiling our evening. She knows it's because of the twins, even though she doesn't ask. I bet she's afraid that if she mentions either of them, all we'll talk about are *them* for the rest of the night. Which is probably true. But avoiding uttering their names doesn't make my concern for them fade. If anything, it makes me retreat deeper into my mind. Heidi is pissed and settles in front of the TV to watch this alien sci-fi show I can't stand. I mean, come on, *all* the characters on the show are whiny and purple.

I go to bed before her but don't sleep while she all but snores next to me. All night, I stare at the red digits on my alarm clock. I try counting my breaths, holding my breaths, pushing air out of my lungs, keeping it in. Nothing knocks me out. At five-thirty, I roll out of bed and go to the gym. I lift weights until my shoulders cramp and my muscles tremble, and then I buy a protein shake from the tiny concession stand on my way out.

Heidi is blow-drying her hair when I get home, whirling a thick brush through her dark blonde locks that look shot with copper and gold.

"Where were you?" she asks, setting her tools down.

"I hit the gym. Do you have time for breakfast?"

"I need to be in class in a few minutes." As she sits on the bed to tie her sneakers, she's quiet.

"I'm sorry about last night. I—"

"It's not just last night, Josh. It's all the time. Since Aster—"

I close my eyes. *Don't go there, Heidi.*

"Since Troy died," she says, "it hasn't been the same."

"I know but I care so much about you. Before all this blew up, we were good, weren't we?"

"We were."

I kneel in front of her and take both her hands in mine. She stares at me through her purple glasses. "Give us another chance. Please."

She sighs.

"I'll do better. Give me a chance to do better."

Her brown eyes become shiny. "Okay."

I shoot up so quickly that we rock backward onto the bed. Her shiny hair fans out around her head, making it look as though she were lying in a pool of melted metal.

I cup her freckled cheek. "You're so beautiful."

She giggles, so I pay her more compliments. It's the least I can do after being so distant with her. Even though she complains that she's going to be late for class, I make love to her, and it's amazing and liberating, and when she suckles my neck just as I'm finishing, I groan with pleasure.

"We should do this more often," I tell her, lying on my back with my arms cradling my head.

She slips her pink thong and jeans back on.

"Like right now. I'm ready," I say.

"I need to get to school." She climbs on top of me for one last kiss. "Dinner tonight?"

"As long as we have a do-over," I say with a wink.

"It's a date, mister."

She grabs her bag from the chair and slings it across her shoulder. "Pick me up at six? I'll be at the dorm."

"You got it."

I don't move for a long time after Heidi leaves. I feel too good to move. I haven't felt this good in days. At some point, I pass out and nap until a strident car horn startles me awake. I peel myself off the bed and take a much-needed shower. Although visiting Aster in prison is the last thing I want to do right now, it's also one of the only things I have to do. So I get dressed and head out, blasting music to make the drive out of town feel less ominous.

Instead of leading me to the visitation area, they upgrade my visit with Aster to the room they keep for attorney meetings. I take a seat on one of the iron chairs and look at the glass wall. A prison guard with a belly hanging over his belt and a mean scar through one of his eyebrows brings Aster to me. When she spots me inside, her blue eyes grow wide with alarm. Her mouth moves with words I can't hear. The guard shoves the door open, then shoves her in.

"You got fifteen minutes, Officer Cooper, then I need to take her to her shrink appointment."

Aster resembles a broomstick with her bristly hair and emaciated body. She jumps when the door shuts behind her. "Wh-what's going on? Is it Ivy?"

"Sit down."

With shaky hands, she pulls out the seat in front of me and sits.

"Aster, did you doctor the photos of Kevin Martin?"

"Who?"

"The contestant who was eliminated. Did you do it?"

"No. Why?"

"Because the media is claiming you might be behind the fake pictures."

"They're fake?"

"Are you playing dumb?"

"No!"

"Wasn't Photoshopping part of your job at the ad agency?"

"Yes, but I didn't do it."

"You promise?"

"Yes! Anything else you came to accuse me of?"

I rub the side of my neck. "How did the quilt end up—"

"Is that a hickey?" she exclaims. Her hands have stopped trembling.

"What?"

"On your neck."

"Oh, that…I cut myself shaving." Heat fills my face.

"Are you seeing someone?"

I breathe slowly, hoping to delay the inevitable. "Do you really want to know?"

Her lower lip wobbles. She bites down hard on it, then releases it and murmurs in a tiny voice, "Since when?"

"Let's not talk about this—"

"Since when?"

"A month." The lie pops out of my mouth. It's been two, but one might hurt less.

"Is it serious?"

"Aster," I whisper softly.

"Well, is it?" She's no longer whispering.

"I don't know."

"Do I know her?"

I rub the spot on my neck Aster is still gawking at.

"Who is it?" she asks.

Honesty is the best policy, right? But what if she goes after Heidi when she gets out of here? I'm an asshole. Aster isn't a murderer. I mean…in normal circumstances. How can I even be entertaining such thoughts? I'm a despicable friend. "Heidi," I blurt out.

"The floozy from Dairy Queen?"

"Don't call her that."

"You're the one who told me she slept around. She's going to give you HIV."

I forget about the hickey and about keeping my temper under control. "God-dammit, Aster! You and I are no longer together. Don't you get it? You are my *friend*."

Aster bobs in her chair, forward and backward. Her mother used to do that when she became angry. The only person who could calm her down was Ivy. She would whisper words in her ear and hold her hands without ever breaking eye contact. She called it "grounding."

I hesitate to reach over the table to ground Aster. She'll most certainly pull away. If only Ivy were here. She'd know what to do. Then again, if Ivy were here, she'd slap me for my insensitivity. I should've kept my yap shut.

Aster is somewhere else. Her eyes are glazed over like the top of Mom's mini donuts that the neighborhood kids love. The door of the visitation room opens and the fat guard steps into the small concrete chamber to collect Aster. I bet he eats tons of donuts.

"What happened?" he asks me.

Our private lives are none of his business. "Is she taking her medication?" I ask instead.

"Yeah."

"It must not have taken effect yet."

He snorts. "Because you really think medication can do much for her?"

I glower at him, animated by a strong desire to punch him. "I'll be back tomorrow. Can you tell her that, once she calms down?"

"Sure."

I stand up and wait for another guard to collect me. A short woman with a long braid down her back arrives a few minutes after Aster is taken away. She leads me back through the musty prison corridors.

My car feels like a toaster oven. As soon as I get the motor running, I pump up the air conditioning until it's louder than the music. I raise the music. Unfortunately, all the noise blasting around me does nothing to quiet my conscience, which is telling me what a total prick I am. It repeats it all the way back into Kokomo. And shrieks it even louder when I park in front of the ad agency where Aster used to work.

I take the elevator to the third-floor offices. Everything is white and clean and smells like air freshener. The receptionist, who sits behind a curved desk that resembles an outsized boomerang, recognizes me right away. She hops out of her chair and wiggles over to me on heels she's obviously not used to.

"How is she? We're all so worried. Did she really do it? Poor little sweetheart." The sentences pour out of her so quickly that I don't have time to answer any of them. "Good riddance. The criminal not Aster. Can't believe she's being convicted for it? What do you guys think at the police department?"

She's stopped talking so abruptly that I imagine she's taking a breath, but she looks at me expectantly.

"It's a complicated case," I say.

"I'd go visit her, but I'm scared of prisons. I've heard about the stuff that goes down in some. Even in the visitation areas. Besides, she'll be out soon, right?"

"We're working on it."

"I watch Ivy. I vote for her everyday. Everyone in here does. And all my Facebook friends and Twitter followers are voting for her. If they don't, I unfriend them."

Maybe I should vote against Ivy so this woman unfriends me. She's one of those people who posts something every hour on the hour, even during the night, be it pictures of cats, quotes about Jesus, or videos of babies burping.

"Wait"—she arches her unnaturally black eyebrows—"why are you here?"

"Um." I stare away from the pink bow with the articulated skeleton clipped into her black hair. "I need access to Aster's computer."

"Is this for the police investigation? Are you subpoenaing her computer? Are you taking away all our computers?"

"Just Aster's." I don't mention I have no police jurisdiction to back up my request.

She breathes a sigh of relief. "Of course. Come with me." She waddles all the way to the back of the open-space layout of the agency. Curious faces pop out from behind computer screens, but quickly duck back.

She taps on the keyboard and enters the company passcode. "All yours." She returns to her desk to greet a deliveryman who's just arrived. I bet she would've stuck around and looked over my shoulder if he hadn't.

I'm not great with computers, but I know enough to locate picture files. I sort them by date and open each one. None of them correspond to the black-and-white pictures of Kevin Martin that were leaked on national TV. I do find an entire file on Ivy's quilts. I click through them. I find the one she gave me: three shadows made of small rectangles. It's supposed to represent us, but sort of looks like my parents' shower tile. But prettier.

As I look through the folder, I come across the quilt Ivy sold Troy. I stare at the embracing figures for a long time, wondering who they're supposed to be. Did my friend have a lover? No, I would've known. It must be an idealized vision of love. That's what artsy people do. They represent ideas. Or maybe it's her mom and dad? I right click on the mouse and print out the image. The printer roars to life on the other side of the room.

I close all the open windows on her computer screen and go collect the printout. As I roll it up, two of Aster's colleagues stop by to ask questions about the case. I tell them I'm not at liberty to discuss it, because technically I'm not, and because they're busybodies. Unlike the receptionist with the skeleton in her hair, they don't care about Aster. And even her, I have my doubts. She cares too much about everyone.

In the elevator, I slip my phone out of my pant pocket to call Fred for news, but an e-mail makes me forget about my partner.

Josh—

The quilt is here...was here. It's the one I auctioned off. There was a rip in it. I think Aster did it. Can you find out why?

How did Ivy send me an e-mail? I thought she wasn't allowed access to the

Internet. I shake my head. That's not what's important. What's important is that there was a rip in it.

I get an awful feeling in my gut that Aster wrecked the quilt to punish Ivy for leaving her behind. That must be why she sent it to the art school. To show Ivy how torn she was herself about being abandoned.

NINETEEN

DAY 4

Brook

Ivy is inside my bedroom. She's been inside for a while now, so I knuckle the door.

"Everything okay?" I ask.

"Y-yes. Almost ready."

The door swings open and Ivy steps out. She's wearing this tiny turquoise bikini that shows off her perfect body. I'm tempted to throw a towel over her, so that nobody else can see how incredible she looks.

"That's a nice color on you," I end up saying, because I've been staring too long at her *not* to say anything.

She lifts her eyes that look as turquoise as the beads sewn on the bikini. "Thanks."

I look away from her so she doesn't think I'm sleazy, especially after last night at the restaurant. My gaze locks on the pile of clothes she's left on the armchair beside my bed. A piece of black lace sticks out.

She turns her head, but I wrap my fingers around her arms to stop her. I don't want her to see what I'm looking at.

"I'm going back to the museum to greet Kevin. Save me a swim, okay?"

"Brook? Your phone keeps—" My brother's voice makes Ivy jump away from me.

Great timing, brother.

"I'll see you outside," Ivy mumbles, stepping past me, and past Chase, who's still holding my phone out.

I swipe it out of his hand.

"It's Mom."

"You're not allowed to take phone calls," I say.

He snorts. "I didn't take it. You have Caller ID." He shakes his head.

We stare at each other for a long while. I can find no trace of the little boy I used to build Lego fortresses with, of the younger brother I would smuggle into R-rated movies when he was still a pre-teen, of the one I'd cover for when he was late coming home from dates with Diana.

Diana.

After their breakup, she came over to my apartment to vent. Chase showed up, supposedly to ask me for advice. He hadn't asked me for advice in years. Anyway, after seeing her, he ran off assuming things, and I was too offended to set him straight.

I walk into my room and slam the door closed behind me. For a moment, I just breathe. Then, when I feel somewhat calmer, I twist the lock and walk over to Ivy's clothes. There isn't much fabric to look through. I swallow hard when my fingers brush her underwear. I need to stop fantasizing about a girl who obviously doesn't like me. I fold everything back and peer inside the bag she brought with her, but it's made of mesh. Not exactly conducive to hiding things. I'm about to leave when I spot my iPad on my nightstand. I unplug it and slip it inside one of the drawers in my bathroom. I can't have contestants using it.

When I leave my bedroom, Chase is no longer in the hallway. He's lying by the pool next to Ivy. *God, is he flirting with her?* I walk up to the sliding glass windows. I can't hear them, but I can see them talking.

She doesn't like him, I reassure myself.

She doesn't like me either, though.

Heart twisting in my chest, I turn away from the pool deck and call my mother back.

"What is going on?" she yells.

"On the show?"

"Not on the show. In our lives. These two men are here from the bank. We are being evicted. Evicted, Brook!"

"Is Dad there?"

"He went out earlier, and now he's not answering his phone." My mother is hysterical. "Can you please come here? Honey, please…" She sobs.

"I'm on my way, Mom."

The elevator takes forever to go down seven stories, and the ride uptown takes even longer. I call Dominic to tell him I have a family emergency.

"Kevin's flight has been delayed anyway. Can you be at the museum in about an hour?"

"I think so."

"Good. Call me if there's anything I can do for your parents."

By the time I get home, Dad has returned too, sweaty from a jog. "You said we had two months," he's telling the bank emissaries.

"I'm sorry, Mr. Jackson, but you must take this up with your account manager. We received instructions this morning."

One of them, a young guy in a suit that's too shiny to be of good quality and a tie with an awful pattern, gawks at me. "Aren't you…?"

"On TV? Yes. Where's my mother?" I snap.

"In the living room."

Dad looks up. His dark eyes are wide with anguish, but it's nothing like the anguish lodged in my mother's face.

I sit down beside her. She leans into me and cries. As I confess everything Dad should have told her, mascara runs down her cheeks.

"How could he not tell me? How could *you* not tell me?"

"Dad was protecting you."

"You don't protect a person by not telling them the truth. Lies make people vulnerable!"

I attempt to calm her down, but it backfires. "He was trying to find a solution."

"And what? I wasn't smart enough to help?" Now, not only is she furious with Dad, but she's furious with me.

"Honey, would you like Carmelina to pack your suitcase?" Dad asks, standing in the doorway.

Mom's green eyes blaze and her mouth flattens until almost no more lip is visible. "How dare you," she shrieks, grabbing a picture frame and chucking it at him. It hits the wall, making the glass shatter and rain down over the worn parquet.

I'm so stunned by her violent reaction that I stiffen. Dad gapes at Mom, then looks down at the broken object. It's as broken as he is…as our family has become.

"I can pack my own suitcase. I have to get used to it now anyway, don't I?" She leaps off the couch and stalks off toward their bedroom.

Things crash and break inside. Ghost-faced, Dad looks to me for help, so I go after my mother inside the gray velvet room. She's staring at the mosaic of pictures of us nailed into one of the walls.

"Mom," I whisper as I wrap one arm around her slumped shoulders.

She leans into me and weeps. The top of her head fits right underneath my chin. It's fit there since I was eighteen.

I stroke her back and she quiets down. She still cries, but they're silent tears.

"I sent Sandra a message. I'm going to go live with her," she whispers, her voice cracking.

"Or you can come stay with me." Not that staying with her younger sister is a bad idea, but I want her to know I'm there for her too.

"You're in the middle of a show, Brook."

"Well at least let one of the chauffeurs drive you over."

"I don't have much of a choice, do I? One of my credit cards was declined this morning. I bet none of them work now."

I sigh.

"I knew things weren't great when we had to sell the beach house, but this"—she gestures around her—"this goes beyond my wildest imaginings." She turns toward me, swiping her palms across her cheeks, smudging the trails of mascara and staining her cheeks gray. "What else don't I know?"

That I've done bad things to keep her and Dad afloat, things I could get convicted for. I feel a presence behind me and turn to find my father standing in the doorway. "Nothing else."

My mother stares at my father for a long, hard time. Decades of shared history and unspoken blame pass like an invisible current between them.

"I'm going to my sister's place," she finally tells him.

"I heard."

"Alone."

"I understand," he murmurs.

"Alone?" I ask, because I didn't realize.

"I need time to think," she says.

Dad hunches over.

I swing my head between both of them.

"Where are *you* going to stay?" I ask Dad.

"Larry offered to lend me his guest bedroom."

That's bound to be weird for Chase since Larry is Diana's father. Then again, living with his ex-girlfriend isn't a permanent arrangement.

Dad gazes at Mom. "When I find a job, I'll start looking for a new apartment."

"A job?" I say stupidly. "Doing what?"

"Whatever I can," he says softly.

She can't leave Dad. Not right now. Not ever. "Mom—"

"Do we have anything left to give Carmelina?" she asks.

Dad takes a few crumpled twenties from his wallet.

"That's it? That's plain insulting." Mom's tone is so harsh it makes Dad shrivel. She walks to the closet, to the safe bolted into the floor.

When I was young and she opened it, I would dig through her jewelry, pretending I was a pirate who'd just unearthed a bounty. Which reminds me of the diamonds I should be searching for in Ivy's room. Screw those diamonds.

"My jewelry is still here." She sounds surprised. She yanks out the open boxes she uses to store her big rings and twinkling earrings, and tosses them on the bed. The stones glitter like the glass that shattered earlier. "Sell them, Henry. Sell everything. And give it to your sons."

"But—"

"I don't want any of it. I don't need any of it." She stares at the glistening pool of jewels, bends over, selects a necklace with a heart-shaped diamond, and walks out of the room.

"That was the first present I ever gave her," Dad croaks. His eyes shine as brightly as the pile of baubles.

"I can't," Carmelina says from somewhere in the apartment. "I can't."

A tear rolls down Dad's cheek. When Mom returns, necklace-free, she asks Dad to leave.

"Carmelina will call you when I'm gone," she says. Her green irises look phosphorescent against their red background.

Dad scrambles out of the bedroom, and I dash out after him, afraid he's going to do something stupid. He trips over the rug in the living room and falls, crumpling to the floor. Glancing back at me with wet eyes, he hoists himself up and limps out of the apartment. Waves of dread slam into me, fill me, rock me. I have just witnessed the fall of a great man.

I can't decide whether to go after him or return to Mom.

"Brook," she calls out, making my choice for me. "Don't tell Chase. I don't want him to worry."

I nod.

"I know it's his birthday the day after tomorrow. Tell him Sandra broke her ankle and I had to go help her out. And tell your father not to burden him with anything."

"How—How long will you be gone?"

"As long as it takes. Will you come out to see me after the show?"

I nod.

"Can one of Dominic's drivers truly take me out to Rhode Island?"

"Yes."

She walks over to me and hugs me tight. "I love you so, so much, honey. I'm sorry you have to go through this. If only I'd known, we could have made plans. Instead—" She breathes in through her nose. It makes her nostrils flare.

"I'm worried about Dad."

She doesn't say anything.

"Are you leaving him?" I ask.

"For a while."

"So not for good?" I feel like a seven-year-old kid, scared his mommy and daddy might not love each other anymore.

"After thirty years, you don't leave someone for good on a whim."

My throat hurts too much to speak.

"Now, go," she tells me.

"The car's downstairs when you're ready."

She tries to smile, but her steel-gray cheeks barely crease with the dimples she passed on to me.

I start walking but turn around. "You'll be okay?"

"I'll be fine. Go."

So I do. On my way out, I find Carmelina sitting in the kitchen, sobbing. "I can't take this."

Like my mother, I try to smile but just can't. "You'll break Mom's heart if you don't."

"But it's yours. For your girlfriend someday."

I shake my head. "I'd have to find a girlfriend first." I go over to her and kiss her cheek. "Give me news from time to time, okay?"

"You too."

I nod and leave. I call Dominic to ask him about using a car to take my mother to Rhode Island. Like I thought, he accepts. He tells me to hurry to the museum. After giving instructions to the driver who brought me uptown, I hail a taxi. Thankfully, the cabbie doesn't recognize me, so the ride crosstown is quiet. I attempt to phone Dad. Several times. He never picks up. Fear twisting in my gut, I tap my phone against my jean-clad thigh and instruct the cabbie to go down into the parking lot.

"It's restricted for show personnel," he says.

"I am show personnel."

"Oh." His eyes dart to his rearview mirror as he drives down the ramp. The security guard stops us, but then sees me and waves the cab through. There is only one other car parked in the underground lot—a silver Ferrari.

Gulping, I pay the cab driver and hurry into the museum and up to the contestants' quarters. The makeup room is dark. I try a switch but still no light comes on. I turn the flashlight on my phone and walk through the black space, hoping there is electricity in the tent, but it's even darker in there. A creak makes me jump.

I lift my phone and shine it right into Dean's face.

"You scared the living daylights out of me," I hiss, clapping a hand over my chest.

His eyes gleam in the darkness, more silver than gray. "I found one."

He grabs my wrist to angle my phone's light on his other hand. A small porcelain box rests in the middle of his palm. With his thumb, he flicks it open. Inside shines a diamond twice the size of the heart pendant Mom gave Carmelina.

"Ivy had it?"

"Yep. Sewn into the lining of her bag."

"Just one?" I'm still whispering even though Dean isn't.

"Don't have to whisper, man. I cut the power and no one's around. And yeah. Just one. She probably brought it to New York to sell it. Wouldn't risk flying with all of them."

"So you think she knows where the rest of them are?"

"I do."

"And if she doesn't?"

"Then her sister definitely does."

"I'm going to give this one to the D.A. as a guarantee that the others are coming, then I'm leaving for Indiana."

"To see the Discolis?"

He snorts. "Hell no. I value my life. I'm going to offer my services to Aster Redd."

"You're what?"

"I'm going to become her lawyer."

"But—Won't that look suspicious?"

"I'll tell her she's my pro-bono case of the year."

"But it's a public trial. The Discolis are bound to find out."

"You are so naïve sometimes." He belts out a sinister laugh. "I won't actually go to trial. I only want the location of the diamonds. You're going to inform Ivy I'll be representing her sister, and then you're going to introduce me to Ivy. I'll work both sisters until I can find my stones. Because I *will* find my stones. Mark my words."

His phone beeps, which makes me jolt.

"Relax," he says without even checking it. "I'm tracking the car Dom sent to fetch Kevin. This was to tell me it's ten minutes away." He smiles. "Things are looking up for us. You might just get your commission after all."

Right, my commission... "What about the pictures?"

"You mean, the ones Sergeant Martin's wife doctored to get her husband disqualified?"

"What are you talking about?"

"I'm talking about the fact that I am a mastermind, and a mastermind finds a solution to every problem."

"Why would she ever consent to take the blame?"

"Why does anyone ever consent to do something?" When I don't come up with the answer, he tips his head to the side. "Why did *you* accept to help us? Besides for our undying friendship, that is."

Something in the way he says the last part irks me. "Money," I admit.

"Bingo. It's magical. I might've also dropped a hint that her husband was gay and sleeping around while in Afghanistan."

"What?"

"Yep. I did some homework on our little undercover buddy. His wife was plenty happy to sign the confession and take my money." He puts his hand on my shoulder and squeezes it, the same way Dominic does when he wants to give more weight to his words. "Heard about your parents. I was poor once too. Until I found my fairy godfather. Dom will take care of you until you can bounce back. Just like he took care of me when he found out about me."

TWENTY

JOSH

My coffee slops out of the Styrofoam cup as I hit the brakes a little too roughly. The security chain-link gates of Aster's prison just stalled at the halfway mark. Even though my car is small, it's not narrow enough to slip out, so I wait until the guard stationed by the DOC's only entry point can fix it. I blot the stain off my navy pants with an old napkin. It's not too visible.

As I wait, I take my small pen and my little spiral notebook out of my shirt pocket and jot down everything I learned before I forget.

- Aster put the quilt back inside the envelope she found it in. It was already addressed to New York: to the Masterpiecers.
- There were diamonds inside, or so Aster told me. She said she left them inside.
- Angela Discoli must have given Troy the diamonds. She must have hid them inside the quilt (that's why she was nervous when I asked her about the quilt). NOT WEDDING PRESENT.
- Aster thinks her sister is involved, but she's not. Right?

I stare at my little checklist until the gate screeches back to life. The armed guard gives me a thumbs up and I go through, fingers tapping my wheel, but not in time with the music blasting out of my speakers—in time with the hectic pace of my heart.

When I get on the highway, I call the police station and ask to speak to Chief Guarda.

"I'm sorry, Cooper," the officer on the phone tells me, "but he's in a meeting and can't take your call."

More like doesn't want to talk to me. I try calling Fred but he doesn't pick up either. Annoyed, I fire the car in the direction of the precinct. I have information they'll want. Which means they'll have to see me. I still want to be reinstated, but right now, it's not about my badge. It's about dismantling an organization that stretches far beyond my reach. Which is something I can't do by pursuing my little investigation alone. I need higher help, and I'm not talking about God, although a divine intervention would be much appreciated.

I park in my old spot and race into the precinct. I don't stop by the dispatch desk, even though the cop on duty—the one I had on the phone—shouts out my name, yelling for me to stop. I run up the stairs to our first-floor offices, and barge into the conference room just as the guard catches up to me.

He digs his fingers into his waist, panting. "Cooper…come on…stop."

The chief rolls the tips of his mustache between his fingers.

"I tried…to…stop him."

"Didn't do too good a job now, did you?"

The officer releases his waist, and straightens up. His complexion goes from red to white in under a second. The fear of losing his job is scribbled all over his face. I'm tempted to pat his back and welcome him to the badge-less club, but don't. Picking on another officer is not my style.

"I have something big for you," I tell the chief.

He studies me, still stroking his mustache.

Fred's tiny eyes, which usually look sunk deep in his tubby face, seem to protrude as he stares at me.

"Close the door," Guarda barks, still looking at me.

My rainbow of hope sinks so quickly through me that I expect to see it pool around my leather shoes, multi-colored and foolishly shiny.

Bowing my head, I start to turn around, but the chief's voice stops me, "Not you. It's the other imbecile I want out."

I snap back around like a rubber band, head held high again.

I'm back!

After the door closes, I take a breath and recite the bullet points on my spiral notebook to Fred, Guarda, and the female officer they replaced me with. No one speaks after I finish enumerating my discoveries. When the chief pushes himself back from the table, I anticipate he's going to walk over to me and pat me on the back. Instead he crosses his legs and leans back. Not the ecstatic, proud reaction I expected.

"By running your little investigation, you disobeyed direct orders, Cooper," he says.

"I—"

"Let me finish. You knew about Angela Discoli's meeting with Troy Mann and you didn't tell us."

"I didn't know who she—"

"I said let me finish," Guarda snaps. "You penetrated the Discoli compound without backup."

I curl my fingers into fists to keep myself from asking how he knows that.

"You keep visiting Aster in prison, posing as a badge-bearing officer. I heard you even dropped by her office yesterday to look through her computer. And now you dare run into my precinct and interrupt my meeting."

I gulp and shut my eyes, bracing myself to be ripped a new one. Instead, there's silence. It echoes louder than the chief's barking.

Finally, his voice rings out again, "What do you have to say for yourself?"

I don't dare open my eyes. I don't dare speak. I barely dare breathe.

"Cooper, I'm allowing you to talk, so talk."

I crack my lids open. All three are gaping at me. "You took me off this case because I was careless about Troy Mann's file. I deserved what I got. I'm not disputing this. However, this is *my* case, and it's become even more so now that it reaches into my private life. Aster and Ivy Redd are my friends, and I can't stand around and do nothing. So whether you want me involved or not, Chief, I will be involved. The moment I figured out who the girl in the motel was, I told Fred. And then I went to visit her because I wanted to understand what she was doing with Troy Mann. She said they were lovers. Maybe that's true. I don't know. What I do know is that she startled when I spoke about the quilt, so I understood that was important to the investigation. And now I know why. They used it to transport diamonds to New York. What I still don't understand is who they were trying to pay off, or what they were buying. And that's why I came here. Because even though I can keep investigating on my own, I don't want to. I want to work with a team. I want to work with you again. You told me you don't play by the rules. Well, apparently, I don't either."

I watch Guarda's lips. I'm waiting for them to curl in displeasure, but instead, they curve upward.

"How long did it take you to come up with that speech?" he asks.

"Uh. I…I came up it with it n-now."

"Well then, bravo. It deserves some applause." He claps.

Hesitant at first, Fred and the blonde chime in. When Guarda stops, the two others stop.

"Sit. We have a lot to discuss," he says.

I scramble into a chair.

"This is going to be hard for you to hear, but if you're going to be part of this task force again, then you need to be aware of our suspicions."

"Okay." My leg shakes and my foot taps the ground.

"We don't think your friends are that innocent."

"What?"

He rocks against the springy backrest of his chair, bobbing like the baby-pink awning of Mom's bakery when there's a lot of wind. "We have two theories. One, that Ivy knew about her quilt being used to launder mafia goods, and that her cut was getting a place on the show."

My mouth gapes. I should snap it shut, but I can't, so I let it hang open.

"And two, that Aster, who's a little genius with computers—but you know that already—well, we think that she forged those pictures to get her on the show."

"I checked her computer."

"We know. We collected it from her office. It's being picked apart as we speak."

"She didn't do it. I checked all the files."

"Did you check the deleted files?" he asks. "Did you check her emails? Did you check the ROM memory?"

"No. I—"

"Well, we are. We're covering all our bases. And Ivy is being interviewed this afternoon by our liaisons in New York."

"Interviewed?" I repeat stupidly, picturing my poor friend in an interrogation room.

"We want to find out how many players we're dealing with."

They're making a mistake. Ivy and Aster are not involved. *Right?* But what if they are? Ivy really wanted to get on that show, and Aster would do just about anything to help her sister. A chill spider-crawls up my spine. "Do you know what the diamonds were used for?"

"Little Diego, Angela's youngest brother, has been convicted in New York for killing a prostitute." Guarda grins. "Although I believe that's the slightest of the crimes that make him rotten, at least he was caught. I'm willing to bet you anything those diamonds are going to pay off a prison guard to help him escape. We've informed the warden at his jail, who says they've tightened security."

"But who at the Masterpiecers is connected to the Discolis?"

Guarda pinches his lips so hard it looks as though he's vacuum-packed them. "The agents in New York are working on that. They don't care to swap info."

"Wouldn't working together be more beneficial to the case?" I ask.

"Why don't you go ahead and tell them that?" he says, his voice as tight as his lips. Slowly, he unseals them. "We don't need them, right, team?"

Fred and my replacement nod.

"*They* need *us*. It might take them a while to realize it, and until they do, we're pursuing our investigation. All they have right now are a bunch of puzzle pieces. What we have is a picture that's missing a few corners. About one of those corners, Claire…have you made any progress tracking down Elise Frothington?"

"Elise Frothington?" I ask.

"She's the woman who bought the quilt at the show's auction."

Claire tightens her long, blonde ponytail. "From the footage I received, she arrived at the museum in a taxi cab. I ran the plates and got us a name and number. Apparently the cabbie picked her up from the Four Seasons Hotel, where she was checked in under Elise Frothington and paid cash. She checked out right after the auction was over."

"Cooper, Claire, get everything you can on this woman, down to the brand of toilet paper she uses to wipe her ass."

I give a jerky nod.

"Fred, you get me an update on Diego's criminal case proceedings, and phone the prison. See how he's behaving." He rubs his hands together excitedly. "Finally, we're getting somewhere."

We *are* getting somewhere, but it's not anywhere I want to get to if the twins are truly, knowingly involved.

TWENTY-ONE

Brook

When two detectives waltz into the museum after today's test, I assume they're heading for me. I back up into the crowd, bumping into someone. The detectives don't even look my way. They approach Ivy, and then they take her away. Being the coward that I am, I don't try to help her. I stay frozen and quiet, unlike Dom, who stands up to the detectives. And then I flee to the second floor and pace the empty galleries even though I'm supposed to be working the crowd below. I can't bring myself to head downstairs and make small talk.

I twirl my phone between my fingers as I stare at the shadowy paintings around me. I crossed paths with one security guard, but it was two galleries down from where I am now. No one is watching me here. I find myself in front of Jasper Johns's *White Flag*, and it reminds me of Ivy. Everything is starting to remind me of her. I drop on one of the benches and yank at my hair in irritation. I would shout or punch something if I weren't afraid it would trigger an alarm.

I should go to the station and confess, but that would mean bringing Dom and Dean down with me. And my parents…what would they do if I were to go to prison? Because that's probably where I'd be sent. After all, I received mafia money. I accepted bribes. Chase would hate me because the show would probably be terminated if Dom were to be convicted. And Ivy…she'd be free, but she would despise me too.

I am *so* close to cracking.

Even though I try to bite back my anger, it rips up my throat and through my parted lips. I ball my fists and punch the bench. Screw the security cameras. Screw everything and everyone!

I call Danny the driver and ask him to go pick up Ivy. "Phone me when she's in the car with you," I tell him before hanging up and calling my father. "Hey, Dad," I say, attempting to temper my voice to sound normal. "How's life at Larry's?"

"Can I call you later? I'm in the jewelry district," he says. He's pawning off Mom's jewels. Which is good. At least he's not dangling off the Queensboro Bridge.

"Sure." I hang up. "I'm fine. Thanks for asking," I mutter after ending the call. I shouldn't be bitter with Dad, but I can't help myself. No one cares about me.

My phone rings. I stare at the screen. When Diana's name pops up, I'm tempted to let it go to voicemail, but maybe talking to someone on the outside is exactly what I need. "Hey, there," I say.

"Brook Jackson, what the hell is going on?" she shouts.

"You mean, Dad moving in with you?"

"Yeah. *That*. And on the freaking show? What the hell is happening on the freaking show? One of the contestants just got *arrested*?"

"She didn't get arrested. She was taken in for questioning."

"For what?"

For nothing. "They're still looking into those doctored photos."

"How's Chase doing?"

"He's fine."

"And you?" she asks, her voice softer. "How are you doing?"

I was wrong. Someone does care about me. My brother's ex. "I'm okay."

"You don't sound okay."

"You can tell over the phone?"

"Brook, I've known you for-freaking-ever. Your father's here with me, your Mom's in Rhode Island, and you're hosting a super messed-up show. Don't pretend you're okay. At least not with me."

Silence stretches between us, interrupted only once by a car horn. Diana must be walking around the city. I lean forward and hang my head in my free hand. I close my eyes, wishing I were outside too…wishing I were far away.

"Is Chase talking to you at least?" she asks.

"No."

"Does he still think—"

"That we hooked up? Yeah."

"Now would be a good time to tell him the truth."

"I'm sick of having to explain myself to everyone."

"So you'd rather let him assume things?"

"He wouldn't believe me, Diana."

"Then I'll tell him."

"I thought you never wanted to speak to him again."

"Your dad is living at my house. I don't think I'll be able to avoid Chase once the competition is over."

My caller ID beeps. Danny's calling. Ivy must be on her way back. "Diana, I have to go. I'll call you soon, okay?"

"Call me whenever you want."

"Whenever I can," I correct her. Perhaps, if I were to go to jail, Diana's father, who's an extremely successful hedge fund manager, would bail me out. The thought winches up the hem of the bleak veil that has settled over my future.

Danny informs me that he's just dropped Ivy off, and I sprint down the large stone stairs into the almost deserted lobby. I spot Ivy entering the elevator and run faster, just managing to slide my hand between the closing doors.

Cara, Ivy's assistant, blinks at me.

"I need a word with our contestant," I say.

It takes her a moment to figure out that I'm dismissing her. She steps out of the elevator while I step in. As the elevator begins to rise, I tug on the red emergency lever.

Breathing hard from my run, I finally wonder what got into me to trap Ivy in a steel box. She must think I'm crazy.

"What?" she snaps.

But I'm not crazy. I'm concerned. I want her to leave the show. Staying will only make things worse for her. "Dominic's worried about you," I lie. "He's worried you have a lot on your plate. Perhaps too much. He thinks that maybe you should…"

"Maybe I should what?"

I gaze at the floor. She's angry—and rightfully so. I flick my eyes upward but still can't bring myself to look straight at her face. *Stop being such a coward…* Slowly, very slowly, I lock my eyes on hers. "He thinks that maybe you should drop out."

"Drop out? Of *The Masterpiecers*? No…no way. I want to stay. I *need* to stay."

"Ivy, you're doing well, but—"

"But what?"

But bad things are bound to happen if you stay. "But there's a lot to think about. Between the media, and Kevin, and your sister. You should see what's being written up in the newspapers." I'm a wuss, that's what I am.

"I'm bringing the show bad press. Is that what you're getting at?"

"Well…not exactly." I rake my shaky fingers through my hair. "Yes."

She tilts her head to the side. "Don't you know journalists love scandals?"

"I know that, but—"

"They don't intimidate me, Brook. And neither does Dominic. I'm sorry about the bad press, but I'm not leaving the show. This is my one chance. Maybe you don't understand because you've never had to worry about where your next meal came from, but I *can't* drop out. And I'll say this again however many times I need to: I had *nothing* to do with Kevin's pictures." She shakes her head, and her glimmering hair flutters against her bare, burnished shoulders. "You know, for a second there, when you cornered me, I thought you were going to ask me how I was doing. I thought you were worried about me. But I guess people like you, like Dominic, like Josephine, only worry about themselves."

"Don't say that." I jolt forward. "I *am* worried about you. The situation sucks, Ivy. Really, it does."

"I'm still not leaving. If you want me out, you'll have to disqualify me."

She shouldn't want to stay; she shouldn't want to endure the media scrutiny and the nastiness everyone on the show doles out on her!

"That wouldn't be fair," she adds, her voice raspy.

Life is not *fair, Ivy.* That's what I want to tell her, but perhaps I should let her dream. Just because I'm living a nightmare doesn't mean she has to take part in it. I could protect her from now on. She's so close I can feel the heat from her body seep into mine. I can hear her heartbeats thunder in the silent, suspended space.

"The public's vote counts for something," she says. "Now, can you please switch the elevator back on?"

Before I let her leave, I need to know what the detectives wanted, but instead of asking her point blank, I mumble a stupid question, "Could Aster have had anything to do with Kevin's pictures?" A question I already know the answer to.

"I doubt it."

"But you're not sure? She's your sister—"

"If I remember correctly, you had no clue your brother entered the competition," she counters.

I frown. "I did know. His girlfriend told me."

"The one you screwed?"

Shocked that Chase would confide something so intimate to her, I blurt out, "You know about that?"

"Yeah."

I breathe in slowly. And breathe out even slower. Anger at my brother fills me so quickly that I want to punch the wall. My hands turn into fists. Dean used to tell me that my brother was a spoiled brat. The few times he came over to visit me at Duke, if he didn't want to do what we had planned, I'd cancel everything for him. I never felt it was a great sacrifice on my part, but Dean saw it as such because, when I returned to New York during holidays, Chase wouldn't alter *his* plans for me.

Thinking about Dean reminds me about the conversation we had yesterday afternoon in the contestants' tent. "I have a great lawyer."

"Are you threatening me?"

I blink. "I meant for your sister, Ivy."

"Oh."

"And he'd be free."

"Really?" She bites her lower lip. In the darkness, her teeth seem phosphorescent against her red mouth. "Is he free even if I decide to stay on the show?"

"Yes."

"Does he work pro bono?"

"No. He's a friend."

"Why would you do that?"

I swallow. Hard. "So you can forgive me for being disrespectful toward you."

"I don't know what to say."

"Just say yes, and I'll make the call."

As I tug the lever back up to free her, she releases her lip and lets out a smooth breath. "Okay."

The lights snap back on, blindingly bright. I lift my fingers to her face and brush a strand of hair off her cold cheek.

"I'll give him a call right away," I murmur.

I tuck the pale strand behind the shell of her ear that's as soft as peach fuzz.

"Thank you," she whispers back.

The elevator doors open. For a second, I hold my breath, hoping she won't step out, wishing there existed a button on the elevator dashboard marked *Elsewhere*.

But there is no magic button.

And wishes don't come true.

Her black lashes swoop down over her glorious eyes as she turns and walks away.

TWENTY-TWO

JOSH

I grab the Chinese take-out Heidi asked me to pick up. It smells like hot oil and sweet garlic. Before I've even made it to my car, a spot of grease blooms on the brown paper bag. I wince, reminded of my awful Hamster days. Fatty Chinese food was my favorite back then. I pull an old newspaper from my trunk, lay it on the passenger seat, and position the grubby bag on top.

As I pull out of the Panda Express parking lot, my phone lights up with a call from Mr. Mancini, the twins' nosy neighbor. I bet he wants to ask me if Aster killed the guy in cold blood, or maybe he wants to complain about the noise his upstairs neighbor's baby makes at night. I'm not a disturbance cop, yet that's how he's treated me since I got my badge. When he calls me again, I assume it's more important than the kid who doesn't sleep through the night.

"Hello, Mr. Mancini," I say politely. "How can I help you?"

"You have to come over right away."

"Did something happen?"

"Would I call you if nothing had happened?"

Yes. "What is it?"

"I can't tell you over the phone. Never know who's listening."

No one is listening. "Can it wait until tomorrow morning?"

"Sure, but the person could be gone by then."

"What person?"

He grunts with impatience. "The one inside the twins' apartment."

"There's someone in their apartment? Who?"

"Would I be calling you if I knew who it was?"

"I'll be there in a few minutes. Stay in your house, okay?"

"Yeah yeah. Just hurry."

So I hurry. Even though I don't have flashers on my personal car, I drive as though I've turned them on. I even go through two red lights. When I come to a stop in front of Mancini's ground-floor apartment, my tires screech.

Before my finger grazes the doorbell, he unlocks the door, holding a rifle in his liver-spotted hands.

"I loaded my hunting rifle," he says, swinging it toward me so I can see it.

I drag the nozzle away. "I'm sure that's unnecessary."

"You have your gun?"

I tap the holster at my waist.

"What is that? A Colt?" He wrinkles his long nose. "I'm keeping mine. Now, let's go." He shuts the door.

"But—"

"Don't you dare tell me to stay inside. *I* saw the intruder, so *I* get to go too."

I open my mouth to say *no*.

"I was a bank manager back in the day," he says, "and we had a hold-up once. And I saved everyone because I brought my shotgun to work that day. And before you ask, I have a license to carry." He's breathing so heavily that his nostril hairs quiver. "The only reason I called you is because I know you got a key to the Redd girls' place."

I nearly snort, but stop myself because Mr. Mancini has narrowed his fog-colored eyes.

"Now let's stop making a spectacle of ourselves. Go open the door."

I dig my keys out of my jeans' pocket. "If we find anyone," I whisper, "you can't shoot them."

"Stop your yappin'. We're gonna be found out," he hisses.

Grabbing my gun, I plunk my key in the lock and twist it. I push the door open carefully, senses on high alert. Gun pointed, I scan the dark living room with my eyes and my ears. No sound. No movement.

Tailed by Mr. Mancini, whose rifle is hazardously swinging this way and that, I creep toward Ivy's studio in the veranda. The place is a mess. All the drawers have been tossed. Fabric litters the floor and her sewing machine is toppled over. The room reminds me of our lawn the night me and my buddies decided it would be fun to TP the large oak tree in our backyard. It had been much less fun the following morning when Mom asked me to clean it all up—even the pieces stuck in the top-most tree branches.

Something crashes. Like glass. Heart punching my ribcage, I run out. Mancini is cursing. "Knocked this vase over with the barrel of my rifle."

I widen my eyes and fling my finger against my lips. Stealthily, I check the two bedrooms in the back. I don't have to open any closet doors as they all hang open already. Clothes are everywhere. The dresser drawers have been pulled out. I race to the small bathroom, the last room in the house. I flick the light on.

The cabinet is wide open and the medication bottles have all been opened and emptied. A rainbow of assorted pills surrounds the tossed toothpaste tubes and face creams on the yellow bathmat. I crouch down and pinch the expensive perfume bottle I gave Aster at Christmas. I hold it up to the light and whirl it around slowly, looking for prints. Nothing. The person was wearing gloves. I lay the bottle back on top of the messy heap. Mancini is standing in the narrow hallway behind me. He peers into one of the bedrooms.

"You think it's a random break-in?" he asks.

"No."

"Anything missing?"

"I don't know." The scattered pills draw my attention. Whatever this person was looking for could fit inside a pillbox— *The diamonds!* I squeeze both sides of my face with my palms, before rising from my crouch.

"What's the point of entry?" Mancini asks.

"Aster's window," I say without hesitation.

I traipse back down the corridor and straight into Aster's room where the butterfly wallpaper has turned yellow and is peeling off the walls. Her hung window is closed, but when I tug on it, it slides right up. "The lock's been broken for ages."

"Not too smart of Aster to leave it broken."

"The only option was to change the whole thing, and that was expensive."

Mancini stares around the room. "She kept it the same."

"The same?"

"As her mom. I came over ages ago. The girls were seven or eight at the time. I helped her fix a leak. It was before she turned loopy. Whatever happened to her? She still in the loony bin?"

"She passed away five months ago."

"Oh. I didn't know."

I cock an eyebrow. The man who knows everything didn't know the twins lost their mother?

"Is that where they took Aster? To the batty house?"

"Aster's in jail. Don't you read the papers?"

"I've been feeling under the weather. You know, pancreatic cancer." He shrugs as though he told me he had a common cold.

"I'm so sorry."

"At my age, it progresses slowly, so I'll probably die of natural causes."

"Do you have any family, Mr. Mancini?"

He rotates his knobby fingers around the barrel of the gun. "I had a daughter." A few tears trickle into his wrinkles. I turn around so he can wipe them. He sniffles once, then clears his throat. "We should call it in."

"We should," I say, holstering my gun.

"Well, what are you waiting for?" He's back to being his usual sweet self.

As I take out my cell phone, he leans against his big gun, which he's rested on the floor like a cane.

"Don't you have a radio-thingy?"

"Not in my off-duty vehicle."

I call the station to report the robbery. Fifteen minutes later, a cruiser careens onto the street. Claire and Fred step out of it. They interview Mancini, and then Claire walks him back to his place and calls another unit to come and run prints and document the break-in.

"Is anything missing?" Fred asks me before the crime scene technician arrives.

I shake my head no. "But it's a mess, so I can't tell. And I tried not to touch anything, but my prints are already everywhere."

"Don't worry, Coop," he says, staring at my hands that I have clasped together.

They're shaking. I'm shaking. I hadn't even realized it. I stuff them inside my pockets and watch as both cops weave around the apartment.

"You think it's connected to the case?" Claire asks, squatting to inspect the pills on the bathmat. Her blonde ponytail swooshes around her shoulders as she straightens back up.

"They were looking for the diamonds," I whisper.

"Didn't Aster say they were in the quilt?" Claire asks.

"I think she lied to me." I grab my car keys out of my pocket and make to leave but Fred stops me. "I need to go see her, man."

"It's the middle of the night. They probably won't let you see her. Besides, what are you planning to do? Threaten her until she breaks? Think this through, Coop."

"I need to know where she hid them, so I can check if they were found, before more people rummage through her stuff."

"Visiting her in the middle of the night will freak her out. And freaked out people don't confess. Especially…" Fred's voice dies off.

"Especially what?"

"Especially if those people are…unstable."

Although I wince, Fred's right. If she lied to me, then her mind isn't functioning right. The real Aster, the one who takes her medication, she trusts me.

TWENTY-THREE

DAY 6

Brook

As the contestants build art from sand and grass and wood, I stare out at the ocean that rolls gray-blue waves onto the shore. I've been to better beaches, I've looked out on more beautiful seas, but being whipped by salt spray and briny sunshine feels, nonetheless, incredible. I can almost forget the show is under scrutiny, that my family is destitute, that my parents split-up, that a PI squats a few feet away weaving a rope while surveying Ivy.

"A thousand dollars for your thoughts?" Dean asks, sidling in next to me with the stealth of a wildcat.

"A thousand dollars would be nice right now," I reply, keeping my gaze on the frolicking waves.

"Here," he says.

I glance down at his outstretched hand. "I was kidding, Dean." We're standing far enough away from the crowd that no one can see the flattened and folded hundred-dollar bills. As he tucks the money back inside the pocket of his pricey pantsuit, I ask, "So what's the plan? You have one, right?"

He stares out at the ocean, which makes his eyes appear steelier, in spite of the bright sunshine. "I didn't find anything last night," he says, instead of answering my question. "I looked everywhere. I checked the freezer, the oven, their underwear drawers, the pill bottles…you should see how many they have. Pills for everything. I even brought some back." He shakes something. I see the name

Aster Redd on the label. "A few of these can knock someone unconscious almost instantly."

I look up at him. "Dean…"

"I'm not going to use them on myself," he says, thinking I'm calling him out on his drug habit. I'm not. Although it would be nice to see him sober. "I'm going to slip some in Kevin's drink. Get him to talk. And then I'll plant the bottle somewhere easy to find. When he comes out of his medicated stupor, he'll have forgotten about me, but he'll have this little reminder." He jiggles the bottle. "It'll get him off our scent." His eyes are wild, like the foamy crests in the distance.

"If you do that—"

"It will get him sniffing around Ivy instead? That's what you were going to say, wasn't it?"

"He's already convinced she's involved."

"Better her than us, right? Besides, if she's innocent, she'll manage to prove it."

I want to tell Dean to go to hell with his pills and Machiavellian plan, but Dominic is staring at us and so is Josephine who's giving an interview. A soft breeze makes her white-blonde hair flutter around her long, pallid neck.

"Introduce me to Ivy tonight, okay?" Dean says.

I drag my gaze away from Josephine. Even though it kills me, after a stilted moment, I nod. "Be careful. There are cameras everywhere."

Far behind Dean, Ivy spins blue beachgrass around slender twigs. She's concentrating so hard that she's biting her lip.

"Josephine asked about Elise Frothington," I tell him.

"Dom told me. She won't find anything. And even if she does, my mother's allowed to purchase art."

"She is, but not under an alias. Why couldn't you have paid someone else to buy it? Someone *not* related to you."

"Because the only person I trust entirely is my mother."

I cast a sideways glimpse at him. I sense there's an insinuation. However peeved I am by it—after everything I've done—Dean is right: his mother would do absolutely anything for him. And not just because he's secured her a generous alimony and a mansion in Palm Beach.

"Where's your ring?" he asks.

I stare down at my bare pinkie. "I forgot it at home."

"You forget it a lot these days. Are you embarrassed to be associated with me?" He fiddles with the gold bar that holds his poppy-red tie flat against his dress shirt. For all the confidence Dean exhibits, deep down, he's insecure.

"I can't believe you're wearing a tie here," I say, to change the subject.

"After six years, you can't believe it?" He smiles, but it seems contrived. "I just spotted Kelley."

"Who?"

"Kevin's lawyer."

"Here?"

"Yeah. As your sugar mama's guest. Dom told her to invite him so I could speak to him."

I bristle. "Madame Babanina is not my sugar mama."

Dean's smile grows wider, taunting. "Perhaps you should ask her to be. You could use a sugar mama right now."

"No way."

Dean chuckles, squeezes my shoulder, then trots toward Mr. Kelley, a ruddy-faced man seriously lacking a neck.

ALTHOUGH I KEEP an eye on my friend throughout the afternoon, I don't see him again until after Herrick gets eliminated, until after I offer Ivy thirty thousand dollars to buy her web—money I don't have.

Her eyes shine at my proposition. When I feed my fingers through hers to shake on our deal, the beach empties. It's an illusion, I know, but what an illusion it is. I wish we were the last ones left on this beach, just me and this beautiful barefoot girl dressed all in white.

"What are we shaking hands to?" Patrick, the photographer, asks, intruding on our moment.

Startled, Ivy pulls her hand out of mine.

"I've just bought my first Ivy Redd piece," I tell him, trying to slow my thundering heart before he can capture it on camera.

Thankfully, he snaps a picture of her—not of me. The flash makes her blink.

"The web?" he asks.

"The Web," I repeat, smiling down at Ivy. "Shall we call it that?"

"Sure."

"I might not be the first owner of a Redd original, but I'm certainly the luckiest because I saw it come to life under my very own eyes. How many collectors can claim that?" I tell Patrick, all the while watching Ivy.

She's looking beyond me now, at Kevin and Mr. Kelley, who are talking with Dean. His gaze slides to mine and he tips his chin. He wants me to bring Ivy over to him. I grip her arm gently, which makes her look away from the three men. I don't want to take her there. I want to drag her off the beach and tuck her away somewhere safe until the night is over…until the show is over. But of course I can't do that. She'd think I was a psycho.

Goose bumps rise on her skin under my palm.

"Excuse us, Patrick," I say, still holding on to her. "I have someone I'd like to introduce to my contestant." Hoping the goose bumps are a reaction to my touch, I rub my thumb over her soft skin, but stop when we reach Dean. And then I let her go. "Ivy, I'd like you to meet Dean Kane, my dear friend and the lawyer who will be defending your sister."

She frowns as she shakes his hand.

"And this is Mr. Kelley," I tell her, gesturing to Kevin's lawyer.

She politely shakes his hand too.

"I should get back to Madame Babanina. She doesn't like to be left alone," Kevin's lawyer says. "Mr. Martin, I am deeply sor—"

Kevin, whose chin is tucked into his neck, doesn't wait for him to finish his sentence before traipsing away. I eye Dean whose lips cock up on one side with a shameless smile.

"Brook, may I speak to Ivy privately? I'd like to discuss her sister's case," he says.

"Sure, but don't bore her with too many details."

I watch them set out along the beach and keep them in my line of vision until they return. This might make me an awful friend, but I don't trust Dean with her. Later, when she parts ways with Dean to sit at the contestants' table, I take a much-needed break from spying and head to the luxury port-o-potties, where I am ambushed by the divorcée. She comes at me so quickly and so suddenly that I find myself locked in her embrace. I try to press her away, but her hands tighten around my back, her sharp nails ploughing into the fabric of my shirt like the talons of a vulture.

"Madame Babanina, please..." I try to say, but she squashes her lips against mine.

I was taught to be polite, but I don't feel like being polite right now, so I shove her off.

Although her bangs cover her forehead, I can tell she's frowning.

"I'm sorry, but I have a girlfriend," I lie.

She smirks. "And I have a boyfriend. Two even." She raises her face toward mine again and plants a short kiss on my lips. "I don't mind."

"I do."

"What a shame. What a shame." Keeping the smile up, she winks and walks away.

I'm so stunned it takes me a moment to gather my composure. And when I do, I almost wish I hadn't, because in front of me, knee-deep in the ocean, my brother has his arms wrapped around Ivy's waist.

And he's kissing her.

My heart holds still, and then it shatters like the frame Mom threw at Dad. I tear my gaze away, but still I see their kiss. I recede into the shadows and stagger away from them, from the crowd. Minutes later, when I think I've succeeded in escaping everyone, I come across Kevin and Dean sitting on the beach, sipping drinks and chatting like old friends. I crouch behind a sand dune to stay out of sight.

Fireworks explode overhead. It's the fireworks I organized for Chase's birthday. My present to him. I hope he hates them, because I certainly do. Everyone on the beach is staring heavenward except Kevin, who's now slumped against Dean's shoulder. Even though more rockets erupt overhead, I keep my gaze on Dean, who is struggling to stand. He pulls Kevin up and slings his arm around his shoulders, then slowly, losing his footing a few times, he walks over to the ocean.

What is he doing? I scream inwardly.

A chill inches up my spine as he wades into the surf, dragging Josephine's private investigator along. When Dean lets go of Kevin and the big man topples facedown into the water, I rocket out of the sand dune. Kevin floats away, drifting atop the waves like an unmoored boat.

He's going to drown!

Dean rubs his hands against his suit that is soaked up to his knees. He scans the beach, and his eyes lock on mine.

No. NO! Killing the PI wasn't the plan! My angry, appalled thoughts teeter on the edge of my tongue, but don't spill out.

As though he didn't just drown a man, he pulls out his checkered pocket square and polishes the pill bottle. Then he drops it on the sand, and plods unhurriedly back toward the thick crowd who's too mesmerized by the glittery sky to realize what's happened.

I tear my gaze off him and stumble across the beach, eyes skirting the water for Kevin, hoping that it's not too late to save him. Between the people swimming and the darkness, I can't him pick out. What I can pick out is the incriminating prescription bottle. I swipe it as the first scream pierces the night.

TWENTY-FOUR

JOSH

"You know, you're making one of my childhood dreams come true," Heidi tells me, as we hop over a stream.

"You dreamt of sexcapades as a kid?" I tease.

"No, silly. Camping."

"You've never been camping?"

"Never."

"So this will be a first for you?"

She nods.

"I like firsts."

She rolls her eyes. I try to kiss her, but instead I stub my toe against a rock and rock backward, taking Heidi down with me. My enormous backpack breaks my fall, and my body cushions hers. I readjust her tilted sunglasses, then wrap my arms around her and enjoy the moment.

She grins down at me. "Nice move, hotshot. Have you been practicing?"

"Yep. At the precinct. On Fred. He's a bit harder to catch, though."

She laughs. She's never met my partner, but knows his weakness for junk food.

I smile, bring her face closer to mine, and place a chaste kiss on her curved lips. "You're real pretty, you know that?"

"I know. Guys throw themselves at me all the time. It's exhausting." I can see her wink through her dark shades.

"At least you're not vain."

"At least there's that."

She kisses me, and her tongue slips into my mouth and caresses mine. Everything in me tightens and hardens, and if it weren't illegal to have sex in a public place, I would have my way with Heidi on our shaded patch of hill underneath the purpling sky with the gurgling stream in the background.

"Should we pitch our tent out here?" she asks, coming up for air.

"Yes." I stand up abruptly, fueled by the idea of getting our shelter up to pursue our make-out session in private.

"Never seen anyone so excited to build a tent," she says, latching on to my extended hand. I pull her up, and she dusts the back of her bare legs and the bottom of her khaki shorts with her freckled hands.

"Setting up camp has little to do with my *excitement*."

She whistles a song as I pull the lightweight dome tent out of the backpack and toss it in the air. It opens up and clicks in all the right places.

While Heidi secures the pegs into the ground, I unroll the blow-up mattress and puff air into it.

"Stephanie told me she was selling Troy's Cadillac. I know you have a thing for vintage cars—"

"I'm not interested." My stomach churns at the mention of Troy Mann.

Heidi nods, but her mood turns gloomy. I tuck a loose strand of hair behind her ear. "For the rest of this weekend, let's not talk about anyone but ourselves, deal?"

She hoists up a small smile. "Deal."

"Did you bring the sleeping bag?"

She taps her rucksack.

I shove the puffed-up mattress inside the tent and cover it with the sleeping bag. When I crawl back out of the tent, Heidi's popping the lid off Tupperware containers and setting them out around a bottle of wine.

"Did you cook?"

"In my dorm room? No. But I tried to buy wholesome stuff since my boyfriend worries about what goes inside his body."

"I'd rather not revisit my Hamster days. Shoot me."

"And I'd rather do other things to you than shoot you."

Grinning, I hold the tent flap up. "Then after you, *mademoiselle*." I don't think I pronounce it right, but it makes the corners of her mouth lift as she crawls inside. I scuttle in after her and zip up the tent.

When she tugs off her tank top before I even have time to lie back, I think sacrificing my cell phone and access to the news for two days is the smartest decision I've made in my life. At any rate, half of me thinks so.

ON SUNDAY MORNING, the sky cracks open and our little tent is battered with so much rain that the air in the tent turns suffocating. In minutes, Heidi and I are packed up and running toward the campsite facilities.

"You kids forget to check the forecast?" the guy behind the desk asks us the second we step inside. He sports a beard my father would kill for, dense and evenly trimmed.

"Yeah," Heidi says. Her long hair is stringy with water that's bleeding into the collar of her tank top.

"Want to rent one of our cottages?" he asks. "I got only one left."

"How much is it?" I try not to make a habit of digging into my savings, but if it can buy me more time with Heidi, then—

"A hundred and twenty bucks. You gotta pay up front."

"What?" I choke. "A hundred and—" My voice dies off when I sense Heidi's disappointment. "Is food included at least?"

"No, man."

"Can you make it a hundred?"

"No. If you don't take it, someone else will. At a hundred and twenty bucks," he repeats, leaning his beefy forearms on the wooden desk. A barbed wire tattoo wraps around one of them.

"One-twenty is perfect," Heidi says.

I wrench my gaze off the guy's inked arms and onto Heidi's hand that's brandishing a credit card. Before Tattoo can grab it, I say, "Put that away, will you?"

After I pocket my receipt and the key to the cabin, I study the layout map scotch-taped to the counter. The door chime rings and a couple that resembles drowned rats dashes in and asks for a cabin.

Tattoo hoists up an eyebrow. I'm expecting him to say he doesn't have any, but instead he says, "Got one last one."

"Last one, my ass," I mutter as Heidi shoves me out of the cabin.

We take shelter under the roof that juts a couple feet out.

"Where's our cabin?" Heidi asks, scanning the campgrounds hidden behind sheets of rain.

"Fifth to the right."

The people who came in after us peek outside. "We're better off waiting it out in here. Did you hear what happened on *The Masterpiecers* last night?" the woman says right as the door seals shut.

My ears prick up at the mention of the show. I touch the doorknob to find out what happened, but Heidi claps my arm.

"You promised."

"But what if—"

"What if Ivy got disqualified?" she supplies.

That's not the thought that entered my mind. Granted she doesn't know about my investigation.

"Will it change anything if you find out tomorrow?" Her lips are squashed together as though she's just sucked on a Sour Power Straw.

With a sigh, I release the doorknob. I pray Ivy hasn't been disqualified, and then I pray even harder that nothing bad happened to her. What if—

"Race you," Heidi says, grabbing my hand and jerking me into the rain.

Shoving all the *what ifs* out of my brain, I run along.

TWENTY-FIVE

DAY 7

Brook

Even though I tried to sleep when I got home from Fire Island, I couldn't. Every time I shut my eyes, Dean was there, leading Kevin into the foamy water, pushing him under. After tossing and turning, I get up, pull on a pair of swimming trunks, and dive into the cool water of my pool. I swim until I'm exhausted, until my muscles hurt more than my head, until I've rinsed Troy and Kevin's blood off of me. No one was supposed to die, yet two people are gone. How many more before this is over?

The sun crests on the horizon, tingeing the city orange and pink and the dark waters of the Hudson River navy blue. Below me, the Highline is coming to life as New Yorkers ford the suspended deck, walking by landscaped clusters of flowers and trees, clutching thermoses of coffee and pastries wrapped in paper napkins. I enjoy the view from up here, just like I enjoyed watching my stick insect slink around his terrarium.

As I pour myself a bowl of cereal, my mother calls. She heard the news. She's horrified. I bet she'd be even more horrified if she knew it wasn't a suicide—that's what it was ruled after Kevin was fished out. I ask her when she's coming home. Instead of answering, she tells me to wish a happy birthday to my brother.

Right...

Even though I have no claim to Ivy, I'm pissed that he kissed her. He should've known, should've sensed I liked her, but my brother only feels what he wants to feel. If he knew me at all, he wouldn't still be convinced I hooked up with Diana.

Dominic phones to tell me we are taking another day off filming that will end with a dinner at "the place I'm lending you." Granted, it's not *my* place, but *the place I'm lending you* sounds downright threatening, like he's reminding me yet again of all he's done for me…all he's still doing for me. Before hanging up, he asks me to pay Patrick Veingarten a visit.

"Review the pictures he took last night. In case you find anything incriminating we can hand over to the cops," he adds, even though he's actually telling me to check for any damning picture of Dean and Kevin.

I walk uptown. It's long, but pleasant and loud, almost loud enough to mask the noise in my head. Birds chirp while people do the same on their cell phones. Metal shop curtains creak up and delivery trucks beep into tight, illegal parking spaces. I'm surrounded by so much life, and yet I'm filled with so much death.

On my way to Patrick's, I pass by the Met, which is still decorated with the outsized publicity banners for the show. In the warm breeze, they puff up like the sails on a ship. There are three: one of Dominic, one of Josephine, and one of me. Seeing my face up there had felt like a leap in my career. What a leap it was… straight into a sinkhole that sucks me under a little more every day.

The block teems with news vans and hordes of teenage fans, yet no one notices me. I speed-walk the last few blocks to the brick firehouse Patrick's turned into his studio and ring his doorbell. Not too long after, the door sweeps open.

"Dominic informed me you were coming. Come in." He leads me into the living room. His freshly shaved head reflects the sun pouring through the round skylight "You want something to drink?"

I sink down on the couch. "No."

Patrick's bare feet plod over the vintage tiles that are cracked in spots. "I know why you're here," he says, taking a seat across from me.

I link my fingers together. "Dominic wants to see if you captured anything…" I can't find the word, but Patrick finds it for me.

"*Peculiar*? You can say that."

My mouth feels as hot and dry as the air outside.

Patrick grabs his laptop from the coffee table and powers it on. Once he stops clicking, he rotates it toward me. In the background of one of his shots stand two shadowy figures. Even though they're grainy, they're recognizable. "I'm guessing that's your friend Dean, right?"

I wet my lips but don't talk.

"And that looks a hell of a lot like Sergeant Martin, doesn't it?"

Again, it's not a question.

He flicks through two more shots. One of Dean entering the water with Kevin and one of Dean in the water, alone. And then he closes his laptop and reclines in the high-backed chair he bought from a flea market. He told me all about it during a photoshoot once, so damn proud of his purchase.

"Tell me, Brook. Why should I turn these pictures in to you instead of to the police?" he asks. "It looks to me like the cops could make great use of them."

I drag my knotted fingers through my hair and sigh deeply. "Your career…it took off thanks to Dominic, didn't it? When he let you be the official photographer of the first *Masterpiecers'* competition three years back, right?"

This time, it's Patrick who stays silent.

"Don't do this for me. Do it for him."

"We'd be covering up a murder," he says.

"An alleged murder," I correct.

"Come on, Brook. I'm not an idiot. Kevin was murdered!"

My eyes go wide when I hear the words spoken out loud.

"We'll pay you."

"I don't want money. I want to know *why* I'd be doing this?"

"Kevin was a PI. Josephine hired him to nail Dom for something, anything, so she could get his job," I say. "You know the art business…it's not always black and white. Dom could've lost everything."

"So he told Dean to kill Kevin?"

"No. Dean chose to. He was trying to protect Dominic."

"Why?"

"I can't tell you."

"Oh, we are *way* beyond keeping secrets from each other, Brook. You're going to tell me right now, or I am leaking these."

"You wouldn't…"

"Do you want to test me?"

Although this is not my secret to tell, it's also no longer my secret to keep. "Dean is Dominic's son."

"Dominic has a kid?" he exclaims.

"Dominic has a kid," I repeat. Once it's sunk in, once Patrick has stopped blinking as though he has dust in his eyes, I add, "Do you have any pictures of Kevin running into the water alone?"

"One. But it was a while before the fireworks."

"Can you darken the sky and add some fireworks?" I ask.

"Brook…"

"If you do this, Patrick, Dominic will give you that private show you've been dreaming of. I'll see to it myself."

The sigh is replaced by a rapid intake of breath.

"It'll double your pictures' worth. Probably even triple it."

Patrick grimaces. He's going to accept. No one turns down easy access to fame and fortune.

I didn't.

"This"—he gestures between us—"this never happened. You got it? 'Cause if it does, Brook, I'll hang your ass right next to mine, and I don't mean on some pretty gallery wall."

I extend my hand to shake on another dangerous deal.

WHEN I LEAVE PATRICK'S, I walk for hours. I don't answer my father's phone call. I'm in no mood to meet him and Chase for lunch. If only I could walk to another town…or to another state. I bob along with the throngs of people clouding Third Avenue. No one recognizes me. After crossing Lexington, I amble through Grand Central, itching to buy a one-way ticket to anywhere, but it's an illusion to think I can escape.

An attractive illusion…

Dominic phones me. Did he sense what I was considering or does he have someone tailing me? I spin around and scan the enormous marble hall, but there are too many people to single out a tail.

Finally, I pick up the call.

"I'm on my way to your house. Apparently you're not there," he says.

Sighing, I say, "I'm on my way."

As I start weaving back through the mass of travelers, Dominic fills me in on Ivy and Lincoln's run-in with the press on the Brooklyn Bridge. Apparently Lincoln insinuated Ivy had a hand in Kevin's death. Detectives are heading over to my house to interview her again. My heart starts pumping, with contempt for Lincoln, with grief for Ivy, and with anxiety for myself. By the time I arrive downtown, I'm drenched in sweat and racked with tremors. Barely acknowledging the camera crew, I steal into my bedroom to shower and change. I don't usually pop pills, but I find a leftover Xanax and swallow it with a mouthful of cold water.

The water slackens the tightness in my shoulders, but does little to level my raging nerves. I pull on a white shirt and a pair of pants, then wander into the hallway. When I find Lincoln standing by the guestroom door, I shoot her a dirty look.

"Is she in there?" I ask, reaching for the handle.

"Yeah. And she's *super* pissy."

"Justifiably so, don't you think?" My hand shakes so badly I have trouble wrapping my fingers around the slender piece of metal keeping me from Ivy.

"Whatever," Lincoln says, blowing a strand of wheat-blonde hair out of her green eyes.

I'm about to tell her to go away when Dominic barges into the apartment through the front door that is wide open since it's part of the "set."

"Where is she?" he asks, his haggard gaze darting over mine. The skin underneath his eyes is puffy and dark, like mine. I wonder what state Dean's in. I can imagine him sprawled out on his thousand-thread comforter, comatose from snorting too much cocaine.

"In here," Lincoln says.

I draw the door open, and Dominic trundles in the bedroom ahead of me. Ivy is curled up on the bed. She looks so fragile and so small. Dominic lifts her feet to make space to sit, then asks me to leave and close the door. I listen to their muffled conversation until Dominic's lawyer and the two detectives erupt into the apartment. My trembling, which had lessened, starts up again. Every nerve in my body twitches at the sight of the two law-enforcement agents. Even my eyelids.

"Where's Ivy Redd?" the female detective asks, looking tightly at me.

My pulse jackhammers as her partner sizes me up too. "Here," I say, hoping my voice doesn't crack.

I press the door open. The two detectives and the Masterpiecers' lawyer troop in. Ivy is sitting up in bed, with her legs gathered against her. Her light blue eyes appear leaden. When they alight on me, my breath hitches. The detectives ask her about Kevin, about her whereabouts, about her drinking. I try to concentrate—what they're saying is important—but their words bounce off my eardrums.

When Ivy says, "He stole something from my room," I snap to attention. Is she talking about me?

I blink and stare at Dominic whose face also spasms.

"Are you sure?" he asks.

Ivy nods.

"What was it?" he asks.

Don't say a diamond!

"A piece of jewelry," she says.

"Why didn't you come to me with that? Or to Brook?" Dominic asks.

My shoulders jerk. I press them back until the blades touch and I've somewhat contained the juddering.

"Can you pull the camera footage?" Dominic asks me.

"There's no camera in the hallway," I say.

"The angle of the one in the living room should be wide enough to see if anyone went into her room." Dominic's forehead glistens with sweat. "This is just absurd! I swear, the show's cursed this year."

"Can we get back—" Detective Clancy begins, but Dominic interrupts her, "When did you notice the theft, Ivy?"

"The night Kevin arrived."

"And you're sure it couldn't have happened before he got there?" Dom asks.

"I'm sure. It was still in my bag when I left for the pool party."

Dominic slaps his thigh. "Absurd, I tell you. Brook, pull the footage of that day."

I swallow hard. "I'll phone Jeb."

"What were you doing in the ocean last night?" Detective Clancy asks Ivy.

"In case you didn't notice, there were a lot of people in the water," Ivy says.

"Yes, but what were *you* doing?" McEnvoy, the detective with the premature gray hair, asks.

A knock resounds in the room.

"Come in," Dominic says.

The door opens, and my little brother treads in. From the sour look on his face, I can tell Dad told him something. What? I don't know. But something. And for a millisecond, I feel better because I'm no longer the only one in the sinkhole. But then that feeling dissipates when Chase provides the detectives with one of Patrick's pictures—one of him and Ivy kissing. It's her alibi; while Kevin Martin drowned, she was busy swapping saliva with my brother. My stomach clenches, so I shut my eyes and work on erasing their kiss from my retina…from my memory.

"Will that do, detectives? Can I be dismissed?" Chase asks.

McEnvoy rips the picture from his partner's hand and ogles it. Then he flicks his index finger against it. "How do we know this hasn't been doctored?"

My brother's jaw clenches.

"Shut up, Austin," Detective Clancy mumbles, eyes flashing over the room.

"Thank you for your time, Counsel, Mister Bacci, Mister Jackson. Miss Redd, I'm sure we'll see each other again soon."

"Why would we?" Ivy asks.

"Just a hunch," she says.

Ivy blanches.

"Let me walk you out," Dominic suggests, ushering the lawyer and the two detectives out of the bedroom. Chase leaves right after them.

I need a stiff drink or I'm going to unravel like the black thread Troy stitched through Ivy's quilt.

"Brook," she calls out.

Wincing, I turn back toward her. Her skin looks like porcelain, like those hand-painted dolls Diana collects. She has an entire shelf of them. I remember lying in her bed about a year ago. She'd needed to discuss Chase's problem with expressing emotion, and apparently I was the right person to talk to about it. I'd stared up at those dolls, wondering how their unblinking ogling didn't freak her out.

"I have a paper to give to Dean. It's for Aster's trial." She slips her hand into her pocket and holds out a folded sheet.

I don't know what I was expecting, but not to be a mule for Dean. Though isn't that what I am? *All I am*… "Okay," I say, taking it from her fingers.

Her nails are shiny red. And long. She has beautiful hands. The sort of hands I would give anything to feel wending through my hair and caressing my bare skin.

I take the paper and tuck it inside my back pocket. "So you and my brother, huh?"

"There is no *me and your brother*."

"But the picture—"

"Pictures lie."

My pulse thrums with hope. *Stupid hope*. I lower my gaze from hers. "Kevin's personal effects are being packed up as we speak. I'll have the cleaners check for jewelry. What was it exactly that was stolen?"

She hesitates. Will she tell me the truth? Does she trust me enough?

"A necklace," she says.

The answer is *no*. Ivy Redd doesn't trust me. "Can you describe it for me?"

"It was a diamond pendant. I kept it in a porcelain box."

I look back up at her. "Why weren't you wearing it?"

"Because the show lends the jewelry. I thought my stylist would make me take it off."

"You should've left it at home then."

"I don't have a safe at home."

Then where did you put the others? I don't say this out loud, although I think it so loudly I think she'll hear me. I study her face, and my gaze is inevitably towed down to her lips, which she moistens with the tip of her tongue. I find myself leaning in, craving to close the distance between our mouths.

"Sorry to interrupt, Mr. Jackson, but we need to get Ivy ready for dinner," her stylist says.

I jolt away from her as though electrocuted.

"Already?" Ivy breathes, eyes cemented to mine.

God, don't look at me like that...not when others are around.

I shut my eyes to sever our connection, and then I nod and leave without turning back. I head to the terrace that's set for dinner and pour myself a glass of wine. I walk to the transparent railing and stare out at the sun setting over the Hudson River. The dark waters are thick with color—peach and gold and sapphire. As I sip my wine, they brighten and dance on the choppy surface, magnificent and vivid and full of life, a piece of art more glorious than any that graces a wall. But it's transient, and when I take my place next to Ivy at the dinner table, the colors have dimmed, smudging together, their glory tarnished by the absence of a sun.

The camera crew's bright lights fall on Ivy, even though she needs none to shine. Unlike nature, she is as stunning in darkness as she is in daylight.

Dominic begins dinner with a toast. "To Kevin, who we hope has finally found peace."

"Amen," I say at the same time as Josephine.

"*And*, to the most eventful, and surely the most memorable, competition." He smiles. How he can smile right now is beyond me. "And to the last two tests! We're raising the stakes."

"Shh...Dom," Josephine says. "Don't give it away."

"And to Chase's birthday...a happy one this time," Dominic adds as servers bring out little glass bowls of gazpacho.

"I'd also like to propose a toast," Josephine says. "*Plus de drame*. No more drama. Okay, Brook?"

Fear blooms through me. I down my glass of wine. I don't look at anything but my wine for the remainder of dinner. The line of liquid decreases then rises almost as fast, then dwindles again. When Josephine excuses herself—apparently she needs an early night—Dominic tugs me aside.

"Pull yourself together," he whispers.

"I'm trying."

"By drinking your weight in wine?" He snorts. "You should be sober, Brook. Alcohol makes people slip up. This is not the time to slip up."

After chastising me some more, he asks about Ivy's "missing jewel." And I tell him what she told me.

"I don't think she knows about the others," I murmur, watching the crew pack away the equipment.

"I'll inform Dean," he says.

"About Dean, Patrick asked—"

"If he was my son. I heard. He already called me to schedule his *big* show."

I cringe.

Instead of asking me what I was thinking, Dominic squeezes my shoulder. "You did good, kid...you're doing good," he adds as an after-thought or as an encouragement. I don't feel like I'm doing good. "Two more days."

"Two more days," I echo.

A tight smile curves his lips right before he leaves.

I return to the table that's been cleared. "Dom has agreed to let all of you hang out a while longer. To decompress," I tell Chase, Ivy, and Lincoln.

Chase eyes me. "Is that what *you're* doing?"

"If you were under the stress I was under, little brother, you'd—"

"I just think you should quit while you're ahead."

Did my father not tell him about our family's situation? "Why don't you mind your own business?"

Chase walks over to one of the lounge chairs.

"Well, this isn't awkward," Lincoln says. "I'm going to go powder my nose." She rises and heads inside.

"I feel like I'm missing something," Ivy says.

Fueled by all the alcohol I ingested, I observe her unabashedly. "Josephine doesn't like me."

"I don't think she likes anyone."

"Yeah, but she really has it in for me."

"Why?"

"Because she's afraid Dominic's going to promote me," I tell her.

"So what if he does?"

"I'd be taking her place."

"Ah. I can see how that would be a problem." She runs her tongue over her lower lip, making it glisten.

I contemplate her mouth. "Remember that day at the airport, when you arrived at the same time I did?"

"Hard to forget when someone treats you like dirt."

"Josephine orchestrated that."

"If you have proof, then she can't use it against you."

I lean in closer. "Exactly."

I lift my hand to tuck a strand of hair behind her ear.

"You shouldn't do that," she says.

"Do what?"

"Touch me. I'm a contestant."

I drop my hand back onto my lap. "Right."

"Crap. Now Lincoln's going to tell the press that you and I are hooking up," she whispers in my ear, tipping her head toward her nemesis.

Pleasure shoots through me. And power. There's not much I can fix right now, but this is within my means. "Watch me take care of that." I stand and walk over to Lincoln. "Want to go for a swim?"

She nods.

"Anyone else up for a midnight dip?" I ask loudly, hoping Ivy will come inside the pool too.

"I think I'm over midnight dips," she says.

I cover my disappointment with a hefty wink.

I change quickly into swim trunks. When I step back inside the darkened living room and spot her lying down on the lounge chair next to Chase, pieces of my heart flake off. I'm suddenly animated with the need to break something. My gaze brushes against the clear, bubble-shaped vase propped on my coffee table. I reach out for it as a hand skims over my back.

Lincoln stands there in a skimpy bikini. "When they said dinner was at your place, I hoped it entailed swimming."

To help Ivy, I was going to kiss Lincoln, but now, it won't be just to help her. I make a fist and dig my nails into my palm. Now, it will be to begin to forget her. She wants Chase; she doesn't want me.

TWENTY-SIX

DAY 8

JOSH

"The wife did it," the chief says, trundling into the meeting room on Monday morning. Claire and I are nursing mugs of hot, watery coffee, and Fred is nursing an extra-large glazed donut. "It's always the wife."

"Did what?" I ask.

"She killed her husband?" Claire asks.

"Which wife? Which husband?" I ask.

"She wasn't on the beach with them," Fred says.

"Someone died?"

All three pairs of eyes converge on me.

"Where did you spend your weekend? In a cave?" Claire asks.

Not too far off. "I was camping."

"Kevin Martin drowned on Saturday night, Coop," Guarda explains, while I stare at him wide eyed.

So that's what that couple was talking about in front of the cabin.

"Yeah…shocking," he says.

And crazy. And unsettling. Ivy must be beside herself.

"And Kevin Martin's wife is the one who tampered with the pictures of him," Guarda continues.

"So Aster is no longer a suspect," I say more than ask. Even though I'm furious with her because she lied to me about the diamonds, I'm relieved she didn't cheat to get Ivy on *The Masterpiecers*.

Guarda tosses a photocopy of what looks like a note on the table. "I went to high school with her lawyer, Mr. Kelley. He sent me this little nugget."

Fred picks up the sheet and scans it, then hands it over to Claire. I get it last. It has a few grease smudges, which makes one of the words hard to read.

"However, she is *not* the one who killed her husband. It was a suicide." He flicks a picture of Kevin running into the water, fireworks exploding over him, reflecting in the ominous black water.

Claire snorts and twirls her mug. Her fingers are thick and her nails are wide and cut off at the cuticles. They look like foreign hands that have been attached to a random body. "That's a pretty drastic move. End his life because of heartache and shame."

"Shame is a huge suicide factor. Depression's number one, but humiliation is right up there," I say.

"Look who's brushed up on his psychology," she says.

I stare down at the brown liquid that reminds me of the pond the twins' mother drowned in.

"Shut it, Claire," Fred says.

Claire grumbles, "Geez. I didn't know it was a sore subject."

"Chief, may I be excused? I'd like to go see Aster. Ask about those missing stones. I have a hunch she took them out of the quilt and hid them somewhere."

"I don't think today's a good day for that."

"Why not?"

"You haven't heard?"

"Heard what?"

"That Aster was locked in a freezer?"

"What?" My hands jerk, which makes my coffee tip over. A brown river flows toward Fred. It stops next to his empty plate. "Is she okay?"

"She's alive."

Ice shoots up my spine. "Was it an accident?"

"Apparently. But it's prison…if you get my drift," Guarda says, while Fred blots the spilled coffee with a paper napkin.

"Do we know why the wife confessed, Chief?" Claire asks. I'm not sure whether to feel relief at the change of subject or irritation.

I want to know more.

I want to know everything.

I want to know which cruel, nasty person could do this to my Aster.

"The wife felt guilty, and wanted to make things right by confessing. Kelley's going to pay her a visit tomorrow. Cooper, want to join him?"

I nod, even though my mind is on Aster. She must be terrified. And what was I doing while she was going through hell? Showing Heidi I could survive two full days without a phone and without Internet. I proved my point, but I also proved I was a great big idiot.

"Fred, what's the status on Diego Discoli?" Guarda asks.

"He's still locked up, but his trial's been postponed."

"Can you find out why it's been postponed?"

Fred nods, and carrying his plate with the small pile of sopping brown napkins, he walks off toward his desk.

"Claire, any leads on Elise Frothington?"

On the TV behind the chief, Lincoln, the pretty blonde contestant on the art show, is apologizing for having blamed Ivy for Kevin's death.

"What the?" I exclaim, walking up to the television screen.

"Ivy, I regret the terrible confusion my words created," the blonde is saying. "I didn't mean you any harm."

"*Ivy* was accused of murdering Kevin?" I shriek.

"Where the hell were you camping, Josh? Under a rock?" Claire asks.

"I turned off my phone," I say, although I shouldn't have to explain myself to my replacement. I'm sort of pissed she's still even on this task force.

Guarda stands next to me as the news channel replays some footage of the night on the beach, shots of Ivy and Kevin together at different moments of the evening.

"That's Kelley," Guarda says, pointing to a man whose head seems screwed right into his torso.

"Who's the guy next to him?" I ask. "The one with the red tie? I've seen him somewhere."

Guarda cocks an eyebrow. "Apparently, he's your girlfriend's lawyer. Dean Kane. Kelley says he's an arrogant prick."

"My—Aster doesn't have a lawyer."

"Are you sure?"

I squint at the screen, as though my retina could run some fancy face recognition system—which it can't, because I'm not a robot, *and* I don't have any fancy spy glasses, although I've been writing them on my Christmas lists since I was six.

"Where have I seen you, Dean Kane?" I ask out loud. When it hits me, I run to Fred's desk, swipe the Discoli file that he has opened in front of him, and run back, flipping through it until I find a picture of the same guy. He's wearing a grass-green tie in this one. I jam my finger on the picture. "He's Diego's lawyer!"

Guarda stares at the picture, then stares at me, then stares back at the picture. Claire's gaze follows the same trajectory.

"Shit," Guarda whispers, eyes and face glowing from the discovery. "Dig up everything you can on him."

Animated by the conviction that Dean Kane is one of our missing puzzle corners, we spend the next hour researching him, and boy, do we find *a lot* of stuff. A young nobody who went from living in a trailer park in Naples, Florida, with his mother, to an all-star Duke University graduate turned lawyer to the rich bastards of the world. In a society column, there's a picture of him in a tuxedo standing next to a woman who looks to be a decade older than him. Instead of a bow tie, he sports a hot-pink tie. How many ties does this dude own?

"Blow the picture up," Claire says, leaning over my shoulder, chomping on a piece of gum that smells like cough syrup. "Well hello, Elise."

I eyeball the woman holding Dean's arm. "*No*…no way."

The caption on the bottom reads, *Dean Kane and his mother, Alaina Kane.*

Claire must have told the chief and Fred to come over, because they're both there, pressing in.

"Troy went to Duke University. That's how they know each other," I say as Mann's file swims through my mind.

Guarda sucks in a breath, then straightens up. "It's time we call New York."

He's the first to leave, and then the two others peel themselves away from the space around me. Buzzing erupts inside my skull, or perhaps it's inside the room. I look at the phone on my desk and pick it up to call Aster's jail. After they authorize a visit, they ask me to hold for the shrink.

"Joshua Cooper?"

"How's Aster?"

"The nurse told me she was okay, considering. Look, I've been—"

"Just okay? Who did this to her?"

"She says it was an accident."

"Yeah, right."

I hear the shrink sigh. "I wanted to speak to you about something else."

"Can you make sure she's not returned with the rest of the prison population? I want better protection and better care. This *accident* is unacceptable! Actually, transfer me to the warden right away!"

"Officer Cooper, please. I have an urgent matter to discuss with you."

"More urgent than my friend's well-being?" I snap. "I don't think so."

"Were you aware that Ivy made her sister sign a document that gives her power of attorney over her?"

"What?"

"Aster signed it without understanding what it meant."

I want to say *what* again—scream it.

"Aster's lawyer emailed it to me this morning."

"Her lawyer?"

"Yes. A Mr. Kane."

I cradle my head, then glide my fingers down my face, squeezing it. Both my head and heart throb long after I hang up with her.

I realize I didn't get to talk to the warden. I'm about to dial the prison again when my phone rings. Maybe I can get a tête-à-tête with the warden after I see Aster.

"Officer Cooper," I say in an exhausted whisper.

"We were told you were the person to contact about the recent burglary at the Redd apartment."

"Yes. And you are?"

"The crime scene technician."

"Did you find anything?"

"Unfortunately, nothing besides your DNA and the twins' DNA. Whoever the perpetrator was, they were careful."

Of course they were. I'm not surprised by the news, but I'm irritated by it.

"You may clean up the apartment now as we are closing this case," the person on the other end of the line tells me. "Have a nice day."

Grumbling to myself, I pick up my cell to tell Heidi not to wait up for me tonight just as Angela Discoli waltzes in—or rather is escorted in by Claire. I jog to the hallway down which they've just turned. They're headed to an interrogation room. Angela's gaze flicks to mine. She doesn't say anything, yet I can hear a thousand words in her hostile stare.

When the door clicks shut behind both women, I jog to the adjoining room from which I can hear and observe the interview. Fred and Guarda are already inside, standing next to the glass, peering in at the pretty blonde and the not-so-pretty blonde. *Sorry, Claire*.

"You didn't tell me you were bringing her in," I say, breathless.

"The motel clerk phoned the precinct. He said she was going through the room she'd used with Troy Mann."

Angela's livid blue eyes find mine through the glass. I jerk back, but then remind myself that all she is seeing is her reflection. She probably knows it's not a mirror, though.

"Miss Discoli, what were you doing at 10:35 a.m. this morning in room 2B of the motel off route 9?" Claire asks.

"I was looking for a lost earring," Angela says.

"An earring?"

"Yes."

"And did you find your missing *earring*?"

Angela smirks, and runs one of her manicured hands through her hair. Her large blonde curls shimmer.

"Definitely took after her mother," Fred says, "because her father is one ugly bastard."

"Why are the hot ones always conniving?" Guarda says.

"Not always," I say, just as a tinny voice says, "Who's hot?" Both Fred and Guarda stare down at the cell phone in my hand. "Josh?" comes the distant voice.

"Crap," I mumble. I dialed Heidi without realizing it. I lift the phone to my ear and retreat to the back of the room. "Hey."

"You forgot me," Heidi says, pain tingeing her voice.

"I'm sorry, babe."

Guarda glares at me.

Cupping my hand over my mouth, I add, "Look I can't talk right now, but I need to go to the twins' place tonight. Clean it up. I don't want them coming back to it looking a mess."

"Want some help?" she asks.

"You must have better things to do."

"Then spend time with my boyfriend?"

I chew on my bottom lip. I can't have her around because I'm not just planning on cleaning it up; I'm planning on finding those diamonds. Plus, she doesn't know it was tossed. "This is something I need to do by myself."

"Fine," she says in a tight voice. "Bye, Josh."

When I return to the interrogation, I ask Fred, "You think she was looking for the missing diamonds?"

"Yeah."

"Did you search her?"

"Claire frisked her. She didn't find anything."

"She could've swallowed them."

"Considering she was still unscrewing the showerhead when we found her, I'd put good money down that she didn't recover them."

"Chief, I'm going to see Aster. The DOC gave me the green light."

Even though his chin is tucked into his neck, Guarda nods.

"Is Claire going to ask her about Dean Kane?" I ask before stepping out.

"We're going to ask her about every fucking person in her life. I'll phone you if we get anything," Guarda says.

I pull open the door and rush out of the precinct toward my car. After pumping the music up, I set out toward the jail. Thirty minutes into the trip, I blow a tire. I slap my steering wheel before driving the car to the side of the highway. Then I mutter a long strand of ugly words. If my mom were here, she'd make me drop quarters into her curse jar.

I get out of the car, pop the trunk, and grab the extra tire and toolkit. This isn't my first rodeo changing a tire, but it is the first time I have to do it in ninety-degree weather on the side of a highway. The last two times were in town, and both times, I'd managed to pull the car into a parking lot.

I set everything out and begin to loosen the lug nuts when this idiot in a Range Rover drives so close to me, I can actually feel the boiling air vibrate against my backside. I jump up and give him the finger but he's already long gone. I bet he was speeding. How I wish I could've pulled him over and fined him.

I squat back down to finish loosening the lug nuts and then wedge the jack under the car body and begin cranking it. Something creaks and I barely have time to jolt out of the way before the jack shatters and my car comes crashing down.

"Fuck!" I explode. Another quarter pings into Mom's curse jar.

I yank my phone out of my jacket pocket to call AAA only to notice that it's run out of battery. I didn't use it all weekend! How could it have run out of battery? I kick the flat tire. Repeatedly. The nearest exit is seven miles away. *Seven miles!*

So many choice words fly out of me that the sound of a Vegas slot machine goes off in my scorched brain. Attempting to calm down, I stare at the highway and debate whether to walk the distance or get a ride. I'm already sweating profusely, so I decide to stick my thumb out. Even though I don't have my patrol car, I'm dressed like a cop. Someone is bound to pick me up.

Or not.

An hour slips by and I'm still standing there with my thumb out, and probably, with the sunburn from hell. Fourteen cars have passed me and none have stopped. They didn't even slow. People probably think I'm a fake cop, one of those who pull you over to rob you. Even though I'm tempted to sit back inside my broken-ass vehicle, and wait for traffic to pick up—I'm bound to find one nice soul then—I start walking.

And I walk.

It takes me almost two hours to reach the exit. I feel as though I've been dunked in a pool fully clothed. Every inch of fabric sticks to my burning skin. I start fantasizing about freezers and ice cubes. The fantasy eggs me on. When a gas station shimmers ahead of me, I blink to make sure it's not a mirage. It trembles in the stiflingly humid heat, but remains right there.

To say the teenager behind the counter is surprised when I walk in would be an understatement. His eyes bulge like anthills. "You okay, sir?"

"My car broke down seven miles back, and then my phone died, or maybe my phone died before my car broke down, and I don't have my police radio, so no, I'm not okay." I don't mean to be rude, but I am pissed at the world.

The teen jumps off his stool behind the cash register and brings me a bottle of cold water, free of charge. "You a police officer?" he asks, as I gulp it down.

"Yeah." I tap the badge hooked onto my belt. The metal part feels like it's just come out from welding and the leather around it is stewing in sweat.

The kid stares at it. "You can use the phone in the back, sir."

He leads me to a back room that's more of a closet than a room, but who am I to complain? There's a working phone and fan. I grab the phone and dial AAA. After explaining where I left the car, I ask them to meet me at the gas station. Planting my face against the fan, I call the precinct and ask to be patched through to Fred. He tells me they got nothing from Angela, and I tell him I got nothing from Aster besides a blown tire.

"But guess who else went to Duke University?" he says.

"Who?"

"Brook Jackson."

I gasp, gulping down so much fan air I start coughing.

"They were all roommates their sophomore year," he continues.

I cough so hard I can't get any air in...I can only push air out. My lungs feel sore and compressed, as though Fred were sitting on them.

"You okay, Coop?"

"He's the—he's—" I hold my breath to calm the spasms.

"Yeah. He's the one linked to the Masterpiecers. Apparently, Josephine already had doubts about him. She even provided proof of his involvement."

"What did she have on him?"

"Don't know. The Feds wouldn't tell."

Damn Feds. "When are they going to arrest him?"

"Tomorrow."

"Why not right now?" I snap.

"They want to interview Dominic Bacci to see if he knew about it, or if he could give them more info. But don't worry. They *will* get him."

"As long as Ivy is out there, and he is too, she's at risk."

"Josephine asked the show's videographer to keep an eye on her. Apparently he's monitoring the security cameras."

"That doesn't reassure me."

After hanging up with him, I call the prison and ask to speak to Aster because there's no way I'm making it out to her jail before visitation hours end, but I'm told she's unable to speak at the moment. Shrink's orders.

"You don't understand. This is urgent," I shout into the phone.

"You take it up with the warden. I'm just following orders," the woman says.

"Patch me through to the warden then."

"Don't you use that tone of voice with me, mister."

The recycled air pulses up my nostrils. "I need to speak to Inmate Redd's warden. This is—"

"Visiting hours start at 8 a.m. tomorrow. Goodbye."

When the dial tone drones in my ear, I growl and throw the phone against the desk. The battery compartment cracks off and the batteries fly out. As I reassemble it, my fingers shake because putting this back together is easy. Putting my life—and the twins' lives—back together is beginning to feel impossible.

TWENTY-SEVEN

Brook

Lincoln is clingy the night of the art heist. It's partly my fault—I shouldn't have kissed her in my swimming pool. But Lincoln is the least of my worries. It's Dean who's at the forefront of my mind. I called him several times to find out how he was doing and what he was doing and didn't even get a text back.

"Any news from Dean?" I whisper in Dominic's ear after he's done greeting the director of the Museum of Modern Art.

Dominic smiles warmly at the retreating man. When he's not looking any longer, the smile washes off his face. "Not here."

"Did you tell him about the detectives?"

Dominic spears me with a dark look.

"Did you—"

He drags me toward the orchestra. The vibrations from the brass instruments throttle my eardrums. "I don't want to worry him. Besides, it'll blow over soon."

I don't see how this is going to blow over; I only see how this is going to blow up.

"In other news, Josephine and I talked this afternoon. She admitted hiring Kevin to investigate me."

"She confessed this? To you?"

"Yes. She wanted to ask for my forgiveness. She realized she'd been wrong in assuming I was part of anything. She had the Masterpiecers' bank records pulled.

Our school has done no wrong." Dominic smooths out my burgundy lapel. "I told her it was unacceptable and asked for her resignation."

Tonight, I didn't get to wear my own clothes. I had to match Dom. My get-up makes me look like I'm part of the circus. "So she's resigning?"

"She has to. After what she's done." Dominic smiles. "You can relax now. Everything's going to be fine, Brook."

I chew on my lip.

"How are your parents?"

"My parents? Uh…I think they're okay."

"Call them tonight. I'm sure they'd like to hear from you."

"O-Okay."

"Now let's go. Our audience awaits. And our contestants."

Sure enough, Ivy, Chase, and Lincoln are taking their places on the stage. Ivy is in black tonight, which makes her look elegant, but also in mourning. Even her face seems strained. She's still beautiful, but she doesn't glow like she did the first night she was up there.

As Dominic begins his show, asking the audience if any of them had guessed that today's test was an art heist, I stare at the Egyptian temples' floor-lit carvings.

Josephine is resigning. Everything will be okay.

The lights dim and the three screens hanging around the room light up with the picture of Chase. He's winner number one. I already knew that. He worked at Christie's, and that's where he chose to perform his art heist, so it was no surprise when he walked out of the auctioneers with his stolen piece tucked under his arm. He says they ate up his lie about our mother wanting to see the piece hung in our family home before purchasing it, but I'm pretty certain Dominic called ahead.

Ivy's hands wring together in her lap. She's nervous because she's not aware she's the other winner. The deserving winner. What a performance she gave in the Museum of Modern Art. To torture her, Dominic asks Jeb to play both her heist and Lincoln's before announcing the second winner.

I watch her performance again, and again I find it exceptional. From the camera hooked into her shirt, I see what Ivy saw when she stepped into the MoMA, when she rode the escalator up to one of the galleries, when she located the painted silk tissue installation she had to steal, when the museum-goers swarmed around her begging for autographs. In part thanks to her cunning and in part thanks to the accidental mob, she surreptitiously pocketed the silken prizes.

Her profile glows from the projection. When the drumroll resounds through the room, she sits up straighter, but there's the slightest quiver in her shoulders, as though the rumble were inside her. And then the room goes dark. I keep my eyes on her as she's plunged in shadows. When the screen flashes with her picture, her mouth curves with a smile that takes my breath away.

If only that smile were for me.

At least it's not for my brother.

Her delight is contagious and loosens the tendrils of angst that locked around me the day her quilt arrived empty.

During dinner—which the contestants attend tonight—I lope around the room, stopping by tables, making small talk with our clients and our benefactors, high on

Ivy's bliss. I save her table for last. When I reach it, I slide my hands over her shoulders.

She tips her face up to mine.

"How many special orders have you received already?" I ask her, grinning.

"None yet."

Her skin is soft and warm. "What? What's wrong with you people? Grab her while you still can."

"We were waiting until dessert to ask such forward questions," the curator of the MoMA says with a chuckle.

Across the table from Ivy, Paul Willows—a blond art dealer who graduated from the Masterpiecers ten years ago and whose father Dad detests—leans back in his chair and folds his arms over his chest. "I'd like to buy your entire collection, Ivy."

I laugh. It's a nervous sort of laughter. I hate Paul. Paul is not touching Ivy's art.

"I'm serious. All of the pieces you've made," Paul tells her, keeping his eyes on me.

My laughter dries up, and my fingers tense against Ivy's shoulders.

"Have you signed with anyone yet?" Paul asks her.

"Signed? You mean with a gallery?" She sits up straighter and shakes her head no.

"But if she wins tomorrow, she'll automatically be represented by the school." If I could get my hands on a microphone, I'd shout it to everyone in the room.

"And if she loses?" Paul asks.

"She'll be represented by me."

Ivy tips her face up again, surprise etched in her blue eyes.

"Are you allowed to take on private clients, Brook?" Paul asks.

My fingers are so tight now they're probably bruising her skin. "Why don't we discuss this matter tomorrow, in private?"

"With pleasure. You have my number. Call me at your convenience."

Because I need to cool down, and because our conversation has created tension, I move away from the table, but keep my eyes on Ivy. When she stands, I wind my way back toward her. I find her talking to some overly done-up woman whose dress looks two sizes too small.

"Excuse me," I tell the woman. I surely know her, but I don't bother retrieving her name from the depths of my memory. "I need a word with my contestant." When she leaves, I say, "Don't sign with that guy, okay?"

Her unsteady breath tickles my jaw. "Are you really going to offer me representation?"

"I've been considering it."

"Are you allowed?"

I make up something about it being a clause I've asked the show's lawyer to implement in my contract. "I just need to get it past Dom."

"And past Josephine," she says.

"Josephine's opinion won't matter."

"It won't?"

"No. Soon it won't."

"Is she leaving the school?" Ivy asks.

"I wouldn't use the word *leaving*, but yes. Something like that."

"Was she fired?"

I've said too much. I need to quit while I'm ahead. "The heist was all Dom's idea," I say, before anyone overhears us.

"What an idea. Anyway, I should get to bed. Larceny is exhausting, isn't it?"

I gawk at her.

"Goodnight," she says, and turns to leave.

I start to follow her. I'm sick of this. So sick of all these secrets. I want to tell her everything. But of course, someone captures my arm and tows me back to discuss some emerging artist before tossing me to his friend like a chew toy. By the time everyone's done trying to scrape information from me about which rising star to bet on, Ivy's long gone.

My confession will have to wait until tomorrow.

TWENTY-EIGHT

JOSH

As the highway blurs past, I rub my temples to combat the headache that's made my skull throb since I found out about Dean Kane and Brook Jackson's friendship.

At least I'm not the one driving. I would've swerved into a ditch or rear-ended another vehicle by now. I flash my eyes to Guarda's friend, Kelley, Kevin's former lawyer. I met him two hours ago, when he came to pick me up from the twins' apartment to drive to Columbus, Ohio to visit the widow.

Apparently, we're not just going to offer our condolences anymore. Guarda thinks Dean Kane is behind the note she wrote her husband. He wants us to get proof so we have solid grounds for an arrest, because apparently being a Discoli louse isn't enough.

"It was her signature on the paper, wasn't it?" I ask Kelley as we pass the sign for Springfield.

"Yeah, but I don't know. Don't you think it was convenient?"

It is convenient. "But she confirmed she wrote it?"

"Yeah. But it ain't right. It just ain't right." With his polo shirt buttoned up to the top, he looks like he has no neck. "What were you doing at Ivy's place?"

"Cleaning it up. It was broken into about a week ago."

"For the missing diamonds?" he asks.

"Chief Guarda told you about the case?"

"My client drowned on a show that's being sniffed out by the Feds, so yeah, I know everything about your case. Did you find them?"

I think of the hours I spent rearranging the rolls of fabric, the bookshelves, the closets, the kitchen cabinets. Fruitless hours. I press my lips together. "No. I didn't find them." And I'd searched underneath their mattresses, in the couch cushions, in places even the intruder hadn't touched. "Dean was on the beach the night Kevin drowned, wasn't he?"

Kelley frowns. "He was. But he left after speaking with Ivy."

"Are you sure?"

"What are you getting at?"

"What if Dean had a hand in Kevin's death?"

"Kevin ran into the ocean. There was a picture of him."

"Pictures can be tweaked."

Kelley spins his face toward me so fast, the car swerves too. Horizontal grooves form on his forehead. "Guarda told me he requested more footage, but there wasn't anymore."

"Brook Jackson could've made it disappear."

Kelley glances my way again. And the car veers to the right, again.

As I seize the grab handle over my window, my stomach squeezes as though it's about to eject the lone granola bar I ate for breakfast. "Could we stop for a sec?"

"I was just about to suggest it."

I buy a sandwich and a cold Coke that help lessen the nausea caused by my lack of sleep and my surplus of stress. They do little to squelch the queasiness from Kelley's erratic driving. To avoid distracting him, I don't utter a single word during the last half hour of our trip. Instead, I pretend to sleep.

Kelley taps my shoulder. "We're here."

We've pulled up in front of a simple one-story house in a cookie-cutter neighborhood. Every home on the block is single storied and painted the same shade of carpet beige. Only the mailboxes planted by the driveways are different. The one in front of the Martins' home resembles a birdhouse. It's probably confusing for the postman…and for the birds.

We park the car on the street, then walk up to the house and press on the doorbell that chirps like cheery birds. *Obsessed much?*

There are no approaching footsteps, no movement of the doorknob. Kelley digs his cell out of his jeans and dials her number. The home phone rings. We can hear it through the plaster walls. At least it sounds like a proper ringtone, not some bird song. Not that I have a problem with birds.

As we wait, I slink along the wall of the house until I reach a set of windows that look into a kitchen. The phone's still ringing.

"Are you sure she's expecting us?" I ask Kelley.

His brow furrows. "Go round the back."

So I take off at a trot and travel around the house, peering into every window. Only her bedroom window is obscured by drapes. I knuckle the glass. She must be asleep. If I'd led someone to suicide, I'd be holed up to lose track of time, too.

I knock again. Harder this time.

I'm about to return to Kelley and suggest we kick the door down, when the shiny eggplant drapes tremble. A set of dark eyes stare out at me. Involuntarily, I jerk back. Mrs. Martin cracks the window open.

"Fuck off," she says. "I'm not giving interviews."

"I'm here with Mr. Kelley…your lawyer?"

The whites of her eyes are red.

"I'm real sorry for your loss, ma'am," I add, to make myself sound nicer, even though I don't think many nice things about this woman. She crushed her husband's hopes. Wives are supposed to be supportive, not destructive. My mother always champions my father. They're a team. That's what she told me once. Teammates in life and for life.

"Mr. Kelley's here?" Her face is mega white and her neck, too. The only color on her body is her neon yellow bra and panty set. "I'm comin'," she grumbles, shutting the window and yanking her curtains closed again.

I scurry back to the front door where Kelley is still waiting. I nod to him as the door swings open.

His eyebrows shoot up in surprise. "Mrs. Martin, I left you a message to tell you—"

"I've stopped checking my phone. Too many fuckin' messages," she says, tying on a silk robe.

Kelley shifts his weight from one white-socked-loafer to the other.

"Well, are you gonna come in, or you gonna stay planted out there?" she says.

His gaze dips to her inner thigh and that bright underwear of hers, which is totally exposed since she didn't tie her robe very tight. I don't think she notices since she doesn't adjust it, or maybe she doesn't care.

Kelley steps in, and I follow suit.

"I'm sorry, Mrs. Martin," he says.

"Yeah, yeah," she mumbles as she leads us toward the couch with a…*wait for it*…bird pattern on it. Various colored-glass birds sit on an otherwise empty bookcase. I wonder if she likes birds or if it was Kevin's passion.

"You didn't come here to tell me that, did you, Mr. Kelley? You came to ask me why I did it, didn't you? It's not a crime to write your husband a letter."

"But it is a crime to tamper with pictures," he tells her.

"I said I was sorry about that. You're my counsel. Why are you even givin' me shit about it?"

"Since I am your counsel, why didn't you come to me with your note? Why did you go to Dean Kane?"

"He came over and told me the Redd sisters were going to press charges if I didn't come clean."

My gaze drifts beyond her, to three packed suitcases. "Are you going somewhere, Mrs. Martin?"

Her ghost-white cheeks flare. "I was going…I was going to visit my mother out in Texas when I received the news of"—her voice catches—"of Kevin's crazy reaction to my letter."

Kelley reclines backward into the couch to dig something out of his jeans pocket. "So you *weren't* booked on a flight to Belize?"

She blinks. I blink too since he didn't breathe a word about it during the two-and-a-half-hour car ride.

"What? No." She shrugs, which makes the robe fall open even more. I really try not to stare.

Kelley points to the printout. "But it says here—"

"Okay, fine. I was going to go away. I wanted to leave Kevin. He cheated on me! And with guys. I should've known what he was…" She shakes her head and her hair whips her almost-bare chest. "Never wanted to have sex with me. Do you know how that feels? I started wonderin' if there was somethin' wrong with me. It effed-up my self-esteem. And before you ask, I didn't mean for my note to make him commit suicide. I'm not some cold-hearted bitch. But I did mean to hurt him. He hurt me so fuckin' much."

"Did Dean Kane give you anything in exchange for the note?"

"Yeah."

I scoot closer to the edge of my seat. *This is it.* The morsel that will help us put him away for good. I'm winded by how easy it was to obtain. I suppose wronged people have no trouble—

"He gave me five phone numbers. Kevin's lovers. You want the list?"

"I thought you modified those pictures because you already knew about his lovers."

She flushes again. "I only knew about two of them."

"Did he give you any monetary compensation for it?" Kelley says, disregarding her offer for the list.

"Are you askin' if he bought my confession?" She drums her hot orange nails against her bare knee.

"It's come to our attention that you've come into a bit of money recently."

She stops the drumming.

"Mind telling me where this money came from, Mrs. Martin?" Kelley asks.

The doorbell chimes before she has time to respond. It sounds like we're sitting in a huge birdcage. The pealing makes my temples throb. Not bothering to pull her robe closed, she walks over to the door and flings it open. The UPS man's gaze zeroes in on her bare legs and sticks there for an inappropriate amount of time.

Since he just stands there, she yanks the oddly shaped package from his arms and begins closing the door in his face.

He finally reacts. "I need a signature."

She takes the small stylus he hands her, signs his screen, then kicks the door closed. She walks back into the living room and plops the bundle down on the coffee table. "At least it's not flowers. I swear, if I get another condolence bouquet…" She picks up a pen and jams it into the sticky tape, then drags it the length of the package and underneath the flaps.

Black eyebrows pinching together, she takes ahold of what's inside and pulls it out. At first, I think it's a snake.

"What is this?" she asks, nose crinkled.

"It's the rope Kevin made on the beach," Kelley explains.

Her throat convulses as she studies her dead husband's work, and tears snake out of her eyes. She doesn't bother blotting them as she walks into the kitchen, still clutching the rope. From where I'm sitting, I see her pull open the drawer underneath the kitchen sink and release it into what I imagine is a trashcan.

She returns and sits back down, folding her legs and jiggling one of her feet. "Could we do this some other time? I'm not feelin' too well."

"Tell me where you got the thirty-thousand dollars and we'll get out of your hair."

She pinches the bridge of her nose. "From a Mega Cash scratchy ticket."

"You have it here?"

"No. You gotta give it in to win the prize."

"Where did you claim it?"

"I don't remember. I was so fuckin' excited that I walked into the first 7-Eleven and they gave me cash for it."

"That's interesting," Kelley says, leaning back into the couch. Kelley proceeds to explain that they wouldn't give her that amount in cash but would've had to write a check.

We caught her. But most importantly, we caught Dean Kane.

"So Dean Kane gave you money?" I ask, point blank.

"Uh. No. I won—"

"Mrs. Martin, please. Stop lying," Kelley says. "The more you lie, the less I'll be able to help you."

She stares at her lawyer, wide eyed.

"Now, tell me the whole truth," he says, and she does.

Dean Kane falsified those pictures to get the PI off the show, then paid her thirty grand to take the blame for them. We phone the local police to place Mrs. Martin under house arrest until we can get her testimony in writing, then we phone Guarda with the news that we can officially put out a warrant for Kane's arrest.

Once I'm done rattling on about what a genius Kelley is, and what a dumbass Kane is, he asks, "You sitting, Coop?"

The blood drains from my face, because no one asks you to sit to give you good news.

"Mr. Kane visited Aster's prison this morning, Joshua."

I swallow. He never calls me by my first name.

"He slipped an inmate a weapon. Told her to threaten Aster with it so she would cough up the location of his diamonds." He stops talking. I don't want a cliffhanger; I want the rest. I want the entire story. I'm about to tell him not to leave me hanging when he adds, "It did a lot of damage. She's in a coma."

I feel hot and cold, I sweat and shiver, and then I dash out of the living room and throw up in the flowerbed on the side of her house until I've poisoned all the flowers like Kevin's wife, Dean Kane, Brook Jackson, Troy Mann…like they've all poisoned my sweet Aster.

TWENTY-NINE

DAY 9

Brook

Finding the right words to confess everything to Ivy kept me up all night. Around sunrise, I turned off the TV, rolled off the couch, and went for a swim. The water invigorated me, and followed by a glass of iced coffee, I almost feel human when I stroll onto the set. I smile politely at Jeb's crew, then mingle with the audience until Ivy and Chase penetrate the Temple room for their final test: finding a fake painting. The catch: the gallery will be full of forged pieces.

Dominic chose this test because Chase would excel at it. I was enthusiastic when he ran it past me, but today, I wish the trial had been to create something, because then, without a doubt, Ivy would win.

As we walk toward the designated gallery, I look at Ivy, and keep staring at her long after we've arrived. Dominic introduces both her and Chase to the two art experts who are supposed to help them understand how to use the advanced technology laid out before them. Both experts are smart and trained at the Masterpiecers. I went on a date with one of them two years back.

When Dominic gives his okay to start, Chase all but pounces onto the one I'd wined and dined. He should've let Ivy pick first. I scowl at him, and he glares right back. This show did nothing to bring us closer.

Ivy is so focused that I don't get more than a fleeting glance from her. As Dominic speaks to me about his projects for the school come fall, I keep my eyes on her. At some point, she reaches for the x-ray binoculars at the same time as

Chase. I half-expect my brother to swipe them, but instead, he grasps Ivy's hand, pries it open, and sets the silver binoculars into her palm. I stiffen as their fingers and eyes lock.

"I suspect those two like each other," Dom whispers. "They're rather sweet together, don't you think?"

I fold my arms in front of my chest so tight I'm cutting off circulation in my forearms. As Dominic explains how their budding romance will bolster the show's ratings, my hands go cold and stiff. He's aware I like Ivy, and yet he salts my wounded ego.

When Ivy and Chase walk up to us with their answers, I tell Ivy to come with me, but I never get to lead her out of the room. Josephine surges out of nowhere, flanked by Lincoln and a man she introduces as her lawyer. My heart hurtles around my chest like a trapped mouse.

Josephine asks to speak to Dominic in private. Seemingly exasperated, he latches on to her elbow and accompanies her out of the room. The contestants are taken away, and the ending of the test is delayed. The upheaval has caused a great amount of uneasiness within the crowd. My head buzzes too loudly to concentrate on their whispered hypotheses of what could be going on. As they're herded out of the gallery and out of the museum, Jeb latches on to my arm and guides me out too.

"What's going on?" I ask before taking the elevator down to the parking lot.

"Everyone's been asked to go home and change, and return at seven o'clock sharp."

My heartbeat picks up momentum. "Why?"

"For the concluding celebration," the short videographer tells me.

"But Josephine—"

"Came to speak with Dominic about her resignation."

"You know about that?"

"I know about everything around here."

Everything? I shiver.

"Go home, Brook. See you at seven."

Jeb unhands me when the doors open. I walk into the elevator, and as it dips below ground, so does my dread. It sinks through me and spreads until I shake so much that putting one foot in front of the other becomes a feat. On my way downtown, I replay Jeb's words, that this is about Josephine's resignation. If she wants her job back, making a spectacle of her demands might get Dominic to fold.

I take the elevator up to my penthouse and pace around it like a caged tiger. My mother phones to ask what's going on, and I tell her the two heads of the Masterpiecers have been on the outs.

"It's just an ego thing, Mom."

"Has Dominic offered *you* her position?"

"No."

"I heard rumors he was thinking about it."

"I don't want her position."

"Don't be a fool, Brook. If he presents you with this opportunity, you take it, you hear me? There's nothing left for you at home."

Her words make my throat tighten.

"How's Chase? He looked confident today."

The mere thought of Chase is like a tornado striking after a tsunami.

"Honey?" Mom says. "Are you still there?"

"I have to go," I whisper. "I'll come up to see you in Rhode Island tomorrow or the day after, okay?"

"Oh, that would be lovely. Bring Chase."

"Sure," I tell her, even though I refuse to take a three-hour car ride with my brother. I've seen enough of him these past few days.

After I hang up, Dominic calls to tell me Josephine decided not to resign.

"What was Lincoln doing there?" I ask him.

"She's Jo's new assistant. Birds of a feather, those two. But don't worry…I'm sure you won't need to see too much of Lincoln. Unless you *want* to see too much of her. I heard you two had a moment in your pool."

A beat passes. "You're misinformed, Dominic."

He makes a sound, like a grunt. "Anyway, wear a tux tonight," he says before disconnecting.

His explanation doesn't appease me. I lie down on my bed to mull things over, but end up sleeping. When I wake, it's a quarter past six. In a panic, I pull on my tuxedo and comb some gel into my hair.

"This is the last night," I tell my mirror image. "Last night."

Grabbing my keys and cell phone, I walk out my door and go down into the street where the driver who dropped me off is already waiting. Maybe he was always there. I climb into the car and send Diana, who's left me half-a-dozen messages, an emoticon of a thumbs up.

When I arrive at the museum, the driver drops me off in front of the mammoth entrance. Along with the other attendees, I make my way inside, dodging one question after another. I spot Madame Babanina a few paces ahead of me, twittering with her high-society friends. Hoping she doesn't notice me, I hurry past them into the Temple room and make a beeline for the stage, watching the small entrance for Ivy and Chase. Without uttering a single word, Josephine sidles in next to me.

"Lincoln's a liar," I say. "You shouldn't associate with her."

"Aren't we all liars?" she asks, keeping her eyes on the entrance.

My heart jabs my ribcage. The temptation to get the hell away from these toxic people almost overpowers me, but again, I stay stoic, slap on a smile, and remind myself that in a couple hours, I'll be free.

Ivy steps into my line of sight, and my breath catches like it did ten days ago. Her blonde braid gleams as it dips over her shoulder and curves over one of her breasts. I hope she'll be able to forgive— My train of thoughts screeches to a halt when I spot her hand entwined with my brother's.

"We've made it," Dominic yells to the enchanted crowd.

I keep staring at Ivy's hand. She's released my brother's, yet I can't shake the image of their fingers overlapping. Josephine jabs me with her elbow. Rigid with rage, I glare at her. I hate her. With all my heart, I hate her. I also loathe Chase, and I don't like Dominic much either.

She tips her chin toward my right side where an assistant is extending two electronic tablets. Stiffly, I take them from him and carry them over to Ivy and Chase so they can write down their answers. I can't bear to look at Ivy, neither when I hand her the tablet, nor when I collect it.

Her hand shakes. If she'd chosen me, I would have held it.

My brother wins, and although I clap his back, I don't feel happy for him. My gloominess is exacerbated when I see Lincoln speaking with Ivy.

Her calculating green eyes lock on mine. Evil witch. "So you're working for the devil, now?"

"If Josephine's the devil, what does that make you, Brook?" She resents me for our meaningless kiss. "Enjoy your evening. I know I will." She winks and leaves.

"Did she really get eliminated yesterday because of...of what happened in your pool?" Ivy asks.

"Is that what she told you?"

She nods.

"She was eliminated because she was careless," I tell her, just as Madame Babanina locates me.

"Brook, dear, you look so handsome tonight," she says, not bothering to address Ivy. Perplexed by Lincoln's words, I don't tell her to leave me alone even though I'm screaming it inside my mind.

"So, this is goodbye?" Ivy asks.

Lincoln is whispering something into Josephine's ear. "I suppose it is," I say distractedly.

The divorcée's curvy bangs bob against my jaw as she slides her hands around my arm. "I have someone I'd like you to meet. He'd like to start a collection, and I was thinking who better to advise him than—"

I start to shake her off when the entire room goes eerily quiet. The lights flare overhead, and then the detective with the prematurely graying hair bursts into the room.

"FBI," McEnvoy yells. "Nobody move!"

Madame Babanina drops my arm and slinks to the back of the room, along with a large chunk of the crowd.

His partner, Clancy, pops into my line of sight, also in navy and yellow FBI garb. She walks straight up to me. "Brook Jackson, put your hands where I can see them."

Terror flares through me. I rock back.

"Hands up, Jackson, now," she repeats.

In slow motion, I raise my arms. I look for Dominic but instead find Josephine beaming with a savage grin.

"Brook Jackson, you are under arrest for colluding with wanted criminals, trafficking stolen goods, and laundering money for the mafia."

"What?" I yelp. "This is fucking ridiculous."

Josephine waves her hands in the air. In one of them, she clutches the empty, torn package Ivy's quilt arrived in.

"What the hell is that?" I ask, even though I know exactly what it is. Frantically, I search for Dominic. I can't find him, goddammit! I glare at Josephine as the room fragments around me. I listen as she accuses me of using art for terrible things. I can't decide whether to yell or bawl. Finally, I spot my boss.

"Dominic, tell them this is a misunderstanding," I plead.

Slowly, hunched over, Dominic shakes his head and walks away. *He walks away!*

"With these rights in mind, do you wish to speak to me?" Clancy asks me.

I swing my face toward her. "I'm not speaking to you, or to anyone else here. I want a lawyer. Chase, call Dean right away!" Might as well take him down with me.

"Dean Kane?" McEnvoy asks.

"Yes!"

"Doubt Mr. Kane can represent you as he'll be needing his own defense." McEnvoy glances at Ivy when he says this. "Once we catch him."

"What are you talking about?" I ask in a shrill voice.

Clancy moves toward Ivy. "Ivy, why don't you come with me?" she says, her voice low.

"Wh-why?" Ivy stutters.

She looks around. Agents are escorting the agitated audience outside.

"What happened?" she asks.

"Your sister was attacked."

She pales. "Attacked?"

Clancy nods.

"Is she…is she alive?" she asks, as Chase winds one arm around her waist. I glare at his arm.

"She's in a coma," Clancy says, then tells her that Dean gave one of the other inmates a blade to attack Aster.

"I don't understand," Ivy says, but I do.

I squeeze my eyes shut.

"Why did Dean order the hit?" Ivy asks.

"To retrieve the diamonds Troy Mann hid inside your quilt."

"Diamonds?" She looks genuinely surprised.

"Dean and Troy were working together."

"But then that would mean—" Ivy swings her gaze toward me. "You didn't send Dean to help her. You sent him to execute her!"

Her words and her expression drain my lungs of air. When she launches herself at me, and Chase holds her back, I freeze.

"Let go of me!" she screams.

"No," my brother says.

"Let go of me right now or so help me God—"

He still doesn't.

"Chase, please," she begs, her voice breaking.

"Did your sister take the diamonds, Ivy?" Clancy asks.

"I don't know," she says.

I start laughing, a nervous, uncontrollable laughter, the sort of laughter that possesses mourners during funerals. I try to stop it, but everything inside and outside of me has become uncontrollable. Tears drip from the corners of my eyes. I shut them to push them out. When I crack my lids open, Ivy's expression has morphed into pure hatred.

Clancy turns to her partner. "Take him away," she says, at the same time as Chase whispers, "He's not worth it," in Ivy's ear.

Those words shatter what's left of me.

PART 3
AFTER

THIRTY

JOSH

Today is the fourth week of Aster's coma. The doctors aren't pessimistic about her remission, but they don't offer guarantees. One of the nurses tells me she's even noticed spikes in her pulse. The EEG waves in her brain are faster, and apparently that's a good sign.

I've spent so little time with Heidi in the past few weeks, I decide to make it up to her tonight by taking her to a fancy restaurant. I don't really feel like it, but it'll probably be good for me. Talk about something other than Aster's coma, with someone other than Ivy.

Although, am I even able to talk of anything else?

I've barely asked Ivy about the show and about Chase. Our conversations somehow always revolve around Aster. Plus, I don't especially enjoy talking about Chase. I've met him, and I don't trust him. Maybe I'm biased, but he's the brother of a convict…that's bad news. When I mentioned it to Ivy, she reminded me she was the sister of a convict. I told her the parallel wasn't amusing.

As I iron my shirt for my date, Ivy phones me.

"I've just spent thirty-five minutes pressing a shirt," I say, lifting the iron. I've created a huge crease along the front of the shirt. "I suck at this."

"Can you come over?" she asks, her voice a mere whisper.

The hot iron slides out of my hand and falls on my foot. Thankfully, I have a sock on so it doesn't burn my skin, but it still hurts.

"Is everything all right?" I ask, as I unplug the damn thing.

"I…I got a package today."

A sour taste spreads from the back of my throat to my palate. This cannot be starting again. "You got to be kidding me."

"I'm scared."

I remember her mentioning Chase was coming over for a visit. "Isn't your boyfriend there?"

"He is, but I need *you*," she whispers.

"Okay. I'll be there in fifteen."

I put the iron back on the board, yank on my shirt, and grab my dinner jacket, wallet, phone, and keys. On my way over to Ivy's, I phone Heidi to tell her I'll be thirty minutes late. "I have to stop by the office to grab something," I lie. I think she'll give up on me if I tell her the truth. "I'll be there at seven-thirty. I promise."

"Okay," she says unenthusiastically, and hangs up.

I drive like a madman over to Ivy's. When I get there, she's standing by the door, a flimsy shawl draped over her pointy shoulders. She's starting to look as skeletal as Aster. I jog up to her.

Shadows press across her pale face. "Come in."

I look for Chase, but don't see him. I hear the shower, so I imagine he's in the bathroom. Wordlessly, the shawl still pulled tight around her, Ivy extricates a small, lumpy envelope from one of the kitchen drawers and hands it to me. Her name is printed on it, along with the hospital address.

"A nurse gave it to Chase, who brought it up to me," she says.

I shake it, and a small, black velvet box tumbles out. I pop it open and my eyes widen. A gold pendant spells Ivy's name and a diamond as big as a blueberry dots the small *i*.

"Christ, is that one of the diamonds?"

She holds a finger to her lips. "It looks exactly like the one that was stolen from me in New York," she whispers.

I suck on my bottom lip and watch the stone wink at me maliciously. I click the box shut. "I'll bring it to the precinct. And I'll stop by the hospital to find out who dropped the package off."

"There's a stamp, Josh. It was mailed."

Right. I look around the living room. "Any new ideas where Aster could've hidden the rest of them?"

"I'm still convinced Brook has them."

"He swore the stones never got to New York."

"Like I would believe a word that comes out of that guy's mouth." Her voice is low and hard. "What else did he say?"

"That he was moving them for Dean Kane."

"Of course…" Ivy mutters. "Why would he ever take the blame? Putting it on someone else is way easier."

"I do believe he was moving them for Dean Kane."

"Are you taking his side?"

"I'm not taking sides," I say gruffly. "It's been a shitty month, Ivy. A real shitty month. Do you know that Heidi is barely speaking to me anymore? I'm supposed to take her out to the restaurant tonight, but now...now I need to deal with this."

"I'm sorry."

The shower stops.

Looking remorseful, she takes the box from my fingers and slips it inside my jacket pocket. "I meant to ask you something...I felt like sewing today, and when I went to pick out some fabric from Mom's special drawer, not only was it unlocked, but the latch was broken and the fabrics were in disarray. Do you know anything about that?"

I unbutton my jacket, then button it up again. "I didn't want to worry you..."

"But now you are."

"There was a break-in."

"A break-in?"

My face goes hot.

"*What* break-in?"

"While you were in New York, someone searched your apartment."

Her eyes have become as round as those translucent psychic balls her mother adored. "What?"

Footsteps resound. I glance at her to see if she wants to continue talking about this, or if she wants me to leave before Chase makes an appearance.

"Whoever broke in probably found the rest of them, then." There's a bitter edge to her voice.

I don't like it, but I deserve it. "I doubt it. A few days later, we caught Angela Discoli rifling through the motel room she'd used with Troy Mann, so my guess is that they're still missing."

I spot Chase in the entrance of the hallway, a towel knotted around his waist. His brown hair drips water along his chest. He's not as scrawny as he looked on TV, but he's far less muscular than me. For some reason, I find satisfaction in that.

"You know those diamonds Special Agent Clancy told us about—the ones Troy Mann hid in my quilt? Apparently they're still missing," she tells him.

I scowl at her. I don't think she should be sharing so much information. What if Chase is working with Brook? After all, he brought the package to Ivy. "It's just a theory."

"Someone broke into my place to search for them," she adds.

Chase strides toward her and wraps an arm around her. He's getting her clothes wet. "You're not safe here, Ivy. You should come back to New York with me."

"Because New York is safe?" I snort. "Give me a break."

"I can't leave Aster anyway, Chase," she says, tilting her face toward him. "I'll walk Josh out. I'll be right back." She breaks away from her boyfriend and steps out ahead of me in the darkness. Once the door shuts, she asks, "Can you go see Brook? Tell him I will press charges if he makes another threat?"

"I'll phone the Feds. Maybe they can send someone—"

"You mean those detectives who interrogated me?" She snorts. "No. I want *you* to go. You're still the only person I trust."

"I'll try to get a flight out in the morning."

One of her neighbors drives down the street. He glares at Ivy as he unloads his sleepy kid from the backseat. "Everyone hates me around here. Maybe it would be safer, at least for everyone else, if I left."

"Don't you dare go anywhere. And especially not with Chase." I don't tell her about my suspicions, but from the way she winches her eyebrows, I think she gets it.

"I won't."

After a quick hug, she goes back inside and shuts the door. I get in my car, but don't drive off. I call the chief.

"She got a diamond in the mail today," I tell him.

"A real one?"

"I…I hadn't even considered it could be fake."

"Bring it to Fred. His wife did some gemology course if I'm not mistaken."

"Okay. And, Chief, I'd like to go to New York tomorrow to pay Brook a visit. You think I can go?"

"I think you *should* go." I'm hoping he says the precinct will fund the trip. He doesn't. "And tell Fred to phone me after his wife's done looking at the stone," he adds before hanging up.

I stare at my dark dashboard. I knew that until we caught Dean Kane and retrieved those diamonds, life wouldn't go back to normal, but the fact that Brook is targeting Ivy with scare tactics bothers me. I get back out of the car and knock on Mr. Mancini's door.

The lights are on and the TV is painfully loud, so I know he's awake, yet he takes a mighty long time opening up.

"Sorry. I got the runs," he explains as he tucks his plaid shirt into his high-waisted pants. "Everything okay?"

"You haven't seen anyone lurking recently, have you?"

He farts, long and loud. I grimace as the terrible smell reaches me. "Besides your pretty cop? Naw. I'm keeping watch."

"My pretty cop?"

"Yeah."

There was only one woman in the precinct who was remotely pretty. A Puerto Rican girl—

"Long red hair, yay tall." He taps his chest.

"We don't have a redhead at the station."

"I asked to see her badge, and she showed it to me."

"When did she stop by?" I ask, scanning the street for movement.

"'Bout ten days ago."

"And you're sure she had red hair?"

"I might be old, but I'm not blind. And her badge was real. I inspected it."

"Did she give you a name?"

"Officer Carella."

Goose bumps crawl over me. There is no Officer Carella. "Can you call me if she stops by again?"

"Yeah."

As I turn to leave, I scan his porch. A tiny red dot catches my attention. I stride over to it. "Did you put this camera up?" I ask him.

"Your guys installed it. For Ivy's security. They did a shitty job if you ask me."

"What guys?"

"I don't know, Josh. You sent them over a couple days after Ivy got home. Even though I didn't feel like piercing holes in my beams, I let them. I thought I was doing you and the twins a favor."

"What did they look like?"

"They looked like your usual security guys. One had a beard, I think."

"Did they mention what company they worked for?"

"Securitox."

I type it into an Internet search page on my phone. "Doesn't exist." I gape up at him, sweat beading behind my ears.

"Well, don't just stand there. Rip it out," he yells.

I raise my arm and tug on it, but it's screwed in tight. Mr. Mancini storms back into his house, then back out, rifle in hand. I'm about to tell him not to shoot it down when he starts hitting the camera with the stock of his gun. After four blows, it falls down.

I was wrong. Ivy isn't safe here.

After asking Mancini to call me if anyone else approaches him, I return to my car and drive over to Fred's with the camera and the diamond. While his wife gets a loupe and a pair of tiny tongs to inspect it, I tell him about the fake cop and show him the camera.

"The stone's fake," she says.

Like the cop, but not like the camera.

THIRTY-ONE

Brook

"Inmate Jackson, you got a visitor." I rise from my seat on a bench in the outside pen they take us into for some fresh air every day, come rain or shine.

As I follow the guard, the other inmates stop lifting weights or tossing a ball to stare at me. Since I was booked almost a month ago, only one guy tried to mess with me, but I beat him to a pulp, bruising my knuckles badly in the process. It served its purpose: the others left me alone.

I half-expected to cross paths with Diego Discoli, but he was moved to another prison upon my arrival. A higher security one. I'd been hoping to run into him since he's one of the reasons I'm stuck inside this shithole, but a meet-and-greet never happened.

Not much has happened at all in the past weeks.

Dad came to visit a few times. Mom comes nearly every day. She's been staying at a hotel nearby. I told her not to spend her money on a hotel for my sake, and she told me to shut up. Carmelina and Diana have also visited me religiously. Chase is the only person who hasn't made the trip. Even Diana's father came up once.

He's been trying to counter the no-bail rule since I'm not innocent of the crimes I was charged with, but no judge is willing to discuss it until my "associate" Dean Kane is brought in.

A few days ago, I took matters into my own hands, and sure enough, when I see who's come to pay me a visit through the bulletproof glass, my plan worked.

I sit down and pick up the phone. The young officer on the other side of the glass has his phone already pressed against his ear.

"Joshua Cooper, right?" I ask.

He nods. "How do you know my name?"

"You investigated me so I investigated you. Only fair."

"Did you send Ivy a package containing a necklace?"

"Yes."

His eyes narrow. "Did you also send a fake cop and have a camera installed?"

"What? No."

"You admit you threatened her with a necklace, but didn't—"

"It wasn't a threat."

"Was it a gift?" he asks sarcastically.

"No."

"Then why the hell did you send her a necklace?" he yells, but then, he glances around him and drops his voice. "Are you some sort of sicko?"

"It was a message." I lean my elbows on the table and stare straight into Josh's pulsing green irises. "I'm done playing games, and I'm done playing nice. I want out of here, Josh…Can I call you Josh?"

"You've been convicted of a federal offense. What makes you think you can get out of here?"

"What if I told you I can get Dean Kane to come straight to you?"

"If you say *you* aren't the one monitoring Ivy, then my guess is, he's already around."

"Have the diamonds been found?"

"That's none of your business."

I grind my teeth. "It's become my business."

"Look, I made the trip out here with money from my own pocket, money I earned the hard way, the lawful way. And the only reason I came is to tell you to strop threatening my friend."

The young cop makes to hang up the phone, but I knuckle the glass to stop him. Reluctantly, he brings it back to his ear.

"I can help you nail Dean Kane for murder."

"Murder?" Of course that gets Josh's attention. "Aster didn't die."

"I wasn't talking about Aster Redd."

"Who were you talking about then?"

"Get me out, and I'll talk. But I'll only talk to you and to Ivy, no federal agent."

"What makes you think I have that authority?"

"*You* don't, but I'm sure you can make contact with someone who does."

"I can't get you out just because you're asking me to."

I close my eyes. "What if I told you where you can find one of the missing stones?"

Josh blinks. He's hooked, sinker and all. "Where?"

I lean forward. "I want an official release paper signed by a judge."

"That could take me days to get."

"Then it'll take you days to find out the whereabouts of the diamond."

TWENTY-FOUR HOURS GO BY.

And then twenty-four more.

Joshua Cooper either didn't bite or didn't have the political pull.

When my mother stops by to see how I'm doing and notices my glummer-than-usual mood, she assumes something appalling has happened to my ass. It takes a while to convince her I wasn't raped.

An hour after she leaves, Joshua Cooper returns with a signed, supervised release form. The paper is my first tiny victory. That very day, I walk out of jail with leg irons, handcuffs, and hope.

He's leaning against the prisoner transport van that's been prepped for my twelve-hour trip to Kokomo. "You better not make a run for it, Jackson, because my chief and I are risking a lot taking you out of here."

"I have nowhere to go, Josh," I tell him as I climb into the empty minibus. "So I'm not running. But my mother needs to be informed. She's the only one who visits me every day. She'll ask questions if I'm not there."

"We're not broadcasting your release," Josh says, climbing in the back with me.

"I wouldn't want you to. Have the prison guards tell my mother I was moved to a restricted area."

He grumbles something, but makes the call. Once he hangs up, he asks, "So where's that diamond?"

"You know the D.A. on the Discoli case?"

Josh's jaw slackens.

"*That diamond* is around his wife's neck. Type Hope Gala and her name in Google's search bar and you'll find several pictures of her wearing it. Ask the D.A. for the stone's certificate. He won't be able to produce any. And then, he'll either tell you it's a family heirloom, or he'll tell you it was a gift. Whatever lie he chooses to go with, you'll have one of your missing jewels."

Joshua stares at me long and hard before calling his chief. He stays on the line a while, probably to verify my information. Finally, he disconnects. "The chief saw the picture. He's calling New York to have someone pick it up." He bites his lip. "So the Discolis sent the diamonds to New York to pay off the D.A.?"

I nod.

"And you only got one to him?"

"*Dean* only got one to him."

"What about the others?"

"They never arrived in New York."

Josh keeps chewing on his lip. "How'd you get the necklace to Ivy?"

"I asked a friend to have it made and shipped to the hospital."

"What friend?"

"There are enough people involved, don't you think?" I ask. "Plus, she wasn't aware of what she was doing. She was just doing me a favor."

"Like someone else I know…"

His comment doesn't rile me up like it would've done a few days back when my future was as bleak and forbidding as that blue hole I dove into during a long-ago boat trip in the Bahamas. Besides, he's right. I *was* stupid. But I'm done being stupid.

"How's Ivy?" I ask after another long bout of silence.

"Like you care."

"I do care."

He shoots me a sideways glance. "She's not doing too well."

"Mom told me Chase was visiting her. Is he still there?"

"No. He left last night."

Frustration at the fact that he *was* there, doing God knows what to Ivy, stings my heart. "So she's alone?"

"I put a security detail on her."

An hour slides by in thick silence. Josh plinks around on his phone. It buzzes repeatedly, and repeatedly he types back messages.

"What happened between the two of you?" Josh asks, and it takes me a minute to understand that we're speaking about my brother again.

"We were both after the same thing."

Josh runs a hand through his short brown hair. "You mean, the art school?"

I nod, even though the Masterpiecers was just the igniting incident. "He wanted the family business, and I would've gladly given it to him if there was anything left of it. But you must be aware by now that my family's bankrupt. It's been all over the news. If I remember correctly, the day after the show closed, the *Times* published an article titled, *The Jacksons: Win Some, Lose Some*."

Josh doesn't respond. After a long while, he says, "I didn't tell Ivy about the fake cop or the camera. I don't want to fuel her stress, so don't mention it when you see her."

"I won't breathe a word of it tonight."

"Tonight? It'll be late. You can see her tomor—"

"Tonight, or I stop talking."

Josh turns away from the window. "How do I know you're not planning on hurting her?"

"I suppose you don't. You'll just have to trust me."

"Trust you?" Josh pounds his fist against the headrest of the seat in front of him. "How am I supposed to trust a felon?"

The bus driver glances into the rearview mirror but doesn't slow down.

"Josh, who has more to lose? You or me?" I ask.

He leans his forehead against the seat in front and shuts his eyes. "You swear you're not playing me?" His eyes are still closed.

"I tried to save my family. That's how I found myself in this mess." Mess sounds too insignificant for what it truly is. "I'm not a bad person, Josh. I'm just a person who did bad things."

He opens his eyes and glares at me.

"I admit I was looking for easy money, regardless of whether it was clean or not. But unlike Dean, I didn't murder anyone to preserve that money."

"*Who* did he murder?"

"How do you think Kevin died?" I say, slipping one of my aces out of my prison-issue jumpsuit sleeve.

Pressing himself upright again, Josh blinks. "I knew it!"

The driver's gaze skirts the rearview mirror again.

"And you have proof?" he asks excitedly.

"I know where to get proof; however, and—this is non-negotiable—the person who possesses the proof cannot be charged with anything. If you don't promise me this in writing, I will not obtain it for you. As I said before, there are enough people involved already."

"Why now, Jackson? Why wait three weeks?"

"I was giving Dean and his father one last chance to save me."

"His father?" Josh says. "You mean mother…"

"No, I mean father."

"Who's his father?"

I don't tell Josh because Ivy deserves to be the first to find out.

THIRTY-TWO

JOSH

When we get to the safe house, it's late. After signing discharge papers for the transport guard, I take hold of Brook's arm and lead him inside the small apartment where Claire is waiting. Guarda ordered one of us to remain with the prisoner at all times, so we're doing eight-hour shifts. Claire starts tonight, Fred comes in tomorrow morning, and then it's my turn.

I help Brook out of the leg irons and the handcuffs, but leave the ankle monitor in place.

"This is for you," Claire tells him, shoving a brown paper bag filled with clothes and some toiletries into his arms. Her gaze lingers on him, and I swear she wets her lips.

As he takes everything inside the bathroom, I turn to Claire. "Are you going to jump him or guard him?"

"Funny, Coop," she says, pursing her lips.

"I'm going to go collect Ivy. I'll be back in a bit. Don't screw this up."

I phone Ivy on my way over to her place and tell her to get ready.

"For what?" she asks.

"Can't tell you over the phone. Just get dressed."

I should probably have specified what she should wear because when I arrive, she's put on this little black dress, sheer tights, and ankle boots. "You have no idea how much I've been wanting to get out of the house," she says, locking her door the minute I pull up in front.

I let her think we're going to dinner during the entire drive. It's way better than telling her about Brook.

"How's everything with Heidi?" she asks, combing her fingers through her long hair. It sparkles each time a streetlight hits it.

"We're taking a break."

"What?" she exclaims. "When did that happen?"

"After I took your necklace to have the diamond inspected, I lost track of time. She assumed I'd stood her up—which wasn't honestly too far from the truth." My fingers clench around the steering wheel. "I'm a lousy boyfriend."

Ivy touches my arm. "No. You're an amazing boyfriend, but you're also an amazing friend, which has made your dating life hell. Do you want me to talk to her?"

I cock an eyebrow at her suggestion. I even raise a small smile.

"I'm the last person she'd want to talk with right now, huh?"

"Not the last. But yeah, somewhere down there."

She makes a face. "I ruined your love life."

"You owe me."

She nods. "How can I make it up to you?"

I slide the car in front of the safe house.

Ivy looks around. "Where are we?"

"You asked how you can make it up to me? Come inside."

"What's inside?"

I don't answer.

"Josh, you're scaring me. What's inside?"

I get out of the car and walk over to her side. After I pull her door open, I extend my hand. "Do you trust me?"

"Of course."

"Then trust me."

She latches on to my hand, because a decade and a half together inspires trust in people. Making her face Brook without warning could harm our bond, but it's a risk I'm willing to take to have this be over.

THIRTY-THREE

Brook

I jerk upright as the door opens. When I hear Ivy's voice, I pull my shoulders back and sit up straighter, attempting to salvage some of the pride prison stole from me.

"Is this a joke?" Her head veers so wildly from me to Josh that her long curls whip her face. She picks the gold strands out of her eyes. "What is *he* doing here?"

Josh looks down at the floor, clearly uncomfortable. "Brook is cooperating with the police to help us apprehend Dean Kane."

"But they're both as evil," Ivy screams. "He laughed at me the day he was arrested! He laughed when he heard Aster had been attacked!"

"I wasn't laughing at you, Ivy, or at your sister," I tell her.

She swings back toward me. "I heard you!"

"When I'm nervous, I laugh. I can't control it. I laughed at my grandfather's funeral. Ask Chase."

The mention of my brother makes her stick out her chin. "Does he know you're here?"

"No one knows except you, and Josh, and his *squad*," I say, gesturing toward the blonde cop who's been ogling me like a tourist in front of a gelato display.

"The name's Claire," she says, twirling the tip of her ponytail around a fat finger.

"Well, I'm thrilled you have some inside help, Josh." Ivy does not sound thrilled at all. "But there's no way in hell I'm talking to him."

"Ivy…" Josh's Adam's apple bobs. "Please."

"Why me? Have I not been through enough?"

I stand up and take a step toward her, but stop when she steps back. She folds her arms over her chest.

"You're one of his reasons for cooperating," Josh says. "Hate me for this later, but help us catch Dean. Please. I worry so much about you and Aster. I don't want to worry anymore."

Ivy's beautiful lips press tight.

"I beg you, Ives."

I keep my gaze on her mouth until the firm line becomes pliable. Then I dare look up into her eyes. They still glow with hatred, but also with reluctance.

"Will you sit?" I ask her.

"I'm fine standing." Her chest heaves, rising and falling underneath her pretty black dress.

I sink down on the cheap, foam couch and explain how I ended up running errands for Dean Kane. As I talk, her arms loosen. She doesn't walk up to me and lay a comforting hand on my shoulder, but at least, when she looks at me after I'm finished explaining, all that's left in those vivid blue eyes of hers is pity. I'm not sure I like the pity, but I like it better than the fierce loathing.

"So where is Dean Kane hiding?" she asks.

"My bet is on Dominic's yacht."

Josh starts at the information. "Dominic…as in Dominic Bacci?"

"Dominic is protecting him?" Ivy's voice is shrill.

My fingers overlap and my palms squash together as I stare up into Ivy's face. Her eyes have grown so wide with trepidation I don't feel the thrill I thought I would at the big reveal. Instead, an ache blooms in my chest at having to tell her that yet another person she trusted deceived her.

"Dominic is Dean's father."

THIRTY-FOUR

JOSH

"No way," I whisper, at the same time as Ivy rocks back on her heels, face incredibly pale.

"Dominic"—her voice cracks—"Dominic and Dean…"

Brook gives a heavy nod, but doesn't gloat. I have to give him that: he doesn't seem proud about all the information he's feeding us. He seems sad. For a brief moment, I take pity on the guy, but then I remember he had a choice, and he made the wrong one. Whatever his reasons.

I'm expecting Ivy to ask me to drive her home, but instead she sits down.

"It's enough for one night," I tell her. "Let's go home."

"I just want to understand—"

"Tomorrow, Ives. Tomorrow, you can spend all afternoon babysitting Brook with me, but tonight, you and I are going home."

Brook glances up at me, his dark eyes shiny. I suppose he's happy at the prospect of spending all day with Ivy, which leads me to wonder if anything happened between them in New York.

"Now," I say when I don't see her move.

She springs off the couch.

Brook stares at her and she stares at him. Those Jackson brothers are bad news. Both of them. She still hasn't moved, so I grab her arm and tow her out, yelling at Claire to stay alert. She gives me the finger, and I'm so riled up against Brook that I growl. Inside the car, I give Ivy a large chunk of my mind.

"Geez," she says, "you sound like your mother." She plops her elbow on the armrest and cradles her head with her fingers. "I can't believe Dominic has a son. I can't believe I didn't realize they were related. How did I not see the resemblance?"

"Stop tormenting yourself."

She sighs.

I stare ahead at the broken white lines that rhythmically vanish and appear around my lane.

"Josh?"

"Yes?"

"If Aster—I mean *when* Aster wakes up, what's going to happen to her?"

"There'll be a trial, which she won't need to attend if we use the power of attorney you made her sign."

"You know about that?"

"Yeah."

She bites her lip. "I did it to protect her…in case…in case prison made her… made her…" She carves her hand through her hair. Her fingers tremble. "Made her worse."

I catch her hand in mine and squeeze it. "Ivy, you thought you were doing the right thing. Turns out, you did, even though you should've discussed it with her."

"She would never have agreed."

"Probably not." I stop at a traffic light. "I'll call Kelley tomorrow. Ask him if he can help out."

"Kevin's lawyer?"

I nod.

"You think he would help us?"

"He's friends with my chief."

"Is he expensive?"

The light turns green. "Don't worry about that."

"How can I not worry about that?"

"Because I'm asking you not to worry about it." I make a left turn into her street. "Maybe he'll do it for free."

"Dean wanted to make her plead insanity. You think that's what he'll suggest?"

"I think that might be her only option."

I park. My fingers latch onto the handle but don't pump it open. "Just because Brook's cooperating doesn't mean he's a nice guy."

"I know, but what he told me tonight…it clears so much up."

"Did anything happen between the two of you back on the show?"

"No." Even though it's dark inside the car, I see color splashing her cheeks.

"Then why are you blushing?"

"I don't know." She throws her hands up in the air. "I always blush. Plus, I'm dating his brother. That would be wrong in too many ways."

"About his brother…are you being safe?"

"Oh my God, Josh! I'm not discussing my sex life with you."

"So you *are* having sex," I say.

"No, I'm not."

"Why not?"

"Because I'm stressed out... He's stressed out. It's never the right time." A weighty sigh escapes her. "And he keeps asking me if I'm sure."

"Well? Are you?"

"I'm nineteen. Even Aster—" She stops talking because she knows who took Aster's virginity.

Me.

"Are you sure you want to have sex with *him*?" I clarify.

"He's my boyfriend. Who else am I supposed to have sex with? And don't suggest you. Yuck."

"Yuck?" I say, right before I burst out laughing. Then she cracks up. Tears stream out of my eyes. After a while, our laughter is replaced by large smiles, and then by weaker ones.

"We needed that," she says, pressing her head back against the headrest.

"We seriously needed that. But really"—I stick out my bottom lip—"yuck?"

"I adore you, Joshy, but you're the brother I never had."

"I love you too, Ives. And agreed; I would never do you either. Even if you begged me."

She opens her car door and steps out. Before shutting it, she asks, "Can you stay with me? Until I fall asleep? I know it's juvenile, but I don't like being home alone."

Never able to say no to Ivy, I go inside and sit at the foot of her bed, and discuss Brook and Dean until I'm the only one talking. Once she's sound asleep, I head over to the hospital to check up on Aster.

It's the middle of the night, yet several cars are parked in front. As I walk toward the dimly lit entrance, I do a double take in front of a powder blue bumper. Running my hand against the pointed tailfins, I circle Troy's Cadillac and peer inside. A lady purse and a discarded blouse lay on the backseat. I assume both are Stephanie's. She mustn't have found a buyer, which leads me to wonder how much she's asking for it. Probably a bunch. Troy kept his ride in pristine condition.

I startle out of my price-assessment. Stephanie hates Aster. If her car is here that means— I sprint through the sliding glass doors toward the welcome desk, point to my badge, and ask if a Stephanie Britton has checked in. The nurse shakes her head no. I describe her. Again, I'm met with a headshake. I take the stairs two-by-two and hold my breath until I reach the guard stationed in front of Aster's room. I ask him about visitors. Like the nurse, he says there weren't any.

She must've sold the Cadillac then. I long to ask Heidi, but how can I call her in the middle of the night to ask about Troy's car when I haven't had the courage to talk to her about us yet?

Breathing deeply, I enter the small room and listen to the rhythmic beeping of the electrocardiograph machine until my pulse evens out. Then I pull up a seat next to Aster's bed and latch on to her hand, and I tell her about Brook, about New York, about Dean and Dominic. If it weren't for the oxygen mask covering her mouth, Aster would simply look as though she were sleeping.

Her hair has been chopped so short it looks fuzzy. I caress it, then stroke her cheek. It's warm and pulsates from the air that's being pushed into her lungs. I rest my forehead against the side of her face.

"I'm going to make your world safe again, Aster. I promise."

I press a gentle kiss onto each of her eyelids. I want her to feel I'm here. Her heart spikes on the EKG. I suck in a breath and watch her face, hoping to see her lids flutter, but they don't.

I take her hand and squeeze it. "I'm going to go home and try to get some sleep. I'll be back in the morning."

As I stand up, her fingers tighten around mine. I shoot my gaze down to her hand. It's definitely curled around mine. The pressure happens again. It's light but it's there.

I jerk my gaze up to her face. Her lids are open.

"Aster?" I whisper, not wanting to spook her.

Her eyes don't meet mine. Instead, she stares up at the ceiling. It's a little freaky. Without letting go of her hand, I move my face into her line of sight.

"Aster," I whisper again. She blinks but her eyes remain focused on nothing. "Hey, you." When her fingers begin slipping out of my hand, I crush them. "Blink twice if you can hear me?" I stare at her eyes. They're lighter than Ivy's, almost translucent, with steel-blue circles around the iris. I've missed those eyes.

They close. I will them to open again, but they remain sealed tight. I don't move for a long time. It's the door of her room swinging open that jolts me. A nurse trundles in and frowns at me.

I think she might ask me what I'm doing visiting at this hour, but instead, she says, "You should go home and rest, honey. You look terrible."

"I'm going," I say with a sigh.

Delicately, I place Aster's fingers back on the bed sheets and rise. I head to the door, but instead of walking out, I stay inside and close it, then I turn back toward the nurse. She's inspecting the EKG machine and jotting something down in Aster's chart.

"She opened her eyes," I tell her.

The nurse looks up. She has all these lines on her face even though she doesn't look old enough to have that many. "When?"

"Fifteen minutes ago…a half hour. I'm not sure. She even squeezed my fingers."

Her lips slope up. "I thought I detected an elevation of the ST segments."

"Does that mean she's out of her coma?"

"It means her chances of recovery have just improved. But, Joshua, she's reaching the minimally conscious state. She could stay in that state a long time before making a full recovery. Your mom told me not to get your hopes up too high."

"You spoke to my mother?"

"She's stopped by a few times to check on Aster. We talked. She's worried about you and the twins. I hear their mother's no longer alive, and the father's not around."

I find myself smiling a little. Even though it's late, I text my mother to thank her for taking care of the girls.

"Can you call me…if she wakes up again?" I ask the nurse. "And don't leak this to the press," I add. "It's really important."

"Deal. But get some sleep. You're going to run yourself into a hospital bed."

"Tell the other nurses, too."

"Okay, Officer. Now, go."

As I take the elevator back down to the lobby, I brace myself against the wall to keep my knees from buckling. The doors open, but I don't get out. And then they close, like Aster's lids. And I just stand there, watching them.

When the elevator goes dark, I tap the back of my head against the wall and let the relief of the day burn away the fear and worry that's been gnawing at me since Aster discovered Troy Mann's file on my desk.

THIRTY-FIVE

Brook

"You want us to do what?" Josh exclaims the following afternoon. He's flushed beet-red and beads of sweat track down the sides of his face.

"I want you to put out a news brief that Aster woke up. If he thinks there's a way to get his hands on those diamonds, he'll be on the first flight back from Cuba," I tell Josh, his boss, Fred, and Claire. "Ivy can give an interview from Aster's hospital room, posing as Aster."

"No way." Josh shakes his head.

"You have to admit, it's a sound idea, Coop," the chief says, rolling the ends of his mustache.

"I'll do it," Ivy says.

"Absolutely not! The guy killed someone in cold blood. Do you think he would hesitate for a second to do the same to you when you can't tell him where the diamonds are?" His forehead is so shiny it reflects the ceiling light dangling over the wooden coffee table.

"She'll have increased protection," the chief says. "They'll both have increased protection."

"It would be *crazy*," Josh yells.

"It really isn't that crazy," Ivy says calmly, glancing at me. I wouldn't go so far as to say she's excited, but she's definitely animated by the idea.

"You don't even have the same hairdo," Josh says. He's nitpicking now.

"I'll crop mine short like hers," Ivy suggests.

This time, I say no at the same time as Josh, because one, I love her hair, and two, no pictures of Aster have been leaked since she was wheeled out of the prison and transported to the hospital.

"I didn't even know her hair had been cut. So Dean probably doesn't either," I say.

"Why don't we just arrest Dominic and force him to bring his boat out of Cuban waters?" Claire suggests.

Josh blinks at her.

"All that would do is spook Dean. The only thing Dean wants is to set things right with the Discolis before they off him. Trust me. We let him think Aster woke up with no memory loss, and he's going to come straight to us."

"How do we know this is not some ploy to get *your* paws on those diamonds?" Claire asks. I almost laugh at the word paws, as she has quite the pair.

Ivy sits up straighter and frowns.

"What exactly would those diamonds do for me, Claire?" I ask in a brittle voice. "I wouldn't be able to sell them. I wouldn't be able to trade them with the bank to cover our debts. They belong to the Discolis, so then I would become a target for the mob family. And let's not forget the FBI…they'd lock me up forever. The only real thing those diamonds would win me is a one-way trip to the graveyard, and I don't care for dying. I still have things I want to do."

"Like returning to the Masterpiecers?" Fred asks.

"I don't plan on returning to that school, or to New York."

"Where are you going to go then?" Ivy asks.

"I want to move to a small town, maybe work with horses on a ranch."

Her lips part in surprise.

"I can picture you in a pair of cowhide slacks and a cowboy hat, chewing on some long grass," Claire says.

I don't enjoy her picturing me in her head.

Ivy snorts a laugh. She claps her hand against her mouth. "A ranch?"

I smile. "What?"

"Can we please get back to the matter at hand?" the chief says.

I nod. We all nod. Even Josh, who's glaring at me.

"When do we do it?" Guarda asks.

"Next week," Ivy says.

"Why wait so long?" Fred asks.

"We are not doing it," Josh says. "I'm going to come up with a better plan. Ivy and I will brainstorm this weekend."

"I can't this weekend," she says, a blush slinking over her nose.

"Why not?" Josh asks her.

"I'm, uh…" She stares down at her Stan Smiths. "There's a party. Remember Maxine? She's throwing a party at her house in the Hamptons for everyone from the show."

The smile snaps off my lips.

"You shouldn't be going anywhere until we catch Dean," Josh says.

"I agree with Josh," I say.

"I need to go. I promised—"

I interrupt her. "How are you even getting there?"

"Um…uh…by plane."

"What plane?" Josh asks.

"Someone's," she says cryptically.

"Ivy, just get it out already. What plane?" he all but growls.

Has my brother chartered a private aircraft with the hundred grand he won? If he has, he's an idiot. Mom and Dad—

She sighs. "An art dealer wants to meet with me. He wants me to bring over some of my quilts. So he's sending his jet over to pick me up." She lifts her eyes to mine. "Brook knows him."

I suck in a furious breath. "Paul? You're going on Paul Willows's jet?"

A blush floods Ivy's face.

"I told you not to sell anything to him. He's as sleazy as they come."

"You should talk," she says, and I recoil, my body, like my ego, taking a hit.

I don't raise my eyes to hers once while the rest of them discuss the safety of leaving Indiana. When the chief stands up, the others accompany him to the door. I stare sullenly at a sticky stain on the coffee table. Specks of lint are trapped on the surface. They shiver in the cool, musty air blowing from the AC vent above my head.

"It came out wrong," Ivy says.

My jaw clenches like a steel trap.

"I know you're not sleazy."

Still I don't say anything.

"I'm sorry."

I pump my jaw to loosen it, and ask, "Is Chase going with you?"

"He's meeting me there."

"Good." I never thought I'd be glad my brother was with Ivy, but I despise Paul that much.

"By the way, what do you mean, he's sleazy?" she asks, picking at bits of flaking turquoise nail polish.

"He has a reputation for sleeping with most of the artists he represents."

She wrinkles her nose.

"Does Chase know you're going on his plane?"

"Yes."

"And he's not worried?" I'd be going out of my mind if my girlfriend were locked in a compartment several thousand feet above ground with a scumbag.

"Paul is already in the Hamptons. Chase has a meeting with him the afternoon of the party."

"Josh," I say, and the cop whirls toward me.

I wave him over. "Can you accompany her?"

"He has better things to do than play chaperone, Brook."

"Dean is out there," I say. "He might've heard about the party. If he corners you there—"

"Why do you even care?"

"Because"—I stare down at the floor—"I just do." When I raise my eyes back to hers, she's contemplating me as though I were some curio in a shop window.

"Brook's right, Ivy," Josh says. "Either I go with you or you don't go at all. Your choice."

Ivy's face goes through several emotions before settling on resignation. "Fine," she sighs.

Even though I would've liked to have been the one to accompany her, Josh cares about her so deeply I know he will do everything in his power to protect her, be it from Dean or from Paul.

THIRTY-SIX

JOSH

As we drive to the private airstrip, Ivy casts a long sideways glance at me.
"What?" I ask.
"Nothing."
She whisks her gaze away, propelling it on the gleaming silver jet beyond the security gate.
"What?" I ask her again.
"Did you have to wear a Hawaiian shirt?"
I peer down at my floral, short-sleeved shirt. "We're going to a beach party."
"In New York, not in Key West."
"You're wearing leggings and a T-shirt."
"I'm going to change on the plane."
"What *was* I supposed to wear?"
"A plain shirt…with long sleeves."
"Well, I didn't have a clean one," I say, feeling as annoyed as when I was bullied back in middle school. I jab my thumb against the window switch to lower it, then punch the call button. When did Ivy become so hoity-toity about dress codes anyway?
Once the gate opens, I raise my window and drive over to the parking area. Still reeling from Ivy's comment, I pop the trunk and grab my duffel bag and Ivy's suitcase. Aster would never have made me feel bad about what I was wearing. We

walk up to the plane, and to the pilot standing beside it. He's wearing a plain white shirt. If I'd cared to fit in, I would've asked him to trade.

He ushers us onto the sleek aircraft that smells of new leather and warm coffee, and seals the hatch. As he takes his seat up front, we settle on two squashy beige leather seats that face each other and click on our lap belts for takeoff. The stewardess introduces herself and asks us what we would like to drink. Ivy asks for coffee while I ask for nothing. I don't want to take anything from these people. I fold my arms together and stare out the small, round window as we shoot upward through a thick layer of clouds. The plane shakes. Ivy grips the armrests while I just squeeze my arms tighter against my chest.

Suddenly my phone rings. I'm so stunned it works at this altitude that it takes me a second to fish it out of my khakis' pocket.

"Can I take the call?" I ask the stewardess.

She nods, so I press it against my ear.

"Cooper," I say.

"Joshua, this is Sabrina, the nurse from the hospital. You told me to call you if there were any changes."

"And? Have there been?"

"Aster started to obey some commands. When I asked her to pinch her nose, she touched it. It's a good sign. Will you be able to stop by to see her today?"

"Not today, but I'll be there first thing tomorrow."

"Good, I think it's important for her to have her loved ones around. It speeds up recovery."

My pulse bleats inside my ears. "Thank you for the news."

"Of course."

After I hang up, I stare at my phone for a long time.

"Who was that?" Ivy asks.

"Claire."

"What did she want?"

"To update me on Angela Discoli's movements," I say, burrowing deeper in my shameful pit of lies. I should tell her the truth, but I don't want to raise her hopes. What if Aster's recovery stops? Or worse, what if the coma returns?

Can a coma return?

"And?" she says.

"Huh?"

"Angela Discoli...has she been on the move?"

"She's, uh...been seen around the motel again."

"They really want their stones back, don't they?"

"The one we seized from the D.A. was estimated to be worth close to five-hundred thousand dollars, so if there are seven more like it, you do the math."

Ivy gasps. "Five-hundred thousand dollars?"

I nod.

"I had half a million dollars sewed into my bag," she murmurs. "If I'd sold it—"

"If you'd sold it, you'd be in jail."

Her cheek dimples; she must be biting it.

"How many quilts did you bring with you?" I ask, to change the subject of jail and diamonds, which is all I've talked about in the past month.

"Four."

"Which ones?"

Her eyes shine with excitement as she tells me about them. Sewing her magnificent quilts is what keeps her sane and happy, even as the world disintegrates around her. A half hour into the flight, she takes out the quilt she's working on and stitches more pieces to it.

"What is that?"

"A sunflower."

I stand up and grip the side draped against her legging-clad leg to see the larger picture.

"You can't see it from this close," she says. "Stand back."

She hangs the quilt over the chair, then pushes me as far back as possible.

"Wow, that's gorgeous," the stewardess says. "The one you did for that show, that one was exceptional, but this is something else."

Ivy's eyes cloud at the memory of her ruined quilt.

"So tell me about this one," I ask.

"It's supposed to represent pieces of my life. The brown petal is for Mom." She points to an oblong pointy shape made of chocolate-colored silks and velvets. "I'm using only the fabrics my father gave her."

I loop one arm around Ivy's shoulder. "A sunflower, huh?"

She turns toward me. "My happiest memories were of the weekends we spent at your grandparents' house. I don't think I've thanked your mother enough for making them happen."

"You don't need to thank her for anything."

"Are you kidding, Josh? Your family saved Aster and me. You were so kind, taking us away from Mom when she had to work…or when she'd *check out*. Most people don't open their doors to strangers, yet your family did. Your parents got us into a better school, helped us with our homework, fed us when times were rough. Whenever I ask your mom why, she tells me it was the normal thing to do. But it isn't the normal thing to do."

"She cares about you girls."

"But why?"

"Because that day in McDonald's, when she found out your mom had left you by yourselves so she could go run errands—and you told her it wasn't the first time—she was outraged. She wanted to call child services."

"But she didn't."

"If she'd called them, Ivy, they would've placed you in foster care. They might even have separated you and Aster. It would've been worse. Plus you'd become my friends by then. I never had any friends before you."

"Stop…you're going to make me cry," she says.

"I'm serious. No one wanted to be friends with the Hamster."

She rolls her eyes.

I squeeze her against me, then shoot my chin to the quilt before us. "What's with the black petal? Does it symbolize your trip to New York?"

She snorts. "Funny. And no. It's supposed to symbolize our swing."

"Ah, our tire swing." The one Dad had hung from the branch of a grand old tree before my grandparents' field was bought back by some multinational and razed, replaced by an ugly gray factory. "Am I going to get a petal?"

"More than one." She glances up at me, then at my Hawaiian shirt. "Maybe I'll even create one from the fabric of your shirt."

I snort a chuckle. "What do you have against my poor shirt? Grandpa gave it to me."

"Was it one of his?"

"Ha-ha."

"Only senior citizens in Florida wear them."

"And me."

"And you." She pecks my cheek. "I'm happy you came. I *am* a little nervous about this trip."

"Don't be. I'm here."

"What if I don't sell anything? I filed a tort claim for Aster's medical bills, but I still have so many of Mom's to pay—"

"Maybe my parents can lend you some money."

"No way am I asking your parents for anything, Josh. I owe both of them too much already."

"You owe them nothing." I squeeze her hand to drive my point home.

As she collects the fabric sunflower from the seat, she asks, "What happened to my quilt?"

"The one on the show?"

She nods.

I sit back down and reattach the lap belt. "Brook told me Dean shredded it."

"Asshole," she mumbles.

I wonder if she means Brook or Dean. "In other news, I called Kelley. He said he would defend Aster. For free. And he said that, considering her current condition, he could represent her without either of you present."

"Wow. That's amazing."

I dip my chin toward my neck. "It's not that amazing, Ivy. He said the best case scenario would be institutionalization."

She takes a sharp breath. "What about a suspended prison sentence?"

"It was premeditated," I remind her softly. "Premeditation cancels any chance of parole."

Tears moisten her eyes. She grinds the heels of her palms against them, but can't stop their fall. When her cheeks are as wet as her hands, she picks up her handbag and disappears into the small bathroom. She emerges minutes before touchdown, looking as though she hadn't cried, and also, as though she were auditioning for a cabaret act.

"You're not wearing that," I say, pointing to her short, backless red dress.

"Then you're not wearing your Hawaiian shirt."

"I didn't bring anything else. You did. Put your leggings back on at least."

"I can't wear leggings with this dress."

I grouse about her outfit until we land, while she just grins. As we're released onto the tarmac, she grabs my arm. At least she's added a jean jacket to her red dress, but it does nothing to cover her long legs.

A sedan is waiting for us. I see two people in the backseat and stall, trying to make out if either of them is Dean, but Ivy keeps striding toward them, a huge smile stretching over her lipstick reddened mouth, so I assume he's not there.

When we get closer, I recognize Chase. And I imagine the other one is the notorious scumbag Brook warned us about. Their driver holds the door open.

Chase's dark eyes narrow as they set on me. "You came with *him*." Being referred to as *him* is downright demeaning. I have a name, which he knows well.

"Ivy's under police protection," I tell them. As I let go of Ivy, I curl my fingers into fists, then stretch them out before I punch something…or someone.

"Why? Did Brook break out of prison?" Chase asks.

Ivy's posture stiffens.

"We're worried about Dean," I reply.

"Party starts in thirty. We should get going. Hop in." Paul pats the space between Chase and him.

As she climbs inside, I see her underwear, and it incenses me, because if I can see it, others can too.

"Nice shirt," Paul says with a smirk right before he shuts the door.

The driver takes Ivy's suitcase from me.

As I settle in up front, next to the driver, Paul asks her about the quilts.

"I brought four."

"You'll show them to me at the Specter property," he tells her. "They have many rooms we can use for private viewings."

I gag. *Dirtball.*

"Okay," Ivy says, in a small voice. The guy probably thinks she's trying to sound cute, but I know the airiness in her voice has nothing to do with appealing to him and everything to do with being frightened of him.

I lower my sun visor so I can have a view of the backseat in my vanity mirror. While Paul chats on his cell, Chase asks Ivy about her week, and she lies quite superbly when she tells him it was uneventful. He has one hand on her bare knee and the other playing with her fingers.

I snap the visor shut and stare out at the flat greenness from which rise ridiculous mansions. The Discoli house would fit right in here. Between the houses, I spy the navy ocean lapping at stretches of white sand and wild grass.

The car finally pulls into a horseshoe-shaped driveway covered in small white pebbles that make a crunching sound under the tires. Round, rectangular, and accordion-shaped, white paper lanterns are strung up across the house's façade. Waiters, all in white, perhaps to resemble the lanterns, wait by the open front door with platters of drinks. I grab a glass of water and down it, then plop it back down on the platter.

As we infiltrate the monstrous front hall, people stare—mostly at Ivy, but my Hawaiian shirt garners a few glances.

"Ivy!" The girl with the buzz cut from the show struts toward my friend in a pair of strappy silver heels that make the long muscles in her calves pulse. She's way hotter in person than on TV, even though she was pretty hot on TV. "You made it!" she says, hugging Ivy, who tenses at the contact. Even her fingers, which are still wrapped around Chase's, whiten.

Maxine kisses Chase's cheek, then Paul's, then starts to lean in toward me, but rocks back on her heels. "I don't believe we've met."

"I'm Joshua Cooper." I'm tempted to add my title, but don't want to alarm anyone. I settle on, "Ivy's friend from home."

"Well then, welcome, Joshua." Her eyes skim my shirt before settling on my face. She smiles. "The others are on the patio," she says, before going to greet some other guests.

"I would go topless, but I don't want to shame all these rich bastards," I murmur into Ivy's ear.

She giggles. "Yes, keep those abs hidden or you'll cause a riot."

The patio is decked out in candelabras and plush couches that don't look suited for the outdoors. I scan the perimeter for Dean. It's probably pointless, but one can never be too careful.

Ivy leans toward me. "Look at that. Another person in a floral shirt."

My gaze bounces to where Ivy is looking. It's the gay dude from the show with the big poufy hair. His shirt is black with miniature purple and red flowers, and it's tucked into his narrow black pants. Maybe I should tuck mine, but I get a vision of my grandpa—he always tucks his in—so I leave it hanging out. I'm not trying to fit in, I remind myself.

"Mine is way cooler," I say over the loud music that streams through the evening air from a live DJ.

After a lengthy round of introductions, where I meet everyone from the show, Paul reappears and takes Ivy by the elbow. "I had the driver set your quilts out in one of the bedrooms upstairs. Shall we take a look at them?"

Ivy gulps. Lincoln, who's standing in the circle sipping a shaded orange and yellow drink, studies Paul and Ivy.

"What did you bring back from Indiana this time?" she asks.

Ivy stiffens, whereas I vibrate with animosity.

"What?" Lincoln says, when she realizes everyone is gaping at her. She sucks on her straw.

"*Wow*...I definitely didn't miss you," Ivy tells her, and I want to pump her hand in the air for her brazen retort.

"Totally reciprocal," Lincoln says, with a smile that makes her large green eyes gleam.

"Can you guys keep the claws in for tonight?" Herrick says. "For Maxine's sake. She's thrown us such a fabulous party. Show a little respect."

Lincoln rolls her eyes and walks away.

"Josh," Ivy says, holding out her hand toward me, even though I would never have let her go alone with Paul, or anyone else at this party.

"I'll go with you," Chase offers.

"No, stay here. Enjoy the party," she tells him. Gloom explodes over his face, darkening his already broody expression. "Josh?"

"I'm right behind you, Ives."

As I trail them upstairs, I sense waves of hatred rippling off Chase. He keeps sulking until this girl sporting a pair of teeny black shorts and a lacy white blouse comes up to him. As she runs her fingers through her long, strawberry-blonde hair, he squares his shoulders and narrows his eyes, which gives me the feeling he knows her.

We've reached the landing, so I can't see him anymore, but my curiosity is piqued. We walk past one door and stop at the next one. Her quilts have been draped over the furniture. One over the bed, one over what I imagine is a desk and chair, one on the floor, and the last is draped over a velvet armchair.

I'm about to step inside, but Paul holds me back. "I have to talk shop with my future artist. I cannot have anyone around. It's not conducive to good negotiations."

Ivy's alarmed eyes find mine.

"I go where Ivy goes."

"Fine. But I don't like doing business like this."

Like I care.

We go inside and he inspects her works, asks her for details and stories, examines the stitching and the fabrics from up close before stepping back. "They are *very* nice." He scratches his chin. "If I remember correctly, you sold the one on the show for seventy-five hundred dollars, right?"

She nods. "But I sold my web—you know, the piece I made on the beach—for thirty thou—"

"Did you ever get paid?"

She frowns. "Brook didn't have time to pay me."

"Because you think crooks pay? Sorry, sweetie, but I have no respect for the guy. I didn't have any before the scandal, but I have even less now. He's a lowlife who belongs behind bars. Even Chase agrees."

Ivy's skin darkens with anger, and tendons pinch in her throat. I rush to her side to prevent her from saying something that could compromise our operation.

"Don't you see he still upsets her?" I blurt out.

"I want fifteen thousand per quilt. Paid immediately," Ivy says, voice as tight as a mooring rope during a storm. "I believe that is not only reasonable, but also a bargain, considering my fame."

Paul smiles. "I'm going to like working with you," he says in a syrupy voice. I expect him to bargain her down, but instead he tells her he wants exclusivity, and then he asks her to sign a three-year contract.

"I need to read it first," she says.

"Of course. When you return it signed, I'll deposit the money in your bank account. Now we should get back to the party before Maxine notices we're gone. Oh, and, Ivy, you can no longer sell your quilts privately or you'll be in breach of contract. Have you ever sold any besides the one from the show that I should be aware of? Just in case they surface on the market...I don't want to think you ignored my demands."

Ivy gulps. "Josh has one."

"Are you planning on selling yours, Josh?"

"No."

"If you ever do, you sell it to me, okay?"

"I'm never going to sell it."

Paul turns to Ivy again. "Anyone else owns one?"

"Just one other person."

"Can you send me his or her name? I'd like to buy it back. If the person isn't too unreasonable, that is," he adds with a smile.

She nods. As we leave him to study his purchases, I ask Ivy about the buyer. A blush streaks her cheeks and nose.

"Is it Chase?" I ask.

"No. It's uh…it's no one important."

"Ivy…"

She fidgets with the bangle around her wrist. "Fine. It's Aster's warden. I gave him one so he would take care of Aster. I can't tell Paul about him. It'll be seen as a bribe. And if Aster ever returns to jail, and he's still the warden, and—"

I squeeze her arm. "First off, she won't go back to jail."

Her eyebrows furrow.

"Second off, I'm pretty sure you can give presents to prison personnel, as long as they're not monetary." I'm not sure at all, but if I want Ivy to relax, I need to act like I am. "Now let's go back down to the *fabulous* party," I say with a smile that makes hers reappear.

"You hate it," she says, as we clamber down the sleek wooden staircase.

"I'm hanging out with you, so no, I don't hate it." I almost bump into Ivy, who halted a few steps from the landing. I follow the direction of her gaze.

In a corner of the living room, Chase is leaning against the wall, talking to the girl with the tiny black shorts and the long hair while stroking her back. Instead of cowering in the opposite direction, Ivy strides over to them. I trot to keep up with her. When he spots her, Chase yanks his hand away from the girl.

"Chase?" His name is the only word Ivy utters, yet I can hear a thousand others in the silence that ensues.

"This is Diana."

The girl's face is stained with tears.

"My ex."

Ivy sizes up Diana, and Diana sizes up Ivy.

"She was just telling me that she tried to go visit Brook today, but apparently he's locked in some high-security cell where he isn't allowed visitors."

Ivy's hands, which were planted on her hips, slip down.

"She suspects it's because of the necklace he sent you," he says.

Ivy rubs her palms against her red dress. "The necklace?"

Chase narrows his eyes. "You know, the one the nurse gave me in the hospital? The one you told me Kevin stole from your room."

Ivy gulps.

"He asked me to have it made for you," Diana says. "I thought it was to make up for what he'd done. I didn't think it was an intimidation technique."

"Why did you lie to me?" Chase asks Ivy.

Her posture shifts from guilty to infuriated. "Because I was freaked out. And you're his brother, and I wondered if maybe *you* had anything to do with it."

He shakes his head. "How little you know me, Ivy…I understand I share the same blood as the guy who ruined your sister's life, but I'm nothing like him. Nothing." He pushes away from the wall and winds his way through the room.

"Did he just break up with me?" Ivy asks.

I'm not sure if she's asking me or Diana.

Diana bobs her head, and her long hair brushes my bare forearm. It's soft, like Heidi's. "A word of advice. Chase holds grudges. If you want him back, you need to go over there and talk it out."

Ivy's shaking. I put my hand on her shoulder to soothe her, but it doesn't work. "Why did *you* come to this party?" she suddenly asks Diana. "Are you an artist? A dealer?"

"No. Chase told me about it when we were driving up to the Hamptons yesterday."

"You guys talk?"

"Not much, but we live in the same house, so we're bound to exchange a few words."

"Rewind. You live in the same house?" Ivy has gone so still that I nearly wish she'd go back to trembling. I don't want her to flip out.

"He didn't tell you?" Diana asks.

She looks at Chase who's chatting with Herrick. "Must've slipped his mind," Ivy says between gritted teeth.

"Chase and his father moved in with us. It's a temporary solution to their... money problems. He's supposed to get a room on campus this week." Diana touches my friend's arm. "Nothing happened between us."

Ivy pins her down with a frigid stare. "I'm ready to go, Josh."

"Then let's go."

"Ivy," Diana calls out. "I don't think Brook was trying to scare you. He felt terrible for what happened."

Slowly, with a neck as stiff as the rest of her body, Ivy nods. "I know."

My eyes bulge.

Diana frowns. "You *know*?"

Ivy shuts her eyes for a second, then she looks to me to save her.

"I went to visit him to understand the meaning of the necklace," I say.

"Is the necklace the reason they locked him in a higher-security cell?" Diana asks.

"Uh. Yeah. Probably. I mean, I'm no expert on the prison world, even though, considering my line of work and my acquaintances, I should be."

"What do you do?" she asks.

"I'm a cop. But I came here as Ivy's friend," I add quickly, hoping it sounds believable.

"Do you have a phone, Josh?"

I cock an eyebrow up. "Yeah. Why?"

"I want to give you my number. In case you need any information I can provide from New York."

"That's kind of you, Diana," I say, handing over my phone.

"It's not kindness; it's revenge. I want Dean locked up and Brook released," she says.

"You're the ex who slept with Brook, aren't you?" Ivy suddenly asks.

Diana's eyes slant toward her perfectly straight nose. "I never slept with Brook."

"Chase caught you," Ivy says.

"Chase did find me at his brother's place. But we didn't sleep together. Brook's the person I run to when my life goes to shit. That's why I was with him. Because Chase had turned my life into a pile of shit."

A muscle ticks in Ivy's jaw. She looks at Chase again, but he doesn't look back at her.

"Thanks for your help, Diana," I say, grabbing Ivy's hand to drag her out before her heart explodes with jealousy…or with sadness.

THIRTY-SEVEN

Brook

I lean against the tiny pantry's wall. "How was last night?"

Ivy stares at the coffeemaker without blinking. "Paul asked for exclusivity. He gave me a contract."

"You want me to look it over for you?"

She peeks at me through the disheveled curtain of hair she's been sporting around her face since she's walked in. She's barely glanced my way—or at anyone, for that matter. Something's up. "Would you?"

"Of course. I'm good at catching the pesky clauses. It was one of the things we learned back in school."

Ivy returns her gaze to the coffeemaker. She presses some buttons. "When you offered me Dean's services, did you know he would attack my sister?" The tone of her voice has changed.

Did I? I think back on that day in the elevator with Ivy. "I didn't want him to show up at your sister's jail without your knowledge of it."

She turns to face me. "That's not what I asked."

"I didn't think he would attack her."

She fiddles with the buttons again, but no coffee drips out. "Why isn't this thing working?"

"Because you've pressed this button too many times."

She lets out an annoyed breath.

I point to the largest button. "Just push once and wait."

She does. After a few seconds, the machine beeps. As she waits for the coffee to trickle out, she turns around to face me. "Were you ever going to pay me for the web?"

This interrogation is worse than any I had to endure back in jail. "I wanted to. Dominic allots a budget to buying art for the school."

Her eyes darken. "When he picked me to replace Kevin, was it based on my talent or because he wanted access to my quilts for his son?"

"Both," I admit, tracing the yellow tiles underneath Ivy's Stan Smiths with my eyes. I'm afraid to look up…afraid she'll see I didn't think much of her quilts back then. Now—and not because of my feelings—I see what Dominic saw.

"God. This is so screwed up," she says, raking back her hair.

"Tell me about it."

I hitch my gaze back on to hers. She doesn't blink as she stares at me. I don't either.

"You told me the other day that Kevin was a PI. Is that why he was eliminated before the show started?"

"Yes."

"Dean paid the wife to doctor those photos?"

"He paid her to take the blame. He and I doctored the pictures." I rub the back of my neck. "Look, I'm not proud of what I did, but I can't change the past. I can only change myself. So that's what I'm doing. I'm changing myself into the person I'd like to be."

She tips her head to one side, observing me in a way she never dared to before. It almost makes me uncomfortable. "Did you help kill Kevin?"

"No!" I gasp. "No. Dean did that all by himself."

"Kevin was a private investigator. Didn't he know about Dean?"

"Josephine hired him to investigate the Masterpiecers. He wasn't aware of the connection between Dominic and Dean. No one was aware of it."

"How did Dean do it?"

"He gave him…" I weigh the pros and cons of confessing it was her sister's medication. The truth will set me free, right? "He gave him some of Aster's anti-psychotic medication."

"How—" She freezes. "*He's* the one who broke into my place?" she exclaims, which wins us a few cocked eyebrows and a stopover from Josh.

"What happened now?" he asks.

"It wasn't the Discolis who broke into my place. It was Dean."

I flatten my back against the wall as Josh gapes at me.

"He's been inside my house." She shivers.

"You have police protection around the clock now, Ivy."

"He knows where I live," she croaks.

"He can't get in."

"I don't want to stay there anymore," she whimpers.

"You can stay here with me. He doesn't know about this place. Plus there's a cop in here all the time," I add, to make my invitation sound less creepy.

Josh surprisingly doesn't say *no*. "It's not a bad idea, considering how often I have to leave you alone."

An incredulous look settles over Ivy. "You'd rather lock me up *in here* with *him*?"

"It would just be for a short while. Just until we catch Kane."

Ivy flinches, seemingly horrified by Josh's suggestion. I'm comforted by it, because it means Josh understands I'm not the enemy. I wish Ivy would feel this way too, but that's a lot to ask from someone I wronged so terribly.

"What if it takes you a long time to catch him?" she says.

"It won't."

She shakes her head. "I'll stay with Aster at the hospital."

Josh blanches. "That's not an option."

"But—"

"No." His eyes are wide, fearful even. He's hiding something.

I lift an eyebrow, which makes his eyes bulge further. Ivy's too busy brooding to notice.

"You can have the bed," I tell her.

She scowls. "Whatever."

"Ivy—" Josh starts.

She raises her hand. "I understand. I don't like it, but I understand."

"Good," he says, right before his chief calls him back to inspect the hospital blueprints. They must have a new plan.

"I met Diana last night," Ivy says.

I startle at the change of subject.

"She told me she's the one who sent the necklace, but she thought she was sending me a gift." She grunts. "Like you would ever send me a gift. You're calculating, not generous."

I narrow my eyes. "When I had money, I was generous."

"You don't have to have money to be generous." When I stay silent, she adds, "Did you know Chase was living at her house?"

I nod.

"Why didn't you tell me?"

"It wasn't my place to tell. Besides, I thought Chase would've told you about it."

"Well he didn't. I had to hear it from Diana."

I lay my palms flat against the pantry wall. "I'm sorry."

"You know what else she told me?"

I shake my head.

"She told me nothing ever happened between you and her."

I stay quiet, attempting to comprehend where she's going with this.

"Why didn't you contradict me in the elevator? Why didn't you contradict Chase?"

"Because Chase only believes what he wants to believe."

She snorts. "Yeah. I learned that about him last night."

I frown.

"We broke up," she explains.

"Why?"

"Because I dared voice my concern that he might be working with you. When I got the necklace, he's the one who brought it up to my room."

"Chase would never do anything for me."

"I realized that. But it made me wonder..." Her eyes redden, unlike her face that's as pale as the dawn that broke over Kokomo this morning. "Would he ever do anything for me? You're his brother. He's supposed to love you, but he never visited you in jail."

My heart twists at her words. "Do you love Aster because you're *supposed* to?"

She shakes her head.

"Unfortunately, I've learned that sometimes you'll love people who won't love you back, and there's nothing you can do about it."

Her eyes redden. Audacity—or perhaps folly—seizes me, and I move toward her and gather her in my arms. I can't erase the pain my brother caused her, but perhaps I can ease it...if she'll let me. I stroke her back and she leans into me, and I realize she's letting me.

"I'd do anything for you," I whisper into her hair, but she's crying, so I don't think she hears me. I sort of hope she didn't.

I press my cheek against her head and rock her until the tears subside.

And then I rock her still.

And still, she lets me.

THIRTY-EIGHT

JOSH

"Hey," I whisper, stroking Aster's icy hand.

"Josh," she whispers. My name sounds like a gush of steam. And feels like it too. It warms me up, straight to my core.

"How are you doing, Sleeping Beauty?" I ask, keeping my voice low. I don't want to overwhelm her senses.

A smile slowly climbs over her face. "Good." She no longer has a respirator taped to her cheeks, and her skin is no longer gray.

"How's the head? Does it still hurt? One of the nurses told me you were in pain this morning."

"A little." Her speech is slow and labored, but articulate. "How…is Ivy?"

"She's fine."

I don't tell her Ivy is now spending most of her days with Brook. Our newest plan was delayed due to an impromptu visit from two federal agents who worked the case in New York. They came by because, after the D.A. was arrested for accepting gifts, they stopped by the prison and were told Brook had been checked out. They came straight to us. Brook has refused to meet with them, but he's aware we're joining forces.

"Mom…stopped by," she says. "I kept…eyes closed."

"Your mother? She's dead, Asty."

Slowly, she points her finger at me.

"Oh! *My* mom?"

She nods heavily, as though her neck were a spring holding up too hefty a load.

"Good girl," I say. I'm relieved that she remembered to appear sleeping. I don't want anyone to know about her recovery. Dean could come back before we're ready for him.

"When Ivy…come?"

"Soon. I promise. Now let's get you up a little."

"Tired, Josh." Her lids flutter close.

"You have to take a few steps every day." The nurses told me it was important to prevent bedsores and muscle atrophy. "Just lean on me, okay?"

Her eyes open again. I drape her arm around my shoulders and heave her up. Holding her around the waist, I guide her around the room. Her feet move as though there was no gravity to seal her soles to the ground. In her white robe, she looks like a fairy. Remembering that one time in prison when she told me I never paid her compliments, I tell her that. I think it's a nice thing to say. And sure enough, it makes her grin.

We turn and go the other way.

"Asty, do you remember those diamonds you told me about once when I came to see you in jail?"

Her eyes brim with tears.

I kick myself for not keeping my trap shut, but finding them could make a huge difference.

"Ivy. One."

I blink. She remembers. *She understands!* "Yes. Ivy had one. Where are the others?"

"I…I"—she starts jerking her head from left to right—"put them…"

"Where?"

"In quilt."

"No."

Sweat coats her deepening complexion, but at least she's stopped shaking her head. "Yes."

"No."

I can't tell if she's trying to keep her secret safe or if her memory is spotty.

"I…I…bed please," she whispers, lowering her eyes to the floor.

"It'll come back to you."

She starts shaking. Even her teeth rattle. Delicately, I help her back onto the bed. She's still trembling, and she's still sweating. I press on the call button, then climb in next to her and tuck her body against mine to soothe her.

Rubbing her arm with my hand, I whisper, "I'm right here, baby. Right here." Still she shivers. I can't seem to supply enough comfort to chase away the goose bumps.

Finally the door bursts open and the nurse called Sabrina strides in. After a glimpse at Aster, she plugs a tube into her catheter. I climb off the bed, but keep one hand wrapped around her wrist. Her trembling lessens, her arm goes limp, and then her lids slam shut.

Sabrina turns her lined face toward me. "What happened?"

I shift from the heels of my feet to the balls and back. "I asked her a question I needed an answer to."

"It upset her."

"But I needed an answer."

"Joshua, she just woke up. Give her some time."

"We don't have much time."

"What's so important?" she asks.

"It's about the case."

"Why don't you tell me, and I'll speak to her when she feels better?" She prods my friend's wrist to measure her pulse.

"It's okay. I'll come back tomorrow."

She sighs. "Well, whatever it is you need an answer to, I hope Aster will recover quickly to give it to you."

"Me too. I need to get to work now. Call me—"

"If there's any new development," she says. "I know the drill."

I kiss Aster's cheek and murmur a promise of returning soon. As I walk out of the hospital room, I check my phone and see seven missed calls from Claire.

I sprint down the stairs, phone pressed against my ear. "What's going on?" I shout.

"My kid's little league game starts in ten minutes and I'm stuck here. You were supposed to be here an hour ago!"

I slap my palm against my hammering heart. "This is about a baseball game? God, Claire, I thought Dean Kane had taken you hostage."

"Family's important to me, Coop. Are you on your way?"

"Yes. I'll be there in fifteen." High on adrenaline, I dash to my car and drive over to the safe house. Claire must have heard my car, because she's already opened the door, handbag swinging from her shoulder.

"I got tied up at the hospital," I tell her.

"Just get inside," she huffs.

I step past her.

"How's Aster?" Ivy asks as I close the door.

"Same old," I lie.

Ivy is sitting on the couch, stitching her quilt. She must be getting to the end because the sunflower almost looks like it has all of its petals.

"Where's Brook?"

"He's taking a nap. Apparently Claire talked to him all night. I suggested that he come and sleep in the room."

"You did not…"

"It's just to sleep."

"You can't invite a guy to share your bed, Ivy."

"You and I do it all the time."

"First off, we don't do it all the time," I say snippily, "and second off, he's going to take advantage of you. Haven't you seen the way he looks at you?"

Ivy blushes. "It's not like that between us." She shakes her head. "Not at all."

"Ives, you're a smart girl, the smartest one I know, but sometimes, you don't act very smart."

The redness recedes from her face. “That’s not a very nice thing to say.”

I squash my lips together, regretting my words. “It’s because you’re innocent.”

“You’re right. I am too innocent. Instead of sitting around here stitching quilts, I should become reckless, go to the Neon Cactus, dance and drink too much alcohol, pick up some guy, do things girls my age do instead of living in constant fear that my sister won’t wake up, that I’ll end up broke and homeless, that Dean will catch up to me and kill me.”

I tread over to Ivy and drop next to her on the couch. “Hey. Slow down. Where is this coming from?”

“He killed Kevin, Josh. He almost killed Aster. How easy would it be for him to kill me?”

“No one’s going to kill you, you hear me?”

Her lips twist.

“I promise,” I whisper. “Promise, promise.”

A door opens. She swipes her knuckles quickly under her glistening eyes and focuses her attention on her quilt.

“Hi,” Brook says, stretching.

Muscles move underneath his skin. I think of Ivy sleeping next to him, and how defenseless she’d be if he decided to have his way with her. If only I could be there to protect her all the time.

His arms drop alongside his body. “Everything all right?”

“Everything’s fine,” I mumble.

Brook cocks a thick eyebrow up at me, but doesn’t say anything. Instead he goes into the kitchen to pour himself a cup of coffee, to which he adds his weight in cold, full-fat milk.

Sighing, I grab the remote control and turn on the news, convinced that watching other people’s lives spiral out of control will beat the present situation. But boy am I wrong.

I try to click the TV off but the remote control slips out of my clammy hand. I bend over to grab it from the floor, but it’s too late.

Ivy has lifted her gaze to the screen.

THIRTY-NINE

Brook

"My sister is awake?" Ivy shrieks.

Holding my mug of tepid coffee, I stride back into the living room and stare at the television, at the reporter gushing about the miraculous recovery of Aster Redd, the girl who was savagely attacked a month ago by another inmate.

Josh's face is as red as the shell of a boiled lobster.

Ivy tosses her quilt to the side and stands up so fast that she sways. "That's why you've been keeping me away from her? Not for my protection but because you didn't want me to find out she was awake? When were you going to tell me?"

"After we apprehended Dean. I didn't want to overwhelm her," he mumbles.

"Overwhelm her?" she shouts. "She's my twin!"

"I was trying to do the sensible thing. The right thing."

"You don't get to decide what the right thing is without discussing it with me!"

"You didn't discuss the power of attorney with me."

Ivy's eyes bulge. "How dare you!" She whirls away from him, dashes into the bedroom, and slams the door shut.

"Is Aster coherent?" I ask after a beat.

"She recognizes me."

"Has she asked for Ivy?"

"What do you think?" he hisses.

His phone rings. As he glances down at the screen, sweat forms on his upper lip. Sponging it away with the hem of his polo shirt, he picks up. From the way he squints throughout the call, I take it his chief isn't tremendously pleased with the news. When he hangs up, he cradles his forehead with his hands before inhaling a long breath and pressing himself up. He paces the small living room, head bowed in thought.

"Why did you really keep it from her?" I ask, interrupting his manic marching.

"Because. I didn't want Ivy to get her hopes up in case Aster's progress stopped or reversed."

"She's a big girl, Josh."

"With a big heart that's gotten crushed over and over. She could do with fewer shattered hopes."

Some time later, there's a knock at the door. After checking the peephole, Josh pulls it open and his squad files in. Even Claire. She looks particularly unhappy to be back. I imagine it's because she's missing her kid's baseball game. She told me all about it while I was trying to sleep.

"I'll go check on Ivy," I say, but no one pays attention to me, too busy tearing Josh a new one. I knuckle the door. She doesn't tell me to come in, but I do anyway.

Sunlight streams around the edges of the flimsy drape that covers the small window, which is more of a porthole than a window. Shutting the door softly, I walk over to the bed where Ivy is lying in the fetal position and crouch down. A slender beam of light falls into her eyes, rendering them as luminescent as lagoons.

She looks at me, and her lower lip trembles. "I didn't think she would ever wake up."

I run my thumb over her mouth to iron away the tremors. She blinks, and then frowns a little, so I lower my hand.

After a long stretch of silence, she whispers, "I should've been there. The moment she woke up, I should've rushed to her side. I don't want her to think I abandoned her."

"I'm sure she doesn't think that."

A tear snakes down her cheek. I lift my hand to brush it away, but stop midway when I see her looking at my raised fingers. Again, her eyebrows tip toward her nose and her gaze connects with mine. When I was coming out of the bedroom, I heard Josh insinuating I'd take advantage of her if she shared my bed. From the way she contemplates me, I fear she believes him.

"I'm so mad at him," she says.

"He did it to protect you."

"Protect me from what?" Her voice is rough with emotion.

"From disappointment in case her progress was short-lived."

"She's awake, Brook! Even if it lasts only minutes, I want to see her, to hold her, to speak to her. Keeping it a secret was selfish." She sits up, flinging her legs over the side of the bed, and stands. "I have to get out of here."

I rise from my crouch. "Not in your state."

"I *need* to see her. It's visceral."

"I understand, but you have to absorb this first. You're in shock. You don't want her to feel your shock. Plus I bet the hospital is crawling with reporters. They'll pounce on you if they spot you. And Dean—" I stop myself from voicing my greatest fear. She's already terrified of him.

"Do you truly think Dean will come back?"

Thinking of my ex-best friend cleaves my heart open. "Yes."

"Do you regret working with the police?"

I shake my head. "Go to the hospital with Josh. Just in case."

Her gaze turns somber. "You didn't care about my safety back in New York, but now you're worried?"

"I did care. I just didn't think Dean was dangerous until…until he drowned Kevin."

"That was two days before the competition ended. Three, if you count the day off. Why didn't you warn me then?"

My lungs contract as though there is no oxygen in the small, dark bedroom. "Telling you would've put you in danger."

"Because not telling me worked out so well?" She backs away toward the door.

There is no fear in her eyes, but there is regret. When I was in prison, I used to think that if Aster made it out alive, Ivy would be able to forgive me once she knew my reasons for doing what I did, but that scenario played out, and the wariness remains. My only hope now is that capturing Dean will sway her.

But what if it doesn't?

What if I'm stuck loving someone who could never love me back?

FORTY

JOSH

Ivy interrupts our frenzied meeting with an insane request to go to the hospital.

"No way," I tell her.

"You don't get it, Josh. This isn't me asking; this is me telling you I'm going to see Aster. Now either one of you can take me, or I call a taxi."

"Claire, can you accompany her?" the chief says, sighing.

Claire grumbles but stands up.

"No, I'll go," I say.

Guarda glances at Ivy for her approval. What he doesn't get is, even if she puts up a fight about me coming, I'm not letting her out of my sight. Now that Aster's recovery is all over the news, I'm expecting Dean or a Discoli to crawl out of their shadowy dens.

In the car, Ivy doesn't talk to me. She doesn't even look at me.

"We're monitoring the airstrips, the state borders, the bus stations. And the hospital is swarming with federal agents. If he comes, he won't make it out."

"What about my house? Are you still monitoring it?"

Hearing her voice makes me giddy with relief. "Since you've been at the safe house, we've stopped the patrols, but Mr. Mancini is looking out."

"So are you just going to wait now?"

I nod.

"That's a shitty plan."

"You have a better one?"

"Yes."

"Let's hear it."

She releases her lip and turns to look at me. "Eyes on the road, Joshy. You're a guy; you cannot do two things at once."

"Is that right?"

"It's a fact."

"You do know that's never been scientifically proven, don't you?" I say.

She snorts.

"So what's your stellar idea, Miss Redd?"

"After I leave Aster's room, I can give an interview that her mind is clear and her memory is intact. Dean will think she told me where to find the diamonds."

"And he'll hunt you down."

"And you'll catch him. Or I can send him a private message to ask him for a meeting through Facebook?"

I smile, but shake my head.

"What?" she asks.

"Inviting him to dinner is cute, but I don't think he'll bite—even if he's hungry. He knows Aster's awake. He'll come. He's probably already here." I think of the camera, from which we didn't get anything. *Stupid digital contraption.*

The hospital comes up on my right. I put my blinker on and wait for the light to turn green, tapping my fingers against my steering wheel to the beat of a P!nk song.

"Do you trust Brook?" Ivy suddenly asks.

"Yes." I glance at her. "Don't you?"

"I want to."

After I park, we walk up to Aster's room. I spot a handful of agents wandering through the hospital. They're conspicuous even though they're in plain clothes.

The guard on duty lets us through. Inside the room, Sabrina is sitting beside Aster. "I didn't speak to the press."

"It's all right."

Her eyes lock on Ivy, but my friend's attention is riveted to her sleeping sister.

"Could you leave us, Sabrina?"

"Of course."

Once the nurse is gone, Ivy strokes her sister's cheek. "Can I wake her?"

Aster's eyes flutter open. They grow wide and wet, and her lips part but no sound comes out.

"Hey," Ivy says gently.

She picks up her sister's hand and presses it into her own, and, as though Aster's palm were connected directly to her tear ducts, tears spring out and trail down her gaunt cheeks. Ivy wipes them off before they reach the small mole over her lip.

"Hey, baby sister," Ivy says.

Aster's lips wobble into a smile. They always bickered about who was the oldest one. Some people say it's the twin who's birthed last. Apparently that means she was created before the other. I never took sides. To me, Ivy and Aster are two parts of the same person. In the womb, a person's right arm doesn't grow sooner than the left.

"Really you?" Aster whispers.

"It's really me," Ivy says, sitting down on the mattress.

Aster's smile manages to stick to her pale lips. While Ivy asks her how she feels, Aster reaches up and touches the ends of Ivy's curls. They're not as flat and shiny as usual. They're more like Aster's—when her hair was long.

"Yours will grow back, Asty," she reassures her.

Aster gives a minuscule nod. "In looong time."

"Time goes by so fast," Ivy says.

"For you."

Ivy fiddles with a slender gold band she wears around her thumb.

"Slow in prison," Aster says, letting her hand fall back against the thin sheet.

"You're not going back there."

Furrows groove Aster's forehead like the perfect rows of sunflowers we used to wander through as kids to reach the tire swing.

"I'm making you a quilt," she tells her sister.

"Really?"

"Yes."

"Can I see it?"

"I can bring it tomorrow."

Aster's lids droop a little, but she heaves them open. It looks difficult.

"She's going to feel groggy for a while," I tell Ivy, whose eyes flash to mine in worry. "It's normal."

Aster's lids collapse again, but she wrenches them back open.

"I was here a lot when you were sleeping," Ivy tells her. "I told you stories. Did you hear them?"

"I like stories," she murmurs. "Tell me…a story?" she breathes. "The faerie one."

"You mean the one I made up when we were eight?"

Her head dips at the same time as her lids. This time they don't come back up. Ivy nestles against her sister.

"Once upon a time," she begins, "there was a little faerie with transparent wings and a translucent body. She was the only one of her kind who was see-through. All the other faeries were big and dark blue, with sharp talons and pointy teeth. She had no such attributes. Her teeth were rounded and her feet soft. The others would laugh at her and terrorize her with their barbed extremities. Some would fly right into her, pretending they hadn't seen her.

"Many times she tumbled onto the forest floor and injured herself. Once, she tore her wing on some brambles and couldn't fly back up into the tall tree they lived in. That day, she learned to walk. It hurt because her feet weren't used to it. She discovered that moss felt nicer than rocks, and that grass tickled. She walked until her wing healed. It took days, weeks.

"By the time it mended, she'd arrived in a big city with big cars and big people. No one saw her, because she was transparent and so small. She was almost stepped on and swatted so often that she took to flying again. And high. She would stare at everyone and everything with her wide, clear eyes. If she'd been navy blue, the humans would have captured her and studied her, but no one could see her, so no one could catch her. It was the first time in her life she felt thankful for being different.

"But after months, it turned lonely. Even though her people made fun of her, at least she existed in the forest. Here, no one knew she existed. So she started her journey home. Tired one evening, she landed on a big green shrub full of flowers that resembled Ping Pong balls. She suckled the flowers, and it was the most delicious nectar she'd ever drunk. It put her straight to sleep and she slumbered until she heard a little voice saying hello.

"She zipped off her leaf, heart beating as fast as her wings. It was silly, because no one could see her, so no one had said hello. But a small girl with wild, blonde corkscrew curls was staring straight at her. Not through her. *At her*.

"You can see me? she asked. The little girl nodded. How? she asked. Because I'm looking, the little girl said, widening her eyes to prove her point. She poked her clear body with her chubby finger, which made the faerie look down. She'd turned a little blue during the night. Frowning, she gazed at the white ball-like flowers, then back down at her body. She checked her feet for talons and felt her teeth, but they had not sharpened…*yet*.

"All her life, she'd longed to be like her kind, but suddenly, she feared it. What if becoming blue turned her into someone mean? She refused to believe it. Looking like someone else didn't turn you into someone else. She decided that if she were to stay blue, she would also stay kind…" Ivy's voice trails off and I startle back into the room, blinking away the little see-through faerie.

She's fallen asleep right alongside Aster. They look so peaceful, so happy, so whole, that I don't dare wake them. I let them enjoy each other's company before they're uprooted and torn apart again.

I call my mother, I call my father, I call the chief. He sounds funny over the phone. Excited. "We have a new plan," he gushes.

When I ask him about it, he says he'll fill me in when I return. I toy with my phone a long while after that. I write a text message to Heidi, but delete it. I stand up and stretch my legs just as a nurse comes to check on Aster. I gently shake Ivy awake and tell her we should get going. She kisses her sister's cheek, then rises and follows me out.

"Aster always told me she hated that plant," I say as we reach the elevator. "The buttonbush," I add, in case sleep erased her memory of her faerie story.

"She did?"

"Yeah."

"That's weird. She's the one who bought it. With her allowance. She even planted it herself."

"Didn't your mother say that it would grow wild and block out all her light?"

Ivy sighs. "That does sound like something Mom would've said."

"Why do you think she was so hard on Aster, but more lenient with you?" I ask as we walk out into the dusk-covered parking lot. I never asked her this before, because I was afraid to bring it up…afraid it would create friction between the sisters, or between us.

"I used to believe Mom was trying to make her tougher, but now I think it's because she saw herself in Aster," she says, getting into my car. "When she acted out against her, she was acting out against the pathology they shared."

"Sorry I brought her up."

"Never be. It's good for me to talk about her sometimes. Even though she wasn't perfect, I don't want to forget her." She grabs a tissue from the car's backseat. After she blows her nose, she says, "Now you owe me a really good dinner and a really strong drink."

"You're underage."

"Josh, silence your inner cop. He's being rude to me."

I chuckle. "Fine. Shall we pick up some roast chicken and potatoes?"

"What about going to a restaurant?"

"When Dean is caught, I'll take you and Aster out, on my measly little salary, to the best damn restaurant in all of Indiana, but until then, we're laying low."

As I drive away from the hospital, my phone rings. I pick up. "Hi, Mr. Kelley," I say. "You're on speakerphone, and Ivy Redd is next to me."

Ivy's eyes grow wide and eager.

"Here's the deal from the courthouse. Your sister was found not guilty by reason of mental disorder. So now she has two options, either she is transferred to an institution for an indefinite amount of time, or she is returned to prison. Considering she was found *not guilty*, if she returns to prison, she could probably get out in a couple of years, once the system deems she's no longer a threat to society."

"So you're saying she's better off returning to prison?" Ivy exclaims, horrified.

"I'm suggesting it might be the better of two evils," Kelley says.

"She almost died in prison!"

Kelley lets out a heavy sigh. "I have two days to inform the judge what we are going to go with."

A tear glides down my cheek. I haven't cried since the first time I was nicknamed Hamster. I sniffle. "We'll call you tomorrow. Thank you, Mr. Kelley."

Ivy is dry-eyed, but her jawline quivers. She's as racked by emotion as I am, but doing a better job at holding it in. "We can't send her back," she whispers.

I nod my agreement.

FORTY-ONE

Brook

"I can't believe I got stuck taking care of the two of you," Josh says, tossing a piece of pretzel at Ivy, who ducks out of the way, but it still lands in her hair, and since her hair is so springy, it gets stuck.

As I pick it out, I say, "You did take Claire away from her son's little league game."

"I did no such thing. That was the chief. He should be here instead of me," Josh says.

"That would be way less fun. He'd probably make us stop drinking," Ivy says, tipping her glass of wine to her lips.

"I should make you stop drinking," Josh says, even though he's downed a couple beers himself.

"Don't even," she says. "After that phone call, I'm allowed as much wine as I want."

I eye them, not privy to the phone call they're referring to.

Ivy spots my curiosity, gulps down more wine, then says, "My sister can choose between going back to jail or getting stuck in an institution for an"—she hiccups—"*indefinite* amount of time." She replaces her glass on the table next to her neat stack of quarters. "Will you also have to go back to jail after this...*job*?"

"It's not a job," I say in a low voice.

She shoots me a wry smile.

"And no. I got a commutation of sentence for meritorious service."

"In English?"

"I won't go back to jail because I'm cooperating with government authority, but I also won't regain my civil rights." I spin a quarter between my index and middle fingers. "If they catch me gambling, though, they might overturn their ruling. I don't think it's too well regarded as a pastime for a reformed conman. I bet gardening would be way better viewed."

Ivy smirks. "Gardening? First a ranch, and now tilling soil? You're so down-to-earth, Brook. A true peasant."

I crack a smile. "Yeah, yeah. Make fun now. When you visit my ranch someday, you won't be laughing."

Although her eyes are bright, the mirth has vanished from her face. "Crap," she whispers, tossing her two cards face up on the table. She stands up so abruptly that both Josh and I frown.

"What?"

"I think I know where Aster put the diamonds."

"What?" Josh and I say at the same time.

"I mean, I have an idea. *Crap.*" She looks for her shoes. Once she locates them, she slips them on. "You have to drive me to my house."

"Right now? I'm a bit tip—"

"Right now," she says.

Josh jumps up, slips his loafers on, and grabs his car keys. I get up too, but I don't have shoes to put on. They didn't think I was going anywhere.

"I'd like to come," I say.

Ivy glances at me, but her eyes are glassy, focused inwards, on her breakthrough.

"It's not like I can leave you here all by yourself." Josh rubs his short hair. "Crap. I shouldn't be driving in my state."

"You had three beers and a lot of chicken," I say. "I think you'll be fine."

He glowers, rubs his eyes, and unlocks the front door. "You're sure, Ivy?"

"No. But it's worth a look," she says.

She's out the door quicker than Josh.

"Will this beep?" I point to my ankle monitor.

"Nah. It will just send your GPS coordinates to the transmission unit."

"Could you maybe phone in that I'm not trying to escape? So that I don't get shot down or anything."

As he locks the door, he calls the precinct and informs them that we're heading over to the Redd place. I scan the dusky street. Any moment, I expect Dean's silver Ferrari with its blinding lights to rev right up, but the cars parked along the sidewalk are as humble as the shadowy buildings next to them. Only one car sticks out from the lot, and thankfully, it's not a Ferrari but a vintage, light blue Cadillac. For some reason, I feel like I've already seen this car, but I can't put my finger on where.

Ivy climbs into the backseat, so I sit next to Josh, who rubs his eyes at least twenty times during our drive. I've never seen where Ivy lives. I'm imagining something minuscule and rundown, but in fact, it's much nicer. At least from the outside.

Josh moves toward her front door, digging inside his windbreaker for keys, but Ivy touches his arm and shakes her head. She leads us to the side of her apartment where a veranda curves out into a tiny yard. She drops to her knees and starts digging under a plant.

Josh crouches down next to her. "She wouldn't—"

"She had dirt under her nails, Josh. Don't you remember?"

"Shit..." he whispers, mouth gaping. He kneels down next to her and digs also.

Minutes go by and the only thing they turn up is wet soil.

"A little help, Earth Boy," Josh says.

A car drives by. I peer into the darkness for it, but all that remains by the time I locate it are burning taillights.

"I didn't think you'd want my help," I say, lowering myself to the ground on the other side of the enormous shrub. I feel hard filaments, which I imagine are roots, and slippery soft bodies, which I suspect are worms, but no diamonds. We dig so long and so deep I worry the plant won't survive our foraging.

As I start to press the dirt back against the spindly roots, Josh gasps.

"Did you find something?" I ask, springing up and rounding the bush.

Ivy rocks back on her heels and extends her shaky hands toward me. In her palm rests a tiny square of yellowish-brown paper that crinkles as Josh plucks it from her. He unfolds the sealed edges with his dirt-coated fingers. Under the moonlight, seven diamonds, the size of the one Dean found in Ivy's room during the show, sparkle.

Josh stares at Ivy, who hasn't moved or said a single word since her discovery. "We found them," he whispers.

He smiles at her. When she doesn't reciprocate, he smiles up at me. I'm too stunned to smile.

At the sound of approaching footsteps, he folds the makeshift envelope back up and stuffs it inside the pocket of his windbreaker. An old man shouldering a shotgun creeps up to us. I stick my hands up because he has it aimed at me.

"You're that guy from TV. The mobster," he says.

"I'm not a mobster."

"But you're that guy from TV, aren't you?"

I nod, swallowing hard as the nozzle gleams in the night, too close to my stomach for comfort.

"Mr. Mancini, lower your weapon. He's with us," Ivy says.

"But he's that guy. The one—"

"I know who he is. Put your gun away," Ivy says, standing up. She steps in front of me, her chest almost pressed against the rifle. "Please."

The old man's lined forehead smushes up, but at least he draws his gun back down. "What are you three doing, digging up a garden in the middle of the night?"

"I lost a lucky penny," Josh says.

"Under the buttonbush?" The old guy narrows his eyes. "Joshua, you promise this guy hasn't taken you hostage?"

"I promise, Mr. Mancini. Thank you for coming to check. I truly appreciate it."

He harrumphs, steals a few shadowy glances at us, and finally treks off. "If I read about your bodies being found buried in some ditch, don't expect my pity," he throws over his shoulder.

Josh's smile widens. I don't know what Ivy's feeling as she still has her back to me. Her hair blows against my neck. I place my hand over her shoulder. She shivers. I raise it but let it hover over her cold skin as I walk around her.

"Thank you," I tell her.

She bites her lip. Her eyes, which sparkle like the diamonds in Josh's pocket, turn up toward me. "This can be over now, right?"

Josh clears his throat. "There's still the small detail of his crazy friend."

"He's right, Ivy. Dean's still out there."

Josh dials his chief. Although he keeps his voice quiet, it's animated. Ivy wraps her arms around herself, as though finally realizing that all she has on is a tank top and leggings. I peel off my long-sleeved gray Henley and drape it over her shoulders. Ivy's eyes travel over my bare chest before climbing back up to my face. She tries to press the shirt back, but I shake my head.

"You don't even have shoes," she says.

"I'm getting ready for my life as a peasant."

She smiles. When her teeth clatter, I drape an arm around her shoulders and walk her back to Josh's car. He beeps it open. I press her into the backseat and sit next to her, keeping my arm around her shoulders. She leans into me, and my heart gallops. I close my eyes and tuck her in closer. Josh is speaking quickly, dizzy with the delight of our nocturnal treasure hunt.

He pumps up the music until the car is filled with a hectic beat that mirrors the thumping inside my head.

"This is incredible. Incredible," he exclaims, whirling around to look at us. The traffic light above the car tinges his hair red.

"That was a clever hiding spot," Ivy says.

Another car is stopped at the sleepy intersection, the vintage Cadillac I saw earlier. Instead of advancing through the green light, it waits.

"Josh, that car was parked next to the safe house," I say, just as the light turns green for us.

Slowly, too slowly, Josh spins back around. The other car crawls over the pedestrian pathway, or perhaps I'm imagining it moving in slow motion. If Josh reverses, the car will miss ours. But he doesn't go backward. He doesn't go forward either. He just stares at the Cadillac as though it were a ghost.

Keeping one arm around Ivy, I lunge forward and latch on to his headrest. "Go, go go!" I yell into his ear.

Ivy's body hardens in the crook of my arm.

He hits the gas. But so does the other car. I spring back and curl my body around Ivy's. And then I wait, bracing myself for impact.

FORTY-TWO

JOSH

A scream reverberates inside my skull. Is it mine? The scream turns into a bizarre, brassy symphony. Metal, glass, air, and light explode around me.

Inside of me.

Shrieks and shouts and sobs sound softly in my ears. An ache blooms in my jaw, in my legs, in my waist. Something cuts into my chest, cracks my left arm, yanks on my neck.

I flip.

I land on a multicolored sea of plastic balls beside the tire swing, and Aster and Ivy laugh, long blonde curls flapping in the sunflower-scented breeze. I reach behind me to push up, but there's no ground beneath the balls.

And soon, there are no balls.

And there is no Aster, and no Ivy.

I fly.

Granddad and Grandma wave as I soar above them, while Mom and Dad blow me kisses out of their palms. Mom's lips are cherry-red, her favorite color, and Granddad has his special flower shirt on. The one he gave me.

The one I never gave back.

I float.

Heidi skips and twirls, and her metallic hair and freckles glint in the bright, pale light. She smiles and whispers my name.

And then I see Jackie again. The flash of her warm, sad smile, of her badge that warded off evil.

She grows smaller and dimmer as I drift higher. Farther.

There is no more sound.

No more gravity.

No more pain.

Only bright…white…light.

FORTY-THREE

Brook

I tuck my chin into my chest and squeeze my eyes shut as the car flips in the air. With no seatbelt to hold me down, my body, still entangled with Ivy's, levitates. Glass shatters and embeds itself inside my bare back like miniature daggers, and metal slices through my thigh. My muscles tauten and my limbs harden as we roll again and again. With every thump, fresh pain stirs inside my wounds; with every scream, my pulse thunders and my heart swells. I sweat, I bleed, I shiver.

When the tires of the car slam back into the ground, I pry my eyes open. Josh's body is bent at an unnatural angle, and his eyes, although open, are veined with blood. Vomit shoots up my throat and burns my mouth. I bounce away from Ivy and lean as far away as possible in our crumpled metal box. Although I grind my teeth closed, the vomit sprays out of me. My ears ring, yet I hear someone cry. *Ivy*. She's alive. I swipe my arm over my mouth, before turning back toward her. Her cheeks are streaked with blood and tears, but there are no cuts on her face, at least none that I can see. It must be my blood.

She shrieks and propels her upper body over the central armrest. "Josh!" Her hands prod and stroke Josh's lifeless body. "He has no pulse," she screams.

I knew that before she touched him. He has the same look Kevin had when he was fished out of the ocean.

His body moves.

Could he still—

Large hands, not Ivy's, run over Josh's windbreaker. I want to think that someone has come to save us, but a gold ring glints on the person's pinkie.

"Dean," I croak. It's not a plea for help; it's a warning for Ivy.

She looks at him, body immobile, face impassive. Unable to predict what his next move will be, I latch on to her waist and yank her back. I kick at the door until it grinds open, and then I shove my entire body against it. Cradling her, I crawl out.

"Josh," she whimpers. "Josh." Pink tears course down the side of her face.

Gravel scratches my knees through my ripped jeans, yet I push forward, taking us as far away from the car as possible. Setting her down gently, I press both my hands into the ground and rise, grinding my teeth to avoid screaming in pain as I straighten my spine.

"What have you done?" My voice sounds unfamiliar to my humming ears.

"Recuperating what is mine." In Dean's hand rests the rumpled, yellow paper filled with diamonds. "I heard you were planning some elaborate scheme to trap me, but a mastermind stays one step ahead. Always one step ahead." He rounds the smoking front bumper. "You disappointed me, brother." He taps the left side of his chest with the butt of a gun. "But I expected it the day you stopped wearing your ring."

I curl the fingers of my right hand into a fist. "That ring tied me to someone I no longer recognized."

"Speaking of recognition…Dominic is terribly upset with you after all he's done for your family. Fabricating and feeding stories to the FBI"—he gestures toward Josh—"that's low of you." He shakes his head from side to side, his silver eyes reflecting the cold gleam of the headlights. "You almost ruined everything when you chose her over me. *Oh*…and you can forget about your commission."

An almost feral sound shoots out of me. I lunge toward Dean, but hands close around my chest and hold me back. A flashback from our boating trip catapults into my mind. "I saved your life once, Dean! Troy and I pulled you out of the water. If I could've predicted any of this—"

"You wouldn't have saved me?" Pain flashes in Dean's eyes.

I gulp as more memories flood me. Toasts to undying friendship and great success.

Our friendship is dead, and so is our futile attempt at success.

"Just leave us," Ivy says, her breath warming my bare back.

Dean laughs. "After what you've done to me, what your sister has done to me, you're deluding yourself if you think I'll let you live."

"Ivy's done nothing to you."

"She stole what wasn't hers to steal," Dean says.

"She had no idea! Her sister gave her that diamond. Besides…it wasn't even yours."

"Oh come on, Brook!" He slaps the hood of the car with the gun, which makes Ivy jump. "Have you seen where she fucking lives? It's a dump. People who live in dumps can't afford diamonds. She knew her sister stole it. Didn't you, sweetheart?"

Her hands tremble and glide down my skin, wet, slippery, and cold.

"Put the gun away, Dean," I say, my voice as cool and hard as the ground beneath my feet.

"When Mom gets here, I'll put it away." His eyes dart to the empty intersection.

"Is she late? Maybe she's busy getting naked with some guy. Isn't that how she makes money these days? Screw anyone with a big wallet and hope for another kid?"

"Fuck you," he says. After a beat, he adds, "She's coming."

"She's not, Dean."

"She's already here." A manic smile curls over his mouth. "She's been in this goddamn town from day one, monitoring the girls' house, speaking to their neighbors. She even stopped by the hospital for some updates."

Ivy springs out from behind my back. "No way. The police would've known—"

"The police *did* know. At least your little cop friend knew. It took him a while to figure it out, but he did."

"That's impossible…" Ivy says. "Josh tells me everything."

"You're sick, Dean," I tell him. "You need help."

His eyes dart to the still-empty road.

"The only ones coming will be cops. They're tracking my ankle bracelet." I want him to feel as alone as I felt the day the Feds burst into the Temple room to arrest me. Alone, and helpless, and petrified. "You better start walking, because I don't think Troy's car is in any shape to be driven." It finally came back to me where I'd seen the Cadi…in a picture Troy sent me after he'd fixed it up. He'd been so proud.

Doubt crosses Dean's face. He takes a step back, then another, but then stops. There's movement somewhere behind him. It's not a car though. It's a person. I squint to see if it's his mother, but my eyesight is blurry, and all I can make out is a shape.

"On second thought"—he grins, resembling the Joker I was so terrified of as a child—"I have no desire to spend my life looking over my shoulder." He points the gun at Ivy.

I leap in front of her, hoping my body will be strong enough to shield hers. The shot rings out, echoing inside my eardrums along with the rest of the quiet world around us.

My jaw cracks as my cheek knocks into the gravel, but nowhere else hurts. Dean must've missed…or I wasn't quick enough and the bullet hit Ivy first.

I open my mouth to call out her name when pain, worse than the one in my face, erupts inside my waist. I can't see anything. There's too much blood, and dirt, and sweat in my eyes to see anything, but I can feel everything. Warm blood oozes out of my mouth, trickles down my lips. Cold hands press against my skin.

Ivy yells, but her words don't make sense.

A second explosion rips through the night.

"Ivy?" I murmur, attempting to stand, but the ground sucks me in, and the world spins.

Something falls…a long, dark shape…a body.

"Ivy?" I croak.

The burning sensation in my waist starts to fade. I can't feel her hands anymore. He must have shot her… A cry rips out of me, and I flatten my palms against the ground and press as hard as I can to turn over so I can see, but something, someone holds me back, cradles my jaw, a gentle voice murmurs my name. I think it's an angel, but I realize that it's Ivy with her backlit halo of curls and her beautiful face.

"He's gone," she says.

"Gone?"

"Dead," she murmurs, then adds, "Mancheenee." I frown, yet in some distant recess of my mind, the word calls back the face of an old man.

Sirens wail. Footfalls echo. I lock my gaze on Ivy's because I don't want to fall asleep. I'm frightened that if I do, I'll never wake up.

EPILOGUE

10 DAYS LATER

Ivy

I've left the hospital twice since Brook was wheeled in, bleeding and unconscious: once to pack a small suitcase of clothes, and once to visit Josh's mother.

I still can't believe he's gone. Every time someone calls me, I expect to see his name flash on my phone; every time I close my eyes, I see his face. I thought after ten days, the tears would subside, but I seem to have a bottomless stock of them.

"He was so handsome, wasn't he?" I tell Aster, scrolling through picture after picture of Josh on my phone. I pause on the one I took the day he made trooper. Just a year ago. "He was so proud of his badge."

I'm not sure showing Aster reminders of Josh is the right thing, but I want her to react. I want her to speak. Ever since he died, she's shut down. Losing Josh destroyed my sister. He meant everything to her. She's stopped talking, stopped smiling, stopped feeding herself, yet she keeps breathing…so I keep hoping that one day, someday, a small smile will bloom on her face like the white flowers of her buttonbush.

I stroke her dry cheek. "Margaret told me she had a beautiful story all picked out for you."

Margaret is Aster's private nurse. Even though my twin is no longer in harm's way—Alaina Kane was apprehended on her way to rescue her son and Dominic was arrested—I don't allow anyone beside Margaret and me by her side. That is… until I have to send Aster away, to the dreaded institution. I haven't told her yet. I don't know how to tell her.

As the cheery nurse seizes the book I laid on the overbed table, I squeeze Aster's hand. "I signed Paul Willows's contract."

Brook was furious about my decision, but I couldn't refuse the money. Besides, it's not forever.

Nothing lasts forever in this world.

"I can now buy you all the romance novels you can dream of," I tell her, hoping for a smile.

Her lips stay limp, like the rest of her. Only her eyes roll up toward me. I can read the wordless plea in them…to let her go…to help her go.

"I can't," I whisper. "Forgive me, but I can't."

A single tear drips out of her eye and travels down her cheek, tripping over her tiny mole before vanishing between her parted, chapped lips. Incapable of holding her gaze any longer, I slide her hand out of mine and flee her room, dashing down the hallway. I slow when I reach the cafeteria. Even though I have no appetite, I force myself to eat.

"Hey, Ivy," Chase says, waving from a table.

I buy a muffin, then wind my way toward him. "How's Brook?" I ask, taking large bites of my breakfast to get it down fast.

"Better. They're talking about releasing him today."

"Oh." My heart draws this strange arabesque against the walls of my chest. "Will he return to New York with you?"

"That's what my parents want."

"How are your parents?"

"Back together, so there's that."

I smile even though I don't feel much like smiling.

He rubs the back of his neck. "There was something I wanted to tell you before I left."

I frown.

"About Kevin."

"You want to talk about Kevin?"

He grimaces. "Remember that day I told you he'd hit on me?"

I nod. The memory of the private investigator feels distant, like he was part of some other lifetime, lived by some other girl.

"Well, he didn't. He questioned me about Brook. Told me about his suspicions. He asked me to help him keep an eye on him…and on you."

"What?" The word shoots out of me like the bullet from Mr. Mancini's rifle, the one that brought Dean down. "*Wow*."

"I wanted to tell you for some time now, but it was never the right time."

"No kidding."

"Don't be mad, Ivy. Please." He gazes at me through brown eyes rimmed with terrible sadness.

"I'm not…mad. I'm just surprised. I thought the great Chase Jackson never lied."

"I'm an ass."

"Can I get that in writing?" Humor returns, because after all I've been through, his lie doesn't hurt much. Doesn't hurt at all, actually. "Is that why you dated me for all of ten seconds?"

He shakes his head, and his copper hair flaps wildly around his blushing ears. "No. I promise. That wasn't why."

"Relax. I was teasing you." I squeeze his arm that feels unfamiliar, even though, once upon a time, that arm kept me upright when life insisted on tipping me over.

"Brook's asking for you," Diana says, appearing next to our table. Chase's face is so uncharacteristically red that she frowns. "You okay, Chase?"

He coughs. "Fine."

"I wanted to go back to the hotel. Can you give me a ride?" she asks.

He nods. "So we're good?" he asks me as I start walking off.

I toss the rest of the muffin into a bin. "We're good." I quicken my pace to reach Brook.

When life finally tipped me over, it wasn't Chase's arms that caught me; it was his brother's.

From his sick bed, Brook shoots me a smile that makes my heart twist again. "Hey," he says as I approach. He's propped the backrest up.

"I heard the big news…" I try injecting some enthusiasm into my voice. "All fixed, huh?"

Dark eyebrows pinched together, he scoots to one side of the bed, then pats the empty space next to him. I climb up and rest my head against his bandaged shoulder. I want to act cheery, but nothing remotely cheerful comes to mind.

"My parents' former housekeeper came to visit me yesterday," he says. "I think she cried more than you."

"I doubt that's possible."

"She brought me tamales. Want one?"

"I'm not really hungry."

His thumb strokes my cheek. "I'm buying my ranch."

I press up to look at him. "What? How?"

His dark eyes turn down to the white sheets. "She kept something safe for me. Something very valuable." He lifts his eyes to mine. "I didn't want to take it back, but she didn't want to keep it."

"What was it?"

He swallows hard. "One of my mother's…one of her diamond necklaces."

I bristle. I hate diamonds. I even hate the word.

"I get to start over," he says.

I nod. "That's great." I avert my gaze. "So you're going straight to Montana, or wherever it is you buy ranches these days?"

"After I stop by Troy's grave, yes."

I close my eyes as Josh's headstone swims into my mind. Even though he was never my real brother, his mother had the words *Beloved Brother* carved next to the words *Beloved Son*. "Everyone keeps leaving me."

"Hey," he says, gathering me in a hug. Maybe our last one.

I inhale a shaky breath. “You’ll call me, right?”

“Why would I call you?”

I press away from him, hurt. “Because we’re friends, aren’t we?”

“I took a bullet for you. So no, Ivy, we’re not friends.”

I think the bullet might have hurt less.

“We’re more than that. And I’m not going to call you because”—he raises his hand to my jaw—“because I’m not leaving without you. I don’t have much more to offer than my heart, but I was hoping it could be enough for now.”

I stare at him.

Just stare at him.

“Please say something.”

I can’t unearth a single word as my wild heart has overpowered my brain. Even though I rue the day Dean shot Brook, it made me realize I wasn’t ready to lose him. Not after I’d just found him.

His gaze turns uncertain. “Ivy?”

A breath whistles through my lips. It doesn’t calm my pulse but it brings oxygen into my faulty brain. “After everything…you still want me?”

“I’ve always wanted you. Even when you didn’t choose me, I kept wanting you.”

My chest clenches. “You weren’t a choice back then, Brook.”

He sits up straighter and tucks a long curl behind my ear. “Well, pick me now.”

“I’ve already picked you.” I gaze at the pale green wall, beyond which lies my sister. I can’t see her, but I can feel her.

My other half.

My sweeter half.

My shattered half.

I nestle my cheek into his open hand, then slide my mouth against his warm skin and kiss it. “But I can’t leave.” His hand stiffens. “I can’t leave Aster.”

“You can’t move into the institution with her. You’ll visit. Often. After I sell the necklace, I’ll put some money aside for your trips.”

“You don’t have to do that,” I start.

“Yes, I do. I don’t want you using any of Paul Willows’s money.”

My lips quirk up at his jealousy.

He tips my chin up, then slowly runs his thumb across my mouth, before pulling me in close. He stops when the tip of my nose touches the tip of his. “I love you, Ivy Redd. I’ve loved you since the first night you walked into the Temple room in your blue dress, and I’m going to love you for a very long time. Forev—”

I kiss him before he can finish the word, hoping that if I seal the syllables between our lips, forever might happen…for once.

ACKNOWLEDGMENTS

The *Cold Little Games series* started with ***Cold Little Games*** (previously titled: *The Masterpiecers*), which has now become the second book in the series. You must wonder how a first book became a second book? Well, the answer's simple: I wanted my readers to get to know Aster and Ivy before they became famous and to see where they came from. It took me signing up to be part of a wonderful mystery and thriller boxed set (MURDER & MAYHEM) to make this happen.

Now, onto the real reason for this part of the book. I'd like to thank, you, dear reader, for spending time with Aster and Ivy. I hope you've enjoyed their tale and will look for the next episode in their lives.

I'd like to tell my beta-reading pit crew how thankful I am for the time they took out of their busy lives to read and critique my work. Your opinions and insights mean the world to me. So thank you, Theresea, Katie, Vanessa, Marina, and Astrid.

Sarah, Becky and Jessica, thank you for your attention to detail and your talent.

And finally, my crazy, loud family, I love all of you (more than I like writing, I promise!).

ALSO BY OLIVIA WILDENSTEIN

PARANORMAL ROMANCE

***The Lost Clan* series**

ROSE PETAL GRAVES

ROWAN WOOD LEGENDS

RISING SILVER MIST

RAGING RIVAL HEARTS

RECKLESS CRUEL HEIRS

***The Boulder Wolves* series**

A PACK OF BLOOD AND LIES

A PACK OF VOWS AND TEARS

A PACK OF LOVE AND HATE

A PACK OF STORMS AND STARS

***Angels of Elysium* series**

FEATHER

CELESTIAL

STARLIGHT

***The Quatrefoil Chronicles* series**

OF WICKED BLOOD

OF TAINTED HEART

CONTEMPORARY ROMANCE

GHOSTBOY, CHAMELEON & THE DUKE OF GRAFFITI

NOT ANOTHER LOVE SONG

ROMANTIC SUSPENSE

***Cold Little Games* series**

COLD LITTLE LIES

COLD LITTLE GAMES

COLD LITTLE HEARTS

Want to hear about what I'm writing next? SIGN UP FOR MY GENERAL NEWSLETTER on **oliviawildenstein.com**

ABOUT THE AUTHOR

USA TODAY bestselling author Olivia Wildenstein grew up in New York City, the daughter of a French father with a great sense of humor, and a Swedish mother whom she speaks to at least three times a day. She chose Brown University to complete her undergraduate studies and earned a bachelor's in comparative literature. After designing jewelry for a few years, Wildenstein traded in her tools for a laptop computer and a very comfortable chair. This line of work made more sense, considering her college degree.

When she's not writing, she's psychoanalyzing everyone she meets (Yes. Everyone), eavesdropping on conversations to gather material for her next book, baking up a storm (that she actually eats), going to the gym (because she eats), and attempting not to be late at her children's school (like she is 4 out of 5 mornings, on good weeks).

Wildenstein lives with her husband and three children in Geneva, Switzerland, where she's an active member of the writing community.

Places you can find me:
www.oliviawildenstein.com
press@oliviawildenstein.com

Lightning Source UK Ltd.
Milton Keynes UK
UKHW012254081122
411848UK00004B/216